THAT FIRST KISS

THREE SIZZLING READS

CHELLE BLISS

THAT FIRST KISS...

This is **NOT** filled with sweet romances.

They're spicy books!

Happy reading.

WHAT'S INSIDE...

Throttle Me - Suzy has her life planned out — until a tattooed bad boy turns everything upside down. Could their one-night stand become the real deal?

Maneuver - Delilah is suspicious when sexy Lucio offers her and her baby a place to live. But soon the muscular bar owner is working his way into her heart — and into her bed...

Flame - Gigi and Pike spent a week in bed together before she took off without a word. But when Gigi starts working at her family's tattoo shop, she's stunned to find Pike is her new co-worker — and their chemistry is as combustible as ever!

Dear Reader,

Thank you for downloading and reading *That First Kiss*, a collection of my USA Today bestselling spicy romance novels, Even if you never read beyond these three ebooks, thank you for grabbing your copy!

Chelle Bliss

THROTTLE me

A MEN OF INKED NOVEL

WALL STREET JOURNAL & USA TODAY BESTSELLING AUTHOR

CHELLE BLISS

CHAPTER
ONE
SUZY

THE MOONLIGHT FILTERED through the pine trees lining the fields, leaving shadows on the pavement. The crisp air that had been missing for months caressed my skin. Cranking up the radio, I sang along to Justin Timberlake's "Rock Your Body." It was just the cool breeze, JT, and me. I couldn't wait to crawl in my bed and close my eyes, getting lost in a dream world that had nothing to do with my current reality.

The night had been perfect. I'd had dinner and drinks with my best friend, Sophia, and although I was exhausted from a long workday, I felt a sense of serenity. Spending time with Sophia always made me happy. She was like a sister to me, especially when she had lived with me for over a year. I felt like part of me had been missing since the day she moved out, leaving me behind.

Dancing in the seat, screaming out the lyrics, I thought about how I wanted someone that would do everything the song described. No one had ever made me feel the way that JT sang about women. The steering wheel shook in my hands and a screeching sound pulled me out of my JT trance.

"Damn it," I said, hitting the steering wheel with my palm.

The orange flash from my hazards blinked against the dark pavement as I pulled off the road and my car sputtered to a stop. Bad luck seemed to follow me. I squeezed the steering wheel, trying to calm my frazzled nerves. I knew the day would come, the day my car would die, but I prayed it would happen after my next paycheck…no such luck.

Resting my head on the wheel, I closed my eyes, taking a deep breath. "Great, just fucking great." I rocked back and forth, feeling sorry for myself, hitting my head on the cool plastic. I thought about whom to call or where to walk. I hadn't passed a gas station or even a damn streetlight in miles. Without picking up my head, I reached for my phone, bringing it to my eyes.

"Shit." The screen wouldn't power on after I hit every button I could think to press. It was useless. It was dead and now I was totally stranded. What else could possibly go wrong? Sighing, I sat up and glanced in the rearview mirror, but only the shadows from the trees filled my view. No cars, neon signs, or streetlights. Fuck.

I placed my hand on my chest to feel the beat of my heart, which was so hard I swear it was audible. Visions from slasher movies flooded my mind. Girl deserted on the side of the road until she's found by a handsome stranger that ends up being a serial killer.

Should I start walking to God knows where? Do I just sit there and wait for a stranger to offer me help? I never liked feeling helpless—I was too smart to be helpless, but it was the only thing I felt in this moment. It could be hours before someone found me in my car.

I grabbed my purse, dead phone, and keys, and climbed out of the car. My feet ached in the extra-high heels I wore. Leaning against the car, I gave my feet a moment to adjust, as I looked in both directions. Neither of my options were good and I was exhausted. My feet fucking screamed from standing still. Thank God I could sleep in tomorrow after the way this evening was ending. There was a gas station a couple miles back—better to go with what I knew than to walk into an uncertain future. I tapped the lock button on my key chain one more time, helping relieve my OCD need to double-check everything, before I started walking away.

Barely clearing the trunk, a single light came over a small hill in the distance, hurting my eyes with the brightness. The roar of the engine grew louder as the distance closed. I waved my arms as a figure came into view, but the asshole biker drove right passed me as I screamed, "Hey! Hey!" The wind from his bike caused the dust on the road to kick up and fill my mouth.

I turned around, coughing, and screamed toward the bike. I knew it was pointless. There was no way in hell he'd heard me yelling above the roar of his bike, but he had to see me. The red taillight lit up the road as he turned the bike in my direction. I swallowed hard, unsure if this was my best idea of the night—but I'd already made too many mistakes to dwell on that. He was my only hope of getting home.

I stood there like a deer in headlights, unable to move, as I gaped at him. My hands trembled as the figure on the bike came to a stop. The engine was almost deafening, as I took in the sight of him on the machine. The bike was a Harley, a Fat Boy, with no windshield, chrome handlebars, and a dark body. He wore black boots, dark jeans, and a dark t-shirt. He was large and muscular, and I sucked in a breath as my eyes reached his handsome and rugged face. A playful grin danced on his lips as he watched me ogle him. Fucking hell.

"Need some help, lady?" he asked, removing his helmet, running his fingers through his disheveled hair. The dark peaks stood up on the top, the sides were short and clipped, and the color matched the sky—dark. I couldn't see his eyes;

a pair of tinted glasses hid them. Could serial killers be so sexy?

"Um, do you have a cell phone I could use to call for a ride?" I asked without taking a step in his direction. *Don't get too close—leave room to run.* Who the fuck was I kidding? I couldn't make it five feet in these damn shoes.

"Sure." As he leaned back on his bike, I studied his body as he dug in his pocket. The skintight jeans showed his muscles through the denim fabric. Everything clung to him. I wanted to poke him to see if he felt as hard as he looked. What the fuck was wrong with me?

I was too busy staring to notice what he was holding out for me. "Lady, you wanted my phone?"

Snapping back to reality with the sound of his deep voice, I took a step toward him, reaching for the phone. "Oh, sorry."

My fingertips grazed his palm, and a tiny shock passed between us. His fingers closed on my hand as I pulled away. My heartbeat, which had calmed, now began to pound feverishly in my chest. It had to be my hormones. I hadn't had sex in God knows how long—I stopped counting after three months. The man in front of me wasn't my type, but his sex appeal wasn't lost on me. He looked like a whole lot of trouble, and I didn't need that in my life.

I stepped back, keeping my eyes trained on him, as I dialed the only person close enough to help—Sophia. The phone rang and his eyes traveled up and down the length of my body—with each ring, my stomach began to turn. I didn't have anyone else to call.

Tapping the end button, I sighed. "There's no answer. Thanks." I gave him a sheepish smile as I handed him the phone.

"Let me take a look and see if there's anything I can do. Okay?" he asked, as he began angling the bike to shine the headlights on the hood.

"Sure." I hit the unlock button on my car key before

climbing in. I put the key in the ignition, but stayed aware of his proximity. No one would hear me scream if he tried to kill me. I couldn't let my guard down.

He put the kickstand down, climbed off the bike, and placed the helmet on the seat. Pulling the hood latch next to my seat, I watched him from the relative darkness of my car, my face hidden by shadows. He was large, larger than he looked sitting on the Harley. He had to be more than a foot taller than me, and looked more solid with the bike illuminating his body. I stared at him, mouth open slightly, my breathing shallow as I looked at him like a piece of meat through the gap between the hood. He oozed masculinity and ruggedness, and I tried to picture him without all the skintight clothes. The muscles in his arm rippled as he touched the parts under the hood.

What would it be like to be with a man like him? Every man I'd dated just didn't work out. They were nice guys, but the spark I wanted was always missing. People think I'm a good girl, and I am, but my mind is filled with dirty thoughts that I could never share with a mate. I'd shared them with Sophia, but she doesn't count. No one had ever done anything fantasy-worthy with me. I can barely speak the words that are needed to describe the things I want done to me, or that I'd want to do to another person in this world.

"Ma'am," he said, snapping me out of the evaluation of my sex life, or lack thereof.

"Sorry, yes?"

"Can you try and start it for me, please?" he said, leaning over the hood, his hands placed on either side of the opening. "Now," he said. The car churned and churned. "Stop," I heard him yell over the screeching noise. He moved methodically around the engine. "Try it again." I turned the key, causing the engine to rattle, but not start.

He stood, rubbing the back of his neck as curses spilled from his lips. The only thing I could see was his crotch. I stared, motionless. His t-shirt covered the belt loops and stopped just above his groin. Damn. He filled out those jeans. He had to be big. Everything about him was big—he couldn't, just couldn't, have a small cock, could he?

The last guy that I'd slept with was more the size of a party pickle. It was the most unsatisfying sexual experience of my life. He was a teacher, and I wanted someone who was educated and self-sufficient, but he was boring in and out of the bedroom. I thought I'd found that with Derek, Mr. Pickle, but I was wrong. He was a wreck, and filled with more mental issues than anyone I'd ever know. He was germophobic, which was problematic when having sex. He'd jump right out of bed immediately after sex to shower and wash the dirty off. I sighed to myself, remembering his need to be clean—never mind that he was an asshole, too.

The hood of my car made a loud thump as the man slammed it. "Your car is a little tricky. Foreign cars can be complicated. I can't seem to get it to start," he said, walking toward the driver-side door.

"It's okay. Thanks for trying." I climbed out, not wanting to be trapped inside. What the hell was I going to do now?

"I was heading to the bar up the road. Want to join me?" He smiled and tilted his head as he studied me. "You can call a tow truck from there. It may take a while for them to get out here."

I couldn't think of any other option. He was my only hope, my saving grace from the dark roadside, and a means to an end. There were worse things than climbing on the back of his motorcycle and wrapping my arms around him. "Okay, but I've never been on a bike."

"Never? How is that even possible?" he asked, shaking his head, a small laugh escaping his lips. His teeth sparkled in the light, straight and white. His jaw was strong, his cheekbones jutted out more when he smiled, and a small dimple formed on the left side of his face.

I looked down at the ground, my cheeks heated. "I don't know. I just never knew anyone that had one and I find them totally scary."

"It's not far from here and there isn't much traffic. I'll keep you safe," he said, holding out his helmet.

My stomach fluttered as I closed the car door and thought about my first motorcycle ride. The black, round helmet felt cool against my fingers as I took it from him. I scrunched my eyebrows together as I studied it. I didn't know if there was a front or a back, or how to put it on.

"Here, let me help you," he said as he reached for the helmet, removing it from my grip. His hand touched mine and I felt the spark again. Not a real spark, but electricity that I felt with every fiber of my being from the slightest touch. My body wanted his touch, but my mind was throwing up the caution flag.

Placing it gently on my head, he ran his rough fingers down the straps, almost caressing my skin, to adjust it to fit my face. I inhaled deeply, trying to fill all my senses with him. He smelled different than any other man I'd smelled. He didn't smell of cheap cologne, but there was a spicy, woodsy scent that reminded me of home. I closed my eyes and relished the feel of his warm skin against mine.

"All done. Are you ready?" he asked.

I opened my eyes, heat creeping up my neck, as I had been lost in his touch. "Yes." I prayed my voice didn't betray me.

He climbed on the bike, sliding forward, making room for me. "Lift your leg and climb on."

Placing my hand on his shoulder to help balance myself, I followed his instructions; my body slid forward, smashing against him. Rock solid. He turned his head, looking me in the eyes. "Put your feet on the pegs and wrap your arms around me. I don't bite—well, unless you want me to." He smirked, and my heart felt like it was doing the tango in my chest as I pressed against his back. He didn't just say that to me, did he? I lifted my feet off the ground, turning over complete control to the stranger I was entrusting with my life. I locked my hands together, completely wrapped around him.

"Ready?"

"Wait! I don't even know your name. I mean, I'm putting my life in your hands and I don't even know who you are." I gripped his body tighter, clinging to him.

I couldn't hear his laughter, but I felt the rumble of it from deep in his chest. "My friends call me City, sugar." He throttled the engine and my heart skipped a beat. Fear gripped me —there was no turning back now.

My grip became viselike, fear overcoming any need to be cool or seem calm in front of him. He patted my hands before the bike began to move, and I couldn't bear to look. I buried my face in his back, avoiding any chance of seeing the road. The wind caressed my skin, causing it to feel like ice compared to the warmth my palms experienced. Did this man have any soft spots? I flexed my fingers against his chest, wanting to feel his hardness, praying like hell I made it seem natural and not like I was molesting him.

The bike picked up speed, and my heart thundered against his back. I gripped him harder, holding on for dear life, the sound of the engine drowning out everything else around me, except the two of us. He leaned into the bike, his ass moving snugly between my legs. I didn't dare move. He was warm, comfortable, and I enjoyed every minute my body touched his. I closed my eyes, trying to not think about the movement of the bike underneath us—the slight shift and unevenness of the road made me feel off balance.

The noise of the engine changed, and I finally peeked over his shoulder. The parking lot of the Neon Cowboy was packed with bikes and was the brightest thing for miles. I'd driven by it dozens of times, but never thought about stopping. This wasn't the type of bar for kids on speedy, foreign-made bikes, but a place for tough bikers to hang out, drink beer, and pick up chicks.

City backed the bike into an empty spot, and I could feel my body begin to tremble from the fear that finally began to seep through my veins. I did it. I rode on a motorcycle, and with a stranger, no less. My breath was harsh as I blinked slowly and tried to calm myself down.

"You can climb off now, sugar." His legs were straddling the bike and he held the handlebars, securing the bike for me. "Enjoy your first ride?"

I released my hands from the security of his body and hoisted myself off on trembling legs. "It was the single most terrifying thing I've ever experienced," I said, thankful when my feet were firmly on the ground. I stood, trying to get my body to stop shaking and my heart to slow down before walking inside the bar with him at my side.

"If that's the scariest thing you've ever experienced, you need to get out more, sugar. I took it slow with you." He grinned, and my stomach plummeted from his sinful smile. I wanted to see him above me naked and moving in and out of my body slowly, almost at a torturous pace. Everything about him made my body convulse and scream for attention. He wasn't my type. I preferred a bookworm and a man that liked to spend an evening inside watching a movie or playing Scrabble, not riding like a bat out of hell on a Fat Boy to hang out at a bar. I wasn't a barfly and never would be.

The outdoor lights gave me a full view of the man that called himself City. His hair was darker than I originally thought, almost jet black, and an inch long on the top, brushing against his forehead as he shook it out. It was a mess from the wind, with the front hanging over his forehead. I couldn't tell the color of his eyes; they were still hidden behind the tinted lenses of his glasses.

"Yeah, lucky me." I chuckled and tried to play it cool, even though my body shook. If that was slow, I didn't think I wanted to know what his idea of fast and hard were—or did I? Fuck me. He had my brain all jumbled.

After removing the helmet, I ran my fingers through my hair, trying to straighten it after the wild ride. He laughed as he crawled off the bike, taking the helmet from my hands, and placed it on the seat. I watched, mesmerized, as he removed his glasses and put them inside a small bag hanging from the side of the bike. I wanted to see his eyes, and the entire man without a mask or veil.

"Ready, babe?" He motioned toward the door.

I wanted to scream no, but I didn't have a choice. I could never walk into this sort of place on my own.

"Yeah, ready as I'll ever be." I started walking toward the door and felt a hand on my arm, stopping me in my tracks. I looked at his fingers wrapped around my arm and turned toward him. "What are you doing?"

"You can't just walk into a place like this. You're an outsider. They'll eat you alive in there. I don't want anyone giving you shit. We have to make them believe you're with me so they leave you the fuck alone. Unless you want the attention?" he asked with a crooked eyebrow.

"I don't." I didn't mind the idea of making everyone in the bar think we were together. City was hot and seemed like a nice guy; he did stop to help me when he could've driven right by me.

"Just stay by my side and follow my lead. I know these people and I don't want them sniffing around you. They look for easy prey," he said, giving me a smile that made my body tingle and my sex convulse.

"Okay, I'll stick to you like glue and follow your lead." Jesus, I sounded like a dork. I've always been a bookworm. I was national honor society member, and when all my friends were partying, I stayed in my dorm to study.

City nestled me against his side, tucking me between his body and arm. I moved with him, trying to keep up with his fluid movements, but my legs were so short I felt like I almost had to jog to keep time with him. He opened the door and I was immediately hit with a smoky smell, loud, twangy music, and a dozen set of eyes looking directly at us.

Randomly people yelled out "City" throughout the bar, giving me a clue that he was a regular. I felt like I'd entered a seedy version of *Cheers* and City was Norm, only sexy and muscular. He leaned down, placing his mouth next to my ear. I felt his hot breath before I could hear his words.

"Stick close and show no fear," he whispered, causing goose bumps to break out across my skin. "Let's say hello then we'll call a tow for you."

City looked big enough to handle any man in this place, but I didn't want to take that chance. I concentrated on breathing, keeping my chin up, and watching where I walked. The floor was filled with peanut shells and dust, and it made the walk in the stilettos even more treacherous than normal. I could barely walk when I bought them, but they looked too sexy to pass up.

We walked to a table filled with men all wearing their leather vests, covered in patches. They were unshaven, as dangerously sexy as City, with mischievous smiles on their faces. "Who's this lovely lady, City?" one man asked. His eyes raked up my body, stopping at my breasts before he looked at my face.

"This is Sunshine. Don't even fucking think about it, Tank, she's with me," City said with a smile on his face as he pulled me closer.

Sunshine? I'd never told him my name and he never asked. I didn't like the way Tank looked at me. Thank God he wasn't the one driving by while I was stranded. He looked at me like I was a piece of meat, a meal for his enjoyment.

Tank put his hands up in surrender. "Dude, I'd never. Chill the fuck out. I'm just enjoying the view," he said, his eyes moving from City to me, and not being coy about his visual molestation.

City squeezed my waist. "Sunshine, this is Tank, the asshole. This is Hog, Frisco, and Bear," he said, pointing to each of the men.

The nicknames didn't seem to fit any of the men, except Bear. His arms were hairy and he was big, huge, in fact, with dark hair and a fuzzy face. He looked huggable and kind, with soft hazel eyes.

"Hi," I said, looking at each of them quickly, but I didn't try to memorize their names.

"I didn't know you were bringing a woman tonight, City," Bear said.

"Wilder shit *has* happened, Bear," City said, pulling me closer, leaving no space between us.

"She doesn't look like your usual taste, my friend." Bear smirked. "I don't mean that shitty, girl, I just mean you're one fine piece of ass and too good for that low-life motherfucker. You should be sitting on my lap." He patted his leg, and I wanted to find an exit. I looked down and studied my clothes. I didn't wear the trashy clothes some of the women in here wore, but I looked classy, sexy even, with not a hint of nerd to be found.

City moved toward Bear, and my heart sank as he began to speak. "Show some respect, you asshole. That's not how you talk to a lady." City stood inches from Bear's face. "Apologize to the lady. *Now*." City towered over him as Bear stayed rooted in his chair.

Bear looked at me, and I could see him swallow hard before he spoke. "I'm sorry, Sunshine. I was just kidding around. I really am an asshole. Forgive me, please."

"No harm done, Bear," I said with a fake smile, hoping to calm the situation.

"We're going to sit at the bar." City looked at Bear, not moving his eyes.

"Come on, dude, sit with us. Don't mind Bear. He's a total dick. Make his ass go sit at the bar," Frisco said.

"Sunshine and I want to be alone. I'll catch you guys another night," City said, pressing his hand against my back, guiding me away from the table and the large bar area.

"I'm sorry. They can be childish dicks. Bear doesn't have a filter," he said as he pulled out a chair for me. City had manners. Not many of the men I dated did something as simple as pull out a chair for a lady—it was a lost art. "He's a good guy, but sometimes his mouth runs and he doesn't think before he speaks."

"It's okay, really…it is. Thanks for sticking up for me," I said to him as I sat down, pulling my stool closer to the bar. "Why did you call me Sunshine?"

"Well, I don't know your name and you remind me of sunshine—your hair is golden and your smile glows. Just sounded right. I had to come up with something on the fly," he said. "I hope you didn't mind." He shrugged and grabbed the menu lying nearby.

"I didn't mind, but my name is Suzy."

"What would you like, Suzy?"

I wanted to say "you," because somehow this man made me lose my grip on reality. "Virgin daiquiri, please."

"Virgin? Really?" His brows shot up and the corner of his mouth twitched.

"I already had a drink tonight. I just want something sweet, no liquor."

"Do you want something to eat?" he asked. "You a vegetarian too?" He laughed.

"Shut up." I smacked him on the arm. "I'm good. I just want to call a tow truck."

"Gotcha." He pulled out his phone and placed it on the bar. "Hey, darlin', can you put in an order for a cheeseburger, a beer, and a virgin daiquiri?" he asked the bartender.

"Sure thing, handsome," she said, walking away, slowly

swaying her hips to grab attention. I turned to City to see if he was watching her, but he was staring at me instead, and my mouth felt dry and scratchy.

"You want to call Triple A or someone else?" he asked without taking his eyes off me. They were an amazing shade of blue, and I couldn't look away. I'd always loved my blue eyes, but his were almost turquoise. I felt like he was staring through me, into me, seeing everything I hid under the surface. I wanted him, but I didn't want to admit my attraction. I *couldn't* admit it.

"Triple A is good," I said, reaching for my purse to find my membership card. I fumbled with my wallet, finding the card behind everything else inside. I could feel his eyes on me; he studied me and it made me nervous. What was he thinking? I dialed the number as I swiveled away from him, needing to avert his stare.

"Hello, Triple A, how can I help you?"

I could barely hear the tiny female voice above the loud classic rock that pulsed throughout the smoky bar. City chatted with the bartender as I tried to drown them out and give my location and details about my car. They wouldn't be able to make it out to my car until morning. Fuck. I thanked her for helping me before hitting the end button.

"What'd they say?" City asked with a sincere look as the bartender sashayed away from us.

"They won't make it out here until morning because they're busy and we're in the middle of nowhere. I'm to leave it unlocked so they can get in and put it in neutral or something. I don't know how it works. I've never had my car towed before." Now what the hell was I going to do? I was stranded at the Neon Cowboy with Mr. Sexalicious and my dirty thoughts.

"I'll bring you back to your car when I'm done eating. I guess you'll need a lift home too?" he asked, sipping his drink as he eyed me.

I smiled at him. Though I hated the thought of him going out of his way, and I wasn't that comfortable with a stranger knowing where I lived, I couldn't say no. "I'd appreciate it, if you don't mind."

"Not at all, Suzy. I can't just leave you here and walk out the door. I got ya, babe." He turned his stool toward me and leaned into my space. "Where do you want me to take you after we leave? Home?" He quirked an eyebrow, waiting for my response, and held me in place with his hard stare.

Home? Whose home was he referring to? City looked to be the type that had different women falling out of his bed every morning...or maybe he kicked them out before he fell asleep. His fingers brushed against the top of my hand and my internal dialogue evaporated.

"Where. Do. You. Live?" The laughter he tried to hide behind his hand made it clear that I'd sat there longer in thought than I had realized.

I cleared my throat. "I need to unlock my car then I need a lift home. I live about fifteen minutes north. Is that okay? I mean, I don't want to—" He put his finger over my lips and stopped me mid-sentence.

"Doesn't matter, I'll take you anywhere," he said with a sly grin that made my pulse race and my body heat. He licked his lips, and I stared like an idiot. My sex convulsed at the thought of his lips on my skin. What the fuck was wrong with me? Every movement he made and word he spoke turned sexual, as if permeating my brain. I needed to get laid; this man was not hitting on me, was he?

"You want some? I can't eat it all," he said as the plate was placed in front of him.

I shook my head and picked up my drink, trying to cool my body off from the internal fire caused by City. The cool, sweet strawberry slush danced across my tongue and slid down my throat.

I swirled the red straw in my mouth, trying to occupy my

mind. His arms flexed as he lifted the burger to his mouth, forearms covered with tattoos. The left arm had various designs woven together—a koi fish, a tiger, and a couple of other nature-themed pieces that seemed to move across his skin, and his right arm had a city skyline. I wanted to touch his arms and run my fingers across his ink. He looked big everywhere, and my gaze drifted down his body and lingered at his crotch. I wondered if his motorcycle and tattoos made up for shortcomings elsewhere, but I couldn't believe a man like him was tiny. There was no way in hell he had a party…

"Pickle?"

I blinked and moved my eyes away from his crotch to his eyes. *Pickle?* He held it and motioned for me to take it.

"No. Thanks, though. You eat it," I said, feeling like he was reading my mind. God, I hoped he didn't see me staring at his crotch. I sucked down the rest of my drink, wishing now that it did have alcohol in it. Maybe then I wouldn't feel so embarrassed. "I noticed your tattoos. What's the one on your right arm?"

"That's the Chicago skyline," he said, as he took another bite.

"You from there?"

"Born and bred, baby." He grunted and continued to chew. I couldn't take my eyes off his mouth. Watching him eat was erotic to me; his lips moved as he chewed, and he sucked each finger in his mouth to clean off the juices that flowed from the sandwich. Damn. It *had* been too long since I'd had sex—when eating becomes sexual. Houston, we have a problem.

CHAPTER TWO

CITY

I COULD'VE EASILY STARTED her car, but I didn't want to. Her beauty caught my eye and I wanted to know more about her. Shit, I wanted to fuck her. I couldn't just drive away and leave her out there to fend for herself. I'm a dick usually, but I couldn't just leave her there.

She looked helpless as I almost drove by her. When the lights of my bike shone on her, dirty thoughts flooded my mind. She had on "fuck me" heels with a short-as-hell skirt and a lacy white tank top that instantly made my dick hard. Her hair fell across the top of her breasts and sparkled in the light. It was golden, and I wanted to pull it while my cock was buried deep inside of her.

I pretended to come to her rescue and try to help, but I wanted to keep her as long as I could. I'd have one of the guys at the bar tow her car back to her place.

I could see fear in her eyes when we walked in tonight. They were large like saucers, her mouth hung open, and she looked around the room like she'd never been in a bar before. The guys here could be assholes, especially when a beautiful woman enters the room. Bear was always a total prick, but he did have a point. I wanted to fuck her and I wanted it dirty.

"How about I buy you a real drink? Just one. You aren't driving tonight, so what's the harm?"

I watched as she chewed her lip. "I guess you're right. My week's been crappy. I could use something...stronger," she said, blowing out a puff of air, causing her hair to move.

"Well, let's change that. Bad date?" I asked. I looked at her shoes before moving up her entire body and stopping at her face. "How can I make it better?"

Her lips parted and her chest heaved as she sucked air in quickly. "It's not so bad anymore. Tonight started out great, I went out with a girlfriend of mine, but it's just my friggin' car that put the icing on the cake."

Friggin'? Did grown women really use that word?

"I'm sure the car is no big deal," I said as I motioned for the bartender. "Know what you want?"

"Martini. A sweet one, please." She polished off her *virgin* daiquiri. She didn't swear and barely drank liquor; she wasn't like most girls I knew—even her clothes weren't as sexy as I'd expect for a girl her age.

"What can I get you, honey?" Sandy asked.

"Sunshine here will take a sweet martini, Sandy. Anything you can make flavored, preferably." I looked over at Suzy. "Right?"

"Yes, thank you." She looked out of place in a bar like this, but I wanted her at my side. She appeared to be a good girl with a clean mouth, but I could tell her mind was littered with filthy thoughts. She looked at me—no, stared at me—watching every movement and studying my entire body. She wanted me as much as I wanted her, even though she didn't want to admit it or couldn't. "You come here a lot, huh? Everyone seems to know you."

"The guys and I hang out here a couple nights a week after work, and it's close to my house. It's just a place I like to come to relax and unwind a bit after a long day."

She licked her lips, and I swear to fuckin' Christ my cock

twitched. I adjusted myself, trying to stop a full-on hard-on from catching her eye. I watched her legs as she shifted in her seat, rubbing them together before crossing them. I had her and I knew it, but the trick was to not scare her off.

"What do you do, City?" She glanced at her hands, trying not to look at me.

"I'm an artist. You?" I left it at that—sounded classier than "I'm a tattoo artist." I was an artist at heart, but my canvas was human skin.

"Teacher. What kind of artist?"

She didn't look like any schoolteacher I'd ever had. I wouldn't have been able to pay attention in class with her walking around in heels and stretching to write on the chalkboard. "Tattoo," I said as I pointed at the artwork on my arm. "You have any?"

"Tattoos?" she asked as her eyebrows rose and her eyes grew wide.

"Yeah, by the look on your face I'd say the answer is 'no.'"

"Oh no." She laughed. "Needles scare the heck out of me." Grabbing her drink, she gulped down half the martini without even blinking.

"Do you swear?" I asked as she set the glass back on the bar.

"What?" She gaped at me.

"Do you swear? Simple question. You've said 'heck' and 'friggin' so far, but nothing dirty."

"Oh, um, yeah, I swear." Her cheeks turned pink and a small smile spread across her face. "I'm just used to watching my words with the kids around all day."

"Prove it," I said, staring in her sapphire eyes.

"What? Why?"

"'Cause I need to know if it's in you. Are you all good girl? Or is there something more underneath dying to come out?" I hid the smile and laughter that were so close to breaking free from my lips. The pink of her cheeks spread across her face. I knew I'd embarrassed her, but fuck, I needed to know if I stood a chance.

"Yes, I swear. What do you think I am? I'm not a child, City." She glared at me as she raised the drink to her lips and wrapped them around the rim. Fuck. I wanted those lips wrapped around my dick, taking me deep and sucking me off.

"Never said you were, babe. Do you drink besides tonight?" I asked, now smiling because I knew she was upset. I liked the fire I saw in her eyes when I pointed out her good-girl qualities—she obviously didn't like being labeled.

"Sometimes. I'm just responsible. I don't drink and drive. My dad used to be a cop, and it was drilled into my head at an early age." The words she spoke hit me like a ton of bricks. Drunk driving was the one thing in the world that caused my blood to boil.

Good-girl teacher with a cop father? Just my luck. "Nothin' wrong with that. Virgin daiquiris aren't always your thing, then?"

"Why? Do I have to be a drinker? I mean, does it make me less of an adult?"

"No, Suzy. Just trying to get a feel for who you are—*what* you are."

Her shoulders slumped and she seemed to relax a bit with my words.

"Want another drink? You downed that one quick." She'd surprised me with how fast she polished it off, so my question about her drinking had been answered, but I wanted to watch her get a little pissed.

"One more and then I'm done," she said.

"You order your drink and I'm going to go talk to my friend over there real quick. He's a mechanic. I'll see what he can do with your car tonight." Standing, I motioned to Sandy and pointed to Suzy.

"Okay, don't leave me alone here too long."

"Promise, two minutes, tops." I walked away from Suzy as Sandy approached. The vultures would swoop in soon enough in my absence.

"Bored with Sunshine over there, buddy?" Tank asked as he kicked back in his chair as the others laughed. Tank's smile was wide, and the laughter only encouraged him further. "I can step in if you'd like. I wouldn't mind spending the night with that sweet flower."

I sat down in my usual seat next to Bear. "You can fuck off tonight." I pointed at Tank. "I don't need your shit." Tank just grinned. I knew he was fucking around, but it pissed me the fuck off. I'd known Tank for years, and although he could be a pain in the ass, he had a heart of gold.

"Easy there, City. What the fuck crawled up your ass and died?" Bear said.

"Nothing, man, long day. Sorry, brother."

"Sweet on that girl, huh? Never knew you were such an uptight dick, let alone overprotective of a woman," Bear said.

"I'm not, but fuck, the shit that comes out of your mouth just pisses me off at times."

"Sorry. Just fuckin' with you."

"We're cool." I slapped Bear on the shoulder, hoping to change the mood. No matter what assholes the guys could be, they were still my friends. They always had my back. "I need a favor, Tank."

"Name it."

"Her car's down the road and isn't starting. It's an easy fix to get it moving again, but there's some other issue with it. Think you could take care of it for me and drop it by her place tomorrow?"

"Sure. Whatever you need. You want me to just get it running or fix it for her?"

"Fix it and I'll pay for the repair. Don't let her pay for anything. Just drop it in her driveway."

"Gotcha, kid. I'll need her keys," he said as he popped open a peanut and threw the shell on the floor.

"I'll get them to you before we head out. Thanks, man." I stood quickly, needing to get back to Suzy. I'd already been gone too long.

"Night. Enjoy the Sunshine. Don't get burned," Bear said. *Motherfucker*.

A man stood over Suzy, invading her personal space, as she backed away as far as possible without falling off the stool. He looked greasy, with long, straggly hair, a dirty top, and stained pants, and he was covered in old, faded tattoos. I'd seen the motherfucker here before, and it never ended well. He always creeped women out, and someone always tossed him on his ass after he had one too many.

"Excuse me," I said as I stood behind him and waited for him to turn his attention toward me.

"What?" he asked without turning around.

"The lady doesn't want to talk to you." I squeezed my hands into fists and tried to keep my temper down for Suzy's sake.

"I didn't ask your opinion."

Her eyes were wide, and she slowly shook her head at me. The anger was clearly evident on my face. I felt like I was breathing fire at this point.

"Get the fuck away from my girl or it won't end well for you." I crossed my arms over my chest and stood there, unmoving. If it weren't for Suzy I would've laid the mother-fucker out by now, but she didn't seem like the bar-fight type of girl.

He squinted at her and looked pissed off, but what the fuck did I care? "I don't see your name on her, dick."

"What's going on over here?" Bear said behind me as I grabbed the bastard by the collar, getting ready to pound his fucking face into a bloody mess.

"This asshole is bothering my girl. I think he needs to be

taught a lesson." I tightened my grip on the material that hung from his body.

I could see his Adam's apple bob as he swallowed. I knew Bear would seal the deal, and the fucker would move on without me having to punch his fucking lights out. "Sorry, guys. You should be more careful about leaving your property unattended. Next time it may not be here when you get back. Would be a shame for something to happen to this beautiful creature." The fucking bastard smirked.

My fist landed against his face before I realized what I'd done. The fucker deserved far worse than a punch to his jaw. He was a sleazy-ass motherfucker bothering someone that obviously didn't want to be touched. "Get the fuck out of here! Now!" I yelled as he lay on the floor holding his jaw.

"Let's go, asshat. Time for you to leave." Bear picked him up and pulled him toward the door with his feet dragging across the wood planks. "Don't fucking show your face in here again if you know what's good for you."

I shook my hand as pain shot through my fingers. I knew I'd feel that punch for a couple of days, but it was worth it to lay that scumbag out and get him away from Suzy. "Are you okay?" I asked her as I flexed my fingers and studied her face.

"Yeah, I'm fine. Thank you for saving me, again." She smiled at me and looked at my hand. Her smile faded as she saw the way I moved my fingers. "Are you okay?"

"Yeah, bastard had a bony-ass jaw, is all," I said, shaking out the last pain in my knuckles.

She reached out and held my hand. "Sandy, can we get some ice over here?" she asked over her shoulder as she stroked my fingers and rubbed my knuckles with her soft, warm hands. I wanted to close my eyes and relish the feel of her skin against mine. I wanted to touch her. I ached to kiss her, but this wasn't the place.

"Really, that's not necessary. I just want to make sure you're okay, Suzy." I didn't stop her from touching me. I could feel the heat from her skin even after her fingers had moved on to another part of my hand. My hands always hurt from working for hours on designs, so the fist to the jaw didn't help them feel any better. I touched her cheek with my free hand, and she moved into my touch and searched for the contact. "You are okay, right?"

"Yeah, that guy was creepy, but he didn't hurt me. Thank you for coming back when you did."

"Sorry, I should've paid attention and shouldn't have left you. I didn't offend you with being possessive and calling you my girl? "

"Oh, no. I've never had anyone say that about me, ever." Her lips turned down as she concentrated on my hands. How could no one ever call her "my girl"?

"Hey." I held her chin and forced her to look at me. "Every girl should hear those words in her lifetime." I didn't smile. I wanted her to know I was dead serious.

"Yeah, well, I haven't." She let go of my hand and turned away from me, pulling out of my grip.

I didn't think I'd ever used those words when speaking of a woman, except Joni. A sharp pain hit me square in the chest as I thought of my ex, the only woman I'd ever loved. I had a reaction to Suzy like I did when I met Joni, and seeing another man bothering her made me see red. I wanted to protect her, unlike I had with Joni. I cleared my throat and shook my head, trying to rid myself of my lost love. "Well, it's not too late for it to happen. I didn't think I'd be sitting in a bar tonight talking to such a beautiful woman, but here I am. Your story has yet to be written."

"I'll never give up on my fairytale," she said as she let go of my hand and picked up her martini, swallowing the last drops. "Is it hot in here?" She pulled on her tank top, moving it back and forth to cool her skin. Every time the material moved away from her flesh, I'd get a peek of breast, and I had to force myself not to stare.

"Want to take a ride on the bike to cool off?" I asked. I wanted to feel her body against mine again, hugging my hips with her thighs, her arms wrapped around me.

She rubbed her forehead. "I'm feeling a bit lightheaded. I shouldn't have had two drinks."

"I'll make sure you don't fall off the bike. Just hold on tight and I'll get you home safely." I touched her knee, wanting to see if she'd pull away from me, but she didn't. The skin was soft and smooth, and I wanted to run my hands up her thighs and watch her head fall back in ecstasy. I wanted to take her home and have my way with her, but I couldn't just ask her.

"What about my car?" she asked breathily as I pulled my hand away. My touch had an effect on her, based on the tone of her voice. She wasn't good at hiding her feelings.

"I talked to Tank about it. He's going to take care of it tonight and drop it off in the morning. He just needs your keys."

"Really? He'd do that for me?" Her eyebrows shot up and her lips parted.

"Yes, and for me. Keys?" I held out my hand to her, ready to ditch this fucking place.

She dug through her purse, pulled out her keys, and placed them in my hand. She brushed her hair over her shoulder. I wanted to sink my teeth into her. I wanted to hear her moan, breathless underneath me. She truly was beautiful. She had an understated sex appeal to her. She didn't flaunt the beauty of her body, and I didn't think she even had a clue how fuckin' hot I found her. She was the girl next door, the untouched bookworm that every guy wanted to conquer. I wanted to make her dirty. I wanted to make her scream filthy words while I fucked her. I wanted to corrupt this girl in the worst possible way. She would be a challenge, and maybe I'd found someone worthy of my time.

"How will he know where I live?" she asked.

"Registration in the glove box." I twirled the keys in my finger and held my hand out for her to take. "Ready?"

"Duh," she said as she shook her head and grabbed my hand. All I could do was laugh. She wobbled on the high heels as she reached out and grabbed my shirt to steady herself. Sex didn't ooze off of her. There was a quirkiness that I couldn't put my finger on, but the sex kitten was there somewhere underneath the surface.

"Home?" I wanted to ask her "your place or mine," but I didn't think she was that type of girl. My life had become an endless parade of those girls, and there wasn't one thing that said "take me home and fuck me" about Suzy.

"Yes," she said.

I motioned to Tank, and he walked toward us before we made it to the door. "Her car is two miles south, man. Can you have it done by tomorrow?" I asked as I placed the keys in his hand.

"Sure, buddy. I'll have it at her place as early as possible."

"Thanks," I said as I shook his hand.

"Crap," she said.

"What?" I asked as we both looked at her.

"I have to cancel my tow," she said.

"Here." I handed her my phone. "Call them back before we hit the road."

"Thanks." She walked away on shaky legs; the drinks must have had a greater effect on her than I had thought. She leaned on a table with the phone in her ear and her ass sticking out. Her skirt rode up, giving me a view of the back of her legs. The muscles flexed and moved as she swayed back and forth. I couldn't imagine being tipsy and walking in those pointy fucking shoes. Women were insane.

"Make sure her car is running good before you bring it back, got it? No shit-ass job, Tank. I don't want her breaking down on the side of the road again."

"Got it. I don't do half-ass work, City. Got a thing for this girl?"

"I don't have a thing for her—my dick does, but she's just another woman. Stop busting my balls and do me this favor."

Tank laughed. "Sure. I gotcha. I'll take care of the car and you take care of her—get her home safely." He winked at me.

I rolled my eyes and spoke through clenched teeth. "I'm always a gentleman, Tank."

"Like fuck you are, man. Kind, at times, a gentleman, never," I heard him say as he walked away, twirling her keys in his fingers.

"Okay, all done. Let's bounce," she said as she touched my shoulder.

Did she just say *bounce*? Fuck me runnin'. I was in trouble with this girl. I knew it from the moment I saw her, but my cock didn't want to be the voice of reason. It never did—traitorous fucker. "Let's get you out of here and out of those shoes, Suzy." I wrapped my arms around her waist and helped her to the door.

CHAPTER
THREE
SUZY

DID I JUST SAY *BOUNCE*? Hello, the nineties want their phrase back. I'd never been the cool girl, the one that attracted the sexy guy, but hell, tonight I was in rare form. My legs felt like jelly as we walked out of the Neon Cowboy into the parking lot. I was thankful for the coolness of night and the fresh air. City made me nervous, and made every part of my body scream for his touch.

I couldn't take my eyes off his fine ass as he grabbed the helmet and turned toward me. "Can you do the helmet yourself or do you want me to do it for you?" he asked with his head cocked and a smile on his lips.

I just wanted him to touch me. "Can you do it, please? I'm worried I won't do it right."

"No problem, beautiful."

I closed my eyes. I could feel my body sway no matter how hard I tried to stand still. I felt amazing, like I was flying on a cloud. I opened my eyes to peek at him as he adjusted the straps. The world seemed to spin faster every time I closed my eyes. His fingers touched my skin and I swear electricity flowed through his hand. I wanted more—needed more.

"All right, sexy. All ready." Sexy? Oh God, I wanted this man. I watched as he climbed on the bike and held out his hand to me.

"Here goes nothing," I whispered before grabbing him and climbing on the bike.

"Hold on tight." He scooted back into my legs; my entire body felt like it was on fire as I wrapped my arms around his torso and locked my fingers together. His muscles moved underneath my fingertips and I wanted to rub them—no, I wanted to lick them. I squeezed my legs together, leaving no space between us as I leaned forward, resting my breasts against his back.

"Where am I going?" he asked as he started the bike and cranked the engine.

Please don't let me be wrong. "Your place." I held my breath as soon as I said the words and waited for him to laugh.

"You sure?" he asked in an even tone, but didn't turn around.

I'd never been so reckless about anything in my life. "Yes, unless you don't want to…" Did I read the signs wrong? *God, what an idiot I am.*

"Are you fucking crazy? I've been dying to crawl inside of you since I saw you on the road. Hold on, sugar, you're in for one hell of a ride."

I tried to control my breathing, thinking about his words, but it was useless. Excitement filled me, and thankfully the couple of drinks helped give me courage to go home with this sexy-ass man…or stupidity, but in this moment all I could think of is what the night held.

I held on for dear life as we cruised down the country roads toward his place. I didn't even know where he lived, and I wasn't paying attention to anything but his body and how it felt against me and under my hands. Images of him naked flooded my brain as my heart raced in my chest almost as fast as the bike moved. I got lost in time and didn't seem to worry as much as I concentrated only on his hardness.

I peeled my face from his back as the bike slowed, and I looked around as he backed up. A small white single-story house with green shutters lay before us. His home was on a large plot of land from what I could see. The street was far away from the structure, with a long driveway connecting the two.

"Change your mind, princess?" he asked.

"No, I meant every word." My voice shook and my entire body seemed to quake.

"Climb off first, use my shoulders."

I grabbed his shoulders and could feel the hardness. He was covered in muscle. I hadn't felt one squishy part the entire time I had my hands on him. I'd always describe myself as a tad fluffy. I wasn't lean and muscular, I did have curves and some softness to my body, but not City—he was ripped. I pushed myself off, using his shoulders as leverage, and the gravel driveway made my ability to stand still and straight almost impossible. The drinks didn't help either, and the killer shoes I had on didn't allow me to grip the ground any easier.

I watched as he climbed off the bike, his muscles rippling and shifting with each movement. My mouth watered at the thoughts of touching him and being his for a night. He moved toward me, and I swallowed hard. The closer he moved, the quicker my heart pounded in my chest, and I closed my eyes out of fear and anticipation. I puckered my lips and waited for him to kiss me, but nothing.

"I need to take your helmet off." *For the love of God, please help me disappear.* I'd forgotten about the helmet, and had to look like a complete idiot standing there with my eyes closed, waiting for a kiss, swaying in the wind, and wearing the damn thing. I'd been so wrapped up in the moment that all I could think about was him—kissing him, seeing him naked, touching him...just him. I smiled and could feel the heat creep into my cheeks. Butterflies filled my stomach, and I closed my eyes, hoping the embarrassing scene that just occurred would be quickly forgotten. I could hear him softly chuckling as he undid the straps and pulled it off my head. "Cute."

I opened my eyes and squinted at him. "Cute? What the heck is cute?"

"You." He tapped my nose, and I rolled my eyes.

"Freaking great."

"Yep, you're cute. Innocent, but fucking dying to be bad." He placed the helmet on the bike, turning his attention back at me. He touched my chin, pulling my face up to look him in the eyes. The rough skin of his thumb glided across my cheek, and I inhaled quickly. "I'm going to make you swear if it's the last thing I do. You're going to be screaming curse words tonight."

Everything in my body ignited at once—my heart pounded, my hands shook, and I stood there on trembling legs, feeling his nearness. The man stole my breath and made me lose all ability to communicate. He wrapped his solid arms around me, pulling my chest against his rock-hard torso, his lips hovering over mine. His hot breath brushed against my mouth as his fingers rested against my throat. My pulse raced under his fingertips, his touch making the rapid beating of my heart increase. Everything ceased to exist as he nipped my bottom lip, sending a jolt of pleasure throughout my body.

An overwhelming craving for more took hold, and I melted into him. A small moan escaped as his lips crushed against mine. Gripping his shoulders, I tipped my head back, giving him deeper access to my mouth. I wanted everything he had to give—all doubts vanished and were replaced by sheer need.

Lust consumed me as he ravaged my mouth and

commanded the kiss, deep, warm, and hard. The warmth of his fingers on the back of my neck sent goose bumps across my flesh. Wanting his heat, needing more contact, I lifted the back of his shirt and swept my fingers across his silky skin. There was a cavern near his spine, the outer edges rimmed in hard muscle that flexed underneath my touch. I brushed the edge of his pants with my fingers, sweeping them inside, grazing his skin with my fingernails. His hold on my neck tightened, and he groaned in my mouth. We fed each other air, leaving no room or moment to absorb anything else but each other.

I wanted all this man had to give. I wanted his promise of making me scream words that I didn't use. Bending down and grabbing my ass, he scooped me into his arms, never breaking the contact with my mouth. My stomach flipped like on a rollercoaster, the movement and excitement taking over my senses. The anticipation bubbled inside me as he carried me toward his house, and eventually his bedroom.

I wrapped my legs around his waist, hooking my ankles together, and felt his hardness against my core. With each step it rubbed against my clit, the friction driving me close to the brink of orgasm, until he raised my body to his abdomen. The key scraping against the lock sent a thrill through me—*I'm doing this... really doing this.* Running my fingers through his hair, I bit his lip before opening my eyes.

"Suzy has claws?" he asked against my lips, his breath warm as it caressed my face. I squeezed my eyes shut, hoping that we wouldn't hold a conversation at this moment. I didn't want to talk or chicken out. City was the most gorgeous man I had ever kissed, let alone slept with. "Want it rough, beautiful, or soft and slow?" he asked with a hard squeeze of my ass, kicking the door closed.

I sucked in a breath, not sure how to respond. No one had ever asked me what I wanted before this moment. "Um," I mumbled into his neck.

Peeling me off his chest, he looked me in the eyes. "No one ever ask you what you wanted before?"

What the fuck? Could he read my mind? "No." I looked down, trying to avoid his gaze. I felt too transparent, and I couldn't stand the thought of being figured out.

He whispered in my ear as he ground his hardness against me: "Tell me what you want and it's yours."

I bit my lip and stared at him. There was no smile or smirk on his face. City looked like a man possessed, and I had no doubts he'd deliver on his offer. I didn't know what I wanted, but I knew I wanted him any way he'd give it to me. What was his idea of rough? Fuck. "Can I have both?"

His eyes sparkled as his smile reached his baby blues. Anxiety filled my body at the thought of him naked and inside me. My breathing became labored with the knowledge that we were inching closer to our final destination. The lights were off as he carried me through the house. He nipped at my neck as I tried to take in my surroundings. His footsteps and our breathing were the only sound as he carried me.

Light filled the room and momentarily blinded me. As my eyes adjusted, I looked around the bedroom before he placed me gently on the bed. The large room had white walls; a large, framed Harley poster hung above the dresser and was the only visible decoration in the room. Dangling my feet over the bed, I noticed that the only color in the room was from the black comforter and the rich auburn wood flooring. City lifted his shirt as he watched me look around, but didn't say a word as he approached. I swallowed hard as I took in his magnificent, tanned torso.

I was speechless, and for me that's a rarity. The six-pack he sported made my mouth water, and my fingers itched to touch it. As he approached, I could clearly see the intricate art on his chest and arms. A black dragon filled his right ribcage, and black tribal designs decorated his right shoulder, looking richer against his dark skin. I never cared much for tattoos, but on him they fit and were freaking amazing.

A twinkle caught my eye, and I leaned forward to get a better view of his chest. There were barbells running through each of his nipples, and I was shell-shocked. Tattoos had become part of the social norm, but piercings still were a bit of a taboo in my mind. Not taboo in that I found them revolting, just the opposite. I wanted to play with them like a new toy at Christmas.

"Still a yes, princess?" he asked as he stood between my legs.

"Yes." My voice was a little stronger now, my resolve more certain than it had been when I'd squeaked out the words before we pulled out of the Neon Cowboy.

He leaned over me, pushing me into the mattress. My face was buried in his chest as he reached toward the nightstand, and I couldn't help myself—I licked the metal around his nipple. As he leaned into my tongue, the sound of his groan filled the room, and the sound of plastic alerted me he'd grabbed a condom. There was no turning back now; I'd be his for the night—at least he was prepared.

"Like what you see?" he asked, his lips twitching at the corners.

He knew he looked good. I was sure he'd never had a moment where he doubted his hotness or sexual prowess.

"Your artwork is amazing and the piercings are just— wow." I didn't know what else to say. I loved everything that I saw and couldn't wait to see the rest.

Hovering over my body, he stared into my eyes and lingered just out of reach of my lips. Placing my hands on his chest, I felt the solidity of his body before digging my fingernails into his flesh. His fingers touched my stomach, and I knew what I wanted. I didn't want slow, but fast and hard…all night long.

The initial softness of his kiss caught me off guard. I expected it to be demanding from the start, but his lips explored mine, testing my resolve to stay the course. He kissed perfectly. A hint of tongue swiped against my bottom lip, looking for entrance, and I willingly granted him access. Our tongues tangled together as his hand explored my body. I wanted him—I craved his touch. I moaned as his hand rubbed against the lacy fabric of my bra. I writhed under his fingers as they skillfully worked my nipple, pulling and twisting.

He broke the kiss, and I felt like I could breathe again. "Sit up," he commanded.

I didn't hesitate. I pushed myself up as he backed away and studied me. His expression made me nervous—but it wasn't critical—as he soaked me in. His lips turned up as his eyes roamed my body, and I could tell that he only had one thing on his mind. He leaned forward, grabbed the bottom of my shirt, and started to lift. "Arms, babe," he said as I sat up in front of him.

I moved quickly as his fingers inched closer to my bra. I couldn't do anything but stare at the cocky grin on his face while he undressed me. He didn't look like any other man I'd ever been with. Having him undress me was the single most erotic moment of my life. His smell surrounded me, a mixture of earth, sweat, and musk. When I thought my heart couldn't beat any faster, his fingertips caressed my collarbone, and it skipped a beat before thundering in an erratic rhythm. I wanted to get down on my knees and pray that I lived through this experience.

"Breathe," he said.

I inhaled quickly, not realizing I'd been holding my breath. I wanted to cover my body, but his lopsided grin made me do the opposite.

He wrapped his hand around my neck and kissed me. My toes curled from the passion in his kiss. I felt a hunger, like I was about to be devoured by him. Pressing my body into his, I became his meal, willingly offering myself.

Our hands and mouths became entwined, and the sound of our hard breath and lips tugging and pulling filled the air. I opened my eyes to look at him, and became entranced by his mouth. I watched as he kissed me, and took in all of his features. His long brown lashes lay against his protruding cheekbones, and were brought out by full, dark eyebrows. A shadow had developed on his jaw line and joined with his sideburns, and I couldn't keep my finger away any longer.

The facial hair tickled my skin as I ran my finger down the roughness to the edge of his mouth. I could feel our lips move under the pads of my fingers. Our hands explored each other feverishly, learning the curves and spots that made one another twitch and shake. There was a delicious torture to the touching and kissing.

My clit ached as his hand inched up my thigh and brushed against my underwear. I gasped in his mouth as his fingers dug into the material and ripped it from my skin. I didn't care that they were my best underwear that I saved for special occasions; I wanted him inside me. He cupped my sex, applying pressure as I moaned and my head fell back. I didn't have the ability to hold it up as he began running his fingers through my wetness.

"Oh God," I said, as my eyes rolled back and my lids fluttered closed.

Warmth surrounded my nipple as his mouth closed around it, and he sucked in a pulsating rhythm. I dug my nails into his skin, needing something to hold. I cried out as his teeth captured the throbbing tip and bit down. Slowly his finger prodded my entrance before slipping inside at an agonizing pace. I needed to be filled and wanted the friction of his palm to relieve the ache between my legs.

I ground my hips into his palm, begging for more, as he pulled his fingers out and thrust them back in. I wanted to palm his cock through his jeans, but his body was too long and his crotch too far away. I grabbed his hair, fisting it in my hand, and he moaned, causing the vibration against my nipple to push me to the edge. His warm, rough palm stroked my clit as he worked his fingers in and out, massaging my G-spot. Pants and moans fell from my lips as he worked my body like a well-choreographed dance number.

I couldn't stop my body from twitching as my release crashed over me unexpectedly. I screamed his name as the ripples of pleasure cascaded throughout me. I gulped for air, trying to catch my breath as my aftershocks squeezed his finger and tried to suck him deeper.

"Jesus," I muttered, wiping a bit of drool from the corner of my lips. I'd never had an orgasm so intense. No one had ever found my G-spot, let alone touched it with such skill. I lay panting with my skirt on as he climbed off the bed and began unbuckling his belt.

"You ain't seen nothing yet, sugar." His deep laugh filled the room.

"Oh, um." My stomach flipped. I needed to move. "No, let me," I said. He moved his hands away from the metal and closer to the bed. Crawling catlike, I positioned myself right in front of him and tucked my feet underneath my ass. I unbuckled his belt slowly, pulling it out of the loops in a teasing motion. Movement caused my eyes to look downward; straining against the restrictive denim I could see a long, thick bulge.

"Like what ya see?"

Fuck. "Uh huh," I said, swallowing roughly. I touched his stomach and slowly slid my fingers down his skin before grabbing for the button. "You sure about this?" I thought I'd turn the tables a bit. He kept asking me if I was sure, but hell, I knew what I wanted, and it was him.

"Mm hmm," he said with a smile on his face and a twinkle in his eye as he rested his hands on his sides.

He grinned like he knew something I didn't. A small patch of hair lined the top of his jeans—happy trail indeed. I unbuttoned his jeans and slowly unzipped them with fingers more steady than I thought possible. The clicking of the zipper passing by each tooth as I took my time and made my heart race. I savored the moment, freeing his hard-on. I leaned forward and pressed my lips to the soft, dark hair that had been trapped underneath the fabric. His body shook at the contact and his fingers tangled in my hair. The denim of his jeans was rough against my palm as I slid up his massive thigh to palm him. A small bump at the tip gave me pause before I looped my fingertips in the sides, licking a path from his belly button to the zipper.

I tugged the material down his skin as I kept my mouth attached to his abdomen. I backed away as the material slid down and his shaft sprang free. My heart stopped and I sucked in a breath, my eyes growing wide.

Jesus. "What the…" What the fuck? I stared in wonderment. Not only was the man blessed with a large member, but also he added to it, decorated it. A large metal loop with a ball hung from the tip. I was eye to eye with it, and couldn't imagine why any man would do that to his body.

"You can touch it." He laughed. "It won't hurt you," he said, moving his abdomen in my direction.

"I've never seen anything like it." I reached out and ran my finger across the shiny metal jutting out. "Will I feel it?" I felt like a complete idiot, but I'd never seen one in person, let alone had sex with someone that had extra parts.

"It will give you a different sensation at first, closest to your opening…some pressure, maybe."

I didn't want to touch it with my finger, so I stuck out my tongue and licked around the cool, sleek hardware. His hips jerked and his shaft lurched from the contact. I reached out and fisted his shaft in my hands, being mindful of the metal protruding from it as I worked it with my hands and mouth in unison. He was rock hard.

"Fuck," he moaned as I slid it out of my mouth and flicked the piercing with my tongue.

I stopped and looked at him, but didn't let go. "Did I hurt you?" His head was tipped back, with his arm outstretched, still with a handful of hair in his grasp.

"Sugar, you can't hurt me. Take all of me."

I smiled at him, and the name "sugar" made me feel all gooey inside. No one had been so forward with me, and it made wetness pool against the fabric of my skirt. I inched closer, stroking him, and held him firm in my grasp. His musky scent was intoxicating.

I knew I couldn't fit the entire thing, but I'd try like hell. I moved forward, allowing more to slide across my tongue, causing his body to tremble and his breathing to turn hard and fast.

"Fuck, baby. That's the spot. Just like that." He fisted my hair roughly, causing my eyes to water.

I moaned against his cock, and he released a shaky breath. I tried to draw him in a little deeper with each stroke of my lips against his warm, smooth skin. I stopped when the metal hit my teeth, flicking it, as his hips shook in my grasp. His hand moved in my hair, pulling and pushing me, controlling the speed as I gagged each time the head hit the back of my throat. I opened my eyes and looked up at him. His mouth was opened slightly, his chest heaved from heavy breath, and goose bumps covered his flesh. Saltiness caressed my tongue as I worked the tip with precision.

"I want to taste you." His words caused warmth to pool between my legs and my core to spasm.

"But I'm not done," I said, looking at him, confused, my hands stroking his shaft. "Don't you want me to finish?" My brows knitted together as I looked at him. He grinned and unclenched his fist from my hair.

"We aren't done. I want to bury my face between your legs and make you scream again."

Well shit, who could say no to that?

"Did I do something wrong?" I shook my head as I looked down at my knees.

His hand gripped my chin, tipping it back, and stared into my eyes. "Suzy, you didn't do anything wrong. Fuck, it was perfect. I want to lick, suck, and then fuck ya, sugar." The words left me breathy and wanton. I felt beautiful and wanted.

He guided my face to his and crushed his lips against mine, sucking my tongue in his mouth as he pulled the skirt down my hips. "Tell me you want me to taste you," he said against my lips.

I swallowed hard; words, again, escaped me.

"Say it, Suzy." With one hand filled with my hair and the other wrapped around my back, he held me in place and left me with nowhere to go. Talking wasn't something that I was used to during sex, and he definitely brought me beyond my comfort zone. "I'm waiting." He bit my lip and brought me back to the moment.

"Taste me," I said, unable to look anywhere but into his dark eyes.

His grip tightened, pulling my head back as he released his hold on my back and began to lay my body back. I felt like a Raggedy Ann doll; I was putty in his hands. My heart hammered in my chest with anticipation as I waited for his mouth to kiss my flesh. He grabbed my legs underneath my knees and pulled my body to the end of the bed as he knelt on the floor. Gripping the sheets, needing something to hold, I tipped my head back and closed my eyes. Heat flooded my cheeks with the thought of him staring at my pussy. I lifted my head and looked at him as he smiled and ran his hands along my thighs, licking his lips, and absorbed the view in front of him. Not in one spot, but all of me; his eyes roamed over my body before his head leaned forward, and I closed my eyes, unable to look. My body convulsed as his lips touched the delicate skin just to the right of my sex, enough to cause my body to crave more. Suckling the spot where my legs met my core, my body began to tremble. His hands slid down my legs, my entire body was on fire, and I ached for more. I needed more, but this felt more like a tease. He gripped my ankles and lifted my legs, placing each one on his shoulders.

His finger ran through my wetness as his tongue flicked my throbbing clit. My body shot up; I was unable to control the movement caused by the pleasure that shot through my body. His mouth clamped down as his finger slid inside me. His hands were large, but I wanted more of him as my core sucked his fingers inside. He drew me into his mouth and laid his tongue against my flesh, moving it around in circles. My breathing sounded shaky and I tried not to cry out in ecstasy, as I was so close to the tipping point.

Adding a second finger made me feel stretched to the limit, almost to the point of pain. How in the hell would I handle all he had to offer? Swirling his tongue around my clit, his fingers caressing my aching flesh, he slid his hand under my ass, his fingers digging into my skin, as he tilted my hips. My eyes rolled back as his fingers and tongue made all coherent thought disappear. I was so lost in the moment that I didn't notice his mouth leave my body as his fingers stopped.

"Do you want me?" he growled against my clit, and my eyes opened and became drawn to his stare.

I trembled and tried to steady my breath. "Yes."

"Yes, what? What do you want?" he asked, his eyes not moving from mine, his entire body still.

"Have sex with me." I knew what he wanted me to say— he wanted me to use the F word, and I hadn't, couldn't.

"Suzy." He drew out my name and flicked his tongue against me. "You know what I want to hear. Tell me exactly what you want." He withdrew his fingers and tongue, leaving me panting for more.

I closed my eyes and exhaled, needing a moment to gather my thoughts. They were just words, and ones I said every day but never during sex. Drawing in a shaky breath, I said, "I want you. Fuck me, City."

CHAPTER
FOUR
CITY

THERE'S something about corrupting someone in the purest form. She didn't swear, or didn't like to, but the sound of it made my cock grow hard. She looked fucking beautiful laid out across my bed with her flowing blonde hair and her blue eyes sparkling in the vibrant lighting of the room. She wasn't muscular from working out, or too thin, like a crack addict, from being strung out. Her body could best be described as a classic hourglass—large breasts and curvy hips joined by a tiny waist. She looked almost angelic, her white skin against the black comforter.

I reached under her torso, cupping the crook of her arms, and tossed her up the bed. "Wow." She laughed as she bounced against the mattress. "You just moved me like I weighed nothing."

"You're like a feather," I said, crawling up her body and reaching for the condom on my nightstand.

She giggled, her eyes growing wide as I tore the condom wrapper open between my teeth. There was something so fucking innocent about her, and I wanted to crawl inside of her goodness and never leave.

I nested between her legs, resting one arm under her body,

trying not to crush her under my weight. "Laugh while you can, sweet girl," I murmured against her lips. "I'm going to make you scream all those dirty words you're too scared to say."

Her eyes were like saucers as I slid the condom over my piercing and down my shaft. Her pussy glistened as I nudged her legs farther apart with my knees. I wanted to tear her up, own her body, and make her mine for the night. I didn't wait for a reply before placing my lips over hers, consuming her, and coaxing her tongue into my mouth. I could spend hours kissing her, exploring every crevice, and be happy, but my balls were heavy and throbbed, needing the release. Capturing her nipple with my fingers, I pinched it lightly and rolled it between the tips. She moaned in my mouth, and my dick jumped to attention, aching to be inside her.

My mouth never left hers as I captured all of the sounds that escaped; those were mine and only mine to devour. Her body writhed under my relentless pursuit of her nipple and the overwhelming onslaught of my fingers against her delicate flesh. I wanted to make her come like this, but I knew there would be time for that later.

Her throat was soft underneath my tongue, and I inhaled the sweet smell of her perfume, stopping near her collarbone before sinking my teeth into her flesh. Her body moved, her hips rose off the bed, and her pussy nudged my cock—an open invitation.

"What do you want?" I said, as I bit down on the flesh of her shoulder.

"You."

"What part of me?" I didn't want to make this easy on her. I got a secret thrill out of watching her squirm with each question or prompt.

"Your penis."

Jesus…seriously? Normally I'd think it was all an act, but this girl was as good as they came, and I'd have my work cut out for me. I liked the idea of a conquest, someone that I could corrupt and make my own.

"The other word. I won't fuck you until you do." I could have blue balls by then, but eventually she'd say it. I wouldn't give in until she did.

I captured her nipple between my teeth, clamping down on the tip as I flicked it with my tongue.

"City, please," she said as she grabbed my shoulder almost breaking the skin with her nails.

I held her nipple with my teeth. "Say it."

"I can't." She pushed her pussy against me. "Just do it." I gave it right back as I ground my cock against her wetness. "Oh, God," she moaned.

"He ain't gonna help you now. Say the word, and it's yours." I sucked the tip harder.

"I want your c…"

"Say it and I'll slide it in that hot, wet pussy and make you scream. That shit I can guarantee." I slid my stiff shaft against her, touching her clit with each stroke. "Say it."

"Cock," she exhaled. "I want your cock."

"That wasn't so bad, was it?" I asked as I smiled against her skin. I knew she was uncomfortable, but I didn't give a fuck. She seemed like the type of girl that lived in a very controlled world; set limits for herself and never crossed them. I'd help her go beyond her imaginary lines.

I kissed her deeply and nudged her opening with the tip of my cock as she wrapped her legs around my back, almost pushing me inside of her. She knew what she wanted. She forced me inside of her with a moan and a whimper.

Her body felt warm and slick, and a shiver ran down my spine as I entered her. I wanted to thrust inside, wanted to be balls deep, but also wanted to be in control of the pace. I licked her lips and stared into her eyes as I pushed in slowly, until I couldn't go any further. I was still for a moment and just relished the feeling of being in her—exactly where I'd wanted to be since the moment I saw her.

She looked beautiful lying on my pillow with her blonde hair framing her face like a golden crown. Her blue eyes shimmered in the light and her cheeks were tinged pink from the excitement, could have been lust. I needed to move. I wanted to make her scream. I pulled out of her slowly as her nails dug into my shoulder, and thrust my dick inside of her, unable to stop myself.

She mewled and moaned with each stroke, as I picked up the pace, unable to take it slow. I wanted to watch her, see her face, as I fucked her. I leaned back and pulled her legs from my back and placed her feet against my shoulders. I smiled at her and licked my thumb.

"Want more?" I said as I pulled out of her.

"Yes." Her voice was breathy and whisper quiet.

I placed my thumb against her swollen clit and began to move it in small circles. "Oh, God," she moaned as her pussy convulsed around my shaft.

"Do you wanna come?" I asked, pulling out again, just leaving the tip inside.

Licking her lips, she looked at me with glassy eyes as she panted, "Yes."

"Do you want me to fuck you?" I asked as I denied her the very thing she wanted most—my cock and her orgasm.

"Please," she whispered.

"Say it." My lips twitched as I tried to stop the smile and laughter that wanted to escape as her face turned pink. "It's a simple phrase. You want my cock? Tell me what you want me to do with it."

She opened her eyes and exhaled before quickly saying, "Fuck me."

"Gladly." I thrust inside of her and moved my thumb rhythmically against her swollen clit as her body twitched and her head pushed deeper into the pillow. I wrapped my free hand around her thigh, gripping it as I assaulted her.

"Your pussy feels so fucking good," I moaned. I didn't go easy on her—she wasn't breakable. I increased the pace as her breathing became more jagged and her body began to glisten in the light. I could feel her body milking me, wanting more, and in that moment I stopped.

"Hey," she yelled, and her eyes opened, showing more passion and hatred than I thought possible. "I was so close."

I didn't speak, but pulled her legs tighter against my torso. Her feet were near my face and her legs were flush against me. I gripped her legs, allowing me to hold her and stop her from moving. I pounded into her, battering her body. I watched in awe as her tits bounced from the force of my body slamming into her.

She began to yell, "Oh, God."

"That's right, sugar. Let go. Feel all of me. I want you so fucking bad."

I used every muscle in my body to fuck her. I wanted her to know I possessed her and owned her orgasm in this moment. Her body began to tremble as her leg muscles tightened and flexed against me. I gripped her legs tighter, not wanting her to move.

"Fuck," spilled from her lips, and I couldn't control myself any longer. I didn't have to coax her into saying the word, but my cock had pushed her over the edge.

"You're so fucking tight," I said as I watched her body on the edge of orgasm—covered in sweat, skin flushed, and mouth open, lost in sensation.

She reached up and touched her breast, pushing herself over the edge as I thrust into her harder than I had before. "Oh God. Oh God, don't fucking stop," she wailed.

Her naked body before me, her dirty mouth, and watching her touch herself caused my balls to tighten, and the orgasm ripped through me. I shook and moaned as I pounded into her, her insides gripping me. Every part of my body tingled, and small aftershocks shook me to my very core.

I needed to catch my breath. The only sounds that filled the room were our gasps for air and the snap of the condom. "Fucking hell. That was amazing," I said as I kissed her ankle, running my hands up her legs.

"I've never..." she said.

"Never what?"

CHAPTER
FIVE
SUZY

"NEVER EXPERIENCED ANYTHING LIKE THAT," I said. How to explain it without sounding pathetic? Damn, nothing in my life had compared to having sex with him. I'd had a few one-night stands in college, but those boys didn't exactly know what they were doing.

City was rough and controlling, and I loved it. I stared at his beautiful body as he knelt before me, his skin glistening with sweat, his muscles moving in unison as he tried to catch his breath. I wanted to take a picture and always remember how he looked—sweaty and sexy as hell.

"That's nothing compared to what I could do to you," he said in a husky tone as he wiped the sweat from his brow. I wanted to lick the sweat off his body. I wanted to do things with him that I normally didn't even think about doing to anyone in my life. He was different.

"Hell," I said, unable to think of anything else. He could do better? Was that even possible?

"Maybe you'll let me show you sometime." A smile crept across his face, but it wasn't a sweet smile. This guy definitely had tricks up his sleeves. My heart raced at the thought of feeling him inside me again.

"You want to see me again?" I asked, unable to believe his words. We were polar opposites, and I didn't know why he'd want to see me again.

"Why wouldn't I?" His eyebrows turned down as his nose wrinkled.

I covered my eyes, feeling like an asshole. "I dunno. I thought this was just a one-night thing."

"I won't lie, I thought it would be just a one-night 'thing.' I wanted you from the moment I blew by you on the road." He moved next to me, wrapping his arm around my body. "You're not like any of my friends or the women I know."

"Well, I've met some of the people you hang out with." I frowned, thinking about some of the guys he'd surrounded himself with. Most of them seemed shady as heck. "They look more like my class full of underachievers or someone I'd see on *America's Most Wanted*. Not my type."

"They look that bad?" he said in my ear. His low tone made my exhausted body buzz again.

"They're kinda scary, City. They remind me of criminals," I whispered.

He laughed. "Funny shit, sugar. They look scarier than they are." He nuzzled into my shoulder, burying his face in my hair. "I don't hang out with all those guys. Many of them are customers—some of them are my best clients. I stop there on the way home sometimes for a drink. Some of them are friendly and, well, some you've seen are assholes."

"You can say that again."

His body shook and I felt the vibration from his silent laughter. "I spend more time with my family than with those douchebags at the bar." He brushed the hair off my cheek and ran his fingers down my throat before he rested his palm on my chest. I felt exposed. "Are you cold?" he asked as I shivered.

"A bit," I lied. I wanted to cover my body.

"Did you want to leave?" He yawned.

"Um, I'm sure you're tired. I can stay if you want. It's up to you." I didn't want to leave this hot, hunky man and go home to my empty bed. *Don't kick me out like a piece of trash.*

He grabbed the blankets and covered our bodies. Yes! Inside I was doing cartwheels and screaming with excitement. He pulled me against his side and wrapped me in his arms. His body felt hard and comfortable. I rested my forehead against his jaw and could hear his heart beating in his chest. The sheets were the softest cotton I had ever felt—not really what I had expected. I thought he'd be more of a flannel guy, or those scratchy sheets you find in hotels.

"Comfortable?" he asked with a long, content exhale.

"Very." I hadn't slept in the arms of a man in years. Usually I didn't fit just right, or they were so bony that my head hurt resting against their body, but City was built to sleep on. He was built for anything that involved two bodies.

I didn't quite know where to rest my hand. Did I put it on his chest or leave it at my side? Sophia wasn't going to believe this story when I tell her. She knew me as the good girl that lived in my controlled environment, unable or unwilling to move, but City was like a tsunami that started slowly and built into a giant wrecking ball of sin.

"Hand, babe."

"What?" I mumbled against his chest.

"Gimme your hand."

I moved my hand from my thigh and held it out to him, trying not to touch his skin. Grasping it, he placed my palm on his rock-hard chest, and put his hand on top. "Perfect," he said.

I didn't have any grand illusions, and I wasn't delusional. I knew I'd only have this night with City. We weren't meant to be—he wasn't what I was looking for. He wasn't the type of guy that was part of my master plan. I'd just lie here and enjoy the night in his arms.

I listened as his breathing slowed and changed. His hand

twitched against mine as he squeezed my fingers and drifted into a deeper sleep. I felt exhausted, but I almost didn't want to sleep. I didn't want to miss a minute of staring at his body.

Thoughts flooded my mind while I listened to his deep breaths. I wanted to see him again, but would it be a waste of time? Did I want to go down a dead-end street and become attached to him? I knew I could fall for him. Even though I wanted to find someone to spend my life with and have that great happily ever after, I didn't open my heart to just anyone. Heartache was something I avoided at all costs. There wasn't a need to risk my heart if the certain outcome would be disastrous. The war of words continued in my head for a few minutes, until I finally decided to enjoy the moment and worry about the rest tomorrow.

***

The sound of metal clinking woke me, and I sat up in a panic. I thought someone had broken in while I slept. Looking around the room, I realized I wasn't in my bedroom. Last night hadn't been a dream. Reaching over, I felt the sheet where he had lain, and it was cold to the touch. Sunlight streamed through the sheer white drapes and bounced off the walls, amplifying the light. The room was tidy, except for our clothing from last night strewn about the floor.

My body ached as I stretched, trying to relieve the pain from my muscles being over used the night before. I needed something to wear and had to find a bathroom. I tiptoed out of bed and wrapped the sheet around my body to keep the cold at bay. A flannel shirt hung on the back of his door, and I grabbed it and held it up to my face, burying it in the soft material. The hint of cologne and the muskiness of his skin made my pussy clench. I dropped the sheet, wrapped the flannel around my body, and rubbed my cheek against the wrist cuff. I felt surrounded by City.

Walking to the door that I thought was the bathroom, I opened it and found his closet. Fuck. It was filled with t-shirts, jeans, and hoodies. I studied the contents, running my hand over the soft materials as they hung, before I closed the door. There were only two doors in his room, and neither of them led to a bathroom.

My reflection in the mirror hanging on the back of the door made me cringe. My blonde hair was in tangles and looked a mess, and my eyes looked tired from the night in his bed. A messy ponytail helped to tame my mane, making me feel presentable. Good enough. Opening the door, I peered into the hallway before tiptoeing into the hall. A loud, long creak filled the air as I took my first step.

"You up?" he yelled from the kitchen.

"Yes," I said, trying not to sound annoyed. "Be right there."

"I'm fixing breakfast. Take your time." I could hear dishes, cups, and all kinds of movement in the kitchen. I didn't think I'd ever had anyone besides my mom, Sophia, and Kayden make me breakfast. The smell of bacon and something sweet drifted down the hall and made my stomach grumble.

An old claw-foot bathtub and white pedestal sink filled the white and black room. He didn't seem too fond of color, which I found odd, since he described himself as an artist. Everything was clean and sparkling. I could tell that he took pride in his home. I searched his bathroom, looking for an extra toothbrush, but tried not to make noise. A knock sounded at the door and I jumped, knocking over some bottles under the sink and smacking my head against something hard. "Shit," I said as I rubbed my head.

"You okay? Did you need something?"

"I'm fine." So not fine. He caught me snooping and probably heard the bang from my head. "I wanted a toothbrush, do you have a spare?" I put my head in my hand, feeling like a fool but thankful that he didn't witness the event.

"There's an extra one in the medicine cabinet. Help yourself." I could hear his footsteps quiet as he walked away.

My face was still red as I left the bathroom and walked into the kitchen, trying to avoid City's eyes.

"Eggs, pancakes, and bacon okay?"

He looked amazing. He wore a pair of black track pants and a smile.

My stomach rumbled over seeing all the food he had prepared. "Did you cook for an army?" I asked.

"Didn't know what you liked, so I made a little bit of everything." He put the spatula on the counter and walked toward me. He was so damn hot. I licked my lips and closed my eyes.

I could feel his hot breath on my lips, and I smelled his scent. "I'm gonna fuck you, right here, right now. Yes or no?"

OMG, OMG, OMG, yes, yes, yes!

I swallowed hard and nodded before I leaned forward.

"Words, Suzy. Now the answer needs to be 'yes, fuck me, City' or 'no, I don't want to.'"

How would I ever say no to this man? I thought about the possibility of never seeing him again, and I wanted one last shot at him.

"Yes, fuck me, City," I whispered against his lips.

His mouth crushed mine and I could taste the coffee and sugar on his tongue. I could only hear our breath as the world around us fell away. His hands trailed up my thighs and cupped my ass. Fuck, this man was pure sin, and I wanted to be his minion.

He broke the kiss and looked in my eyes. I could hear his breathing, fast and hard. "Hands on the counter," he said with a commanding tone. *Yes, sir. Gladly.*

I turned my back to him and placed my palms on the edge. He pushed down on my back and lifted my hips. I rested my head on the cold tile and waited. Looking behind me, I watched as he pulled down his pants before palming his shaft. I heard a crinkling noise coming from his pocket. He'd planned this—he had a condom ready to go. *Lord, help me with this man.* Could I resist him?

I started to stand up when I heard, "Back down, sugar." I closed my eyes and followed his command. I felt him stroke my opening, and I sighed. When did I turn into a big ole pile of mush with a guy? He slid inside of me easily; I was slick and ready for him.

He grabbed my hips, holding me tightly as his hardness worked like a machine inside of me. I gripped the counter and my fingers began to tingle from my death grip. He felt amazing, caressing my insides with the metal piercing. My muscles ached as I stood on my tiptoes. He pounded into me, the sound of our skin slapping filling the air, his grunts ringing in my ears. His grip intensified and became almost painful.

"Fuck, your pussy is so damn tight," he growled.

"I love your cock," I moaned. That just slipped out—like it was something I said every day.

"I love being buried in your sweet pussy, sugar."

All the dirty words and the feeling of him stroking my depths pushed me over the edge. My body began to shake, and I moaned, "City."

I heard a loud crack and my ass began to sting. Did he just slap my ass? The pain began to radiate throughout my body and made my orgasm grow and build. My grip began to slip as my insides clenched against his length. *Crack.* Fucking hell.

"Fuck," he yelled as his stroke became more intense and erratic. I could feel him grow harder inside me as he slammed me against the counter. He rested his head against my back as we both stood there immobile for a moment.

"You got me all kinds of crazy, Suzy," he said, breathing heavy.

"Makes two of us." I was thankful the tile was cold. My body was covered in moisture and my skin was hot from the pounding I had just taken. He pulled out, and I instantly felt the loss of him. I waited for my feet to uncramp before trying to stagger to a chair. He removed the condom with a quick snap and tossed it in the trash. I swayed to my seat, thankful that it was only a few steps away. He adjusted himself inside his pants and walked to the stove with a devilish grin on his face.

"Pancake?" His blue eyes stared into mine as he held the pan up, asking permission to slip it on my plate.

I forgot how hungry I'd felt when I walked in. How did the man just fuck me like a maniac and now he was cooking like Guy Fieri?

"Yes. I never met a meal I didn't like." I silently prayed to God the jitters that filled my stomach would subside long enough to eat the giant meal he'd prepared.

"I love hearing shit like that. My sister is so fucking picky it makes me batshit crazy."

I buttered my pancake and watched him out of the corner of my eye as he grabbed the pan of eggs off the stove. An awkward silence filled the room as I looked at my plate. He'd just had his cock in me as the food sat on the stove, and now what? I wanted to keep the conversation flowing, and figured I'd follow his lead.

"Just one sister?" I asked.

"Just the one, but I have three brothers too. Eggs?"

"Everything," I said, moving my pancake to make room for the eggs and bacon. "Five kids, wow, your mother must be an amazing woman."

"Yeah, I think we caused most of the gray hair on her head, which she now dyes to keep her youthful appearance. We aren't the traditional Italian family. You have any brothers or sisters?" he asked, plopping the eggs on his plate and then putting the pan back on the stove.

"A sister, she doesn't live here. She's still up north, where we grew up." I poured the syrup on my single golden pancake before cutting a chunk.

I envied City. He had a big family and they had a bond that I'd never had with mine. He had something I always wanted.

"Ah, I can't imagine only having one. We're kinda a gang. We do everything together." He stuffed the eggs in his mouth and grabbed a piece of bacon. "You've missed out."

I loved that it seemed easy between us; we were comfortable, and he made me feel that way. "I guess so, but I have some friends that I'm closer to than any of my family." I placed the forkful of buttery goodness in my mouth and let it sit on my tongue a minute before I chewed it. "My mom's kinda a flake, and my dad works all the time, so I just have my friends."

"Damn, that fucking sucks. My family gets together every Sunday for dinner, and it's usually a bit loud."

"Every Sunday?" I saw my parents every week, but sometimes it was only for an hour, and dinners only happened on holidays.

I tried to go slow, not wanting to eat everything on my plate. I didn't want to look like a pig, but I was starving.

"Every Sunday. It's required, or my parents think something is wrong. Sometimes my grandparents come over and it turns into an all-day affair. Mom usually wakes up early to make the sauce and meatballs. We're required to be there at one for an early dinner."

It sounded nice. I'd never had anything like that in my life —never knew families did that kind of thing, besides in the movies.

"Hmm, that sounds like fun." I ate my breakfast and thought about all the family things I'd missed out in my life. My parents seemed too busy to deal with us at times, let alone have me over for dinner every Sunday. I knew they loved my sister and me, but we didn't have the close-knit family that City had described.

"It is, but I work with my brothers and sister and sometimes it gets to be too much. So, babe, do I get to take you on a proper date?"

"Oh, sorry," I said. "I'd love to go on a date with you. I mean, we already…" I moved my hand around, lost for the right word to describe what we did the night before.

"Fucked." He laughed. "I don't know if I will ever get over your good-girl thing you have going on."

"I'm not a good girl, City." I wasn't, and I knew it. Good girls didn't think about the things I did. They didn't want the things I wanted, and they sure as hell didn't go home with strangers. "What we did last night wouldn't have happened if I was a good girl." I smiled at him.

"You're a woman, Suzy. Sex doesn't make you a bad girl; it makes you human. That shit was explosive last night, and this morning I needed to be in you again. I wouldn't change a goddamn thing." He must have sensed I was uncomfortable with the entire conversation. "I don't think you're bad. If someone does, then fuck them. I don't give a shit what anyone thinks about me."

"I know. It's not always so easy." I wanted to change the subject. "Do you want me to call my friend to pick me up?" I didn't want to dissect my qualities at the moment.

"I'll take you home after you're done, okay?"

"Thank you. I have a ton of things to do today." I had to grade papers—it was the end of the grading period, and grades were due on Monday morning. I had to make lesson plans and pay the bills before the weekend ended. My work never ended, not even on the weekends. Teachers don't walk out the door on Friday and leave it all behind—we work on the weekends and walk through the door on Monday prepared to teach the budding students not always so interested in learning. I sighed, thinking about all the work I had to do, but I was the only one that could get it done.

"No problem. I have to get to work by noon, so no rush."

I wiped my mouth unable to consume another morsel. "Where do you tattoo?"

"Inked. Ever hear of it?"

"I drive by it every day on the way to work, I think." I remembered seeing the sign, but had never set foot inside. "Looks like a nice place."

"Ever been?"

"Oh, no. I meant from the street. Doesn't look like the other shops in the area. Yours is pretty. How long have you worked there?"

"I don't think I've ever heard it described that way. My sister does all the decorating. We own the shop and opened it about five years ago."

Well, maybe he wasn't the starving artist I thought he was.

"Why don't you stop by sometime? I'd love to pop your cherry." I started choking. "Ink, babe, I'd love to give you your first tattoo." He laughed.

I patted my chest and coughed. "Maybe someday I'll let you. My parents are just anti-tattoo, and I never found anything I'd want to look at for a lifetime. How'd you pick yours?"

"Each one signifies something in my life." He pointed to the city skyline on his arm. "This is a reminder of where my family comes from, Chicago. It's where I grew up, and I go back every summer to visit my friends. It's part of me in more ways than one." He laughed and rubbed the tattoo on his arm.

"And the fish?"

"Ah, the koi. Well, that one I had my brother, Anthony, do when we opened the shop. It's a symbol of determination and power to achieve goals. We always talked about opening our own shop, and we'd finally achieved it. Plus, I fucking love the color orange."

"Looking at your house, I'd think you loved white."

He picked up my plate and laughed. "This place is only

temporary. I don't see a point in splashing color on the walls. I'm surrounded by color all day at work. It's calming to come home to an empty canvas." Artists—complex creatures.

"I understand. My walls are actually white except for one blue wall in my bedroom. I'm not the typical bubblegum-pink girl."

He began to clean the kitchen and put the dishes in the dishwasher. His muscles rippled and flexed with each movement. My mouth watered as I remembered what it felt like for him to be above me and in me—I wanted more of him.

"I'll finish cleaning up. You go get ready to hit the road, okay?"

I could get used to being waited on. Mind-blowing sex? Check. Good cook? Check. Sexy as hell? Check. Manly, yet nice? Check. He had all the right qualities and kind of reminded me of Kayden. I didn't want Kayden, but I wanted someone that cared enough to take care of me.

"I'll just be a minute," I said as I stood from the table. "I don't want to take up any more of your time."

"Take all the time you want. I can't get fired if I'm late." He laughed as he kicked the dishwasher closed. "By the way, is Suzy your full name?"

I hated my full name. It sounded stuffy and old. "No."

"Spill."

"It's Suzette."

"Now that's sexy as fuck. *Suzette.*" It rolled off his tongue, and I felt the moisture from my core begin to pool. Fuck, he'd made me a total cock-loving whore, and I wanted to hear him scream my name.

"Right." Looking over at his beautiful skin and taut muscles, I drank him in—memorized the picture before I walked out the door, leaving him to finish and to get the hell out of here. He could definitely become a weak spot if I didn't put distance between us. That yin and yang bullshit didn't really work in real life.

CHAPTER SIX

CITY

I SHUT the bike off and waited for her to climb down. She tried to remove the helmet on her own and stood there looking as drop-dead fucking gorgeous as she did last night. She fumbled with the straps, trying to pull it off, but she frowned and her fingers began to move frantically. "Lemme get that for you," I said as I motioned for her to move closer.

"Sorry," she said, blowing a puff of air out.

"It's my pleasure, trust me." I winked and watched her cheeks pinken. I worked the straps apart slowly, trying to prolong the ending to our time together. I felt like she was going to give me the brush off. Her body language didn't match the last twelve hours. I needed to set another date with her and dig deeper into the woman she was instead of who she pretended to be.

"Thanks," she said, trying to look me in the eyes.

"There. So, about the real date. How about tonight?" I asked. I didn't see a point in wasting time. I wanted her in my bed again—or against the counter.

"Um, I guess tonight is good." She looked at me and then to her feet.

"Sugar, it's just a date. A real date—no strings attached." I grabbed her chin to look into her sky-blue eyes. "We kinda missed that part of getting to know each other before I took you. I'll pick you up at nine. Wear something warm."

"Okay, I'll be ready. Want me to drive?" She looked at my bike, wrinkling her nose, and then noticed her car. "Wait, how did my car get here already? I totally forgot about it breaking down. What the heck?"

"Tank fixed it for you and delivered it about an hour ago. It's all ready, but to answer your question, no. We're taking the bike."

"Oh. Do you have his number so I can pay him?" she asked, her eyes wide as she chewed her lip.

"I got it. He did it as a favor to me."

"Oh, I couldn't. Let me pay you for it, then."

"Suzy, let me do something nice for you. Really, it wasn't a problem. Tank and I worked it out. I don't want you broken down again on a dark country road."

"I know. I just try and watch my money. I was going to get it fixed."

"Well, now it is. Nine tonight, and warm clothes." I leaned forward and kissed her lips. I grabbed the back of her neck and drew her closer. The light, sweet scent of her perfume filled my nostrils, as I tasted her lips. Everything about her was fucking sweet, and I wanted more. I consumed her mouth and commanded her body with my kiss. I wanted to leave her weak in the knees and wanting more when I drove away. I broke the kiss, but kept my hand in place and watched her as she stood there with puckered lips and her eyes closed. Exactly the response I wanted.

"Sugar," I said, smiling at her as her eyes fluttered open.

"Oh, sorry. I say that a lot around you." Her cheeks turned pink as she bit her lip.

"We'll finish that kiss later. I can't wait to crawl back inside that delicious pussy of yours tonight. Digits," I said before she had a chance to walk away. I programmed her number in my phone and sent her a text as she walked in her house. She'd be back for more.

I started the engine, revving it a couple times before pushing backwards and down the drive. She waved with a sweet smile on her face. My cock ached as I thought about all the dirty shit I wanted to do to her. I watched her in my side mirror as she watched me drive away. I had her.

***

"Where the fuck you been, Joey?" Mikey said as I walked through the door of Inked.

We opened Inked about five years ago. Everyone in my family has an artistic streak, and we didn't trust outsiders with our money. Growing up, my father had drilled that mantra in our heads. Don't trust others when you can do it yourself. We agreed that there would be no outsiders unless absolutely necessary. Problem with it, though, was that you could never fire family, especially when they're part-owners. Mike had the spaz gene. He was known for overreacting.

"I had to drop someone off, shithead. Who made you boss?" I asked as I set my stuff down at my workstation.

"You're typically here early. I started to get worried. You could've called or something, asshole."

"Don't get your panties in a bunch, Mom. I'm here now, so shut the fuck up."

Mikey threw his hands in the air—showing his surrender or disgust, I couldn't tell. He was the shop manager since he had absolutely no artistic talent, but he was one hell of a piercer. His real passion was fighting. He had joined the circuit years ago and often traveled out of town for a fight. Fighting with your hands and tattooing do not mix. My hands were precious to me. I needed them to work my magic and see the smiles on the faces of my customers.

"Mom called to remind us about tomorrow," Anthony

said as he walked out of the employee-only area. Anthony is my oldest brother and probably the most unsettled. He's an amazing tattooist, but he's a musician. He dreamed of hitting it big, but for now he was ours.

"What the fuck?" Mikey said.

"How could we forget? It's only been the same day for thirty years," Izzy said as she unpacked her machine.

Izzy's the youngest and the only girl beside my mom. My parents kept trying until finally they had the little princess they always dreamed about, after having four boys climbing the walls and roughhousing. She was girly and kind, but if you crossed Izzy, she'd kick your ass. We were all overprotective of her, but we were scared of her too. In my family, the ladies ruled the roost and weren't to be crossed. She got that commanding personality from my mom, and led with an iron fist.

"Let's run down the schedule before I open the doors," Mikey said, leaning over the counter, looking toward the work area.

I listened to Mikey babble on about the clients of the day. I already knew my lineup. I had to finish a back tat I'd been working on for months, and a girl wanted me to fix her bad choice in a tramp stamp.

My mind kept wandering to Suzette. My mom would be happy if I brought a good girl home for once—someone that could give her grandchildren someday. I was not ready for that. My dick was doing the thinking instead of my head. *Get your head on straight, man—too much pussy out there to settle.* I was getting a little ahead of myself, but Suzy may have been the first respectable girl I'd met in a long time. I never brought women I'd dated or slept with around my family. None of them had a future with me, and I didn't feel the need to subject my family to an intruder or an outsider.

"Joey." My sister stood, her face invading my personal space.

"What, Iz?" I looked up and noticed her squinty eyes as she studied me.

"What are you grinning about?"

"Nothing."

"Oh, bullshit." She pointed at me and tapped me on the forehead. "You've met someone. Spill it, brother."

"There's nothing to tell. You think you're a mind reader, but you aren't, sis."

"I've known you my entire life. You walk around here all moody and serious, but today I'd say you're almost glowing, ya big pansy ass."

"Fuck off, love."

"Ooooh, jackpot. Who is she?" A giant smile crept across her face as she leaned forward and stared in my eyes. She wasn't going to let it go. Everyone stopped what they were doing to listen to what I had to say, and Isabella's impending inquisition.

"Fine, Iz. I met her last night and I'm taking her out tonight. Happy?"

Iz twirled around and giggled like a schoolgirl. "Extremely, big brother." She kissed me on the cheek. I leaned back in my chair and watched as my sister celebrated like I was about to walk down the aisle.

"Don't get ahead of yourself, Iz. It's just a date."

"Oh, now come on. I can tell by the look on your face that she's a little bit more than just a simple date. I want the deets."

Grunting, I crossed my arms over my chest. "She was stranded and I stopped to help her. I brought her home and I'm taking her out tonight, simple as that."

"Hmmm."

She came closer, not believing a word that I spoke.

"Izzy, leave it at that."

"Who is she?"

"She's a school teacher, but I don't know much about her."

"You've had sex with this girl. I can tell." Izzy poked me in the chest. "You can't hide anything from me."

"Well, shit, Iz. That's none of your business, really." The door chimed as my client walked through the door. I was thankful that I had a reason to end the conversation and save the grilling for another day. But I wouldn't get too comfortable. I knew my sister's interrogation would happen sooner rather than later.

***

The shop had a buzz today. Everyone had smiles on their faces. The fall weather always made people happy. I had been coloring in a beautiful flower that I had inked on a client, Michelle, a week ago, but she couldn't take any more pain to finish it that day.

"It's healing nice, darlin'." I wiped the blood and ink off her skin.

"Yeah, I can't wait to see it finished. Sorry I pussied out the other day, City." She closed her eyes as the needle poked the still-healing skin.

"Hey, it's cool. I've seen huge men in tears getting a tattoo. I rather you walk away than pass the fuck out."

Her eyes opened and she started to laugh. "Really? Guys have actually cried?"

"Yes, like little babies. So no worries. Now hold still so I don't fuck this up." I patted her leg with my rubber gloves and set out to finish the beautiful tattoo.

I loved working with color. Flowers weren't normally my thing; I loved animals and intricate designs, but flowers were a challenge and were laced with bold colors.

My phone vibrated on the table and I glanced at it as I dabbed the needle in the pink liquid.

Suzy: I can't make it tonight. Sorry, City.

Fuck, she was brushing me off. I couldn't stop and text her

back. Little Ms. Suzy would have to wait. I'd have to remind her of how good it felt inside her and how fucking hard she milked me.

"Something wrong, City?" Michelle asked.

"Nah, darlin'. Just thinking about something."

"Didn't mess up my tattoo, did you?"

"Hell no. I don't fuck up."

"Thinking about a girl?" Her eyebrows wiggled up and down.

"A woman." I didn't look up as I spoke to her, and I kept my eyes glued to her tattoo so I didn't have to eat my fucking words.

"Lucky cunt," she muttered.

"What?" I'd heard her loud and clear, but just wanted to see if she'd 'fess up.

"Oh, nothing. Wanna talk about her?"

"Nope. I'm good. Shit's between her and I, Michelle."

I had to get in that pretty little head of Suzy's. I knew I scared the fuck out of her and I should. I wasn't her type or some clean-cut cocksucker. I knew how to please a woman, take care of myself, and have a good time. I just couldn't give her a chance to run away like a scared little princess.

Time felt like it stood still as I colored in the same area over and over again to get the shade just right. A small hint of gray near the pistil and I had finished this flower of torture. I wiped off the ink and patted her calf. "All done. Take a look."

She glided her hands down her legs in a seductive manner, but I didn't take the bait. "It's beautiful. You're fucking amazing." Not going there—not with this one.

I grabbed my phone, needing to change Suzy's mind about tonight.

Me: Come on, it's Saturday night. Live a little, sugar.

I washed my hands as Michelle sat back down and stared at the finished masterpiece.

"You remember what I said last time about taking care of

the tattoo? Stay out of the sun, don't go in the pool or ocean until it heals, and keep it clean. Let me cover it for your trip home first. You can pay up front. Iz can check you out." After grabbing a new pair of gloves, I covered the area with a dressing.

"Don't you want to check me out?"

I could hear the hurt in her voice, but fuck no, I didn't want to check her out. I only had one person on my mind, and it was Suzy Goodie Two-shoes.

"Pfft, fine." Michelle stomped off as I grabbed my phone and typed another message.

Suzy: I don't think it's a good idea. I had a great time with you. Thanks for your help.

Like hell I'd let her off that easy. She was going to be mine again.

Me: I'll be there at nine—be ready. No ifs, ands, or buts.

Suzy: City—No.

Me: Boyfriend?

Suzy: No. I'm not a cheater. I don't think we'd work out— we're just not right.

Me: Sugar, it felt right this morning when my cock was buried inside of you and you screamed my name. Nine. No strings—just FUN. You know the word, right?

I cleaned my workstation and prepped for my next willing victim. I wouldn't let her weasel out of a night of fun. She didn't respond right away, but I knew that she would. She had to be thinking about the way she looked at me when I was buried inside her. I knew I had her. I just had to get beyond all her brains and rules. I had to reel her in. I knew my last sentence would agitate the hell out of her. I didn't think people besides the fuckheads in her class challenged her very often. I wasn't a boy and didn't know how to take no for an answer.

Suzy: Nine.

Gotcha.

***

Suzy opened the door with a smile on her face and a killer outfit. "Hey. You look amazing." She had on furry boots, skintight jeans, and a fluffy, oversized sweater.

She eyed me up and down, studying my outfit. "I guess I'm dressed okay."

"I'm not a fancy guy. I wear my jeans, t-shirt, and boots or sandals."

She made a face at me—what the fuck was that about?

"You never dress up?" she asked, as she locked the front door and turned to face me.

"Only when necessary. Tonight it isn't." I sat on the bike and held out the helmet. "Want to do it yourself?"

She plopped it on her head. I laughed as she fiddled with the straps. "Want help?"

"No...I'm perfectly capable of doing it myself." She fastened the buckle under her chin. "See?" The helmet slid forward, covering her eyes. "Damn it."

I couldn't help myself; I burst into laughter. "Come here, lemme help."

Her lips pursed with annoyance.

"Don't worry, sugar, you'll get the hang of it."

"I'm not used to all this..." She motioned to the bike, her eyes still hidden as I pulled her toward me.

"Live a little. Learn to let go."

Her lips turned up in a smile. "Not that you know, but I'm a total control freak."

"We'll work on that." I pushed the helmet on top of her head and grabbed the straps.

"I'm perfect just the way I am." She squinted at me, which made it harder for me to stop laughing. The pissed-off-teacher look made my dick rock hard and my balls ache.

"I didn't mean it that way. I mean you need to learn to

have some fun," I said, grabbing her chin after fixing the fasteners.

"I have plenty of fun, for your information."

"Climb on, sugar." I patted the seat. "What do you like to do for fun?"

Her hand touched my shoulder as she hoisted her leg over the bike. "Well, I like to read. I go out with my friends some-times. Um, I like to hang out at the pool. I like to play games. I do plenty of fun things." Her body rested against mine and I closed my eyes. *Down, boy—not tonight.* She didn't mention one thing that resembled fun in my book.

"What about a club? Concerts? Parties?" A girl her age should've experienced a couple things in her life. She went to college and had to live a little...I mean, fuck. "I know you've never ridden a bike before."

"I don't dance. Concerts, a couple of times in college, and parties? Do work parties count?" She clasped her hands around my chest and sealed the gap between our bodies.

"Everyone can dance. I saw how your body moved last night, babe. You can dance." I turned the key and throttled the engine.

She swatted my chest. "Hush."

I'd embarrassed her. Good—I needed to push her. I wanted to learn what she was really all about. The good-girl bullshit worked for me, but I needed to know there was a sinner underneath that polished veneer.

"Well, tonight we're going to add a few check marks to your life." I moved my body, leaving no space between us.

"What are we doing?" she asked against my back, already hiding her face.

"Heading to the beach."

"It's dark, though."

"Exactly."

I drove slowly through her neighborhood, waiting for the right moment to pay her back for the smack on my chest. I hit the open country road at the end of her development and gunned the bike. Glancing in the side mirror, I could only see her blonde hair blowing in the wind.

I sped up, and she pinched my pec and yelled, "Stop!"

I didn't listen, pretending the wind made it impossible to hear. I pointed at my ear and shook my head. "I can't hear you."

"Slow down," she yelped.

Stopping at the red light, I turned to look at her. "There's no one around. We're safe—I promise."

"I don't know if I can ever get used to riding on this dang thing."

"Do you trust me?"

"What?"

"Trust, sugar. Simple question."

She sighed. "I do."

"Then enjoy the ride. It's freeing and there's nothing like it in the world. Ready? Hold on." I gunned the bike, but not enough to lose control, as she screamed in my ear. I couldn't stop myself from laughing.

She still had a stranglehold on my chest as we rolled into the beachfront bar. I squeezed the bike into the only single space available. Charlie's was the place to be seen on a Saturday night, and by the looks of it, half of the town was there.

"Can I open my eyes now?" she asked, her voice muffled from my jacket.

"We're here. Off you go." I pried her fingers apart and patted them.

"Charlie's?" She climbed off the bike and unlatched the helmet quicker than I thought possible.

"Yes. Have you been?"

"No." She looked around the parking lot.

"Hey," I said as I grabbed her chin. "It's okay. I'll give you plenty of firsts." I smiled at her. "I like the idea of showing you new things." There were so many things I wanted to do to her. I wanted to ruin her in every possible way. Fuck the lawyers and the boring motherfuckers.

"I rarely come down to the beach, let alone at night."

"Well, tonight there's a DJ, and I want to dance with you."

"Oh," she said, her eyes wide in shock. "I told you, I can't dance."

"You can and you will. Might take a couple of those sweet drinks you like, but you'll do it."

"Oh, suck it."

"I plan on it." I smirked at her and grabbed her hand.

CHAPTER
SEVEN

SUZY

DID I know what a good time was anymore? I went to college and knew how to live it up and let go. My life had become so wrapped up in work and finishing my master's degree that I kind of forgot what it meant to let go and unwind. I'd always put more pressure on myself, wanting to get ahead in life, not wanting to worry about paying the next bill. I lived comfortably and I was happy with that. I enjoyed staying home and reading a good book. Hell, it was cheaper than going out to a bar and drinking. I needed to watch my pennies, and drinking them just felt silly.

"I'll take a margarita," I said to the bartender, reaching in my purse, but City put his hand over mine.

"I'll take a Yuengling, please," he said to the bartender, and then he looked at me and said, "I got this, Suzy."

"I can pay for myself."

"We're on a date, sugar. I pay when we're on a date. Put your money away—I'll find another way for you to pay me back." Butterflies filled my stomach as he said the last word in my ear close enough that I felt the vibration.

I grabbed my drink, letting the cool liquid slide down my throat. I needed liquid courage if he thought I would dance with him tonight. Dancing and me didn't mix, never had. I never knew what to do with my hands, and I always felt like everyone watched me—it freaked me the hell out. If he wanted to dance, I'd give him exactly what he asked, and make an ass of myself to prove him wrong.

City picked up his beer and studied me. Why did he have to be so damn sexy? I didn't want to like him, but I did. His cockiness wasn't like the other men I'd dated; it had nothing to do with his career or his material possessions. No, his was natural and sexual.

"I'd like to say you should slow down, but fuck it, I like when you're tipsy." He sipped his beer and leaned against the bar.

"I don't see you tearing it up."

"I can't, I'm driving and I don't drive drunk. Have to keep a clear head when you're on a bike." He ran his finger over the rim of the bottle, and all I could do was stare at him.

The band took the stage, and everyone clapped as the lead singer began to speak. "Thank you. Thank you," he said as he motioned for the crowd to quiet down. The guitarist began to play, and the crowd grew quiet. A soulful melody filled the air as the lead singer began to sway. The rhythm was intoxicating, and if I were home, I'd be dancing around my living room making a total ass of myself without any witnesses.

"Finish your drink." City's lips were set in a hard line, and I knew what he wanted.

"Think you can handle all this?" I motioned up and down my body. Fuck, how else could I stall?

"I know I can." He licked his lips, and I didn't want it to affect me, but he got to me. "I remember the way you moved against my cock, sugar." He brushed the hair off my shoulder, and my spine tingled.

My face grew flush as images of last night flashed in my mind. I didn't respond to him as I polished off the last sip of my margarita. "I warned you." I shrugged and smiled. *Here goes nothin'—let's show this big boy whatcha got.*

Holding hands, we walked to the middle of the dance floor. The music wasn't the right tempo for a slow dance or to shake my booty, as Sophia used to call it. I didn't really know what to do as I stood there and looked around. He wrapped his arm around my back and pulled me close. "Feel the music. Follow my body."

Every inch of his front touched mine as he began to move with the music. Wrapping my arms around his neck, letting his body guide mine to the beat, it struck me how well the man could move. His body rubbing against mine caused my nipples to harden, and a familiar ache between my legs returned. The memory of how he felt inside me, moving in the same rhythm, made my knees feel weak as he held me against his torso. I let him move my body—I became pliable in his hands.

"See? You got moves," he said in my ear as I buried my face in his chest.

I didn't know if the liquor had given me the ability to move with the music or if it was the man holding me, but I'd never moved this gracefully in my life. I looked up into his eyes, and he stared at me with the side of his mouth turned up in a grin. Why did this sexy-ass man, who lived life totally opposite of me, want me? We didn't fit—we didn't make sense on paper, but that didn't stop my body from reacting to him, no matter how hard my mind said to ignore his charms.

"You think too much. Stop making a list of why you shouldn't be here. Feel the reasons you should," he said, and kissed my lips, distracting me as he pressed his erection into my stomach. My doubts vanished. I leaned into his body and grabbed his pecs, toying with the piercings underneath his shirt. "Don't start something you don't want to finish, Suzette," he whispered against my lips.

"I always follow through, City." I smirked and winked

before pressing my lips against his. I couldn't resist him, at least not in person. I'd live for tonight and deal with the fallout tomorrow. Our bodies slowed as we kissed. He ran his fingers through my hair and then fisted it, tipping my head back to give him deeper access.

I breathed his air, no room left between us, as he held my body to his. He pulled back and left only a small gap between us, not releasing his hold on me entirely. "I want to taste you."

Fuck me. Every bit of my body felt hot and damp. I wanted City more than I had last night. "You do?" No one had ever talked to me like he did.

"I will." I could see his eyes change with his words, his pupils fully dilated. "I don't make false promises."

I swallowed hard, unable to stop the barrage of sexy images from invading my thoughts. Why can't he be a lawyer or something other than a biker tattoo guy? He probably wouldn't have this effect on me if he was anything other than who he was —City.

"Stop thinking and dance." He released his hold on my hair and swung me out, pulling me back against his body with a thump. *Christ have mercy on my soul.*

For once in my life, I felt like I could actually dance. The music was slow and sensual, and let me move without feeling like an idiot. We touched each other constantly and didn't lose eye contact.

The music slowed and everyone began to clap. "For our next song..." the lead singer said.

"Want another drink, sugar?"

"Yes, I'm parched." City had me all kinds of crazy. I felt like I was drooling, but my mouth screamed for something cool, and my body needed a break from the foreplay on the dance floor.

City motioned to the bartender, snapped his fingers, and pointed at me. "Aren't you getting one?" I asked.

"Just a water. I'm driving, remember." I respected him for sticking to his original plan. "Plus, I'd rather get you a little liquored up. We have an appointment down on that swing." He pointed in the distance to a dark object.

"What's out there?" I asked, squinting and trying to get a better look, but the beach was shrouded in darkness except for the glimmer of the moon on the ocean.

"Darkness."

"And?"

"You. Me. Darkness." The corner of his mouth tipped up, and I swear to God his eyes almost twinkled.

The bartender placed the margarita in front of me and I picked it up, needing a diversion. I ran my tongue along the salt before taking a mouthful of the cool, sweet liquid in my mouth. I swallowed fast, and the alcohol burned my throat on the way down. I looked at City, and he was watching me intently, curiously. I licked the rim again, letting the salt dance on my tongue, and saw his chest expand as he breathed in quickly.

"Keep doing that, sugar, and I won't let you take another sip."

"What? This?" I licked the rim again, keeping my eyes trained on him, and let my tongue drift as far as I could.

"Fuck," he muttered, running his hand across his face.

Two can play a naughty game, City. I may not be the hussy he was used to being with, but I knew how to get a man's attention.

Smiling against the glass as I took another sip and looked away, I pretended to be uninterested. The salt tasted good, mixed with the sweet, tangy drink as I let the liquid linger on my tongue before swallowing it. My legs felt tingly as the liquor spread throughout my system.

"Damn," I said, my face becoming flushed.

"What's wrong?" He raised an eyebrow, cocking his head.

"Strong drink. Guess the first one never left my system," I

said, tipping it back again and sucking down the last bit of liquid.

"That's it. Come on, Suzy. I got something for you to lick." He grabbed my hand and started to tug me away from the bar.

"I can't," I protested as I set the glass on the bar.

"Oh, yes you can. You said you always follow through, and I'm cashing in on that promise, sugar." Butterflies filled my stomach with the knowledge that we were not going to be watching the waves. City had plans for me, and I couldn't back out now.

We reached the last step on the deck, and I stopped before my feet hit the sand. "Wait." My hand fell from his. "My boots. I don't want them to get ruined." I tried to give an innocent smile. I really didn't want to ruin them. They cost me more money than I wanted to admit.

He grunted and moved closer to me. We were eye to eye, with him flat on the beach and me perched on the step. He didn't say a word as he reached down and picked me up. I laughed as he pulled me against his chest. "Wrap your arms around me."

My laughter stopped as I wrapped my arms around his neck and stared at his face. City was beautiful; his dark features and ice-blue eyes that looked clear in the moonlight stole my breath. His jaw had a shadow from the stubble, and I ran my fingertips across it, remembering the night before. His lips were full and beautiful and screamed to be kissed. His eyebrows were manly, yet neat—no waxing, but he groomed them. His dark hair flopped with each step, and I couldn't help but smile. He was everything I wanted and exactly the type I ran away from.

City sat down on the swing, still holding me in his arms. "Straddle me," he growled in my ear as the swing moved back and forth.

"But people can see us." I looked around as my heart thumped in my chest.

"Could you see the swing from up there?" He smirked.

"No, I couldn't, but if someone catches us we could get in trouble."

"Sugar, we won't get in trouble and no one's going to find us. Trust me. Now straddle me."

I scanned the deck area, and he was right—no one was looking for us, or even seemed to notice that there was anyone on the beach.

"You a regular here, big boy?" I said as I adjusted my body.

"I only come out here to be alone. You're the first girl I've ever brought here."

"Hard to believe that I could be your first in anything."

"Sugar, no bullshit. You gonna kiss me or what?" he asked, grabbing my chin.

"Depends on the what," I said giggling, as he squeezed my waist, pulling me close, our noses touching.

"You talk big, little girl. I'm going to get that taste I've been looking forward to."

CHAPTER
EIGHT
CITY

I COULDN'T STOP the thought of Suzy moaning on my lap, facing away from me last night as I finger-fucked her. She was hesitant at first, nervous someone would see us, as I unzipped her pants enough to slide my fingertips inside. I wiped any thoughts out of her mind with a few strokes of my fingers. I watched her face as she rested her head against my shoulder—I watched her eyes roll back, and a small sound escaped her lips. "Quiet, sugar," I whispered in her ear, and she obeyed. Stroking her insides, circling her clit until her body shook and her pussy clamped down on my fingers.

She didn't move at first as I withdrew my fingers from her lace panties and brought them to my lips, wrapping my lips around them as I sucked her juices, and she stared at me with an open mouth and wide eyes.

"Mm. Taste yourself on me." I bent down and pressed my lips to hers, dragging my tongue across her bottom lip.

"City." She moaned in my mouth.

Reaching up and pulling her face to mine, I crushed my lips to hers.

"Joey. What the fuck?" Something hit my shoulder, and I blinked.

"What the fuck, Iz."

"Your dopey ass has been sitting there in fucking La-La Land for ten minutes grinning like a fucking mental patient. Snap. The. Fuck. Out."

"Couldn't just leave me there?" I asked. "And Iz, stop fucking hitting me. You're the only person that I let get away with that shit. You're always poking me with those bony-ass fingers."

"It's time to eat. Mama's been calling for everyone to come to the table." She rolled her eyes at me before walking away.

"I'm coming, Ma." I adjusted my dick in my jeans. My mind had become a little too engrossed in my fantasy, and the relief I needed would have to wait. I climbed off the couch and slid my hand in my pocket, looking for the phone that vibrated against my dick.

Suzy: I love your idea of or what.

Based on her message, I could tell I wasn't the only one thinking about our time on the beach.

"Iz, what the hell do you call the what, where, when, why, and how in English?"

She looked at me confused as I sat down at the table. "Trying to impress the teacher?" She giggled.

"Just answer the question, please." I sighed and stared at her, placing the phone on the table.

"What teacher?" Ma asked.

"Iz, what's it called? Throw me a bone."

"Interrogatives." My sister rolled her eyes before turning to face our mother. "He's schtuppin' a teacher, Ma."

"Isabella! That's not appropriate at the dinner table." My mom set the lasagna on the table. "I want details, Joseph." Ma winked at me.

Me: Wait until you feel the rest of my interrogatives.

I placed the phone on the table and looked around the room. Everyone had their eyes glued on me instead of the meal, as they usually were. "What?"

"You're smiling as you type—who is she, Joseph?" Ma said as she dished out the first steaming slice of heaven to my father.

"Just a woman, Ma." I held up my plate as I waited to be served. My mother was traditional in many ways, refusing to let us serve ourselves. She was the one to dish out the food and to sit last.

She held the lasagna over my plate. "I've never seen you like this. You want your piece, baby? You hungry?"

"Hell yes." I licked my lips and moved my plate closer to the piece hovering just out of reach.

"Then you're going to tell me about her, yes? No information means no food." She held the slice of lasagna to her nose and inhaled it. "Mm, it would be a shame for you to miss out on this meal."

I sighed. Women—the root of the evil in this world. If pussy wasn't so fucking perfect I'd swear off them for eternity.

"Fine, Ma. I'll tell you about her after we eat. Can I please have a piece now?"

"Sure, baby. You can help me wash the dishes and tell me all about *her*."

Fuck. "You're an asshole, Iz." Throwing me under the bus with Dean? Still seeing him?

"Bella, you better not still be seeing that man. He's nothing but trouble," my mother said.

Iz glared at me across the table. Served her little gossipy ass right for airing my shit at the dinner table.

The conversation turned to sports and football, as it always did on Sunday. My grilling was soon forgotten as my brothers and Dad stuffed their faces and rubbed their stomachs. I finished my lasagna, wiping my plate clean with a piece of garlic bread, before picking up my phone again.

Suzy: WTF. I teach math—no clue what an interrogative is. Hello—I don't get your angle.

Me: At the end of my linear path I have a point for you.

Did that make sense or did I just make a complete ass of myself? Fuck. This girl had me all fucked up. My parents always wanted their children to "settle down" and make babies, but I'd always been more interested in perfecting my skills and not wanting to get tied down, at least not after Joni. We didn't marry young and follow their path in life, and I thought my parents were secretly proud of us for waiting. They were happily married and have been for over forty years—they tied the knot right out of high school. Times were different.

Suzy: Oooh, you know just the right things to say to a girl.

Me: Tuesday night = (dinner) + my linear path + your diameter

"Joey, grab your plate. We have a date with a sink and some dishes," Ma said from behind me. I looked up at her and saw her smiling and reading over my shoulder. Fuck.

Suzy: No can do—grad classes. I'll take a rain check.

I turned off my screen and placed it in my pocket. Nothing was secret or sacred in this fucking house.

"Everybody bring your plates in the kitchen. Come on. Clear off the table," Ma said. The room filled with grumbles, but we all knew the drill. Thirty years later we didn't need to be told what our roles were in this family. My father was the figurehead, my mother told everyone what to do, and we did as told without giving lip.

Ma waited for me by the sink as I set my plate on the counter. "Did you find someone?" She was beaming.

"I just met her, Ma," I shooed her to the side so I could start tackling the dishes.

She threw the dishrag over her shoulder and eyed me. "Baby, the heart knows what the heart wants. Your sister told me you've been acting differently. It's written all over your face. Sometimes fate steps in and throws you off the course we've set in life."

"Don't go crocheting baby blankets yet, Ma."

She placed her hand on my shoulder as I scrubbed and avoided eye contact. "Joseph, I know the man you are. I know you're guarded with your heart after Joni, but you have to open again sometime. You need to find someone to trust in life. Is this girl worthy of that trust? Is she worth the risk?"

"Ma, I barely know the chick."

"Tsk, tsk. Someone doth protest too much." She kissed my cheek, ruffling my hair. That shit made me crazy, but with my hands full of soap I had no other option but to let her do as she wished.

"I can see you're not going to stop. She seems like a good person. She's different, Ma. She seems genuine, but I'm not rushing into anything."

"What about her? Is she madly in love with my baby boy?"

"Ma." I should hate her calling me her baby boy, but my mother could call me anything in the world. I adored the woman. "She isn't jumping on the Joey train. I don't think she really wants to see me."

"What? Why not?" She leaned against the counter, crossing her arms. "You're perfect."

"That's 'cause I'm your kid. I'm hardly perfect, Ma." I cleaned the last dish and placed it in the rack to dry. "You don't really know everything about me, no matter what you think."

"I know more than you think, sweetheart. Iz has loose lips, you know." I could beat my little sister's ass. I'm sure she doesn't tell my ma about all her love affairs. "I know you're quite the ladies' man. I'm not judging you, Joey. You never bring any girls around, but I know you."

Fucking Iz. "When and if I find the one, Ma, you'll be the first to know." I kissed her cheek, and her radiant smile lit up the room. "Suzy sees me as a tattoo artist that rides a motor-cycle and hangs out in shithole bars. I don't exactly rank up there on her boyfriend material checklist."

"I kinda like this girl already." She giggled. I loved hearing the sound of her laughter. "She doesn't know every-thing about you and our family?" She raised her eyebrow.

"No, I don't tell anyone about us, Ma."

"Checklists are made to be changed. She needs to know the Joey I do. Are you going to ask her out? Make her yours?"

"That's what I was trying to do at the table, but she has class."

"Ah, a smart girl too. Joey, don't ask a girl out through text message. That's what's wrong with you kids today. She needs to hear your voice when you ask. Texting is too impersonal, and I'll never understand it. Call the girl."

"I will. I'll call her later. Happy?"

My ma wrapped her arms around me and said, "Very."

CHAPTER
NINE
SUZY

I COULDN'T GET him out of my mind, and it had been less than twenty-four hours since he dropped me off with a soul-stealing kiss. His cocky smile, his muscles, the way he touched me stayed with me long after he left. No one had made me want to break a rule more than he did. No matter how hard I tried to concentrate on my lesson plans for the upcoming quarter, my mind drifted to him.

Trying to quiet my brain, I flipped on *Catfish* as I crawled in bed. It had been my guilty pleasure since this show began. I loved watching the train wrecks and the broken hearts of those that thought they fell in love with someone, only to find out that they weren't who they pretended to be.

I used to tease Sophia and Kayden, my old roommates, mercilessly about how different their little tryst in New Orleans could've turned out. Their situation was different; they had mutual friends and had checked each other out, so they felt it was a sure thing.

On paper, Kayden and Sophia didn't work—it wasn't a match made in heaven—but their love was undeniable. It was electric. Sophia followed her heart, and his pull was inescapable for her. She fell for him hook, line, and sinker. I never understood it until I got to know Kayden. He wasn't anything like I thought—his heart was pure, but his path in life had been different than mine. I'd never believe Sophia would find a guy without a college education and a criminal record to fall in love with, but they were the happiest couple I knew, and I wanted that kind of love.

My checklist had been realistic in theory, but City had me questioning my method and requirements. I'd dated men that fit on paper, but the chemistry lacked. City was just so City. I was approaching the end of my twenties, sitting in bed, eating bonbons, and watching *Catfish* alone.

I am happy, aren't I?

My phone began to move across my nightstand. I popped the last morsel of chocolaty goodness in my mouth. "Herlo?"

"Hey, Suzette." The vibration of his voice through the phone made my heart skip a beat as I swallowed the chocolate slowly. Damn, why did I have to eat that last piece before I answered? *Herlo?* I sounded like I had a speech problem.

"Oh, hey. How are you?" I grabbed the water on my nightstand and washed down the last bit of candy.

"I'm well, sugar. Whatcha doin'?" I heard rustling in the background. Were those his sheets? Was he naked?

"Just watching television, and I'm about to go to sleep, you?" I wiped the chocolate from my lips and licked my finger. These little bitches were so damn tasty.

"I just crawled in bed. What are you wearing?" he asked in a smooth timbre.

OMG, he didn't just ask me that. I looked down. I had my ratty go-to clothes for when I lounged around the house. "Um, a tank top and flannel pajama pants."

I could hear him laughing. "Really?"

"Yeah, why? What are you *wearing*?" *Please don't say you're naked.*

"Nothing, sugar." *Damn it all to hell.* "You still there?"

"Yeah." I knew he could hear the change in my tone, as it came out all breathy and quiet.

"When can I see you again?" he asked.

"I don't know, City." I wanted, *God* how I wanted to scream now, but I needed to think about him—us.

"Don't deny you want me, Suzy. I can hear it in your voice. You're thinking of my cock inside you and your lips on mine."

My breath hitched as the images played like a movie in my mind. "I won't deny it, but that doesn't make it right," I said, moving down in the sheets and turning off the television.

"I'm not asking you to be my girlfriend, Suzette. I remember you having an earth-shattering time yesterday. I can still hear the sound you made when I made you come against my fingers." A small moan escaped his lips.

My heart ached when he said he didn't want me to be his girlfriend. What the hell? *Stay on course—do not waiver from the list.*

"It was the sexiest fucking sound I've ever heard, sugar. The way your eyes rolled back and your body rocked into my hand. Fuck."

I squeaked. *OMG, lemme die.* "City."

"The taste of you on my tongue after. Fucking perfect. I'm rock hard thinking about you."

"You are?" I whispered.

"Rock fucking hard." His breathing changed like it had when he fucked me. I could never forget the sounds the man made when he came. "Friday night, Suzy. No excuses this time."

"Okay. Friday."

"Good. I'll be thinking about that sweet pussy all week, sugar. Sweet dreams." His words were drawn out and his tone was sexy as hell.

"Night," I whispered back before the phone went quiet

and his harsh breath disappeared. Listening to the man turned me on, and I wanted to run to his house and have sex with him, but I didn't. Reaching into my nightstand, I grabbed my trusty battery-operated boyfriend of the last five years and thought of City as I climaxed. The orgasm didn't compare to the one I'd had under his deft fingers. He fucking ruined one of my simple pleasures.

***

Fuck Monday mornings. I never wanted to get out of bed. I pulled in the school parking lot five minutes late before throwing my bags down in my classroom, and I headed to the copier to be prepped for class that started in ten minutes. Damn. I hated being rushed.

I tapped my finger against the copy machine as it slowly churned out each piece of paper. People walked in and out of the teacher work area with quick hellos and "happy Mondays."

"What are you grinning about? It's Monday and you never smile, bitch," Sophia said behind me.

"I wasn't smiling." I turned around to see her grinning like a loon that had just escaped the funny farm.

"Oh, you were, sister. What happened?" Sophia always looked so put together and breathtaking.

"I have so much to tell you. I'll come see you during my planning period."

"By the look on your face I'd think you got laid this weekend. I'm not talking about a boring bullshit fucking either. You got *fucked*," she whispered in my face. I felt my face flush. "You did, don't lie, and I want every last detail."

The homeroom warning bell blared, and I started to panic, grabbing my papers in a crazy heap. "I'll be up third period. I'm going to be late, Sophia. I gotta run, babe."

"I'll hunt your ass down if you don't show up," Sophia said as I reached the door.

"I'll be there, whore. Shut it."

***

Sophia shut the door to her office. "Tell me, and I mean all of it."

Sitting on the comfy old couch in her office, I rested my head against the wall. "What do you want to know?"

"Don't play coy with me. You know more about my sex life than anyone else in the world. I want all the information, starting with who and when."

Sophia sat at her desk and rested her head on her hand. "I met him Friday night."

"Friday night? I don't remember you meeting someone," she said, her eyes looking upward as she replayed our time at the martini bar.

"After I left you. My car crapped out and this drop-dead gorgeous man stopped to help me."

"Helped you out of your panties too, I presume?" She giggled and slapped the desk.

"Eventually." I laughed. "I called you, but you didn't answer. I went with him on his bike to call a tow, and ended up having a drink or two."

"Bike? Like the ones the drunks ride around here with the electric motors, or are we talking smokin' hot Harley action?"

"Smokin' hot."

"His name?"

"City, but it's a nickname. When we left he asked where I wanted to go, and I told him I wanted him to take me to his house. I'd had too much to drink, because you know that just isn't me."

"Whatever. You're dying to be naughty but those uptight

pricks you date are missionary men. Bleh. Keep talking," she commanded.

"Pushy wench, aren't you? When he undresses, girl…" I sighed. "Oh. My. God. His body is covered in tattoos, his nipples are pierced, and he, and he…" I covered my mouth and tried to hide my grin.

"Breathe, Suzy. He what?"

"His penis was pierced too." I swallowed, remembering how it looked.

"Oh, now I'm enthralled. So your ass breaks down, is rescued by a sexy-ass biker with tats and piercings, and…"

"I slept with him. More than once. I stayed the night, and he had me before breakfast too."

"Have you talked to him since?"

"Yes, we went on a date Saturday night, and he wants to take me out again on Friday."

"I know that look. What's the problem?"

"He's just not…isn't what I'm looking for." I frowned.

"Suzy, baby, listen to me. Do you like this man?"

"Yes."

"As you would say, did he make your body tingle and make you scream?"

"Yes, more times than I can count."

"Do you want to see him again?"

"I do, but—"

"Fuck buts, girl."

"He's a tattoo artist and lives in an old house. He just doesn't fit my checklist. He's a biker, Sophia. What could we possibly have in common?"

"You and your damn lists. If I had a list I wouldn't have Kayden and Jett. I can't imagine my life without them. We can't always control everything in life; sometimes life jumps up and smacks us in the face."

"I know, Soph. He scares me," I whispered.

"Has he hurt you?" She stood and walked toward me with

her eyebrows drawn together and her mouth set in a hard line.

"No. I mean, I'm scared I could fall for him. I've never been with anyone like him, and I want to see him again. I've never had *that* spark, and with him it's like lightning."

Sophia sat down next to me and grabbed my face. "You listen to me, Suzy. You're young and have your whole life ahead of you. If you want to be with him, then do it. Stop trying to fit everyone in your mold. Rules are made to be broken. Give the guy a chance, babe. He's not asking you to marry him, is he?"

"No, he said he's not asking me to be his girlfriend either."

"Kayden wasn't looking for a girlfriend, but here we are, engaged with a baby. Sometimes life doesn't give us what we're looking for, but it gives us what is supposed to be. We just have to be willing to take the plunge. Live a little. Take a risk for once."

I smiled and hugged her. "You're right, Sophia, but I need some time and distance. So, Kayden still makes you happy even after everything?"

"I wouldn't trade a moment I've had with him. He's everything to me. My life's complete, Suzy. You need to find that guy that makes you feel whole. The one that gives you a reason to wake up each morning."

"So I should just enjoy the ride?" I wiggled my eyebrows at Sophia and laughed.

"In a matter of speaking, yes. Was it beautiful?"

"What?"

"His dick, Suzy. I've never seen a pierced one in person."

"Oh my God, it was the most beautiful thing I'd ever seen."

"I'm so excited for you, Suz." She bounced on the cushion, causing both of our bodies to shake. "When are you seeing him again?"

"Friday night. He didn't give me an option to say no."

"Smart man. You're such a pussy at times—listen to your heart and not your mind for once, got me?"

"Yes, Mom. I understand."

"Oh, and Suzy?"

"Yes?" I turned and looked at the grinning Sophia.

"I want pictures."

"You're such a whore." I laughed as I walked out the door.

CHAPTER
TEN
CITY

ME: *Are you in bed?*

Suzy: Yes, you?

Me: Yep, just lying here thinking about you. 24 hours until I hear you scream my name again.

We'd been texting all day. I never looked forward to a simple phone call or text from any chick. I ached for her. I lived with a perpetual boner now. We didn't have an exclusive deal, but the other girls didn't seem to do it for me anymore. My dick didn't ache for them. It wanted Suzy and her tight, sweet pussy.

Suzy: What's your real name?

I thought I told her my name, but maybe I hadn't.

Me: Joseph.

Suzy: Can I call you Joe or Joey?

Me: You can call me anything you want, sugar.

Suzy: Joey. It suits you.

I never felt like a Joey—it seemed childish, and the nickname City seemed to fit me better.

Me: Tank top and PJ pants?

Suzy: Yes. Y?

Me: Just want to know how to picture you as I stroke myself.

Craving the release, I stroked quicker, gripping it in my hand. I didn't want to come too quickly tomorrow night—I wanted to savor her and feast on her body.

Me: I'm going to picture you with your legs on my shoulders and your beautiful tits bouncing from my dick, slamming into you.

I stroked myself as I waited for her reply, caressing the tip, toying with the ring, giving it a tug.

Suzy: That's sexy. I can't wait to suck on you. Feel your velvety hardness in my mouth.

Oh, the little girl could be dirty. Time to push the envelope.

Me: Tell me one of your fantasies.

I wanted there to be a bad girl underneath—someone that wanted to get dirty with me. I stroked my shaft slowly and pictured her tight cunt milking me.

Suzy: Really?

Nothing was easy with this one.

Me: Yes, pick one.

Suzy: I always wanted someone to take me from behind and for him to hold my wrists at my side so I can't move.

Fuck me, it was a start at least. I wanted to pound her into next week. I wanted her so bad I thought my dick would break in my hand.

Me: What else? More.

Suzy: I always heard choking was amazing.

I stroked my cock faster and harder than I had before. I pictured my hands wrapped around her throat, watching her face turn pink, and feeling her clawing my chest as I rammed my cock into her. The warm liquid spurted, landing on my abdomen before I could stop.

Me: Fuck, sugar. You just made me come so fuckin' hard.

Suzy: OMG.

Me: Are you touching yourself?

I grabbed my shirt off the floor and wiped up the mess that I created lost in my mental fuckfest.

Suzy: Yes! You do things to me, Joey, things I've never felt before.

Me: Wait till tomorrow, sugar. Put a finger inside yourself.

No reply. She must be following my command. *Fucking perfect.*

Me: Don't type; just watch the screen, Suzette.

Me: I'm going to fuck you from behind and hold your wrists so tight in my grip that your fingers will go numb. My cock's going to throb inside of you—hit every spot that makes you scream, sugar.

How in the fuck was I getting a boner already?

Me: When I see your body grow flush and dew on your skin, I'm going to wrap my hands around your throat from behind and apply pressure until you're gasping for air and milking my cock for more.

Me: Come for me, sugar.

I lay in bed and pictured her touching herself. *Down, boy —fuck.*

Suzy: You're bad for me, Joey.

Me: Who the fuck wants to be good? Sweet dreams, beautiful.

Suzy: Night, Joey. I'm looking forward to the ride tomorrow night bahaha

I turned off my ringer and stared at the ceiling. I planned to give her more than she could handle and make all of her fantasies come true. Suzy was getting to me and cracking the well-built wall around my heart I'd created after Joni's death. *Air—I need air.* I jumped out of bed and put on a t-shirt and jeans. I needed to think, and I did that best on the open road.

I revved the engine a couple of times, put on my riding glasses, and cracked my neck. The roads were clear. The cold weather kept most of the snowbirds that traveled south off the roads, especially at night. I kicked the bike in top speed and felt the wind lash my exposed skin and blow through my hair.

I rode for over an hour, winding through the country roads before pulling in my driveway after midnight. My muscles vibrated and I felt exhausted. My mind was too tired to think of anything but my bed.

***

After grabbing my keys and jacket off the couch, I headed outside. Even though the calendar read October, the air was sticky and the sun made my skin burn—but I knew there would be a chill in the air tonight. Florida's winters were bipolar. Sometimes hot, sometimes cold—a totally fucking guessing game to keep you on your toes.

I tried to use Suzy's crazy-ass fucking method—I made a mental checklist while I drove. She had pros—fucking beauty, smart as hell, kick-ass career, independent, kind, innocent— but she also had cons. She was too fucking innocent and she could crush my heart into a million fucking pieces. *Think, man. She has to have other fucking flaws.* I liked the geeky girl underneath the hot, beautiful body. She wasn't used up and bitter from her experiences.

I walked in the shop early to find Mikey sitting at the front desk, rifling through the papers. "Morning, Mikey."

"Hey, bro, how's it hanging?"

"Little to the left," I said, adjusting myself.

"Never pegged you for a lefty. Thought maybe down the middle."

"Fucker, how could it hang down the middle? You need your head checked or some shit?"

"You know, maybe you weren't blessed with the Gallo family genes. Just sayin.'"

"Dumb fuck. You've seen my dick—you pierced the motherfucker for me."

Mikey chuckled. "I know, fucker. Just yanking your fucking chain. Touchy this morning, aren't we?"

I threw my bag next to my chair and walked up to the desk.

"Not touchy, Mike. This fuckin' girl is stuck in my head."

Mikey shook his head and started to laugh. "Ah, she's cracking that cold, dead heart of yours?"

"Fuck, I don't know. I'm seeing her again tonight. What the fuck am I doing, man?"

"Pussy. She got good shit, huh?" He grinned.

"Platinum pussy. Has my brain all fuckin' jumbled up, man."

"Never thought I'd see the day."

"Makes two of us," I mumbled.

"Listen, you want anyone else fucking her?" he asked as he placed his hand on my shoulder. He was always into love and touching, and it made me batshit crazy.

The thought of anyone else touching Suzy made me want to fucking vomit, or beat the shit out of the bastard. "Fuck no, I want to be the only one inside her. I don't like sloppy seconds."

"Well, there's your answer."

"Fucking hell." I shook my head and stared at the floor.

"Doesn't mean you have to marry her, Joey. Just make sure she doesn't want to fuck anyone else. Make her yours—take the leap."

"For once, Mikey, you're right. Fucking miracle." I couldn't deny it anymore. I wanted her and couldn't stand the thought of anyone else touching her or kissing her beautiful lips.

"You know I always got your back. It's been years, man. Joni would want you to be happy." He grabbed the schedule off the counter as the door chimed and the rest of the Gallo pack walked through the doors. "Would they have been friends—Joni and this girl?"

They had some similarities. Joni would think Suzy was funny as hell and sweet. "Yeah, they probably would have liked each other."

"She doesn't want you alone, wherever she is."

"Thanks, Mikey." Waiting for everyone to get settled, I grabbed my phone and sent Suzy a message about tonight.

Me: You're mine tonight, Suzette.

CHAPTER
ELEVEN

SUZY

THE DAY DRAGGED ON, and the students were in a foul mood. I needed the weekend to start. When the lunchtime bell rang, I walked in my office, plopping in my chair as I let my head fall back. "Jesus," I muttered. I closed my eyes for a moment and listened to the stillness in the air, since the kids had cleared the building. Two more class periods—I could do it.

I opened my drawer, grabbed my container of leftover pasta, and searched for my phone. I hoped City messaged me —I needed something to brighten up this shit day. I looked at the screen and my stomach fluttered. I was "his" tonight. What did he mean? Sexually?

I never liked to be called Suzette, but the way it sounded coming out of his mouth made my breath hitch. He always seemed to whisper it in my ear or say it against my lips, and it drove me crazy. I wanted to hear him say my name tonight.

Me: Only tonight?

Hell, did I just sound needy?

City: All things are possible.

What the hell did that mean?

"Hello. Suzy, you in here?" I heard Sophia calling from the door.

"In my office," I yelled, grabbing a forkful of noodles.

Sophia stood in the doorway and made a sound of disgust. "I don't know how you eat that Ragu shit cold. Bleh." She scrunched her nose, opened her mouth, and stuck her finger inside, pretending to gag.

"Hey, Mama Guido, what are you doing slumming it down here?" I stuck the noodle in my mouth and made a face at her.

"Kayden and I were talking, and we wanted to know if you and the cock piercing wanted to come over for a barbecue tonight?"

"You just want to molest him with your eyes."

"No, I don't. I have my hunk. Kayden still makes me tingle thinking about him." She made a silly face and shook her body like just the thought of him brought her pleasure. "I want to meet this guy and see if he's worthy of my little Suzy. Plus, Kayden could use a little pick-me-up. Maybe they can be friends and we can double date." She rested her body against the door with her leg crossed in front of the other and her arms folded. I always had a hard time saying no to Sophia.

"Well, I'd have to ask him. I don't know what he had planned."

"Send me an email after you ask him. It'll be fun. Don't take no for an answer. You've piqued my curiosity about this man that has you all types of insane. I mean, sweetie, I've always known you were crazy, but he has you questioning everything in your perfect little mapped out life. I must meet him."

"Fine, Soph. Let me ask him."

Me: BBQ at my friends' place tonight. You game?

"There, I asked. It's up to him now. Happy?" I grabbed a

huge forkful and slowly placed it in my mouth—anything to gross Sophia out. She was the queen of sauce and meatballs. I missed when the house used to fill with the smell of her cooking. I'd come home after a long day and Kayden would have something divine on the stove. Now it was Ragu and me against the world.

"Ugh, I can't stand here and watch you eat that shit."

My phone chirped. "Wait," I said as she walked away from my office. "Incoming."

"So?"

City: Sounds fanfuckingtastic. What time shall I give you a "ride"?

"Um," I said as I felt the heat creep into my cheeks. "He wants to know what time we should arrive."

"He talks all proper like that?"

"Nope, but that's all you're getting. Time, please?"

She sighed. "Eight, okay? If you're gonna be late just let me know, whoreface. Bye," she said as the door closed behind her.

Me: Sophia said to be there at eight. Pick me up around ten till to be there on time—Sophia doesn't do late.

I knew that Sophia would take one look at City and practically be doing cartwheels. She'd never liked any man I had seen since we became friends. I flipped through the paperwork from my mailbox this morning as I waited for City to respond.

City: I'll be there at six thirty. Be ready for me, because I'm hard as a fuckin' rock. I have plans for that pussy before we go to the BBQ.

OMG, OMG, OMG.

Me: I'll be waiting with bells on.

Five minutes left before the next barrage of hooligans walked through the door. My afternoon classes were murder. They weren't bad kids, but they were challenging and mentally draining.

City: Naked—no fucking bells.

A fire ignited in my body as I read the screen. *It's on like Donkey Kong.*

CHAPTER
TWELVE
CITY

"COMING," a female voice from inside yelled.

"I remember you saying those very words twenty minutes ago," I growled in Suzy's ear.

Her cheeks turned a rosy shade of pink as she bit her lip, trying to hide her smile. Suzy pushed her hair off her shoulders and fixed her shirt, as though she wanted everything perfect and in place.

"Stop fidgeting, sugar."

"Oh my God, I can't. Sophia is going to take one look at me and know what we did," she said, dabbing her fingers at the corner of her lips.

"If she doesn't, then I didn't do it right."

A beautiful brunette opened the door with a smile. She looked me over, starting at my face, and then her eyes raked over my body. I felt almost violated by the way she appraised me. She looked at Suzy with a devilish grin and opened her arms. The girls exchanged hugs and whispered words that I couldn't hear, but Sophia's eyes didn't leave mine.

"Sophia, this is City."

"Nice to meet you, Sophia." I extended my hand to her.

Sophia's hair was pulled back in a sloppy bun that sat on top of her head. She had a bright white smile and kind eyes.

She placed her hand in mine. "Nice to finally meet you, City. I've heard *all* about you." She winked.

A grin crept across my face—I guessed I got the thumbs-up from her friend. "Nice things, I hope."

"She spoke very *big* of you." She giggled, and I felt my cheeks heat. I could tell these girls together were going to be a handful. "Come on in. Kayden and Jett are out on the patio starting the grill."

I extended my arm for Suzy to walk in front of me, and I watched both girls walk inside as I stayed close behind. They lived in a small apartment that was decorated with mismatched pieces that all worked. *SportsCenter* was on the television, and baby things were scattered everywhere.

"Don't mind the mess. Children have a way of overtaking everything, no matter how small." Sophia waved her hands around and picked up small toys off the floor before tossing them in a basket near the television stand.

The door to the patio opened and a tall, muscular man holding a baby walked into the living room. His head was clean-shaven, and he looked like someone that I'd find down at the Neon Cowboy—or a guy who would walk in my shop for some work.

"Kayden, baby, Suzy brought her new beau, City."

Kayden eyed me warily. I held out my hand to him. "Nice to meet you, Kayden. Suzy talks very highly of you and Sophia."

Kayden placed the baby in the crook of his left arm before extending his right hand to me. "Glad to meet you, City." He squeezed my hand tightly, almost to the point of pain, but I didn't dare pull away. I knew the fuckin' macho bullshit. He was staking his claim on Sophia and giving me a silent warning with Suzy.

"Oh, Jett, come here, baby." Reaching for Jett, Suzy plucked him from Kayden's arms.

"No hello, Suzy? How are you, Kayden? I've missed you, Kayden. Just oooh, Jett." Kayden laughed.

"Oh now, Kayden, you know I love you. Gimme a kiss," she said, puckering her lips and closing her eyes.

My heart raced with the thought of Kayden placing his lips on hers. I squeezed my hands into fists. They were just friends. Kayden planted a kiss on her cheek as he rubbed the head of his child before walking into the kitchen and wrapping his arms around his wife.

"He's gotten so big," Suzy said as she bounced the baby in her arms, patting his butt. She looked natural with a child in her arms, like it was something she did every day. Her eyes lit up as Jett gripped her thumb.

"He's growing like a weed," Sophia said from the kitchen. "What do you guys want to drink? City, what can I get you?"

"I'll take a beer if you got one."

Suzy's eyes grew wide and her nostrils flared, and I didn't know what I said, but obviously I'd fucked up somehow. "But it's okay if you don't. I'll really drink anything."

"Coming right up. Suzy? Virgin daiquiri, babe?" Sophia snickered as she opened the fridge and began to dig around.

"What did I say wrong?" I whispered in her ear.

"Kayden doesn't drink. He's an alcoholic and has been clean for about a year now." She looked at Kayden and Sophia before returning her attention on the cooing baby in her arms.

"I didn't know. Shit, you should've given me a heads-up, sugar."

"I'm sorry. It just slipped my mind."

"It's okay, City. It's not something the ladies like to talk about. It's always the giant elephant in the room," Kayden said as he handed me the beer. "I can be around alcohol and not drink." He sat down on the couch and put his feet up on the coffee table. "Sit down; let the ladies work their magic in the kitchen. We'll take care of the meat, like God intended."

"I don't want to hear about your meat, Kayden." Suzy snickered.

"Kitchen, Suzy, but let Sophia cook." He pointed at her then toward the kitchen, and snapped his fingers.

"I can cook, Kayden," she said as she rubbed her nose against the baby's face before handing the baby to Kayden and walking away.

"City, Suzy can't cook a lick. She's the queen of pre-made. Just an FYI," he said as he cradled the baby and ran his finger along the chubby cheek.

Sitting on the couch, I set my beer on my knee and relaxed. "Eh, I can cook, so it's not a deal-breaker for me. Bucs fan?"

"Fuck no, Browns fan born and bred." He stretched out, placing his free hand behind his head.

"No shit? You like an underdog or abuse?" I smiled before lifting the beer to my lips.

"I stay true to my roots, you?"

"Bears fan. No other way to be."

"They've had some fuckin' horrible seasons, but the Browns have the market cornered on losing."

"Give ya that," I said as I tipped my beer toward him. "Suzy said you three lived together."

"Yep, for a while. She was a lifesaver, and I owe her. Don't fucking break her heart—I'll beat the fuck out of you." He laughed. "Seriously, you'll have a few more holes to match the ones you currently have."

What? I could see the girls had talked about me in detail. "Not my plan," I said. "Suzy isn't like other girls."

Suzy leaned against the counter and watched Sophia as they chatted. They looked over at us and started laughing.

"No, she's not. She's kind, pure, and too trusting. I feel

like she's my little sister, and I'll protect her like she's my family."

"Gotcha. Loud and clear."

"You boys done with your pissing match?" Sophia said as she walked in the room with a plate of burgers. "These won't cook themselves."

"Let me handle the meat," Kayden said, handing Jett back to Suzy.

"That's what she said." Sophia chuckled. Kayden grabbed the plate from her and kissed her on the lips. She looked at him with a dopy grin as he backed away.

"If you're a good girl, I'll let you handle my meat later."

"Not in front of our guests," Sophia said as she smacked him on the shoulder.

"They're kind of nauseating aren't they?" Suzy stood next to me and rocked Jett in her arms. His eyes were almost closed as he sucked his fingers.

"A bit." I felt content with the three of them. I could almost feel the bond that they had, the love for each other.

"They've endured more than most people have in a lifetime, and they came out on the other side with an unbreakable bond. Someday I'll tell you their story. If fate is real, they're the perfect example. They were made for each other." She smiled as she watched them on the patio.

They touched each other and kissed, never moving apart. His actions portrayed adoration for his woman. "Are they married?"

"Not yet. Someday, I hope. They've both been married before, and they use that as an excuse not to *rush into things*." She curled her lips up and rolled her eyes. "I remind them that they have a baby. I guess I'm old-fashioned." She shrugged.

I made sure not to fuck that up. I never fucked without a condom or took that kind of risk. "I was brought up that way too, but you can't deny what they have. I'm sure they'll do it in time."

***

The evening was relaxing, and I liked talking with Kayden. He didn't bullshit, and Sophia was something else. She was a spitfire, and loved to tease Suzy mercilessly. "Did I pass the test with your friends?" I asked as we climbed on my bike.

"You did well. You got the thumbs-up from Sophia."

"She's not the one I'm worried about."

"Kayden? Oh, please. He likes to talk all his macho crap, but he's the sappy one. He just wants me happy, City."

"He said he'd kick my ass if I broke your heart, sugar."

She wrapped her arms around me as I walked the bike away from the building, trying not to be too noisy. "Kayden's been known to take matters into his own hands, but I'll set him straight about us," she said in my ear, chuckling.

"Whatcha mean?" I said as I started the engine.

"Oh, nothing." She rested her head against my shoulder and toyed with my nipple piercing. It was the first time I didn't feel her tense against my body when riding on the back of the bike. Maybe she was finally letting go and enjoying herself without overanalyzing the situation.

CHAPTER
THIRTEEN
SUZY

I HAD BECOME USED to being the third wheel around Sophia and Kayden, but tonight everything just felt right. Kayden and City had laughed and talked about sports for hours as Sophia and I talked about work and Jett.

I didn't want to be alone anymore, and I couldn't waste time with City. My heart ached around Kayden and Sophia, and I envied them, wanted what they had—that great love, the one that you can feel and almost touch, and I wouldn't settle for anything less. I had to walk away from City and move forward in my life.

Tears formed in my eyes while I thought about having to give him up as we pulled in and I climbed off the bike. I put my helmet on the bike and started to walk away from City. I didn't want him to see the glistening in my eyes.

"Where you hurrying off to?" Reaching out, he grabbed my wrist, pulling me into his arms.

"Nowhere, I was just going to unlock the door." I shrugged, keeping my arms down and not melting into his touch.

"You okay, sugar?" he asked, looking at my eyes with a question on his face.

"Yeah. The wind made my eyes water." I smiled at him.

"Glasses will block the wind. We'll have to get you a pair."

Thank God he bought that crock of shit. He wrapped his arms around me, smashing my face in his t-shirt. I inhaled, enjoying the musky scent in the material. I closed my eyes and luxuriated in the smell of him.

"Maybe." I felt shitty and my heart ached. Why bother buying me glasses? I didn't plan to spend the rest of my life riding on the back of his bike. Although Sophia and Kayden were opposites, they worked, but City and I didn't have a future.

"What's wrong?" he asked, squeezing me tighter.

"Nothing. I'm just tired." I squeezed him back and relished in the feel of his tight muscles. *Don't say it; don't look like a girl whose head is filled with fairytales.*

"Sugar, that's bullshit. You've never walked away from me or been snippy. Your sparkle's gone. Spill."

Don't do it. He isn't your knight in shining armor riding in on a white horse.

Shifting my weight, I stared at the ground, trying to avoid his gaze. "Nothing, City. I just need sleep. I swear." That lie felt easier than I'd thought.

"Look me in the eyes and say that." He pulled my chin up, forcing me to look into the clear azure eyes that showed sadness. I swallowed hard and steadied my breathing. I knew he could read me like an open book, everyone could, and I had to pull this off. *Don't cry or blink, girl—breathe.*

"I'm just tired, really." I stood on my tiptoes and placed my lips against his. This would be the last time I'd kiss him. I couldn't spend more time with him without risking my heart. I could fall in love with him easily, but I wouldn't risk the heartbreak that would follow. "Call me tomorrow?" I said as I backed away.

"You don't want me to come in, beautiful?" he asked, drawing his brows together and studying my face.

"Not tonight, City. I want to crawl in bed and drift off. If you come in, I know what will happen." I grinned at him as a sly smile spread across his face. He ran his finger down my cheek, and I wanted to lean in to it—I wanted more. "No, no. Don't even think about it." I giggled as he tried pulling me into a kiss. "Down, tiger."

"Tomorrow then," he said as he kissed me on the lips.

I instantly felt the loss of his heat as he let go of my body, and I looked at him. He really was beautiful. He looked like every girl's fantasy with his bike behind him, hard muscles, dreamy eyes, and kindness. I couldn't let myself fall any deeper for him. Every time my phone rang, my text alert chirped, or I stood in his presence, my heart raced. My heart and body responded to him, but my mind kept saying *run*. He wasn't the type that settled down and had a family, and I couldn't blame him. He was a playboy that led a different life than I did. He was on a different path.

I stood at a fork in the road—travel down the path of heartbreak and further immerse myself in his world, or make a clean break and continue on my journey to my ultimate destination of happiness and the love I couldn't live without.

"Tomorrow, big boy," I said with a meek smile, and waved to him before disappearing inside the house without watching him drive away. I threw my keys on the table, walking through the darkened house to my bedroom. My eyes felt heavy, and they burned from the tears that wanted to break free.

The roar of his engine made the walls in my bedroom rattle. I'd never hear that sound again without thinking of him and feeling butterflies in my stomach. He'd altered my thoughts and invaded my mind.

I undressed and put on my favorite comfy pajamas, catching a glimpse of my reflection in the mirror. I wanted to turn back the clock to a time when life felt simpler. When I didn't know the pure animal magnetism and sexual chemistry like I felt with him, but I couldn't. He ruined me and stole that from me.

My phone vibrated as I turned it in my hand and caught a glimpse of his message.

City: It's tomorrow—one minute after midnight.

Setting the phone on my nightstand, I stared at the empty bed and thought of how different the night could've been.

Me: Night, City. Drive safely.

I crawled under the sheets, loving the crisp material against my skin. I stared at the ceiling and watched the fan whirl, causing a shadow to form against the white background. I couldn't fall asleep, and turned on the television, praying that the mindless entertainment would help calm my thoughts and help me forget him.

My phone danced across the wooden surface. *Don't pick it up.* I couldn't do it. I wanted to see if I could break free of him —quit cold turkey like a junkie. I had to try to put distance between us. I'd only known him a week, but he invaded my life.

Flipping through the channels, I stopped on a show about a group of bikers. I'd heard about the show but never found interest in it until now. I couldn't bring myself to turn it off. Every man on the screen reminded me of him. The roar of the engines made my heart flutter and my stomach hurt. Curling on my side, I hugged the pillow as tears poured out, plopping on the material. I wanted to feel the wind in my hair and my arms wrapped around his body, but it could never happen again. My eyes burned as I gave in and drifted off to the sound of roaring engines.

***

I woke to a couple of messages from City wishing me good morning and asking when I could see him again. Leaving my phone on my nightstand, I made a glass of tea and sat on my front step sipping the warm cinnamon liquid. The neighborhood was quiet as a few couples walked down the sidewalks and children played in the front yard down the street. I stared at the sun shimmering off the wet grass and thought about him. I couldn't sit here all day and think about him. I had to find something to do today to keep my mind off him and move toward my future.

I needed a shower, had to wash his scent off me and start my day. No more wallowing in self-pity and the whirlwind that I'd lived for the last week. I grabbed my phone off the nightstand, but there were no new messages from City. Maybe he got the hint after I didn't send him a good morning text.

The ringing of my phone made me jump as I waited for the water to warm. I walked to the phone slowly and peeked at the screen—relief flooded me as I saw that it was Derek and not City.

"Hey," I said, as I stood there naked, staring in the mirror, the fog blurring my reflection.

"Hi, Suzy. What are you doing later?" Derek had a deep voice, but it didn't have half the effect on me that City's voice did.

"Not much, just about to jump in the shower. What's up?"

His sharp intake of air made it evident that he had just pictured me naked. "I wanted to know if you wanted to go to dinner tonight and maybe play some mini-golf. Do you want to go with me?"

"Oh, well..." I gnawed on my thumbnail and debated a date with Derek. He worked on paper, and we ran in the same circles. Our worlds were similar and we could relate to each other. Maybe he was the path that I needed to follow—or at least he'd help keep my mind off City.

"Come on, Suzy. We'll have fun. What do you say?" His voice was hopeful. Couldn't blame a guy for being persistent—he'd never taken no for an answer.

"Okay, Derek." I ran my hands down the bare skin between my breasts, loving the feel of the softness. I instantly felt like crap for saying yes when all I wanted to do was run to City.

"It's a date. I'll pick you up at six."

"See you at six."

"Great. I can't wait to see you tonight. Bye for now, Suzy."

"Bye, Derek." I heard him celebrating his victory before the line went dead.

I stood in the shower and daydreamed about City before touching myself, relieving the ache between my legs. The orgasm wasn't as satisfying as I had hoped. It dulled the need I felt for City. I craved the earth-shattering orgasms I felt under his deft fingertips, but I couldn't let my sexual desire cloud my judgment.

City sent me two more text messages before Derek picked me up for dinner. I ignored the urge to reply and finished my makeup, smacking my red lipstick together before running the brush through my hair one last time. The tight black miniskirt and yellow tank top helped show off my fading tan. Soon the winter cold and weakened sun would cause my skin to return to its almost ghostly shade of white. Grabbing my strappy black stilettos out of the closet, I thought of that last time I'd worn them—the night City rode into my life. I put my favorite Reef sandals in my purse for later, when my feet ached and we played mini-golf.

The chime of the doorbell snapped me out of my memories of the first night in City's bed. Opening the door, I took in the sight of Derek in a pair of khaki dress pants and crisp white linen shirt, with his toes peeking out from the fabric around his feet. His smile beamed as his eyes roamed my body, taking in my outfit before stopping on my breasts. He licked his lips before he settled on my face with a goofy smile.

"Wow, you look sexy, Suzy." His nostrils flared as his gaze drifted down my body again.

The way he looked at me made my skin crawl. "Thanks, you look great too." He did look nice, but not heart-stopping or panty-dropping.

He held out his hand to me. "Ready?"

I placed my fingers against his smooth palm, "Yeah," I said, although I was anything but.

Derek opened the door to his beat-up Nissan Altima, waiting for me to climb in before he kissed my hand and slammed the door.

I sighed as I watched him walk around the car, a brilliant and victorious smile on his face. "God, this is a horrible idea," I mumbled to myself as he opened the door and climbed in.

"What did you say?" he asked as he climbed in, closed the door, and looked at me.

"Just saying how hungry I am. Where are we eating?"

He brushed the hair off my shoulder, gliding his fingertips across my skin, lingering longer than felt comfortable. My body involuntarily moved away from his touch. "Sorry," he said as he turned away and gripped the steering wheel, his knuckles whitening from his firm grasp. "We're going to Paesano's for some Italian, if that's okay with you?"

"Sounds great."

I stared out the window, watching the trees pass by as Derek chattered about work. I looked forward to my weekends and escaping the stress and my job, but that was all Derek wanted to talk about. I listened to his words and answered when asked a question, but he already bored me. Thankful that the drive to the restaurant wasn't long, I climbed out of the car as Derek jogged to me and grabbed my arm, hooking them together.

The conversation during dinner was stagnant. We didn't have much in common besides work. It became evident as he talked about video games. My idea of a great night did not involve playing a mindless game on the television. When the food finally arrived, I found myself thankful for the silence as he shoveled the food in his mouth without care. He ate like a pig, with sauce from his pasta dribbling on his chin and resting at the corners of his mouth. I moved the food around on my plate, trying not to stare.

"You want to go for some drinks after here or you want to go to mini-golf?" he asked with a full mouth, a small piece of pasta falling in his lap.

Why the hell did I think this was a good idea? "Drinks sound great." I prayed that a few drinks would make him interesting and have the evening end on a high note.

We skipped dessert and headed to Club Karma for drinks. The club had opened a couple months ago, but I hadn't set foot inside. It had a big-city feel, not like the typical small-town hangouts. The walls were blood red, decorated with black-and-white photos of couples in various sexual positions and states of undress. Colorful lights bounced off the shiny black tile floor as dancers moved their bodies against each other. There were small seating areas with couches filled with couples laughing and touching, and a large bar on the opposite side of the entrance.

"Drink first?" Derek asked. I nodded and looked around as he guided me through the overcrowded space. Derek rested his body against the bar, his arm touching my skin. "You want to dance?" he shouted in my ear above the music.

I shook my head and waited for the bartender to come in our direction. A large mirror hung above the liquor bottles on the wall behind the serving area. Watching people dance with such erotic and methodical moves made me think of City and our dance last weekend. I never felt sexy on the dance floor, but with him I had been able to feel the music instead of thinking of my next move.

I ordered a martini, wanting the alcohol over a virgin daiquiri, needing to forget City and find a way to make Derek more palatable. His arm brushed against my back as he rested his hand on the bar, effectively trapping me. I ignored him, staring into the mirror as the bartender placed my drink on the bar.

I took a sip, testing the sweetness of the raspberry martini. This whole night had been a bad idea. I knew it from the moment I accepted his invitation to dinner. I wouldn't have said yes to him if I weren't trying to forget the tall, muscular Italian man.

"Suzy," Derek whispered in my ear, further invading my personal space.

"What?" I said into the glass still pressed against my lips.

"Drink up, babe, because I can't wait to get you out there." Derek bobbed his head like a character in a skit from *Saturday Night Live*. I could see his reflection in the mirror, and my cheeks felt heated at the thought of someone seeing me with him.

"Uh huh." I didn't turn to look at him but kept my eyes on the scene in the mirror, like I was watching a television show. I'd find a way to stall. I couldn't go on to the dance floor with him. No way in hell would that happen. He didn't have the ability to make me dance like City had, and his awkward movements would only draw more awareness to us, when all I wanted to do was blend in.

His fingers touched the skin of my arms and hand as I fought every urge to kick him in the balls. He rambled on about his clubbing days in college and how he mastered the dance floor and people would stop to watch him "bust a move." Almost spitting my drink out, I broke out into laughter, tears forming in my eyes. I could imagine the scene. Derek thought people stopped to admire his ability, when in actuality they were stunned or entertained beyond belief.

"What's so funny?" His lips were turned into a frown as he moved his head away from mine and stared at me.

"Oh, nothing, Derek. Just something I remembered from college." God, I had always been a shitty liar, but I didn't want to hurt his feelings. The man had confidence, and who was I to kill it?

"Ah, okay. I thought you were laughing at me." He shrugged before sipping his beer and wiping his lips on his shoulder. "Come on, just one dance," he begged, and released me from my human cage.

I sloshed the pink liquid in my glass, now half drained, and lifted it to my lips. I owed him at least one dance for his efforts. I swallowed the last mouthful and placed it on the bar. "Just one."

His eyes lit up as he grabbed my hand and pulled me toward the writhing bodies in the middle of the room. The beat of the music made me unable to feel my pulse, even though I knew it had to be hammering. I wanted to throw up at the thought of anyone watching me make an ass out of myself. Just as we reached the spot that Derek wanted, dead center, the DJ switched songs. Fuck, why me? A sad, slow melody filled the air as Derek pulled me into an embrace. I'd rather make a complete asshole out of myself with a wicked beat that didn't require touching.

"Perfect," he said, wrapping his arms around me, his hands resting a little too close to my ass.

Placing my hands on his shoulders, I tried to keep some distance between us, but Derek didn't get the hint. His body felt nothing like City's; there was no hardness to it. Derek's hands roamed my back as he swayed our bodies side to side to the music, and I gave in, letting him control our movement. He didn't speak as he moved us back and forth to the beat. Time passed slowly, and I felt like I had been wrapped in his arms for hours with no escape.

When the song ended, Derek broke the embrace and backed up to look at me. He gave me a silly grin, "Thank you."

"For what?" I yelled as the music began to thump through the speakers.

"The dance, Suzy. I loved having you in my arms," he said, as he reached for my hand and kissed the top.

"You're a sweet guy, Derek." I blushed. He wasn't a bad guy—he just wasn't City.

"Another drink?"

"If I didn't know any better, Derek, I'd think you're trying to get me drunk."

He smiled, his face turning pink as he pushed on my back and led me off the dance floor. "Can't blame a guy for trying."

We passed a set of couches, and something drew my attention. There before me was a woman in a skintight, barely there dress with red stiletto heels and long brown hair. The woman didn't draw my attention, but the man whose lap she sat on was City. He didn't notice me as he talked to her, giving her his total attention. His hand rested on her ass as she nibbled on his lips. I wanted to throw up. He didn't seem to have a problem forgetting me.

Bile rose in my throat at the sight of the two of them together. I'd spent the entire day trying to forget him without success, but he had moved on to someone else. "I'll take you up on that offer, Derek." No longer able to watch City with another woman, I walked to the bar with Derek right behind me. Derek only had eyes for me tonight, and the smile on his face made it clear that I had made him happy with my response.

Even though I had been the one that ignored him, it still stung to see him enjoying the company of another woman. "What'll it be, sweetheart?" the bartender asked me as she leaned against the bar with a smile.

"Shot of anything sweet and another raspberry martini, please."

"I'll have another Miller," Derek said before she walked away. "A shot, huh?"

"It's Saturday night and I could use a little something stronger."

"I didn't know you were a drinker, Suzy." He grabbed our drinks, pushing mine in front of me before throwing down a twenty for the bartender.

"I'm not, but what the hell. Why not?" I shrugged before picking up the shot and smelling it. Raspberry something or other, but I wasn't quite sure. It would do the job and help dull the pang of jealousy I felt from seeing City with the girl in red. "To life and love," I said, raising my glass before swallowing the sweet concoction.

Derek tipped his beer in my direction and watched me as he raised it to his lips. "Why aren't you taken?" he asked from behind the brown bottle.

I shrugged. "Looking for the right one." The martini sloshed the glass as I brought it to my lips too quickly. One drink and a shot and I didn't give a fuck that some of it splashed on my breasts. Tears stung my eyes as I gulped the martini and hoped that it would put my brain in a temporary haze. The feel of a hand touching my breast caused me to jerk, sending the last bit of raspberry heaven to the floor. "What the fuck?" I said, looking down to see Derek's hand move away from my breast.

"Sorry." He grinned. "Just thought I'd help you with that little spill." He sucked on his fingers as he stared at my chest.

I snarled as I put my face close to his. "No matter how drunk I am, you don't touch me without asking. Am I clear?"

"Yes, ma'am," he said, raising his hand to salute me.

What a cocksucker. Poking him in the chest, I spoke very slowly. "I mean it, smartass. Do. Not. Touch. Me." Turning away, I looked in the mirror and saw the red dress still sitting on City's lap, and my fingernails dug into the wooden bar.

"Okay, Suzy. Let me make it up to you, since I made you spill your drink. Let me buy you another?"

I closed my eyes, rubbing the bridge of my nose, before turning my attention back to Derek. "I don't think so, Derek. Will you just take me home?"

"One more, Suzy. I swear I'll keep my hands to myself. I don't want the night to end like this. Please."

I studied his face, and he looked genuine, with a sad smile and pleading eyes. I held up my index finger to him. "One more and then I want to go."

"Excellent." He raised his hand in the air and snapped his fingers, grabbing the attention of the bartender.

As I leaned against the bar, my eyes kept wandering back to the mirror. The third martini was easier to drink; my legs felt weak and the bar became necessary to keep me from tipping over. Derek chattered in my ear and kept his distance as we polished off our third drinks.

"Ready?" he asked as he set the empty bottle on the counter.

"Are you okay to drive?" I asked. I may be drunk, but I knew enough to ask.

"Yeah, I can handle more than three beers, babe."

Hearing the word "babe" come out his mouth when he spoke made me want to throw up on his shoes. Everything about him made me crazy, and I knew that I'd never go on another date with Derek. On paper he seemed right, but in person he was a creepy mess that revolted me and did nothing for my libido.

"Okay, let's go." I grabbed my purse and walked on unsteady legs toward the door, leaving Derek to walk behind me.

"You want to hold my hand?"

"Why?" I stopped and turned to face him, almost falling over. I'd had too much to drink and didn't realize it until now.

"Because you're walking funny. Just hold on to my arm until we get to the car." He held out his hand and waited for me to take it.

He didn't grin or smile, and I believed he was sincere in his offer. Clearly the alcohol had made my brain fuzzy. I didn't hold his hand, but snaked my arm through his and leaned on his body as I swayed through the parking lot, thankful when we made it to his car.

Leaning against the car, I waited for him to open the door. I closed my eyes and soaked in the feel of the cool air against my warm, clammy skin. The air inside the club had felt stagnant. My anger and hurt over City made my body feel flushed and caused me to sweat. I had done this. I pushed City away. I had been an idiot, and I knew it when I saw him with her in his arms.

Derek's lips were on mine before I could react. I pushed at him, hitting his chest as he trapped me between him and the car. My arms felt like jelly, and I couldn't gauge how hard I was hitting him as the beat of my heart filled my ears. "Stop," I mumbled between breaks in the kiss, but he didn't stop crushing his body against mine harder. His lips moved over my cheek to my neck as he grabbed my breast and squeezed. "Derek, stop, damn it!" I yelled, hitting him in the ribs.

"You know you want it, Suzy," he said against my neck.

"I don't! Stop!" I pushed against him again, but his weight was too much. I swung and connected with his face with a loud smack. My hand stung from the contact.

His face moved away from my neck, and he looked me in the eyes. He glared at me with his mouth set in a firm line. "You hit me. What the fuck? I'm just giving you what you want, baby."

Clearly I had sent the wrong signals, or he was just a dumbass. "Get the fuck off me."

"You're such a prick tease in this outfit tonight. You can deny it all you want, but I know you want me."

"I do—"

His lips were on me again before I could stop him. I struggled against him, bending my knee up to make contact with his balls, but hit nothing as his body flew backward.

City held Derek by the throat, bringing him to eye level.

"Why don't you pick on someone your own size, motherfuck-er?" City said with a look of pure hatred.

"This has nothing to do with you, man," Derek spat. "This is between the lady and me." Derek clawed at City's hands, trying to escape his grip.

City turned toward me. "He your boyfriend?" His eyes moved over my body, taking in my outfit. I shook my head, my hands gripping the car, not moving. "You want him to touch you?" He looked at Derek and back to me.

Derek's face had turned a deep shade of red, on the verge of purple, as City's grip increased. "No! I told him to stop!" I said. "But I work with the scumbag. Don't hurt him."

City growled; his chest heaved with rough breaths while deciding his next action. "Fuck," he muttered before drop-ping Derek to the ground.

Derek gasped for air as he tried to stand, but collapsed on his hands and knees. Air filled my lungs, and I realized I had held my breath, waiting for City to beat the hell out of Derek before my eyes. Did he deserve it? Hell yes, but I didn't want to witness it or deal with the aftermath.

City stood in front of me, his hands clenched at his side as he stared at me. The hard features of his face looked more pronounced by his anger. His cheeks flexed, his nostrils flaring as he studied me. "What the fuck, Suzy? I called you and you don't fucking answer and then you're here with this fucking prick and almost let him maul you in a parking lot." Running his fingers through his hair, he turned and looked at Derek before returning his attention back to me.

"I'm sorr-ry." I didn't know what else to say. I didn't have an excuse. "I didn't know I had to answer to you. You seemed to have your hands full inside, anyway." I snarled as I spoke.

"What the fuck are you talking about?"

"Brunette, red dress, almost dry-humping you on the couch. Ring any bells?" Who the fuck was he to question my actions?

"Fuck." His arms flexed as he clenched his hands into a hard fist at his sides. "Kaylee means nothing to me."

"Neither do I, I suppose."

"Woman, you have no idea what the fuck you're talking about." He stepped closer, and my body instantly registered his nearness, moisture pooling between my legs.

I swallowed, the dryness in my mouth making it hard to move anything down my throat. "I saw your hands on her ass as she kissed you. How the hell do you explain that? It seems women have no value to you."

"Shut your mouth, Suzy. I followed you out here because I saw you stumbling out of here with someone I didn't know. I came here to check on you. Kaylee is no one, hear me now, *no one*. I didn't come here with her or ask her to sit on my lap. I was trying to be nice to her."

"Well, if nice means you feel her up, I'd say you were very kind to her."

"Suzy, listen to me. I called you and asked you back out. You blew me off. What was I supposed to do? Sit home and wait for you to call?"

Breath escaped me as he closed the small space between us.

Tears began to stream down my cheeks as I took in the enormity of the situation. If City hadn't stopped Derek, would I have been able to get away from him? He just saved me, and I was being a total bitch. The sob tore through my chest as I broke down. City wrapped his arms around me and kissed my forehead. He felt so right against my body. I felt safe and comfortable with him, no matter how much we didn't seem to fit on paper. He said nothing, but made sounds to calm me as I buried my face into the soft material of his t-shirt. My fingers found the piercing on his nipple as I toyed with it and tried to catch my breath.

"Can I take you home, sugar?" he asked with his face buried in my hair.

"Yes," I whimpered, clinging to him like a lifeline.

Without speaking, he drew me into his arms, carrying me across the parking lot. I melted into him, resting my head against his shoulder. The thought of Kaylee still stung, but I couldn't be mad at him anymore. He saved me from a totally fucked-up night, and for that he'd earned my forgiveness. The jostling movement as he placed my bottom on the cool seat of his bike made my stomach churn. I said nothing as he put the helmet on my head and fastened the harness against my chin. He had the right mix of pissed-off male and swoon-worthy alpha to make any girl's heart go pitter-patter.

"Can you hold on?" he asked as he held my chin between his fingertips.

"Yes." My tone was breathy and betrayed me with the sound of need.

He climbed on the bike, scooting his ass between my legs and gripping the handlebars. I molded my torso against his and interlaced my fingers. The usual jitters I felt anticipating the ride ahead didn't register.

"Hold on, sugar." He throttled the engine and took off for the short drive to my house. The cool air whipped my hair around as I nuzzled against his warm back. My mind grew blank with the movement of the bike and the roar of the engine. I allowed myself to get lost in the moment and the sensation of the vibrations from the bike—and the feel of City between my legs.

Lost in the City coma, I didn't notice as we pulled into my development and weaved through the winding streets to my house. Maybe I'd drifted off, but I wanted to stay like this forever—wrapped around his body, in a stress-free haze of contentment. I mumbled against his shirt as he turned off the bike, placing his feet on the ground, securing it and tapping my hands. "Sugar, we're here."

"Mm hmm," I said into his back before raising my head and looking through blurry eyes at my house. I sat up, letting go of his chest before wiping the drool off my lips. "Thanks, City. I don't know what would've happened tonight if it weren't for you." I started to climb off the bike but didn't have the energy, and plopped back against the seat with an "oomph."

City laughed as he climbed off, pulling me off the bike, cradling me in his arms. "Can I come in?" he asked, brushing his nose against my cheek.

"Depends. You mad at me?" I asked, praying he said no.

"I'm not mad. We gotta talk, Suzy." His eyes begged me to let him in as his brow furrowed.

"Okay." I rested my head against his hard chest and rubbed my palm against his pec.

I handed him the keys as we approached the door. Anger was no longer visible, but the tilted grin I'd grown accustomed to had vanished. He kicked off his boots before he walked across my white carpet, placing me on the couch. The couch dipped from his weight, but I couldn't look him in the eye. I fiddled with my fingers as the silence became deafening. The alcohol-induced haze had started to wear off, and I felt a small buzz.

"Why the hell didn't you call me today? I thought we made plans. What the fuck did I do wrong?" His words made me cringe; sadness was evident in his voice.

"I wanted to put distance between us. You didn't do anything wrong." I shook my head, meeting his eyes.

"Distance? What for?" His eyebrows drew together as the skin wrinkled in between.

"I just don't think we'll work out." I shrugged.

"Woman, you think too damn much, and it's fucked up. Blew my ass off for that douchebag tonight, and how'd that shit turn out for you?" He paused before continuing. "What makes you think we don't have a shot?"

I looked away from him, unable to look him in the eyes. "We're just so different, City. I don't see a future between us, and at my age, I'm looking forward. I don't live life by the seat of my pants like you. We have nothing in common and we run in different worlds." Water clouded my vision as I stared at the wall across the room. I blinked, trying to clear the tears from my eyes.

Sighing, he reached for my face, touching my cheek and pulling my face in his direction. "Look at me, sugar." His eyes moved around my face. "I don't know how you think I live, and you sure as hell don't know who I am. We're getting to know each other, but you shut me out without a reason. You said it yourself, Sophia and Kayden are opposites but they work. Why couldn't we?"

I drew in a shaky breath, his words making my heart ache. "I know I said that, but I don't know, City."

"What don't you know? Talk to me." His hand closed over my fist in my lap as he stroked his thumb across my sensitive skin.

"I like you a lot. So much that it scares me, and I don't know if I could deal with the heartbreak when you walk out of my life." A tear slid down my cheek as I spoke.

"You never gave us a chance to see if we could work." His finger slid across my skin, wiping the tear away.

"You're not a one-woman man. I could tell that about you, and I don't work that way. I don't want to share you."

"Suzy, I'm not a whore. Since I met you last week I haven't been with anyone else. I don't want anyone else, just you."

"I'd like to believe that, but you looked a little too cozy with Karen tonight."

"Kaylee, not Karen. I'll be totally honest with you about her. I had sex with her twice in my life. Not my proudest moment, but she offered and I accepted. She wants to be my girlfriend, and I've told her no. I'm very clear with her that she and I are nothing and never will be. Should I have pushed her ass on the floor when she sat on my lap?"

"No, I guess not." I didn't want to think about the visual I had of another woman sitting on him and fawning.

"I wanted to be with you tonight. You blew me off. We had such a nice time last night, and as soon as I brought you home, you shut down."

"I don't know, City," I said.

"Joey."

"Joey, I watched Kayden and Sophia all night. They reminded me of what I want someday. I want someone that's going to love me and be mine alone. I want to be important to someone," I said, staring into his eyes without blinking, worried another tear would slip down my cheek.

"It's what everyone wants—"

"Let me finish." I shook my head. "I like you, Joey. No one has ever made me feel the way you do, but I can't risk falling for you. I can't have my heart broken." I bit my lip, trying to focus on pain instead of sadness. I didn't want tears to flow freely. "I think it's best if we stop now. The time we've spent together has been amazing, but I can't do it anymore. I can't lie to myself."

"May I speak now?" He smiled at me, but it was a sad smile.

"Yes."

"Do you think I'm incapable of love?" He stared at me, waiting for an answer, his mouth set in a firm line.

"No, I just don't think it's who you are *now*, and I can't wait around for that part of you. It wouldn't be fair to either of us."

"Suzette." Formal names always meant something serious. "I never allowed myself to think of a future with anyone, but last night I saw a world of possibilities. I realized what I was missing out on—I want what Kayden and Sophia have." He squeezed my fingers, and I watched his thumb rub the back of my hand. "Look at me. I've never allowed myself to get close to anyone in years, but your innocence and sweetness have pierced my heart."

"Oh," I said, my eyes growing wide with surprise.

"I didn't want to rush into anything with you. I don't want to ruin anything, but you need to understand where I'm coming from. You need to know my past." His Adam's apple bobbed in his throat as he swallowed before continuing. "I have been in love before. I had a fiancée and I thought my entire life was made. Plans don't always work out exactly as we think."

"I'm sorry," I said, breaking a hand free from his grip, touching his cheek, running my thumb across the rough stubble.

"It was a long time ago. We were in college and her name was Joni. We were high school sweethearts." He closed his eyes, and I could see the pain on his beautiful features. "I loved her more than anything in the world, and she was ripped from my life."

My heart skipped with the thought that anyone could break his heart.

"A fucking drunk driver hit her on her way home from work and she was killed instantly." He hung his head, hiding his face from my view. I could only imagine the pain that he'd felt losing his love that day in such a brutal manner. "I've never allowed myself to get that close to anyone after she died. It fuckin' wrecked me, and I didn't know if I'd ever fully heal."

"I'm sorry, Joey." I kissed his cheek, allowing him the time to gather his thoughts and hide a small part of himself.

His eyes rose to meet mine. "You remind me a lot of Joni... your kindness and playful nature. It's infectious. You two would've been good friends. She was my light, and I couldn't remember life without her until the day she died. I thought the heartbreak would kill me, Suzy. I've been so scared to open myself to anyone again, but you made me want to try.

Don't shut me out. I can't promise forever, yet, but I want you to be mine, Suzy."

My breath caught. "What do you mean?"

"Woman, I swear sometimes I have to spell shit out to you. For a smart girl, sometimes you amaze me." He chuckled. "I want you to be my girlfriend. Mine and only mine. I'd planned to ask you tonight before you blew me off."

Yes, yes, yes! "What about you?" I asked. Would he see other girls? My heart couldn't take that.

"Just you, Suzy. I want a full commitment, and it's a two-way street. Your body is mine...no one else's. I haven't wanted to be with only one person in a long time."

"Okay," I whispered, a smile creeping across my lips. My body vibrated with excitement as his words sank in. City wanted me to be his girlfriend. Wow.

"So, you'll be my girlfriend?" he asked.

"Yes," I said as I crawled into his lap. "I've never wanted anything more," I said against his lips.

"Mine," he growled as he crushed his mouth to my lips. The kiss felt different than the others. There was a hunger behind it—a claiming.

City lifted my body as he stood. Wrapping my arms around his neck, I kissed him back with more passion than I had before. I wanted him more than I ever did. I wanted to make love to him and convey all the passion I felt for him—I wanted to heal him. He may have been broken, but I'd help his heart heal and show him all the love I had to offer.

CHAPTER
FOURTEEN
CITY

SHARING the loss of Joni was easier than I'd thought. I rarely spoke about her, and only my family knew about my past. I felt Suzy needed to know to understand. I owed it to her. I'd let it go beyond a casual relationship by meeting her friends and seeing her more than once. Fuck, I'd seen her more than any woman that I'd allowed in my bed since Joni.

Placing her feet on the bedroom floor, she slid down my body before standing, leaning against me. Her soft eyes stared into mine as the corners of her mouth turned up into a smile. Cradling my face in her hands, she rose on her tiptoes and touched her lips to mine. She tasted sweet, and my body craved more. We kissed with our eyes open, and I watched as her pupils dilated and her blinking slowed. Her hands began to move, and I heard the fabric of her shirt rustle as her knuckles brushed against my abdomen. I grabbed her hands, stilling them. "I undress you," I said, and her hands went slack at her side.

She swallowed, smiling at me before lifting her arms. Pulling up her shirt, I exposed her soft belly before the white lace of her bra became visible, her hard nipples calling for my mouth. I dropped her shirt to the floor behind her and ran my hands down her still-raised arms, over her collarbone, over her breasts, stopping at her nipples. I palmed her breasts in my hands and felt the heaviness in them. Her breathing changed as I ran my thumbs over her hardened nipples and stared in her eyes. Her mouth opened, and she sucked in a quick breath as her head fell back.

I wanted to take her hard and fast, but after the talk we'd just had, I knew I had to show her the gentler side of sex. I couldn't be rough with her, not this time at least. I had to show her that I cared for her and didn't think of her as a fuck toy.

I forced my hands to leave her breasts and moved them over her soft stomach, hooking my fingers inside the cloth hugging her hips, as I pulled her skirt down her legs, to reveal matching white lace panties. I kissed the delicate material and placed my knees on the floor. She stood there and swayed, but didn't move.

"Feet, sugar." I tapped the tops of her feet as I waited for her to react. I could hear her giggle above me as she crawled out of her skirt, and the sound of it made my heart skip a beat. Innocence and bliss. I grabbed her hips and moved her body until the back of her knees hit the soft mattress. She sat down and looked at me with wide eyes.

"Lie back," I growled as I held her knees, spreading them wide. "I want to taste that sweet pussy of yours. I'm going to devour you until you're begging for my dick, sugar." I grinned at her. I could hold out an eternity feasting on her body—worshipping her center with my tongue.

She rested on her elbows and smirked at me as I sat between her knees. "All the way down, sugar." I squeezed her knees in warning.

"Damn, you're pretty between my legs. I just wanted to watch you," she said with a playful grin on her face.

"Keep your eyes on me." I reached for her lace panties and wrapped my fingertips inside the material.

"Wait," she said as I began to move the material away from her body.

I pulled quickly, and the material disintegrated in my hands.

"Well, crap, those were expensive." She blew out a breath.

"I'll buy you new ones, sugar. No more talking; my mouth has other things to do that are more important." My hands glided down her legs, pulling them apart as they reached her knees. I moved my mouth to the soft, sensitive skin of her thigh and licked, causing her body to shudder.

I could smell her arousal, and the sweet scent of her pussy made my dick ache. I kissed and licked to the V where her leg connected to her body, only inches from her pussy. Sucking her flesh in my mouth, I lapped at her juices as I twirled my tongue over the smooth skin and listened to her tiny moans. Continuing the slow, sensual assault on her body, I gripped her knees as I ran my tongue across her pussy, but didn't stop to pay her engorged clit any attention. I stopped at the same exact spot on her right leg, pulling the skin into my mouth to leave a mark. I hadn't given a hickey since high school, but I wanted to leave something to remind her of who owned her body.

"You're killing me," she said, all breathy. I smiled against her skin as I bit down on the flesh and she flinched. "Jesus," she yelped, and the bed dipped as her back dropped against the mattress.

My tongue soothed the red skin where my teeth had left a mark, leaving no doubt where I'd been and to whom she belonged. I couldn't wait any longer to taste her and feel her on my tongue as I moved toward her heat, inhaling her scent before my mouth descended on her body. I buried my nose in her blonde hair and smelled her sweetness. My flat tongue rested against her clit as I began to circle it with my tongue, but I denied her the contact she wanted. I sucked her lips into my mouth, like a starved man, tasting her wetness on my tongue. Her fingers laced in my hair and pushed my face into her core.

I dipped my tongue into her wetness and swallowed her arousal. I didn't think I could ever get enough of her taste. I wanted to hear her scream and couldn't wait any longer. I licked upward, capturing the last drops from her pussy as I sucked her clit hard.

She moaned, pulling my face harder against her body, writhing under my touch. I pushed two fingers inside her and her body stilled. Her pussy clenched against my fingers as I thrust them inside her. Her body arched and she gripped the sheets as she moaned. Moving my palm against her skin, I placed my fingertips on her nipple. Pinching it, my grip pulsated against her stiff peak, and it tipped her over the edge. She lifted her head, and her body grew rigid as her breathing became erratic and shaky.

I stared at her face, watching her fall into oblivion, overcome by the orgasm gripping her body. She dropped her head on the pillow as her eyes opened, sucking in a shuddering breath. Listening to her ragged breaths, I grabbed the condom from my back pocket before standing and removing my clothing.

The look on her face was one of a predator staring at their prey. I stroked my cock and stared at her body, waiting to be filled. Her mouth opened as she stared at my hand, and I stroked it with a firm grip, catching the piercing as I touched the tip.

"You want me inside you, sugar?" I asked in a slow, deep tone as I stood at the foot of the bed stroking myself.

"Well," she said, caressing her skin and licking her lips. "I mean, your fingers are magic and your mouth is divine…"

I held up my free hand. "Shhh, sugar. No more talking. The only sound I want to hear is you screaming my name as you come on my dick."

"Oh," she said, her eyes still glued to my shaft like she'd

never seen it before. She was so easy to fluster. I tore the condom wrapper open with my teeth and rolled it over my aching member. I couldn't wait any longer to be inside her luscious cunt and seek my release.

I moved up her body and nestled between her legs. "For the first time, I'm taking you as mine." I laid my palm against her pussy, cupping it as I gripped it in its entirety. "No one else gets to touch you understand, Suzette?" I asked with my lips against hers.

"Yes, Joseph. It's yours and only yours," she said, staring in my eyes.

I kissed her and claimed her body as mine, fucking her with passion. I took her slow and gentle, showing her body the attention it deserved, and worshipped her in a way she'd never experienced before collapsing on the mattress.

I stretched out in bed and stared at the ceiling as she went to get ready for bed. She walked out of the bathroom in a t-shirt, but I wanted to feel her skin against mine as we slept. "No clothes."

"What do you mean?" she asked as she touched the edge of the mattress.

"When you sleep in bed with me, I don't want you wearing clothes. They're a barrier I don't want to deal with—I want all of you whenever I want you, even in the middle of the night." I patted the mattress.

"Underwear?" She smiled and lifted the shirt.

"No underwear either. Strip and get your fine ass in this bed." She didn't move, looking at me with a silly smile. "Do it," I said, eyeing her.

"But—"

"No, buts, sugar. I've seen every inch of your body, even that beautiful little asshole of yours. That'll be mine someday too."

Her smile faded, but her eyes twinkled as she stepped out of her panties and threw her nightshirt on the floor. She curled against my body and rested her head on my shoulder.

"Hand, sugar."

She placed her hand on my chest, not forgetting where I'd put it the first night we spent together. My heartbeat thudded below her palm as I rested my hand on top of hers. I placed my lips against her forehead. "Sweet dreams, beautiful."

"Night, Joey," she said as she yawned. Her breathing changed quickly as she drifted to sleep.

I listened to her tiny breaths as she slept beside me, wrapped in my arms, and curled into my body. I held her hand against my chest and felt her fingertips rub my skin. I felt my eyes grow heavy as I rubbed her hand and tangled my fingers in her hair.

***

I felt someone staring at me as I opened my eyes in the darkness. "You awake?" she whispered.

"I am now," I said, moving my fingers in her hair. "What's wrong, sugar?"

"I couldn't sleep. I didn't want to wake you, but I…"

"What's bothering that pretty little head of yours?" I moved my fingers out of her hair and rubbed the soft skin of her arms, thrumming my fingers back and forth rhythmically.

"I'm just scared," she whispered.

"Of me?" I moved my head away to see her face barely lit by moonlight cascading through the blinds.

"Not really." She rubbed my chest. "I've had boyfriends, but only a couple. I've never felt about them the way I feel about you, Joey. It scares the piss out of me."

"How did you feel about them?" I asked, more curious about how she felt about me than the previous men in my shoes.

"They were nice, but I didn't get butterflies every time I

saw them. We'd go days without talking, and I was fine with that, but with you I'm always checking my phone for a message. I'm feeling needy with you, Joey, and I don't like it."

"Sugar." I reached for her chin, drawing her shadowed eyes toward my face. "That's not needy. Needy and clingy is if you're up my ass all day and want to know my every move. Needy is when you show up at my house all hours of the night and at the shop during the day." I shook my head and smirked at her. "You're not needy. Wipe that shit from your mind."

"If you say so. It's just a new feeling for me. If I overstep or act like a crazy person, please tell me." The worry in her eyes began to ease.

"Deal." I kissed her forehead, lingering over the soft flesh with my lips.

"What was your longest relationship?" I asked. I hadn't been the pillar of normal relationship behavior since I lost Joni, but I had an inkling that she had been just as unlucky in love as I had been.

"Four months," she whispered.

"Did you love him?"

"I think I loved him, but a week after I said those words to him, he left me. He's the only man I've ever said that to—he broke my heart."

I rubbed my hand up her arms to soothe her while she spoke.

"I've never really allowed myself to get that close to anyone after that. It was during my freshman year in college, and after that breakup, I just spent my time studying and avoiding anything that felt like it could lead to a relationship." She yawned and burrowed her body a little closer to mine.

"I understand heartbreak and wanting to guard your heart from the pain. I've lived it for more years than I'd like to admit." I pulled her closer, leaving no space between us. "Let's just take this slow. It's best for both of us."

"Slow," she said, as she reached up and rubbed my face. I pulled her hand back to my chest and held it against my heart.

I could hear her breathing change as sleep took her. I closed my eyes, content and happy for the first time since Joni had last slept in my arms. I looked forward to what tomorrow held.

CHAPTER
FIFTEEN
SUZY

"HOW'D it go with Mr. Piercings?" Sophia chuckled in the phone as I chewed my bagel.

"He gave me a little going-away present this morning before he headed home to change." I chomped down, letting the cream cheese slide across my tongue.

"Oooh, someone had a sleepover. I like him, Suz. He looks badass, but I can see a kind heart underneath. Reminds me a bit of Kayden, but I hope without the other bullshit."

I swallowed down the dry leftover bagel. "I almost messed everything up with him, Sophia." I grabbed the glass of milk off the counter, taking a sip, while I waited for her to scream at me.

"Are you fucking crazy? Why in the hell would you do that? What happened?" she yelled, her shrill voice causing my ear to throb.

"I just didn't see us going anywhere, and I didn't want to get too attached to him. I ignored him yesterday and ended up going on a date with Derek instead."

"Derek? What the fuck, Suzy? You know that guy gives me the creeps."

I sighed as I leaned against the counter, wanting to smash

my head into the gray Formica for being so stupid. "I know. I just wanted to forget City—epic disaster that I'll tell you about someday. Anyway, City came to my rescue and took me home."

"Well, thank Christ for small miracles."

"He asked me to be his girlfriend, Sophia. Can you believe that?"

"I do. You're an amazing girl, little mama. Any man would be lucky to have you as his woman. City was smart enough to realize it. Kayden was the same way with me, but his hard exterior melted. Sometimes you just have to roll with it to get to the good stuff. Nothing in life is risk free, Suzy."

"I know, Sophia. My entire body vibrates when I'm around him, and my stomach fills with butterflies. I've never felt that way with anyone, and it scares the crap out of me. I tried to push him away, but he didn't let me."

"You must have some fine shit."

I choked on my milk, and it started to come out my nose as I wiped my face. "What in the heck are you talking about, woman?"

"Well, you tried to get rid of him, and I know you usually hold true to your plan, so I know you didn't relent first and he came to you. Most guys would just say fuck that and walk away without looking back, but you must have something special that made him come back for more. Huh, who knew?" She giggled.

"Shut it, whore. We had a long talk about relationships and love when he brought me home. He's been hurt before and hasn't had a real girlfriend in years."

"We've all been hurt before. It's part of love. If you never hurt, then you've never truly been in love before, Suzy. What happened to him?"

"His fiancée died," I said, putting my cup in the dishwasher. I leaned against the counter and rested the phone against my shoulder.

"Wow, that's horrible. I couldn't image losing Kayden. I'd be a complete and total mess. I don't know if I'd love anyone the way I love him. I couldn't allow myself to love anyone that way again if he was ripped from my life."

"Yeah, I just wonder if he'll be able to make room in his heart for me. I'll always be competing with her for his love, I'm afraid."

"It's not a competition, sweetheart. There's room for both of you. He's taking a risk with you—just give him time to deal with his feelings. Don't rush into the L-word."

"You did with Kayden," I said, smiling even though she couldn't see me.

"I know." She sighed. "I couldn't imagine anyone else in my life. Kayden was it for me, babe. He ruined me and I could never be without him—I knew that after our first weekend together. It felt like all the planets aligned. I was finally with the man I was meant to be with my entire life."

"I'm just going to enjoy his glorious body filled with extra holes and pretty pictures. Jesus, girl, you should see his fine ass naked."

"Did you say ass?" she asked, sounding shocked.

"I am an adult, Sophia. I do swear."

"I think City's dick stirred your brain and altered your thought pattern. My Suzy sunshine never uses profanity," she bellowed.

"Suck it."

"What am I sucking?" she asked.

"Kayden's dong." I started laughing at how immature that sounded.

"Listen, whore, no matter what you do—do not fucking say 'I want to suck your dong' to City. His hard-on would vanish, as he would fall on the floor in a fit of laughter. It's not sexy, not at all. Funny as fuck? Yes, but not come here and fuck me talk. Got it?"

"I know. Just wanted to see what you'd say."

"Silly, girl. Oh, and don't call it a penis. Use the dirtiest, crudest words you can think of when you speak to him. Men love it dirty and raw. If you can find it in the health teacher's textbook, avoid it like the plague."

"Got it. All right, I'm going to go get ready."

"Where you going so early? Your ass usually isn't out of bed before noon, and it's only eleven."

"I have grocery shopping to do today, and I feel like browsing at a couple of stores. I plan to look at all the things I'll never be able to buy. A girl can dream, right?"

"Grocery shop today and window browse tomorrow. I'm so glad we have a long weekend, and I want to go shopping and have a girl's day out. We need to practice your dirty talk."

"Don't you want to stay home with him and Jett?" I asked, walking in my bedroom, searching my closet for something to wear.

"Nah, let them have some male bonding time. What time you want to pick me up tomorrow?" she asked.

"Noon, okay?"

"I'll be waiting for you, my pretty." She cackled as she hung up the phone, and I shook my head. Sophia was going to make it a very long day.

***

"Come on, you big pussy, let's go inside," Sophia said, yanking my arm as we sat in the parking lot of Inked. Once Sophia had something in her mind, she was like an Italian woman I knew—totally unbendable.

"Sophia, please. It's not nice to surprise him at work. What happen with the 'no cling' stuff?" I shook my head and put all my weight on the seat.

"It's not clingy. I want a damn tattoo. I want to surprise Kayden, and I never get a chance. I either have the baby or him with me. I'd rather him do it than some stranger. Please get out of the car before I pull you out by your hair."

Her hands were on her hips and she was giving me the pushy teacher look that always cracked me up. Sophia was just as much of a softy as I was, but her look was nastier and usually made people do as they were told.

"Fine, but when it all implodes I'm blaming your bossy butt." I closed the doors and hit my remote twice, making sure that no one could steal my collection of vintage hip-hop cassettes.

Sophia whistled as we approached the door. "This is a nice shop, not like most of the shit-ass tattoo places around here." She grabbed the door handle, and my palms began to sweat as my heart pounded in my chest, causing my breathing to grow ragged.

"Can I help you ladies?" a man asked. He looked like a younger version of City. His muscles bulged from under his shirt; his arms, covered in tattoos, flexed as he rose from his chair.

"I'd like to get a tattoo today. Any possibility of that?" Sophia asked.

Looking around the shop as Sophia spoke with the one of the Gallo boys, I took in all the vibrant colors on the walls—reds and oranges with yellow on the ceilings. No white space invaded this realm of his life.

I walked over to the beautiful artwork on the walls to get a closer look. The pieces on the wall were body parts that had been decorated with some of the most stunning work I'd ever seen. I turned my head and my stomach dropped. City was sitting next to a beautiful brunette with his hand on her breast and his face only inches away. They were laughing and talking, but he didn't see me. They looked comfortable together, like there was something between them, or maybe there had been at some point. My heart thumped against my chest and I felt flushed looking at them.

I walked back by the desk quickly and grabbed Sophia's arm. "Can we go, please?" I asked quietly.

She turned around and gave me a confused look. "What's wrong?"

"He's touching some girl's boob and I just can't look at it. It hurts to see it."

She touched my shoulder. "Babe, it's a boob. He's an artist and some girls like tattoos on their breasts. It's like a gynie looking at a snatch; it's just another body part. Don't get caught up in what you think you see." She smiled.

"You're crude. It was more how they were looking at each other." I shrugged.

"Was he looking at her or what he was doing?" She eyed me.

"He was looking at her breast, for Christ's sake."

"He was looking at his lines. Calm the fuck down before you have a coronary. Lemme see." She pushed me back and peered through the doorway to the tattoo area. "Look," she said, yanking my arm and pulling my body to see what she saw. "He's concentrating on his artwork." She held my body so I couldn't move, and forced me to view City touching someone else.

"Call me a prude, but I don't want to see it." I pulled away from her grip. "I'll go wait in the car—you get your tattoo or whatever. I can't be in here, Sophia."

"God, you're so dramatic. Get over your shit. He's not fucking the bitch in the chair, he's creating a masterpiece." She looked pissed at me. "Suit yourself, go wait in the car and I'll be out in a bit."

I pushed the door open as I heard Sophia say, "Hey, City."

Damn it. I wanted her to leave with me. I knew she was going to spill her guts, or should I say mine, and tell him everything that happened. I sat in my car and waited for over an hour. I tilted the seat back and closed my eyes, enjoying the warmth of the sun. I cracked the window an inch so I could feel the cold rush of wind on my face every so often.

"What are you doing, sugar?"

I jumped, his voice waking me from a nightmare. His face was buried in someone else's legs, kissing them with his mouth like he had done to me the night before.

"You scared the crap out of me. Jesus." I placed my hand over my eyes to block out the sun as I looked out the window to see his beautiful body.

"Why aren't you inside with Sophia? What the fuck are you doing out here alone? You didn't want to see me?" He looked hurt, but I couldn't get the visual of him with the woman's boob out of my mind.

"I thought it was best if I waited out here."

"Are you going to open your door so we can talk face to face? Or am I going to talk to you through glass like it's a prison visit?"

"You looked like you had your hands full," I said, and looked out the front windshield, avoiding his glare. "I'm sure you have more boobs to fondle." What the hell was wrong with me? The pang of jealousy hit me hard, and it felt foreign. I had never been a jealous person. No one had evoked this kind of emotion before him.

"Open the damn door, Suzy." He pulled on the handle, bending down to peer through the window. "So that's what it is. You're jealous?" He laughed.

I wanted to smack that shit-eating grin off his face. He looked so smug. "I'm not jealous." When had I reverted to acting like a childish crazy person? *Get a grip.* I knew it was only part of his job, but it was foreign to me, and I couldn't wrap my mind around the image and reality.

"Sugar, come on. I wasn't looking at her breast. I was working, for shit's sake. It's a piece of canvas to me. Don't be jealous—although I kinda like that emotion in you. Shows me that you care."

"I need time to process it all. Did you start Sophia's tattoo?" I asked, wondering how long I'd have to sit here.

"She needed a break. I won't go back in and finish until you get that fine ass out of that car and we talk about this."

The man knew how to hold me hostage. I closed my eyes and took a deep breath before unlocking the door.

City pulled on the handle, opening the door before crouching down next to me. "Sugar, look at me." The grin on his face made me want to smack him. "Only you. She's a married woman with children, and I've known her for years. I wasn't staring at her nipples—I watch my lines. If I make a mistake, it can't be fixed. Outta the car, Suzy." He backed away and waited for me to climb out.

Closing the door behind me, I leaned against it before he placed his arms on either side of my body, pinning me against the car. Rubbing his crotch against my stomach, he said, "You're the only one that does this to me."

I wanted to stake my claim and ward off any woman that thought he could be theirs. His hand snaked around my neck, gripping me roughly as he crushed his lips against mine. My lips parted, granting him access as he pushed his stiff shaft against me.

He broke the kiss and searched my eyes. "Are we good?"

"I just didn't like seeing it, City, especially so soon after seeing you with Kaylee. It's going to take some getting used to for me." I could get lost in his crystal blue eyes. "I'm sorry I was so childish," I said as I leaned my forehead against his cheek.

"Childish and jealous," he stated. "I'll be patient with you, but I'm going to make you pay later for your little temper tantrum." He laughed.

"What do you have in mind?" I asked with a cocked eyebrow and a grin.

"It's on a need-to-know basis, sugar, and you don't need

to know...yet." He licked my bottom lip and grabbed my hand, pulling me to the shop door.

"That's not fair, City."

"Sometimes life isn't fair, sugar. I can guarantee that you'll be screaming through it, and it won't be out of pain, unless you're into that sort of thing." He waggled his eyebrows and chuckled.

Oh, hell. I knew trouble when I saw it, and it was standing right in front of me. City would be the death of me, but hell, at least I could say it was fun while it lasted. I did the thing I never, ever did—I took the plunge and jumped in feet first without holding my nose.

CHAPTER
SIXTEEN
CITY

I HAD plans for my little darling. She needed to pay for her temper tantrum, but I wanted to give her plenty of time to think about her actions and worry about what was ahead of her.

Suzy stared at the ground as we walked through the door of Inked. Mikey sat at the desk and was engrossed in his work until I cleared my throat. He looked up, a smile breaking out across his face.

"Suzy, this is my brother Mikey."

"Michael," he said, holding out his hand.

Suzy smiled at him and placed her hand in his. "Nice to meet you, Michael."

"Pleasure is all mine." He brought her hand up to his mouth and kissed it.

"Hey, dickhead, break this shit up. Suzy's mine." I smacked his shoulder and gave him a glare.

"I'm just giving her a proper welcome, bro. Chill the fuck out," Mikey said, looking at me with a smarmy grin. *Asshole.*

"Do you want to come in the back or stay out here with *Mikey*?" I emphasized "Mikey" just to get under his skin.

He'd always been Mikey, but he didn't like the nickname when women were nearby.

"I'll keep you company," he piped in, and I turned to give him the look of death.

"Um, I don't know. I don't really like blood. Is it bloody?" she asked.

"Not too bad, sugar. Tattoos are done with needles, so there's some." I pulled her close and buried my face in her hair, inhaling her sweet, flowery scent.

"I think I better wait out here," she said into my chest.

"I'll keep her company—no worries, Joey." The fucker winked at me, and I wanted to punch him in the face. I knew he was just fucking with me, because one thing my brother sure as fuck wasn't was a woman stealer. He wouldn't try and fuck Suzy or take her from me, but it still grated on my fucking nerves.

I'd never felt so territorial over someone, and especially not as quickly as I had with Suzy. Maybe it was her similarities to Joni or her kind heart, but I didn't want anything bad to happen to her, and I sure as hell didn't want to lose the opportunity to get to know everything about her.

"I'll be done soon with Sophia. I just have to finish the color." I kissed her, making sure to leave her breathless and her mind only filled with thoughts of me before I left her in the capable hands of my wanker little brother. "Don't let Mikey fool you. He's not as innocent as he looks."

"I figured that. I'm not completely naïve." I chuckled, because she *was* that naïve. Mikey had the look of a kind-hearted person, with his charming, boyish good looks, but I'd seen him beat the piss out of men almost twice his size.

"Okay, sugar. Just don't believe a goddamn thing that comes out of that mouth of his, got me?" I smiled at her, and all I wanted to do is take her home and fuck her brains out, but I had to finish Sophia's tattoo and leave these two to talk.

"Gotcha, big guy. Go finish that tattoo so I can get her

home to Kayden before he starts blowing up her phone. I'll be okay."

"I still have plans for you, sugar. I haven't forgotten. Catch ya in a few." I slapped her ass hard enough for it to sting. She yelped and jumped from the quick swat.

"Dang, City," she said as she rubbed her ass, and I laughed as I walked to the back of the shop.

Sophia was typing on her phone, and looked up as I approached.

"Get the pussy out of the car?" she asked as I pulled on my gloves.

"Yeah, we had a little talk." I laughed. I sat down and grabbed my machine and dipped the needle in the yellow ink.

"You have to understand her, City. She's not like most girls. She's in a class all her own," Sophia said as she looked up from her phone.

"Whatcha mean, darlin'?" I asked, rubbing the salve over the design before placing the needle against her skin.

"She hasn't really had a boyfriend or been in love. Shit, I'd never been truly in love with someone until I met Kayden. She's not used to any of this. God, I'm so fucking this up, but you're fucking killing me with that needle, City." She giggled.

"Just a little bit longer. Tell me more about her, Sophia. You guys were with each other, like, twenty-four-seven there for a while. What don't I know about her? What won't she tell me about herself?" I looked down and shaded in the beautiful hibiscus on her hip with shades of pinks and yellows.

"Well, where should I start? I'm sure you've figured out she doesn't swear, but trust me, that girl has one dirty-ass mind." She laid her head back in the chair and her body grew less tense. Talking seemed to help people get their mind off the needle scraping against their skin.

"Really? This I gotta hear."

"I don't want to give away all her secrets, but she needs a guy like you."

"What's that mean?" I had an idea, but I wanted to hear her best friend say it.

"Suzy is a control freak. She needs someone that won't give in to her, but—and this is a big but—she also needs someone that's going to care about what she wants. She's been with men that don't really live up to the promises in the sack, or make her feel like a freak."

Now she fucking intrigued me. "What would make her feel like a freak?"

"She has this fantasy about being kidnapped and sold into slavery."

She whispered the last words, and I looked up at her. I almost fucking choked. "Suzy?"

"Don't be so shocked, Joey. She just wants to be owned, if you know what I mean. She may be a control freak, but in the sack she wants to be used and controlled. Think you're up to the challenge?" She moved her eyebrows up and down, with the biggest smile plastered on her face.

"I think I'm just what the doctor ordered. Tell me more—this shit is good."

"She has fantasies, but will probably never share them with you."

"Why not?"

"No one has ever asked her, so don't expect her to just cough up that shit. You have to pull it out of her."

"Got it."

"Just don't break her heart, City, or I'll crush your balls. Got me?"

"Loud and clear, and I think you'd do it too, Sophia." Sophia didn't seem like the type to not follow through on her words. She reminded me of those strict teachers that you didn't want to fuck around in class and get that pissed-off-teacher look from, but I knew she was sweet too, 'cause Suzy wouldn't be friends with someone who wasn't.

"Oh, I have no issues inflicting bodily harm when necessary."

"Kayden must be one hell of a guy to handle you, Sophia."

"He's complicated."

"Suzy mentioned something along those lines about Kayden." I dipped the gun into the black to finish the shading as I hit the home stretch on the design on her leg.

"I normally wouldn't take as much shit as I did from him, but when you love someone and you know you're meant to be with them, you stick it through. I couldn't abandon him in his time of need. Someday I'll tell you the whole story, 'cause it's a long fucking tale."

"Almost done, just a few more lines. Was it worth it?" I knew the answer, but I wanted to hear her say it was worth the struggle that I feel she had to endure to find the love of her life.

"I wouldn't trade a moment of our fucked-up journey. We were meant to be together. I don't regret a second of my time with him."

I liked hearing about Kayden and Sophia. All my friends and siblings were single and had been put through the wringer. I wanted to hear that it was possible to find love in today's jaded world.

I put the machine on the table and began to wipe the tattoo to clean her skin so she could get a good look at it. "There ya go, darling. Hop up and look in the mirror." I leaned back in my chair and stretched my back.

Sophia jumped up and walked up to the mirror, holding the side of her pants down. It was beautiful and permanent.

"Whatcha think?"

"Oh my God, City. It's amazing. I fucking love it." She

turned to the side and stood closer to the mirror. "The color's amazing."

"Will Kayden like it?" I asked. I was sure he'd love it; what man wouldn't love their woman to have their name on their skin? She was marked and his forever.

"He's going to freak out. The guy has a thing for tats, and he has my name on him. I can't wait to show him." She just stood there and stared in the mirror with a giant smile across her face.

"He does?"

"Yep, huge down his leg. There's no way to cover that shit up, either. He's mine forever and I'm his," she said as she walked back over to the chair.

"I never advise anyone to tattoo a boyfriend or girlfriend's name on their body. It's asking for disaster. You're brave."

"Brave? I'm never leaving that man, City. No one will ever love me like he does."

"I've seen the chemistry you two have. I did my part in warning you, but I can't deny you the design you want." I rubbed the salve on her skin and covered it to keep it clean. "You know how this works and about after-care?"

"Yep, it's my fifth tattoo. I got this shit."

"Well then, darling, you're all done."

"I have to use the ladies' room. Where is it?" she asked.

"Down the hall to the right. I'm going to go check on Suzy." I wanted to see her and make sure Mikey kept his paws off her.

I pulled my gloves off with a snap and threw them on the table. I cracked my neck and rounded the corner to see Mikey and Suzy sitting in the chairs talking and a little closer than I'd normally feel comfortable with—but this was Mikey.

They began to laugh. "Oh stop, Michael, you're killing me." She covered her mouth and slapped her knee.

"I shit you not," Mikey said, then looked up at me and cleared his throat. "Oh, big brother. How'd things go?"

"What the fuck are you two talking about?" I knew Mikey wanted to find any way to embarrass me; my family was fantastic for that shit.

"Nothing at all."

Suzy's face turned red, and she could barely look me in the eyes without breaking out into a fit of laughter. "Don't you worry, we're just sharing family memories."

Cocksucker. Someday I'd make him pay for this shit. I wouldn't normally give a fuck, but I didn't want Suzy to think of me in the way Mikey had probably described me. Thank the motherfucking gods that the rest of the group wasn't here today. Izzy would be all over Suzy, grilling her and filling her head with stories that should stay in the past. "That's what I'm afraid of."

"No worries. Michael was just reminiscing," she said between her fingers, trying to hide her laughter.

I wanted to choke the motherfucker. I knew he had a knack for making shit up just for his amusement and my embarrassment. I rubbed the back of my neck, trying to stop myself from punching him in the face.

"Where's Sophia?" Suzy asked, getting up from her seat.

"She's using the ladies' room. Go back and see the work I did on her." I kissed her, patting her ass as she walked away. "What the fuck did you tell her?" I said to Mikey.

He started to laugh as he stood. "Oh, nothing."

"Bullshit. What lies did you fill her head with, asswad?"

"I told her you slept with a teddy bear and sucked your thumb until you were ten." He doubled over in laughter, and I saw red.

"You're a dickhead, Mikey. Why do you always do this shit to me?" I closed my eyes and calmed my breathing.

"You never got all worked up before. You must really like this one." He plopped his ass in the chair and pulled himself up to the desk.

"Fuck you."

"Oh, testy. Definitely a boner for that blonde bombshell. Hey, you told my last girlfriend that I pissed my bed until high school. All's fair in love and war, rat bastard."

I burst into laughter. That was the last time that woman came around the family. She broke up with Mikey shortly after our Sunday dinner. "You didn't even like her. You were just fucking her." I heard the door creak, and Suzy and Sophia emerged with smiles on their faces. "Guess you're right, I deserved it, but for fuck's sake—I really like this girl. Don't fuck it up for me. Got me?" I said, leaning over the desk so only he could hear.

"Righto. Don't get your panties in a wad, man." Mikey stood quickly, and smiled as the ladies walked up to the desk. "Everything okay, ladies?"

Sophia's smile couldn't be any bigger. "Fabulous. You did such an amazing job, City. I fuckin' love it, and Kayden's going to be shocked as hell."

"Kayden?" Mikey said, his voice filled with curiosity.

"Yes, Kayden, my boyfriend and father of my baby."

"Fuck, all the good ones are taken," Mikey muttered as he walked away.

"I'm glad you're happy. Let me know what Kayden thinks about it."

Sophia wrapped her arms around me and said, "Thank you."

"Anytime, babe. I'm your man if you ever need any more work. Give that some time to heal. You're going to be sore for a couple of weeks. The hip is tender. Watch what type of clothing you wear, too."

Suzy stood off to the side and smiled at us both. I couldn't wait to get her alone later, but I still had work to do. "Come here, sugar." I held my hand out to her, and she placed her tiny fingers in my palm.

I wrapped her in my arms and pulled her body against mine. "I haven't forgotten that I owe you for your little display earlier." Her eyes went wide as she stared at me. "I never break a promise, either, sugar." I kissed her and rubbed my dick against her stomach. I couldn't wait to bury myself in her pretty little cunt. "I'll be over around eight. Be ready." I smiled and said goodbye as the two girls walked out of the shop in a fit of giggles.

CHAPTER
SEVENTEEN
SUZY

I COLLAPSED ON THE BED, exhausted, sweaty, and out of breath. City stretched out next to me, hands behind his head, a smug-ass grin stretching his lips. "What's that look?" I asked.

"I fuckin' rocked your world."

"Cocky much?" He fucking did, too. I'd never come so hard or as much as I had with him. He knew all the right things to do and all the perfect places to touch. "If that was your punishment, it didn't work."

"Oh, I don't know about that. I heard you yelp a few times when I smacked your ass." He laughed.

I stared at the ceiling and thought about his words, remembering the stinging feeling of his hand landing on my ass. It set my skin on fire and made everything more intense.

"More out of shock than hurt. You surprised the heck out of me."

City turned on his side, rested his head on his hand, and gazed at me. He ran his fingertips across my stomach, and my flesh broke out in goose bumps. "I hope it's not the last surprise I ever give you."

I closed my eyes and wanted to stay in this moment forever.

"Whatcha thinking about, sugar?"

I opened my eyes and looked into his beautiful blue eyes. "You, Joe. You're just so, so...I don't know how to describe you." I sighed.

"Unlike anyone you've ever been with?" He arched his eyebrow.

"Yeah, and I don't know if that's a good thing, either." I didn't want to say that he also made me half neurotic. The jealously I'd felt in the tattoo shop was something foreign to me, and I didn't like it—not one bit. I barely knew him, and it gutted me to think of him with someone else. I was starting to question my sanity.

"Oh...it's good. The way you screamed my name couldn't be anything but good, sugar."

My face flushed, and warmth crawled down my skin. I had never been a yeller or made much noise at all, but then again, I'd never had a reason to before.

"Don't be embarrassed." He pulled me against his body and kissed my temple as he fisted my hair.

I couldn't escape him—his smell, skin, and warmth. Everything about him made me want more, and I couldn't block it from my mind or wish it away.

"Want me to go?" he whispered in my ear.

"No!" I opened my eyes quickly, turning toward him. My lips brushed against his. I didn't close my eyes and neither did he—we stared in each other's eyes for a moment as I melted into his body.

"Stop overthinking shit, Suzette. You want to be with me?"

"You scare the hell out of me, honestly."

"Why?" He brushed the hair from my face, and my skin tingled from the innocent touch.

"Like you said—you're unlike anyone I've ever known. You're like one giant damn mystery to me."

"I'm an open book. I don't hide my feelings and I don't pussyfoot around shit. I do what I have to and I say what's on my mind."

"I guess I'm just not used to someone being so…so…"

"Cocky, sexy, manly?" He chuckled and started to grab my side, causing me to break out into laughter.

"Stop!" I couldn't catch my breath.

"You think too damn much instead of saying what's on your mind."

"Okay, okay," I puffed out through my giggle, with tears running down my face. His hands stilled at my side and his tongue darted out and licked the tear from my cheek.

"Like that. No one has ever done that."

"Sugar, maybe I need to ask what they have done to you. I feel that list is shorter than what they did do. Have you come during sex before?"

I didn't want to answer that question. "Um."

"Yes or no?" I felt like his azure eyes were staring into my soul and trying to unwrap all of my secrets.

"Not really." I gave him a shy smile, not wanting to divulge that no one had ever gotten me off like he did. City was cocky enough without thinking he was my own personal sex god.

"Hmm. Did you come with me or were you faking that shit?"

Oh, here we go. "I did and I sure as hell wasn't faking—I never fake it."

"Besides me, ever? Without having to do it yourself?"

"No, no one has ever really cared if I did."

"Fucking assholes." He shook his head. "Why do women date assholes like that? I know no one's ever smacked your ass. What do you want that no one has ever done to you?"

Oh my God. I couldn't be any more embarrassed than I felt in this moment. "I don't know."

"That's bullshit, sugar. Everyone has fantasies." He nuzzled my hair, and I didn't feel so under the microscope, but I didn't want him to laugh at me.

"Tell me one of yours." I stroked his arms and traced the tattoos on his skin. The artwork really was beautiful. My parents always told me that tattoos were trashy, but on City they were works of art. They were a timeline of his life, and I wanted to peel back the layers and hear the story.

"I want to fuck you on my bike."

My breath caught in my throat. The thought of him taking me on his bike hadn't even crossed my mind, but now the image was burned into my brain.

"I want you spread eagle, my face planted between your legs, licking every ounce of wetness from your body before sinking my dick in you." The vibration of his words in my ear caused wetness to pool between my legs. Damn him. "Your turn." I knew he had a smile on his face without even seeing it. *Bastard.*

I sighed. "Where do I begin? God, this is so embarrassing."

"Sugar, if you can't share your fantasies with your boyfriend, who can you?"

One point, City—Suzy, Zero. "I swear I need to have my head examined." I covered my eyes with my hands. City would think I was nuts.

"Out with it. Sophia told me you two read a lot of those smut books. Fantasies can become reality, sugar."

"It's just so weird. You're going to think I'm completely insane."

He stroked my arm as I tried to cover my face. His body shifted as he moved my hand away from my eyes.

"I gotta know now. I can call Sophia and ask, or you can tell me. Give me the naughtiest thing you've always wanted."

I swallowed and shut my eyes. I didn't want to see his reaction when he heard this one. "Fine. I have this fantasy of being taken against my will."

He didn't gasp or scream, but very calmly said, "Rape or kidnapping?"

I opened my eyes and turned to look at him. He had a grin on his face, and the butterflies dancing in my stomach calmed. "Kidnap. I know it's weird," I mumbled.

"No, Suzette. It's not weird at all. We all have our kinks and fantasies. Okay, so kidnap and then what?" He looked so damn eager to hear the rest, like he was hanging on my every word. How could I not share the rest?

"Do you honestly want to know?"

"Yes."

"I've read so many amazing books that deal with kidnapping and being owned by someone. I don't really want some crazy person to kidnap me, but the books make it seem appealing and sexy as heck."

"I'll see what I can do to make that happen."

"Oh, God."

"I won't surprise you, you'll know when it's coming—when I'm coming for you."

He pulled my body against his, our skin touching, his hands pressed into my back; he made me feel normal about wanting something so taboo. He smelled so good. His masculine and musky scent mixed with the smell of sex. I didn't think I could ever get enough of him.

His hand glided up my back, on to the nape of my neck as he grabbed a fistful of hair. The feel of his calloused hands against my skin and the prick of pain on my scalp felt like electricity throughout my body. Holding my head still with his firm grip on my hair, he looked into my eyes. The brilliant blue of his almost glowed in the light and burned with passion. "As for being owned, I plan to own every inch of your body. You *are* mine, sugar, don't forget that shit. I'm going to fucking ruin you."

Why the hell did that sound so amazing? Damn trashy books altered my sense of right and wrong. I wanted him to own me—ruin me.

I was lost in thought until his lips crashed against mine. His kiss wasn't gentle or kind, but demanding and all-consuming. My body molded around him as I wrapped my leg around his waist.

"I'm going to be rough, Suzette," he said against my lips.

I searched his eyes and could see the lust and need within. "I'm yours," I whispered.

He grabbed my torso and flipped me on my stomach. He moved faster than I thought possible, and he was behind me in a moment. He grabbed my hips and pulled my ass in the air. "Stomach down, sugar." He pushed on the small of my back. "Head too, only your ass in the air." I buried my face in the sheets and could smell him on the fabric.

I started to hyperventilate. I'd had sex doggie style, but this was something different—new. His fingers raked through my wetness, stroking my clit and squeezing it lightly. A jolt coursed through my body, and I cried out.

Smack. "Don't move," he said, rubbing my ass with one hand and pinching my clit with the other. "Unless you want another swat on the ass."

I wanted to squirm or rub against him like a cat in heat, but the sting of his last swat kept me rooted in place. His hand left my ass, and I turned to look at him. His tall, muscular body stood on the bed, and he stroked his cock. The metal piercing at the tip would disappear in his hand. His beautiful black hair was a mess and lay across his forehead, and the light reflected off his eyes. I could stare at him for hours—he was everything my mother told me to steer clear of in life. Just looking at the man made my panties wet. *I'm so screwed.*

I was so exposed in this position. My ass and pussy were on display for him. He pumped his hardness in his fist as he positioned himself behind me. I could feel the head rub through my wetness. His cock was hard as it poked at my entrance. I closed my eyes and held my breath as I waited for him to fill me. I instantly felt the loss of his body, and opened one eye to see what he was doing.

"What's wrong?" I asked, staring at him just standing there, stroking the shaft as he looked at me.

"Relax, sugar. I'll make it fanfuckingtastic." He rubbed my ass, and I knew his words were true.

I relaxed my muscles and closed my eyes as I felt his hand on me again. The head of his dick touched my opening, and I wanted him inside me. I gripped the sheets and braced myself for the impaling I was about to endure. He rested his hand on the top of my ass as he pushed himself inside. I felt stuffed, and I knew he wasn't fully seated inside. I squeezed the sheets tighter as the sensation of him became overwhelming, and more intense than I'd felt before.

His body slammed into mine as he pumped in and out. His body worked like a well-oiled machine, and his shaft was the piston battering my insides. The tip hit parts of my body that had never been touched before, and I wanted to crawl away—the fight-or-flight instinct started to kick in. My ass stung as the sound of his hand striking my ass filled my ears.

"Ass up, Suzette," he growled, grabbing my hips and molding my body exactly how he wanted it without going out of rhythm.

I bit my lip. I wanted to cry out. I wanted to crawl away. I didn't know if I could take one more minute as I reached back and grabbed his ankles. I dug my nails into his skin and grounded myself. I had to fight every urge in my body to flee.

I could feel every inch of him as it moved inside my body. His breathing was harsh and quick, and I buried my face in the sheets to stop from crying out. My muscles tightened as I felt an orgasm building inside me, but how? He hadn't even touched my clit in this position, and I hadn't touched myself.

His speed increased and his hips slammed against the sore spot left by his hand. He grabbed my hips and pulled me closer, allowing himself to be buried to the hilt.

"Fuck, your cunt is so tight." His fingers dug in my hip as I was held captive by his hands. "I can feel it squeezing my cock. Fuck, sugar," he said as he pulled my body against him to meet his thrust.

I squeezed my eyes shut as a moan escaped my mouth that I could no longer hold. I needed to yell as the orgasm crashed over me, my body becoming rigid. My core gripped his shaft as the aftershocks tore through me, and his rhythm became more intense, and eventually more erratic. He moaned and my body became limp, but I kept my ass in the air because of his rock-hard grip.

His body twitched against me before he pulled out and collapsed on the bed. "Fuck," he muttered.

My body ached. Rolling over, I stretched out across the mattress and rested my arm across his body. Our labored breathing filled the air. My hand rose and fell with his chest as I gulped for air and tried to swallow the cotton taste from my mouth.

Neither of us spoke as we lay there. City had been more than I could ever imagine. I liked being with him. He was easy to be around. He made me feel beautiful and wanted. I needed to turn my brain off and stop thinking of the reasons I should run away from him and enjoy our time together.

I felt like I was in a dream world, half awake as City rolled over and placed his arms around me. He kissed my face and whispered, "Night, beautiful," in my ear.

CHAPTER
EIGHTEEN
CITY

WE SPENT a few nights together during the week—work took up our days and kept us apart, but the evenings were filled with fucking her raw and leaving no doubt in her mind of my feelings toward her. Saturday she had a wedding to attend that she'd already RSVPed to and couldn't change.

As I locked up the shop, my phone chimed.

Bear: Get your pussy ass over to the Cowboy. Where the fuck you been, man?

Suzy would be gone until around midnight, and a drink with the guys was in order.

Me: Headed that way, asshole. Save me a seat and you better have a fucking cold beer waiting for me.

Shoving the phone in my pocket, I climbed on the bike and headed toward the Neon Cowboy. Steam rose from the dampened streets as the tires parted the mist. The moonlight flashed through the trees lighting my path. The cool breeze felt good against my flesh as I barreled down the road to hang with my guys.

Walking in the bar, I took in the familiar smell of smoke, the sound of the country guitar, and the murmur of the crowd, and I realized how much I'd missed this place.

"Yo," Bear yelled, grabbing my attention. "I almost sent a search party looking for your ass," he said as I approached the table. Tank and the others laughed.

"I've been busy, fucker." A frosty glass sat waiting for me, as I'd hoped it would be.

"Busy nestled between that sweet blonde ass, I assume," Tank said as he twirled the beer bottle between his fingers.

"You're just jealous because you gotta pay for your pussy, shithead."

He shrugged, bringing the bottle to his lips. "Less complicated that way. I just wanna bust a nut without the cuddling and whining."

"You're an asshole." Frisco laughed, slapping Tank on the shoulder, causing the bottle to move from his lips.

"Fucker, you made me spill my beer."

Frisco covered his mouth with his hand as his eyes turned into small slits. We called him Frisco because he hailed from sunny California and grew up in the San Francisco area. His features were unique—his Chinese mother and American father were both evident in his features. His eyes were almond-shaped and dark, his hair pin straight, cropped at the top, and coal black. He was taller than me, and thin with a slight, muscular build.

"So, City, tell us about the li'l woman? How are things going?" Bear asked.

I leaned back in my chair and rested the beer against my knee. "Fucking perfect."

"You're serious about this one?" He raised an eyebrow and studied me.

Everyone at the table stopped, turning their attention to me. "Serious as a motherfuckin' heart attack." I sipped my beer, looking at their faces. Frisco smiled, Bear's mouth hung open, and Tank scowled. "What?" I said, moving the bottle from my lips.

"Didn't think I'd see the fucking day, dude," Bear said with a sappy grin.

"She's too pretty to be with your loser ass," Tank piped in before I could speak.

"Fuck off, Tank."

"I'm happy for you, man. This calls for another round." Tank raised his fingers to his lips and whistled. He was so crass, but the girl always ran when she heard him call. "Another round, sweet cheeks," he said as he patted her on the bottom.

"Hey, City. Nice to finally have a gentleman back in here." She winked at me before turning her attention back to Tank. "Anything for you, handsome?" she said, running her fingers down the side of Tank's face. He blushed as he placed his order.

"You know your ass would give up this shithole for a piece of that every night," I said to Tank as he watched her ass swaying in her Daisy Dukes as she walked toward the bar.

"Won't deny that shit." He laughed before slapping the table roughly, causing all the bottles to jump.

We talked for hours about motorcycles, tattoos, women, and, of course, the bar. The guys filled me in on the events of the last week. It was always the same old bullshit—bar fights, hook-ups, and booze. The town was so small that everyone knew each other's business, and word spread like wildfire.

"Fuck," Bear hissed. "Speaking of bitches, Kaylee was in here looking for your ass."

"What the fuck? When?" I gripped the bottle in my hand, trying to control my anger.

"Last night. Mumbling some bullshit about how she was yours. Spreading that shit around here like it was the gospel. I told her to fuck off," Bear said, leaning back like he was about to beat on his chest.

"She's a fucking train wreck. Stuck my dick in her twice and she won't let me fucking forget it. I'll set her ass straight, unless one of you boys wants to take her off my hands?" I looked around the table and waited for someone to accept.

"Fuck no, that bitch makes my skin crawl. Hate clingy women," Frisco said, shaking his head.

"My dick, my problem," I said, feeling the phone vibrate in my pocket. Pulling it out, I glanced at the screen under the table.

Suzy: Drunk and tired. Sophia's taking me home, but you're welcome to join me.

"Ball and chain wrangling your ass in?" Tank asked.

"Such a ball buster. It's late and I worked all day. I'm heading home. Thanks for the drink, Bear." I shook his hand and turned to Frisco. "Good to see you again, buddy. Tank, it's been real."

"Whipped," Tank mumbled as I stood to leave.

I left the guys to end the evening how they always did. Bitching about life and women. Thankful that my night wouldn't end like it had for countless years, I sent Suzy a text.

Me: Leave the door unlocked. I'll meet you in bed.

When I arrived, Suzy was half dressed and passed out across the bed. Her mouth hung open, hair was half covering her face, and her dress was halfway off, exposing her breasts. It took everything in me not to snap a picture of her and remind her of it later, but I didn't want to be a dick.

"Wake up, sugar." I grabbed her leg, pulling her body down the bed. She mumbled but didn't wake. I pulled the hem of her dress, removing the clingy material. I rarely had the ability to just stare at her body without her trying to cover her skin. I stood and looked at her—white skin, perky breasts, and long, muscular legs. She was a vision.

Gathering her in my arms, I placed her head on the pillow before I removed my clothes and climbed in next to her.

"City," she muttered as she shimmied her ass into my dick.

"Fuck." I sighed. My cock throbbed from the warmth of her soft cheeks rubbing against it. "Go back to sleep, sugar." I pulled her tighter, burying my face in her hair before drifting off to sleep to her soft snores.

**

"How's the shop doing?" my father asked as we sat around the dining room table. Today was gnocchi, and it always sat in my gut like a ton of fucking bricks.

"We're doing good, Pop. We're turning a profit and we're constantly booked when I can get everyone to show up for work," Mike said before shoveling in a heaping forkful of gnocchi.

"Mike, you aren't always there either, so don't be a martyr and skip the bullshit." Anthony pointed his fork at Mikey before stabbing the gnocchi on his plate.

"We all have other shit to do. The shop is for fun and to have something of our own, so get off our damn backs, Mike. You aren't the *boss*,'" Izzy said emphasizing the word to sound like a great big "fuck you." "You just aren't an artist like the rest of us." She picked up the wine glass and brought it to her lips to hide her smile. Izzy always had been a spitfire.

My mother and father sat at the opposite ends of the table and exchanged looks as my siblings had a war of words. As children, we battled with our fists and usually one of us ended up bloodied, but now we used our mouths. Sometimes words leave a greater mark than any punch ever could.

"I'm every bit an artist as you are, baby sister. I just prefer to use my hands for other things. I may not draw pretty pictures, but I can pierce anything and knock a bastard on their ass in a single punch."

My father cleared his throat. "Is the shop too much?" he asked.

I needed to speak up. The shop was doing great and we all got along. Sundays often made us crabby because we wanted to do anything but be trapped in this house. A one-weekend reprieve would be fucking mind-blowing—and a totally bullshit improbability. "Pop, the shop's great. We're packed. Everyone shows up on the days they have appointments. I'm there more than anyone and I know the business the best. Mike may organize shit, but I know what happens inside the walls of Inked." I soaked my garlic bread in my mother's homemade sauce, which had spread out around my plate. "We need to keep ourselves busy during the day, and the shop has more than done that."

"Good, son. I'm proud of all of you. You could be sitting on your asses at home, but you're business owners and successful—not to mention your other hobbies." *Oh fuck.* Everyone hated to have their true passions and dream careers referred to as a "hobby."

I heard forks drop to the table and clatter off the dishes. Such drama queens in this goddamn room.

"Sorry about that. It's not what I meant." My father looked down at his plate, concentrating on his food, but I could see the smile on his face. He loved a good punch to the gut and ego whenever possible.

"I have a big fight coming up after the first of the year," Mikey piped in, to show my dad how far he'd risen.

"Around here?"

"New York. I got the call yesterday. I've been training for months for this opportunity."

"That's fantastic, son. Wish your mother and I could see it."

My mother looked green at the thought of her son being in a closed ring beating the piss out of someone—or getting the shit beat out of him. I'd put my money on Mikey in any fight, but I know my mother still thought of him as her baby. Fuck, we were all her babies.

"Michael, why can't you be like your brother? Go into music or something without violence and bloodshed?" She dabbed her lips with her napkin and then placed it on the table.

"Ma, I'm great at it and I love it. It's my dream to be a well-known ass kicker."

Pop reached over and slapped him on the back. I was surprised he didn't start beating on his chest at how proud he was of his ass-kicking son.

"I just don't like the whole idea. Become a musician or something else."

"Tone deaf," Mikey mumbled as he placed more food in his mouth.

My mother sighed and fidgeted with her fork on the table. "I was fine with it when I thought it was just a hobby or a passing phase, but now, I'm scared for you, Michael."

"No worries, Ma. I got this shit. You'll see." He grinned at her and flexed his muscles. "It's going to be on pay-per-view, so you'll be able to watch, Pop. I'm not the headliner, but they show all the opening fights before the main event."

"I'll have to have the guys over to watch my son kick some ass."

I rolled my eyes and hoped someone would change the conversation.

"Anyone talk to Thomas this week?" Mom asked.

Not the topic I would've liked, but anything to not hear about Mr. Badass and his upcoming match.

"I did, Ma, he texted me. It's hard for him to call with work," Anthony said.

She sighed and closed her eyes, pinching the bridge of her nose. "I worry most about him. He's in such danger every day, and I don't like him being so far away. I need all my children around this table every week."

I could see the pain on her face. She worried about my brother. He'd been an undercover cop for the last year. He was trying to infiltrate a motorcycle group notorious in Florida for drug trafficking and gun smuggling. He rarely called or texted in order to keep his cover, otherwise his life would end.

Why the fuck my brother risked his life was beyond me. It's one thing to work the streets every day walking a beat, but to go undercover and be discovered was something cops rarely fucking came back from. If something happened to him, my mother would never recover. Tommy had always been an adrenaline junkie, but this was extreme. Jump off a fucking bridge or skydive like normal people; don't risk being shot in the fucking head when they realize you're there to help bring them down.

"He said he's fine, Ma. He said not to worry and he's well and living the life. You know, Tommy would have made a great actor. He can bullshit the best of them." Izzy always tried to console my mother about Tommy's work, but it was always there—the worry. We all felt it like a ton of bricks, waiting for the phone call that he was missing, but thankfully it hadn't happened.

"I know, baby girl." My mom smiled at Izzy. "He could always charm the ladies."

"Speaking of charmer, Ma, Joey's girl was at the shop yesterday and I missed it." Izzy pouted and winked at me. She knew she'd just thrown me under the goddamn bus, and my mom would have a shitload of questions…again.

"Still seeing her, Joseph?" Her face lit up. I knew she was already picking out the baby names, but fucking hell, I wasn't ready for that shit.

"Yes, Ma." I hated talking about this shit with anyone, especially my mother.

"Is she your girlfriend?"

I sighed, wanting to reach over and choke that shit-eatin' grin off Izzy's face. "Yes."

"Don't chase her away because she isn't Joni. You hear me?"

"Yes, Ma."

"I met her, Ma." *Fucking Mikey.*

"What's she like, Michael?" My mom knew she wasn't going to get much more out of me than she had last week in the kitchen. She knew to ask the blabbermouth of the group.

"She's beautiful and deserves so much better than that punk." His head moved in my direction, and I wanted to bitch-slap him.

"Better as in you, Mikey?" I eyed him.

"Calm down, bro. She's a nice girl, Ma. Reminds me a bit of Joni. Innocent, and her laughter is infectious. You'll like her." He grinned at me.

What a fucking asshole.

"You'll have to bring her for Sunday dinner soon, Joseph." Exactly what I didn't want to do. I didn't want her to be around my crazy-ass siblings, especially Izzy. Iz was dying for another girl, since the testosterone to estrogen level was off balance.

"Maybe soon. I don't want to get ahead of myself."

"The holidays are coming up. Christmas, maybe. Is she a Catholic girl?"

Already planning the wedding ceremony. Religion weighed heavily in an Italian family—christenings, baptisms, weddings…everything seemed to revolve around the church.

"Ma, you haven't been to church in years," I said flatly.

"I know, but it's still important. It makes life easier. Is she Italian?"

"I never asked." I grabbed my plate and headed for the kitchen. I could hear the giggles from the table as my mother and sister always liked to rag on me most of all. No one was in a relationship in the group, but for some reason I was always the target.

I didn't know where Suzy and I stood and what the future held for us. She was always so wrapped up in her fucking thoughts and second-guessing our relationship. She couldn't get beyond the tattooed façade and the beat-up shack I called home. I needed to know that I was enough for her. I wanted to be liked for me—the good, bad, and the ugly.

CHAPTER
NINETEEN

SUZY

I COULD HARDLY CONTAIN my excitement all week. City and I talked every night on the phone and texted during the day. I couldn't stay away from him and couldn't get him out of my mind. I tried to keep myself busy and find reasons not to be with him, but it didn't work. I was falling for the man, and falling hard.

Growing up, my mother had drilled in my head that I needed to find a man with a stable job. I needed to settle down, have a family, and live the American dream. I tried for years to find that man, the perfect mold, but all of them were just...boring as hell.

I'd never been willing to settle for anything less than perfect. A picket fence and a beautiful home are worthless if you dread going home to the one you're supposed to spend your life with. I prefer being single to the doldrums in which some of my friends currently dwelled. Sophia and Kayden were the happiest couple I knew, and they were complete opposites—they were the yin to the other's yang.

The students cleared the building as soon as the last bell blared at two in the afternoon on Friday. I had another thirty minutes left and couldn't seem to function. All I could think of was tonight and what could be—what would be. I couldn't stare at the clock and watch another minute tick away. I knew Sophia would be tidying up the library, and I needed to talk to her. She'd questioned me all week about City and when I'd see him again, but I hadn't told her the plan we had. I needed her opinion.

The lights in the library were dimmed, but I could see her wandering around, returning books to their rightful spots. I took a deep breath and walked through the door to the torrent of questions I knew I'd face.

"Sophia," I called out. I didn't want to scare the hell out of her. I knew most of the staff had snuck out early, but the two of us never took the chance at losing our jobs for a few minutes of our time.

She turned the corner with a stack of books in her hand and a smile on her face. "Hey, Suzy Q, what are you doing up here? Don't you have any big plans for tonight?" She winked at me. I couldn't hide the smile on my face. I felt like the electricity and joy radiated off my body. "How many hours until you see him?"

"Maybe I'm not going to see him tonight." I was so full of shit, and I knew I couldn't fool Sophia, but sometimes I hated that she could read me like an open book.

"Whatever, whore. It's written all over your face. You're going to get some cock tonight, and by the red creeping across your cheeks, I'd say it's fucking amazing."

"Do you hear how you talk in a school?"

"Prude ass. Every child has run away from this place screaming at two. There isn't a soul within earshot except for us. What time are you meeting him tonight?"

"We're meeting at seven." I plopped down on one of the comfy couches as Sophia placed the books on the table and sat down next to me.

"My feet are freaking killing me in these damn heels." She

kicked off her shoes and rubbed her feet. "What's the plan tonight?"

"I don't even know if I can repeat it." I shrugged. My stomach was a jumbled mess from just thinking about the possibilities.

"You can and you will. This is me, girl. I know all your darkest secrets. Shit, you used to lie in bed with Kayden and me and grill us on our sex life. We have no secrets. I know you're a kinky bitch underneath that polished veneer."

"It's your fault. I was happy with my bland sex life and you had to go and ruin me with all those trashy novels."

"Stop changing the subject. What's the plan with the sexy-as-sin City?" She grinned and waggled her eyebrows up and down.

I'd always wanted sex that was worthy of girl talk, and for years, I'd lived off the stories that Sophia and my other friends had shared with me. City had made sex worth talking about; I'd finally have some wild stories to share.

"I kind of shared one of my fantasies with him and he's going to make it happen tonight." I covered my eyes with my hand, avoiding her stare. I was scared to tell her any more, but she knew every fantasy I had and always reassured me that I was normal, that my sanity hadn't been replaced by impure thoughts.

"Oh my God. Tell me, tell me." She practically bounced on the couch cushion. "Don't hold back now, bitch." She slapped my arm.

"I told him the darkest one."

"You didn't?"

I grinned, and my cheeks almost hurt from the smile that had been plastered on my face all day. "I did, and he said I'd have it."

"Kidnapping?" She looked shocked, but I saw the twinkle in her eye.

"I can't believe I told him, but yes. Oh my God, it's happening tonight, Sophia."

"I'm so proud of you." She wrapped her arms around me. "My baby's all grown up." She squeezed me and ran her palm down the back of my head. "Tell me more. I want to hear about him. Now."

"We're going to meet at the Neon Cowboy, that biker bar out in the country. We're going to have some dinner and drinks before I leave alone and he makes it become a reality."

"You're going to chicken out. Oh God, he's giving you time to change your mind." She stood up and started pacing the room.

"Calm down, Sophia. I'm not going to chicken out. I've wanted someone like him, and tonight I'm getting more than I could ever dream of—my fantasy becoming a reality."

"You've never done this shit. You're like I used to be—Ms. Missionary Style. I expect details tomorrow, and I mean a full report."

"Yes, ma'am. I'll give you a full briefing."

"I want every last fucking detail too, got me?"

"I got ya, Sophia. I better go get my stuff and head home. I want to rest a bit before I see him."

"Good luck with resting." She snickered.

"I know. I could barely sleep last night." I sighed.

"I used to get that way when I would see Kayden after time apart. There's no feeling like it." She smiled and hugged me. "Now go. I have to finish up and get home to my fantasy man."

"You still feel that way about Kayden after all this time?"

"I still get butterflies when I see him, Suzy. That's the difference, you know—that feeling has never gone away. I'm still get excited like the first time we met."

"I envy you, Sophia."

"You'll find your Kayden, babe. I think you may already

have, if you don't let your stupid OCD checklist get in the way." She tapped me on the forehead.

"I got to go. We'll debate my sanity and compulsions another day." I waved to her as I walked out the door. "Later, Soph."

"Don't forget to call me, Suzy, or I'll hunt your ass down," she yelled to me as the door closed behind me.

***

"Hey, sugar." His voice filled my car via speakerphone, but he didn't sound as excited as I felt.

"Hey, City. I'm almost to the bar."

"I'm going to be fifteen minutes late. Fuck, I'm sorry. The tattoo I was working on took longer than I thought. Can you wait for me in the parking lot?"

Damn. That bar gave me the heebie-jeebies, and I didn't fit in, not even in the parking lot. "Yeah, City. I wouldn't dream of walking in there alone." I felt sick. "This isn't part of your plan, is it?"

"Hell no! We're still having some drinks first. I need you to not overthink everything tonight. I want you a little tipsy for what I have planned." He laughed.

The excitement took over, and all second thoughts vanished. "Okay, City. I'll be waiting for you."

"Do not go inside alone. Understand me?"

"I won't. I promise."

"See you soon, sugar."

After tossing my phone on the passenger seat, I rolled down the window, welcoming the cool air against my clammy skin. The events of the night played through my mind. City would be my kidnapper. My lungs burned as I screamed along with the song on the radio, "Dark Horse" by Katy Perry, the bass causing my windows to rattle with each beat.

Pulling into a spot hidden in the shadows, I turned off the lights and waited for City to arrive. In the rearview mirror I saw my face glistening from the humidity in the air, and I wanted to look flawless. City had seen me at my worst, but I wanted to look beautiful for him in front of his friends.

The lighted mirror behind my visor was more forgiving as I blotted my face with an old napkin I found in the glove box. My lips lacked color as I smacked them together, making kissy lips. After slathering on some Buxom lip gloss from my purse, I rubbed my lips together with a pop. They tingled as the peppermint oil started to plump my lips, soaking into my skin.

A loud knock on the window made me jump, and I hit my head on the visor. "Shit," I said. I turned to get a glimpse at my knight in shining armor, but it wasn't City outside my car. It was a guy that looked vaguely familiar. He stood there staring at me, and alarm bells went off in my head.

I cracked my window an inch, thankful I had rolled them up when I arrived. "Can I help you?"

"Why's such a pretty lady sitting out here alone? Come inside, beautiful."

Hell, he creeped me out. "I'm waiting for someone." I didn't want to hold a conversation with him. His hair was a mess, gray hair lined his face, and dirt was smeared across his tattered t-shirt. A sour smell caused me to wrinkle my nose—he was the asshole that wouldn't leave me alone the first time I came here, until City and Bear stepped in. Shit, where was City?

"You can wait inside, let me buy you a drink." His face came closer to the window, and I could smell the alcohol on his breath, mixing with the body odor that I couldn't escape. My heart raced and my palms started to sweat. *Just stay in the car.*

"Thanks, but I'm going to wait here." I couldn't stand looking at him anymore. Why won't he just go away? I heard a motorcycle pull in the parking lot and come to a screeching halt next to my car. Peering through the passenger window, I saw City climbing off his bike quickly and coming at the scumbag outside my window.

"Get the fuck away from her," City roared as he stood toe to toe with the asshole.

"I just asked her to come inside for a drink." He looked City in the eye and didn't move. He must have had a death wish.

"She doesn't want to be bothered. Go the fuck home, you drunk bastard. Stop bothering all the ladies here, or at least *mine*. Do I need to beat that message in your stupid-ass head?" City grabbed his shirt, crumpling it in his fist.

The man threw his hands up in surrender and tried to back away, but City had a firm grip on his shirt.

"Come on, man. I didn't know she's yours. You need to keep better track of her. Pretty things disappear all the time around here." He grinned, and my skin began to crawl.

"Beat it, jackass. Next time I won't speak. I'll just bash your fucking head in so the only thing you can do with that mouth is drink through a goddamn straw." City released him and shoved him backward. The man stumbled before falling on his ass.

City opened my car door and held out his hand, but I couldn't take my eyes off the guy on the ground. The look he gave me was pure hatred.

"Come on, sugar. I'm here, he won't bother you."

Placing my hand in his, I didn't say a word as I closed my door. I stayed close as we approached the bar. My nerves were shot, and I needed that drink more than ever.

He stopped, grabbing my arm and turning me to face him. "Are you okay, Suzy?"

"Yeah, Joey. He didn't hurt me, but he's creepy as hell."

He wrapped his arms around me, cocooning me. Melting into him, I buried my face in his shirt. Unlike the man from the parking lot, City smelled amazing—the mix of musky cologne with his natural scent. My hand drifted across his chest until I found the piercing I'd become fond of touching.

"Sugar, keep doing that and we won't make it through the first drink before I take you in the bathroom and fuck you raw."

I leaned back with a smirk on my face. "I can't help myself. It's nice to finally touch you after such a long week." I buried my face in his shirt again, not letting go of the little metal object attached to his body.

"I have another piercing that could use some attention," he said through clenched teeth as he ground his cock against me.

"Nah, I'm good. Drink first, then you can do anything you want to me."

Did I just say that? I needed to learn to filter my promises —he was not a bland and boring lover, he liked his sex hard and fast, and he had mentioned my ass. *Don't even think about it.*

"Anything?" he whispered.

"Within reason." I smiled against his chest—thank God my face was hidden.

"That's my girl. Always thinking." He laughed and wrapped me under his arm before walking through the doors of the Neon Cowboy and into the firing squad of males that had egos to protect and manhood to show off. *Lord, help me.*

***

The guys I'd met the first night insisted that we sit with them. I reassured City that it was fine as long as he never left my side. The asshole in the parking lot had already put me on edge, and a tableful of strangers didn't help put my mind at ease.

Bear and Tank talked me into lemon drop shots and beer. I

couldn't exactly order my virgin daiquiri sitting at table full of bikers. I tried to fit in, calm my nerves, and get in the right frame of mind for my "kidnapping." I listened to them talk about bikes and tats—a world foreign to me, but still entertaining. They looked scary, but they were good guys that just wanted to hang out, drink beer, and bullshit.

Bear looked just like his nickname—wild, curly, overgrown hair; a beard; big and burly. When he stood, I could picture him like a grizzly bear on its hind legs ready to attack. When he spoke about his kids and old lady, he reminded me more of a teddy bear. I quickly learned my first impression of him had been wrong, and I needed to be more open-minded. Wilder shit had happened.

"What are you two kids doing tonight?" Bear asked as he washed down the last sip of beer.

I felt the heat crawling up my face, and I couldn't answer his question. I sat there and stared at City. I'd let him field that question.

"Nothing much, Bear. Just going to kidnap this beautiful creature and use her how I see fit." He winked at me and looked at Bear with a cocky smile.

I glanced around the table, and everyone was staring at me. I was sure the picture in their mind was accurate, minus the actual kidnapping part.

Bear slapped City on the back. "That's my boy," he said with a laugh.

City leaned over and nuzzled his face in my hair. "Why don't you head out and I'll find you, sugar," he whispered in my ear. I shivered at his words. I wanted him to play this game.

I turned my face and kissed him on the lips. "Yes, sir. Catch me if you can." The guys at the table started to hoot and holler as I stood from the table, almost knocking over my chair as City caught it. "Sorry about that," I said as I stood on shaky legs.

"Get going, sugar." City swatted me on the ass, and I yelped. I shouldn't have done that last shot.

I kept my eyes on the floor, making sure not to trip on my way out the door. My eyesight felt fuzzy, and my head was cloudy from the vodka. I turned to look back at City before walking out the door. Every man at that table stared at me. City looked excited as he winked at me with a tilted grin that made my panties wet, but the rest of them looked in shock. Maybe City had clued them in on our little role-playing adventure that lay ahead.

I smiled and waved; the cool air touched my skin as I walked outside to wait for my captor to find me. My heart thundered and my stomach gurgled as I made my way toward my car. I was ready for him.

CHAPTER
TWENTY
CITY

"WERE YOU BEING FUCKING SERIOUS?" Tank leaned forward.

"About what? Using her?"

"Fuck, all of it," he said with an eyebrow raised and one side of his mouth curved in a smile.

"All of it. I got to go, boys. Time to go find my victim for the night." I stood from the table and threw a fifty down. "You gentleman have a good night with that image rolling around in your head right now."

They couldn't even begin to process what we were really going to do. They thought "kidnap" was just a nice way of saying I was going to take her away from the bar and have sex with her, but I was going to literally kidnap her.

"Can one of you take my bike home tonight and I'll grab it in the morning?" I asked before walking away.

"I'll take it," Bear said. "I'll tow it to Tank's shop."

"Thanks, man—my dick thanks you too." I laughed as I tossed him the keys.

"At least someone's prick will be happy tonight," Bear mumbled as he placed the keys in his jacket pocket.

I didn't say anything, but couldn't stop laughing. Poor bastards.

I rolled my neck as I headed for the door, cracking it almost like I was prepping for a game. I'd give Suzy everything she wanted and more.

"City!" a voice rang through the crowd. *Fuck.* "City!" A hand waved above the crowd, and I knew the voice but pretended not to hear her.

I didn't turn around, but walked faster until a hand wrapped around my arm.

"Oh, Kaylee, I didn't see you."

"I was screaming your name," she huffed, trying to catch her breath.

"Didn't hear you, either. I'm in a hurry and got to go."

"I've missed you, City." She tried to wrap her arms around me, but I grabbed them and forced them away.

"Stop, Kaylee. I really don't have time for this shit."

"You've always had time for me before." She pouted and tried to play the guilt card.

"I don't now. I have to go meet my girlfriend," I said, hoping she'd get the fucking hint.

"Girlfriend? Since when?" She looked in shock as she held my arm, digging her nails into my flesh.

"Bye, Kaylee. I don't have time for a goddamn chitchat. My girl's waiting for me, and I don't mean you."

I left her there with her mouth open and gulping for air like a fish. I needed to get to Suzy. I'd already left her entirely too long outside by herself. Damn it. She had to be in knots by now, but then again, it probably helped build her excitement.

Rubbing my face as I walked outside, I couldn't believe fucking Kaylee. I was supposed to be only moments behind Suzy; she'd fumbled with her keys trying to unlock her car when I grabbed her from behind. She could've changed her mind and gone home with the amount of time that had elapsed.

Her car was parked in the same spot, but her door was open and she wasn't inside. I looked around—where the fuck was she? I studied every inch of the parking lot, but couldn't see her. My heart thundered in my chest. I felt sick. I heard a muffled cry, but couldn't tell where it came from over the street noise. "Suzy," I screamed, panic taking hold.

Her purse lay on the ground near her car; I just had to find her. I couldn't stand there and wait any longer. I had to move. I ran into the woods behind her car and surveyed the area. I listened for any sound; a man's voice caught my attention— faint but enough to pull my gaze to behind the bar.

I ran in the direction of the noise and saw a man on top of a woman, Suzy, raising his fist before striking her. "You bitch," he seethed. It was the motherfucker that had bothered her earlier when I arrived.

I grabbed him by the throat before he could land another blow and slammed his body to the ground. The force of his head connecting with the concrete made a horrific sound from his skull cracking. Straddling him, I pummeled him with my fists, feeding off the sound of his jawbone crunching underneath my knuckles. He moaned, but I didn't give a fuck. He hit a woman, *my* woman. I punched him again then grabbed his head, and I wanted to bash it into the cement to watch all of his blood ooze out, but a pair of hands began to pull me off him, stopping me.

"City, you're going to fuckin' kill him," Bear said as he tried to pull me back.

"Fuckin' bastard deserves to die." I moved my hand to punch him again, but Bear grabbed my wrist.

"Goddamn, man. He's out cold. Get the fuck away from him and take care of your girl."

Suzy. I had been so busy beating the fuck out of him, lost in my anger, I forgot to check on her. She lay on the cement with her eyes closed, not moving. She was limp in my arms as I cradled her against my chest. Blood dripped from her lip and nose, and I brushed the hair from her eyes to look for more damage. She had a red mark that would turn into a bruise near her temple.

"Suzy," I whispered, brushing my fingers across her face. "Suzy, wake up, sugar." I gathered her legs off the cold ground and placed her in my lap.

I looked at Bear as he stood over me with wide eyes. "Call an ambulance, Bear."

"On it, buddy." He stood over the asshole lying on the ground unconscious, and I saw Bear kick him. "The attacker is knocked out on the ground. I'll keep him restrained," Bear said to the person on the phone.

"Suzy, come on, sweetie. Wake up, beautiful." I kissed her warm lips. This was my fucking fault. "I'm so sorry, Suzy." *Fuck.* Her clothes were in place, nothing was torn, but they had dirt on them from being on the ground.

Her eyes started to open, and I felt like I could breathe again. I smiled at her, touching her cheek. "City," she said with a shaky voice. Her arms started to move, reaching for me.

"Don't move, sugar. Wait for the ambulance." I didn't want her to injure herself worse than that fucker may have already done.

"What happened?" She stared at me with her big, beautiful blue eyes. I could see the confusion and hurt in them.

"I'm sorry, Suzy. I got held up inside and I showed up too late. This wouldn't have happened if I didn't force you to live out one of your fantasies."

She smiled sweetly at me. "Ouch." Her tongue slid across her lip and stopped on the blood.

"You're bleeding, sugar. Just lie still until the paramedics can check you out."

"What about?" She didn't have to finish the sentence—I knew what she wanted to know.

"He won't hurt you anymore."

She closed her eyes and a tear slid down her cheek. "What did you do, City?"

"I gave the fucker a taste of his own medicine. He's out cold." I wiped the tear away from her cheek with my thumb.

"Is he"—her lip began to tremble—"dead?"

"He's alive. I wanted to kill the prick, but Bear pulled me off him." Sobs tore through her as her body began to shake. "Shh, I got you. No one's going to hurt you ever again, Suzy."

I held her until the paramedics arrived, and a second ambulance pulled in a moment later. Two men pulled her from my grasp, assessing her injuries before placing her on a stretcher and completing their evaluation. I watched as they checked the fucker's body on the ground. Fuck him. I hoped the bastard fucking died.

"We need to take her to the hospital. She's sustained some head injuries and we want to make sure it's not serious," the EMT said. "Would you like to meet us there?"

"I'll follow you." I looked over his shoulder and saw them loading Suzy into the ambulance. "Can I speak to her first?"

"Yes, quickly, so we can leave."

I climbed in the ambulance and crouched down next to the stretcher. Her body was strapped in and machines were attached to her arms. Suzy looked worse with the lights shining on her face. "Sugar, you want me to go with you or follow them?"

"Take my car, City. I don't want it here, please."

I leaned over and kissed her. My heart felt like it was going to explode in my chest. "I got it. I'll be right behind you. Don't worry," I said, not wanting to leave her, but wanting to obey her wishes.

She gave me a weak smile before I climbed out and headed for her car, moving as fast I could to be by her side. I had to beg for her forgiveness, and I prayed her injuries weren't serious. I could never live with myself. I found Suzy's phone lying by her purse, and I knew what I had to do. I dialed Kayden and Sophia and knew there would be hell to pay.

CHAPTER
TWENTY-ONE

SUZY

TIME SEEMED to pass in slow motion as a flurry of doctors and nurses poked and prodded me. I repeated the story of what happened so many times I could've recited it in my sleep.

"One more time, ma'am. What happened to you tonight?" the doctor asked as he placed a small light in my eyes.

I sighed and wanted to tell him to fuck off as he moved the light back and forth, momentarily blinding me. "Do I have to say it again? I've told you the story already." My patience was wearing thin.

"I need to make sure you have no memory issues from the blow to your head. Last time, I swear."

"You said that last time we did this." I rolled my eyes.

The doctor snickered. "I guess there's no short-term memory problems."

"My boyfriend and I were at a bar tonight, and I walked out before he did. I thought he was right behind me, and when I unlocked my car someone grabbed me from behind. By the time I realized what was happening, I was already on the ground and tried to fight back, but it was no use. I don't remember much else."

A police officer stood in the corner and scribbled on a little notepad as I spoke.

"I remember waking up in Joey's arms and then the ambulance arriving."

I couldn't give the truth. My boyfriend was supposed to kidnap me as we played out my fantasy for him to abduct me and make me his sex slave. Who did shit like that?

"We're just going to keep you here overnight for observation. You have a couple of bruised ribs, the laceration on your lip, and a concussion, but nothing that will cause long-term damage," the doctor said, staring at his clipboard. "We'll get you into a regular room as soon as possible so you can rest. We will release you in the morning."

"Is anyone here to see me?" I couldn't believe that City hadn't shown up, or anyone for that matter.

"Yes, but he's been instructed to wait outside until we complete your assessment."

"Can he come in now, please?"

My body ached, my face throbbed, and my head pounded from the aftereffects of the attack. I wanted to rest my eyes and turn off the light, but I needed to talk to City. I had to find out what happened, and why he wasn't the one to find me alone in the parking lot.

"Yes, I'll have the nurses talk with him and send him in. I'll see you tomorrow, Ms. McCarthy."

"Thanks," I said with a fake smile. I had nothing to be thankful for. All I wanted to do was crawl in my own bed and sleep against City's body. Crunchy hospital sheets, plastic mattresses, and thin blankets were not my idea of comfortable.

I threw my head back onto the thin pillow, squeezing my eyes shut. I wanted to cry, but I didn't have tears left.

"Ma'am," the officer said, and cleared his throat. "I've taken down your statement, but I may need more details. We have your attacker in custody and the statement of Joseph

Gallo and another gentleman, but we may still need your side to fill in the gaps. Here's my card. Call me when you can talk. It can wait until you're home and more comfortable." He smiled at me, and I could see he was genuine.

"I'll call you, sir. I just don't feel like talking about it anymore tonight." I rubbed my eyes. The lights were making my headache worse, and I wanted to sleep.

"No problem, ma'am."

Drawing back the curtain to leave, I caught a glimpse of City. A frown was visible as he looked at me. I could see the pain on his face. His hands appeared swollen, and red dotted his knuckles—blood from the pounding he must have given to the asshole.

"Hey," he said as he approached my bed.

"Hey yourself."

"Are you okay, sugar?" He sat down on the bed and held my hand.

"I'm okay, City. They're just keeping me for observation." I shrugged.

Touching my cheek with the rough pads of his fingers, he studied my face. His eyes roamed over every inch, stopping on my lips and cheekbone. "God, I'm so sorry, Suzy. It's all my fault." Deep lines appeared on his forehead.

"It wasn't your fault. You meant well. I give you an A for effort, but a D in completion, big boy." I smirked. I couldn't really be mad at him.

"Don't make jokes, sugar." He tried to keep a straight face, but I saw a small smile tug at the corner of his lips. "I could've lost you tonight." He squeezed my hand.

"What happened to you? You were supposed to be only a minute behind me, Joey." Closing my eyes, I remembered the fear I felt when I realized it wasn't City grabbing me from behind.

"I was on my way out of the bar after joking with the guys, but I got held up. I tried to get away as quickly as possible. I didn't want you to be outside alone. I should've never taken you to that bar. Fuck." He rubbed his face, "What happened before I got there, sugar?"

Tears began to fill my eyes as I spoke. I couldn't hold them back. "I pretended to drop my keys when I heard someone behind me. I thought it was you. As I bent down to pick them up, he grabbed me by the hair and knocked me off balance." I paused, trying to steady my voice. "He pulled me by my hair behind the building, and I tried to get free of him. I kicked and screamed, but no one heard me. He hit me in the face and called me names. I could taste the blood in my mouth. I don't remember anything else until I woke up in your arms." I cuddled into City, needing the feeling of safety.

"Shh, sugar. I'll never let anything bad happen to you again." He crawled in the bed and wrapped his arms around me. I cried in his chest until there were no more tears left. He stroked my hair, kissing my head, rocking me until I calmed.

"Where is she?" Sophia's voice woke me from my peaceful slumber. "I don't give a shit, I want to see her now."

Jesus.

"Ma'am, you can't go in there."

The curtain opened in one quick motion, and a scared Sophia appeared. "Oh my God, Suzy. I've been worried sick about you." She rushed to my bedside.

I saw movement out of the corner of my eye—Kayden. He looked pissed. More pissed than I'd ever seen him, and I'd seen him pretty crazy at times over the years.

"I'm okay, Sophia. Just some scrapes and bruises. I'll heal."

"You could've been killed, for shit's sake. And you." She glared at City, pointing at him. "You were supposed to protect her from shit like this. How could you let her go outside alone?"

"It's not his fault," I said, but she held up her hand.

"Well?" she asked.

"City, may I speak to you for a moment?" Kayden asked in a calm voice.

I didn't like pissed-off-looking and calm-sounding Kayden. "You both need to back off," I said.

"Suzy, this is between City and me. I won't keep him long," Kayden said.

I looked at City, silently pleading with him not to go. He squeezed my hand as he slid off the bed. "I'll be right back, don't worry." He gave me a wink and a smile before leaving with Kayden.

"Let the boys talk. What the fuck happened, Suzy?" Sophia sat down next to me, tilting her head before she grabbed my hand. "God, I was out of my mind when City called. This is all my fault."

"It's no one's fault, Sophia. I walked out and everything was going perfectly. I guess City got held up for a second, and that's all it took." I wiped the remaining tears off my cheek. "The same creep had bothered me before and must've been waiting for me. It was stupid to think we could live out that fantasy. It's not as sexy as it sounds anymore."

"Fuck, it's my fault." She hung her head.

"Sophia, why would it be your fault?"

"I kinda told him about your fantasy." She didn't look me in the eyes.

"You did what?"

She stood up and moved out of reach. "When he was doing my tattoo, I told him that you don't like to share your fantasies, and told him about your kidnapping thing you've been dying to live out."

Jesus Christ. "Sophia, I know we're best friends and all, but that was between you, me, and Kayden." I took a deep breath and tried not to be angry. Sophia loved me, and so did Kayden. We always talked about sex, and they were the two people in the world that never judged me. Kayden was the only male that let me pick his brain on the subject, and he answered honestly without making me feel like an idiot. "I'm a little embarrassed here. I thank you for trying to give me what I want, but that was my secret to tell."

"If it would've worked out, he would've knocked your socks off, babe. City is exactly the type of guy you need to be with. Don't let this experience put doubt in that pretty little head of yours. He was a wreck, Suzy. I feel a little shitty now that I got bitchy with him. He really cares for you, my little OCD friend."

I laughed. I always made Sophia insane with all my little quirks and lists. The woman lived life by the seat of her pants, and I wanted everything planned. I had lists for my lists, and I would even include her on my lists when we lived together. "I know he cares, Sophia. I saw the pain in his eyes tonight. I don't think I've ever seen anyone so afraid for me before."

I could hear the murmured voices of Kayden and City but couldn't make out the words. "What is he saying to City?"

"You know Kayden is very protective of you. He's just having a man-to-man."

"I'm not a child, Sophia. Kayden better be nice." I crossed my arms over my chest.

"Kayden's always nice. They're just chatting." She smiled, but I could see the worry on her face.

Life had become so complicated, and my plans seemed to unravel before my eyes. I felt like Sophia on the rollercoaster she experienced when falling in love with Kayden. She put her hands up and screamed through the ride, while I wanted to jump off and keep my feet on the ground.

CHAPTER
TWENTY-TWO
CITY

"HOW IN THE fuck could you let her walk outside alone?" Kayden stood toe to toe with me. I didn't blame him—he cared for Suzy.

"Kayden, I know, man. I was supposed to be right behind her. Everything got fucked up." I kept eye contact with him. I wouldn't show weakness, even though I knew the entire thing happened because of Kaylee and my past. My fucking cock always caused trouble.

"Yeah, I'd say. If anything happens to her, City, I'll kick your ass. I may look small compared to you, but I'll crush you. Hear that shit."

I clenched my hands, stopping myself from beating his ass right here in the hospital. I knew he wouldn't hit me. Throwing down with Kayden would only drive a wedge between Suzy and me. I'd let him say his piece. "Got it loud and clear, Kayden. I'll protect her with my life."

"I know you didn't mean for any of it to happen, City, but I expect more." He stepped back. "She's like a sister to me. Just protect her and we won't have an issue. I don't want to be a dick, but I had to tell you that you fucked up."

"I know, and I will, Kayden. I'm happy that you love her

and you'll look out for her if I'm not around. I know I fucked up and I'll do everything in my power to make it up to her."

"Are you planning on breaking her heart, man?" He crossed his arms over his chest and stared. "If this shit is just a game to you, then you need to end it now."

"Fuck no, but I don't know where her head is right now." I rubbed my eyes, exhausted from the events of tonight.

"Don't give her a choice, City. She's quick to overthink everything. She needs a little push sometimes."

"I'm happy to show her the way. Are we good, man?" I asked. "I need to get back to her."

"Yeah, we're good." He held out his hand to me.

"Thanks, man." I shook his hand.

I walked through the curtain to the girls whispering on the bed. "Hey, ladies," Kayden said behind me. "Suzy, how are you, love?" He walked in front of me and stood next to her bed.

I stood at the foot of the bed and watched them as they interacted. They were a family, anyone could see that. There was a love and a shared past that brought them together. They chatted as I stood there, transfixed. Suzy looked battered, with bruises and a split lip. It would take forever for the effects to fade from her beautiful face.

"We have a room ready for you," a nurse said as she entered the small space.

"Oh, great," Sophia said. "We better head home, Suzy. Sleep well, and we'll stop by tomorrow to see you." She kissed Suzy on the cheek, and Kayden did the same.

"Night, Suzy." Kayden turned to me. "City, make sure she's okay tonight. Don't leave her alone." He wrapped his arm around Sophia.

"I wouldn't be anywhere else, Kayden."

"I love you guys. City will take good care of me. Go home —Jett will be up soon."

"Bye, love," Sophia said before they walked out.

I sat down next to her as the nurse started to unhook the machines. "Hey, sugar. How are you really feeling?"

"Sore." She winced as she moved her limbs. "Can you find a mirror? I want to see my face."

Oh God. Her face was swollen, with a small amount of dried blood in the corner of her mouth. I didn't want her to see herself all bruised. "I'll find one soon. Wait until you're moved."

"You can follow, sir. We're taking her to the second floor for the night." The nurse removed the brake on the bed as I stood and moved out of the way.

"I'm not leaving her side, ma'am," I said as Suzy laid her head on the pillow and smiled at me. I wouldn't leave her tonight.

The trip to her room was quick, and the nurse left us alone and didn't ask any questions. I sat down in the chair next to her as she yawned. My eyes felt heavy and my mind cloudy.

"Will you sleep up here with me? I mean, there isn't much room, but I want you to hold me tonight. I need you."

How could I say no to anything she asked? I'd stand on my head all night if it made her fucking happy. "Anything you want, sugar." I kicked off my shoes, climbing in the small twin bed before lying on my side, pulling her face to my chest. "Try to sleep. I'm not going anywhere."

The tiny bed was perfect as I cradled her in my arms. She gripped my shirt, resting her face against my shoulder. I enveloped her in my arms, I wanted her to feel safe, and I needed to know that she was okay.

Listening to her breath as she slept, I smelled her hair, but it had the scent of the cigarette smoke from the bar, and dirt. Her body twitched as she whimpered in her sleep. I wanted to crawl inside her dream and rescue her.

I flexed my hands; the stiffness from the bruises and small cuts made me wince. It wasn't anything I hadn't felt before, but I couldn't work for a couple of days until they healed.

After pulling my phone from my pocket, I adjusted her body without waking her then sent Anthony a message. My other siblings would be in a panic and the entire crew would be here, but Anthony I could count on to keep the information low key—at least for tonight.

Me: Won't be in tomorrow. Tell Mikey to reschedule my appointments. Thanks, bro.

Anthony had a gig in Clearwater, and he was a sure bet to get the information.

Anthony: I told him, he's with me.

Fuck. Might as well have put it on the evening news or taken out a fucking billboard. Mikey would have a million questions and would want details.

Anthony: What the fuck happened? Not like you to not work.

I didn't want to give them the details, but I had to give enough to get them off my back. I didn't have a fucking choice in the matter. I'd have to cancel dinner with the family. My mother would want to know why—no one got out of dinner without a legitimate excuse. I wanted to stay with Suzy for the weekend and make sure she was okay before I let her be alone.

Me: Situation at the bar tonight. I need to stay with Suzy. Tell Mom I can't make it and clear my schedule for a couple days at least.

Anthony: WTF happened? You okay?

Suzy didn't move as I typed with one hand, trying not to break the embrace.

Me: Beat the shit out of some fucker that attacked her. She's in the hospital for the night and I want to stay with her after she's released. Don't tell anyone. I don't want them to flip out.

Anthony: Gotcha, but Mom is going to want details. Which hospital?

Me: County Hospital, but we're okay. My hands are just swollen. I'll be fine.

Anthony: Gotcha. Mum's the word.

Nothing stayed a secret in my family. It was like the mafia party line. I knew Mikey had probably read over Anthony's shoulder, and soon the entire brigade would be on high alert. I set the phone above my pillow and closed my eyes, wrapping Suzy in my arms.

I tried to think about happy things, Suzy's laugh or how she kissed me, but all I could think of was her limp body and bloodied face in my arms. I kept opening my eyes to remind myself that she was okay. I waited for exhaustion to take me and wipe that vision from my mind.

The sound of plastic squeaking against the tile floor woke me early in the morning. "Sorry, I didn't mean to wake you," a nurse said as she moved to the IV stand.

I grunted and waited for her to leave before closing my eyes again. Hospitals aren't the place for rest. The movement outside the room is constant, alarms and announcements echo through the halls, and people talk loud enough to wake the dead. I felt like a Mack truck had hit me. My back was stiff, my eyes burned, and my hands throbbed. I wanted to get the fuck out of here and crawl in a real bed with her.

A quiet knock caused Suzy to stir, and my mother stood in the doorway. Fucking brothers—always mama's boys.

"Hey," she said, smiling.

I held put my finger to my lips, hoping not to wake Suzy as my ma entered the room. "It's early, Ma. What are you doing here?" I whispered.

"Your brother told me something happened and that you were here with Suzy. You know I can't sleep good when I worry about my children." She stood next to the bed, looking at Suzy's face against my chest.

"I'm fine, Ma. I couldn't leave her and I want to stay with

her when she gets out for a couple days. I didn't think Mikey would put out an all-points bulletin."

"Always so quick to blame Michael, aren't you, Joseph? It was Anthony that texted me. I just wanted to stop and see if you two were okay." She shook her head at me.

When did my mother learn how to text?

"We will be as soon as we get out of this shithole."

"What happened, son?" My mom pulled up a chair and waited for my answer.

"Someone assaulted her. When I found her, I kicked his ass." I didn't want to meet my mother's eyes. She was the only person in the world I never wanted to disappoint. I wasn't a mama's boy, but in an Italian family a mother is the queen bee, top dog, and wore the pants. Even my father bowed down to her and cherished the ground she walked on. He wasn't a pussy, and could kick ass in his youth, but Mrs. Gallo wasn't a person any of us wanted to piss off. "Trust me, Ma, he looks worse than me."

She wrinkled her nose; she never liked to think of any of her children fighting, even Mikey. "Where were you?"

"Neon Cowboy, and we were on our way out after having a couple drinks." I definitely didn't want to share that I'd planned to kidnap my girlfriend. Sex wasn't something I talked to my mother about, and usually not even my father.

"I told you I hate that damn bar. There's nothing but trouble in *those* types of places. Haven't you learned anything from Thomas?" She wasn't mad, but I could see the fear in her eyes.

"Yes, Ma. I have friends there, clients even, and I like it there. I'm not going to stop hanging out there because of the what-ifs."

"Is she okay, son?" She peeked over my shoulder, her eyes growing wide as she took in the sight of Suzy's face.

"Yeah, she'll heal. Just waiting for the doctor to come and

release her. I won't be there Sunday, but I promise to be there next week."

"Sure, baby. Can I drop off food, at least? That way you can spend time taking care of her without having to cook."

How could I say no to my mother? When she offered food it was the highest honor. She lived to cook and take care of her family. If I said no, it would be an enormous insult and there would be hell to pay.

"Sure, Ma. I'd love if you'd stop by with some food." I didn't entirely mean that statement, but I knew it would make her happy.

"I'm going to go and let you two rest. I don't want to wake her. I'll call you later, Joseph." She stood up and kissed my forehead. She was the only person in the world that I'd let treat me like a child. No matter how many times I told her I wasn't, she just made it all the more unbearable, smothering me with her love.

"Okay, Ma. Thanks."

"I love you, Joseph. Take care of that one."

"Love you too, Ma."

She walked out of the room and I ran my fingers over the bruises on Suzy's face. They were brighter in color and more visible than they had been the night before. She began to stir at my touch, and her eyes opened. The side crinkled from the smile on her face.

"You stayed?"

"Where else would I go, sugar?"

She closed her eyes and made a sound like "I don't know" as she smashed her face in my chest and inhaled. "Can we get out of here?"

"I'll go see if I can get the doctor to discharge you. Let me get up."

She winced as I helped her move out of my arms and climbed off the bed. "You're going to spend all day in bed when I get you out of here."

"Oooh, that sounds so sexy." She laughed and held her side.

"Bad girl, you're injured—rest only." I was happy to see that her spirit hadn't vanished with the attack. "Be right back or I'll break you out of this joint."

I found a nurse sitting at a desk and pleaded with her to process the paperwork quicker than normal. "You can help her get dressed to speed up the process if you'd like, sir," the nurse said as she typed.

"Sure, we'll be waiting, ma'am." I returned to the room to find Suzy trying to climb out of bed. "What the hell are you doing?" I said, rushing to her side.

"I needed to pee." She looked up at me with a shy, embarrassed smile.

"I'll help you, sugar. Then we got to get you dressed."

"Fine. I hate having to need help to walk, City. This is a little ridiculous."

"It's what I'm here for. You're *mine* and I'm going to take care of you this weekend. No arguments. Got it?" I waited for her reply before taking her hand.

"Yes, sir. I'm yours for the weekend. I thought it would be a bit different, but..." She shrugged.

"Makes two of us. Come on, sweetheart." I helped her to the bathroom and then grabbed her clothes. I hit them a couple times to get the dirt off before she dressed.

"I need a shower," she said as she hobbled out of the bathroom.

"I'll help you as soon as we get you home."

"You're the boss."

I liked the sound of those words coming out of her mouth. I wouldn't take any lip from her this weekend. She was *mine*.

CHAPTER
TWENTY-THREE

SUZY

I SETTLED IN MY BED, thankful to be home, and watched City as he undressed. I'd never been with a man that I couldn't stop staring at. I wanted the image etched in my brain. His muscular build flexed as he took off his pants. The tattoos on his torso and arms moved, and I was mesmerized as if watching a movie. I ached to tug on the bar that hung from his nipple, salivated to taste his flesh, and shivered at the thought of him inside me.

He kicked his pants in the air and caught them. "Don't look at me like that, sugar." His shaft bobbed, catching my attention; my mouth suddenly felt dry.

I blinked and looked at his face. "Like what? I was just thinking about how skilled you are at catching your pants." I giggled.

"You just looked at my dick in a way that makes me want to jam it down your throat." He grinned at me, and even though my face hurt, I wanted nothing more than for him to do that to me. "Not today, sugar."

"Tomorrow?" I raised my eyebrows, hoping that I could entice him, or at least get a promise of something before the weekend ended.

"We'll see. I decide when and how. What can I get you?"

"Your cock." I knew when I said dirty words that he couldn't resist me. If he continued to deny me, I sure as hell wouldn't make it easy on him.

He rubbed his face and muttered something I couldn't quite make out. "Want something to drink or eat?"

He stood there, buck-naked and mouth-wateringly delicious, and waited for my answer. How could I think of water when his beautiful body was on full display? I shook my head and patted the mattress with a crooked smile.

"Tomorrow, sugar."

A pout hung on my lips, but inside I was happy to at least get a concession. "Good enough. I don't have anything in the fridge, City. I didn't think I'd be here much this weekend." Admitting to an Italian man that you lacked even the staples in your pantry wasn't easy.

"My mother wants to drop off food later. Are you okay with that?"

"Really?" My mother had never brought me food, even when I had the flu. I always fended for myself, even if it meant crawling to the kitchen to grab a glass of water. His mother, a woman I'd never met, would bring me food, and I had a twinge of jealousy. What would it have been like to grow up in a house like his?

"I can call her anytime and she'll drop something off. You just say the word."

"Word, word, word! Does your mom use Ragu like mine?" My mother never cooked from scratch. As a child I thought Chef Boyardee was the bee's knees, until I grew up and realized it was closer to vomit in a can.

City laughed, and his smile made my chest ache. "Don't even mention the word Ragu to her. She'll have a mental breakdown."

"Good to know," I said. "Remind me to never cook for her, okay?"

City grabbed his phone as he crawled in bed. "Hey, Ma. Suzy's going to rest for a bit, but we'd love for you to drop by with some food." I could hear her talking on the phone, and it reminded me of Charlie Brown's teacher. I couldn't make out the words, but I heard a garbled voice as I put my head on his chest. I played with the piercing, which earned me a stern look. "I'll text you her address. Thanks, Ma."

He put the phone down and stared at me, but I just smiled. "What?" I asked innocently.

"You must've hit your head harder than I thought."

"Maybe." I kissed his nipple, tugging on the hoop with my lips. He inhaled sharply as I bit down.

"Sugar, not now. I'm trying to be real good here, and you're not in any shape right now to do the things to you I want. Later, when you've rested and had something to eat, I'll give you more than you can handle…*if* I feel you're up to it."

"Party killer," I said, as I laid my head back down in the crook of his arm.

"Be a good girl and sleep." His fingertips trailed down my back, leaving a wake of warmth against my skin. I closed my eyes and enjoyed the feel of his hands on me, even if it wasn't the way I wanted.

***

I didn't know how long I slept, but when I woke up, I was alone in the bed. His side was still warm. My muscles rebelled and ached as I stretched. "Damn," I whispered, wanting to move without pain.

The doorbell rang and my heart started to pound—*his mother*. I didn't look presentable, and my face had to be a mess. I'd stared at it in horror this morning at the hospital. This wasn't the way I wanted to meet his mom.

I could hear them talking in the kitchen. The door cracked

open and I turned my head, praying it was City. "Hey, sugar, ma's here. Do you want to meet her?"

"I look like crap, City. I can't have her see me like this."

He sat down next to me. "Sugar, she was at the hospital this morning. She's seen your face. She's not going to stare at you."

I sighed. "You didn't tell me."

"Sorry. Come on, just a quick hello. She made you lasagna." He brushed the hair away from my face, following the curve of my cheek.

I'd do anything this man asked me to. A smile, touch, or kiss and I was totally and utterly his. "Let me get dressed and I'll come out."

Meeting parents always scared me to death, and it meant a step deeper into a relationship. His mother obviously loved her son enough to bring us food, and I wanted to at least thank her for her kindness.

I looked into the mirror, touched the stitching on my lip with my tongue, noticing the coppery taste of blood. There was no need to bother with makeup. I couldn't look any worse than I did, and if she liked me now then I'd knock her socks off when she saw me at my best. Dressed in my favorite hoodie and sweats, I walked out to meet Mrs. Gallo.

"There she is," City said, standing from the couch with a smile plastered on his face.

Mrs. Gallo stood up and turned around. Her face was lit up and she looked like the mom I always wanted. She had long, wavy brown hair, big brown eyes, and a kind smile. "Suzy, it's so nice to finally meet you," she said as she wrapped her arms around me. "I'm sorry for how we're meeting, sweetheart. How are you feeling?"

"Thank you, Mrs. Gallo, I'm feeling much better." I moved to sit next to City, and grabbed his hand. "Thank you for making me lasagna. It's one of my favorites."

"My pleasure. Food always helps make everything better," she said.

"Italian motto," City muttered, and I laughed.

"I'm going to get going now and leave you two kids to enjoy your food. I just wanted to say hello. Is there anything else I can do before I leave?"

"No, ma'am, you've done more than I can ask for."

"Mrs. G or Maria, please. You need anything, just have Joseph call me."

"Joseph." I laughed. It sounded so serious, and fit him well.

"Watch it," he said in a playful tone, and squeezed my hand.

We all stood and hugged his mother goodbye. We walked to the door and watched her leave. I pictured her climbing into a minivan, even though she didn't have small children. I never pegged her for a woman that drove a Mercedes. I dreamed of a new Honda and knew it would be a budget killer...maybe someday.

"Your mom is great," I said as I wrapped my arm around his waist.

"She can be, but she's a pit bull when you cross her—just ask my father," he said. "Want some lasagna?"

"What's for dessert?" I asked as he closed the door.

"Anything you want, sugar."

"You know what I want," I said.

"Are you up to it?"

"Question is, big boy, are you up to it?" I wanted him, and I figured that if I challenged his manhood, he'd finally cave. All men are the same in that regard.

He laughed. "Don't ask questions if you can't handle hearing the answer. Eat your food and I'll show you how *up* to it I am, sugar."

He placed a giant piece of lasagna with cheese oozing out in front of me. My stomach growled at the smell, and the feeling of hunger finally registered. I cut into the slice and watched all the insides squish onto my plate. The hot lasagna spread across my tongue, and I wanted to moan from the taste.

"That good, huh?" City asked as he scooped a chunk in his mouth.

"What? Did I?"

"Yep, you moaned, sugar."

My face became heated. "Well, I'm used to Stouffer's lasagna. This is amazing, City. You don't know how lucky you were to grow up on this type of home cooking." I slid the fork across my tongue and slowly chewed, letting all the flavors dance on my tongue.

"I never thought about it." His fork stopped near his mouth as he looked at me with piercing eyes. "Suzy, you keep making noises like that and I won't let you finish the next bite." He set the fork on his plate and leaned back.

"I need my fuel to get better." I placed another sliver in my mouth, closed my eyes, and made a small sound in the back of my throat.

"You have thirty seconds to finish what's in front of you before I take your ass in the bedroom and give you something to really moan about." He crossed his arms over his chest and looked at his watch.

I shoveled the food in my mouth. I felt torn in this moment, but the lasagna could always be reheated.

"Fifteen." He smiled at me, and I felt everything in my body convulse and scream to be touched. I chewed like a maniac.

"Five."

"Wait!" I held up my hand. "I need something to drink," I said as I hopped off the high-top café chair.

"I got something for you to wash that down with, sugar. Time's up."

***

"Slower, Suzette," City said in my ear as he rocked in and out of me. "It's not a marathon. I want to savor being inside you."

"I've just missed you. Missed this."

"We have the rest of the weekend. I don't want to hurt you. Slow." He grabbed my hips and held me still as he slowed his pace. I wanted to scream and claw him, but I knew it wouldn't help to fight him.

He rested his forehead against mine as he encased my body and assaulted my senses. This was more than just sex. He expressed his feelings, and I felt them seep into my body. I stared in his eyes as he stared into mine before he kissed my lips. The pain of the kiss didn't stop me from returning it with fervor.

My fingers dug into his shoulders and I felt them flex under my touch. Each thrust brought me closer to the release I craved. His breathing grew harsh as he curled his arms under my body, tilting my hips.

My hands rested on his hips, unable to reach his ass, as I felt them relax and constrict with each thrust. I wished I had a mirror to watch his ass and back as he moved with my body. I squeezed the soft skin and hard muscle as the orgasm tore through my body. It was stronger than anything I had felt before. My toes curled and my muscles clenched around him as his pace quickened, before he slammed into me one last time, reaching his own bliss.

He nuzzled my neck and kissed the soft skin, making a trail to my lips. "I don't know what I would've done if something happened to you, sugar."

I ran my fingers through his hair and pulled his face to mine, forcing his eyes to see me. "I'm fine, Joey. You saved me." I kissed him and didn't give him a chance to respond.

He flipped us over, and I straddled his body before breaking the kiss.

"No more fantasies that don't involve me by your side, but I still want to make them come true."

"I'm looking forward to it." I smiled against his chest as I kissed the skin over his heart. I listened to his heart thud in his chest. I had never felt so content with any person, let alone a man.

City spent the rest of the weekend helping me. Even though it started rocky, it ended with me feeling more loved and adored than I ever had. I couldn't deny my feelings for him any longer. My checklist no longer mattered. He showed me that he would take care of me and treat me in the way I'd always wanted. My doubts about if he was the "one" had vanished, and were replaced by a fate that had been sealed.

CHAPTER
TWENTY-FOUR
CITY

"YES, sir, how can I help you?" the older lady at the reception desk asked. She leaned forward and rested her head on her hands.

I gave her my devilish grin and a wink. "I'm here to see Ms. McCarthy, ma'am."

"Oh, please, call me Kathy." She batted her eyelashes. "You're here to see Suzy?" She looked surprised, and her voice ended on a screechy high note. Her eyes no longer looked at my face, but traveled down my arms.

"Yes, I'm here to see Suzy, *Kathy*." I arched my eyebrow as she soaked me in, undressing me with her eyes. She looked like a nice enough lady, but I didn't like how she said Suzy's name, and I certainly didn't particularly enjoy the fantasy she must be having in her head. I cleared my throat, needing to pull her out of her lust-induced haze.

She blushed as she started fumbling with papers at her desk. She asked me for my identification and to sign the visitor's log. The school day had ended, but a few students milled around the receptionist area. I could feel their eyes on me. I wanted to laugh, but didn't want to be a total asshole.

Kathy gave me directions to Suzy's classroom in the next

building. I needed to make sure she was okay on her first day back to work since the attack. I was sure she'd had to explain the injuries to her face over and over again. People could be fucking merciless.

I checked the sign on the door, and it read "101—Ms. McCarthy's Class." The large classroom had tables set up in neat rows, with cabinets lining the opposite wall. There was no chalkboard in the room like there had been when I was a kid, but a dry-erase board hung on the wall. Math problems that made my fucking head spin were written on the shiny white surface.

I didn't see anyone, but could hear voices talking from an attached room.

"I'm fine. Stop it," Suzy said. I picked up my pace to find out what the fuck was going on.

Entering the small office space, I saw Suzy pinned against the wall with Derek cutting off her escape. She looked like she wanted to become one with the wall and couldn't move farther away from his body. Her eyes grew wide as I reached for the prick and grabbed him by the shirt collar.

"What the fu—" he said, his eyes traveling to my face.

"The lady said stop. I think we've already had this conversation once before, dumbfuck." We were nose to nose, and I'd knock the motherfucker out.

"Suzy didn't mean it," he snarled.

He sure had a pair of brass balls, but my fists were made of platinum. I fisted his pansy-ass dress shirt, pulling his body to mine. "She's mine, you fucker, and when the lady says *stop* it she means stop and back the fuck up."

"I should've had your ass arrested the first time you hit me. Hit me again and I'll call school security."

"Need someone else to fight your battles, sissy boy? You pick on girls, but can't handle a man all on your own?"

Suzy had tears in her eyes as I looked at her over his head.

"Listen here, buddy, I don't know who the fuck you think

you are, but Suzy and I have a thing. She's not yours. Right, Suzy?"

She began to shake her head as her eyes grew wide. He turned his head to look at her, and I couldn't hold back my fist any longer. I punched him right in the jaw and watched the spit and blood fly out of his mouth. Served the bastard right. I held him upright with my grip as he wobbled on shaky knees and his eyes watered.

If we weren't in her office at a school, I'd beat the piss out of the motherfucker. He deserved to be taught a harsher lesson than one simple fist to the face, but I had to tamper down my anger for Suzy's sake.

I let go of him with a shove and watched him stumble before catching himself on her desk. "I'll have you arrested for this." He wiped the blood from his lip with the back of his hand and glared at me.

"I'll share the little tidbit with security. I'll tell them how I walked in on you sexually harassing Ms. McCarthy in her office. I heard her telling you stop. Who do you think she's gonna back, asshole? You've touched her for the last time. Do it again and I'll bury you."

Suzy walked to my side and put her arm around me. "Derek, you mention a word and I'll make sure they fire your ass. I'll have no problem telling them about this and the other times." Smiling at me, she squeezed my waist. "I have Joseph and Sophia to back me up. Sophia knows all about you and your bullshit." Did she use two swear words in that speech? *That's my girl*, I thought as I beamed with pride.

"You wouldn't?" he asked, smoothing out his shirt, wiping the last bit of blood tricking down his chin.

"Try me, Derek," she snarled, showing the slightest hint of teeth.

"I'd put my money on the blonde." I smirked at the jackass as he stormed out of the room. "You okay, Suzy?" I asked, wrapping her in my arms.

She squeezed my waist and buried her face in my shirt. "Mm, you smell good."

"Answer me, sugar. Are you okay?" I kissed the top of her head.

"Yeah, I'm fine. Derek's an asshole. I don't think he'll be bothering me again." She laughed into my chest.

"I don't want you working with that dick anymore."

"I think he almost peed his pants."

"Promise me, Suzette? You need to go to the administration about him. He shouldn't work here or be near you."

She patted my stomach. "I love when you get all tough guy and use my full name." She laughed, and I squeezed her ass hard enough to make her jump. "I promise, Joseph."

"You seem to like it when I'm buried balls deep inside you, sugar, I don't hear you laughing then," I whispered in her ear. She shivered in my arms as the vibrations of my words touched her ears. "Why don't we put your desk to good use?"

She smacked me in the chest, but I could see the twinkle in her eye. She thought about it for a second before she answered. "No way, mister. I'm not getting fired."

"I thought maybe you went all bad girl on me, using all those curse words on Derek." I ran my finger over her bruise, but she didn't flinch.

"Two? I swore twice?" Her mouth hung open.

"You did, sugar. I'm proud of you."

"You must be rubbing off on me." She pulled away from my arms and smiled.

"Speaking of rubbin'." I looked down, wiggled my eyebrows, and moved my hips.

"Absolutely not." She looked away and started to move the papers on her desk.

I wrapped my arms around her and placed my face in her hair. "Whatcha gonna do, baby, give me a detention?" I asked. I couldn't help but laugh. God, if she was my teacher in high school I would've been all over her. My wet dreams would've been filled with visions of Ms. McCarthy leaning over my desk to help me with my math problems. I'd pray that her blouse would just happen to fall open and give me a glimpse of her beautiful tits.

She smacked my hands. "You're a naughty boy."

"You have no idea, Ms. McCarthy." I kissed down her neck, making my way to her shoulder before sinking my teeth into her delicate flesh. "You've smacked me twice, and I think I need to teach you a little lesson tonight." Her breath caught, and I heard a small moan escape as I ground my dick into her ass.

"Whatcha got in mind, Mr. Gallo?"

"I'm going to make sure you know you're mine." I cupped her breasts, squeezing them, and ran my palms across her hard nipples. "I'm going to fuck you so damn hard my cock will be the only one you'll ever think about. I'm leaving no inch untouched, no pore not kissed, and no hole unfilled."

"Um." She swallowed loud enough for me to hear. *Perfect.*

"Lost for words?"

"Not here," she whispered as she closed her eyes.

"My place, sugar. I don't want anyone to hear you scream when you think you can't come again, but I'll make you."

"Your punishment sounds so much better than detention."

"It's more like a retention program for at-risk little girls," I said as she turned around with a smile on her face.

"You know how to win a girl's heart." She stood on her tiptoes and kissed me.

I smacked her ass and she bit down on my lip, but not hard enough to break the skin.

"Oh, sorry, baby," she said.

"I'll get ya back, sugar. Let's get the fuck out of here or I'm tearing your clothes off right here." I pinched her nipple and felt her sharp intake of breath against my lips.

I needed to get the hell out of the school and take her to

my bed. I kissed her goodbye after walking her to her car. I walked to my bike on the opposite side of the parking lot after she drove away. It would be hard as fuck to ride with the raging hard-on in my pants—I needed the walk to cool the fuck off.

CHAPTER
TWENTY-FIVE
SUZY

RUINED. It was the only word that came to mind when I thought of Joseph Gallo, a.k.a. City McPierced Cock. He'd ruined me for any other man that could've had a place in my future. How could I go back to a boring anybody with a party pickle penis when I had Joey Sex God Gallo?

Joey made me scream in ecstasy; he'd been the first man I didn't have to fake it with. His voice alone made my skin break out in goose bumps, his kiss made the world vanish, and his cock—well, it was just damn unique and felt fucking amazing.

The idea of punishment didn't sound terrible coming out of his mouth. Anyone else and I would've run for the hills, but not City—he made my body feel like it was on fire. I wanted him to claim every inch of my body. What girl wouldn't want all the pleasure that would involve? I'd be an idiot not to want it.

I studied his body as he drove ahead of me on his sexy-ass Harley. I could see him watching me at the stoplights, and I never wanted the man to have eyes for another woman. He was everything I wanted, but never thought to include in my life plan. His muscles moved underneath his shirt as he hugged the road and gripped the bike. My mind kept replacing my body with the bike as we made our way to his house.

He became an addiction. He didn't ruin just my body, but he found a way to make himself a part of my life in a very short time. He invaded my dreams, and every thought I had involved him.

Watching him reminded me of the first time I saw him. I thought he would murder me on that country road. He looked mean and dangerous, but the only casualty would be my heart. Did I love him? It was a strong word to use in such a short amount of time. Could I go without him? Hell. No. Did I want him in my life? Damn straight. Love was a word I reserved for very few people in my life, and I wouldn't mess this up, no matter how fantastic his cock moved and how hard he made me scream. Love would come someday if he didn't fuck me to death first. Death by dick. Didn't sound half bad.

By the time we pulled into his driveway, my body buzzed with anticipation. It had been less than twenty-four hours since City had been inside me, but this felt...different. Turning the car off, I stared at him as he climbed off the bike and removed his helmet. He approached my car—his movement was like a lion stalking its prey—and I felt my cheeks flush with excitement. He looked handsome. Uniquely perfect.

His beauty wasn't only external. He had that nailed at first glance, but internally he was Prince Charming. Nobody had ever treated me like he did. He had just the right amount of caveman and Casanova to be destructive to a girl's mind—particularly mine.

"Come on, sugar. If I have to wait any longer, I'll fuck you right here in the driveway."

Although his words held promise, I'd never had sex outdoors; I wasn't ready to check that off my bucket list.

Grabbing his hand, I followed him inside the small white farmhouse. I kicked off my shoes, and he grabbed me and pushed me against the wall.

His soft, wet lips crushed against mine as I gasped, and his tongue took that as an open invitation. "I can't decide which part of your body to assault first." His tongue slowly glided across my bottom lip. My heart pounded in my chest and he had to feel the rapid pace of the thump. "Do I start with this pretty little mouth?" He nipped my lip, causing a small moan to escape with the thought of my tongue wrapped around his cock. "Do I use this in your tight little cunt or your beautiful, tight ass?" He squeezed my ass, and I could feel his hardness against my stomach. I thought about all the ways he could and would take me, and a tingle ran down my spine.

"Perfect choice. Your mouth it is…to start." His eyes crinkled from the smile on his face. Fuck, I didn't make a choice.

"What? Wait."

"Not your decision. Watching you suck that lip in your mouth makes my cock ache to feel your tongue tugging at my piercing. On your knees, sunshine." The use of the nickname from our first meeting, when my world changed forever, made my insides warm.

Placing his hand on my shoulder, he pushed me on my knees, and I came face to face with his giant bulge. This time I knew what I would see, but it didn't dull the excitement I felt. Reaching up to unzip his pants, I peered at his face. The grin playing on his lips and the twinkle in his eye made my core pulse. His shaft bobbed and brought my attention back to the task at hand: sucking his beautiful cock and bringing him to his knees.

I unzipped his pants and began the task of unleashing his hardness. I rarely felt in control when City had me naked, but I felt empowered kneeling before him. Springing free, the tip glistened with a drop of moisture. My mouth watered as I palmed his cock, squeezing it, feeling the heaviness and hardness of his silky-smooth erection in my hands. I licked the tip, capturing the wetness on my tongue before taking him fully in my mouth. I loved the feel of the piercing, and every time I brought the tip back to my lips, I'd run my tongue over the metal, giving it a light tug. His body quaked with each thrust and pull. His fingers tangled in my hair. He gripped it roughly, trying to control my movement and depth.

I ignored his grip, welcoming the pain as I controlled the depth and speed. "Fuck, sugar, your mouth feels amazing." I squeezed his ass and felt a shudder take over his body. Pulsing my grip, I sucked harder and quickened my pace, and I squeezed my legs together, trying to relieve the ache. He moaned and twitched, and I could almost taste how close he was to losing it. I focused my effort on the tip of his cock, running my tongue along the underside, flicking the sensitive flesh and capturing the ring between my lips as I worked his length. "Fuck," he moaned, and he increased the grip on my hair. "Stop, sugar."

Screw that. I wouldn't stop until his body shook, he screamed my name, and I milked him dry. I grazed his shaft with my teeth and he hissed. "Fuck." I didn't stop in my relentless pursuit of his release. I watch his face as I sucked and licked like a starved woman on a mission—his eyes were closed, head tipped back, and mouth open. I gripped his ass with both hands, digging my fingernails in his skin, taking him fully in my mouth, hitting the back of my throat. I swallowed and tried not to gag. I clamped down on his cock as a moan escaped his lips, driving me forward, seeking the moment he'd say my name.

The feel of his rock-hard ass beneath my fingers, flexing and twitching, made me crazy. I wanted him, wanted to feel him inside me, but I wouldn't stop what I started. I felt in charge for once.

"Suzette," he hissed as my mouth filled with his release.

When his body stopped shaking and his cock stopped pulsating, I released him. I grinned at him, with his wide eyes looking at me with adoration. Swallowing, I licked my lips and captured a small drop seeping from the tip. His eyes had a twinkle in them as he watched me.

"You don't fight fair, sugar," he said with a shaky voice as he kicked off his jeans.

"I didn't see you stopping me," I said, pushing off the floor. He reached out, grabbed my neck, and pulled me to him, as he crushed his lips to mine.

He felt soft and warm. I wrapped my arms around his neck and soaked in the feel of his hands gripping my waist. He pulled my legs around his waist and I wrapped my arms around his neck, wanting the connection. We moved as one toward the bedroom where we'd begun weeks ago—my life hadn't been the same since.

He leaned over the bed, but my body stayed attached to him like Velcro. "It's your turn to scream my name, sugar." He unlatched my hands from his neck, placing them at my side. "Don't move." He smirked as he moved down my body, running his finger across the exposed skin of my stomach from the bunching of my shirt.

His touch felt like electricity, a tingling sensation spreading throughout my body as he traced around my belly button. "Elastic?" The word pulled me back into reality after I'd been lost in my dreamlike state.

"What?" I could barely think, let alone form a coherent sentence.

"You're wearing pants with an elastic waistband." He eyed them with curiosity. "Never met a girl that wore dress pants like these." His fingers grabbed the waistband and released it, snapping it against my skin.

Oh, shit. I had my granny panties on too. I didn't think I'd see him today. I just wanted to be comfortable, since I walked into a barrage of questions about the bruises and busted lip. I covered my eyes. "They're comfortable," I said as I swatted his hand.

He raised an eyebrow at me as he looked at the material. "I'm sure. I think that's why my mom wears them too." His chest rumbled with a hearty laugh.

"Fuck off, City." I chuckled, kicking him with my foot.

"Watch the goods, princess." He grabbed my foot as I made another. "I have a fighter on my hands." He gripped the bottom of my pants and gave them a hard yank, exposing my underwear. *Fuck.* "You're full of surprises today, sugar," he said.

"Hello… didn't think I'd be seeing you today."

"Guess not, based on your attire." *Smug bastard.*

"This is who I am, City. I'm not a floozy and I don't like a string up my ass all day while I teach."

"Oh no, it's sexy. The best part about you is that you're not a floozy. Makes me feel special that you break out the sexy shit just for me."

"Well, since it's sexy, then I can stop with all the lingerie when I see you." I giggled. I'd never do it, but if he wanted to pretend it was a turn-on…

"I don't give a fuck what you wear, sugar, as long as you end up naked."

I didn't want to be the granny-panty-wearing girlfriend to the hot biker. I wouldn't change what worked. I'd wear my sexy lacy shit when I saw him, but maybe, just maybe, I'd throw him for a loop with innocent little pink flowers every once in a while. "You going to shut up and fuck me or sit here yapping about clothing all night?" I snapped.

"Oooh, I got a feisty one on my hands tonight." He moved his body as he covered mine before settling between my legs.

"You got a horny one that just sucked you off. She deserves a reward, and I can think of a million other things you can do with your lips than talk," I said, running my tongue across his bottom lip.

Lust filled his eyes as he tugged at my lips with his teeth. He pulled his shirt over his head as he balanced on one arm. I'd never get tired of seeing his body.

His fingers wrapped around the side of my underwear before he ripped them from my body with one quick jerk. "Hey," I yelled.

"I won't be buying you new ones, so don't ask." He laughed before nestling between my legs and licking his lips. The need I felt for him never waned like I'd experienced with other men—it only intensified.

I closed my eyes as his mouth closed around me and his tongue flicked my clit. The heat of his mouth made me melt into the mattress. I gripped the sheets, needing something to hold on to keep my body firmly planted. He didn't rush as he caressed and sucked every fold and inch of my core. I looked down, wanting to catch a glimpse of his beautiful face between my legs, and I was met with his blue eyes staring at me. His eyes didn't leave mine as he brought my body to the point of release. My body glistened as every muscle tensed.

"Please," I moaned. I was wound so tight; I sat at the tipping point and needed just a little bit more to tip me over the edge. I released the sheets and pinched my nipple between my fingers, rolling it back and forth. His eyes grew wide as he watched my fingers move against my skin.

The orgasm ripped through me, stopping my breath; I was paralyzed through the explosion of sensations. He moaned and lapped at my body as I screamed something that wasn't audible to my ears. My heart thundered in my chest as I tried to catch my breath. I opened my eyes to a very happy looking man.

"Sexy as fuck, sugar. Watching you touch yourself, coming on my tongue, and babbling all kinds of incoherent shit—priceless. You made me hard again. I want to feel you come on my cock."

City ripped open the condom wrapper before settling

between my legs. The piercing nudged my insides, causing my body to tighten. I felt the pressure building inside my core as he pumped inside of me. He cradled my ass with his hand, and my world exploded around him—and he followed me over the edge.

Multiple orgasms had always been a myth, something I read about in books, but with him they were a reality. What had started as a journey of lust and carnal exploits had now turned into something more. I saw the man behind the muscles, tattoos, and piercings, and I didn't want to let him go. I didn't want to be Suzy Q, the goody two-shoes anymore. I wanted to be a woman that could let her hair down and be who I wanted instead of what everyone expected.

I wanted to do something that I'd enjoy, or at least I hoped I would. City would freak out if I told him what I had planned. I kept it a secret. I contacted Mikey to see if he'd help me pull it off.

CHAPTER
TWENTY-SIX
CITY

THERE WAS a chill in the air as I walked toward the doors of Inked. Fall rolled into winter in Florida, and that meant cold nights and days that felt like the Chicago of my childhood. It was a nice change, but I craved the warmth of summer on my bike instead of the coolness that stung my skin.

I pushed the door open to see an empty shop desk as the bell above the door chimed. Mikey wasn't at his usual post to greet me, like he had been for more fucking mornings than I could count. I could hear a female voice and Mikey whispering from the piercing room in the back of the shop.

I put my ear to the door to listen to their conversation, but the voices grew quiet. I knocked. "Hey, can I come in?"

"In a minute," Mikey yelled. "Kind of got my hands full." I heard laughing as I walked away.

I checked my schedule for the day and listened to the voicemail messages. My first appointment called to cancel due to the flu, so I had some extra time. I kicked back on the couch and sent Suzy a message. Last night I'd left her exhausted in bed before making my way home. We'd been spending almost every evening together and usually never slept apart. The poor thing, I had been exhausting her with middle-of-the-night sex. She'd asked me if it was okay to sleep apart for a night and I agreed, although not happily. I understood, but I didn't fucking like it. The boner I woke up with this morning could've used some attention, but I did what needed to be done.

Me: Morning, beautiful. Sleep well?

I felt like a pussy-whipped fool, but for once I didn't mind feeling that way.

Suzy: Not really. I missed you in bed.

I smiled, knowing she felt the same. Never in a million fucking years would I have thought that I'd find love again in my life. Joni's sudden death had left me raw and reeling, not wanting to ever experience that hurt again. Suzy had changed that.

Me: Move in with me?

Did I really just type that shit? We'd been together only a couple of months, but I'd been with enough women in my life to know when it was right. I thought I'd get a quick response, but nothing. I was a fucking moron. I'd probably just scared her away.

The hinges on the door creaked as Mikey poked his head out. "Yo, bro. Wanna come see my handiwork?" He looked a little too happy for this time of morning.

"Who you working on off books?" There wasn't a name on his schedule before ten.

"Special request. Get your lazy ass up and come look, you prick." His head disappeared, and I could hear a hushed conversation.

"Mikey, I've seen every piercing out there." I climbed off the couch to make my brother happy, because he'd harp on me like a bitch in heat for the rest of the day. Plus, he could kick my ass if I didn't. "What's so special about this one?" I asked as I walked in the room and stopped dead in my tracks.

What the fuck?

Sitting in the chair was Suzy, *my* Suzy, with her breast exposed and a small metal hoop through her nipple. I couldn't breathe as I stood there staring with my mouth hanging open. Mikey looked excited and proud of himself, but I wanted to rip his fucking throat out—fighter or not.

Suzy had a sly grin on her face. "You like?" she asked.

Should I be happy or pissed? I blinked, but I couldn't fucking respond. My brother had his hands all over my woman, even if it was for my benefit, and I wasn't there to supervise.

"Earth to City," Mikey said, and I swear to fucking Christ I wanted to knock his happy ass out of the chair.

"You don't like it, do you?" She frowned at me, and her eyes began to glisten.

"Oh no, sugar. It's beautiful. Sexy as fuck, actually." I grabbed her chin and kissed her. "I'll have fun tugging on it like you do mine. It feels amazing."

"You scared the crap out of me. Are you mad?" she asked as I rested my forehead against hers and stared in her eyes.

"I'm not mad. A little pissed my brother had his paws on your gorgeous tits and that you didn't let me be here for it." I turned my head and gave my brother a scathing look.

"Hey, seen one breast, you've seen them all. It's work, bro."

Dickhead.

"I wanted to surprise you, Joey."

"Well you fucking did that in spades, sugar." I kissed her forehead and inspected the piercing closely. "Next time you touch my woman, I get to be here, brother. Got me?"

"Got ya. I swear to God it was all for you. Get that stick out of your ass and look how well it turned out. She has the perfect nipples for piercings."

Did he just fucking say that to my face?

"Mikey, watch it."

"I look at it as another body part to be decorated. Chill the fuck out. I know she's yours."

"As long as we're clear on that fact."

"Crystal." He stood to leave.

"Mikey," I said, stopping him in his tracks. "I wouldn't trust her in anyone else's hands. You did well."

"Means a lot coming from you, Joe." He slapped me on the shoulder and gave us a moment alone.

"You're not feeling sick are you?" I asked. She looked flushed.

"Perfect. I thought it would hurt more than it did, though. I want to get the other one done eventually."

"It takes a while to heal. You're still riding the adrenaline high, but you'll be sore for a long time. Thank fuck you still have one nipple I can touch."

"Oh, just touch?" She smirked. I closed the door and locked it. I had time to kill, and Suzy sat before me with her breast exposed and a look of want in her eyes. "What are you doing?" Her eyes twinkled—she knew exactly what I had in mind.

"We're going to have a chat about my text you didn't respond to, and then I'm going to fuck you bent over that chair."

I loved her surprised face. "What text?"

"Look at your phone." I crossed my arms over my chest and waited for her to read it.

"You want to move in together?" Her eyes grew wide and her mouth hung open.

"Yes, sugar. We spend every night together, so why should you have to make a house payment when I have a place of my own?"

"Don't take offense, City, but your place isn't really my taste. The man cave, barren walls, and cottage feel. Can't do it. You can move in with me, though."

"Whatever makes you happy. As long as I have you in my bed and my bike in the garage, I'm a happy man."

"So that's it? We're doing it?"

"Oh, we're doing it. Undress, sugar. You're not leaving here until I've erased any scent my brother left behind and my cock is satisfied." I started to unzip my pants, and watched her carefully as she began to undress. Her nipple was red and slightly swollen from the piercing, and I'd have to remind myself not to touch it.

"Grip the headrest, ass out." I stroked my cock as she kept turning her head to see what I was doing. I liked to make her wait.

When she turned back around, I smacked her ass, causing her to jump and yelp. "What was that for?"

"Next time, ask before you change your body forever. I won't say no, but I'd just like to be clued the fuck in. I would've given that nipple a little extra attention before you took it off the market for a couple of months."

"Yes, sir." She smiled and rested her forehead against the leather.

***

Packing up my house didn't take long. We decided I would move my things during Thanksgiving break. I didn't put my house up for sale. It was paid off and I didn't see the need to get rid of it. I loved the land that the small farmhouse sat on. I bought it for that reason, and thought that someday I'd build my dream house on the property.

I moved my clothes into her spare room. She bought a small drawing table for me to use in the evenings, and I decorated the space with my work and my Harley memorabilia. I didn't want to invade her space. Moving in together was a giant step, more of a leap of faith.

"Are you sure you don't want to put your clothes in my

closet?" she asked, leaning against the doorframe in a tiny purple silk nightie.

"No, sugar. My things are just fine in here." I unpacked the last box of clothing, sliding them in the dresser drawer that she'd emptied for me. "You need your space, especially your walk-in closet."

She sighed as she pushed her body away from the door and walked toward me. "Be patient with me."

"Sugar, come here." Holding out my hand to her, I pulled her in my lap. "Don't do anything different because I'm here. I'm easy to live with. I don't require too much. Your body is the only thing I'm impatient about. It's mine."

Her eyes twinkled and her smile widened. "It's yours, City."

"Whenever I want?" I raised my eyebrow, giving her a sly smile.

"Yes." She giggled as I grabbed her by the waist, lifting her ass on the dresser. "What are you doing?"

"Taking what's mine." My hands drifted up her legs, spreading them, and raised the nightie to her abdomen.

The smile fell from her face and all giggles disappeared as I licked her clit. Her body relaxed, resting against the wall, as a small moan escaped her lips. My dick ached to be buried inside her, straining against my track pants. Her breath hitched as I dipped my tongue inside her. The sweetest nectar didn't compare to the taste of Suzy, and I always wanted more.

Her legs tightened around my head, as her breathing grew shallow. Her thighs began to tremble underneath my grip. I sucked harder, flicking her clit with my tongue to drive her over the edge. Her hands fisted my hair as she pushed my face deeper, and I growled, relishing in the prickling sensation of her tugging my scalp.

"Oh, fuck. City," she screamed as I sucked harder, drawing her entirely in my mouth. Her body twitched, and she shook under my tongue as she came on my face. I could never get enough of her. She gasped for air, swallowing with wide eyes as she looked down at me. The grip on my scalp lightened as she grew limp and her back collapsed against the wall. Her nightie had slipped off her shoulder, exposing her breast and the small silver hoop that I'd been dying to touch, but couldn't.

Adjusting my dick as I stood, I kissed her lips, sucking the last bit of air she had into my mouth. "I'll never get enough of you, sugar." Our tongues tangled, her juice mixing with her saliva. She drove me wild. The feel of her small hands on my shoulders, gripping toughly, her nails digging into my flesh, made me rock fucking hard.

"More," she whispered against my lips.

"Insatiable." I pulled her body forward as I opened the top drawer, pulling out a condom.

I fucked her hard and fast. The wooden dresser slammed against the wall, thumping with each thrust. I prayed it didn't collapse from the abuse. Her legs rested on my shoulders as I gripped her ankles, pumping inside her. Each thrust forced a moan from her lips. My balls tightened as her pussy clamped down on my shaft. Her eyes drifted closed as I tipped over the edge, spiraling into an orgasm so intense my legs almost gave out.

My chest heaved as I tried to catch my breath. Her eyes fluttered open, and her cheeks were redder from the second orgasm.

"That's how to start a day."

"Promise." She smiled at me, running her hands down my bare chest.

"I'd fuck you all day, but we wouldn't get much accomplished, sugar. Your pussy is fucking addictive."

"Ha, your cock isn't so bad either."

"You know what your dirty mouth does to me."

"No, we have too much to do, big boy." She pushed against my chest before hopping off the dresser.

I grabbed her around the waist, pulling her back to me. "I'm not done with you yet, sugar. I own your ass," I whispered in her ear.

"I love you," she said, as her eyes grew wide and she covered her mouth.

"What did you say?" I tried not to smile, but the corner of my mouth twitched; I was unable to hold back my happiness. As her hand fell from her lips, I gathered her face in my hands to look her in the eyes.

"I love you, Joey."

"Sugar, I love you more than I thought I could ever love another woman. I've wanted to say those words to you, but I didn't want you to freak the fuck out."

"I do, City. I love you for everything you are. You're everything I wanted and the only one I think about. You've invaded my heart, and I can't go another day without saying the words to you."

"Say it again," I said as I brushed my lips against her mouth.

"I love you." The whisper of her words on my lips warmed my body and sent a shock through my system.

EPILOGUE
SUZY

CHRISTMAS

The transition of having someone live with me again had been easier than I thought. After Sophia and Kayden moved out, I didn't think I would ever allow someone else to live with me. Not because they were such a problem, but because I didn't think I'd find someone I could get along with. I know I'm not the easiest person in the world, and it's a fact that I'd always accepted. We talked about moving into a bigger place, but I didn't think we could afford it. My place was perfectly adequate.

It had only been a couple of weeks, but it had been wonderful. My house was small, but everything seemed to fit okay—with some adjustment on both our parts. I was thankful that it was Christmas break and that I'd get to spend the holidays with City and his family. My parents decided to go on a Caribbean cruise and leave me behind this year, and my sister had her fiancé's family to be with. If it weren't for City and the Gallo family, I'd be the third wheel at Sophia's apartment.

City had spent the morning making a special breakfast for us before heading to his parents' house. He told me that his mother always made panettone French toast every Christmas, and he wanted to treat me to his mother's recipe. It had been the best Christmas morning since my childhood.

I still hadn't mastered cooking, and stuck with the few dishes I could make edible. His mother had shown me some of her techniques and made notecards for me to follow, but it was useless. She would say, "No worries, love, you'll get the hang of it. It just takes practice." It was nice of her, but I knew that either you had it or you didn't—and I clearly didn't.

"Ready to go, sugar?" City asked from the bathroom doorway as I finished applying my lipstick. He looked handsome in a black pair of jeans and tight gray sweater. I wanted to unwrap him like a present.

"Just about, Joey. Do I look all right?" I turned to face him, and watched as his eyes traveled up the length of my body before he stared into my eyes.

"Always beautiful." He grabbed my face and kissed my lips, and the familiar want filled my body. I didn't know if I'd ever lose that feeling with him. I hoped I never did. "No time for what you're thinking, sugar. We can't be late today."

"I can wait. I'm not a total fiend." I laughed. "Did you load all the gifts?"

"Just waiting on you, sugar."

"Okay, I'm ready."

He held my hand and stroked it with his thumb as he drove. He looked happier than he did when we first met. He didn't look sad back then, but the happiness didn't radiate off him. It made me happy to know that I had put it there.

His parents' driveway was packed with cars as we parked on the curb. "Looks like a full house."

"Sugar, Italians do it big. My mom cooks for an army and invites all the neighbors to dinner."

"Oh, that's nice of her. I didn't get presents for everyone, though." A panicky feeling overcame me. I had met his family a couple of times and just started to feel comfortable, and now I'd have to sit in a room full of strangers.

"We do our gift opening later, after everyone leaves. Stop worrying—everyone loves you as much as I do."

City opened the door to a house of people; it looked to be bursting at the seams. His mom came toward the door with a smile on her face. She had on reindeer antlers and a cheery Christmas sweater. She looked like a mom, and one that any child would've been lucky to have.

"Suzy, love, merry Christmas." She enveloped me in a hug. City cleared his throat, and she chuckled in my ear and ignored him. "I'm so glad you came."

"Thanks, Mrs. G. I wouldn't want to be anywhere else. It smells amazing in here."

She held my shoulders and looked at me. "I made all the classic Italian Christmas dishes. Got to fatten you up, my dear." She rubbed my shoulder and stopped on the bone that sat below the skin.

"Not too much, Mrs. G, but I'll have some of everything."

"I knew I loved you, and yes, we do. Someday you'll be carrying my grandbabies." She smiled at me and made a face at Joey.

He choked and wrapped his arm around her to pull her off me. "Ma, let's not get ahead of ourselves."

"Just looking toward the future, Joseph. I want little ones running around. I'm too old not to have at least one. Try and make me happy for next Christmas, will you?"

"In time, Ma. Just give me a hug and we'll talk about it another day." He made eyes at me over her head, and I knew he was embarrassed, but I thought his mom was cute. Her words scared the piss out of me, but it was something nice to think about. I wanted him all to myself as long as possible.

"Come in and grab something to munch on before dinner's ready. Joseph, go introduce her to everyone."

"Yes, Ma." He wasn't always the most patient man, but

that changed when he was around his mom. The reverence that was paid to a mom in an Italian family was something to watch. No one fucked with her or went against her word.

We walked around, and Joey introduced me to the family members that flew from Chicago for a warmer holiday, and the friends of the family. In my family, handshakes were the norm, but here hugs were expected. There was a warmth in the house and love could be felt in the chatter of the guests. I felt at home.

"Suzy," Izzy yelled above the crowd, and I could see her hand waving in the air.

"I'm going to go say hi to your sister. I'll be back," I said as I reached up and kissed his cheek.

He smiled at me with loving blue eyes. "I'll join you in a minute," he said before turning his attention back to the neighbor. They were discussing football and the possible Super Bowl teams. Boring didn't even begin to describe how I felt about the topic.

Izzy looked amazing, like always. Her long, flowing black hair framed her face perfectly. She had on a skintight dress that hugged her curves and showed off her beauty.

"Hey, Iz, it's good to see you."

"Merry Christmas, Suzy. I'm so happy you made it. How's my brother doing?"

"They're talking about football. Thank you for rescuing me." We both laughed and looked over at the two men waving their hands as they spoke.

"Boys and their sports. Did you guys exchange your gifts yet?" The look on her face told me that she knew what City had bought me, and she couldn't wait to get my take on the gift.

"Not yet. Do you know what it is?" I squinted at her. I never liked surprises, and maybe I could get it out of her.

"Oh, I know, and my lips are sealed, babe. City would be pissed if I spoiled his surprise."

A surprise. That means it was something big, and not a frilly dress or casual gift like we'd agreed on. I had purchased clothes and a cross pendant for him, along with new leather riding gloves. He was impossible to buy for, but I threw in some ultra-sexy lingerie that would have to wait until tonight.

"I hate surprises," I grumbled.

"This one you won't, trust me." She smiled and giggled, and my heart began to pound in my chest.

We hadn't discussed marriage, and I didn't know what I'd do if he bought me a ring and asked me in front of his family. *Breathe—you can do it.*

"Hey, big brother, merry Christmas." She wrapped her arms around Joey and they whispered in each other's ears.

The clinking of glass caused everyone to turn toward the kitchen. His mother stood, her antlers shaking with each stroke of her hand. A hush descended over the crowd as she began to speak. "I want to thank everyone for coming today. It wouldn't be Christmas without my family and friends. Dinner's served—feel free to help yourself."

"Your mother is really adorable," I said to Joey as he wrapped his arm around my shoulder.

"Yeah, she loves the holidays. Anytime she can get people to eat, she's a happy woman. Hungry?"

"I just ate a ton of appetizers, but I don't want her upset so I'll figure a way to eat more."

"Better get used to it, sugar. Food's the name of the game in this house," he said as we moved toward the kitchen.

A line had already formed, and he stroked my back as we waited to grab a plate. Every granite countertop in the expansive kitchen had a dish of some sort filled with food. The woman should've opened a restaurant with her culinary skills. Every type of pasta dish, braciole, chicken Parmesan, and meatballs were waiting to be consumed.

We found an open space on the lanai and chatted with the

table guests until we couldn't eat any more. I kept eyeing the bottles of wine on the table—Gallo Family Vineyard. Gallo was a common Italian name, and I was sure out of pride they chose this label above the rest. I could hardly move. If they celebrated every holiday with this much food, my waistline would be in serious jeopardy.

The ladies cleaned the kitchen, and I was told under no circumstances was I allowed to help. His mom wanted me to enjoy myself, since I was a guest, while she and her sisters did the dirty work. I dozed off on Joey's shoulder during the chitchat and screaming at the football game on the television, but was woken up for the next round of eating —dessert.

The guests left a couple of hours later, after coffee was served and the football game ended. After the last person walked out, his mother yelled from the foyer, "Who's ready for gifts?"

"Anthony, get your ass in here," Izzy yelled from the floor.

His mother sat down next to the tree and waited for everyone to take a seat. "I love you all, but I miss Thomas. I wish he could've been here with us this year." The smile on her face faded as she wiped her eyes with the back of her hand. I knew little of Thomas, and he was the only sibling I hadn't met. "He called this morning and spoke to your father and I. He promises he'll be here next year." She cleared her throat. "I'm thankful that Suzy could join us."

She pulled a gift from under the tree and held it out to me. "For you," she said.

I placed it on my lap and looked around, noticing that all eyes were on me. "What?"

"We all take turns, sugar." City patted my leg.

"Oh, sorry. My family, it's more like a free-for-all. Not used to this, but I'll learn."

It took hours to open gifts. They ranged in all sizes and shapes. I watched the family in front of me with joy. I'd never experienced something as loving as the Gallo family Christmas.

"I love everything you got me, sugar. I'll use it all." He kissed my cheek.

I smiled at him and whispered in his ear. "Wait until you see your last gift, but it's at home—for your eyes only." I bit his earlobe and was rewarded with a deep kiss.

"Hey, I know I want grandbabies, but not right here on the couch, please. There's one more gift under the tree, and it's for Suzy." His mother beamed as she handed the last present to me.

The box was small, but not a ring box. City leaned back and stared at me to gauge my reaction. I looked around as I undid the ribbon It's a horrible feeling to be the one left out—to be the surprised and not the one doing the surprising.

Tucked inside was a small business card. I read it, but didn't know what it meant. "You gave me a business card?" I asked, confused.

"No, sugar. Read it. Turn it over."

Mrs. Perkins

Florida Real Estate Specialist

I flipped the card over and recognized Joey's handwriting.

Something to call "ours"

Merry Christmas, sugar

"I don't understand," I mumbled as I turned the card over again.

Joey grabbed my hand as he spoke. "I want to buy a house for *us*. I want you to pick out your dream home, or we can build on my land."

"Joey, we can't afford that, but it's a nice thought." I knew his gesture was sincere, even if it were a fairytale.

His mother started to giggle, and the entire family laughed. I didn't get the joke. "Tell her, Joseph," his mother said as she sat down next to his father.

"Suzy, we can afford it. I can afford it."

"How?" I felt like an idiot.

"Jesus Christ, son. Suzy, our family owns a vineyard in Italy. We've owned it for generations. Joseph doesn't flaunt his wealth, but he has the ability to buy five homes."

I looked from his father to Joey, who sat there with a grin. "Is he telling the truth?"

"Yes, sugar. We all own a portion of the vineyard. We run the tattoo shop because we don't want to sit on our ass all day. We wanted something that was entirely ours and separate from what we inherited."

"Why didn't you tell me?" I felt awkward having this discussion in front of his family, but I figured they knew his reasons.

He stroked my face. "I like my little farmhouse. It was enough for me. I also don't like people to know my business. Too many people want things when they know you have money. Sugar, you have to understand. I thought if I ever— and I didn't think I would—found someone that I loved, I had to know they loved me for me and not my money."

"I do love you for you, Joey." The words came out with ease, and even though I knew he'd lied to me for months, I could understand why. "I'm happy in my home, though. No need to buy another."

"Exactly—'your home,' sugar, not ours. I want something that we pick out together with room to grow. We're cramped, but happy. Anything you want is yours. All I ask is for a big garage for my motorcycles and a space for the guys to hang out."

His mom clapped her hands. "Get lots of bedrooms too. I want an army of grandbabies." Even though the idea of a horde of children made my body break out into a blotchy rash, a big house would be wise.

"Not helping, Ma."

Her laughter filled the room. "Sorry, a girl can dream, can't she?"

"So what do you say, sugar? Can we buy a home for us? It can be a fresh start, the beginning of an amazing journey. We'll take our time until we find the perfect place. I love you, Suzy McCarthy, and this is what I want for *us*."

I didn't really have anything to think about. My last wall had crumbled. Everything I had on my impossible checklist had come true, and Joey was the man I'd always wanted. His family waited for my reply, and the air felt heavy. "Yes, Joey. I'd love to find *our* home and look to the future. I love you too."

His kiss stole my breath, as it always did. I thought back to the words Sophia told me not long ago. Butterflies—I still felt butterflies every time I saw him. The nervous energy never left my body, and I felt the electricity when we touched. When it's right, you know it.

He was the one.

Mine.

———

The Gallo Family Saga continues with Michael Gallo in Hook Me *or visit* menofinked.com/hook-me *for more info.*

Michael Gallo found his calling in life. He works at Inked as a piercer, but spends his mornings training and dreaming of winning a fighting championship. Michael is the road to achieving his goal when a chance encounter alters his world forever. The title is no longer enough – he must capture the woman of his dreams.

Tap here to download Hook Me *or visit* menofinked.com/hook-me *for more info.*

MANEUVER

MEN OF INKED SOUTHSIDE BOOK ONE

WALL STREET JOURNAL & USA TODAY BESTSELLING AUTHOR

CHELLE BLISS

CHAPTER
ONE
DELILAH

"GET THE FUCK OUT." My father pulls over at the corner and slams on the brakes.

I gawk at him with my mouth hanging open as he puts the car in park. The look in his eyes is nothing short of ice-cold, devoid of all emotion and completely loveless.

"Dad, just let me drive." I don't move even though I know he won't back down. He never has when he's drunk. I keep my eyes on the flashing red traffic light in front of us, trying to keep my voice even and nonjudgmental. But really, I am judging the hell out of him. How dare he kick us out like trash? "You're drunk, and it's not safe for anyone."

"I'm done with you and your self-righteous bullshit. Survive on your own two feet, Delilah."

I jerk my head backward as my mouth falls open. I'm used to his drunken ramblings and angry fits, but he's never been as cruel as he is tonight. "What about Lulu?"

Lulu is in the back seat, oblivious to everything and somehow sleeping through my father's tirade. My father has kicked me out plenty of times, or at least, that's what he'd say, but I always had my credit cards and bank account to fall back on. He has never cut me off completely.

It has been over a year since his last outburst. Well, before Lulu was born. I thought her birth would change things. I thought he'd stay sober for her, but I should've known better. He never found it in his heart to stay clean for me. The invisible pull of his addiction outweighed any love for his child. Why would his granddaughter be any different?

"Leave her with me," he snaps and leans over me, pushing open my car door. "But you gotta go." His lip curls as he says the last word, showing the wildness the alcohol has soaked into his veins as he settles back into the driver's seat.

My eyes fill with tears, and my vision blurs. I hate this side of him. When my father was sober, he was a nice guy, but when he was drunk, he could give the devil himself a run for his money. Lately, he's spent more and more time drinking, and the old him, the one I loved, barely surfaced.

"I'm not leaving her with you," I tell him and shake my head. I don't care if I have to steal to make ends meet, I would never subject my daughter to my father's alcohol-induced treachery without being there to protect her.

He leans back against the door, holding the steering wheel with one hand while balling the fingers of the other into a tight fist as it rests on his leg. "Both of you are ungrateful little bitches. You have five seconds to get the fuck out and take the little bastard with you."

I move quickly at that point, but I don't dare step out of the car without Lulu. I turn in my seat, avoiding all eye contact with the maniac next to me and pull her from the car seat. Without saying another word, I cradle Lulu in my arms and climb out of the car. Before I can grab my purse, my father speeds away, fishtailing down the wet pavement with the door still open. He swerves around the corner at the end of the desolate street, and the car door slams shut on its own.

"Fuck," I groan, realizing not only did he take my purse, but my phone too.

Here I am with my little girl, no money, no credit cards, no way to call anyone, and it's well after midnight in the middle of nowhere-good downtown Chicago.

I press my lips to the soft skin of her forehead, letting the tears roll down my cheeks as I whisper sweet words to replace his vicious comments. "Mama's got you, baby. I'll always protect you."

Holding Lulu close to my chest, I shield her from anything and everything as I turn around, hoping to find someplace to make a call. I can't stand on the street corner too long. Not in this neighborhood. There is bound to be someone walking by and probably not the type of person I want to ask for help at this hour of the night.

The sound of a bell and laughter down the street draws my attention as a young couple, probably my age, staggers onto the sidewalk, practically hanging off each other. I walk toward them but don't yell out. They look nice enough, but they are clearly in the middle of something and in the middle of a lip-lock.

Walking quickly, I head toward the doorway the couple just walked away from, glancing from side to side because, in all honesty, I am scared as hell. Light from inside streams out of the windows lining the front of the building, falling on the sidewalk near my feet as if signaling to me like a beacon. I step forward, peering through the glass to get a better look before I dare walk through the door.

Gallos' Hook & Hustle South Side.

The place looks nice enough. Not swanky or anything I'd find on the North Side, but not a complete shithole either. But it's still a bar and the last place I'd want to walk into, especially with my daughter. I step backward and glance both ways, hoping to see the faint glow of a nearby gas station or drug store, but there's nothing but darkness.

I take a deep breath, hold Lulu a little tighter, and reach for the handle. For a moment, no one seems to notice us as we step inside. They're too busy talking and drinking to even look up. These are not the type of people I'd see at my father's country club, sipping martinis and other pretentious drinks while holding their noses high in the air as they try to one-up each other with the size of their bank accounts. Nope. Not even close.

The door closes behind me, and the bell rings overhead, and sure as shit, half the bar turns around. No one yells or shoos us away. They're too busy staring at and judging me for having an infant in a bar at this time of night. It's like I can practically read their minds by the way their eyes are zeroed in on Lulu.

I was thinking so far, so good, but then Lulu lets out a blood-curdling scream like she just saw the boogeyman in her dreams, and I think about bolting for the door. Instead, I softly bounce her tiny body in my arms to quiet her down and smile nervously.

The gentleman sitting the closest to me holds his beer near his lips, looking me up and down in much the same manner my father often did when he was drunk. "It's a little late to have a baby out, don'tcha think?" he asks, tipping his head and completely judging me as a shit mother.

"I just need to make a phone call." I bite my tongue to stop myself from saying something about his late-night middle-of-the-week drinking, clearly doing it often based on the size of his beer belly. Instead, I look at the floor and head toward the other end of the bar.

The woman behind the bar is handing someone a drink and paying no attention to me or the sleazeball hitting on me. "Excuse me," I say, tapping Lulu's bottom as I bounce her to keep her from crying out again, but the bartender doesn't give me the time of day.

"I'm talking to you, beautiful," the same man says, but the word comes out like *beauful* because he's had one too many. He tries to touch me with his dirty, chubby hands, and I step sideways.

"Ma'am," I say, but this time a little louder.

"C'mere," the guy says again and moves faster than I expect, finally touching my arm.

My skin crawls from the contact. "Stop. Please," I beg, trying to inch away from his hold, but he only tightens his grip.

"Harry, get your filthy paws off her, or I'll put your ass on the ground."

I jump and let out a little squeak at the sound of another man's voice I hadn't been expecting. If Harry wasn't scared, I was enough for both of us.

Harry's lip curls as his eyes finally leave my breasts to somewhere behind me. "Sorry, Lucio. No disrespect, man. Didn't know she was yours."

Didn't know she was yours? For a second, I think about not looking. If someone's claiming me, I'm not sure I'm ready to know who he is. I glance over my shoulder with one eye closed, almost too scared to turn around even though I want to get far away from Handsy Harry.

My eyes land on a huge chest, traveling upward to a wide set of shoulders before finally settling on a handsome face.

"You okay?" he asks.

For a moment, I can't seem to form words. I just stare at him with my mouth hanging open. "I…" I pause, not sure if I am okay and too caught off guard by him to finish the rest of the sentence.

Lucio, at least that's what Handsy Harry called him, raises one eyebrow, looking at me funny when I don't say anything more. When he cracks a smile, I'm a total goner.

"Are you hurt?" he asks as his gaze slowly travels down my body. I shake my head, still rendered mute. "Is the baby hurt?"

I shake my head again. *Earth to Delilah.* I better find my voice quick because I can't imagine a guy like him has much patience for a strange woman walking into a bar at this hour.

"I was wondering if I could use your pecs," I blurt out, and my stomach instantly knots.

He tilts his head to the side and laughs. "Come again?"

Gah. I want to hide or at least go back about ten seconds and get a do-over. I've never been so embarrassed in my entire life. Where the hell did that come from? It doesn't help that he's built like a brick shithouse and the only part of him at eye level are his pecs, extremely large and, based on the looks of them, rock-hard too.

"Your phone. I'd like to use your phone," I correct my earlier statement, but the damage is done.

"You only want my phone?" he teases.

I swear his pecs move up and down, taunting me, but my eyes may be playing tricks on me. I nod, but I don't dare speak. I've already done enough damage and don't trust myself to say another word.

"Daphne," Lucio calls out, pulling his backward baseball cap off his head and running his fingers through his dark brown hair. Everything in the room seems to slow as he drags his long, thick fingers through the wavy strands. "She needs to use the phone."

The woman, Daphne he called her, reaches under the bar, lifts a glass, and sets it on the bar near me. "It's for paying customers only. What can I get you to drink?"

I close my eyes, wishing I could be anywhere but here. "I don't have any money." The words are bitter on my tongue and harder to say than I ever imagined.

"No drink, no phone," the woman says without an ounce of remorse and ticks her head toward the doorway. "The police station's down the street. You could try there."

God, she's a bitch. Cold as ice and not an ounce of sympathy for a woman without a dollar for a shitty beer, holding a baby.

"We don't treat people like that," Lucio tells her, stepping around me and staring her down. "You know better than that."

"Whatever, Lucio." She rolls her eyes and walks away like her shit doesn't stink.

Lucio takes a step toward me, looking down at Lulu, and I force myself to stay still and keep my mouth shut. "Follow me." He motions for me to go with him as he heads toward a hallway at the side of the bar.

Where the hell does he want to take us?

"What's wrong?" he asks, walking back toward us when I shake my head and stay still.

"Why can't I use the phone here?"

Every nightmare scenario I've ever seen in a horror movie plays through my head. Maybe he's secretly a serial killer, or he could be a human trafficker and my kid and I are the perfect prey for his lucrative business.

"He's taking you upstairs to our mom's apartment," Daphne, the bitch bartender, says as she tosses a white towel over her shoulder. "He's too nice."

"Oh," I mutter and feel like a fool.

"You can stay down here with all these drunk shitheads, or you can make the call upstairs in the comfort and safety of my mom's place. This really is no place for a baby," he says.

He has a point.

I have to wait for the car service to come, and they are never quick. I don't want to wait on the street or in the bar being hit on by drunken strangers either.

"Lead the way," I tell him and finally take a step forward, hoping like hell this isn't some sort of trap.

CHAPTER TWO

LUCIO

THE WOMAN DOESN'T TAKE her eyes off me as we enter my mother's apartment. I can't tell if she's scared of me or completely infatuated. I've seen the look before—wide eyes, parted lips, barely able to speak.

"The phone's in the kitchen," I tell her, pointing toward the old rotary dial telephone my mother refuses to get rid of. They've been out of date for over twenty years and sit in museums, but she hates change.

The woman walks toward the mustard-yellow telephone hanging on the wall across the room. "Wow. I haven't seen one of these in..."

I keep my distance. The last thing I want to do is spook her. I know from having a sister, every man is a potential threat. I've taught them as much, and I try to remember how they'd feel in the same situation.

"Yeah. I know," I say, shaking my head because my mother is a special bird. "My mother is a little stuck in the good ole days." I smile, trying to put her mind at ease.

She holds the baby in one arm, grabs the phone with the other, and stares at me. I don't move a muscle. I'm barely breathing at this point. I imagine her fear is more for her baby than herself. She has no idea if I am some crazy person or the harmless semi-asshole I really am. Her gaze sweeps across my body, focusing on my arms at first and then my feet for a moment.

She's hot as hell for a mom. The woman doesn't look to be more than mid-twenties. Tall, though not as tall as me, but she's wearing heels which make her appear bigger than she really is. Her brown hair is wavy, ending near the middle of her back, but the top is pulled back and away from her pretty face.

The blueness of her eyes is unlike any I've ever seen before. They're almost turquoise, matching Lake Michigan on a sunny day. For her just having had a baby, her body is smoking hot and her tits are freaking spectacular. I almost feel like a total sleazebag for checking her out the way I am, but I'm a guy and I'm turned on because she is totally a MILF.

She takes her eyes off me for a moment to dial each number, but in between each swish, she glances back at me. We stay like this—her holding the baby, waiting for me to pounce, and me barely breathing—as she cradles the receiver on her shoulder. "Hello," she says to whoever is on the other end. "This is Delilah Miles, Roger Miles's daughter. I need a car as soon as possible."

I tip my head to the side, looking at her in a totally different light. She is a rich girl and definitely not from this part of town. I wonder why she is slumming it so late with her kid in tow. Her clothes are fancier than most of the customers in the bar. She looks like one of the wealthy, hipster kids who come down to Hook & Hustle for a dose of culture and reality every once in a while.

Her eyebrows draw together, and for the first time, she turns her back to me, hiding her face. "Excuse me?" she whispers, dropping her voice so I can barely hear her. "I have an account. I don't understand." She tips her face upward and grunts.

My mother walks out from her bedroom, wearing the most hideous pink robe and bunny slippers with her bright red hair in curlers because she has some weird aversion to curling irons. My mom looks at Delilah and then to me, raising an eyebrow. I shake my head and wave my mom off, because I'm not about to explain the little bit I know while Delilah is talking on the phone.

"Please," Delilah begs quietly. "I can pay for your car service myself. You should have my credit card on file." Delilah pauses and glances over her shoulder at me for a second, not seeing my mother standing nearby. "Fine, but I'll have your ass along with your job for refusing service to me." Delilah slams the receiver down and lets out a little grunt as her shoulders hunch forward.

My mother clears her throat and marches into the kitchen, bunny slippers and all. "Would anyone like anything to drink? I'm parched,". Ma says, trying to be cordial even though it is after midnight and way past her bedtime.

Delilah nearly jumps a foot off the floor and spins around, clutching the baby for dear life. As soon as she sees my ma, her entire demeanor changes. My mom looks like someone straight out of a comic strip, not a murderer ready to do harm to a fly, let alone a person like Delilah.

"Since we're having a party, I have tea or whiskey. Pick your poison." Ma smiles, standing near the sink with the streetlight cascading through the window, giving her an angelic glow.

"Nothing. Thank you," Delilah replies as her eyes rake across my mother's outfit, and the corner of her mouth twitches. "I'm Delilah."

"I heard," my mother says sarcastically, letting a little of her devilish side show. "I'm Betty—" Ma motions toward me "—this big lug's mother."

Delilah's gaze moves to me, and there is almost a smile on

her face. "It's nice to meet you, Betty. Thanks for letting me use your phone."

"Tea or whiskey?" Mom asks again like it isn't well past her bedtime. She seems oblivious to the fact that Delilah isn't sticking around.

"I can't stay. I have to get Lulu to bed." Delilah turns toward me and peers down at the floor. "Do you think you could give me a ride?"

I scrub a hand down my face. "I only have a bike, and my mom doesn't drive." Times like this, I regret not having a car of my own.

"Those things are deathtraps," Ma says quickly, adding to her crazy factor and reminding me again how much she hates my motorcycle.

"It's fine." Delilah waves her hands in the air. "I'll just catch a taxi."

Ma fills the kettle before placing it on the stove, still ignoring the fact that neither of us is staying. "Why don't you sit down for some tea, and Lucio can go downstairs to find someone's car to borrow?"

I nod, liking that idea because there is something about Delilah that fascinates me. She's like a tragic story. Rich girl, stuck in the hood with no way out. Maybe I can swoop in and be the hero of the story. Who am I kidding? I could at least have a night with the hot chick before she rides off into the sunset with some other guy.

"I'm sorry to be so much trouble. I lost my purse and phone, or else I wouldn't be such a bother."

"Oh dear," my mother gasps, covering her mouth with her hand and being overly dramatic like only Betty Gallo can.

My blood pressure skyrockets as I imagine someone stealing Delilah's shit and almost hurting the tiny, beautiful creature in front of me or her baby. "Did someone hurt you?"

"No, no. It's a long story, but we're fine," Delilah says as my mother points toward the couch for her to sit.

"Will you be okay up here?" I ask as Delilah sits down, resting the baby on her knees as the plastic underneath her crinkles. "I won't be gone long." I give my mother the same look she gives us as a warning. While I love my mother, she can be a tad bit overbearing.

"Just go. We're fine," Ma tells me, answering instead of Delilah.

"I wasn't asking about you, Ma."

Delilah laughs softly and relaxes on the couch, pulling the baby into her lap. "We're safe and warm. We'll be just fine."

I glance over my shoulder before closing the door, and I catch sight of Ma grabbing two teacups from the cupboard. I know they're going to be more than a few minutes because once you get Ma talking, there is no stopping her until she is out of things to say. I hope Delilah is in the mood to listen to the sage wisdom of Betty Gallo because, like it or not, she is about to get some.

"Where's the chick?" Daphne asks as soon as she sees me.

I point toward Ma's apartment and shake my head at the strange turn this night has taken. "Having tea with Ma."

Daphne's eyes widen in horror, being just as dramatic as my mother. "You woke her up?"

"We were quiet, but she heard us anyway." I rub the back of my neck, hating the idea of asking Daphne for a favor. My darling sister will want to be paid back, and her favors are always enormous and costly. "You think I can borrow your car?"

"Dude." Daphne quirks an eyebrow as she folds her arms in front of herself. I can tell by the way she tilts her head that she is about to read me the riot act about her precious baby.

"Please. You know I'd never ask to borrow it, but this is important."

"This about her?" She juts her chin toward the stairwell to our mother's apartment.

"Yeah. She needs a ride. I can't take a baby on my bike."

"Bet you never thought you'd say those words." She points at me with her skinny index finger, totally mocking me for buying a motorcycle. She's always hated the damn thing. She told me I wasn't being practical and that someday I'd need to grow up, but the girl drives a vintage Jeep, so she has no room to talk.

"Just get the damn keys," I tell her and hold out my hand, wiggling my fingers.

"Don't get your panties in a bunch. Watch the front of the house. I'll grab them for you, Big Daddy." She giggles as she hands me the damp towel she's been using to wipe down the bar half the night.

"The girl gone?" Johnny, a regular and one of my father's oldest friends, asks as I take away his empty beer glass to give him a refill.

"She's upstairs with Ma."

Johnny jerks his head backward like I am insane for leaving them alone. "Alone?"

"Uh, yeah, man. She's fine."

"You don't know that girl. She could be a murderer. Think about your mother."

"I don't know too many killers who bring their children with them when they want to off someone." I lean forward and stare him straight in the eyes, sliding his fresh beer across the bar. "Did you ever bring yours?"

His eyes narrow into tiny slits as he grumbles under his breath and grabs the beer, busying himself and not bothering to answer my question.

Johnny isn't only my dad's dearest friend, but he is a longtime business associate of my father's. I've always stayed out of their business dealings, but I'm not a complete fool. I know Johnny is, or maybe was, my father's number two, and he did some pretty shady shit in his time. I don't doubt for a minute that he's murdered a person or two over the years.

Daphne places the keys next to me but keeps her hand on top of them. "Let me go over a few things with you first."

"It's a Jeep, Daph. I think I can figure it out." I cross my arms and lean against the bar because I have a feeling this isn't going to be a quick conversation.

"No, she's special," she tells me, putting me in my place and reminding me she's just as crazy as our mother.

I roll my eyes, but she is dead serious.

"You want it or not?"

"Fine. Go ahead," I tell her and throw my hands into the air, giving in to her insanity.

"Sometimes the brake pedal sticks. You have to be very careful how hard you handle her. Ease off the brake slowly, but don't take too long, or she'll stall."

"Seriously?"

"Yeah." She nods at me like I am a complete moron. "She's temperamental."

"Shocking," I mutter because the car sounds a lot like my sister. "I'm sure I'll figure it out."

"If the baby pukes on the seats, you're cleaning it up." She points at me again, twisting her lips. "Got it?"

"Yeah, sis. I got it." I reach for the keys, but she moves them out of the way before I can grab them. "Fill her up too before you bring her back, but none of that low-grade crap either. She needs premium gasoline."

"Anything else?"

She finally moves her hands, leaving the giant keys along with a freakishly large fuzzy heart on the keychain. "Nope."

I'm going to look like an idiot carrying around her set of keys, but at least it's dark, and I don't have to worry about running into any of my friends. I try to jam them into my pocket, but the heart's too big to fit, and the damn thing dangles near my hip for the world to see.

My mother's waiting at the top of the stairs, standing outside the door. "What's wrong?" I ask as soon as I see her.

"She's asleep."

"The baby?"

She shakes her head. "The girl."

Well, fuck. "How? It's only been a few minutes."

She shrugs. "Babies are exhausting, and she's going through something. One minute she was talking, and the next…"

"I'll wake her up."

My mother puts her hands up in front of herself, stopping me from moving past her. "No. Let her sleep. You can take her home in the morning."

"The baby, Ma."

"We'll set up a little sleeping area for her too. I need you to carry Delilah to the bedroom for me."

Somehow, I'm the only one who sees a problem with this. I want to argue, but this is my mother, and I know there's no way I'll win. This girl who we don't know is going to wake up in the morning and totally lose her shit. I know I would if I were in her shoes, but my mother doesn't feel the same.

"I'll stay too, then. I'll move the girl and then be back after I help Daphne close up for the night."

"Before you get busy working, go down to the corner store and grab formula and a bottle."

"Is there a certain type?" I ask, knowing nothing about what babies eat. I've never had to buy a baby bottle, and I didn't think I'd ever have to either.

"Just get one with a decent nipple."

I stop myself from making a joke because I don't feel like getting smacked upside the head as my mother follows behind me and has the perfect opportunity and angle. Ma gently lifts the baby out of Delilah's arms. I hold my breath, waiting for her to wake up and start swinging, but Delilah just mumbles under her breath for a moment before going still again.

"We can just leave her here, no?"

Ma rocks the baby, sniffing her hair like she often did when my niece and nephew were little. "I miss that smell," she says with a look of sorrow and happiness all at once. "No, I want her to be comfortable. The poor thing couldn't keep her eyes open. She deserves a good night's sleep. Being a mother isn't easy, Luc."

"I know, Ma. You keep reminding me."

Thankfully, Ma has her hands full, or I'd get a smack upside the head for my smartass reply.

I watched my three-year-old niece and one-year-old nephew for a week after my sister-in-law died after a short battle with cancer. I have never been so exhausted in my entire life. I could barely find time to shower with the two of them around, but it was something I did for my brother and the rest of the family so they could grieve.

Delilah's lighter than I imagine as I lift her into my arms. Her head rests on my chest and tips back, giving me the perfect view of her delicate, soft features. She has a set of freckles on her left cheek, and they almost form a tiny heart. Her skin is flawless and without makeup. She's nothing short of a natural beauty. I'm so used to the girls at Hook & Hustle with their layers of makeup. Sometimes when I wake up the next day, they don't even look anything like the girl I banged the night before.

I walk carefully, taking small, steady steps toward the bedroom so I don't startle her awake and earn myself a black eye.

There are so many ways this could go bad, but I do it anyway. Delilah can lay into me tomorrow. Scream. Yell. Whatever. I can take the anger from a stranger and move on, but there is no way I'm going to go against my mother on this one.

I place her on Daphne's old bed just below her poster of Mandy Moore that's started to curl at the corners. I grab an afghan from the dresser and cover her under my mother's watchful eye.

"Formula and a bottle. Don't forget, babies like big nipples."

"We all do," I mumble as I walk out the door, typing out a message to cancel my date for later.

CHAPTER
THREE
DELILAH

FOR A BRIEF SECOND, I don't have a care in the world. The room is dark, warm, and it's nice to be wrapped in such soft blankets. I blink a few times, stretching my muscles, but then it hits me.

Bar. Strange guy. Woman in bunny slippers. Lulu.

I leap out of bed like a superhero, and all tiredness and comfort leave me in an instant. I race out of the bedroom, peering in every room as I run down the hallway and grip my chest, trying like hell not to lose my mind.

Don't overreact. I inhale slowly, telling myself she's perfectly fine.

If Lulu's gone, I will tear apart the entire city and bring the wrath of God down on these people. I'm flooded with guilt at the fact that I fell asleep, leaving my baby vulnerable and without my protection in the presence of complete strangers.

How could I have been so irresponsible and stupid?

Rounding the corner to the kitchen, I see the guy from last night, holding Lulu and whispering in her ear. I stop dead, watching the two of them from the hallway.

Seeing Lulu being held in a man's arms does something to me I hadn't expected. When her father skipped out, leaving me high and dry six months into my pregnancy, I told myself good riddance. Who needed him anyway? We sure didn't. But somewhere deep in my heart, I knew Lulu would be missing out on something special. Not that Dwight Jones, the spineless, tiny-dicked man who'd knocked me up, was a prize, but still—she needed a male figure in her life.

My father was worthless. No. He was less than that, and I turned out okay, after all. But there have been so many times in my life when I wished I had a real dad...someone who would treat me like a little princess and make me feel like his number one.

Instead, I had a drunken asshole who left me on the side of the road with his granddaughter and not a penny to my name.

My eyes fill with tears as I watch Lucio and Lulu together. He's so sweet and tender with her, and it's probably the first time I've seen a man be that way with Lulu in her short little life. I slap my hand over my mouth when I feel the sob crawling up the back of my throat.

Lulu's staring up at him, sucking on her bottle and completely captivated by the man. I don't blame her either. He's dreamy in a blue-collar beefcake kind of way.

Last night, he was wearing a tight-fitting long-sleeved white dress shirt, but I barely noticed much about him besides his size. But in the light, with Lulu in his arms, I can see his entire upper body clear as freaking day.

Damn.

His torso and arms are covered with ink. The pictures on his skin almost dance with each movement of the muscles underneath. I've never really been into guys with tattoos, but on him, they are absolutely perfect. I grip the wall, trying to keep myself vertical as my knees start to go weak.

Get yourself together, woman. It's just a guy holding your kid.

"Aren't you a pretty little thing?" he says, bouncing her up and down in one arm as he sets the bottle on the table.

I take a step back, still holding the wall, and I'm careful not to make a sound. I can't stop the stupid smile on my face from spreading as I wipe away my tears.

He places his ankle on top of the opposite leg, creating a little pocket before placing Lulu in between his huge thigh muscles. "So beautiful like your mommy."

Heat creeps up my chest, and I fumble with the collar on my T-shirt. It's been ages since anyone has called me beautiful and even longer since I'd felt that way. I'm too busy in mom-mode with a messy bun, no makeup, and smelling like rotten formula to think I'm even remotely pretty.

I never thought being a mother would be easy, but I didn't think it would be this hard either. There's nothing in the world which could've prepared me for the lack of sleep. And don't even get me started on the stretch marks lining my body like a topographic map. I don't have time to worry about the way my body has gone to shit and how my tits are unrecognizable after Lulu fed off them for the first three months of her life.

Lucio takes a sip of his coffee, still carefully bouncing her, but keeping a close eye on her. I want to rush in and tell him to burp her, but he seems to have things under control. I don't know why I don't step forward and snatch my kid away from his muscular legs which are probably harder than the wood beneath my feet, but I don't.

Lulu makes a little noise, reaching upward and blowing spit bubbles tinted white from the formula at him. He laughs and scoops her in one arm, holding her tiny head in his giant palm, and places her on his shoulder. He does everything so gracefully that I can't stop myself from watching in amazement and a little in awe.

He sets his coffee aside and gently rubs her back, tapping her a few times. I want to tell him to watch out because Lulu is a world-class puker. She doesn't just burp. Nope. Not my kid. She's ruined more outfits than I care to remember, and her baby formula has become my new perfume, which is something I'm not entirely proud of either.

Lulu lets out a burp that's so loud, Lucio starts to laugh, but then it happens. As if everything is moving in slow motion, the burp turns liquid, and a pretty big splash of formula vomit lands on his shoulder before dribbling down his back. I cringe, waiting for the moment when he loses his shit. I mean, here's this hot-as-fuck guy, covered in muscles and tattoos, trying to do me a favor and taking care of a kid who isn't even his, and she pukes on him.

"Well, aren't you a messy little princess?" he says, his laughter getting a bit louder when he brings her face-to-face with him. He's holding her with ease like she doesn't weigh more than a sack of potatoes, and using one finger, he wipes away the formula left near her mouth. "Feel better?"

God, why does he have to be so freaking hot holding her?

The blush that had started moments ago has now turned into a full-blown furnace, radiating from the inside out. I haven't wanted to touch a man since Dwight left town, but Lucio, the hottie with my kid, makes my hands itchy to reach out and touch him. It doesn't matter that he's covered in Lulu's throw-up. I'd happily help him get clean.

Stop being a whore.

The words my father had said to me when he found out I was pregnant echo in my mind as I let my thoughts wander to dirty and dark places about the handsome stranger in front of me.

Betty, the lady with the bunny slippers from last night, walks through the front door, going right to Lulu and Lucio. "Delilah still sleeping?"

"Yeah, Ma," he tells her. "Want me to wake her?"

"You will do no such thing. A mother needs her sleep, and besides—" Betty leans forward and grabs Lulu out of Lucio's arms "—look at this darling face. I could give her a million kisses."

"Ma, she's not yours."

"She could be. I need some more grandkids, honey. I'm not getting any younger, and neither are you." She gives him a funny look, and I cover my mouth to stop myself from laughing. "Why don't you settle down with a girl like Delilah? You'd already have a head start in the grandbaby department, and it would make you my favorite child."

"Ma."

"Lucio."

"Ma, come on. A girl as pretty as her, she probably has a husband, and it doesn't work that way. If I dated her, that doesn't mean this is your grandbaby by default."

"If you were her man, would you let her be out on her own that late at night? And besides, blood isn't required to be a family. You bring her in, and they're both my kin."

I don't know why, but the floodgates open, and tears start streaming down my face like a torrential downpour. No one in my family talks this way about each other, let alone about complete strangers. Even with my father and me sharing the same blood, he treats me, and Lulu too, like trash. My mother is no better after running off with a guy half her age, never to be heard from again.

"She's a rich girl. Why would she want some schmuck from the South Side?"

"You're handsome, and don't even get me started on your heart. Anyway, money doesn't matter when it comes to love."

"You're crazy," he tells her as she gives Lulu a soft kiss on the forehead.

"You keep dating these cheap and easy bimbos who are more interested in what you can buy for them than they are in you, honey, and you deserve better than that."

He pinches the bridge of his nose and leans forward, resting one elbow on his knee. "What am I supposed to do? Just ask her out?"

"Yes, son. It's that easy."

Oh my God. Oh my God.

Is he really going to ask me out because his mom told him to? Does that mean he wants to, or is he being strong-armed by his bunny-loving red-haired mother?

I don't want a pity date, not even from the hot, shirtless guy holding my baby.

I step backward, heading toward the bathroom, leaving Lulu with them for a moment while I try to pull myself together. When I get in front of the mirror, I look worse than I ever could've imagined. My normally tame locks are a hot mess and tangled, the little bit of mascara I managed to wear last night is smeared down my face, making me look like something straight out of a horror movie. On top of that, all the sleep I got last night did nothing to alleviate the bags under my eyes.

Quickly, I scrub my face, grab some toothpaste and use my finger as the brush, and try to pull myself together, making myself as presentable as possible. I am officially lame. I've done this routine before, but usually after a night of hot sex. Never after falling asleep because I was exhausted.

I grab the handle, ready to walk out in yesterday's clothes and feeling worse than yesterday's trash. As soon as the door opens, I come face-to-face with the half-naked hottie looking like someone straight out of the *Magic Mike* movie. Not only that, but I walk straight into his chest, unable to stop myself.

"Hi," I squeak like a teenage girl with a crush as I gaze up into his eyes.

"Hey." He smirks down at me, holding on to my arm.

I go dumb with the way he is looking at me. I stare at him without being able to form a thought or say a single word. How can I? The guy is more like a Greek god with his rippling muscles, perfect skin, haunting green eyes, and a smile that could make any girl, even a nun, have the dirtiest thoughts, leading to a stint in hell for sinning.

"Sleep okay?" he asks, still holding on to me.

I nod my reply, because words are too complicated with him being half naked. That's the problem when you've been basically celibate for well over a year. Something as small as a shirtless man can make a girl, even me, stupid. If it were another man, maybe one with a dad bod, I probably could stammer out a response, but not with this hot hunk of man meat.

"Hungry?" he asks then, but I'm too busy staring at the ink on his chest to bother with a reply.

That song "Your Body is a Wonderland" had to have been written about a guy like Lucio. My fingers want to play now too. Skate around that fleshy amusement park, touching every inch, until I've explored each curve and splash of art across his body.

I don't think I've been staring long, but when he touches my chin, bringing my eyes to his...I know he caught me. The smirk from a few moments ago is bigger and more devilish.

"Are. You. Hungry?" he asks the words again, but he is speaking each one slowly like I have trouble understanding the English language.

In all fairness, I am having trouble processing even the simplest questions. But in my defense, my girl parts are long overdue for a tune-up or at least a quick adjustment.

My lips fall open a little, just enough to draw his attention, and I'm thankful for a momentary reprieve from his watchful gaze. "Yes," I finally say, trying to pull off a totally sexy, seductive voice, but I sound more like my aunt Maud, which, trust me, will never be hot.

He drops his hand from my face, and somehow, I don't whine. But I want to... Oh, how I want to. "Ma's making breakfast."

"Where's Lulu?" I ask, playing dumb and doing a bang-up job.

"My ma has her in the kitchen. I just wanted to wash up." He turns around, giving me a full view of the mess Lulu left down his back, adding to her long list of victims. "Your little girl has quite the appetite."

"Oh my God. I'm so sorry." Somehow, I manage to get the words out, but nothing about speaking is easy. His back is just as magnificent as his front and on full display. Even with Lulu's mess, the damn thing is a masterpiece.

"It was no trouble. Don't be sorry. She's a kid. They throw up. No big deal."

I stare at the floor as he turns back around. I can't look at him anymore and get more than a few words out. The carpet is a much safer focal point. "It's so sweet that you fed her. You should've woken me up. She's not your responsibility. I feel awful." I finally look up because I realize I'm acting like a weirdo, and I'm more than a little embarrassed.

He shakes his head and holds up a hand, stopping me from the verbal diarrhea I'm in the middle of. "You were tired, and I enjoyed spending time with her. And besides, my ma is over the moon to have a baby in the house."

"Oh." I try to hide the excitement in my voice, but it's impossible. On top of being hot as fuck, the guy says everything a single mother wants to hear. It's like he fell out of the sky, landing straight in between my very available and needy legs.

Don't be ridiculous.

This guy probably has a list of chicks he bangs on the regular. The old-school yellow pages probably have nothing on Lucio. What girl could honestly say no to him? He's not even my type, but I'd drop to my knees and pray for salvation later.

"Why don't we eat something, and then I'll give you a ride?"

My eyes widen, and there's no hiding right where my mind went. The blush creeping up my chest and scattering around my neck doesn't help mask the way his words affect me either.

He smiles again, probably knowing exactly where my dirty-ass mind went. I can tell by the way his eyes sparkle he's getting a kick out of my unease. "A ride home," he adds.

"I'll call a friend to come get us. There's no need to put out." I cough and pound on my chest because, again, I can't seem to speak like a normal person around him. "I mean, I don't want to put you out. I'm sure you're a busy man."

Fuck my life. Seriously. I'm in the presence of a hot guy, who held my daughter and stared at her with such adoration that I've gone all stupid.

"Spending a little time with two beautiful girls..." He steps back, his eyes traveling up my body and rumpled clothes. "I can't think of a better way to spend my morning."

I blink a few times, wondering if I heard him wrong because he seems a little too good to be true. Even his mother, the way she talked about Lulu, is like something right out of a weird, inner-city *Brady Bunch* episode.

I need to eat and get the hell out of here because this hot playboy won't lead anywhere I need to go. Yeah, I wouldn't mind a ride or two, but in the end...all men disappoint, including this one.

CHAPTER
FOUR
LUCIO

"THIS IS SO GOOD." Delilah moans softly before shoving the last piece of blueberry scone into her mouth. Crumbs fall from her lips and drop onto the plate, but she gathers them on her fingertip. "Your mom is an amazing cook. I've never had something so delicious." She places her finger in her mouth, sucking the tip, and I'm a complete goner.

The semi-hard-on I'm sporting underneath the table suddenly becomes a huge issue. I can't get comfortable, and it's impossible to think about anything other than sex. I shift in my seat, trying to find a position to relieve the ache, but nothing helps. Just when I am about to start picturing something horrific to try to take care of the issue, my ma walks into the room, and all horniness I feel dies instantly.

"I'll pack some up for you to take home," Ma says, bouncing Lulu on her hip like she did with her own grandchildren when they were small.

Delilah's face changes as soon as she hears the word home. Every ounce of pleasure and joy the scones brought her evaporates and dies in that second. Delilah pushes the plate forward, twisting her mouth before chewing on the inside of her lip.

I want to ask her what happened, why she was on the street so late at night, but it isn't my business, and she isn't mine to pry into her personal life or about her family.

I know all about complicated families. Hell, mine has never been a walk in the park or like any sitcom family I've ever watched on television. Maybe the Bundys from *Married with Children*, but our level of dysfunction sometimes far outweighs even their insanity.

Ma sets a bag of scones next to Delilah, and her eyes dip to the bag, noticing the bakery label as she reaches for them.

"My ma is an awful cook. Be thankful they weren't hers." I laugh and earn the evil eye from my mother. I duck just as she tries to smack me in the head.

"Your father has never complained," Ma adds, as if his opinion matters the most. Just because my father's taste buds are dead, doesn't mean the rest of the world's are too.

"Well, I better get going. I'm so sorry for intruding, but thank you for the great night's sleep and breakfast," Delilah says as she stands from the table and reaches for Lulu who was playing with the pearls around my mother's neck.

My ma whispers something in Lulu's ear before kissing her forehead and closing her eyes.

Delilah practically has to pry Lulu's hands off my mother's pearls. Ma laughs, eating up every moment of baby she can. "I'm so sorry," Delilah keeps saying as if she thinks my mother is upset, even though Ma's clearly enjoying the entire situation.

"Don't apologize, dear. She's precious," my mother tells her and kisses Lulu one last time before Delilah is finally able to wrangle her away from my mother completely.

"She's not usually so attached to people so quickly."

"We're lovable," I tell her for some odd reason. "I mean, at least my mom and I are. The rest of the family... It's debatable."

Ma waves me away, but we both know it's true. "Oh, be nice, Lucio."

"How many siblings do you have?" Delilah asks as she rubs Lulu's back in small, gentle circles.

"Well, three that I know about."

Delilah's beautiful face scrunches, and the smooth space between her perfectly shaped eyebrows wrinkles. "Know about?"

"Well, there could be a few I don't know about. You never know what's hiding in the branches of our family tree."

This time, I'm not so lucky to avoid my mother's smack to the side of the head. "Be respectful to your father."

"Sorry, Ma," I say, but I'm not.

My father was a world-class asshole back in the day. As he grew older, he slowed down, but I know for a fact that he had more than one side piece when I was a kid. I watched as he cheated and snuck around on my mother. I promised myself I'd be nothing like him when I grew up. So far, I've kept my word, but I haven't settled down yet either.

"I like your mom," Delilah says with her lips turned up in a big smile. Why women always like to see a mother put her son in his place, I'll never know. But every single time it happens in mixed company, it always brings some laughs at my expense. But seeing Delilah's face light up again is entirely worth the embarrassment.

"Betty's a bit crazy." I stand, avoiding the second shot that was headed my way for calling her by her first name. "You ready?" I ask Delilah as I reach out to fix the collar on Lulu's dress.

"I can call a cab," she says softly, watching my hands closely.

"I can't allow you to do that. I'll take you home. I won't be able to relax until I know you're safe."

My ma stands behind Delilah and gives me a thumbs-up along with a goofy smile. In her head, she's already planning our wedding day, and while I like Delilah, my ma seems to be getting ahead of herself.

Delilah bites her bottom lip as her cheeks turn a pale shade of pink. "It's very kind of you to put yourself out in that way."

"It's not a bother."

It's not like it's a hassle to spend a little extra time with a beautiful woman. Even if she has a baby, I still like her. There is something that draws me to her. Maybe it's the sadness in her eyes and my always wanting to fix things that make her more alluring.

"I already installed the car seat, so we're ready to roll."

"Oh," she mutters, cocking her head to the side. "You have a car seat?"

"My nephew's. Ma used to babysit, so she had one in the basement. I dug it out while you were sleeping."

To a sophisticated woman who uses a car service to get around, we probably seem like a bunch of middle-class crazy people. Here, she spent the night above a South Side bar in a part of town very few people in her economic class even drive through for fear of losing their lives. My ma's apartment is a decent size, but a complete throwback to the 1980s, complete with her love of plastic coverings on all the furniture. We are not *her* people, but Delilah didn't seem to mind in the slightest.

"If you're ever in the area again, please drop in and say hello," Ma tells Delilah as she gives her a hug.

"I'd love that, Betty." Delilah smiles and wraps one arm around my mother with poor Lulu smashed in the middle.

I'd love that too...and that shocks the hell out of me.

———

Delilah lives on the North Side in one of the largest high-rise buildings on the lakefront. Swanky doesn't even begin to describe the place or the neighborhood. There isn't a beggar on the corner, hustling to sell water or some other small item to pay for their liquor later, like in my neighborhood. Everyone walking on the sidewalks is in a business suit or some variation.

"Thanks for the ride, Lucio. I really appreciate your help and kindness," she says as she gathers Lulu from the back seat of my sister's Jeep.

"It was my pleasure."

I want to say something else, but I can't. We barely spoke on the way to her place, or at least, not about anything substantial. I didn't learn much about her in the thirty minutes it took to head up Lake Shore to her condo. We kept everything general, and I was okay with that. I didn't want to pry and come off like an asshole. I knew she was already embarrassed about the phone call last night, and I didn't want to make her any more uncomfortable with the entire situation than probably she already is.

Delilah stands outside the Jeep on the passenger side, holding Lulu, and she smiles at me for a moment. I want to ask for her number, but hell, she's a mom with no time for an asshole like me. What mother from the North Side, swimming in cash, wants to date a South Side guy who owns a bar? I'm not hurting for money, but I'm probably not the type she was brought up to marry.

"I'm going to wait here to make sure you get in," I say instead, trying to be a gentleman like my mother raised me to be.

"We'll be fine. The doorman will let us in."

"I'll feel better if I stay and know you're safe," I tell her, memorizing her beautiful lips and deep blue eyes.

She backs away slowly with her eyes locked on mine, maybe trying to remember every inch of my face too. A few seconds later, she turns her back to me, and I shake my head, chastising myself for being such a fool. I always ask women for their phone numbers. Never had an issue with it before, but there's something that stopped me today. Hell, I still don't know if she is married or single, and the lack of a wedding ring means nothing in my book.

She looks over her shoulder and gives me a small wave before pushing through the revolving door, disappearing.

"Way to be a pussy, asshole," I grumble to myself and tap against the steering wheel, trying to stop myself from running after her.

My ma has hated every woman I've ever brought home. And while Delilah isn't a girlfriend and just happened to wander into my bar, Ma took to her immediately. Well, she took to Lulu, and that's all that seems to be needed to win her over.

Not that I need my mother's approval, but it makes shit a hell of a lot easier when Betty likes the girl sitting across from her. My ma may be a tiny thing, but her mouth most certainly is not. I can't live out the rest of her life with her hating the woman I decide to marry. I would rather spend eternity single than listen to Ma go on and on about my poor partner choice.

My phone pings from the center console, and I lean forward to see my mother is sticking her nose in my business...again.

Ma: Get her phone number.

I type out my reply, erasing and retyping it three times before hitting send.

Me: She's already gone.

Ma: How could you mess this up so badly?

Me: She has a kid.

Ma: That means she's stable and a good choice.

Clearly, my ma doesn't know some of the girls from the neighborhood who have children and are more off their rocker than many of the people in the mental ward at County Hospital. Popping a tiny human out of your vagina does not mean you're a good person, normal, or stable. It only means you got laid and nothing more.

As I slide my phone back into the center console, I notice Delilah coming out of the revolving door with Lulu on her hip and tears streaming down her face. I rush out of the Jeep and stalk toward her, calling her name.

When she sees me, she cries harder, practically falling against my chest as I touch her arms. "I got you," I tell her.

Whoever her family is…they are pieces of trash. I grab Lulu from her grip and wrap an arm around Delilah's back, ushering her toward the Jeep and away from this place. "Let's get out of here."

CHAPTER
FIVE
DELILAH

LUCIO PLACES LULU back in the car seat without asking me any questions. I stand on the sidewalk, staring up at my father's penthouse and hating him more than I've ever hated another human being. Lulu's father is a piece of shit, but at least he had the decency to leave before she had any memories of him crushing her heart like I do with my father.

I wipe away my tears, trying to collect my thoughts and calm down before I throw myself into a full-blown panic attack. Eli, my doorman since I was in kindergarten, said he was under strict orders not to let me upstairs. I begged him to let me get my things, and although I saw the pain in his eyes, he still turned us away.

My knees start to grow weak as I think about everything that's happened in the last twelve hours. Suddenly, I'm not only a single mother, but homeless and penniless too.

Lucio opens the passenger door and grabs me by the waist, basically placing me in the car with as much care as he did Lulu. "In you go, sweetheart," he says softly, and I move with him.

I don't put up a fight and push his arms away. Besides being completely devastated and in shock, I like him...and the way he treats my daughter. He is a total stranger, but in the few hours I've known him, he's shown me more kindness than my father has in the last ten years.

Sitting in the front seat, I fiddle with the hem of my T-shirt and stare down, waiting for Lucio to climb inside. I don't know what to say or where to tell him to take me. I have nowhere to go and no one else to ask for help. I don't have any identification, and probably by now, not a dollar in the bank account I shared with my father.

"You can just drop me off at the nearest shelter," I tell him because I assume that's what happens in situations like this. I mean, where else does a penniless person go with a baby? I can't live on the streets, and without any family, I have nowhere else to turn.

Lucio leans against the door of the Jeep and turns in his seat. "Absolutely not." He shakes his head as I start to open my mouth to say something. "I'm not taking you and Lulu to a homeless shelter. That's out of the question."

"It's just for a few days. We'll be okay until I figure out what to do," I explain, figuring what I'm saying makes complete sense. But he isn't having any of it.

"Have you ever been in one of those places?" He raises an eyebrow.

I shake my head, twisting my fingers in my lap. "I don't have anywhere else to go," I whisper.

"You have me."

My belly flutters. "We're not your problem."

"Not another word," he tells me. "The place next to mine is empty. You can stay there."

My mouth falls open immediately, and my hands still. "I don't have any money, Lucio. Like, not even a penny to pay for a place."

"Lucky for you, I know the landlord." He smirks and makes everything seem so easy when it isn't. "Do you have a job?"

I shake my head, totally embarrassed. I wanted to stay home with Lulu for as long as I could and live off the trust fund my grandmother left me that I got when I turned twenty-one.

"You can help out at the bar if you'd like to earn some cash. You know, to get back on your feet."

I widen my eyes for a moment before they fill with tears again. I don't know what to say to this beautiful man sitting next to me, offering us a roof over our heads and a place to work. He doesn't owe me anything. He definitely doesn't have to be nice. Lord knows, my own father couldn't find it in his heart to be kind to me or his granddaughter.

"I don't know what to say," I mumble between my sobs. I'm somehow happy, thankful, and crushed all at the same time. I don't know what else to do but cry and fling myself into his arms. "Thank you." I plant a big kiss on his cheek, finding comfort in the warmth of his skin and the hardness of his body. "I don't know how I'll ever repay you."

Lucio rubs my back, soothing me in the same manner I often do Lulu when she is upset. "It'll be nice to have the little squirt around. Life's been way too quiet anyway."

Even through my tears, I smile. This beautiful mountain of a man is lying through his teeth, but I'm not going to call bull-shit even though I know it is. For now, I'll take Lucio up on his offer and try to stay out of his hair as much as possible so we don't ruin his life. "I promise you won't even know we're there."

"Sweetheart, you're doing me a favor, not the other way around."

I back away, untangle my arms from his body, and stare up into his deep green eyes, completely confused as I wipe away my tears. "How's that?"

"The place has been empty for far too long. I need someone to live there to keep everything working until I can find a new tenant."

"Oh." I nod, pretending like I understand, when I don't have a clue what he is talking about. "So, you want me to fix things?"

He rests his thumb against my cheek and brushes away a few tears I missed. "Absolutely not, but if a place is empty too long, things start to go bad. I just want you to make yourself comfortable for a while and not worry about anything."

I gaze up at him, not moving away from his touch because it's nice to have someone be there for me in a way no one else ever has been. "We'll be gone as soon as I can save enough money to give you your place back."

"Or you can just stay there and rent the joint from me. Don't have one foot out the door the entire time." When he smiles, it's like the entire world shifts and the dark cloud that's been following me around moves away.

"Thanks, Lucio. You're almost too good to be true." I grimace, knowing that's a shitty thing to say. I don't mean the words in a bad way, but where the hell did this guy come from?

Out of all the places on the South Side of Chicago I could've walked into, I went into his bar...a guy who's more like a knight in shining armor than a super-muscled, womanizing hottie.

"I mean..." I stammer, trying to think of a good recovery, but fail.

"Listen, Delilah. I have no doubts about how people look at me and what their first impressions are because of my good looks and hot body—" he waves his hands in front of himself and flexes at the same time "—but I'm not some asshole who bangs everything with two legs and kisses his own reflection in the mirror every day."

"You sure about that?" I laugh because this man does love himself. He can deny it all he wants, but there is no getting around his ego. "I mean, not many guys say they're good-looking and have a hot body."

He lifts his chin at me as one corner of his mouth turns upward. "They just don't say it out loud, but they're all thinking it."

I roll my eyes and swat his arm. "Well, at least I know."

"Know what?" He quirks an eyebrow and somehow looks even more handsome.

"That you're not just a pretty face." I shrug and try to maintain a straight face, but I can't with the way he looks at me. Lucio is nothing short of drop-dead gorgeous, but the problem is…he knows it too.

"I'm totally yanking your chain, Delilah. All men are dicks. I'm no different, but I was brought up to respect women and do a little good in the world while I'm here."

"So, you don't think you're good-looking and have a hot body?" I resist the urge to let my eyes drop to his very well-formed muscles peeking out from the sleeves of his T-shirt. Even worse, I want to feel them with my fingertips.

"Do you think I'm good-looking and have a hot body?" he asks, turning the tables.

"You're all right," I tease, because Lucio is, in fact, all of that and more. But at his core, he's a good guy who is willing to help me out when no one else will.

"So are you," he says with a wink before he picks up his phone and sends a text message. He starts the engine without another word and takes off for wherever I am going to call home.

Lucio has a way about him. At one of the lowest points in my entire life, he is able to make me forget the shitshow and laugh. No matter what, I'll forever be grateful to him for giving me a moment's peace and a little security, as well as a place to sleep.

"Where's the apartment?" I ask as we pass the bar I wandered into last night.

The neighborhood looks different in the daylight. Way less scary than I let myself imagine on the moonless light with nothing illuminating the two- and three-story buildings except the nearby streetlights.

"It's a block away from the bar, and it's a house, not an apartment."

I turn my head toward him and try not to ask too many questions because I don't want to seem ungrateful. "So, we're going to share a house?"

"I live downstairs, but the upstairs unit is empty. Don't worry. There's a door with a lock at the top of the stairs for your privacy."

I wasn't really worried. I mean, how could I be? He didn't ask anything of me. He hasn't even come on to me and has barely flirted. Who really wants a homeless chick without a penny to her name? He could probably have any woman he wanted flat on her back in under five minutes, me included, so why would he bother with me? Nothing in my life is easy, and he seems like the type of guy who likes everything easy...including his women.

"That's good to know."

"You'll have everything you need to get started. The place is even completely furnished, and my ma is bringing over some hand-me-downs, so there's no need to worry."

I almost let out a sigh of relief, but although the physical things are being taken care of, I have no way to feed either of us. I can't even afford a container of formula for Lulu. I couldn't care less about myself. I could go a few days without eating and survive, but not my baby girl. Nothing in the world is more important than her.

When we pull up to what I assume is his place, there are two cars and no less than four people unloading groceries, boxes, and a crib. "What the..." My voice drifts off because I can't believe my eyes.

Who does this? What kind of people help out strangers? My family never did. Definitely not my father. Sure, he gave to charity, but they were always nameless, and the entire thing was only to get a tax write-off at the end of the year.

"We got your back," Lucio says as he puts the Jeep in park and tips his head forward. "This is how my family is. When someone's in need, we rally."

"But…"

Lucio places his finger against my lips and stops me from speaking. "Don't say another word. Grab Lulu, and we'll head up to your new place."

I can't wipe the smile off my face. Less than an hour ago, I thought my entire world had ended and Lulu and I would spend the night in a shelter huddled together for safety. Now, we have an apartment, food, and an entire group helping us out when I'm not sure what we did to truly deserve it.

CHAPTER
SIX
LUCIO

DELILAH HASN'T MOVED from the landing at the top of the stairs. She's just gawking at the upstairs apartment with her mouth open as my two brothers, sister, and mother walk around her, dropping items on every available surface before they head downstairs to grab more.

"I just can't believe this," she whispers before she takes an uneasy step forward, as if she moved too fast, everything would disappear.

"This is the last box," Vinnie says as he pushes past me, knocking into my shoulder just like he did the last three times he made the trip up the steps. The once punk-ass teenager is now a college kid with more muscles than brains. "Where would you like this, ma'am?"

Delilah's eyes sparkle as she stares at the box in my kid brother's hands marked *Little Kid Shit*. "Anywhere you'd like." She looks almost as happy as she did this morning when she ate the blueberry scone.

Vinnie grunts, lifting the box higher because he always likes to show off his strength, even if the woman is way out of his league. As the star quarterback in high school and now the sophomore starter for one of the biggest football colleges in the area, he thinks he's God's gift to all humanity, especially women. Delilah might have thought I was full of myself, but she doesn't know Vinnie and how his ego barely fits in the room with the rest of us at Sunday dinner.

My ma grips Delilah's shoulders, and Lulu instantly grabs at Ma's pearls again, but my mother doesn't seem to mind. "Dinner's at one tomorrow. You know where I live, honey."

"What?" Delilah's face scrunches up again, the tiny wrinkles returning toward the tip of her nose. She turns to me, looking for help, but I only shrug.

I'm not about to say anything. Family dinners have always been a special time and a requirement if you were born into this ragtag group of people I call my family. Although my mother seems warm and fuzzy, she doesn't often invite people we just met to sit down at our table. But Ma being Ma, she is doing her best to make Delilah feel included, and I'm sure she's pushing us together in some way. As if living under the same roof and working at the same place isn't enough, Ma wants to make sure we don't spend a moment apart.

"Family dinner is always on Sunday at one."

"But I'm not…"

"Don't say it," Ma tells her, beating me to the words, and gives Delilah her very stern, motherly, don't-mess-with-me look. "The more, the merrier. Family is more than blood, baby."

Delilah seems to eat it up, smiling bigger and brighter than she has before. "Thank you so much, Betty. It's very kind of you to offer, but I think it's going to take me days to unpack everything and get settled."

"Hush now." My ma waves her hand in my direction. "Lucio will help, and besides, you need to eat. One o'clock. Don't be late."

Delilah only nods.

"We'll be there, Ma," I say, saving Delilah because she looks overwhelmed.

Ma walks over to me, throwing her arms around my shoulders and putting her mouth right next to my ear. "Don't fuck this up," she whispers as I stare at Delilah and she stares at me. "You help this girl and keep them safe."

"I know, Ma," I whisper, but neither of us is speaking softly enough for Delilah not to hear us.

Ma doesn't say anything I don't already know or think. In the short amount of time Delilah and Lulu have been around, they've grown on me, and I feel responsible for their safety.

As quickly as my family gathered to save the day and fill the upstairs apartment with so much baby stuff the place looks like we robbed the going-out-of-business sale at Toys "R" Us, they disappear, leaving us alone.

"So, your family is…" Delilah looks around the room and pauses with wide eyes. "I don't know how to describe how I feel."

I rub the back of my neck and start to laugh. "They're crazy at times, but—"

"They're amazing, Lucio. You're so lucky to have them."

She moves into the small, well-stocked kitchen which I had outfitted with new appliances after the last tenant moved out. I follow, keeping my distance because I don't know what type of traumatic shit she's been through, and we don't know each other well enough for me to start looming over her.

"This place is beautiful. Are you sure you don't want to give it to someone else?"

"And what, put you guys on the street?"

She turns then, facing me with little Lulu staring at me too. "You could've." Her eyes dip to the floor, but I stay quiet because I wasn't trying to be a hero in this situation. I did what most people would do when someone is in need. Especially when they have a baby in tow. "I mean, my father didn't have a problem doing that to us."

"Listen." I move forward, closing the space between us now because I want her to understand I want them here. "I don't know what bad shit you had happen or what type of people you're used to having in your life, but you needed help, and I had a place. I couldn't sleep at night if I dropped you and Lulu off at a shelter when I had the means to help."

Lulu holds her hand out, reaching for me, and I take her from Delilah's arms without thinking. Even Delilah doesn't put up a fight and just hands her over like we've known each other for years.

"I'll repay you for everything."

"Stop right there," I say sternly. "I'm not looking for money." I laugh as Lulu touches my lips, plucking at them with her tiny fingers and blows her own raspberry.

"Everyone's looking for money."

"I have a house, a bar, a great bike, and a nice family. I got everything I need. You're helping me out by keeping the place in working order and lending a hand at the bar."

I feel like a broken record, repeating the shit I've already told her, but she doesn't seem to get it.

In her world, the one flooded with so much money they practically drown themselves in decadence, she probably doesn't understand how someone could open their home to a perfect stranger. But as Lulu plays with my face like I'm a Mr. Potato Head toy, Delilah finally seems to relax and let everything sink in.

"We're done talking about it," I say to her, but not like an asshole. I don't want her to continually thank me or think she owes me something for helping her out. "There's two bedrooms over there." As I try to tip my head, Lulu's grip intensifies, and those tiny little nails dig into my skin.

"Oh Jesus. I'm sorry," Delilah says, moving toward me to take Lulu back. "I should probably feed her and put her down for a nap before she gets cranky."

"I don't think this kid ever gets cranky."

"Trust me, she does, and it's like the nine circles of hell when she has her moments." Delilah laughs softly before kissing Lulu's head.

"I have the bottle and formula from earlier. Just relax on the couch, and I'll get it ready. Once she's asleep, we'll start unpacking."

Delilah tilts her head and stares at me like I am part of some freak show act at the cheesy carnival that rolls into town from time to time.

"I can't let you do this all alone," I tell her because I know what she's thinking.

"Cause your ma told you to?" she asks.

"Because I want to, and to be honest—" I rub my hands together, knowing I am going to drop something on her she may not care to hear "—I like you and the kid."

Her eyes widen like my words are a shocking revelation.

I want to ask her if she has a boyfriend or anything, but I assume she doesn't. If she does, he is a piece of shit for not helping out her and the baby instead of me. If she were mine, she wouldn't be dealing with any kind of stress and certainly not living with her asshole father.

"Go sit," I tell her, angling my chin toward the couch behind her. "I got this."

She stares at me with her mouth hanging open, not moving as I walk toward the kitchen and start to prep Lulu's bottle. A few moments later, Delilah walks through the living room and peeks into the two bedrooms. "The crib's already set up."

"We work fast," I say as I measure the formula and heat the water. It has been years since I prepped a bottle, and my mother did it this morning, but it isn't any more complicated than making a drink at the bar.

The leather of the couch squeaks as she sits down. I finally turn around, catching sight of her holding Lulu across her lap and looking comfortable for the first time since she walked into my life. Her eyes are moving fast, checking out the place and all the boxes of God knows what my family decided to drop off.

What kind of idiot would fuck this up?

Hot chick. Cool baby.

Not too much is complicated about the situation. I could never abandon my kid and baby mama, but that's just how I was brought up. Then there's the fact that my mother would have my balls in a vise for doing that shit to my own blood.

I shake the bottle, mixing the chalky formula with the water as I walk into the living room, watching them. "I'll start unpacking while you feed her."

She looks up at me with her big, beautiful blue eyes and long eyelashes, blinking for a second like she is trying to process what I said. "I'm sure you have things to do."

"I don't." I kind of lie. I didn't have anything solid planned, but I was supposed to play a game of football with the guys.

I hand her the bottle and make myself busy, giving her some space and time to think while she feeds Lulu.

I've done some fucked-up shit in my life, but never once did my family turn their backs on me. I can't imagine what is going through her head after her father basically disowned her, leaving her without any money or a place to live.

I don't even make it through the first box when she starts to speak. "I just want you to know no guy is going to show up on your doorstep, demanding to see me or Lulu."

"I'm not worried," I tell her and keep my back to her, slowly pulling out the baby items and placing them on the counter. "You're allowed to have anyone over you'd like."

"Lulu's dad took off before she was born. I haven't heard from him since and have washed my hands of him entirely. I haven't been in a relationship with anyone since, so…"

"It's not my business, Delilah." My heart hurts for Lulu, and Delilah too. Not only do I want to beat her father's ass, I want to strangle the prick who knocked her up and then abandoned them both.

"But I want you to know because—" she pauses as I finally turn around to face her "—I like you too." She speaks so quietly I almost don't hear her, but those words change things forever.

CHAPTER
SEVEN
DELILAH

SAYING those words wasn't easy either. I didn't want Lucio to think I only said I like him because he's helping me out. Of course, that is part of the reason, but not the only thing I like about him.

Why wouldn't I love the guy who swooped in and rescued us from the clusterfuck that's become my life?

But it's more than that.

Here's this drop-dead gorgeous guy, muscles for days, owns his own house and bar, and he's willing to help some woman he just met, along with her baby. Lulu's father couldn't even be bothered, and I dated him for over a year before he knocked me up. Lucio has the qualities every woman's looking for but rarely ever finds.

Clearly, it isn't just his physical appearance that draws me to him, but damn, it is impressive nonetheless. Even standing in the kitchen, holding a teddy bear in one arm and a little girl dress in the other, he is hot as fuck. His tanned skin, bulging arms, and tattoos scream sexy stripper guy. I probably would've made that judgment about him if we'd crossed paths on the street. But he isn't any of that. He is the only person in the city who didn't turn his back on me.

"Give her here," he says, motioning for Lulu. She's fast asleep in my arms with the bottle still in her mouth. "I'll put her down."

I hand Lulu over without saying a word. I stare at him, and he meets my gaze but doesn't acknowledge what I just admitted. Maybe he doesn't like me in *that* way, and I'm totally off base. He could've meant he liked me as a sister or a good friend. Not that he wanted to jump my bones in quite the same way I want to hop on him.

"What the fuck? Way to go, Delilah," I whisper to myself as he disappears into Lulu's bedroom down the hallway.

Pushing off the couch, I scrub my hands down my face and try to overcome the embarrassment as I kneel on the floor. I open a box of baby clothes sitting next to the couch as Lucio walks back into the room. I don't dare look up because I don't want to throw myself at him again and make an even bigger fool of myself.

We work in comfortable silence, stealing glances at one another as we unbox all the items his family brought over. I rarely get flustered around people, but Lucio has me all kinds of off-kilter.

"Are you hungry?" he asks as he stops in front of me.

"A little," I lie, because I am starving.

"Stay here. I'll go grab something."

"Okay," I say as he runs down the stairs, leaving me alone.

Without him here, I walk around and check out my new, but temporary, place. Opening cabinets and drawers, I find the place filled with everything we need. The clean, modern kitchen has stainless-steel appliances, white lacquered cabinets, and black granite countertops. It's stuffed with pots and pans, dishes, and anything else I'll need to whip up a feast.

The decent-sized bathroom has a bathtub with a shower, pedestal sink, and everything else I'd expect to find, including towels, soap, and even bubble bath. The bedroom where Lulu sleeps has a crib and a dresser, but not much else.

My room has a comfortable queen-sized bed, nightstand, dresser, and even a small walk-in closet.

What more could a woman ask for? This isn't my father's penthouse, but it is absolutely perfect for Lulu and me. But I don't want to make myself too comfortable. I know this is only temporary. Lucio is a good man, but I don't want to overstay our welcome.

I lie on the bed, staring up at the ceiling and listening to the sirens screeching down the street below. They will take a little getting used to, but Lulu can sleep through a hurricane…thank God. I close my eyes, moving my fingers across the soft comforter and humming to myself when it becomes too quiet.

"Comfy?"

I jump off the bed and grab my chest as soon as I hear his voice. "You scared the shit out of me," I say as my heart pounds underneath my hand. "Jesus."

"I'm sorry. I was quiet so I wouldn't wake Lulu." He leans in the doorway to the bedroom, arms folded in front of his wide chest, watching me with a devastatingly beautiful smile. "I got pizza. Is that okay?"

My stomach growls and flutters at the same time. I've never felt anything like that before. "You look like a meat kind of guy, yeah? Lemme guess. You got sausage," I say as I follow him into the living room and hope he's not the pineapple type. Because pineapple on pizza is a total deal-breaker.

"Pepperoni. It was the only one they had ready, and I didn't want to make you wait." He opens the lid of the box, and the smell smacks me right in the face.

"It's absolutely perfect," I tell him as my mouth starts to water just looking at the gooey masterpiece. The cheese is perfectly melted, a little brown near the crust, and covered in loads of pepperoni, without a slice of pineapple in sight. Thank God.

"You okay with sitting on the floor?" He looks to the coffee table across the room. It's the only surface in the apartment that isn't covered with boxes or items that need to be put away.

"Of course." I nod and can't hold back my smile.

How could I have a freaking problem with the floor? I don't have a literal pot to piss in without him. I'd eat on the roof if he wanted. I grab two plates from the cabinet along with napkins before kneeling down next to Lucio. He grabs a slice and motions for me to take one too.

"So, tell me about you," I say as I hold the slice near my mouth, moving slowly, trying not to shove the entire piece of pizza in my mouth out of sheer starvation.

He takes a bite, swallowing down the first mouthful with a shrug. "Not much to tell. Grew up in this neighborhood, and I own the bar with my brothers and sister. It used to be my parents', but we bought them out a few years ago after my father ran into some legal issues."

I cover my mouth, feeling like a complete asshole. "I'm sorry," I mutter with a mouthful of food.

"Don't be," he laughs and waves the pizza slice in the air. "Santino knew his house of cards would come crashing down someday. He was into some pretty shady shit, but I'm happy we were able to save the bar before the government had a chance to seize it."

My heart flutters at the way he stares at me. It has been ages since anyone has looked at me like that. Having Lulu in my arms is always a surefire way for no man to see me as anything but a mom. But Lucio is different; he gazes at me like I'm a woman and not a breeding machine.

I set my pizza down and place my hand on his arm. "You didn't have to tell me that. I really am sorry."

He shrugs it off, but I can tell the entire thing bothers him. "He did the crime and has to do the time. I'm not proud of him, but he's still mine. He was always a good dad, just did some questionable stuff we all knew would catch up with him someday."

"He's still a better man than my father," I tell him, going back to my pizza to stop myself from touching him again. I already let my hand linger a little too long.

"Do you mind telling me what happened?"

Typically, my personal home life is private, but Lucio deserves to hear the entire gruesome story. He opened his home to us and needs to know what happened and why. I spend the next ten minutes spilling my guts about my alcoholic father, my missing-in-action mother, and the downward slide of my father's career and how it changed him into an unforgiving and sometimes reckless asshole.

"That's some pretty fucked-up shit, Delilah." This time, Lucio reaches out and touches my arm, sweeping his thumb across my skin. "I'm so sorry you had to go through all that with him."

Goose bumps cover my flesh, and my heart, which is already in overdrive, speeds up a little more. "I'm just sorry I stayed as long as I did. I should've moved out a long time ago. I wouldn't be in this situation if I had."

His fingers still, and he tightens his grip on my arm. "But then you wouldn't be here," he says without even blinking.

All the air I have in my body evaporates as I stare into his dark green eyes. The small apartment suddenly feels even smaller as he stares at me, touching my skin. I swallow down the lump that has settled deep in my throat and try to regain my composure. Something I've failed at multiple times with him. "You'd probably be out having fun on a Saturday instead of saddled with me and my kid."

I regret the words as soon as they come out of my mouth. I sound like I'm fishing for a compliment, and I hate people who do that. I really meant what I said and wasn't looking for him to say anything about how spending Saturday with me is far better than hanging out with his buddies. We both know that isn't true.

Lucio moves closer, and I hold my breath, leaning forward. Part of me is hoping he's going to kiss me. Our bodies are still connected. He's still holding on tightly to my arm. I close my eyes as he moves his face near mine and wait for the moment.

"Delilah," he says softly. I barely hear him whisper my name over the whooshing of my pulse in my ears and the rapid beating of my own heart.

"Yes?" My voice sounds needy, and I am. My body is on fire, the nearness of him and his scent overpowering my common sense. The fact that I haven't been touched by a man in so long amplifies everything.

"Lulu's awake."

My eyes fly open, and I realize he wasn't moving in for a kiss. He was trying to get up because Lulu is crying in the other room. I'd been so wrapped up in him, I hadn't even heard her.

I cover my face with my hands, letting out a little groan as Lucio disappears into Lulu's room. My face is red and heated. All I want to do is crawl under a blanket and hide. I'm sure Lucio knows I expected a kiss. How could he not? I had my mouth open, leaning forward, eyes closed like a dumb-ass teenager waiting for her first kiss.

"You're an idiot," I whisper to myself.

"Delilah," he says as he walks back into the room with Lulu in his arms. "I'm going to kiss you, but not until the moment's right, and definitely not over a box of pizza."

I don't know if I want to spin around the room, celebrating the fact that Lucio does, in fact, want to kiss me, or if I still want that blanket to hide my embarrassment over sitting on the floor with my eyes closed and my lips puckered. "Right," I say, going back to my pizza and keeping my eyes off Lucio as he sits down with Lulu in one arm.

"Hey." He touches my face, forcing me to look at him. "You're hot, li'l mama," he says as his thumb brushes near the bottom of my lip. "I don't want to rush things. You've been through a lot. When the time is right, if it is, I'll kiss you. I don't want to ruin you just yet."

"Ruin me?" I ask, almost choking on my pizza.

"Once I kiss you, you'll never want another man again."

I wish I could say something witty about how he is full of himself, but something tells me Lucio isn't lying.

CHAPTER EIGHT

LUCIO

"MAYBE I SHOULD JUST GO BACK HOME," she says as we walk through the front door of Hook & Hustle.

"No, no. My mother wants you here." I wrap an arm around her back and curl my hand over her hip, stopping her from leaving as she tries to take a step backward. "I want you here," I admit, shocking her as much as myself.

"Oh." Delilah blushes and smiles, tucking a strand of brown hair behind her ear.

"Besides, if you leave now, Betty will track you down."

"She will?" she whispers as her eyes grow wider.

"She's been known to do crazier shit."

She lets out a nervous laugh before glancing around the empty bar. "Where is everyone?"

"We're closed on Sunday afternoons. It's Gallo time until eight when we reopen again."

"It looks so different in the daylight."

"Not as scary?" I try to make light of the situation. I know the other night she was practically shaking in her shoes when she walked through the front door of Hook & Hustle.

"Definitely not as scary." She rests her head on my chest

like she's done it a million times before. I have to remind myself she isn't mine—well, not yet, at least.

Last night, we flirted. I knew she wanted to kiss me more than once, but I was trying to play it cool with her. And that had never been my thing. I'd forced myself to give her space, but it was almost like torture.

I had the worst night's sleep in my entire life. Every time I heard Delilah walking across the floor or Lulu crying, I wanted to run upstairs to see if they were okay. Somehow, I stopped myself from doing just that because the last thing I wanted to do was scare her away.

Especially after the things she told me about her family. It was awful. They are awful. There hasn't been one person in her life she could depend on. I didn't want to be added to the ever-growing list of assholes who'd fucked up her life.

"Lucio," she says as she turns her face upward, piercing my heart with her baby blue eyes. "I…"

I know shit is about to get heavy, and whatever she is going to say is something I'm not sure I am ready to hear. "We better get upstairs. We're already late."

She nods and drops whatever she was about to say. I reluctantly release her from my grip, letting her walk ahead of me up the stairs. I can't help but stare at her perfectly round ass and the way her hips sway as she slowly walks in front of me.

Delilah's foot doesn't even land on the top step when the door flies open. My ma looks down at us with the biggest smile. "Finally," Ma says, holding out her arms and motioning for the baby. "Let me see that angel."

Without hesitation, Delilah hands Lulu over to my mother. "Jesus," Delilah whispers when she gets her first full look at everyone busy setting the table and preparing the food. "This is a small army."

Sometimes, I forget not everyone has a big family like

mine. "You saw almost everyone yesterday, but I never formally introduced you."

"It was kind of hectic," she snorts and somehow makes the noise sound adorable.

"That's Vinnie. He's the baby." I tick my head toward my little brother who is standing in the kitchen and the only one not helping with dinner.

"Yo," he calls out, barely looking up from his cell phone.

"Hey." Delilah gives him a small wave, but Vinnie is too busy to even notice or wave back.

"He's an asshole and thinks he's God's gift to women," I tell her because there's no better way to describe my little brother.

"Must be genetic," she mumbles and starts to giggle, getting in her small little dig about me.

"I'm God's gift to everyone," Vinnie corrects without making eye contact.

Daphne rounds the kitchen counter, walking toward us. I know Delilah was most nervous about seeing her because, let's face it, my sister can be a complete bitch. "Hey. I'm so sorry about the other night."

"It's not a problem," Delilah says and shakes her head.

Daphne grabs Delilah, pulling her into a giant hug. "You got to understand. We get a bunch of assholes who wander into the bar all the time asking for shit. You'll see. It was nothing against you." Delilah doesn't hug her back immediately, but Daphne isn't letting her go. My sister is relentless in everything, including her hugs. "I was in a shit mood, and I wasn't feeling overly friendly. Please forgive me."

"It's okay, Daphne. I do understand," Delilah says, finally putting her arm around Daphne. Maybe Delilah knows she isn't getting out of my sister's grasp without accepting the apology and hugging her back.

"I swear I'll make it up to you. We'll have a girls' night."

Delilah glances back at me, looking for a rescue, but I have nothing to give. My sister is a pit bull, and I'm not about to get into an argument over a girls' night out. "We'll see. I don't go out anymore. Lulu takes all my time."

Daphne waves her hand in my direction as she finally releases Delilah. "Lucio can babysit," she offers without even asking me first.

"I couldn't ask him to do that."

"We're not asking," Daphne laughs. "He'd be happy to do it."

"I'll watch the tiny squirt any time. Everyone needs to blow off a little steam every now and then," I tell Delilah without even thinking about it because I like seeing her happy.

Plus, she could use a friend, especially someone like my sister. I haven't heard Delilah mention one girlfriend she could count on, and there is no one quite like Daphne. She'd happily kick any guy in the balls without a second thought. My brothers and I probably did too good of a job preparing her for the onslaught of men we knew would go after her as she grew up.

Delilah turns to face me, holding her chest. "You'd do that?" she stammers.

"Of course." I'd rather stay in and entertain her, but I keep that shit to myself.

Delilah lunges forward, wrapping her arms around my neck. "Thank you, Lucio," she whispers, standing on her tiptoes with her mouth so close I could've kissed her.

I hug her back, enjoying the way she feels in my arms. Even with her mouth almost touching mine, I don't kiss her. Daphne is too busy staring at the two of us, and I don't want our first kiss to be in front of my entire family, especially Daphne.

"Come on." Daphne grabs Delilah's hand, pulling her toward the kitchen. "Let me introduce you to everyone."

"Go," I tell her when Delilah hesitates, looking to me for permission.

"You're whipped already, huh?" Angelo, my oldest brother, says as soon as the girls are across the room and out of earshot.

"I think so," I mutter, rubbing the back of my neck, unable to take my eyes off Delilah. "I know I don't want anyone else touching her."

"Then claim her," he tells me, like it is the most natural thing in the world.

"Dude, she's not a prize."

"The way you're looking at her, I'd say she is."

His words render me speechless. I've never really looked at someone the way I look at Delilah. That much is true, but I've never really had a girlfriend either. I am more a play-the-field type of guy. Not because I am a playboy or an asshole, but I saw my father struggle to stay faithful for so long, I was scared I had some of him in me.

"She's got a kid, man."

"What's your point? I'm sure you've slept with other mothers."

I don't want to tell him I don't even really know because I've never bothered to get to know them well enough to find out. "Yeah, probably."

Angelo places his hand on my shoulder, doing the big brother crap. "Well, I think your whoring days are numbered, little brother."

I blow out a long breath, knowing what he said is probably true. "Fuck, this could be bad."

Angelo laughs, squeezing my shoulder rougher this time. "Might be the best damn thing ever to happen to you."

"Says the unattached guy," I mumble.

"I think Pop fucked you up in a way. We're all scared of commitment because of the way he was when we were kids, but he's not that man anymore, and neither are we."

"It's hard to be a cheater from behind bars," I remind Angelo.

"He stopped a long time ago. I think he was scared Ma was going to kill him in his sleep if he kept up with his bullshit."

"He finally wised up, and I have no doubt Betty could've offed him."

"Johnny probably would've done it for her," Angelo says.

"The man has never gotten over her picking Dad instead of him," I agree as I glance at my mother, who is still holding Lulu.

Angelo steps in front of me, blocking my view to make sure he has my undivided attention. "If you like this chick, make her yours."

"You make it sound so easy."

Is it really that simple? Life is already going to be complicated. With Delilah living above me, working at my bar, nothing is going to be easy. Our lives are about to become so intertwined I'm not sure if a relationship is the smartest route, but then again, I've never been known for making the best decisions.

The one thing I know for sure is I want Delilah. In the short amount of time she's been in my life, I haven't thought about anyone or anything else. Nothing seems to matter except for her and Lulu.

I want them safe.

I want them happy.

I want them with me.

"I see the war going on inside that head of yours." Angelo nudges me as I space out. "Stop thinking and just do it already. If you don't, I will."

"You're a bastard," I hiss, knowing he's pushing my buttons and it's working.

He laughs and slaps my back. "I'm a motivator."

"A fucker, maybe."

"Careful or I'll be a mother fucker."

I hate him.

CHAPTER
NINE
DELILAH

THE GALLOS ARE nothing like my family.

Growing up, dinner was always a silent affair with only the adults allowed to speak to one another. When I finished the food on my plate, I had to remain seated, waiting for my parents to finish eating before being excused.

Lucio's family is the exact opposite. They don't stop talking. Not only that, more than one person talks at a time, making it almost impossible for me to follow any single conversation. I spend most of the time trying to memorize everyone's names and details because trying to talk is useless.

I asked Lucio to tell me about his siblings before we came to his mother's house. When they dropped everything off yesterday, I was too in shock to process anything. Plus, they came and left so quickly, I barely got to say hello.

Angelo, the oldest brother, is just as tall as Lucio, not as freakishly large, but not small by any means. His eyes are a beautiful shade of ice blue, popping against his olive skin and dark hair. He seems to be more serious than everyone else, but maybe because of everything he's been through, especially losing his wife and being a single parent.

Vinnie, the youngest Gallo brother, is super cocky and

probably a lady-killer. He is the golden boy and star quarter-back, winning the state championship three years in a row in high school. Although he is a part owner of the bar, he is gone most of the year but sometimes comes home on weekends. He's just as handsome as his brothers, but he still has a boyish quality which makes him appear to be innocent when he is the furthest thing from it.

Daphne is two years older than Vinnie. She is pretty straightforward, speaks her mind, and doesn't take shit from very many people. She either likes you or she doesn't, and she makes her feelings very clear.

"What do you think, Dee?" Daphne asks, but I am so lost, I have no idea what she wants my opinion about. She's staring at me, and I shift in my seat, feeling the weight of her gaze.

"Sure," I say because I don't want to seem like I'm not paying attention. Hell, I am paying as much attention as I possibly can to every conversation around the table and failing miserably.

"Yeah?" She looks shocked, and I know I'm in trouble.

When Lucio turns to me with his eyebrows almost to his hairline and asks, "You really want to do that?" I pretty much know I'm fucked.

I look at her and then back to him. "What am I missing?"

"A whole lotta skin," Daphne replies with a wicked smile, pretending to spank the air with her palm. "And muscles for days, girl. Dat ass, though."

"I think she has to work," Lucio says, rescuing me even though I didn't ask him for help from something that doesn't sound like all that much fun.

Strippers used to be fun before I had Lulu. But now the very thought of a bunch of gyrating, naked men doesn't seem as interesting or exciting as a nap, due to my current state of exhaustion.

"Yeah. I heard the boss is a real prick too," I add, giving

Lucio a sideways glance as I bounce Lulu on my lap and try to be funny.

I should've been pissed he answered on my behalf, but I'm not. Sitting around, getting drunk, and watching half-naked men doesn't sound like as much fun as a quiet evening at home alone with Lucio. But I know I am being delusional. The dancers and Lucio have one thing in common...they aren't the type to settle down with a single mother.

"He totally is," Daphne laughs. "But the other boss, the more beautiful one"—she points to herself—"says you can have the night off."

Somewhere along the way, Daphne and I became total BFFs. The woman behind the bar is nothing like the one sitting across the table from me now. Maybe there's a work version of her which is tough as nails and takes no bullshit. Daphne Gallo at her mother's dinner table is sweet as pie. Either that, or she's trying to get me into a world of trouble.

"She has a baby to take care of," Lucio tells Daphne like I'm not even in the room, let alone sitting next to him.

"I'm sure Ma will watch Lulu," Daphne shoots back before staring at her mother, waiting.

I think all hope is lost for a second, but then Betty speaks.

"Although I love Lulu already, I'm busy next Saturday."

Everybody in the room goes silent, turning toward her with their mouths hanging open. It's the first time since I walked through the door there's not a single sound.

Vinnie shakes his head like he can't believe the words that just came out of her mouth. "What the hell are you doing Saturday, Ma? You never go out on the weekend," he asks, finally laying down his phone next to his dinner plate.

Betty stabs at the chicken on her plate, pretending she doesn't hear the question, but she doesn't look at anyone either.

"Ma." Angelo taps on the table in front of her. "Where are you going on Saturday?"

"I have plans," she says between bites.

"Plans?" Daphne cocks one perfectly plucked eyebrow and leans back in her chair, staring in her mother's direction. "You never have *plans*."

"I have a life too, honey." The features on Betty's face tighten suddenly. "Drop it. End of discussion. I can't watch the baby. Delilah will just have to stay home."

Why do I get the sneaking suspicion Betty doesn't have a damn thing to do next weekend? I remember the words she said to Lucio. She seems to want to push us together, and so far, it's worked.

"Fine," Daphne sighs and tosses her napkin on her plate.

"Thanks for asking me to go. It means a lot to me." I try not to seem overly happy I can't go, even though I am relieved.

"You're welcome." Daphne smiles, sitting up a little straighter and pushing her long brown hair behind her shoulder. "We'll do it another weekend."

The momentary silence evaporates, and everyone starts talking again, but no one presses Betty any further.

"So, Delilah, do you have any waitressing experience?" Angelo asks from the other end of the table.

I glance down at Lulu's smiling face and think about lying for a second, but I know he'd be able to tell as soon as I started on the job. "I don't. Is that okay?"

"It's fine." He waves me off and almost cracks a smile. "I'd be more than happy to show you the ropes."

I peer up at Lucio as he sits next to me, but he is staring at his brother, paying no attention to me at all. "I'll be training Delilah," Lucio states quickly.

"If you think you can handle it," Angelo says with a small smirk and returns his brother's stare. "I know how much you hate training new employees."

Lucio's eyes narrow, and he still doesn't look at me. "We haven't had a new employee in four years."

"Dudes," Vinnie interrupts and points at himself with his thumbs. "I'll train the new chick." He winks in my direction and is immediately smacked in the chest with the back of Angelo's hand.

Part of me wants to laugh because Vinnie is adorable, but Jesus, the way Angelo and Lucio are glaring at each other, I am ready to duck for cover.

"I don't want to be any trouble," I say softly as an uneasy feeling settles deep in my stomach.

Without looking down at me, Lucio places his hand on top of mine. "It won't be any trouble. I want to train you."

"I'm sure you want more than that," Vinnie whispers under his breath and is again met with the back of Angelo's hand, but this time a little harder.

"Delilah." Betty breaks the awkward silence and changes the subject pretty quickly. "Want to take Lulu for a walk with me?"

Just as quickly as Lucio placed his hand on top of mine, it's gone.

"Sure," I say and try to hide the sadness from my voice.

"The kids can clean up." She smiles as the *kids* grumble. "I usually take Angelo's kids for a walk after dinner, but they're with their other grandparents."

"That's so sweet." Neither of my parents has ever taken Lulu for a walk. My father barely held Lulu, and my mother still hasn't bothered to see her once. "They must love that."

I am envious of the people around this table. I would've given up growing up with money if it meant I'd have half the support system they do. All the money in the world means nothing without love. I know that firsthand after my parents pawned me off on nannies and boarding school as I grew older. Even when they were physically present in my life, they weren't truly there.

"Lucio, can you get the stroller for us?" his mother asks him.

Lucio stands with me, finally making eye contact. "Want me to come?" he asks.

"No. You stay here and relax," I tell him. He looked so hopeful before those words left my mouth, but I am being selfish. I want a little time alone with his mother, someone I would've loved having as my own.

"I promise to be on my best behavior," his mother says.

Lucio doesn't look convinced. "I think I should go too. Make sure you two are safe." He takes a step forward, but his mother places her small hand on the middle of his giant chest and stops him.

"You'll stay here. Give the girl a little room to breathe, son. Let your momma handle this," she says as if I'm not even in the room, listening to the entire conversation.

It seems to be a theme in this family. I don't know if it's because I'm the new girl or maybe they just like bossing each other around, but it's starting to drive me a little crazy.

"Delilah, why don't I show you where we store it in case you want to use it again?" Lucio motions for me to follow, and I glance at his mother.

"That's a splendid idea. I'll just run and get my hat." She smiles and shoos me toward the stairwell where Lucio is waiting. "Gimme that sweet girl," she says, taking Lulu from my arms before I can take a step.

We don't speak as I follow him through the bar, down a hallway, and to the storage closet where I think they keep the stroller.

Before I have one foot in the doorway, Lucio has his arms around me, pulling me in closer until there's no space left between us.

"I'm sorry," he says as he leans forward, staring into my eyes so intensely my knees start to go weak.

"For what?" I ask as he moves his mouth closer to mine. My voice is so soft I'm not sure he heard me because he doesn't answer right away.

"For this." He presses his soft, full lips to mine and holds me tighter, stealing my breath. He sweeps his tongue across my bottom lip, and I tip my head back, opening to him. In this moment, as our tongues tangle together, I know one thing for sure. He was right.

I *am* ruined.

CHAPTER
TEN
LUCIO

"I CAN'T QUITE PLACE the look on your face," Daphne says as I stand behind the bar, looking out across the room filled with customers.

I know where she's going with the statement. I've been walking around in a haze ever since I kissed Delilah, but I didn't think it was noticeable. I should've known Daphne would be all over me, sticking her nose exactly where it didn't belong.

I fill a pint at the tap, trying to busy myself. "Shut up, Daph."

I walk to the other end to get away from my sister's prying eyes, but she follows me. "You really like this chick, don't you?"

I set the beer down in front of Johnny before I turn to face her. I know she isn't going to back down. That's never been my sister's style, especially when it comes to her brothers and our love lives. "I do," I admit, turning to face her and crossing my arms in front of my chest.

"Huh," she mumbles and shakes her head slowly. "Never knew you had it in you."

My muscles tighten, and I'm instantly defensive. "Had what?"

"The love gene." She punches my shoulder playfully and laughs. "I'm pretty sure it's the end of the world."

"I'm not in love, Daphne. I just met the girl." I may not have been there yet, but I could easily fall in love with Delilah. My ma was right about one thing; Delilah is more stable than most of the women I've dated. She doesn't ask for much, and even though she grew up with a silver spoon in her mouth, the smallest things seem to make her happy.

"You doth protest too much."

I roll my eyes, stalking away from her, done with the conversation. But Daphne's not ready to move on. She follows me, almost face-planting in my back when I stop too quickly. "What are you doing?" I ask, trying not to lose my cool as I glare at her over my shoulder.

Daphne comes around in front of me, blocking the path to the back room and wags her finger in my face. "You had sex with her already, didn't you?"

"Not that it's any of your business, but I haven't." I don't know why I tell her. She doesn't need to know everything that happens in my life. Working together has added a new level of brother and sister closeness I never expected when I agreed to buy the bar with them.

Daphne staggers backward, holding her chest like she's heard the most shocking news. "You haven't? Oh. My. God. It *is* the end of the world."

"Stop being overdramatic." I push her aside and stalk toward the office.

"You sleep with everyone, Lucio. She's been under your roof for more than twenty-four hours, and you haven't nailed her. That can only mean one thing."

"Don't say it," I tell her as Michelle, my sister's best friend and our best waitress, walks into the office just behind us.

"What the hell are you two doing?" She places her hands

on her hips, staring back and forth between the two of us before tipping her head toward the door. "We have a bar full of customers waiting."

Daphne waves her hand at me. "Lucio hasn't slept with Delilah yet," she says, not answering Michelle's question and totally selling me out to Michelle.

My sister says I sleep with everyone, but I don't. Hell, I haven't slept with Michelle even though she's smoking hot and totally my type. She's way too connected with my sister for me to even think about sleeping with her. Something about the very thought has always grossed me out.

Michelle's eyebrows shoot up, and she steps inside the office, forgetting about all the waiting customers she came in here to tell us about. "Oh, do tell me more."

"Both of you get out," I tell them, shooing them toward the door.

They step backward in unison, giving each other a look before laughing. "Someone's got it bad," Daphne teases and nudges Michelle's arm with her bony elbow.

"Get. Out," I repeat as I push them into the hallway, needing some time alone to get my head on straight.

———

I head home early, leaving Daphne and Michelle to clean up because they wouldn't get off my case. I tiptoe through the front door finding Delilah sitting on the steps to her apartment, leaning against the wall, and sound asleep. She doesn't even flinch when the front door clicks and I engage the lock. She looks so peaceful, so beautiful as she sleeps, but in no way does she look comfortable.

Delilah mumbles something as I lift her into my arms, and her face falls against my chest, making it impossible to understand her words. I'm tempted to carry her to my bed, but I know we may not hear Lulu crying, so I take her upstairs instead.

My life went from carefree to complicated the moment Delilah walked into the bar. I've never been one to turn my back on a friend in need, but strangers are a different story. Not that I'm a heartless bastard, but I have too much other shit to deal with on the daily to put a whole lot of thought into helping someone I don't know.

If she had been alone, I might have reacted differently, but I couldn't turn my back on her and Lulu both. Lulu is an innocent in the entire situation, and as far as I can tell, so is Delilah. In all probability, I wouldn't have turned my back on Delilah either because I'm a sucker for a pretty lady, especially one in crisis.

My ma has said more than once that I attract the crazy chicks, but there's a reason for that. They're safe. I never worry about falling in love when the girl is one step away from a padded room.

Delilah isn't safe. Not for my heart, at least, and it's a scary place for me to be in, as well as totally uncharted territory.

"Lucio," Delilah whispers as I place her on the bed.

"Shh," I say softly as she stretches. "Go back to sleep, sweetheart."

I expect her hands to fall away from my neck, but she tightens her hold. "Lie down with me," she begs, and in that moment, I can't say no.

I crawl under the covers, placing my front against her side. She curls into me, smashing her face back against my chest again. I'm not sure where to put my hands, not knowing her well enough to touch the parts I really want to. Instead, I set one hand against the small of her back and use the other to prop my head in my palm.

"How was work?" she asks, pulling her face away from my body and staring up at me with sleepy eyes.

"It was good. You okay?"

She looks sadder than usual, but she nods. "I'm fine. Just had a long night. Lulu wouldn't stop crying."

"Is she sick?"

"No. She was just fussy. Thank God she's sleeping." Delilah groans and brings her hands between us, wrapping her fingers around my T-shirt and holding on to me tightly. Her breasts press against me as she shifts, and no matter what I do, I know my body's going to respond to the feel of her.

I move my face and bury my nose in her hair, recognizing the lavender scent of the baby shampoo my mother gave to her after the family dinner. "Is there anything I can do to make things easier?"

She peers up, tightening her hold on my shirt. "Kiss me," she whispers.

I don't know what I thought her answer would be, but I like where she takes my offer. I'm not sure kissing her again will make things easier, but I know it sounds like way more fun than anything else.

I don't hesitate in moving my lips to hers, our eyes locked on each other as our breathing grows harsher and more labored.

I struggle to keep my composure as my mouth crashes down on hers for only the second time since I met her. The feel of her lips is no less spectacular or mind-blowing than it was the first time I kissed her.

She slides her arms around my shoulders, pulling me on top of her as I tug on her lip with my teeth, teasing her and myself in the process. She lets out a small moan, making it damn near impossible for me to take things slow.

I slide a hand under the hem of her T-shirt, finding the soft skin near her waist. It takes everything in me to keep my fingers there because I want to slip the thin fabric from her body and mine, removing every obstacle between us. The only noise in the room is our lips smacking against each other, and it sounds like pure heaven.

"I want you," I murmur against her lips. God, I want her more than anyone I've ever wanted before. But restraint is key with a girl like her. A single mother needs to be treated with kid gloves. Having her as a roommate makes everything more complicated. I know once we go down this road, there's no turning back.

She laces her fingers through my hair, holding my face and lips to hers. I wasn't going anywhere, though. Nothing could stop me from taking what she had to give.

I slide my tongue across her bottom lip, feeling her softness and tasting her sweetness. Her tongue meets mine, sending shock waves through my system, and the haze I've been walking in for most of the day seems to vanish.

I don't know what I was thinking when I kissed her in the bar, but in all reality, I wasn't thinking at all. I let my body lead the way, and I'm doing it again. I know I shouldn't be touching her, but I can't stop myself.

"I want you too," she admits, and when she wraps her legs around my back, the small sliver of resistance and common sense I had slips away.

I kiss her harder, loving the way she responds with soft moans and by tightening her legs around my body, pushing my cock into her.

She wants me. I want her.

This should be simple, but I know nothing about what's about to happen is.

Just when I'm about to make my move, Lulu starts to wail from the other room. For a moment, we don't stop. It's like some invisible force is holding us together, but as Lulu's cries become louder, we both pull apart. I roll to my side, staring up at the ceiling with my cock hard as a rock and throbbing with need.

"I'm so sorry," Delilah says as she crawls off the bed.

"Don't be," I tell her before she walks out of the room to grab Lulu.

Lulu may have saved me from a big mistake. I don't want to sleep with Delilah because I'm horny and she's barely awake. I want the moment to be right, the feelings to be there. Once it happens, there's no turning back.

I already know I can't imagine them walking out the door, never seeing them again, but can I get over the worry I've carried around my entire life about being too much like my father? I owe it to Delilah and Lulu not to go any further unless I know I can be the man they both need.

CHAPTER ELEVEN

DELILAH

IT'S OFFICIAL.

I'm going to be the world's worst waitress.

"Again," Lucio says as he sits in the back corner of the bar, pretending to be a random customer.

Lucio's been patient with me, setting up the afternoon for us to train, and he hasn't complained once. But I know I'm bad. Bad isn't even a good enough word to describe the level of awful I am at taking orders and serving drinks. Carrying a tray is easy when it's empty, but add a few drinks, and I'm a hot mess with absolutely no balance.

Thankfully, the bar is almost empty. There're a few regulars hanging around, but they're too busy arguing about politics to watch how epically I'm failing.

I turn around, trying to regain my composure before facing him with a kind smile. I've already spilled three drinks and dropped the tray half a dozen times. "Good evening. Can I get you a drink?" I say, changing up the script we've gone over a hundred times.

"Good evening?" He raises an eyebrow.

I drop the straight face I've been able to maintain. "What? It sounded good." I shrug. "No?"

"Delilah, look around the bar." He waves his hand across the table toward the few guys sitting on the stools near the bar. "What do you see?"

I peer over my shoulder. "Some guys."

"What kind of guys?"

"Regulars, I assume."

"Yeah, but do they look like the type to say good evening?"

I peer down at the floor and kick the hardwood with the toe of my shoe. "Well, no."

"This isn't the country club, and the men who come in here don't wear a suit and tie. Keep it casual."

I shrug and blow out a breath. My feet hurt, and I'm irritated with myself. "Whatcha wanna drink?"

Lucio covers his mouth, but I know he's laughing. The words are so foreign coming out of my mouth I can't even stop myself from laughing too.

"That's closer than good evening. Just be yourself."

I go right back into my role, taking his advice to be casual and act more like myself. "So, whatcha want? I don't have all day, mister."

"I'll take a gin and tonic."

I have my tray tucked under my arm, scribbling his drink order on a pad of paper. "How about a double for three bucks more?"

"Nice touch and upsell. Make it a double. I'll also take a Sex on the Beach and a Blow Job."

I blink a few times with my pen hovering over the pad of paper, but I can't seem to write out the words or make enough saliva to swallow without sounding like an idiot. My face heats, and I can't deny both sound pretty damn good about now. I imagine the sun bouncing off his tanned skin as the waves splash over our bodies.

I'm so lost thinking about screwing Lucio, the tray falls from under my arm and bounces off the floor, bringing me right back to reality. "You want a what, again?"

"They're drinks, Delilah. Sex on the Beach and a Blow Job."

Last night, we were so close to having sex until Lulu used her magical kid powers and put an end to mommy time. It was probably for the best, but I can't stop thinking about what could've happened and what the repercussions would've been today.

"Oh." I'm sure he hears the disappointment in my voice because Lord knows I do nothing to hide it. "Coming right up." I snatch the tray off the floor and march toward Angelo, fanning myself with the tiny pad of paper.

Angelo's leaning against the bar, watching me as I approach. "Lucio being too hard on you?" he asks, giving me a kind smile as he stops whatever he's been doing to give me his full attention.

I shake my head and blow the hair out of my eyes that had fallen when I bent down to pick up the tray. "No. He's great. I just suck at this."

"You don't suck. Give yourself some time to adjust. Why don't you lose the tray and leave the paper in your pocket? Only use it when you have a large order you're worried you won't remember."

"I can do that." I somehow muster a smile through my embarrassment. "I hope I don't mess things up tonight."

"You won't. Strangers are easier to serve than someone you know."

"Lucio makes me nervous," I blurt out and instantly regret letting that little nugget of truth slip.

Angelo's ice-blue eyes sparkle as his smile widens. "I think the feeling's mutual, Dee."

His statement makes me feel better. Lucio always seems to have his shit together, while I'm a mess of emotion. "I don't know about that. He's a pretty smooth talker."

Angelo leans forward, closing the space between us. "I'll let you in on a little secret," he says as I lean in closer too, dying to know what he's about to say. "My brother is a smooth talker, but you fluster the hell out of him. I've never seen him so unlike himself around a woman until you walked through the door."

"Waitress," Lucio calls out from across the room. "How's my drink coming?"

"See," Angelo says as he backs away. "He doesn't even like me talking or getting that close to you."

I peer over my shoulder at Lucio, who's watching us carefully and doesn't look one bit happy. "Coming, sir." I smile in his direction, but he doesn't return it.

"What did he order?"

"Double gin & tonic, Sex on the Beach, and a Blow Job."

Angelo rolls his eyes and grabs three glasses before filling them with water. "Carry them without the tray and try not to spill more than a few drops this time."

I carry the shot glass in one hand and the other two drinks in the opposite, walking as smoothly as possible toward Lucio.

His eyes never leave me as I get closer. "Here're your drinks, sir," I say, sliding them onto the table without being covered in water.

"Thank you." He grabs the tallest glass and guzzles down the water like he's been walking in the desert for days.

"Did I do better this time?"

"You did." He wipes his mouth with the back of his hand, green eyes still on me, blazing.

I resist the urge to grab a glass of water and down the damn thing too. The way he's looking at me makes me want to crawl into his lap and beg for his kiss again.

"Grab the credit card reader from Angelo and make it quick this time."

Is Lucio jealous of his brother? I never would have pegged

him for the insecure or jealous type, especially not when it comes to his family.

Angelo has the credit card reader on the bar top by the time I make my way across the room. He dips his head but doesn't say a word. I give him a small smile, not lingering too long because I know Lucio's patience is already wearing thin.

I'm halfway to the table when the door to the bar opens with the familiar little bell chiming overhead. "Can I help you, sir?" Angelo asks the person, and I continue walking, ignoring everyone in the room except Lucio.

"I'm here to see my daughter."

I can't stop the credit card reader from slipping from my grip and crashing to the floor near my feet. All the blood drains from my face, and all the playfulness I was feeling is gone when I hear his voice.

"Your daughter?" Angelo asks as I turn around with wide eyes, seeing my father standing near the doorway.

"Delilah," my father says, rushing in my direction with his hands outstretched. "Thank God you're okay."

I back up, moving closer to Lucio and farther away from my dad. He's the last person I want to see. My eyes are already filling with tears, my vision blurring, and I can't seem to walk away fast enough.

When my father grabs my arm, I pull away and glare at him. "Get the hell out," I snap, not caring who hears or what kind of scene I'm making. I figure the few guys sipping beers only a few feet away have heard worse. "You're not welcome here."

"Baby, don't say that," he says, trying to touch me again, but I jump backward, slamming into a wall of muscle.

"You heard the lady. Get out." Lucio's voice is loud and deep. He wraps an arm around my waist and moves himself in front of me. "You're not welcome here, Mr. Miles."

"I'm her father. I have every right to speak with my

daughter. She's none of your concern, boy. This is family business."

My father looks normal, dressed in one of his best suits with bright eyes and no slur to his words. He's sober and doesn't look as disheveled as the night he kicked me out of the car. So any hatred he spews is coming from a clear head and not the alcohol.

I grip the back of Lucio's shirt, hiding my face as I wipe away the tears with my free hand. I don't want my father to see me crying. He's hurt Lulu and me enough to last a lifetime, and I'm not about to let him have another round at bruising my heart.

"Family business?"

I can't see Lucio's face, but every muscle in his back is tight, and there's a low rumble, almost a growl, deep in his chest.

Angelo rounds the bar and starts to walk in our direction, when Lucio holds out his hand, stopping his brother from entering the fray.

"You have five seconds to get out before I toss you out on your ass," Lucio tells my father.

God, I love this man for the way he defends me when no one else in my life ever has. My father should've always been my protector, but he's been nothing but a nightmare. I'm done being his whipping post.

"Wait." I yank on Lucio's T-shirt and peer up at him.

Lucio looks over his shoulder, and I can see the anger in his eyes, but it's not toward me. "You want to talk to him?"

"I need to say my piece," I tell him. I know that I need to have closure and leave my father in the past. "Let me have this."

It's the only way I can move on and start over again. Pushing him out the door will only make him come back, and next time, he'll probably be shit-faced.

Lucio nods, stepping aside without another word or an argument.

"Outside," I say, not moving until my father starts toward the door first.

"Hey." Lucio grabs my hand as I take a step forward. "I won't be far."

"Thanks." I muster a smile, but inside, I'm shaking like a leaf. "I need to do this."

He releases my hand, and I walk toward the doorway, where my father's waiting. There's pain in his eyes, but it's always there after he has a drunken episode like the other night. Next, he'll beg for forgiveness and promise to attend meetings, but this time, I won't believe a word that comes from his lying mouth.

My father paces on the sidewalk in front of the bar, dragging his hands through his hair as I lean against the wall near the entrance. "You wanted to talk, so talk," I tell him and pick at my nails because I can't bring myself to even look at him.

I've had a lifetime of dealing with his drunkenness, so you'd think I'd be better at handling the aftermath by now. I've always forgiven him in the past. I never forgot, but I found a way to move on, especially after I found out I was pregnant. He made so many promises, and stupid me thought he'd clean up his life for his granddaughter, but I should've known better.

He comes to a stop and faces me, but he doesn't bring his eyes to mine. "I'm sorry, Delilah," he says and runs his fingers through his perfectly combed hair. "I was having a bad night."

"You have a lot of those." My voice is even, which is surprising because my insides are burning with rage.

The hurt in his eyes would've probably affected me a week ago, but standing here now, I feel nothing.

"I want you to come home," he pleads.

"No," I say firmly.

He looks up at the building and makes a face of disgust. I know what he's thinking. He's always looked down at people who didn't fit his perfect, wealthy mold. "You don't belong in a place like this." He waves his hand toward the bar.

I push off the wall, walking toward him quickly, and I stick my finger right in the middle of his chest. "The thing I didn't deserve was being tossed out on the street with my daughter, your granddaughter, without a penny to my name. What I didn't deserve was a narcissistic father who was more worried about getting his next drink than his own family." I poke him a little harder this time because it feels good, and my anger's rolling harder and deeper than it ever has before. "What I didn't deserve was putting up with an asshole like you for the last ten years. I never walked out on you, Dad."

"I know."

"Mom left because she couldn't deal with your drinking, but I stayed." My voice grows louder because my anger is at a boiling point, and I'm close to blowing.

"She left you, too," he says, reminding me of the fact that my mother couldn't even be bothered with me, choosing the hot pool boy over both of us.

"Shut up!" I push him backward using my finger, and he doesn't fight back. "I will not go back home with you because it has never been anything more than a shelter. There's no love between us. You don't give a single shit about Lulu or me. You made that perfectly clear when you left us here."

"I need you," he says, but I don't believe a word of what he's telling me.

"Hire a housekeeper. I'm sure someone will put up with your drunken tirades for enough money. I'm done with you. I've spent enough of my life dealing with your verbal abuse, and I will not subject my daughter to it too." He steps backward, trying to get away from my finger, but I follow. "If you really feel bad, put my money back in my account. It's not yours to take. It's mine and Lulu's. If you really care, you'll make sure at least her future's secure."

He stares at me, and there's a flash of emotion on his face, but I'm not sure if it's sadness or something else. My father's never been one to share his feelings unless he's filled with a bottle of vodka.

"It's my account too," he says like he's justifying his theft of well over a million dollars that was left to me.

I pull my finger away from his chest and take a step backward, glaring at him. "Because I was under eighteen when Grandma died. It's not yours."

"Come home, and I'll return the money. Or stay here, and see what it's really like to survive on your own."

"I would rather live on the streets than live under the same roof as you again. Unlike you, my daughter is my first priority."

"Don't be a fool, Delilah. These aren't your people," he scoffs, and his facial features tighten. "I brought you up better than this." He waves his hand through the air again, motioning toward the bar.

"*These* people have been kinder to me in a few days than you have been in the last ten years. I'd rather Lulu be around people who shower her with love than throw money at her in hopes of winning her affection."

"Already sleep with one of them?" He throws the familiar words in my face, but this time, he's wrong.

"Just go, Dad. Don't look for me. Forget I even exist."

"You'll always be a whore just like your mother. Your bastard child will always be a reminder. I was sorry for what happened, but I can see you have no forgiveness in your heart. You're no better than her."

His words are meant to hurt me, but they don't mean anything anymore. I'm nothing like my mother, or my father either. I will always put Lulu first. I will never let her feel like less than the amazing little girl she is, and I will never allow her around anyone who's willing to hurt her.

Whether they're blood or not, no one will have that power over her or me again.

I glance to the side and see Lucio peeking around the corner of the building. I shake my head, waving him off. I know he wants to rush to my side and physically remove my father, stopping the last words I hope I'll ever speak to him. I want this moment. I want the goodbye to be final and leave no room for him to come back.

"Goodbye, Dad," I say and turn my back to him. "Don't come back. We're no longer your problem or your family."

He curses at me as I walk back through the door to the bar. The few people inside scramble back to their seats, clearly having been listening to the exchange and sticking their nose in my business.

My face turns red, and I'm completely embarrassed, ready to sprint toward the bathroom to hide. But then the guys in the bar start clapping.

"You did good, kid," one of the men says, punching me lightly in the shoulder as I walk by.

"You have some balls, little girl," another one adds and dips his head. "Lemme buy you a drink."

"No, no." I half smile and laugh because they're so happy and sweet, although a little strange. "Thanks."

The sadness I would've felt in the past isn't there anymore. I'm not sorry for the things I said to my father or the fact that I cut him out of my life once and for all. I was done being his carpet to step on when he felt his life wasn't going the way he wanted. He has shit to deal with, and I'm not going to be there to watch him crash and burn.

CHAPTER
TWELVE

LUCIO

"I'M TAKING her home for a while," I tell Angelo as Delilah runs into the bathroom, probably crying her eyes out.

"Take all the time you need. Delilah needs you." He nods, tipping his head toward the mostly empty bar. "We won't be busy tonight, and Michelle's coming in soon."

"Tell Ma we'll be back for Lulu later."

"Don't rush," Ma says as she comes down the stairway, holding Lulu in one arm. "I heard every bit of that nasty man. You take that girl home, and don't let her out of the house until she's ready. Words like that don't leave a child's mind, no matter how old they are."

"I know, Ma."

My father may not have been the best partner, but he was a great dad. He was always kind and patient, even when we probably didn't deserve it. Raising four kids couldn't have been easy for either of my parents, but they never made it seem like a hardship or a duty.

Never once, no matter how many times we fucked up, did they talk to us the way Delilah's father just talked to her.

"Go make her whole again, baby." Ma kisses my cheek as I run the back of my finger down Lulu's soft, pudgy cheek, hating the idea of her ever hearing such hateful words. "Lulu and I are fine together. We're about to go for a walk. Now, get moving. There's a woman who needs you back there."

Delilah's sitting on the floor, leaning against the wall of the bathroom as I walk inside to make sure she's okay.

"He's such an asshole," she says as soon as she sees me, but there're no tears on her face. "I'm sorry you had to see that."

I sit down next to her, touching her shoulder with mine. "Don't ever be sorry."

"I'm so mad right now, I want to punch something."

I push against her shoulder and point at my chest. "You can hit me if it'll make you feel better."

She glances up at me with a small laugh. "You're the last person I want to punch, Lucio."

"You won't hurt me," I promise her and pound on my chest to prove how solid I am.

"I can't," she tells me.

"You'll feel better, though." I'm pretty sure her punch would barely make me flinch. Delilah's so tiny, and her hands are so dainty, I'm not even sure she could hit much harder than a little girl.

"Don't be ridiculous."

"Let's get out of here, then." I stand and hold my hand out to her, hoping she'll take me up on my offer to help her relax a little.

She slides her hand into mine without hesitation, and I pull her to her feet. "But what about work?"

I shake my head and pull her tightly into my arms. "I know the boss. We're good."

She laughs a little and rests her head against my chest. "I can't say thank you enough."

"Hush now," I tell her as I press my lips to the top of her head. "Don't thank me. I haven't done anything heroic."

"You treat me better than my own parents."

"Well, I want in your pants," I joke, but my words aren't entirely false.

I want more than that from Delilah. I can see much more than a great fuck. I see a future. I see a woman who's fierce, kind, and willing to take a risk instead of bowing to someone else's will for a boatload of cash.

She slaps at my chest playfully. "Don't be a dick."

"It's so difficult, though. Sometimes you make it so easy to let that side of myself shine."

She peers up at me with a soft face and kind eyes. "You're really a good guy, Lucio."

"Don't tell anyone. I don't want to ruin my reputation around here."

She rolls her eyes and stands on her tiptoes, trying to bring her face closer to mine. I cup her cheeks in my hands and press my lips against hers. There's nothing hungry in this kiss. I don't rush through the action because this is about emotion, not lust.

"I'll be by your side, Delilah. No matter what happens, I'll never turn my back on you," I promise her.

———

"Why are you so nice to me?" Delilah's blue eyes never leave me as I carry the dishes to the sink.

"Why wouldn't I be nice?"

Delilah shrugs and plays with the napkin in front of her. "Your family may be the only genuinely nice people I've ever met who weren't looking for something in return."

Leaning against the countertop, I stare at the woman who's been beaten down but refuses to be broken. "Maybe it's all a ruse, and I'm secretly going to sell you into sex slavery when you let down your guard."

"Stop being silly. I mean it, Lucio. People aren't nice."

"Maybe where you come from. But down here, people

tend to be kind and look out for each other. That's why I never moved out of the neighborhood."

She sighs. "I wonder what it would've been like to grow up like you. Loving parents, siblings, and nice people. I bet it was the best ever."

"Don't get me wrong. There're some real assholes around here too, but I don't ever regret where I come from. I'm proud to be a South Sider."

She stands and rounds the island, coming to a stop in front of me. "Do you like me, Lucio?" she asks point-blank.

"I do," I answer honestly as she steps between my legs. "I thought I made it pretty clear."

"Do you like me as a friend or…"

I place my finger under her chin, forcing her eyes back to mine when she glances down. "I want to be more than your friend, Delilah. I don't make a habit of kissing my friends."

"Thank you for this," she says, pressing her body to mine and pushing against my cock.

Sliding my palm along her cheek, I run my thumb across the bottom edge of her lip. "For what?"

"This," she states and leans forward, taking a play right out of my book.

The air's knocked out of me, just like the first time I planted my lips on hers. I said I'd ruin her, but in reality, she devastated me. Changed me forever. There was no turning back. No other kiss in the history of kisses could compare to kissing Delilah Miles.

Grabbing her by the waist, I lift her into the air and place her on the countertop before pushing her legs apart. "I want you," I murmur against her lips, not wanting to miss a moment of her sweet taste.

Her fingers find their way under my T-shirt, and her nails scrape the tender flesh of my ribs. "I need you," she moans as I gently pull at her bottom lip with my teeth.

My eyes search hers, looking for any signs of hesitation,

but her blue eyes burn for me. My thumbs slip under the hem of her T-shirt, sliding across the soft skin near the waistband of her jeans, and she shudders. I deepen the kiss, needing something to focus on before I tear her shirt over her head and move too fast. I want to savor every inch of her body and enjoy every dip and curve, reveling in the taste of her flesh and the softness of her skin.

But when she moves her hands down the front of my stomach, slipping them into the waistband of my shorts, I just about lose control. Her fingers are met by the tip of my cock, begging for more than a little attention.

"Oh my God," she whispers and pulls away, glancing down. "Is that…"

"Pierced, baby."

"I've never…"

"I'm about to blow your mind."

"I gotta see," she says and slides off the counter, yanking on my shorts on the way. Her head's against the cabinets, and she's staring at my package, which is currently waving at her, hoping she's going to do more than look. "Can I touch it?"

I'm like a proud peacock, showing off my goods and hoping like hell she digs the fuck out of the piercing. "As much as you want," I say with a smile, stroking her hair and stopping myself from pulling her lips toward my mouth.

Using the tip of her finger, she traces the metal piercing, scraping my super-sensitive skin with her fingernail. I suck in a breath and close my eyes, rocking forward toward her touch.

"It's amazing," she whispers, and her warm breath glides across the tip of my cock, turning the throb into a full-on ache. "Can you feel it?"

"My cock?" I ask, tangling my fingers in her hair and praying for a little mouth action.

"No, the piercing. Does it feel different?"

"It'll pull a little when I'm in you, but you'll feel more than I will because of it."

She glances up, lips parted. "I'll feel it?"

"Wanna find out?" I waggle my eyebrows, hoping the show-and-tell portion of the evening is over.

She licks her lips, and my knees go weak. She grabs on to my ass with one hand, digging her fingernails in, and steadies me like she knew I was about to go down. "It's so..." She moves closer, and I can feel the heat of her skin. "So shiny."

I don't care if she thinks it's blazing like the Statue of Liberty on the Fourth of July, as long as it makes her happy and doesn't scare her away. Between the size of my cock and the piercing, I've had more than one woman walk out the door practically in tears.

"Touch it again," I tell her. "Explore all you want." I'm being an asshole, but God, I'm so horny I'm on the verge of pulling her off the floor, tearing off her jeans, and ramming my dick into her warm, wet pussy.

She leans forward, and I hold my breath and squeeze my eyes shut. I can't watch. I can't move. I'm too turned on to do anything but stand here, waiting for the moment her...

Fuck. Her tongue tugs at the piercing, and shock waves radiate through my system. Every muscle in my body tightens, and for a second, I can't breathe. When her lips close around the head, colors explode behind my eyelids, making me think I found heaven on earth. I'm so turned on, I know I won't last long, and I don't want this to end before we have a chance to really get going.

I grab her shoulders, hauling her up from the floor, and instantly, I miss the warmth of her mouth as her lips slide off the tip. "I need to taste you," I tell her and lift her shirt upward.

She raises her arms as the material easily slides over her head, exposing a white lace bra and a perfect set of tits. My mouth waters. My hands itch to feel their weight in my palms, but I want to explore her with my mouth and have her begging for my cock.

I slide her bra straps down her arms as she stares at me, barely breathing. She moves her hands in front of her stomach and grimaces.

"What's wrong?" I ask, seeing nothing but perfection.

"I have stretch marks." She closes her eyes, and I cradle her face, wanting her to know how I feel.

"Baby, look at me," I say, waiting for her to open her eyes. "I see nothing but a playground built for me. Don't hide what I'm dying to explore."

I fall to my knees and push her hands out of the way, exposing the tiny lines across her belly. The very lines that once held Lulu deep inside her. They're not scars, but a badge of honor…a reminder she gave someone life. "They're beautiful," I say as I lean forward and kiss the edge of the largest line.

She tangles her fingers in the top of my hair and sighs. "You don't hate them?"

My lips glide across her stomach, following the lines as I moan my appreciation for the softness of her skin. She's perfection no matter what's on her skin. "They're like my tattoos," I tell her, my head level with her stomach, but looking up into her blue eyes. "They're a reminder of a life experience. They mean something. They're not scars. They're life."

She doesn't move to cover them again as I run my tongue across her skin this time, tasting the saltiness of her skin and smelling her need. Unable to wait any longer, I unbutton her pants, and she lifts up as I pull them downward along with her panties before tossing them both across the room.

She's nervous. I can see it in her eyes. "Say you want me," I tell her, needing to hear the words from her lips once more.

"I want you, Lucio," she says, clear as day.

I pull her forward, sitting her ass on the edge of the

counter and giving me the perfect view of her beautiful, glistening pussy. She leans back, resting her palms on the countertop, readying herself.

Reaching up, I palm her breast, wishing I had more time, but I know what she needs and how to make her feel good. My thumb brushes against her nipple, and she pushes her chest into my touch.

My mouth waters, and I lick my lips. There's nothing more beautiful than a naked and needy Delilah. I lean forward, placing my head between her legs, close enough that she can feel my warm breath moving across her skin.

She rocks forward, silently pleading for my mouth. I give her what she wants, dragging my tongue through her lips, capturing her wetness on the tip. "So fucking sweet," I say, causing her to moan.

My fingers tug on her nipple as I bury my face between her legs, sucking her clit into my mouth. The salty sweetness of her explodes across my tongue and makes my cock even harder than it was before. The way she moans my name as the tip of my tongue flicks against her spurs me on.

I devour her skin, lavishing her most needy part with every bit of my mouth until her fingers curl around the edge of the counter and she grinds her cunt against my face. She's moaning, screaming, as her body quakes in pleasure.

"Fuck!" she shouts and throws her head backward, jutting her tits out more.

I don't let up. Don't stop sucking until she's limp and gasping for air.

"Jesus." She licks her lips with her eyes still closed.

I give her pussy another kiss before making my way up her body, positioning my cock between her legs.

"Condom," she says as her eyes fly open.

"Of course," I tell her, fishing one out of the drawer next to us. She looks at me funny but doesn't ask me why on God's green earth I keep condoms in the kitchen.

I rip open the package with my teeth before cautiously pushing it over the tip of my cock, careful not to catch the latex on my piercing. She grabs my face, crashing her lips to mine, ending all conversation. When she spreads her legs and presses her ankles into my ass, I know I have permission to bury myself deep inside of her.

Her legs tighten as I slip the tip of my cock along with the piercing inside her. She moans into my mouth, and I swear my eyes almost roll backward. I take it slow, moving a little deeper with each thrust until she's pushing me forward and grinding into me.

Then I'm buried deep inside her, and I know I'll never be the same again.

CHAPTER
THIRTEEN
DELILAH

"ARE YOU FEELING BETTER TODAY, my dear?" Betty asks as she takes Lulu from my arms before I'm even three steps into the kitchen of her apartment.

"I am. Thank you."

Better doesn't even begin to describe how I feel. Waking up next to Lucio, tangled in a pile of sheets and limbs makes me feel more than better... I feel like a new woman.

"I was worried about you after your father stopped by." She motions for me to sit, and I do without hesitation because I'm not crazy enough to argue with her. "Even though you handled him like a pro, I wanted to make sure you're okay."

"I've had a lifetime of practice."

I thought I'd wake up this morning feeling awful about everything that happened, but I don't. For the first time in a long time, I'm hopeful. There's a new sense of freedom I've never felt before. I'm no longer walking on eggshells, waiting for the next drunk tirade from my father.

She sits across from me, rocking Lulu back and forth. "If you don't mind my asking, why did you stay so long?"

I lean back in my chair, trying to figure out why I did stay as long as I did. "I've asked myself that very question a million times."

"We all do what we feel is right at the time, sweetheart. Don't be too hard on yourself."

"I didn't want to abandon him like my mother did to both of us. At first, I was too young to leave. And then I stayed with him through college because I was barely ever home anyway, so it didn't matter. He still got drunk, but I couldn't be his whipping girl if I wasn't around."

She nods her head but stays silent, listening to me spill my guts. The look on her face isn't judgmental, and I'm comfortable talking to her. She's been nothing but gracious and kind, treating me better than anyone in my family ever has. So, I keep going, figuring I could use a little motherly advice on where I go now and if I'm headed in the right direction.

"When I found out I was pregnant with Lulu, my father promised he'd change if I'd only stay with him to raise his granddaughter. He remained sober through my entire pregnancy, going to every doctor's appointment with me after Lulu's father took off."

Betty gasps. "He just left?"

I nod. "I haven't seen him since, and he's never even tried to contact me. Dwight is no better than my father, but at least he gave me a beautiful daughter out of the situation and has left me in peace."

"She's a dream," Betty says as she leans forward to kiss Lulu's head. "This baby girl deserves all the love and kisses."

I smile and keep talking so I don't start crying over all the love Lulu's missed out on already. "For a few months after she was born, my dad kept up his sobriety. But slowly, one drink turned into two, and then he'd down an entire bottle. Somehow, his temper didn't return with the drinking like it had before. Not at first, but over the last week before he kicked me out, he became more aggressive and rarely had a sober moment."

"Did something change?" she asks.

"Yeah." I pause and chew on my bottom lip, remembering the job offer in California for the first time in days.

"How about some tea?" she asks before I can answer.

"I'd love some," I tell her and stop myself from asking for whiskey instead.

I could use a drink, but I've never let myself use alcohol as a crutch or to relieve stress. I didn't want to end up like my father, and I knew enough about alcoholism to know, typically, it is passed on through genetics.

She carries Lulu on one hip like she's been doing it a lifetime, grabbing the teapot and filling it with one hand. "We don't have to talk about it anymore," she says as she turns the stove on, and the flame licks the bottom of the pot.

"I'm fine. I want to talk about it."

"I never want to make you uncomfortable."

"You have never done anything but make me feel welcome and comfortable, Betty."

She leans against the countertop, and Lulu grabs at her pearls. "We love having you here."

"I took Lulu out of town for a few days for a job interview on the West Coast."

"Oh." Her eyebrows shoot up, and I know the information is something I haven't shared before. Betty seems to have grand plans for Lucio and me. While I like the idea, and could probably be happy here forever, I'm not sure we'll work out in the long run.

"Anyway, after we left, he started drinking more and more. He'd call at all hours of the night, yelling and cursing me for leaving him." I blow out a breath, still hearing the scathing words my father strung together over the phone echoing in my ears. "The day before we were scheduled to come back, he went to a meeting and promised he'd get his life back together."

"People make grand promises when their backs are

against the wall, but they never seem to remember to follow through during the small moments. Those matter the most," she tells me.

"They do." I nod. "When he picked us up from the airport after a long flight, I didn't think he was drunk, or I never would've gotten in the car with him. But after a few blocks of him swerving, I knew he was too drunk to drive. He couldn't even keep his promise for twenty-four hours and pick us up sober."

"I'm sorry, dear."

I wish my father could be half the person Betty Gallo is. Even on his best day, he couldn't hold a candle to her love and charm.

"He didn't just put our lives in danger that night, he cleaned out my bank accounts and cut me off completely."

She lifts the teapot, removing it from the hot burner and placing it on a cool one as soon as it whistles. "Earl Grey?" she asks, and I nod. Using one hand, she carries two teacups with little pink flowers around the rim and sets them down on the table before grabbing the pot along with two tea bags. "Would you like cream and sugar?"

"If you're having it, yes." I've never been a tea drinker and I'm not sure what proper etiquette is when sipping tea, but I'll follow Betty's lead.

"So, what about the job on the West Coast?" she asks as she pours the hot water in the cups, watching me as she does.

"I was offered a position at an entertainment company. It's entry-level, but perfect for someone like me. I can't take it, though."

"Why not?" She plops two cubes of sugar in my cup along with a splash of milk before doing the same to hers, but her eyes are on me and I feel the weight of her stare.

I tug on the tea bag, waiting for her to sit before I continue. Lulu's too busy playing with Betty's necklace to care that I'm in the same room. It's nice to have someone else she's comfortable with because, any other time, she doesn't want to leave my arms. "Without the money I had in the bank, I can't afford to make the move and earn the small salary they were going to give me to start."

She tilts her head to the side. "Is that the only reason?"

I frown and peer down at my tea. "I don't know, Betty."

"What about my son?" she asks.

"He's kind of great," I say and can't stop the goofy smile from spreading across my face.

She places her hand over mine. "He really likes you, Delilah. I know Lucio's heart, and it's the biggest of all my children. Sometimes he's hard to read, but when he loves, he loves deep."

"I've never had someone treat me the way he does," I admit.

Before I left California, I wanted to take the job, but something had stopped me. I asked for a little time to think over their offer, and they agreed, giving me one week to make my final decision. The only reason I applied was to get as far away from my father as possible, and now that he's out of the picture, I can't imagine uprooting my life and moving clear across the country.

"Lucio has never fallen in love. He's been so scared he'd be like his father that he wouldn't open his heart, but he's different around you."

"You're not the first person to say that to me."

"Angelo?" she guesses.

"Yeah."

"He's the only one of my kids to have already fallen in love, but when his wife died, I think it scared everyone. My relationship with Santino already had them skeptical. But after Angelo found someone who made him happy and she passed away, no one wanted to put themselves out there."

"Do you regret being with Santino?" I ask even though it's none of my business.

She sighs as she sets down her teacup. "No. Even though our love wasn't always easy, there has never been a time when I regretted being with him. How could I?" She cradles Lulu in her arms, rocking her gently. "He gave me four wonderful children."

"Were there moments when you wanted to leave?"

"Sure. I think there's a point in every relationship when people could walk away. Sometimes it's easier than fixing what's wrong and building a stronger foundation."

"But he's in prison, right?" I grimace as soon as the words leave my mouth. "It's none of my business."

"Santino is in prison for a little while longer, but I never thought about leaving him for that or the long, drawn-out trial that was splashed across every newscast and paper in the city."

Suddenly, I put two and two together, realizing why the name Gallo sounded so familiar. The trial of Santino Gallo was one of the biggest news stories a few years ago. Many people in Chicago claimed organized crime was dead and there was no such thing as the mafia, but after Santino's arrest, they could no longer make the same statement.

"I remember now," I tell her, and my face heats. "I'm sorry."

"Santino did the crime, and now he has to do the time. He knew what could happen, leading the life he did. I turned a blind eye to his business dealings, but I never let him slide when it came to his extracurricular activities."

"Lucio mentioned that."

"There's so much my children don't know. They think I was complacent with his behavior when I wasn't. For a long time, I believed Santino was faithful. No one wants to think otherwise. But I wasn't a fool either. I'd smell the cheap perfume on his clothes when he came home at night. I got sick of it and took matters into my own hands." She laughs, and there's nothing sweet about it.

"Yeah?"

She nods with a smirk. "He knew if he wanted to keep his vital organs, he'd leave the broads in the past and learn to be a faithful partner. I wouldn't leave him, but I wasn't above torturing him. He knows my temper better than anyone, and he came to his senses after a little convincing."

"Convincing?" I swallow, almost choking on the word. I'm not sure I want to know the lengths Betty would go to in order to rein her man in.

She pats my hand, still laughing. "It's best if some things stay a secret, dear."

"I think you're right," I whisper. "You're an amazing person, Betty."

"Delilah, if you want to go to California, we'll understand," she tells me, but while I feel she's being sincere, I don't hear the conviction in her voice.

"You would?"

"I wouldn't be happy, but I'd let you go. I'd love to see you with my son and sitting around my dinner table with this bundle of joy every week. But you need to do what's best for you and your little one."

"Betty," I tell her, covering her hand with mine and squeezing. "To be honest, I've never felt more complete and content than I do here with Lucio, you, and the entire family."

My words bring the smile back to her face. "Does he know?"

I shake my head, because I didn't really know until I just said the words. "I don't think so."

"If you want to love my son, love him fiercely, but don't wait too long to tell him."

"Don't you think it's a little soon for me to love a man I barely know?"

She laughs softly and shakes her head. "I knew Santino

much of my life, but we were never more than acquaintances, growing up on the same block. He was older and I always knew he was a player, but after one kiss, he asked me to marry him."

"Really?"

"I told him he was crazy, but every night, he'd come to my house, crawl onto the roof of my parents' front porch, and knock on my window to ask me again."

"And you said yes?"

"After thirty nights and not a single date, I said I'd move in with him."

"Move in with him?" My mouth falls open. "Why didn't you marry him?"

"I knew marriage wasn't for me. I don't know." She shrugs.

"But you have the last name Gallo."

"I went to court and had my last name changed. I wanted the same name as my children."

"Why not just marry him?"

"His business was complicated. We knew he'd eventually get caught—everyone always does—and this was the best way for me to protect what's mine."

"Will you ever marry him?"

"Maybe. As we get older, I do regret not being his legal wife."

"Well, it's not too late," I tell her, trying to picture her in a wedding dress. "He sounds like he's romantic. He swept you off your feet."

"I was young and stupid back then. But every day, I'd wait for the sun to set so Santino would come to my window. Nothing else mattered. I couldn't even look at another man because I was so smitten."

"So, you kissed him, and that was enough?"

"He was relentless in his pursuit of me. No one else went

to the lengths he did. It didn't matter how many times I said no, he wasn't going to give up. He was foolish and so was I, but sometimes our heart wants what it wants. There's no rhyme or reason to any of it. You can't overthink love, baby. You just got to jump."

CHAPTER
FOURTEEN
LUCIO

"PLEASE, LUCIO." Daphne begs me for permission like it's mine to give.

"Why are you asking me?"

Although I hate the idea of Delilah going out to a bar with God knows who hitting on her, I have no right to say no. She could use a break from me and everything that's happened.

"Someone has to watch the baby," Daphne says, batting her eyelashes at me because she knows I'm a sucker.

I point to myself, drawing my eyebrows down. "You want me to babysit?"

"Well, duh." Daphne rolls her eyes. "Do it for Delilah," she tells me, knowing I can't say no when she puts it that way.

"I don't like this," I tell her and rub the base of my hands into my eyes.

"No strippers." She uncrosses her fingers and shows them to me like the childish gesture means a damn thing. "I promise."

"I'm trusting you, Daphne."

"Come on now. I know you love this girl. I won't do anything to mess that up."

"Fine, fine. I'll watch the baby. Just don't have too much fun."

Daphne throws her arms around me, peppering my face with sloppy kisses. She knows I hate when she does that, but she doesn't stop. "You won't regret this," she tells me, but I already do.

"You're sure about this?" Delilah asks for the fifth time as she slips on the high heels Daphne let her borrow. She's leaning over the couch with her cleavage on full display, but only because of her current position. Her outfit is tasteful, which is surprising because Daphne gave her the dress. I never would've thought my sister had something that didn't reveal too much skin, but somehow, Delilah found the only such dress in my sister's closet.

"We'll be fine," I tell her, not really answering the question. I'm not sure about the entire thing. Spending the night with Lulu should be easy, but imagining what's happening at the bar is a different story. "Go and have some fun."

At least she's going with Daphne. My sister knows how I feel about Delilah and hopefully will have my back, not letting anything get out of control.

Delilah gives me a quick kiss as she reaches for her purse, but I don't let her get away so easily. I wrap my arm around her back, hauling her body against mine and crash my lips down against hers. I want her to feel my kiss all night, remembering who's waiting at home for her.

Maybe it's a dick move, but in that moment, I don't care. I've slept with dozens of women and never cared what they did afterward, but Delilah's different. The thought of another man touching her makes my skin crawl and sends my temper into overdrive.

When I pull away, her eyes are still closed, and her lips parted. "I'll wait for you," I say.

She blinks slowly and licks her lips, making me want another taste. "I won't be late."

Daphne walks into my place without so much as a knock. Much like she did when we were kids. She never cared much for boundaries or privacy, unless it was her own being stepped on. "Ready?" she asks in the most annoying and cheery voice. "Don't want to keep the others waiting."

"Others?" I ask as my stomach knots.

"Michelle's coming and a few other girls from the neighborhood."

"Like who?"

"Colleen and Carmen," Daphne says, glancing around the room because she knows I'm not going to be happy.

Fuck. More than half the women going out together I've slept with. This could be a complete shitshow and the end to Delilah and me. I wasn't a saint. I never claimed to be, but no woman wants to come face-to-face with someone their partner has shared a bed with.

"Maybe you should stay in." I pull Delilah backward before she gets too close to the doorway.

"Don't be an asshole. She's coming. She already knows about Colleen and Carmen."

"You do?" I squeeze my eyes shut for a moment and groan.

"There's nothing to be sorry about, Lucio. We all have a past," Delilah says with an easy smile. "I don't care what you did before I got here. I'm sure it'll be fun."

Fun isn't the word I'd use to describe the conversation that will no doubt be taking place tonight. I'll be the main topic and won't be there to defend myself. Although Colleen and Carmen are nice and hella good in bed, I didn't give either of them the relationship they both begged for in the end.

"Have fun, but not too much," I tell her.

"I've never been drunk, remember?" She places her hand on my chest, peering up at me with her baby blue eyes. "Don't worry so much."

I give her a soft kiss, and my sister grunts, practically gagging behind us. "Let's go," Daphne says, tapping her foot against the marble tile in the entryway. "We're wasting precious time."

"Bye," Delilah whispers, holding my hand as long as possible as Daphne starts to pull her out the door.

When they're gone, I look around the house, rubbing the back of my neck and wondering what I'm going to do with my night off. A few weeks ago, I would've called any number in my contacts, finding some hottie to spend a few hours with to pass the time, but with Delilah around, that's a no go.

I collapse onto the couch, keeping the volume low enough so I can hear Lulu in case she starts crying. I never thought this would be my life, at least not without doing the marriage thing first.

I flip through the channels, surf the internet on my phone, and grow so freaking bored I text a few of the guys and invite them over for beer and pizza. They quickly remind me that they're out for the night, busy living the life I'd been taking part in up until a week ago.

My life before Delilah wasn't better. I have already grown used to hearing her pad around the upstairs apartment and the tiny cries and giggles of Lulu I hear even from my bedroom. I never realized how empty my life was until she came into it.

But I wouldn't change a damn thing. That's the funniest part. I loved my life before Delilah walked into the bar. There wasn't a part I didn't enjoy the fuck out of either. But now, all I want to do is spend the night eating pizza on the floor with Delilah and Lulu. Nothing sounds as perfect or as sweet as something that simple.

Just when I start feeling the weight of the silence in the house, Lulu begins to cry in the other room. I rush in and pluck her tiny body from the crib.

"Hey, doll," I whisper, rocking her in my arms as I hold her tightly against my chest. "Don't cry, baby girl. I got you."

I spend the next twenty minutes heating a bottle and watching Lulu as she sucks down every drop like she's never eaten before. I don't know where she puts it, but I'm quickly reminded when she spits up all over the back of my shirt.

"I still haven't learned."

Based on the smile on her face, she's happy with the way the evening is turning out. There's not much I can do with an infant, so I do the only thing I can think of, throw on some cartoons and stare at the clock.

"Yo," Angelo says, walking through the front door just like Daphne. "I was heading home from the bar and saw your light on. Thought I'd stop in and check on you."

"I don't know how you did this alone, man." I shake my head. I've been with Lulu for only a short time, and I can't imagine handling two kids, nonstop, day after day, with no end in sight. My brother makes everything seem easy, and even through his grief, he's never once complained.

"There's nothing easy about it, and without Marissa, everything is harder." He plops down on my couch, in no hurry to leave. "But I thank God for the month in the summer when her parents take the kids. I need the time to recharge and feel human again."

"Have you thought about dating again?" I ask, still standing because I'm covered in Lulu's sour milk. We've had the conversation more than once, and he's always quick to change the subject.

He rubs his forehead, clearly hating this conversation. "I don't think it's fair to the kids."

"Angelo, don't be ridiculous. You can't hide behind those kids forever."

He juts out his chin, and I know he's about to say something shitty. "And what are you hiding behind?"

Bingo. He's always turning the tables, trying to draw the attention away from himself, but I won't let him this time. "They deserve two parents."

"Lucio, I know you think you know best, but you don't quite understand what it means to be a parent."

"Enlighten me, then."

He stands and takes Lulu from my arms. "Go shower. You smell like shit. And then we'll talk."

I don't argue. With Delilah gone and Lulu not on a regular schedule, I don't know another time I'll be able to shower without someone else to watch the little squirt. "I'll be out in five."

"Take your time," he calls out before I disappear into my bathroom and think about the question my brother asked me.

What was I hiding behind?

———

"Figure it out, Einstein?" Angelo asks as soon as I walk back into the room. "What are you hiding behind?"

For a moment, I feel like I can conquer the world again with all remnants of baby vomit removed from my body. But it's short-lived as soon as Angelo starts playing twenty questions.

"I always thought you were a pussy," he says with a cocky smirk on his face because he knows just what to say to get me going.

"I'm not a pussy," I tell him as I plop down on the couch next to him and pull Lulu from his arms. "You know Dad was an asshole when we were kids, and I don't want to be like him." I pause for a minute and look down at Lulu as she wraps her tiny hand around my finger. "Look at this kid. Am I really a father figure?"

"Did you think I would be?" he replies quickly, raising a single eyebrow.

"You know you're a great dad." Angelo's like Super Dad. If there were a medal given out for that type of shit, he'd get first place. There isn't a thing he wouldn't do for his kids, and somehow, he's managed to keep them alive and thriving even after losing Marissa. I'm not so sure I could've done the same in his shoes.

"Maybe I should be with Delilah. We both have kids. We can make our own Brady Bunch-type family. It'll be perfect."

I stand quickly, pointing toward the door with Lulu in my other arm. "Get the hell out!"

Angelo laughs and shakes his head as he stands. "You got it bad, brother. Make her yours. Stop thinking, and just act for once. Let your heart do the talking." He pats me on the chest before he steps away. "But don't wait too long. I'm sure I won't be the only guy to try to take her off your hands."

"Fuck off, Angelo," I mumble as he walks out the front door. I can still hear his laughter as he jogs down the front steps and onto the sidewalk.

"No one's taking you," I tell Lulu, and she smiles, pulling at my cheeks. "Your momma and you were meant to be with me."

CHAPTER FIFTEEN

DELILAH

IT'S after three a.m. by the time I stumble to the front of the house. I'm drunk. So drunk I'm almost seeing double and can barely feel my legs as I make my way up the stairs.

I turn and wave at Daphne, Michelle, Carmen, and Colleen as they wait on the sidewalk, making sure I can actually make it inside on my own. They were taking bets on how many times I'd fall in my high heels because they had to hold me upright for the last two blocks.

I want to hate them for laughing at me, but I like them, even if they didn't warn me that a Long Island Iced Tea didn't really have any tea in it at all.

"Bye!" I yell, waving and leaning against the front door for a little support.

"Bye, girl. Don't do anything we wouldn't do!" Michelle yells back, and all the girls giggle.

"Or haven't done." Carmen reminds me of the fact that she's slept with Lucio. I can't even hate her for it. She explained it was years ago, just after high school, and he wasn't all that good, but she was sure he'd argue that point.

"Jesus," I mutter as I try to focus on the handle and take a deep breath. I can pull this off. I can pretend to be sober, right?

I nearly trip over the threshold but catch myself on the doorframe, nearly slamming the door into the back wall. "Shh," I tell it and hiccup through the laughter.

I lean over, holding the door handle to stay as steady as possible, and pull off my high heels. The lights are off, but there's enough of a glow from the television for me to make my way through the living room without knocking over any furniture.

Peeking over the back of the couch, I see Lucio asleep with Lulu sprawled out across his massive chest. Her tiny cheek is resting in between his pecs, drool running down the side of her face and pooling against his skin.

Holding on to the arm of the couch, I make my way to the wooden coffee table and sit. I blink a few times and wait for the room to stop spinning as I rest my chin in my palm and my elbow on my knee.

The way he's holding her with his hand against her back, making sure she doesn't slip or move, brings a smile to my face and tears to my eyes. I find it hard to believe Lucio doesn't think he'd be a good father. He's been more than amazing with Lulu, and tonight is proof.

Her little leg twitches, and I hold my breath, trying hard not to wake either of them. I wish I had a camera to capture this moment forever, but I still haven't replaced my cell phone. Lulu stills for a moment before her hands flatten and her tiny fingernails bite into his skin.

He doesn't open his eyes as he removes her claws from his chest with one hand and rubs her back in small, soft circles with the other. I can't stop staring at the way he loves my daughter. I want that type of love for her. I want her to have something I never did, a man who will always put her first.

Lucio could be that guy. He may not believe in himself, but I do. Daphne made it quite clear tonight that her brother has feelings for me, but she didn't tell me anything I didn't already know. She told me, no matter what I hear, to remember he's the most loyal guy she knows. No one would fight harder or defend me stronger than her brother. Part of the night, I felt she was pitching me on all the reasons I should love her brother, but I didn't need her input to know how I already felt.

"You're home," he says softly as I wipe away my tears. "What's wrong?" He reaches out and touches my knee, leaving Lulu balancing on his chest.

I shake my head and bite my lip, wishing the tears would stop streaming down my face. I'm acting like a fool, and the alcohol isn't helping. "Nothing," I whisper and place my hand over his. "I'm just so…"

"So, help me God," he says, placing his other hand under Lulu's bottom as he sits up.

"No. Nothing happened. I'm just so happy," I tell him, waving my hands around because I know I must seem foolish. "Coming home and finding the two of you snuggled on the couch, I realize all the things we've missed."

"Baby." He touches my cheek, wiping away a few tears with his thumb. "I like seeing you happy."

I turn my face, capturing the pad of his thumb between my teeth, suddenly overcome with need. "I want you," I murmur against his skin. "I need you."

His lips part and his eyes close as I pull his finger into my mouth and suck hard, twirling my tongue around it like I've done with his cock. He sways back and forth as his breathing grows more ragged and labored with each passing second. "The kid," he says like I forgot he's holding Lulu.

"Upstairs," I say around his thumb and waggle my eyebrows because I'm more than ready to put my daughter down and get busy taking Lucio to bed.

He groans as he pulls his finger from my lips, and I suck harder, teasing him as much as possible. He's on his feet, almost gliding up the stairs as he takes them two at a time. I'm not as fast, the alcohol still working through my system. I hold on to the railing, swaying just like Lucio had on every step, but somehow, I don't fall backward.

He's waiting for me, having already put Lulu down, watching with a mix of laughter and horror as I make my way to the landing. Before I get my feet flat on the floor, he scoops me into his arms and stalks toward the bedroom.

"Eager little beaver, aren't you?" I snort because I'm a drunken idiot.

"You got the eager beaver, baby." He laughs. "Greedy thing too."

"It's that damn piercing," I say and try to reach down and grab his dick.

He shakes his head, probably wondering what the hell got into me, but I'm sure it's pretty obvious. Any type of shyness or worry I had about sleeping with Lucio again has vanished. Thanks to the Long Islands, I don't care about anything other than feeling his cock buried so deep inside me I can't even breathe.

"You like it that deep?" he asks as he sets me down on the bed and slips the spaghetti straps of the dress down my arms.

"Did I say that out loud?" I'm momentarily horrified, but I forget everything as soon as his lips close around my nipple.

He pushes me backward and hovers over me, holding himself up with his thick, muscular arms. I tangle my fingers in his hair and hold him against my skin. God, his tongue is like magic, sliding across my breast and bringing me one step closer to heaven.

I hum my approval, hoping this feeling never ends. When he starts to move down my body, I pull him back up by his hair and look him straight in the eye. It's like I'm possessed by a sassy version of myself. "Don't," I tell him, and his eyebrows draw downward. "I don't want your mouth. I want your cock."

He gives me a smug smile and climbs back up my body. "You like the piercing, don't you?"

"I like your dick, Lucio. Pierced or not, it's all I want." I don't know where the words are coming from, but he seems to enjoy this side of me because his smile grows.

He pushes himself up and stands at the foot of the bed. All I can do is watch as he shoves down his shorts, revealing that perfectly straight cock with the shiny tip. If I hadn't drunk so damn much, I'd crawl down there and use my tongue to tease him, but I'm not sure I could pull it off without falling off the bed.

"Fuck me," I say instead, hoping it's enough.

"You don't gotta ask me twice." He leans over and grabs his wallet as his cock bobs like it's doing a dance of pure joy.

"How deep you want it, baby?" he asks as he tears open the condom and slides it down his shaft.

"Deep." I barely get the words out because the throbbing between my legs is so intense I'm not sure I won't orgasm as soon as his body slides against mine.

He crawls between my legs, placing the tip of his glorious cock against my pussy, and hovers above me again. He slips his hand between my legs and touches my clit, causing my ass to rise off the bed and shock waves to shoot across my body.

"So wet," he says, telling me something I already know.

"Fuck me, Lucio. Fuck me hard."

I don't have to ask again. He thrusts deep in one push, stealing every ounce of breath in my lungs. He grinds his hips, hitting every inch of my insides before pulling out. "Like that?" he asks, toying with me.

"Harder," I tell him, wanting more. Needing more.

He leans forward and closes his lips around my nipple as he slams into me, pushing me up the bed a little. I scream out with nothing but joy and pleasure coursing through my veins.

His deep green eyes bore into me. "You're mine, Delilah."

"Yes!" I cry out. His words wash over me, sending tiny sparks throughout my body.

"Only mine," he tells me, driving the point home as he pumps into me.

No one's ever kissed me like him. No one's ever fucked me like him. And Lord help me, I never want another man again.

CHAPTER SIXTEEN

LUCIO

WHEN EVERYONE'S left the room, Angelo finally decides to speak to me. "Did you lock it in?"

I look at Angelo funny. "What?"

"Delilah, dumbass. Did you lock her down?"

"You can put your dick back in your pants. She's mine, bro," I tell him, pointing my finger right at his face.

"Good," he says with a big smile. "Maybe you're not as foolish as I thought you were."

I lean back, throwing my arm on top of the chairback next to me. "I'm never foolish when it comes to women."

"Wait." He pauses and narrows his eyes. "Did you have an actual conversation with her about your relationship, or did you just fuck her?"

"I told her."

"Smooth." He shakes his head and glances up at the ceiling.

"Well, we're not in high school anymore. What was I supposed to say to her? 'Delilah, would you wear my class ring?'" I wave him and his silliness off. "Get out of here with that bullshit."

"Make sure there's no doubt in her mind."

"Did I miss the memo that we're back in the fifties?"

"Listen." He leans forward, resting his hands flat on the table and looking at me with one of the most serious faces I've ever seen on him. "I'm telling you this because I love you. I know what it's like to love a woman—and to lose one too."

It's hard for me not to listen after he makes a statement like that. I loved his wife from the day I met her. She was the best woman I'd ever known and the perfect match for my brother. We were all devasted by her death, but no one more than him. I watched my brother's easy, carefree attitude turn serious and sometimes sour. It's hard to stay happy when the one person who brought you the most joy disappears.

"I'm listening," I tell him, being respectful because he's been through more in the last few years than I have in my entire lifetime.

"You can't just tell a woman she's yours. I'm sure that's the dumb-ass shit you did. You need her to know you're hers too. She needs to understand there won't be another Carmen or Colleen."

"You heard about that?"

"Daphne has some balls on her." He scrubs his hand down his face and shakes his head. "I've already had the talk with her."

"How'd that go?"

He laughs and shrugs. "How do you think?"

"Well, I don't see any claw marks."

"What are we talking about?" Vinnie asks, walking in the room before plopping down in the chair next to Angelo.

"Women," I say.

He suddenly perks up and sets his phone down. "About Delilah?"

"Yeah." I nod.

"Did you lock it down?" Vinnie asks, sounding just like Angelo.

"What is this? Now you two are talking the same."

Vinnie looks at Angelo, and they both shrug.

"You lock it down with any of those girls you're always messaging?" I ask, putting some of the pressure on him instead of focusing only on me.

"I have them all on lockdown, Luc."

My eyes widen, and so do Angelo's. "All of them?" he asks, turning toward our youngest brother, staring at him like he has three heads.

"I don't want them with any other guys."

"Dude—" Angelo smacks him in the chest "—that isn't cool."

"Hey, don't hate the player."

We both roll our eyes at the little egotistical asshole who takes pride in stringing girls along. "How does that work?" I rub my forehead, trying to figure out the logistics of the entire situation he's put himself in. "I mean, you have to get caught eventually. Then what?"

Vinnie smiles proudly. "I never say I'm committing to them. I just let them know they're mine and no one else's."

Angelo points at Vinnie, but he's looking at me. "This is what I'm talking about."

"I get it. I get it," I tell him and realize the error I've made. "I'll lock her down."

"Speaking of lockdown," my mother says, startling the shit out of all of us as she walks in, "your father called yesterday." She sits down at the head of the table but doesn't say anything else.

"And?" Angelo rolls his hand in the air.

"He's been granted early release. He'll be home in a few months."

"That's amazing, Ma," Vinnie says, but Angelo and I aren't as overjoyed as my little brother.

"I've missed him," she says, looking back and forth

between Angelo and me. "I know you two have issues with your father, but I want you to bury that in the past."

I've never had issues with the man as a father, but as a partner, he treated my mother like garbage for too long for me to turn a blind eye to it. Angelo feels the same way, but Vinnie is too young to remember our father's shenanigans.

"We'll make it work," Angelo says quickly, knowing it'll make my mother happy, and always trying to keep the peace.

"There's another thing." She plays with the clean spoon still left on the table in front of her but doesn't look at any of us.

"We're listening," Vinnie says, a little too enthusiastically.

Angelo and I are staring at each other, knowing whatever she's about to say none of us is going to like. I ball my hand into a tight fist, hoping it'll be enough for me to keep my mouth shut. The last person in the world I want to piss off is my mother.

"As part of his parole, he'll need a job."

Angelo kicks me under the table, opting for using me as a punching bag instead of his own hand like I'd planned to do. I flinch and bite down on my tongue to stop myself from swearing after his size-twelve shoe smacks against my shin.

Ma looks at me, waiting for me to say anything, but I don't dare open my mouth. "I'd like you to hire him on at the bar to keep him in compliance. He received special permission from the parole board to live above and work in the bar."

"No problem, Ma," Vinnie tells her like he's the only one making the decision. He owns twenty-five percent of the business, and he's barely there, so his vote doesn't even count in anyone's book but his own.

"We'll talk to Daphne about it," Angelo tells her because he knows my answer will be no. "We can't say yes until we're able to talk it through."

"Talk with everyone, but I don't ask for much and I'm

asking for this favor," she states, letting us know that we better say yes, or there'll be hell to pay.

Either way, we're totally screwed.

———

I take Delilah by the hand after she puts Lulu in her crib. "Sit down, baby."

She moves slowly, touching the couch with one hand as she lowers herself onto the cushion. Her eyes never leave mine, and I can see the fear in them plain as day.

"It's nothing bad. I swear. We just gotta talk," I tell her as I touch her face to calm her nerves.

She smiles nervously, watching me with those beautiful blue eyes as I sit on the coffee table in front of her. "Is everything okay?" She fiddles with her long brown hair, wrapping the strands around the tip of her finger. "You're making my stomach hurt, Lucio."

"There was a lot going on last night, and you were drunk."

She covers her mouth and gasps. "Oh God. What did I do? Did I say something stupid?" She pulls at her bottom lip, and her eyes roam around the room. "I remember we had sex, but not much else."

I mentally slap myself because I realize my brother is right. I hadn't even thought about the fact that she was totally shit-faced when I told her she was mine. I thought by the time I told her, she'd sobered up enough she'd remember, but that was my mistake.

"Yeah, baby. We had a lot of sex. It was hot too." I smile.

She blushes. "Well, that's good to know, at least. If you're going to tell me you don't ever want to do it again."

I place my finger over her lips, stopping her from finishing that sentence. "I love you," I blurt out, laying my cards on the table.

"Say that again," she says against my finger before chewing on her bottom lip.

"I love you, Delilah Miles. I want to be yours and for you to be mine."

Her eyes fill with tears again. "Yeah?"

I reach out, cradling her face in my palms, and stare into her eyes so there's no question where my loyalty and love lies. "Yes. There's no one else for me. I only want you. I want Lulu. I want us."

"You're sure?" she asks, tears streaming down her face and her lip trembling.

"I know it's quick and crazy, but I've never been happier in my entire life. I want you here, by my side, in my bed, with me—forever." I scoot forward, leaving very little space between us until I can feel her warm breath skid across my face. "I want that little girl as my own. I want to shower her with love and be the father she needs. I don't want to be alone anymore, and I don't want you to ever be afraid of anything for the rest of your life."

Delilah throws herself into my arms, grabbing my face with her small hands and kisses me so hard I'm sure I'll have a bruise. "God, I love you," she murmurs against my lips. "So, so much." The words come out garbled because she's too busy kissing me to let me speak.

I pull her closer, wrapping my arms around her back, and tangle my hand in her hair. "You love the piercing," I tell her when she finally lets me up for a little air.

"It's a bonus." She says those words with a straight face. "But that's not the only reason. Kiss me again. Mark me," she says, and that's all I need to hear.

I grab her by the waist, flipping her over the edge of the couch and lifting her skirt to expose her beautiful ass. "I'm going to bury my cock so deep, you'll never forget I've been here," I say as I cup her bare pussy in my hands.

She peers over her shoulder with a wicked grin. "Who do I belong to?" she asks quietly.

"You're mine, sweetheart. Now and forever. I own this pretty little pussy as much as you own my cock."

"Forever," she repeats my words, and nothing has ever felt so right.

CHAPTER
SEVENTEEN
DELILAH

"HEY LADY," a woman says from table three, snapping her fingers in the air and looking me up and down like I'm a piece of trash.

I walk up to the table and smile, somehow keeping my composure even though I want to dump a glass of water over her head. "Can I get you something?" My voice is so sugary sweet and about an octave higher than normal.

She's chewing gum and popping it between her teeth in the least classy way I've ever witnessed. "We'd like another round." She runs her fingers through her black hair, catching her fingers a few inches away from her head in the tons of hairspray keeping the nest in place. She recovers well, pretending she meant to do it when she fluffs the bottom of the strands with her palms. "Can you handle that?" she asks when I don't reply right away.

"I can handle it," I tell her before repeating their earlier drink order back to them to make sure I remember. "Sound about right?"

"It's right," another woman at the table answers before the Aqua Net queen practically shoos me away.

I grumble under my breath, knowing these bimbos are

going to leave me a shit tip. If Angelo or Lucio were serving them, I'm sure they'd get more than a few bucks, but I can tell these women are going to be cheap because I don't flip their switch.

"What's wrong?" Lucio asks as I walk up to the bar, mumbling under my breath.

"Nothing." I give him a fake smile, pretending that my night is going amazingly well.

For the most part, it is. I've only spilled one drink. Thankfully, I was still at the bar when it happened and managed to keep the orders straight. I'd call it a victorious night in my book, except for some of the customers.

The men who have walked through the front door have been nice. Some were overly flirtatious, but I was able to shut them down pretty quickly. No one got handsy either, but the night is still young and the customers haven't consumed enough alcohol to get too aggressive. Besides the table of bitchy girls with their teased hair and long, fake nails, I've enjoyed mingling with the crowd at Hook & Hustle.

"I know that look," he says, studying my face closely. "You're upset about something."

"No. I'm fine. Everything's fine," I tell him.

"What's their order?" he asks, pointing his head toward the table of women currently gawking at him.

"Two Whiskey Sours, a Long Island Iced Tea, and a Screwdriver."

He grabs the empty glasses and starts to make their drinks, but he keeps looking at me, waiting for me to spill my guts. "They giving you shit?"

"Nope. I swear. I'm fabulous." I'm not telling him anything. I refuse to complain about a couple bitchy women. I'm sure they won't be the last group of classless hussies who walk through the door of Hook & Hustle.

He pushes their drinks forward, and I snatch them up, walking off like I've been doing this a lifetime. Carrying four drinks isn't hard, but resisting the urge to dump them over their heads is the bigger struggle.

"Who's the tall drink of water?" the gum-popper asks as soon as I set the drinks down on the table.

"The owner," I tell them before walking off, done talking to them. There's no point in being nice and overly friendly when they already hate me. The fact that they're staring at my man just adds to my level of agitation.

"Doll," a man says, wrapping his arm around my legs as I try to walk by. "Why don't you bring me something cold?"

I glare at him, my eyes going from his arm to his face and back again. "You better remove your hand if you want to keep it."

"Oh, I like'm feisty." He laughs. "I'll throw in an extra twenty if you bend over and show me your panties."

I smack his arm away and move out of arm's reach. I have my hand in the air, ready to slap him, when Lucio touches my arm.

"Out you go," he says, hauling the guy up by the collar of his shirt. "There's no touching the ladies."

The guy tries to twist out of Lucio's grip and swings at him, but Lucio's too fast and his arms are too long for the guy to connect.

"You ever come back in here again, you won't walk out on your own two feet." Lucio pushes the guy out the front door, kicking him in the ass at the very last second.

The room erupts into cheers, and Lucio bows to the right and then the left. Within seconds, the bar goes back to normal with loud voices talking about everything and anything as they drink.

I stalk toward him, a little upset because I don't want him to step in any time someone gets a little too touchy-feely with me. "I could've handled him," I tell Lucio with my hands on my hips.

I shouldn't be so upset. He saved me a lot of trouble, and

it was nice to have someone come to my rescue. But I wasn't sure Daphne or Michelle were given the same treatment. No way did I want to be treated any differently from the other girls at the bar.

"He was bigger than you."

"And?" I tap my foot, crossing my arms over my chest.

"What were you going to do with that hand? Slap him?" He raises an eyebrow.

"Of course."

"And then what would've happened if he hit you back?"

I blink a few times, thinking about what he just said. I never thought about someone actually coming back at me. I was defending myself, after all. "Well, I..."

"If he would've hit you, I would've murdered him right here in the middle of the bar. For your safety and my sanity, I took out the trash before this place became a crime scene."

"Thanks," I say slowly, changing my tune because I hadn't thought about how Lucio felt about the entire situation, or the fact that the guy could've cracked me back.

"If any man touches any of the ladies in this bar in an inappropriate way, they'll get the same treatment. Don't ever try to handle it yourself."

I nod, feeling a bit like a fool. I had become used to taking care of myself. Lord knows my dad was never there to rescue me from uncomfortable situations. Then there was Dwight, but besides being a bad lay, he was one of the biggest pussies I knew.

"Are you okay?" Lucio asks, following me behind the bar when I go to pour myself a little water.

"I'm fine, Lucio," I tell him. "I've handled assholes before. He didn't hurt me."

"But he could've," he reminds me again, driving the point home.

"I got it." I keep my back to him and guzzle down an entire glass of cold water before I face him again. "I'm sorry,"

I say after I've cooled down a bit. "I just want to make sure I'm treated no differently from anyone else."

He brushes my hair over my shoulder. "I can't help it if I treat you a little different, Delilah. I love you, and no one gets to touch you or be mean. I'll always step in to protect you."

"Give me a chance to handle things on my own first, okay?"

"I'll try."

"If I can't, I'll call you in as backup. Deal?"

He holds on to my arm for a few seconds, his green eyes searching mine. "Deal," he says before releasing me.

"I have to get back to my tables," I tell him with a sigh before heading back to work.

Aqua Net knocks into me as I make my way across the room. She doesn't say excuse me or even seem to notice that she almost makes me lose my balance. I turn, watching her as she stalks toward Lucio like a woman possessed.

A new couple sits down at my table near the window, and I try to give them my full attention. "Good evening. Welcome to Hook & Hustle. Do you know what you want, or would you like a few minutes?"

Somehow, I get the sentences out even though I can't stop looking toward the bar as Aqua Net primps her hair and applies another layer of lip gloss. She's a few feet away from Lucio, staring at him like he's her next victim.

"I'll take a pint of Guinness," the man says to me as I finally make eye contact. "She'll have a glass of Moscato."

"Anything else?" I ask, glancing over at the bar again.

"Peanuts or chips, if you've got them."

"Coming right up." I give them both a quick smile before marching toward the bar. But this time, I go to Daphne for the drinks.

"I need a Guinness and a Moscato," I tell her when she stops in front of me.

Aqua Net's talking to Lucio, tossing her petrified strands

behind her shoulder, shamelessly flirting with him. He's not smiling or laughing, but she seems to be enjoying herself.

Daphne follows my eyes and snaps her fingers in my face when she realizes who I'm staring at. "Ignore them," she tells me.

"She looks like she's about to jump his bones." My lip snarls out of reflex.

"Lucio isn't enjoying himself." She tips her head in their direction. "Look at him."

"That tramp hasn't been nice from the moment I waited on her, and now she's all over my man." I narrow my gaze, and I imagine myself grabbing her by the back of the hair and hauling her ass to the door like Lucio did to the scumbag.

Daphne places the two drinks on the bar and smiles at me. "I like this side of you."

"What side?" I glance at her for only a second, because if Aqua Net touches him...all bets are off.

"The bitchy, territorial side. If I didn't know better, I'd think you were born here." She laughs and smacks my arm. "I like it."

Lucio catches my gaze from across the room and smiles, giving me a little wink. Aqua Net turns to see who he's looking at, and her nostrils flare.

He says something to her and she turns around, but he isn't there for more than a few more seconds before he walks away. Aqua Net watches me as she walks back to her table and says something to her girls before picking up her purse.

I walk quickly, sliding their bill down on the table before they can walk out. They look every bit the type to leave without paying their tab.

"The guy said it's on the house," Aqua Net tells me with a straight face.

"He did not."

"Yeah. He did."

"Listen, lady. You owe the bar money and you're gonna pay up, or I'm calling the cops."

She looks me up and down, her lip curling at me in disgust. "I don't know who you think you are, talking to me like that, but I don't owe you anything."

"Just pay the bill, Jinny," her friend tells her, yanking on the side of her black leather coat.

Jinny swats the woman's hand away. "Fine, but the bitch isn't getting a tip."

I'm not even the least bit shocked. So instead of being upset, I give her my best smile and say, "It's okay, Jinny. I'm taking the owner home, and that's reward enough for a hard night of putting up with your bullshit."

Jinny's mouth falls open, and her head snaps backward. "I'm sure you're a lousy lay. He'll come to his senses eventually, and I'll be around to make sure he gets what he needs."

"He's not into bimbos, Aqua Net. Sorry to burst your bubble, but you'll never get that man. He's mine. Always will be. So you can move on to your next victim and spread your infection elsewhere."

She throws a twenty on the table and bares her teeth. "You're nothing more than a high-class cunt," she says, trying to wound me.

"He loves my cunt too," I tell her with an even bigger smile.

She stalks away, giving me the evil eye as she slams her hand against the door and walks outside. Her girlfriends follow, whispering to each other and looking at me over their shoulders.

"Wow." Daphne slaps my back. "Definitely a South Sider now. Those country-club folks would've had a stroke if they'd heard that shit coming out of your mouth."

"Fuck them," I say, but I'm not just talking about Jinny, I'm talking about all the people in my past. No longer am I anyone's doormat, and I never will be again.

"My girl," Daphne says and throws her arm around my shoulder. "It's worth coming out of my own pocket to pay the rest of their tab for that kind of entertainment."

"What happened?" Lucio asks, coming toward us with a concerned look.

"Delilah's got a mouth on her," Daphne tells him, laughing as she talks.

"I know." He winks, and I about die of embarrassment.

God, I love every person in this family, even his crazy-ass sister. I finally feel like I'm part of something bigger. Something more. Something lasting.

CHAPTER
EIGHTEEN
LUCIO

I'VE BEEN STANDING against the back wall, arms folded, watching the ticket counter move at an excruciatingly slow pace.

We'd already spent a few hours applying for a new Social Security card and getting a copy of her birth certificate, so she could get a new license. The DMV is my least favorite place, but it's unavoidable in Delilah's current situation.

She waited a few days, hoping her father would at least send her things so she wouldn't have to replace everything. But the bastard hadn't returned her purse or her money.

I'm fuming over the entire situation, but Delilah begged me to let her handle things. Me being me, I work in the background, trying to figure out how to get her money back along with all her stuff out of her father's penthouse.

My phone buzzes from the lawyer I contacted, a regular at Hook & Hustle, asking him to figure out a way to make her whole again, while avoiding court.

"The letter will be delivered today," Sal says without even so much as a hello.

"Thanks, Sal." I tick my chin at Delilah as she bounces Lulu in her lap, watching me. "I hope he comes to his senses."

"I'm fairly certain he'll want to remain out of the public eye and avoid court."

"If he has any brains, he'll do as you asked."

"He has no legal standing and will lose if we end up in court. But," he says, drawing the word out and lowering his voice, "you can probably convince him somehow if he drags his feet."

"Sal, I can't." I know where he's going with this. There's no way in hell I'm asking Johnny or any of my father's people to step in and strong-arm Delilah's father.

Not that he deserves better treatment, but I already promised Delilah I'd let her handle things. And shit would blow up in my face if Johnny used his special methods.

"The guy isn't going to want to go to court. He has a reputation to uphold, Sal. Just handle that shit."

"You got it. I'll contact you as soon as I hear from him or his lawyer."

"Thanks, Sal," I say, disconnecting the call because I know Sal isn't one to say goodbye. Drives me crazy too.

"What's wrong?" Delilah asks as she walks toward me with Lulu in her arms.

"Nothing, baby," I tell her as I pull her into my arms and have her lean against me. "Why don't we go shopping after this? I know you and Lulu could both use some of your own clothes."

"Lucio." She peers up at me and shakes her head. "I made forty-three dollars in tips last night. Forty-three. I'm not buying much with that amount of money."

"I have money."

She pulls away, sliding Lulu to her hip and staring at me. "I'm not letting you buy me clothes."

"I know you're not letting me, but I'm doing it anyway."

She narrows her eyes, and I ready myself for an argument, which I have no doubt I'll win. "I can't let you."

I tap her nose with my finger and smile. "You're cute, doll."

"I'm serious, Lucio," she says sternly, as if her mom voice has any effect on me.

"While you look hot in my sister's clothes, I don't think cutoff shorts, heavy metal T-shirts, and dresses cut so low you can almost breastfeed without actually moving the fabric aside is quite your style."

She glances down at the worn-out Metallica T-shirt and twists her lips. She knows I'm right. I can see by the look on her face she hates what she's wearing. "Only if I can pay you back."

I grab her waist and pull her forward again. "We'll add it to your tab."

"Number 156," a woman calls out.

"That's me," Delilah says, handing off Lulu to me before she sprints toward the counter, weaving through the sea of people.

"Does Lulu want some pretty dresses?" I ask the kid like she has the ability to talk back. "I know Mommy does." Lulu smiles as she reaches up, playing with my lips again.

Delilah pulls out a wad of ones and sets it on the counter next to her paperwork, pushing it toward the woman on the other side. The lady rolls her eyes, throwing all kinds of shade at Delilah, not knowing everything she's been through in the last few days.

Delilah looks over her shoulder and smiles, but I know the entire situation has to sting. She's not used to any of this, but she takes it all in stride and doesn't complain.

A lesser woman would've caved and run back to daddy to cash in on her trust fund, but not Delilah. Maybe it's her attitude which drew me to her the most. She was a damsel in distress but didn't let any of it beat her down. She seemed to pick herself up, brush herself off, and move on without a bit of trouble.

When the woman hands her the driver's license, Delilah has the biggest smile, thanking the woman like she'd done something grand for her rather than just her job.

"Lookie what I got," she says, swaying her hips as she approaches. By the way she's acting, you'd think she won the lottery, not had her identification replaced.

"Let's go try that bad boy out," I tell her and slide my arm around her shoulders as we make our way to the door.

"Try it out?" I can see the confusion in her eyes, and I know she wants clarification, but I'm not going to give any.

"We've got a big day ahead of us," I say, leaving it at that. Delilah doesn't press me for more as she takes Lulu back into her arms and we walk outside. "First stop, the biggest department store in Chicago."

"Lucio," she says. I can hear the warning in her voice. "I don't need new clothes. These are fine."

"If you're a teenage girl from the nineties maybe, but not a grown-ass woman and a mom."

She narrows her eyes while she glances up at me as I open the door for her. "Do not put me in mom clothes. So help me God, I'll…"

"You'll what, sweetheart?" I tease.

The last thing I want on her body is a bunch of frumpy clothes, but she deserves to have nice things.

"We won't go crazy, but I'd like to see you in some grownup clothes, showing off that banging body, but in a classy way."

She leans over, placing Lulu in the Jeep while I check out her tight little ass. "I thought you liked the dress I wore the other night."

"I did, but not so much with you wearing the flimsy thing without me around."

"Jealous?" She smiles as she turns around.

"Greedy." I shut the door before pressing her against the

side of my sister's Jeep. I grab her waist, digging my fingers into her skin. "I don't share, sweetheart."

She places her hand on my chest, curling her fingers into my shirt, and smirks. "I don't either, baby."

———

"What about this one?" she asks when she walks out of the dressing room and twirls in a circle as the skirt lifts, showing off her lace panties.

"Not for work," I tell her quickly, and Lulu claps her hands, mesmerized by the way the fabric moves, "but it has a lot of other possibilities."

My ass is numb from sitting in the tiny chair inside the dressing room area for the last hour, but the smile on Delilah's face is entirely worth the pain.

"I love the fabric." She runs her hand over her bottom, smoothing the material. "Wanna feel?" She grins.

"You're torturing me today." If I feel the fabric, I'll touch her ass. If I touch her ass, it won't lead anywhere good but probably a trip down to the police precinct because I won't be able to stop myself. "I'm good. Just take that fine ass back into the dressing room and put something else on."

She sways her hips as she walks, laughing at the way I adjust myself in the seat. "You sure you don't want to touch it?" She shakes her ass before turning around to face me. "Just a little?" she teases, raising an eyebrow along with the front of the skirt.

I cover Lulu's eyes, and her hands immediately go to my fingers, trying to pry them free. "The kid, Delilah."

Delilah practically cackles as my gaze heats, and I know I'm going to make her pay for this. I hate shopping, but with her, it's a mix of pleasure and pain.

"You have five more minutes, and we're out of here," I tell her, done with the fashion show and ready to get her home.

"Patience is a virtue." She smiles, slowly closing the door and staring at me with a sexy smirk on her face through the crack.

"So is generosity, baby." I watch under the door as the skirt drops to the floor. "And you're about to understand how generous I can be."

"I said I don't want you to buy me clothes." She slides on her shorts, and the dressing room door opens again. "I never asked for this." She grabs a hefty stack of hangers with all the items I liked, and I can see this bothers her.

"I'm not talking about clothes."

"You want me to pay you back in sexual favors?" She fakes disgust, but I know she's going to love every inch of what I'm going to give her.

I grab her chin between my fingers and move my lips within an inch of hers. "No, sweetheart, I'm going to be the one doing the pleasing."

Her blue eyes sparkle as she tips her head up, staring at me with so much need I can feel the heat coming off her in waves. "I like your style, Mr. Gallo."

"Baby, you haven't seen nothing yet." I pull on her bottom lip with my teeth.

Lulu smacks my arm and lets out a little grunt, reminding us both she's there.

"Let's go home," I tell her. "The kid needs a nap, and I need some Delilah."

"Fuck," she groans as she pulls away. "Between work, Lulu, and you, I get nothing done."

"Baby, we're all you need doing." I swat her ass as we exit the dressing room, already pulling out my wallet because I can't waste another minute. All I want to do is to be on top of her, touching her, consuming her.

CHAPTER NINETEEN

DELILAH

LUCIO CRAWLS out of the bed, and I roll over, too comfortable and exhausted to bother getting out of bed with him. There's someone pounding at the door, but I don't care if it's God himself, I'm not leaving the warmth.

The birds chirp outside the window. They're a little too cheery for me. I open one eye and stare at the clock, groaning when I realize Lulu will be up any minute.

Suddenly, I can hear the loud rumble of Lucio's voice, and I jump to my feet, padding across the floor to the window. I pull back the curtain, trying to hide my face because I don't want him to think I don't trust him.

My heart stops as soon as I see his face. Dwight's on the walkway to the front door, waving his hands at Lucio and yelling back. Lucio takes a step forward, and Dwight backs up, knowing he's no match for Lucio's size and power.

I grab a pair of jeans off the floor and slide them on before I find a clean T-shirt, pulling it over my head as I walk to the living room. I'm practically stomping my feet with every step, marching toward the door and the man who abandoned us.

I'm so pissed my hands are shaking, and I'm breathing so fast I'm on the verge of hyperventilating. It's been nine months since Dwight vanished into thin air. I'd say he has a huge set of balls for showing up now, but I know that's not even remotely true.

I can hear Dwight's voice clear as day from the living room as he yells at Lucio. "I want to see my kid!"

"Daughter or son?" Lucio asks. I can't see his face, but his arms are crossed in front of him and he looks like the Hulk compared to Dwight.

Dwight stares at him but doesn't say anything back. The fucker doesn't even know because he left before I found out we were having a daughter, and he's never so much as called or texted to see if either of us survived.

My hand's on the doorknob, but something stops me from going outside. I hate him so much, but I'm thankful he left when he did. Lulu never had a chance to get attached to him and will never know the hurt of being abandoned.

"I want to see my son!" Dwight screams, putting the nail in his coffin.

"You have a daughter, asshole."

"Fuck you. She's my kid, and Delilah's my girl."

"You lost that right long ago. They're mine now."

A thrill runs through me when I hear Lucio say those words. I don't think I will ever get sick of hearing him call me his. The fact that he claims Lulu too makes my heart swell with pride, love, and hope.

"Where's Delilah?"

I turn the knob and step onto the front step, feeling stronger than I ever have. I'm no longer the timid girl, always trying to be proper and kind. "What do you want, Dwight?"

His eyes travel up my body, looking at me like I'm a prize he's already won. "I came back for you, baby."

I tip my head back and laugh as I hold my stomach. "What makes you think I want you?"

"We made a life." He takes a step toward me, but Lucio

holds out his arm and presses his palm into Dwight's chest. "We are in love."

"We are?" My mouth drops open, and I widen my eyes, totally fucking with this worthless human. "Was that before or after you ditched me?"

Dwight's eyes narrow and he tries to push Lucio away, but he's not strong enough to even make him sway. "Don't be that way. You know I had to go."

I step forward, descending the cement stairs as slowly as possible with my eyes locked on him. "Did you get arrested?"

"No."

"Did you get called away on some secret mission?" I ask as I stand a few feet away from them, letting Lucio stay between us.

"Don't be ridiculous."

I tap my chin and glance at the sky. "That's right. You couldn't handle having a baby. You were a coward and decided you needed to live a little, like somehow I was trying to trap you."

Dwight drags his hand through his dirty-blond hair and stares at the ground. "I..." He starts to speak, but I don't give him a chance to come up with another lame excuse.

"I'm not your woman." I point toward Lulu's bedroom window. "She's not your daughter. You're nothing to us, just like we were nothing to you."

When he tries to move toward me again, Lucio grabs him by the arm and holds up a finger. "Take one more step, and I'm knocking your ass out."

"How the hell did you find me anyway?"

"Your dad told me where you were," he says as he reaches out his hand. "We can make us work again. You can't want this." His eyes go to Lucio and back to me. "You're better than this, Delilah."

I touch Lucio's shoulder, knowing he's about to knock Dwight's lights out with one punch to the jaw. I should let him, but I've never been one to use my hands when my mouth will do the trick.

"Sweetheart, can you give us a minute?" Lucio turns to me with worry all over his face. "I'll be fine," I tell him, trying to make him comfortable. "I need to do this."

Lucio shakes his head and keeps his hand wrapped around Dwight's arm. "I don't think it's a good idea."

I touch his face, and his eyes close. "Please," I beg. "She's probably awake and hungry by now." I don't dare say her name. Dwight doesn't deserve to walk away from here knowing anything about Lulu.

Lucio nods before turning around and leveling Dwight with his gaze. "I see you try to touch her, and you're not leaving this front yard without a broken bone."

Dwight swallows, turning pale as a ghost, but he nods slowly. Lucio releases him but not before lunging forward, causing Dwight to flinch. There's a smirk on Lucio's lips when he turns to face me.

"Dwight won't hurt me." I slide my hand across Lucio's cheek. "He's never been that kind of man. He's a coward, for sure, but not a hitter."

"You have five minutes, and then I'm coming back out."

I lean forward, popping up on my bare tiptoes to give him a hard kiss. "Understood," I murmur against his mouth. "But I won't need that long."

Lucio touches my waist, holding on to me as he walks away. His hand slips away as he makes his way up the stairs, and I watch him, waiting for him to go inside before I lay into Dwight about his disappearing act.

I turn, narrowing my eyes, and stick my pointy finger square in his chest. "How dare you show your ugly face, you bastard."

His eyes widen as he backs up, clearly not expecting me to be pissed off and ready to vocalize every bit of that anger.

"You take off, leaving me with my father and a baby on

the way. I know you were scared, but be a man, for fuck's sake. I was scared too, but I couldn't just walk away from the situation like you did." He tries to touch my hand, but I swat his arm away and keep going, pressing harder into his chest. "You need to forget we exist. You did a good enough job with that since the day you left, so it shouldn't be that hard to do it again."

"But she has a right to know her father."

"You were a sperm donor, Dwight. Let's not fool ourselves. Your name may be on her birth certificate, but—" I turn for a second, seeing Lucio watching from Lulu's bedroom window "—this man has been more of a father to her than you could ever be."

"Delilah, please."

"I don't know what you were thinking showing up here, but you're not getting a happy ending. I'm going to a lawyer and getting papers drawn up for you to relinquish your parental rights. Sign them. If you don't, so help me God, I'll go to everyone at the country club and tell them you knocked me up and took off."

His mouth hangs open, and I know I'm hitting him right where it hurts. "What will your daddy think when he finds out you ran away from your responsibilities?"

"I'll tell him." He steps forward and tries to touch me again, but I back away. "I'll make him understand. Don't cut me out of her life. Out of yours."

My hand slams into his chest, knocking him backward and causing him to stumble, almost losing his footing. "Sign the papers, Dwight, or…"

"Or what?" He challenges me, finding a pair of balls I never knew he had.

"Or I won't be able to stop what happens to you."

"What's that mean?" His lips twist.

I have no idea what it means, but I'll find a way to make

him pay. The only thing I need right now is for him to believe I know of ways to hurt him that stretch beyond the law.

"I know people," I say simply, wondering if I could get Johnny to strong-arm Dwight. I'm sure he'd do anything for me; he seems to have taken to me like the rest of the family.

"You know people?" He looks confused.

"Never mind," I tell him, knowing the only thing Dwight cares about is money. "You know what?" I stalk forward. "I don't have any money anymore, but I sure could use some child support. What are you making now? Ten thousand a month?" I smile as his face pales. "I'm sure I can make a case to get a hefty payment from you each and every month."

The last thing I want is his money, but it's the only motivator I have for his dumb ass.

He jerks his head back. "You're broke?"

"Not a dime." I draw out the word, following him as he's already heading toward the sidewalk. "My father stole it, but I'm sure you can help us out, right? We could use all that back child support to get a new place."

"Back child support?" He almost chokes on the words, and I know he's doing a calculation in his head.

"Yeah. I figure you owe us about—" I tap my chin and stop near the sidewalk, but he keeps moving "—about thirty grand by now."

"What? That's insane!"

I'm lying through my teeth. I have no idea how much I'd be awarded by a judge for child support, but Dwight is too stupid to know any better.

"Sign. The. Fucking. Papers."

"Fine," he says, throwing his hands up in the air. "You're nothing but a broke-ass hood rat anyway."

I roll my eyes, not feeling the sting from his country-club, cardigan-wearing, dumb-ass words.

"Fuck off, Dwight. Thanks for the lousy lay and the great

kid," I hurl at him as he walks around the corner and out of my life again.

This time, he's not coming back.

Lucio's out the door before I have a chance to turn around. "He gone?"

"He's gone," I say, turning toward him and burying my face in his chest as soon as he gets close enough. "He's an asshole."

He wraps his arms around me and holds me tightly. "I'm proud of you."

His words warm my insides, making me feel better than anything else in the world. Lucio does that to me. He makes me feel better about myself, more confident, and tougher than I've ever been in my entire life.

CHAPTER
TWENTY

LUCIO

"I GOT THE SHOTS," Daphne says as she rounds the bar and heads toward the middle of the room.

We're cleaning up, readying the bar for tomorrow's service. The bar was busy tonight. More crowded than we've been in a long time.

"I'm exhausted," Delilah says, wiping off the last table.

"It's Saturday night. We can't go yet." Daphne sets down the bottle of vodka, along with a plate of cut-up lemons and sugar. "I'm putting my foot down and requiring us to do a team-building activity."

Angelo raises an eyebrow and glances in my direction. "It's my last weekend without the kids," he says like he's justifying something.

"That's exactly why you deserve to get shit-faced," Daphne tells him and motions toward the table. "We have a new employee, and this will be great for team building and morale." When I groan, Daphne stalks across the room and grabs me by the hand. "We could all use a little downtime before the shitshow starts."

She's referring to my father. As soon as word got out that

he was going to be released from prison soon, people started showing up in droves to get a glimpse of the local mafioso.

Delilah walks toward us, sitting down first and slipping off her shoes to rub her heels. "My feet are killing me," she says and makes a noise so close to the one she makes when I slip my cock inside her, I almost go rock hard. "We have time for a drink, Lucio, don't we?"

"One hour," I say and take the seat next to her.

"Come on, everyone." Daphne claps her hands. "And I mean everyone."

"What's your team-building activity?" Angelo asks, knowing it's useless to argue with her.

"Two Truths and a Lie." She smiles and stares down at us. "It's the best way to get to know each other."

I don't know how this will help anything. Most of us grew up together, and there isn't much we don't know about each other.

"This might be your dumbest idea yet," Angelo grumbles.

Daphne sits down, ignoring our brother's grumpy mood and starts to pour the shots. "We have a new employee. Wouldn't it be nice to get to know her a little better?"

"I'm all about a drink to unwind, Daph, but shots are a little much," Michelle says as she takes the seat next to Daphne and pulls the glass in front of her.

"You're not a lightweight. Stop complaining."

Everyone's finally seated except for Vinnie. He's not here. Not like he ever is, but it's his final weekend home before he returns to school to finish out the spring semester.

Delilah places her hand on my leg and rests her face in her other palm. "I've never played this," she admits.

"Oh, girl. It's easy. You come up with two truths and a lie about yourself. You tell the table, and we have to guess which one is the lie."

"Where's the drink come in?" Delilah asks, staring at a shot glass filled with vodka.

"If you guess wrong, you gotta drink."

"I'm a human lie detector." Delilah smiles. "Prepare to get slaughtered."

"You got a lot of shit talk for a little girl," Angelo teases. "I can see why you two work so well." His gaze bounces between the two of us. "I'll go first." The table gives him their full attention. "I lost my virginity at fourteen, I was once with a woman twenty years older than myself, and I haven't been touched by a woman in two years."

I raise an eyebrow. I know his first two are true, which means the last one is his lie. He's been with someone, which is surprising because he hasn't bothered to mention it to anyone.

Delilah tips her head to the side, studying my brother's face. "That's easy. The last one's your lie," she answers like she's known him his entire life.

"Why d'you think that?" Angelo asks, leaning back in his chair.

"There's no way you've been celibate for two years. You're not grouchy enough. I mean, you're intense and everything, but not near enough for that to be true."

The entire table bursts out laughing. Daphne suddenly stops and slams her palms down on the table. "Wait." She turns and gawks at him. "Who have you been seeing behind our backs?"

"None of your business," he says before downing the shot and grimacing. "You don't need to know everything about my life." I catch the subtle glance he gives Michelle from across the table, but I don't say a word because it's none of my business who my brother is sleeping with.

"Delilah, it's your turn," Daphne says, but her voice isn't as cheery as it was only a minute ago.

Daphne hates not being in the loop. She's used to having her nose so far up in our business that the revelation has to sting.

"So, wait. You slept with a woman twenty years older than you?" Delilah looks shocked. "Who was that?"

"Mrs. Kinsey," I answer for him because all the guys had a turn with her as we grew up.

"Who?" The tiny lines between Daphne's eyebrows deepen. "Who the hell is that?"

"It's a dude thing, little sister." Angelo pats her on the shoulder, and she stiffens.

"The old lady from down the street?"

"She wasn't so old back then," Angelo says.

Mrs. Kinsey was a widow in her forties, but damn if she didn't look a day older than thirty back then. The boys in the neighborhood knew about her and her wild sexual appetite.

"You banged her, man?" I ask Angelo because I couldn't do it. I tried, God how I tried, but she didn't do it for me.

"I let her blow me." He smirks.

"Today her ass would end up in jail." Daphne turns toward Delilah, already a little hot under the collar. "Go." She waves her hand.

"I speak three languages, I met Brad Pitt, and I was once arrested."

"Shut the fuck up, you met Brad Pitt?" Daphne says quickly with wide eyes. "Tell me everything."

Delilah laughs and pushes Daphne's drink in front of her. "Drink up."

"Fuck. Seriously?" Daphne's lip snarls as she takes the shot glass. "What the hell were you arrested for?"

I'm just as shocked as everyone to hear the news. I never pegged Delilah for someone with an arrest record. I'd been booked into County more than once, but I was a minor and had a bad temper.

"Public nudity." Delilah smiles.

There's not a sound in the room, and everyone's staring at the prim and proper Delilah Miles.

"You can't just say that and not explain," I tell Delilah, and I am fascinated once again by my girl.

The entire table is just as interested as I am. We all have our opinions on Delilah, and so far, every single thing we assumed about her has been wrong.

"It's no big deal. It was freshman year in college, pledge week." Delilah sits up straight and twists the shot glass between her fingertips. "The sisters in the sorority thought I was a stuck-up prude."

"Shocking." Michelle giggles.

"Shut it," Delilah tells her like she's been here for years. As far as I can tell, the girls bonded the night they went out, but thankfully, Carmen and Colleen haven't decided to come around. "Anyway, as part of my initiation, I had to run across the football field naked during warmups."

"Impressive." Daphne waggles her eyebrows. "Never knew you had it in you."

"I hadn't planned on the security guards practically tackling me on the fifty-yard line and being hauled out of the stadium in handcuffs."

Daphne downs the shot and clears her throat, not bothering with the lemon or sugar. "Okay." She pauses, and I can almost see the wheels spinning in her head. "I once puked on a guy in the middle of having sex, I've never seen *The Notebook*, and I hate when guys call me baby."

I rub my hand down my face, hating everything about playing this game with my sister. The last thing I want to know about is her sex life. I like to pretend she's celibate, preferring to live like a nun than the wild child she's always been.

"Easy," Michelle says as she starts to laugh. "You've never seen *The Notebook*."

"You're not allowed to play when it's my turn," Daphne tells her, pointing her skinny little finger in Michelle's face. "You know all my secrets."

"Wait, you puked on someone while you were doing it?" Delilah's mouth is hanging open.

"Move on. I'll go," I say because I've learned way too much already, and I don't want the gory details.

"I once danced for money, I've never done drugs, and I have never lied to Ma."

"What about me?" Ma says as she walks down the staircase, scaring the shit out of all of us.

"Lucio says he's never lied to you," Angelo tells her, throwing his hand in my direction.

"That's some bullshit," Ma says, ending my round of Two Truths and a Lie.

"You dance?" Delilah's eyes light up as she looks at me. "Like a stripper?"

"Don't lie, man. You did that shit more than once." Angelo's so quick to throw me under the bus.

"I was young."

Delilah squeezes my leg and winks. "I want to see your act later."

"Baby." I lean over and touch her cheek. "I'll show you what I got anytime."

"I'm gagging," Daphne says and pretends to hurl on the floor next to her.

"I'm done. I want to get Lulu home and my girls to bed." I stand and hold my hand out for Delilah.

"Damn, I wanted to play," Ma tells me, giving me puppy-dog eyes like they're going to work on me.

"I'm already scared enough after tonight. My heart can't take much more." Delilah's laughing as she takes my hand, and I help her up. "You guys play. I'm sure it'll be enlightening."

"Nope. I gotta go. I have a date," Daphne says suddenly.

"Me too," Angelo stands, and so does Michelle, leaving Ma sitting there alone.

"One o'clock tomorrow. Don't be late," Ma calls out as we head in opposite directions.

"I'll grab Lulu. Wait down here for me," I tell Delilah before kissing her on the lips.

I'm halfway up the stairs when I hear my mom tell Delilah, "Once when I was younger and much more flexible, Santino would…"

I cover my ears, taking the steps faster because no way in hell do I want to hear the rest of that sentence. There's such a thing as too much information, and tonight, I've already hit my limit.

CHAPTER
TWENTY-ONE
DELILAH

I'M TOWEL-DRYING MY HAIR, sitting on the edge of the bed when the music starts. I'm barely awake, not having had nearly enough coffee to be coherent or energetic for a Monday morning.

Lucio comes sliding into the room, wearing a pair of black athletic pants, a white tank top, and a baseball cap. My mouth waters the moment I see him, and suddenly my hair isn't so important.

I'd know the song anywhere. It's the theme song from *Magic Mike,* and based on the way he's moving his hips, he knows the routine by heart.

I'm mesmerized as he turns his baseball cap around, exposing his beautiful face and deep green eyes. His gaze meets mine, and my stomach flutters. All I can do is sit here, watching him as he dances around the room, thrusting his dreamy cock in my direction.

I reach out, trying to grab a hold of his waistband, but he pushes my hands away and waves his fingers in my face, telling me no.

He turns his back to me, teasing me as he slowly lifts his shirt over his head. The muscles of his back ripple, moving to the beat of the music. I'm impressed by his ability to control his body the way he does. Sometimes I can barely walk in a straight line, but he has such control, I'm envious and totally turned on.

"Take it all off," I say, careful not to scream too loud because Lulu's still asleep. "Show me whatcha got."

He spins with his feet together, running his hand down his abdomen as the muscles of his arm flex and become more defined. When he grabs his crotch, I almost slide off the bed, so turned on I want to throw myself at his feet and beg for his cock.

But then he jumps on the bed, placing his feet on both sides of me and grinds his dick in my face. I bite through the thin material, teasing him as much as he's teasing me.

I can imagine him doing this in a room full of women, the money flying in his direction because he's that damn good and so freaking sexy. I grab his ass and try to pull his pants down, but he's off the bed, dancing again before I have a chance.

But I'm not in the mood to play fair. I pull my robe open, exposing my breasts, and palm one in my hand. His eyes are locked on my movement, watching as I swipe my thumb across my nipple. His dancing slows a bit when I open my legs and slide my other hand down, running my fingers through my wetness.

He moves toward me and pushes me backward, dancing his way between my legs. I watch down the length of my naked body as he twists down to his knees, bringing his beautiful, lush licks right to where I ache the most.

I close my eyes as his tongue runs over my clit, sending waves of pleasure through my entire body. My fingers close around the comforter, balling the material in my palms as he lifts my thighs over his shoulders and closes his lips around my clit.

I cry out, loving every second of the way he loves me with

his mouth. He's an expert and has learned my body so quickly, but I'm not surprised since I'm not a quiet lover.

When he moans, matching my own, the vibration joins his tongue in delivering a one-two punch. The orgasm comes quickly, way faster than either of us expects, especially me. The air in my body vanishes, and my toes curl along with my legs, burying his face in my pussy. I grind against him, smothering him, but he doesn't seem to mind as he sucks harder. The waves crash over me like a thunderstorm rolling through a mountain valley, overshadowing everything in sight.

"Fucckkkkk," I moan, sucking in a breath as my head spins. "That was so…"

"Amazing and the best you've ever had," he says with a smirk, before running his tongue across his lips, taking in every last drop I gave him.

He tries to help me up, but I push him down and mount him. "That was quite the performance," I tell him as I rub my pussy against him with only his pants separating us.

He smirks, showing off his stunning white teeth against his tanned skin. "Which parts?"

He's cocky, but damn if he hasn't earned the right to be. "All. Of. It." Leaning forward, I lick his lips, tasting myself.

"But the tongue…"

"That's my favorite, but…" I pause and slide down his body. "I think I like this part best." Putting my hand over his cock, I stroke his hard length through the material.

He moans, lifting his ass off the bed just like I do when he licks my pussy. As soon as I pull down the waistband of his pants, his cock springs free, moving through the air as if it's greeting me.

"It's still so fucking pretty. No cock should be this hot," I say, grabbing it with my hand and staring at it.

"None are," he tells me. "Show me how much you like it."

My tongue flicks the piercing, and I'm just about to close my lips around the tip when Lulu starts crying. Lucio's entire body tenses, and I freeze, praying she'll fall back asleep. But we both know it's not going to happen.

"I'll go," he says, pulling me up his body and tossing me onto the bed next to where he just lay. "But you're finishing this later."

"Naptime can't come soon enough," I say through my laughter.

I almost feel bad for him as he pulls his pants up, trying to jam his hard cock underneath the thin fabric. The material does nothing to contain his erection as he stalks out of the room like he has a third arm.

I roll off the bed, closing my robe as I climb to my feet, and I remember there's no time for me to finish what I just started because I have an appointment with an attorney this afternoon.

As promised, Dwight was given paperwork to sign, revoking his parental rights and any future ties to Lulu. After today, there's no reason for me ever to see him again.

Someday, when Lulu's older and has questions, I'll tell her what I can without making her feel bad. I know this is what's best not only for her, but me too.

"Baby."

Lucio lifts Lulu into his arms like he's been doing it since the day she was born. The way he holds her makes my heart skip a beat. He's so tender and gentle even though he's large and covered in muscle.

"Don't forget I have to go to the lawyer's today."

"I'm coming," he says as he rubs Lulu's back, trying to quiet her tears.

"You don't have to. I'm sure you have things to do."

"Delilah." He gives me that look. The one that says I'm being crazy. "There's nowhere I'd rather be than with my girls."

He always includes Lulu. It's not just about me anymore, and Lucio somehow respects and embraces both of us.

"Okay," I tell him, wrapping my arm around his back and leaning forward to kiss Lulu. "I want you to come with me more than anything."

"Hey." He pauses, waiting for me to look at him. "You'll never have to go through anything else alone. I'm here and not going anywhere."

I'd say thank you, but the words don't seem adequate enough for how I feel. I've never truly had someone I could depend on who didn't let me down. Lucio's only been in my life a short time, but I can't imagine ever being alone again.

CHAPTER
TWENTY-TWO

LUCIO

"SAL," I say, shaking his hand as we walk into his office.

"Looking good, man." Sal takes a step back and stares at me. "It must be because of this beautiful lady."

Delilah blushes and smiles, but when Sal reaches out and sweeps his finger down Lulu's pudgy cheek, she laughs.

"Of course, I'm talking about you, Ms. Miles, but I know Lucio's fondness for little Lulu too." He motions toward the small table near the window. "Sit, please."

"Thank you for taking this case so quickly." Delilah walks at my side, holding my hand. I pull out the chair for her, being a gentleman, and wait for her to sit before I take the seat next to her.

"Anything Lucio ever needs, I'm always there for him."

Delilah looks at me and places her hand over mine. "I don't know what I did to deserve him."

"I think you have it backward, sweetheart. I'm the lucky one here."

Sal's watching me with a funny look. We go way back, and he knows my past better than anyone. Neither of us is innocent. We did some pretty dumb shit as kids, but somehow, he went to law school and passed the bar even though I never would've guessed he was smart enough. I guess he hid his intelligence and learned to fit in, because on the South Side, in our neighborhood, muscles beat out smarts every day of the week.

"Did you have any trouble with Mr. Jones?" Delilah asks as she turns to face Sal.

"None." Sal shakes his head. "I called him, and he came into the office the same day to sign the paperwork."

"Not surprising. The bastard." Delilah whispers the last part and covers her mouth, trying to hide her disgust.

"He understood that he'd lose if the case was brought in front of a judge. He abandoned you and your daughter." Sal slides a manila folder in front of Delilah, and she takes it. "He may have been able to get supervised visitation, but he'd have to start paying child support immediately."

"He's too cheap to part with his money. Even for his daughter." Her hand's lying on top of the folder with her and Lulu's names written in black ink on the front. "So, it's done?" she asks.

"You just need to sign the paperwork too, and I'll file it with the court."

She peels back the cover and studies the first page before flipping to the end where Dwight has already signed.

Sal sets a pen down in front of her. "Do you need a moment alone?" he asks.

"No," she says, waving her hand before snatching the pen off the table. "There's no sadness in my heart. No regret about doing this. He doesn't deserve to be her father even if it's only on paper." Delilah scribbles her name next to Dwight's, almost stabbing the dot over the "i" in her last name. She drops the pen and pushes the entire folder back toward Sal. "How long until it's final?"

"The courts are slow and backlogged, but it should only take a few weeks."

"Perfect."

I turn to Delilah and grab her hand. "I want to ask you something," I say, and her eyes widen. "Not that."

I wasn't too smooth with that sentence. If I were going to ask her to marry me, it sure as hell wouldn't be in Sal's office.

"I love you."

"I love you too," she says quickly.

"I love Lulu."

"She adores you."

"What do you think if I..." God, I'm about to say words I thought would never come out of my mouth, and my stomach is knotting and my pulse quickens. "What do you think if I adopt Lulu?"

Delilah only blinks as her lips part, and she stares at me. I'm not sure she quite heard me right because she doesn't say anything right away. Her lips move, but no words come out.

"She needs a daddy, sweetheart. I want to be that for her. I love her like she's my own and never want her to think she wasn't wanted."

"Wait." Delilah turns a little more in her chair, and I can already see the tears forming in her eyes. "You want to adopt her?" she repeats like she really didn't believe the words I just said.

"Yes." I nod, squeezing her fingers between mine. "More than anything in the world."

"You want to be her father?" A tear runs down Delilah's cheek as she blinks. "Like, forever?"

"It usually works that way."

I know this is a huge step and she might tell me I'm completely insane and refuse to let me adopt Lulu, but I have to try.

"I had a long talk with my ma. She agrees with me on this. We all want Lulu to be part of our family forever."

"I don't know what to say," she whispers, and more tears start to fall.

I brush away the tears with the back of my hand before

resting my palm against her cheek, cradling her face. "I've never loved anyone like I love you, Delilah. But Lulu, she has me wrapped around her little finger. I want her to be mine. If you say no, I'll understand, but I..."

I don't get the next words out before Delilah's mouth is on me. Her hands come to my face, and she peppers me with kisses. The tears haven't stopped. She's crying harder than before, but she's happy.

"Yes!" she exclaims, causing Lulu to jump in my arms and scream for a moment.

"You sure?" I ask between kisses.

"You're already an amazing father to her, Lucio. Better than my own ever was to me, and more of a man than Dwight will ever be. Lulu would be lucky to have such a wonderful man as her daddy."

"Sal," I say, peering over at him without turning. Delilah's still attached to my face, kissing me a dozen times. "Draw up the papers."

Sal nods and claps his hands loudly, and Lulu cries this time, startled by all the excitement in the room.

Delilah takes her from my arms and hugs her tightly. "You have a daddy now," she tells her, and I almost choke up.

"As soon as this form is accepted by the court, I'll start official adoption proceedings." He nods and is all smiles. "One more thing," Sal says and pulls another folder off his desk. "Lucio told me about your father, and as a personal favor, I sent him a letter to restore the money he removed from your account."

"You did?" Delilah gazes at me, and I give her a nervous smile.

I may have overstepped my bounds with that favor, but fuck her father, he did not deserve to keep the money which rightfully belonged to her.

"Yes, and I received a letter of response yesterday along

with proof that your bank account has been made whole again."

Delilah's eyes widen as Sal slides the folder in front of her, peeling back the front to show her the deposit slip.

At least the prick had enough sense to give her every dollar back. I wasn't going to let a sleeping dog lie. He was going to pay her back one way or another, but I'm glad it only took a strongly worded letter to scare him into action.

She runs her fingers over the paper, staring at the number. "I can't believe it. I don't know how to thank you both for everything."

"No thanks needed," Sal says, taking the words right out of my mouth. "It's always nice to help someone who deserves it."

Delilah's eyes are filled with tears, and she's so choked up she can't say another word.

"I'm going to take my girls to lunch to celebrate," I say as I stand and hold out my hand to shake, thanking Sal for his help.

He comes around the table, capturing me in a giant bear hug. "I never thought I'd see the day you'd go all soft on me, buddy. It suits you."

I don't even grumble. There's nothing in the world that can bring me down from the high of knowing I'll be gaining a daughter and, hopefully soon, a wife too.

———

Lulu's asleep in the stroller next to the table. She's worn out from the excitement of earlier. The sun's shining overhead as we sit on the patio at the Park Grill overlooking Grant Park.

My finger's in my pocket, and I'm fiddling with the diamond ring I picked out yesterday with a little help from Angelo. I went overboard, but I couldn't help myself. I didn't want Delilah walking around with a shitty ring. No matter how many times someone says size doesn't matter, I know it's a crock of bullshit.

"Champagne," the waitress says, holding out the bottle to us for approval.

"It's perfect," I tell her before she pours two glasses.

"I can't believe we're celebrating," Delilah says, and she still hasn't come down from the high of earlier.

"I was worried for a second," I admit.

The entire thing could've blown up in my face. Delilah could've shot me down, going on with our relationship just as it had been. Other people would think we're crazy. We've only known each other a few weeks, but I can't imagine letting her or Lulu walk out of my life at this point.

"I'm sorry I scared you." She touches the base of the champagne flute and gazes at me from under her lashes. "I was just so in shock."

I know what I'm about to do is going to be another shock to her system, and I pray to God she says yes. We're both in too good of a mood to have something destroy the happiness we both deserve.

I'm almost certain she'll say yes. I've never seen her smile as easily as she does with me. When she first showed up at the bar, she was an entirely different person. It took a little time for her to relax and open up, but once she did, there was no turning back.

A noise across the way draws Delilah's attention, and I know it's my one shot to surprise her. I slide to my knee and pull the ring from my pocket before she turns back around.

When she looks across the table and I'm not there, she almost panics. But when she sees me… God, when she sees me on one knee, holding a giant ring that's sparkling in the sun like a beacon, her eyes widen and she gasps.

"Ms. Delilah Miles, would you do me the honor of being my wife?" I say quickly because I know she's about to cry again, and hell, I might too.

My heart's pounding, and all the voices around us seem to quiet. Everyone's watching, waiting with bated breath as I kneel before her, praying she'll say yes.

"Fuck. Are you kidding me?" she says.

"No jokes, sweetheart. I've never loved another person more than I love you. All I think about every day is you and Lulu. The only place I want to be is by your side. I want you to be mine forever. I want to marry you in front of my family and God. I can't imagine another day on this planet without you."

"Yes! Yes! Oh my God. Yes!" she yells, and the tears start falling as I slide the ring onto her finger.

She doesn't even look at it or notice the size. I agonized for hours over the perfect one. Learning everything I could about cut, clarity, and all the other bullshit that comes along with diamonds.

She leans forward and wraps her hands around my neck. "I love you, Lucio. I want nothing more than to be yours forever."

The people sitting around us clap and smile, feeling the excitement in the moment. Engagements always make people happy, even if they're miserable in their own lives.

I pull her into my arms and know this is meant to be.

CHAPTER
TWENTY-THREE

DELILAH

"LEMME SEE," Daphne says as soon as we walk through the front door of the bar.

I hold out my hand and wiggle my finger, showing her the extravagant ring Lucio bought for me. I would've been happy with a small rock. Size never really mattered to me. How could it when I have a guy like Lucio by my side?

"It's so beautiful." She stares at the ring, bringing my hand closer to her face. "He did damn good. I'm impressed."

"Where is she?"

I turn as Betty comes down the stairs with the biggest smile on her face. She's wearing the most magnificent black-and-white polka-dot dress with her hair styled like a 1950's pinup. She's absolutely stunning and smiling bigger than I've ever seen before.

"There's my girl," she says, holding out her arms. For a second, I think she's going for Lulu, but when she wraps her arms around me, I can't help but smile. "You've made me so happy." She pulls back and grabs my cheeks. "So, so happy."

Lucio clears his throat, getting his mother's attention. "I wouldn't let you down, Ma."

She pats his chest, always proud of her son. "I never had any doubt, baby. Now let me see my granddaughter."

"Ma, it's not official yet."

She rolls her eyes as she takes Lulu from my arms. "I don't need a court to tell me she's one of my own." Lulu laughs, grabbing for those pearls again, just as attached to Betty as she was the very first time she held her.

"When's the wedding?" Daphne asks, almost chomping at the bit to know more.

"I don't know." I look to Lucio because we haven't even talked about when we'll actually say I do.

"As soon as possible," he answers easily.

"We must book the church immediately. No child of mine is getting married at city hall. Father Michael must be the one to marry you."

"I'll let you ladies plan everything," Lucio says and shakes Angelo's hand as soon as he walks over.

"Finally growing up," Angelo teases him. "Locked it down like I told you."

"Locked it down?" I ask.

Lucio leans over and kisses my cheek. "Made sure I never let you go, sweetheart."

"Oh." I laugh. It's a bit cavemanish, but I kind of like it.

Angelo grabs Lucio by the shoulder and announces to everyone, "My brother's getting married. Beer's on the house."

The few regulars, people I've come to truly like, erupt into cheers, congratulating us on our upcoming wedding; although they are probably more excited about the free drinks.

"There's so much to do." Daphne grabs me by the arm and ushers me to a nearby table. "Dresses, reception, invitations."

"We can keep it small. I don't really have anyone to invite." The words sting a little, but besides my father and mother, there's no one left in my family who hasn't been driven away.

"Girl, our family is huge."

"How big?" I ask.

"Between the cousins, we're talking well over a hundred people."

My mouth falls open, and all I can do is blink. "For real?"

"Italians always show up at weddings."

"Always?"

"Always. I can bet my mother is going to invite everyone from the neighborhood, then we have the customers, and the family too. It's going to be enormous."

I'm suddenly nervous, thinking about all the strangers staring at me as I walk down the aisle. "Maybe we should just keep it small. Do it right here in the bar." I like my idea. It sounds simple and more intimate.

"Don't be crazy. We have a wedding shower to plan and so much to do. You're going to look like a princess on your big day," Daphne tells me, and my mind's reeling from all the information she's hurling at me.

I was so excited about the engagement, I didn't even think about all the things that would come with it.

"I'm planning the bachelorette party," Michelle says, coming to sit with us finally.

"I'll let you, but you better make it good."

I smile because I don't know what else to do.

I'm so overwhelmed by their love and excitement I can't even talk anymore. I just look around the bar, watching their happy faces and know I've found my forever home.

Michelle places her hand over mine as I watch Daphne walk away. "You okay?"

"Yeah. Just overwhelmed."

"The Gallos don't do anything small, but I promise we'll be there to help. Don't get scared. You're about to be part of something amazing."

"I know," I tell her, and my smile comes easily. "I've never been so happy in my whole life."

"Daphne and I have been planning our weddings since we were kids. We're excited about this and hope we can help you."

"Of course. I want your help in everything."

I don't even know where to start. After watching my parents' marriage end in spectacular fashion, I never thought I'd be willing to take the plunge. I didn't have the best role models, and the thought of making the same mistakes scares the shit out of me.

———

"Do you want to postpone the wedding?" Lucio's standing in the doorway to my bedroom, watching me.

"No. Why would you ask that?"

He walks across the room and sits next to me on the bed. "We can elope, then."

"We can't do that."

He grabs my hand and kisses my fingers. "You seem over-whelmed."

I stare at him and smile. "I am, but I've also never been more certain about anything in my life either."

"What can I do to make this easier for you?"

God, how is he always so great? So patient. So under-standing. "My parents were a terrible example, and"—I lean over and put my head on his shoulder—"what if we mess the entire marriage thing up?"

He turns on the bed and grabs my face between his giant hands. "Listen, sweetheart. My parents were basically a shitshow most of my life. I know how my mom talks, you'd think they had the type of love you only see in movies, but it's not true. I never want to be like my father. Never."

"His actions don't define who you are," I tell him as I place my hands on his thighs.

"And neither do your parents."

He has a point.

He slides his hands to my shoulders, and he strokes my neck with his thumbs. "I promise to love you and only you. I've always been so scared to commit to someone because I thought I'd be like my father, but I know now, I'm nothing like him."

"I'm nothing like mine," I say.

"Even though my father wasn't the best partner, he was a great dad."

"Neither of my parents was spectacular in any area of their life."

"But you're an amazing mother," he tells me, and I smile, happy someone has noticed.

"Thank you, Lucio."

He turns his eyebrows inward. "For what?"

"For everything."

"Sweetheart." He pulls me into his lap and wraps his arms around me. "Don't thank me. I should be thanking you. Until you showed up, my life was empty."

"Looked pretty full to me," I say and giggle.

He peers down at me and shakes his head. "I'm being serious." His finger finds the engagement ring and moves it. "I never let myself get close to anyone. Never had any real connection. But then this scared girl turned up, and nothing else mattered but keeping her and her baby safe."

"So, we were basically a pity case?" I'm totally joking. Well. Sort of.

"I wouldn't ask you to be my wife out of pity. I've never loved another person as much as I love you."

I sit up straighter and slide my arms around his shoulders. "I love you too, and I don't want to postpone the wedding. I want to be married to you more than anything in the world."

He tightens his hold and presses his lips against my forehead. "As soon as the adoption paperwork is ready, we'll get married. I'll talk to Sal and find out when everything should happen, and we'll plan around it. I don't want to waste another day without you being mine."

I peer up into his beautiful green eyes. "I am yours, silly."

"Forever," he tells me before he moves his face closer and steals my breath in a devastating kiss.

All doubt. All worry. Everything disappears as his mouth covers mine. I know where I'm meant to be. Whom I'm meant to be with. Nothing else matters. The past is the past, but our future is just beginning.

EPILOGUE

LUCIO

THREE MONTHS LATER...

My palms are sweaty, and my heart's pounding so hard I'm sure the entire church can hear the crazy rhythm over the piano music. When the church doors open and Delilah steps out on Angelo's arm, my heart practically stops for a second before beating faster than before.

She looks stunning in the all-white gown with her hair pulled up off her shoulders and the lace veil down over her face. I can't take my eyes off her as she makes her way up the aisle, almost floating over the hardwood.

When she steps up to the altar and I pull back the veil, revealing her tearful but happy face, a sense of bliss comes over me. It's like the entire room disappears, and only Delilah and I exist.

Her hands are in mine as we stand in front of the altar, listening to the priest. The entire church is filled with our family and friends, dabbing at the tears in their eyes as we say our vows.

I haven't taken my eyes off Delilah since the moment she walked into the church. How could I? She's everything I ever wanted but never knew I needed. I can't imagine a day without her or Lulu in my life. My heart's filled with so much joy, I'm not even sure how I can stand as still as I am.

I turn to Angelo on cue and take the ring from his finger. He smiles, but his eyes are teary too, maybe remembering the day he married Marissa. I touch his hand before I turn back around, and he nods, giving me the sign to move on.

The platinum band seems too small as I hold it between my two fingers to face Delilah, one step closer to her finally being my wife.

The priest clears his throat, reminding me of what we rehearsed last night. I slide the ring onto Delilah's finger, staring into her eyes as I see my future come to life. "Repeat after me," he says quietly.

"Delilah, receive this ring as a sign of my love and fidelity. In the name of the Father, and of the Son, and of the Holy Spirit."

I don't speak right away. My fingers are holding the ring and Delilah's hand as I stare into her sparkling blue eyes. "Delilah, receive this ring as a sign of my love and fidelity. In the name of the Father, and of the Son, and of the Holy Spirit."

She bites her lip, holding back the tears I know are about to fall again, only harder this time. Even I can feel my nose tingle, but I take a deep breath, pushing any tears away.

Delilah turns toward Daphne and takes the ring from my sister. She's smiling when she faces me again, looking more confident and beautiful than I've ever seen before. I glance to my mother, who's holding Lulu in her arms. My daughter.

"Repeat after me. Lucio, receive this ring as a sign of my love and fidelity. In the name of the Father, and of the Son, and of the Holy Spirit," the priest says again as Delilah touches my hand.

She keeps her eyes on me as she starts to slide the ring on my finger. "Lucio, receive this ring as a sign of my love and fidelity. In the name of the Father, and of the Son, and of the Holy Spirit."

I squeeze her hands, wondering if that feeling of peace washes over her like it does me in that moment. We've said our vows before the eyes of God and my entire family. Even though the priest hasn't said the words, we're officially husband and wife.

We kneel, waiting for the silent blessing, and our hands are connected. I can't stop turning the ring on my finger, still a little shocked that I'm married. I'm not scared for the future. Not worried I'll mess up like my father anymore.

I sneak a glance at Delilah, and she has her head bowed, but she's watching me too. The mass seems to take forever when all I want to do is take my wife out of this place so I can show her exactly how much I love her.

"Please stand," the priest says, closing the bible in his hands as soon as he's done with the prayer. He nods at us when it's time to face the crowd.

I smile at Delilah, happier than I've ever been as we turn toward our family and friends while they rise to their feet too.

"I present to you Mr. and Mrs. Lucio Giovanni Gallo. You may now kiss the bride."

I know my mother's praying I keep it tasteful. And while I want to abide by her wishes in theory, the ceremony has been entirely too long, and I'm dying to give my wife a real kiss. One that she'll remember forever. One that's bigger and better than any I've given her before.

As Delilah turns toward me, I place my hand against her neck, sweeping my thumb across her cheek as I wrap my arm around her back. She stares at me, tears hovering in her eyes as I lean in. She holds her breath, and I hold mine as I pull her close and fuse our mouths together.

The cheers of the crowd die away, and my mind and body buzz with excitement as she places her hand over my heart and kisses me back. The moment's one I burn into my brain, never wanting to forget how I feel in this moment when we've become each other's.

When I pull back, I gasp for air and my head spins, knowing the ceremony's over and the good hasn't even begun.

As I walk down the aisle with my family looking on, I know the best is yet to come.

———

"Why are Carmen and Colleen here?" I ask, leaning over and whispering in Daphne's ear as we stand in the receiving line, greeting the last few guests.

"Delilah invited them." Daphne shrugs. "Honestly, if we couldn't invite any woman you've been with, there wouldn't be many people here you aren't related to."

Only my wife would give the okay to invite everyone from the neighborhood. I heard her say something about making it clear to every female in a five-mile radius that I was officially off the market. I didn't expect her to invite them all to the wedding. I just had to shake my head and know I probably would've done the same.

"What's wrong?" Delilah asks as the last wedding guest steps down the stairs to the dining area.

"Nothing, sweetheart." I touch her face and resist the urge to haul her into the storage room to officially consummate the marriage.

"I'll announce you to the guests after the wedding party, as you make your way down the stairs, and then we'll go right into your first dance as husband and wife," the DJ tells us so fast I can barely understand his words. Thankfully, I've been to enough weddings to know the spiel without being told.

"Sure," I say, still holding on to Delilah.

He heads toward the dance floor, and Delilah and I finally

look out over the crowd, which has more than doubled since church.

"Holy hell, who are all these people?" she asks with wide eyes.

"Your family," I answer simply.

"I never thought I'd have a family quite this big." She squeezes my hand, and I can see the tears coming again.

"Don't cry, Mrs. Gallo." I like how her title sounds coming out of my mouth. I'm not sure I won't say it on the daily because it's still too damn unbelievable.

The wedding party, which consists of Angelo, Daphne, Vinnie, and Michelle, marches down the stairway, forming a line for us to walk through as the DJ plays the theme music to *Rocky*, even though I told him not to.

But I can't be mad. It's my wedding day, and I married the girl of my dreams. "Ready?" I ask her, bringing her hand to my mouth and pressing my lips to her soft skin.

"Yes." She smiles, and it's like my whole world is complete. "I've never been more ready for anything in my life."

I raise my hand, along with hers, in celebration as we make our way down the stairs, going slowly so she doesn't fall over the ridiculously long dress and her crazy high heels. Everyone in the room is standing, clapping loudly, probably still not believing I actually tied the knot. Hell, I have a hard time believing it myself sometimes.

How the hell did I get this damn lucky? Of all the places her father could've left her, it was in front of my bar. Anywhere else and we probably never would've crossed paths. I'd still be alone, and she'd be... I put the thought out of my mind, trying not to think of what could've happened when that bastard abandoned them.

Angelo slaps my shoulder as we walk by, and for the first time in a long time, he looks happy. Ma's waiting at the end of the line, just before the dance floor, with Lulu in her arms.

Lulu's smiling as she looks at us and holds out her arms. I take her and hold her tightly, bringing my mouth close to her ear. "My baby girl. I love you so much. I'll always love you. Always protect you. You're mine now too. Forever and always."

She makes a little noise, blowing out a raspberry before grabbing on to my ear and giggling. Over the last few months, she's grown so much, and every day's like a new beginning. Watching her grow up, seeing her personality come alive, has been something I never could have explained to another human being without experiencing it.

"I think she needs a little brother," I tell Delilah as she touches my arm to lean in to kiss Lulu.

"Getting ahead of yourself, aren't you?" she says.

"Oh no. I want a house full of little ones running around." She pales a little, and I laugh, giving Lulu a kiss on the cheek before handing her back to my mother.

"Nothing would make me happier," Ma says, looking more than excited about the possibility of more grandchildren.

"Think of all the fun it'll be," I say as I usher Delilah toward the dance floor.

"What? A house full of kids?"

"Making all the babies," I correct her as I pull her into my arms, and the music starts.

She laughs, swinging her arm around my shoulder and taking my hand. When Luther starts to sing, her smile almost touches her eyes. She let me pick the song, and there's no one more romantic than Luther Vandross singing about love.

I hold her closely and sing the words to "Here and Now" to her. Every damn word of this song is exactly how I feel about Delilah.

She doesn't take her eyes away from mine as we dance around the floor. Everyone else in the room doesn't seem to exist. Just the two of us, moving as one to the words of Luther.

My heart's pounding as the realization comes crashing down on me. Delilah's mine forever. As I sing about loving her faithfully and promises for the future, I know when I look into her eyes, I'm the luckiest son of a bitch in the world.

With Delilah and Lulu by my side, anything's possible. I thought I had it all before they walked into my life, but I realize I had nothing. I was a shell of a man with no real purpose or future.

But now, with them, I have everything I ever could've wanted and more.

Delilah places her chin on my shoulder and brings her mouth close to my ear. "I love you," she whispers.

"I love you too, sweetheart," I tell her before singing the words to the song in her ear. I want her to hear the promises, the love, the way I plan to love her forever.

Her thumb strokes the back of my neck, brushing the skin just under my hair. As the song comes to an end, I start to back away, but she pulls me back. "We're not done," she says in my ear.

Luther melts into Celine, and Delilah takes another page out of my book, singing "Because You Loved Me" in my ear. I listen to every word, holding my wife tight, and close my eyes, reveling in the moment.

She thinks I gave her strength, but I didn't. It was always there, waiting to break free. She gave me a daughter, love, and more than I could ever give her. But damn it, I'll spend the rest of my life trying to show her what she means to me and how grateful I am for her to become mine.

As she sings the last word and our bodies stop swaying to the beat, I grab her face and cover her mouth with mine. The moment's sweet, slow, and everything it should be.

We turn to take a bow, and I see him. Standing in the back

of the room, clapping slowly and leaning against the wall with a smile, is my father.

"Fuck," I mutter, and I know shit's about to get crazy.

———

The Men of Inked Southside family saga continues in <u>Flow</u>.

The moment I looked into his eyes, I knew I was in trouble. The second I heard his name, I knew I should stay away.

Our fathers were enemies—Chicago crime bosses from rival families.

But that didn't stop him from pursuing me. Being together was dangerous, reckless, and totally hot.

He wanted me. I wanted him. What could possibly go wrong?

Tap here to read FLOW or visit *menofinked.com/flow* *for more info.*

FLAME

A MEN OF INKED HEATWAVE NOVEL

USA TODAY BESTSELLING AUTHOR

CHELLE BLISS

PROLOGUE
GIGI

*Mistake: an error in action, calculation, opinion, or judgment
caused by poor reasoning, carelessness, or insufficient knowledge.*

LIFE IS A SERIES OF MISTAKES. I've made my fair
share of them. Some were grander than others, but each time,
I tried to learn a new lesson, driven not to make the same one
more than once.

Falling for the wrong man has been my problem. Sure, I'd
done stupid things like every young person. Things that
could've changed the way the rest of my life had played out.

I didn't fear much. I also didn't think too far into the
future, wondering how my newest mistake would alter the
rest of my life. That's the thing about youth. We spend so
much time in the now, we rarely think about the future
because time seems infinite while we feel so indestructible.

Mistakes are how we learn and evolve. At least, that's
what my father told me, trying to get me not to make the
same mistake twice.

But I didn't listen. I'd made the same mistake twice. I'd
loved two boys in my life—Erik and Keith.

Both said they loved me.

Both cheated.

Both broke my heart.

The only thing I got right with Keith, my high school sweetheart, was that I didn't sleep with him. Just before graduation, I caught him cheating and later found out it wasn't the first time he'd done me wrong. *C'est la vie.*

I thought Erik, mistake number two, was the real deal. I thought we'd go the distance, but again, I was wrong. Although I gave him my virginity, trusting him more than anyone in the world, he couldn't keep his dick in his pants either.

I seemed doomed, weaving a web of ex-boyfriends and cheaters to carry with me, altering the way I'd feel about men for the rest of my life.

I didn't want to be that girl.

I didn't want to be bitter and untrusting of every man for the rest of my days. I knew there was goodness in the world.

My parents had been married for over twenty years. Happily married at that. My mother was everything to my father. She could do no wrong in his eyes. He worshiped her. Treated her like a goddess. I grew up watching that goodness, seeing how a man should love a woman. But no matter where I looked, all I seemed to attract were cheaters.

After cheater number two broke my heart, I vowed to myself never to let it happen again. I'd either have to learn to keep things casual with the men in my future or hone my man-picker and try to weed out the slimeballs from the good guys.

How totally laughable is that?

But then I met the man, the one I thought was number three. The one I couldn't imagine getting it right with because everything about him screamed error in judgment.

He was different from any man I'd ever opened my heart

to before. He was different from the boy I'd first given my body to.

...But that didn't mean he wouldn't become mistake number three.

CHAPTER
ONE
GIGI

"HE WANTS YOU." Tamara, my cousin, elbows me in the ribs while she gawks at a guy across the bar. "And he's hot, bitch."

I glance in his direction and look away quickly when our eyes meet.

Holy shit.

The guy isn't just hot, he's Freaking Fine with capital Fs.

But the last thing I need is more complication in my life, especially after what happened with Erik.

I tear my gaze away from him and roll my eyes at my cousin. "I'm not here for a hookup, Tam. I'm here to be with my girls, not some…"

"Hot piece of ass?" She finishes my statement and shoots me a smug grin.

"He's not *that* hot." I throw the thin red straw from my drink in her direction, hoping she'll change the subject.

I'm completely lying, of course.

This guy is hot as fuck. He's not a pretty boy…although he is handsome. He's a little rough around the edges and probably couldn't pull off the corporate look to save his life, but that doesn't make him any less hot. There's no way a guy like him rides his bike on the weekends and sits in a cubicle all day to pay the bills.

He lives *the life*.

He's all in.

Balls deep in the biker world by the looks of him. This isn't a getaway weekend to let his shit hang out and cut loose for a few days. Nope. This life—the drinkin' and ridin'—is part of his core.

On a hotness scale of one to ten, he's totally a twenty. But Jesus, he's a little scary too.

I've known plenty of bikers in my short twenty years walking this earth. Growing up with a biker dad who had biker friends, I've been around guys like the hottie my entire life. Since I worked at Inked during my summers, my circle of bikers grew, but they were all good guys...at least in their own fucked-up ways.

Mallory lifts the shot glass in front of her lips and stares over the rim at me. "You know how to get over a douche like Erik?"

I shake my head. "Don't say it," I warn her.

She slams back the shot and winces before the liquid has even slid down her throat. "Fuck, tequila is no joke," she grits out and coughs into her hand until tears are in her eyes.

"I told you," Mary, her identical twin sister, says and shakes her head in judgment. "You never listen."

"I'm fine. Anyway, what was I saying?" Mallory pauses as she slides the empty glass across the table. "Ah. I was telling you how to get over Erik." Her lips tip up. "Get under someone else."

Ugh.

That's totally Mallory, but not Mary. They are like night and day. Yin and yang. I'm not sure the world could take two Mallorys anyway, so it is a good thing they're so opposite. One's a wild child, and the other is a bookworm.

Tamara nudges another shot of tequila in my direction.

"Have a drink. Maybe you just need a little liquid courage to go talk to Flame."

I raise an eyebrow, glaring at my not-so-innocent cousin. "Flame?"

"Well..." She glances in his direction again and shrugs. "He's hot as fuck, so Flame works. Like, he's so hot, you'll get burned." She laughs, finding herself funny even if no one else at the table does.

I tap my finger against the table, staring at her in disbelief. "You know what happens when I drink tequila, Tamara?"

Her smug smirk grows bigger. "I do, and I'm counting on it." She waggles her eyebrows.

Oh boy. Tamara is supposed to be my voice of reason on this trip. We lied our asses off to our parents about spring break. We told them we were staying on campus to catch up on homework and to study for final exams. They would literally shit a brick if they knew we were here, especially during Bike Week.

"Was Erik even a good lay?" Mallory asks out of the clear blue because her mind always seems to be thinking about sex, even if it isn't her own.

"He was good." I grab the tequila because if my mouth is full or I'm coughing from the burn, I can't talk about having sex with Erik.

I don't know if he was good or not. He was good for me, but he was also the only person I'd ever gone all the way with. Sure, I fooled around with other guys, but my experience wasn't as impressive as some people's.

My answer to Mallory's question isn't a complete lie, but hell if I know if anyone else would say he was good or not.

I wince before the tequila even touches my tongue.

"Good or great?" Mallory asks.

I tip my head back, letting the liquid slide to the back of my mouth before it makes its way down my throat. My eyes tear up immediately, and I almost regret choosing the liquor over talking about my lack of sexual experience with my best friends.

"Does Erik look like he'd be great?" Tamara asks Mallory, saving me from answering.

Tamara knows all about my sex life and everything that happened with my exes. We've always been open and honest with each other. I know she's been with a few more guys than me, but she doesn't judge me. But Mallory doesn't have a clue because she'd totally judge me. She judges everyone.

"He looks like he'd be a lame lay," Mallory says, totally judging Erik.

"Oh, stop, Mal. He does not," Mary replies and pushes a chunk of her long red hair behind her shoulder.

"I've been with enough guys to be able to spot a bad, good, and great fuck a mile away." Mallory turns her attention toward the hot guy who was staring at me. "And he—" she tips her head in his direction "—would be a great fucking lay."

Mallory has no problem putting herself out there with men. She's unapologetic about her sexuality and goes after what she wants. I envy her, but only a little bit. Not the part where she sleeps with any guy who is even mildly good-looking and wants to get in her pants. But the part where she's so self-assured and gives no fucks what anyone thinks about her or her activities.

Mary purses her lips and looks at her sister in disgust. "You can't tell by looking at someone. Stop with your bull-shit, Mallory. Just because you're easy doesn't mean you're better than the rest of us."

Mallory sits up straighter and tilts her head, turning her attention toward her sister. "Sweetie, I'm not easy. Trust me. I make men work for this." She waves her hand in front of her chest. "I don't give it away to just anyone."

Mary, Tamara, and I laugh, but Mallory is shooting

daggers at us, looking like she's ready to lunge across the table and wrap her skinny fingers around our necks.

"You guys can kiss my ass," Mallory snaps. "We're talking about Gigi and the sexy beast over there making goo-goo eyes at her. Is Miss Priss too good for a biker guy like that? Or maybe you're too much of a prude to even talk to a hot-ass guy like him."

I grind my teeth and glare at Mallory. Sometimes, I hate her. She can be such a bitch. If it weren't for the fact that she is Mary's sister, she wouldn't hang around us. But wherever Mary goes, Mallory's right there with her. They're a package deal.

"I am not a prude," I hiss and return her glare.

"Mal, by your standards, everyone around this table is a prude," Tamara says, coming to my defense.

Mallory tips her head back and cackles. "Tam, I know you're not a prude. My sister might as well be a nun, and sweet little Gigi over here—" she waves her hand in my direction, and I do my best not to slap it away "—is well on her way to sexual boredom."

The two shots of tequila I've already downed along with the beer I've been nursing are starting to work their magic. Between Mallory's annoying words, the hot guy across the bar, and the alcohol running through my veins, I'm ready to blow.

I curl my fingers around another shot glass, and I know I'm going to regret everything about tonight when I open my eyes tomorrow. But right now, I don't give a shit. I'm over the conversation, and I'm so totally over Mallory, I'll do anything to shut her up.

"Fuck you, Mal. I've been around men like him my entire life. I didn't grow up like you, in a mansion surrounded by overprivileged assholes. A badass biker guy like that doesn't scare me."

"Put up or shut up, sweetie." Mallory grins, thinking she's

proved her point because she's always the unpredictable one in the group, while Mary and I play shit safe.

The chair scrapes against the floor and my knees wobble as I stand, but I can't stop now. If I falter in any way, I'll never hear the end of it from Mallory. The last thing I want to give her is more ammunition.

I lift the tequila to my lips, pouring it down my throat and barely wincing this time because it's already working its magic. "Don't wait up for me tonight."

Tamara's hand is on my wrist before I have a chance to storm away in dramatic fashion. "Do you think this is smart?" She stares up at me with wide eyes. "Don't listen to her. You know she's a bitch, Gigi, and she's just trying to piss you off."

I pull my arm away, feeling surer than ever that this is, in fact, the right thing to do. I'm going to prove them all wrong.

I can be wild.

I can be reckless.

I know how to have fun, and I can most certainly talk to a hot, badass biker guy without turning into a mumbling idiot.

"I'll be fine, Tam. I won't be back at the hotel room before the sun rises."

"Gigi, don't do this," Tamara begs, reaching for my hand again and missing.

"One second." I take another step backward.

Mallory's face is covered in a shit-eating grin, and Tamara and Mary both look horrified before I turn my back to them and make my way through the crowded bar.

Goddamn Mallory and her self-righteous bitchiness, making me do crazy shit. Well, it's not entirely her fault. A man named Patrón is just as much to blame as the bitchy redhead sitting at my table.

My eyes lock with the handsome stranger's, and all rational thought and any reason to stop what's about to happen go right out the window. God, he's beautiful. He has the sexy bed-head thing nailed with his light-brown locks going all different directions, begging to be touched and smoothed. The way his lips curve at the side, exposing just a hint of white teeth renders me a little stupid, and I almost trip over my own two feet, but I somehow stay upright.

Reaching into my back pocket, I grab my phone and unlock the screen as I take the final steps to the guy who's freaking hot.

This man isn't a college boy, looking to guzzle beer and make out at a frat party. Nope. Not this guy. He looks like the type who would have a different chick on the back of his bike every night of the week and make zero fucking apologies for it, offering nothing but a good time.

"Hey." I try to sound upbeat and excited instead of terrified and pissed off. "What's your number, handsome?" I lift my phone, moving my gaze from his face to the phone and back to him.

The corner of his mouth ticks, and I ready myself for a barrage of questions, but they don't come. "Hey, darlin'," he says smoothly.

Oh my God.

His voice is like velvet sliding over my skin, deep and gravelly. I stand there, unable to move, staring at his mouth, surrounded by that killer beard.

I've never kissed a guy with facial hair. I wonder what it would feel like to press my lips to his. Would the beard tickle? *Get ahold of yourself, girl.*

"Name's Pike." He tips his head back, tilting it a little to the side as his gaze sweeps over me.

I open my mouth and close it because, for a moment, I can't think of a damn thing to say. I can't stop staring at him and all thoughts, rational or not, just seem to vanish. I don't know how many seconds I stand like this, staring at him while he stares at me, but it's more than a few and entirely too long.

"Gigi," I finally mutter like I'm a complete and total imbecile, unable to say more than a few syllables. I can't seem to stop staring in his eyes. They're beautiful, but I can't tell if they're blue or green in the shitty lighting of the bar.

"Still want my number?" he asks, moving his hand across his face and partially covering his mouth to hide the smile he's sporting.

I nod because somehow, I'm still mute. *Way to go, Gigi.* In this moment, standing in front of this hot biker, who I now know is named Pike, I am indeed everything Mallory said I am.

Pike gives me a chin lift, and I raise my phone before he rattles off a set of numbers.

"Be right back." I smile, or at least, I think I do. With the tequila, it could very well be a grimace.

Thankfully, Pike doesn't ask me anything else. He just dips his head, those beautiful lips still quirked before I turn my back to him and hustle away as quickly as possible.

My eyes are wide as I stalk back toward the table where Tamara, Mary, and Mallory are all sitting, staring at me in complete disbelief.

"Tam, take down his number. If I die, you know where to start."

"Don't do this," she pleads and covers her face with her hands.

"Just take down his number."

"Don't listen to Mallory, Gigi," Mary tells me, but I shake my head.

"You want his number or not?" I stare at my cousin, ignoring the other two. "This is happening, so you can either have my back or not, Tam."

"If you fucking die," Tamara says as she fishes her phone out of her purse, "I might as well die too, because my daddy and your daddy will kill me. They'll find out about our fake IDs, underage drinking, and me letting you walk out of here with a scary as fuck biker."

I tap my foot. "Just open your contacts and type, Tam. I don't need a lecture."

She snaps her mouth shut and nods. Her fingers move fast as I read his number off the screen.

"His name is Pike."

"Of course it is," she mutters into her phone screen. "I still think—"

"Don't," I snap as I jam my phone into my jeans pocket while she stares at me with her mouth hanging open. "I'll be fine. You have his name and number. He's not going to murder me. I mean, look at him." I look over my shoulder, catching those beautiful eyes again.

"I'm looking, and he's fine," Mallory adds like any of us give two shits about her commentary or opinion.

I swallow hard, suddenly feeling like I haven't had a drop of liquid in my mouth for days. "Don't wait up for me. I'll see you when I see you." I turn on my heel and head toward Pike.

"Gigi," Tamara yells out, barely audible above the music and chatter of the people around me.

I don't stop, though. I walk straight up to Pike, taking in his vintage T-shirt, torn jeans, road-worn black biker boots, sexy bed head, and just fucking spectacular beard and eyes and say, "Wanna get out of here?"

He pulls the beer bottle back from his lips, eyes sweeping up my body before his lips curve again. "Thought you'd never ask."

CHAPTER
TWO
PIKE

"FANCY PLACE," the girl says as she walks into my hotel room, glancing around like she's waiting for something to jump out and bite her because it's a shit hole.

"I can take you back to your friends if you want." I can see she's not comfortable.

The chick—Gigi, I think she said her name was—drops her purse on the green carpet and turns to face me straight on. "I don't want to go. I'm right where I want to be." She sways as she speaks, clearly on the verge of drunk.

Why in the hell she asked me to take her to my hotel is beyond me. I'm not looking a gift horse in the mouth, though. When a hot chick asks me to get out of somewhere with her, I'm no fool; I take her wherever the hell she wants to go.

Drunk sex can be fun, but drunk sex with such a young chick may not be all it's cracked up to be. Besides being plain fucking stupid. I'm not an idiot. I've been with enough women, drunk and sober, to know when they want it and when they aren't quite sure.

Right now, the way she's looking at me, I'm not sure she wants what she's asked for. I grab the bottle of Jack Daniel's and pour two glasses, one for her and one for me, as she walks toward me. I push one in her direction, lifting the other one to my lips.

She takes the glass, staring at me as she moves slowly, lifting the rim to her mouth. "Pike, right?" she asks.

"Yeah, darlin'," I mumble into the amber liquid, gazing at her as she tips the glass back and takes a mouthful.

"I don't usually do this," she says, wincing as the burn slides down her throat and mine.

Those words, I believe. There's nothing in her body language that screams one-night stand. She didn't leap into my arms, attaching her lips to mine as soon as we walked through the door. I almost feel guilty having her here even if she asked me to bring her exactly where she's standing.

"Figured as much." I move to the bed, sitting on the edge, resting the glass of Jack on my knee as I look at this mint-ass chick with the wild brown hair, big blue eyes, and killer rack. But the thing that gets me most is those long-ass legs, smooth and shiny, dark from the sunshine kissing her skin.

"But I want to be here," she says quickly, moving to stand in front of me, but not close enough to where I could reach out and touch her.

"How old are you?" I ask, noticing the flawlessness of her skin as she stands near the bedside light.

"Twenty-two," she says, not meeting my eyes.

She's right at the edge of my limit. At twenty-six, anyone younger feels just plain wrong. I don't care how much they push their pussy in my face, I ain't looking for jailbait.

I take another sip, eyes locked on hers as she stares at me, shifting from foot to foot just a few feet away. "We can watch TV or just talk," I offer, trying to be a gentleman.

This wasn't exactly how I imagined the night going. When a chick like Gigi leaves a bar with me, I always assume there's pussy coming my way. And before tonight, I've never been wrong.

"You want to watch TV?" she asks softly, finally stilling

and staring at me with her head cocked and one eyebrow higher than the other.

I shrug, staring at the beautiful creature before me. She's like a Greek goddess, wild yet subdued, with hair rolling down her shoulders, covering her breasts in long waves. "Wasn't how I planned the night to go, but I'm down with whatever. This doesn't seem like your thing."

Her foot starts tapping, fast and loud. "What's that mean?"

"Just what I said. We don't have to have sex. We can just hang out."

Why is this girl busting my balls so damn hard? Usually, a girl's already in my lap, lips on mine, riding my cock through my jeans and begging to be filled. But not this one. She's staring at me, putting more than a few feet between us, not moving a muscle or throwing herself into my arms. I'm trying to be a gentleman, but she's making it damn hard to keep my shit together.

She slams back the Jack, slides the glass onto the nightstand, and moves in front of me with her legs touching my knees. I glance up, and it's my turn not to move.

"I want you," she says softly, placing her hands on my shoulders. Her eyes warm as her fingers touch the tender skin on my neck near my collar, stroking slowly back and forth. "I want you to fuck me, Pike."

I don't know what I said that made her flip a switch. Thirty seconds ago, I could've sworn we were going to watch a movie, or at the very least, we'd be heading back to the bar.

But now... Now she's staring at me with hungry eyes and nothing but determination.

She moves forward, lifting her legs one by one, planting her knees near my thighs as she climbs onto the bed. I slide my hands to her waist, steadying her as she settles onto my lap, pressing her sweet pussy against my dick.

The kiss is sloppy, her lips tasting like Jack but her breath laced with tequila. Her movements aren't smooth, sending up red flags all over the place.

I glide my hands up her sides to her arms before hauling her backward. "Are you drunk?"

"No," she says quickly, gasping when I tighten my hands around her upper arms as she tries to get to my mouth again. "Are you?"

She's a sassy thing, ready to throw words back in my face without hesitation.

"Darlin', it doesn't matter if I am. I'm a sure thing. But it matters if you are."

She tries to wriggle free of my hold, but I keep her pinned, my hands on her arms with her body moving in my lap, making my hard-on worse. "It doesn't matter for me either. I just want to have sex."

The last thing I want is to be someone's regret. Tomorrow, when she wakes up, I don't want to be the biggest mistake of her life or even this week. I want to fuck a woman because she wants me, not because liquor gave her the courage to step outside her comfort zone for a walk on the wild side.

In one swift move, I have her in the air and then flat on her back in the bed. But I don't dare join her. I stand quickly, moving away from her as she blinks up at me in shock.

"What the fuck?" she hisses, trying to sit up but falling backward. "What's wrong with you?"

"I don't do drunk chicks." I run my fingers through my hair, pacing a path in front of the bed.

She grunts. "I'm not drunk."

By her behavior, I can tell this isn't her typical scene. Throw in alcohol, and this shit could blow up in my face big-time.

"Fuck."

"Well," she says, waving her hands over her body. "Hell yeah, baby. I'm waiting for that."

I grab the bottle of Jack, walking toward the table and two

chairs near the window. "I need a minute to think." I'm trying to buy some time and a way out without pissing off this chick completely.

She's not timid or meek. She's quick with her words, and I know if I say the wrong thing, she's liable to go off half-cocked, completely losing her shit.

"Pour me one," she says, trying to sit up again, but she falls back down, letting out a loud sigh.

I fill my glass, collapsing into the chair after I set the bottle back on the table. "No. I think you had enough for one night."

"You're not my father," she snaps, fisting the comforter in her thin fingers and squeezing her eyes shut.

"It's a good thing I'm not. I'd tan your hide for doing what you're doing."

She throws up an arm. "Now he has a conscience."

"I always have a conscience." I bring the glass to my lips and look toward the doorway, wondering if I should just leave her here or take her back to the bar.

I'm leaning toward leaving her, letting her sleep off the liquor. The last thing I want is for her drunk ass to be on the back of my bike, sliding onto the pavement because she's too fucked up to stay on.

"Mr. Badass Biker Dude has a conscience," she says before she starts to laugh. "Mr. McHotterson doesn't want to fuck me because I had a few drinks." She pauses, and her laughter turns into loud giggles. "Maybe more like five or seven drinks."

I slide my gaze to her, but her eyes are still closed as she lies flat, unmoving except for her laughter inflating her chest. "However many you had, it was too many."

Her eyes open for a moment, still unfocused as she looks to her side, watching me. "That's priceless coming from you."

I down half the glass of Jack, trying to get my shit under

control because this girl is seriously getting on my nerves. "Coming from me?"

What the hell is wrong with me? An hour ago, I didn't give a shit if she was annoying or not. I wanted to fuck her until I passed out. But now she's lying in my bed, hurling insults and compliments in my direction because I'm trying to do the right thing.

"Well, yeah. You're a badass biker dude."

"What the fuck with that badass biker dude shit? I'm just a man looking to fuck."

"See." She waves a hand in my direction before dropping it to the bed like a ton of bricks. "Totally a badass biker dude thing to say." She closes her eyes again, and I stay silent, knowing the argument is useless. "I just wanted to get laid and get Erik off my mind. Is that so much to ask?"

She wanted to have breakup sex. She wanted to forget. I can understand that even if I've only had a handful of women who ever came close to breaking my heart.

I don't bother asking about Erik. I don't give two fucks about the guy, and at the moment, I don't give a fuck about the mouthy chick in my bed either. I sit here in complete silence, pouring myself another drink as she keeps on talking.

"There must be something wrong with me. Erik was awful in bed, or was I the one who sucked so bad I couldn't even get off?"

She's clearly way beyond tipsy based on the way she's spilling her guts. I'm not engaging in this conversation, but she has no problem continuing.

"If the badass biker dude won't even fuck me when I'm throwing myself at him, maybe I'm the problem. Two guys. Two cheaters. What else can it be but me?"

I'd love to tell her it's in no way her fault. She's beautiful even if she is a pain in the ass. I don't know a guy in his right mind who wouldn't explore her body for hours on end until he gave her a damn orgasm—or so many orgasms she passes out from lack of oxygen.

I lift the glass to my lips again, mumbling into the liquid as quietly as possible because I don't want to engage in her ramblings. I'm thankful when she doesn't say anything else and nothing but her soft snores fill the room.

"Thank fuck," I whisper, glancing toward the ceiling and wondering what I did to deserve this shit tonight. "Dodged that fucking bullet."

All I wanted was a good time. And instead, I'm saddled with a girl I don't even know passed out in my bed, snoring away like she's got no cares in the world.

I'm tempted to leave, go back to the bar, and finish the night the way I'd planned. But I can't bring myself to do it. We may not know each other, but I can't leave her in this room alone. When she wakes up, the last thing I want her to think is something happened when it didn't.

I'm not a gentleman, but I'm also not a complete asshole. I don't need any more trouble in my life. I had enough of that growing up and trying to break free of my parents.

I tip my head back, downing the rest of my drink before climbing to my feet and making my way toward the closet.

"Way to go, Pike." I pull out the spare blanket, ready to bed down on the shitty couch near the door.

This may be one of the longest nights of my life. And I have a feeling tomorrow morning isn't going to be any better.

CHAPTER
THREE
GIGI

"OH SHIT," I whisper, turning my head to the side, seeing the hottie from last night passed out on the couch.

Did we do it?

That's a big nope since I still have on my clothes from last night and they reek of tobacco and the day-after drunk stench.

My head throbs as I start to sit up, and I instantly collapse backward, wishing I hadn't had the tequila. "The bad news is, I have a headache. The good news is, I'm still alive," I whisper again, staring up at the ceiling.

Maybe I can slink out of bed and make it across the room without waking up the badass biker. I place my foot on the floor, my body still flat against the mattress and comforter that probably hasn't been washed since before I was born. I push that thought right out of my mind as my toes dig into the dirty shag carpet, and I slide out of the bed like I'm doing a fire drill. It reminds me of the old stop, drop, and roll they used to teach us during fire safety week in elementary school.

I keep my head up, trying not to focus on the damn stickiness of the carpeting on my palms as I inch closer to the door while crawling on my knees. I hold my breath, trying not to wake the guy and wincing the entire time because it feels like there's a little garden gnome playing the drums inside my skull.

I glance at the guy as I reach for the door, still on my hands and knees, holding my breath. My fingers are an inch from the metal knob when I lift up into a crouching position, feeling my escape almost at hand.

I don't want to be here when the guy wakes up. He's probably pissed because we didn't do it last night. I came back here fully expecting to bump uglies because Mallory had pissed me off so much, and I figured it was spring break and the perfect time to do something reckless.

"Where ya goin', darlin'?" asks the voice from last night, still sounding like sin, but deeper from sleep.

I freeze. "I thought I'd let you sleep."

He reaches behind his head, arm thrown over the back of the couch, and grabs my wrist before I can turn the handle. "You in a rush?" His touch is light. "I figured we could get some breakfast."

My eyes widen and my mouth falls open. "You want to have breakfast?"

His fingers tighten around my wrist, but not painfully. He's holding me with such a light touch, it catches me completely off guard, and I do nothing to pull away. "That's what people usually do in the morning."

"But..." I swallow, hating to bring up last night but thinking it needs to be out in the open. "But we didn't do it."

"Do it?" He repeats my words, rolling his body without letting go of my wrist until we're eye-to-eye. "Seriously?"

I nod and shrug, feeling like a bigger moron than I probably look. And that shit is pretty hard considering I'm on my hands and knees, trying to sneak out of his room without even brushing my hair.

The guy laughs. "No, darlin'. We didn't *do it*, but I'm

hungry, and I'm sure the hangover you're nursing needs some hair of the dog, along with something greasy."

I blink a few times, wondering if I'm hearing him right or if I'm still drunk and not quite understanding what he's saying. "You want to take me to breakfast?"

He lets go of my wrist and rubs his forehead, leaning over the couch with his elbows resting on his knees. "Clearly she isn't as smart as she seemed last night," he mutters to himself. "This is what I get for wanting to bang the hot girl."

I rise up higher on my knees, my back straight, still blinking at him with my mouth hanging open. "I'm the hot girl?" I ask.

He lifts his head enough to see my eyes. "Are you shitting me with this?"

"Pike, right?" I ask because last night is a little fuzzy, which is odd because I didn't have *that* much to drink. But it had been a while since I'd drunk something stronger than beer. He nods, and I continue as I finally climb to my feet. "I am not shitting you. Are you shitting me?"

He throws his body back into the couch and runs his hand through his still hot-as-fuck bed head. "About breakfast?" he asks.

"About everything."

His gaze intensifies as he stares up at me with those dreamy green eyes. "I'm hungry. Are you?"

"Yes."

"Then let's eat."

"Okay…" I whisper as my stomach growls.

It won't be so bad sitting across from Pike and sharing a meal. We don't have jack to talk about, but at least I'll be full and can buy a little time before I go back to my room and have to face Mallory.

"And, babe," he says and pauses, sitting motionless.

"Yeah?"

He's on his feet, hand on my jaw, eyes locked on mine.

"You were one of the hottest chicks there. You're a little fucking loony and can't hold your liquor worth shit, but you're off-the-charts hot."

My knees wobble a little like I'm drunk on his gaze and the words he just spoke. "Now you're really shitting me," I whisper, swallowing hard because I suddenly want to launch myself into his arms and finish what we started last night. "But I could eat."

The corner of his mouth twitches as his thumb grazes my bottom lip whisper-soft. "I could eat too."

Oh, fuck me dead. I know he's not talking about breakfast.

"So, breakfast..." My mouth's suddenly dry. My stomach isn't growling anymore; it's fluttering like a horde of tiny butterflies have taken flight inside it. I start toward the door, but he hauls me backward and in front of him again.

His eyes move down to the floor, but mine are firmly planted on his face. "You're probably going to need shoes."

I close my eyes, wishing I could start the last twelve hours over again. There's so much I would do differently, and maybe I wouldn't look like such a newb in front of this hot-as-fuck badass biker guy.

My face heats, and I want to crawl into a hole and die. "Yeah. Shoes would be good," I whisper, unable to take my eyes off him.

He releases me, but I don't move right away. It's like he's cast an invisible net around me, holding me to him. Maybe it's the fact that I haven't had any action in months, or the fact that every time he looks at me, I can see the hunger in his eyes...and he's not thinking about bacon and eggs.

"Sandals," he says as he sits on the couch and pulls on a boot.

"Yeah," I say, still not hauling ass because I'm too busy watching his every move. The way his muscles dance under his ink-covered skin is completely hypnotic.

"Do you need me to put them on your feet?"

"Yeah," I whisper again because my brain is fried, and I'm not thinking straight. "Wait, no." I wave my hands when he starts to stand. "I got it."

"Thank fuck for small miracles," he teases, putting his ass back on the couch as he grabs the other boot.

I silently chastise myself as I walk around to the side of the bed, finding my sandals placed neatly together, facing outward like he cared. I slide my toes between the plastic and close my eyes, trying to calm the fuck down. "Is it a far walk?"

"Nope. We're taking my bike. That a problem?"

Something about that makes me smile. Erik and Keith didn't have bikes. They both preferred their souped-up sports cars to the roar of a motorcycle. But they were boys, and Pike is all man.

"Nope," I repeat his words and tone. "Just let me make myself halfway presentable."

I don't wait for his approval before I take off toward the bathroom and shut myself inside. Leaning against the door, I allow myself a moment to freak out. Once I've whispered "Holy shit" for the tenth time, I move toward the sink and get a glimpse of my post-tequila face. I scrub away the smeared mascara with the little soap that is still in the wrapper next to the sink. As soon as my face is dry, I almost squeal when I find his toothpaste and place a drop on my finger, scrubbing my teeth and the rancid taste of last night away. "It'll do," I say to myself in the mirror, wiping away the toothpaste from my lips.

"Let's hit it," he says near the doorway, ticking his head toward outside as soon as the bathroom door opens. "I'm starving, and the day is wasting."

"What time is it?" I ask him as I brush past him and shield my eyes from the blazing sun.

"One."

"One?" I gasp, realizing I slept half the day away. "In the afternoon?"

He's right on my heels, laughing because I'm an idiot and making no moves to try to hide how stupid I can be, especially around him. "No, darlin'. The sun decided to come out at night just for you."

I slap his chest as soon as he's next to me. "Don't be a dick."

"Don't make it so easy."

"I don't make shit easy, Pike."

He reaches into his pocket and taps the cigarette packet into his palm. "No shit. I'm learning that quickly, and the hard way," he teases with a smirk, and it takes everything in me not to smack him again.

"Um, Pike."

"Yeah?"

I tuck a lock of hair that had fallen free behind my ear. "Can you not smoke?"

"Seriously?"

"Uh. Yeah. I don't like it, and it's not good for you."

He tilts his head but doesn't put up much of a fight before putting the cigarette back in the pack. "It can wait."

I try not to smile at my victory.

An hour later, we're jamming pancakes down our throats like it's an Olympic sport and we're both aiming for the gold medal.

"How old are you?" I ask Pike.

"Twenty-six. You?"

"I told you last night I'm twenty-two." Which was a lie, of course, but I'm not going to tell him the truth now after everything that's happened. I am a month shy of my twenty-first birthday, even if the fake ID in my pocket says otherwise.

Pike nods, shoving another forkful of pancakes into his mouth, chewing slowly as he stares at me across the table. I squirm in my seat because I expect him to call bullshit, but he lets it go. "Where ya from?"

"Miami. You?"

"Up north."

"Northern Florida?"

"A little farther."

I roll my eyes. I lied about my answer, but at least I was more specific than "down south."

"Are you a badass biker for a living?" I set my fork down, knowing if I don't stop eating soon, I'll need a nap and probably assistance wobbling out of this dive.

Pike laughs, and it's the most beautiful thing in the world. Serious Pike is hot as fuck, but laughing Pike takes my breath away. "Nah, darlin'. I'm not a biker in that way. I ride because I love it. I'm not in an MC or anything."

"So, what do you do?" I ask again because he's cagey, and I'm not getting much out of the guy.

"I'm a tattoo artist."

My eyes widen because I know the community is both big and small. Sounds like an oxymoron, but I know the probability of most tattoo artists in the South knowing my family is pretty damn high. Inked is one of the most well-known shops in the South after being featured in dozens of magazines over the years.

"That sounds fun." I lean back in the booth, fidgeting with my napkin.

"What do you do?"

"I'm between jobs right now, but I'm looking for work as a graphic designer." Technically, I'm not lying. I am between jobs, but I leave out the bit about my college classes. I will be doing graphic design, but not on paper or in a digital format. I'll be tattooing skin just like him.

"What's your medium?" he asks, running his last forkful of pancakes through the lake of syrup on his plate.

"I'm a traditionalist. I like drawing by hand."

"Me too. Those girls from last night old coworkers?"

"Shit. I forgot about them." I pull out my phone from my purse, but I don't look down at the screen. "One is my cousin, but we all work together and figured Daytona was the place to be this week."

I glance down, finally seeing the five missed calls and ten text messages from Tamara. My eyes widen at the level of crazy in her text messages.

Are you okay?

Hey asshole, I'm getting worried.

Are you alive or dead?

Fucker… You better reply to me!

I know you're busy sucking cock and all, but use those fingers to text me back, bitch.

Goddamn it. Should I call the police?

Your ass better be dead since you're not replying.

I'm going to kill you when I see you again.

OMG. If you're dead, your father is going to kill me, and then my father will kill me.

I'm too young to die. I hate you.

"They lookin' for you?" he asks as I chew on my bottom lip, typing out a reply.

At breakfast. I'm fine. Great, even. Don't worry so much. I'll text you later, and we can meet up for drinks.

"Nah. They're good. They know I'm always safe."

"You know that shit last night was *not* safe."

I lift my gaze to Pike. "I'm alive, aren't I?"

He nods. "If you'd have gone with someone else, you might not be. You can't just walk up to a stranger in a bar, ask if they want to get out of there, be shit-faced drunk on top of it, and think you're definitely going to walk away unscathed."

"But I did." I shrug as my phone vibrates in my hand.

Thank fuck. I was about to call Uncle James or Uncle Thomas.

"You didn't look like a serial killer."

Pike's face grows serious as he kicks back into the booth, crossing his arms over his chest, showing off that ink and those muscles. "And what does a killer look like?"

"Fuck if I know, but not you." I smile because he's right, but I feel a lecture about to start, and I'm not going to listen. "I'm alive and breathing."

"Because it was me you left with. Anyone else and shit could've been way different."

I lean forward, pushing my empty plate to the side, and stare at the hottie who's now preaching to me on personal safety. "You're not my father, Pike, and while I appreciate the lecture, it's not needed. I was looking for a good time, and while it didn't end the way I'd planned, shit turned out just fine."

We're headed to Froggy's in an hour. Meet us there, and bring the hot guy and his friends if he has any.

"Fair enough."

"Now, my friends are going to Froggy's if you want to go too. But I imagine after last night, you probably want to ditch me for someone else. So, if you can just drop me there, you can do your thing and I'll do mine."

"You going to pull that shit you did last night with someone else tonight?"

I shrug and give him my best poker face. "I don't know. The day is young, and the night is long."

Pike's jaw tightens and his eyes flash. "I'm coming," he says quickly.

"Don't put yourself out or anything. I don't need a bodyguard, especially not someone I don't even know. I've survived this long without you watching over my shoulder. I think I'll last another night."

Pike leans forward, our knuckles touching on top of the table. He studies me. "I know you don't need me to watch over you, but if you're going home with anyone, it's going to be me, darlin'. We never finished what we started last night, and I'm a man who likes to follow through."

"That's so romantic," I tease, rolling my eyes.

"You want romance, I'll give you romance. You want to fuck, I'm the man to fuck you. Whatever you want, I'll be the one giving it to you."

"Why?" I blurt out, wondering why this hot-as-fuck biker guy wants to saddle himself with me all day.

"Because you seem hell-bent on a good time, and there's no one more equipped to give you that good time than me. You want to let your hair down and get wild, baby, I'll be right there with you. The one thing I won't do—" he touches his hand to his chest "—is let another man be the one to give it to you."

I suck in a breath, feeling like he's punched me straight in the gut. I should hate him. I should tell him to go to hell. I can have fun with any guy here. And trust me, there're thousands of them here this week to pick from.

"Okay." He's hot as fuck, and like Mallory said... The best way to get over Erik is to get under someone else.

That someone else might as well be the hottie across from me, who's staring at me like he's starving even though he ate a stack of pancakes it shouldn't be humanly possible to consume.

He leans back and reaches into his pocket. "Let's blow this joint and get the party started, yeah?"

"I don't want to go to the bar."

The thought of drinking right now makes my stomach turn.

"I'll take you anywhere you want."

"Take me back to your hotel room."

CHAPTER
FOUR
PIKE

I OPEN the door to the bathroom, tucking the edge of the towel around my waist and stop dead. Gigi's standing in the middle of the room with her towel still wrapped around her body, hair damp and wild as she pushes her fingers through her locks.

"Do you have a brush?" she asks.

My gaze travels up her body, taking in her long, tanned legs as she turns to face me.

"I don't." I barely get the words out because she's still in the damn towel.

She said she was going to get dressed before I headed into the bathroom to wash off yesterday's grime. When she left the bathroom, she had her dirty clothes pulled tight against her chest like she was using them as a blocker between us.

"Figured you wouldn't with that hair." She ticks her chin upward, smiling at the mess that's on my head. It's always in a state, and I gave up a long time ago trying to tame the style in any way.

I rub the back of my neck, trying to do something with my hands besides ripping the towel off her body and having my way with her. "I can run and get you one."

"No," she says, taking a step closer to me. "Don't go."

I still haven't moved from the doorway to the bathroom. It's like my feet are glued to the floor. Besides my chest heaving and my heart pounding frantically, the only other thing moving on my body is my cock.

She reaches for my face, but I grab her wrist, needing to set her straight. "Darlin', don't start something I'm not sure you want to finish."

The warning is gentle and soft, but necessary. After last night and standing here in our towels now, I want her so badly, I'm aching to bury myself deep inside her.

Her eyes burn with just as much need as mine do. "What if I don't want to stop?" she challenges, stepping even closer so her towel brushes against my chest. "Maybe I want this just as much as you do."

"Maybe isn't a yes, Gigi. I don't want there to be any miscommunication about what's going to happen. I'm wound so tight right now, I might break."

Her free hand moves to my towel, groping my cock through the rough fabric. I suck in a breath and close my eyes, tightening my hold on her wrist. "Gigi."

She moves her fingers up and down my shaft, causing my legs to tremble. "I want you, Pike. I've wanted you since the moment I laid eyes on you."

I open my eyes, peering down at her beautiful face and soft smile. "You don't know what you're asking."

"I'm asking you to fuck me." She tightens her grip, moving her hand faster until I'm so hard, I'm almost panting. "I know exactly what I'm asking, Pike. But if you can't give it to me…"

"I can give you everything." I lift my hand to cup her face and angle my mouth close to hers. "I want to taste your mouth." I run my thumb along her bottom lip. "I want to taste you everywhere."

She moves her hand to the top of my towel, pulling the

material apart as my lips crash down on hers, getting the taste I've been dying for since last night. I slide my hand into her hair, holding her face to mine as I swallow her moans and my own. Her towel falls away, pooling near our feet as her skin touches mine. It's like a million little electric shocks go off at once.

Her hands are on my hips as I slide my other hand to her back, memorizing the dip of her spine as I move my palm to her ass. "So fuckin' soft," I murmur against her lips.

"So fuckin' hard," she murmurs back as her fingertips move up to my abdomen, toying with my V.

My stomach clenches at the way her fingers trail over my flesh, sending goose bumps scattering across my body.

She's hesitant. I can tell by her movements this isn't her usual thing. Most women would be grabbing at my cock, but not her. She's busy touching my body, exploring what I have elsewhere and not what's the usual main attraction.

I pull my lips away, knowing I have to give her another out. She's a big talker, but maybe the reality of what we're about to do has finally sunk in. "We don't have to do this."

She shakes her head, staring up at me with hooded eyes. "I want this. I just need to take it slow, okay?"

"I'm not looking for fast, darlin'. You take all the time you want because I know I will." I smirk, our faces only inches from each other.

There's something so intense about staring at someone this close. Something so intimate about it. Rarely have I ever done this with anyone. I never care about the emotion in their eyes or the tenderness they need. But Gigi is different. I am different with her.

She lets out a shaky breath, lifting up on her tiptoes to give me her lips again, and this time, I don't hold anything back. I slide my tongue along her bottom lip, loving the way she tastes of mint and strawberries.

Then she pulls away. "I have to be honest with you," she

says, holding my sides but keeping her eyes locked on mine. "I haven't been with a lot of guys, and I was always in a relationship if I slept with someone. This is all new to me. I need you to know…"

"I don't need to know anything."

"But what if I'm bad?" She blinks up at me like she's surprised by my words.

"You can never be bad at anything. There's no such thing. Do what feels right and good. Do what comes naturally, and I promise you it'll be good for the both of us."

She nods, seeming satisfied by my statement. I've never understood that way of thinking. I've never had a bad time in the sack, no matter the level of skill or number of partners the person has had before me. I don't care if she's been with one or a dozen guys as long as her mind, hands, and body are only on me.

"No more talking." We've already said too many words, and I can't go another minute without my body attached to hers in some form.

Her tits press against my chest as I take her mouth again, claiming her long and deep with the kiss, showing her how I feel and how badly I want her, experience be damned.

She slowly slides her hands over my stomach, moving to my abdomen before gliding them across my trail of hair, finding my hard cock. The moan that escapes her lips along with the soft warmth of her skin makes my dick twitch in anticipation.

"You're big," she mumbles against my mouth because I don't give her a chance to get away this time. I knead her ass cheeks, humming my appreciation at the way her hand strokes along my shaft. When her fingertips find my piercings, she freezes.

"Oh. My. God." She pushes me away with one hand, cock still firmly in her grasp with the other. Her eyes are glued to my dick and are wide, her mouth hanging open. "I didn't know you had…"

I move my hips toward her, and my cock bobs, showing off the shiny jewelry that has often gotten a mixed reaction from the ladies.

"Can I?"

I don't think anyone's ever asked for a better view, but if that's what she wants, she can do whatever the fuck she pleases. "Anything you want."

She folds her legs, kneeling before me on top of the towel that had fallen near our feet. I place my hands on my hips, stopping myself from pulling her in and jamming my dick, piercing and all, across her pretty pink tongue.

"You've never seen a pierced dick?" I ask.

She shakes her head. "Not this close, but I have seen them. Never touched one, though."

"Figured all the college boys were into shit like this."

"Shh," she says, peering up for a moment with her eyebrows drawn together before she goes back to staring at my cock. "It's an apadravya, right?"

"For a chick who hasn't seen many, you sure got the name nailed."

She shrugs, toying with the metal. "I know a little about this type of stuff. It's always fascinated me."

I can't take my eyes off her fingers as they move around the tip of my dick. The girl is a conundrum. She's innocent. There's no denying that. It's not an act either. But she knows shit too. Shit someone with her level of innocence probably shouldn't know. I don't ask because I don't care. There's a hot chick on the floor, eye-to-eye with my junk, touching me. That's all that fucking matters.

Her tongue pokes out of her mouth, sweeping across her bottom lip, and I grip my sides harder, trying to control myself. "I've heard it's pleasurable."

"There's one way to find out." I'm about done with show-

and-tell, but then I remember I have to be patient. Something I've never been known to be.

"Can I lick it?"

Oh. My. Fucking. God. This girl is too much. "Of course." I'm not a fucking idiot. "Deep-throat it if you want."

She gazes up the length of my body, looking small kneeling before me. "Let's not get extreme."

"A guy can hope." I smirk and then hold my breath as she leans forward, that cute-ass soft tongue coming out from between her lips, reaching for a taste of my cock.

I can't take my eyes off her. The curve of her breasts as she moves toward me. The slenderness of her fingers as they wrap around my shaft, milking me as she tentatively touches the tip of her tongue to the head of my cock.

My body rocks forward, wanting her warmth and the wetness only her mouth can deliver. I close my eyes because watching this sweet, pure girl take me into her mouth is too much for me to handle.

"Fuck," I hiss as she slides her tongue over the tip, across the shaft, taking me slowly, inch by inch between her lips.

The warmth is instantly gone. "Did I do something wrong?"

I blink down at her in confusion. "Don't stop, darlin'. It was the closest to heaven I've ever been."

She smiles, liking the praise, but then something passes across her face. "I've been told I suck. Not in the good way either."

"Whoever told you that should be shot. There's no such thing as a bad blow job." Technically, I'm lying. There is such a thing, but I doubt this girl could do anything wrong.

Her tongue's back on my dick a moment later, and I breathe a sigh of relief. If there's any more talking, I might lose my mind.

Her lips close around my shaft as she sucks me deep. No teeth with the perfect amount of suction and tongue. I'm in heaven, loving the way she uses her hand, not leaving an inch of my cock untouched.

"Just like that, baby." I tangle my fingers in her hair. I can't keep my hands to myself anymore. I want to touch her. I need to touch her.

"Darlin'," I say softly in a shaky breath as her tongue dances around the piercing, sending shock waves throughout my system. "Up, baby."

She blinks up at me with my cock still nestled between her lips, eyebrows drawn inward like she's confused.

"I want to taste you."

The corners of her mouth tip up, grazing the underside of my shaft with her teeth. I don't wince or grimace at the sensation because the last thing I want this girl to think is that I'm not enjoying myself.

I reach down, helping her stand before wrapping my arm around her back, hauling her toward the bed. My mouth is back on hers as our bodies fall backward, bouncing when we hit the bed. She lands on top of me, but she never stops kissing me as her hands slide across my shoulders, holding on to me.

I roll, pinning her underneath me, careful not to crush her with my weight. I kiss a line down her jaw to her neck, licking at the soft skin below her ear. Her fingernails dig into the skin of my upper back as she arches her back like she's offering her chest up to me and not satisfied with my mouth anywhere else.

Lifting up on one elbow, I stare down at her tanned skin, shining like a beacon underneath me. I slide my finger across the swell of her breasts as her breathing accelerates, and her eyes are fixed on me.

"You're so beautiful." I gaze down her body, letting my eyes linger on her wonderland of flesh.

"I could lose…"

I shake my head. "You're perfect the way you are."

Suddenly, I'm a Chatty Cathy too, whispering sweet nothings to a girl I'll never see again.

She's fierce, yet unsure about everything sexually, almost like she's a virgin. I gulp at the possibility, hoping like fuck she's just had dipshit college boys in her life and that she's not entirely new to sex.

"Have you really done this before?"

She nods, giving me a small smile. "Yes, Pike. I'm not a virgin. I just…"

"Had shit boyfriends."

She nods again. "It was never like this."

"Like what, darlin'?"

"Slow and soft."

Fuck.

The last time I took it slow and soft was back in high school when I didn't know my ass from my dick. But here I am, going slow and soft for this girl because she needs it. Lying here naked with her, I'd do anything she asked without question.

"But I ache, Pike." She shifts her legs, rubbing her knees together and driving me crazy with desire. "I ache for you like I've never ached before."

"I'm going to make you feel good," I promise, leaning forward and swiping my tongue across her nipple.

She gasps, pushing her tits upward and against my mouth as I run my tongue around the outside edge of her nipple.

She burrows her fingers in my hair, pulling my head down against her skin. "Don't tease me, Pike."

I gaze down at her, noticing her rosy cheeks and the sheen of sweat across her skin. "I'm not teasing, I'm savoring, darlin'."

She growls a response, but I ignore her, going back to what I was doing and enjoying the fuck out of it. Her skin is warm and smooth against my lips, but her nipples are hot and hard on my tongue. Her body shakes as I close my lips around the tip, sucking with the right amount of pressure to drive her wild and have her on the brink.

Her nails claw my skin as her legs rub together, her body begging and needing more as she writhes underneath me.

I slide my hand down her side, making my way to her brown curls before slipping between her legs. Her knees fall to the sides, meeting the bed and giving me access to all of her.

The girl is wet. Almost dripping with need and I've barely touched her. I have to test her and figure out what she can take before I try to fuck her. The last thing I need is to hurt her, and she seems so sketchy and unsure about sex, I'm not sure I believe her depth of experience.

She rocks into my hand as I slide my fingers through her folds, parting her skin and stroking the pad of my thumb over her clit. She gasps, jumping like I shocked her at the contact.

I glance up, but she smirks with hazy, lust-filled eyes. "Don't stop," she begs me.

I mumble words against her skin, nipple still in my mouth, so I don't make a bit of sense and I don't care. I'm too busy exploring her flesh, tasting her body, and enjoying the fuck out of myself to speak or stop.

She tenses as I slide a finger down through her wetness and around the promised land, but as soon as I start to push inside, she relaxes and spreads her legs even wider.

She's tight, but not virginal tight. She may not have been with too many guys, but I'm not the first one to enter this territory. She doesn't even grimace as I push my finger all the way inside her body, relishing the warmth of her skin on mine. She moves with me, meeting every thrust of my fingers as her pussy contracts around me.

I pull out, adding a second finger, going slower this time and sucking harder on her nipple. She moans, pushing her ass upward and head backward like she's in heat.

"God, Pike. I want you so bad. Fuck me. Fuck me, please. I can't wait any longer. Don't make me beg."

I lift my head, fingers still buried inside her, rubbing her G-spot. "I'll never make you beg." I smirk, loving the way this girl reacts to everything I say and do. "Unless we're playing that game."

"Not now. Please."

I reach across her, grabbing the condom I'd left there last night when I thought I had a sure thing coming back to my room. Gigi moves both hands to my cock, jerking me as I place the wrapper between my teeth and tear it open.

"You want the honors?" I ask her, loving the way she touches me.

She shakes her head and pulls away, leaving my cock feeling cold and alone. "Not with the metal. You do it."

I lean back, watching every movement. I make quick work of the condom after years of practice, barely noticing the piercing as I roll it down over the tip and shaft, readying myself for what I know is going to feel like heaven.

She places her feet on the bed, spreading her legs open as I slide between her thighs and line up our bodies. I can't take my eyes off her face as I lean forward on my elbows, ready to fuck this girl, but knowing I have to take my time.

I lower my mouth to hers, kissing her soft and gentle as my cock nudges her opening. She moans again as I press inside slowly. Inch by inch, I sheath my cock in the warmth of her pussy, causing my eyes to roll back from the tightness and pressure I haven't experienced with anyone else in a long time.

Her fingernails are on my skin, raking across my back as I push all the way inside until I'm fully seated. She gasps into my mouth, and I swallow down her pleasure, taking it as my own.

I rock my hips, thrusting in and out as slowly as I can with as hard as I am. Sweat breaks out across my skin as the mix of pleasure and torture washes over me. She locks her ankles around my ass, holding me to her, not giving me much leeway to be aggressive.

I roll my hips, moving any way I can in this position. She pulls her lips away, staring up at me as I rock into her. I thought our moment was intense before, but it's nothing compared to this. Being buried balls deep, staring into each other's eyes, I'm momentarily winded from the intimacy.

My heart pounds as I realize I could like this girl. Not just like her, I could spend more than one night staring into her big blue eyes, listening to her babble about whatever she'll talk about. I could spend forever between these legs, fucking her, and never get bored.

I push my thoughts out of my mind, needing to stay in the moment and not think about tomorrow. We never promised each other more than this. More than a fuck at a shitty-ass motel in Daytona. She's a career girl with hopes and dreams that probably didn't include a guy covered in tats, working nights at a tattoo shop.

Get a grip, Pike. My mind keeps straying, and I have to remind myself to let shit go. Gigi grounds me, bringing me back to the moment when her tongue runs along the skin near my collarbone.

"Harder," she pleads, digging her heels firmly in my ass.

I pull back, breaking the bond her ankles have around my back and slam into her.

"Yes!" she screams, bucking against me, grinding her pussy against my body. "Fuck yes!"

It doesn't take but a few more minutes for me to teeter on the edge of orgasm. With one hand, I reach between us, rubbing her clit as I thrust inside her, deep and sharp, quickening the pace each time.

She gasps for air as her body locks up, following me over the cliff into bliss. "Jesus," I murmur as I nearly collapse on top of her.

"Again," she says almost immediately.

"Little tiger," I whisper, staring down at the most beautiful girl I've ever seen.

"I hope you're up for more, big boy, because I'm nowhere near done."

"I could go all night."

She pushes me backward, climbing on top of me. "Let's see if you mean what you say."

I slide out from underneath her as she paws at me like she's going to pull me back to the bed. "I'm going to need to get rid of this condom and get another."

"Take your time. I'll just stare at your ass and touch myself."

I turn, looking over my shoulder to see she's a girl of her word. "Fucking incredible," I whisper, running to the bathroom because I'm nowhere near done fucking her.

CHAPTER
FIVE
GIGI

FIFTEEN MONTHS Later

The day I stepped off the stage with the diploma in my hand, I felt like I was finishing a chapter and starting a new one. The grown-up part of my life I'd been waiting for since I was a little kid.

The only thing I'd ever dreamed about was working at Inked. My artistic skills, I clearly got from my dad. He'd sit with me for hours when I barely reached his hip, watching me draw picture after picture as I tried to copy his work. He was a patient teacher and an even better father. There isn't a time in my life I remember art not being part of my world.

My poor mother didn't have a creative bone in her body. She was a numbers girl, and math bored the crap out of me... much to her disappointment. She dreamed of me growing up and becoming some dull corporate suit, slaving away for someone else instead of being tied to Inked.

After four years of college and four summers interning at Inked, I am finally ready to take my rightful spot, or should I say chair, at the shop.

"I don't understand why you need to move out," my mom

says as I sit down at the kitchen table with a cup of coffee, trying to get time to pass a little quicker.

I can't wait to get to the shop. My uncle Bear decided he would be my first official customer, and I couldn't be happier. But I could probably ink a piece of shit on him, and he'd still love it.

"I love living here, Ma, but I want to have my own place. You're great and Dad is the best, but I haven't lived under your roof and with your rules in four years. I just think it's the next step I have to take in my new life. Living here feels like taking a step backward, and I'm all about moving forward."

"Can't you stay a few weeks? I've missed you." She leans against the counter and sips her coffee, looking just as beautiful as ever.

"I'm picking up my keys before work today, but it'll take me a few days to get everything in order, so I'll be here until the place is ready to move in."

"Take your time, baby," she says softly before letting out a long and very dramatic sigh. "Make sure it's perfect before you officially move out."

I want to tell her that I moved out four years ago, but I don't. My mom is a big softy, and by the way she's looking at me, she's about to cry.

"Did you move back home after college?" I ask her.

She shakes her head. "I love my parents, but there was no way I could ever live under their roof again. I knew once I left for college, I'd never go back."

"Even if they were great parents, could you have gone backward after having a taste of freedom?"

She slides onto the chair next to me and places her cup on the table. "I don't think I could've gone back." Her lips pull downward because she realizes where I'm coming from, and no matter what she says, I won't change my mind. "Maybe we could build a guesthouse out back for you."

"Mom, come on now. I already signed my lease. And I'm sorry, I love you both, but living in the backyard won't work for me."

It's a sweet gesture and completely my mom, but in no way, shape, or form will that type of living arrangement ever work for me. I'm already going to be spending all day working with my dad. The last thing I want is to see him every night, checking up on me, and living under the Gallo microscope.

"I worry about you living alone."

"I'll be fine, Ma. Tamara is going to live with me for the summer, and when she's home on break too. If all goes well, when she graduates next year, she'll move in with me too. Where's Dad?" I change the subject because there's no way I'm living at home, and I know the mention of my cousin's name will get Mom off my back...at least for a little while.

She wraps her hand around her coffee mug and stares out the window overlooking the backyard. "He went in early. There's a new artist starting today, and he wants to train him before everyone gets there."

"Maybe I should be there too. Why didn't Dad ask me to go?"

Mom laughs. "Baby, you grew up in that place, and you've been working there for four summers. I'd hardly call you a new employee." She laughs and brings her gaze back to me. "I'm pretty sure you could train this boy yourself."

I push away from the table, about to stand, when she covers my hand with hers.

"Stay a little longer. You don't have to be there for thirty minutes, and I feel like we never have quiet time like this together."

"I don't want to be the last one there on my first day, Mom. How about we go shopping on my day off and buy some stuff for my new apartment?"

I'm grasping at straws here, but the last thing I want to do is sit here another twenty minutes, listening to my mother hem and haw about how I shouldn't move out. I figure if I ask her to help decorate my new place, she'll feel more invested, or at the very least, like she helped me.

That's the thing about Suzy Gallo. She's not one to sit idly by when her loved ones are in need. It doesn't matter that I only need help to pick out the perfect throw pillow or the best pots and pans, she wants to be included.

Right on cue, her face lights up. "I would love that. I know all the best places we can go too. We'll make a day of it."

"It's a date, Mom. I'm off Friday, if that works. But if not, I completely understand."

"Luna and Rosie have cheerleading camp starting on Wednesday," Mom says, looking pained and moderately horrified that her two daughters are cheerleaders. "So, I have all day on Friday to be with you."

"Perfect." I push away from the table and walk toward the sink. "I better run. The landlord is probably waiting for me, and I want to make a good impression."

Mom follows me, leaving her coffee mug where it was sitting on the table. She leans against the counter, staring at me as I rinse and place my mug in the dishwasher. "I'm proud of you, sweetheart. I'm proud of the independent woman you've become."

My insides warm. "That's because I had two kick-ass parents."

Her smile falters.

I know she wants to chastise me for my crude language, because she's never been one for cussing.

"We want nothing but the best for you."

I lean over and kiss her cheek because, hell, I love my mother. "I couldn't have asked for a better mother. I mean it, Mom."

She wraps her arms around me, hauling me close. "I love you, baby. I can't believe you're old enough to move out. I never wanted this day to come, but now that it has, I couldn't be prouder."

That's my mom. She's full of all the goodness in the world. She never has a mean thing to say about anyone or anything. She wears rose-colored glasses when it comes to life. There are times where she's a little overprotective and worried about everything for no good reason, but I wouldn't change a thing about her.

"I have to run, Mom." I pull away from her embrace even though she tries to squeeze me tighter. "I don't want to be late on my first day."

Mom laughs. "Well, at least you know the owners. I'm pretty sure they won't fire you if you're a few minutes late."

"Mom, I don't want to be treated any different."

"Different from whom, baby girl? Besides Kat, everyone is family and works by their own rules."

I shrug. "The new guy. I don't want to set a bad example, ya know?"

She nods. "Go and have a great first day at work."

It's all silly. I'd worked at Inked for four summers, but interning is entirely different from earning my seat at the shop. Today feels like the first day of my adult life. No more school. No more classes. No more homework. Only freedom and time lie before me.

I had the same feeling the day my parents dropped me off at college. I watched their SUV pull away, and I waved at them frantically, filled with excitement and possibility. I had so much freedom, I didn't know what to do with myself the first few days. I didn't have a schedule. No curfew. No reporting my whereabouts to anyone. The only rigidity I had in my day were classes, but they were a breeze and mildly interesting.

But this, my first job and new place, will be the first time I get to make all the rules. I set my own hours at Inked, have my own place, and don't have to walk around my apartment in anything at all if I don't feel like getting dressed.

By the time I make it to the leasing office, Mr. McNamara is waiting at his desk, paperwork ready and keys lying right next to the pen. "Are you ready to sign, Miss Gallo?" he asks as I slide into the seat across from him.

"I've never been more ready for anything in my life, sir."

Five minutes and a dozen signatures later, I have the keys in my hand. I thought graduation was the sweetest moment of my life, but I have to admit, being officially handed the keys to my new place tops even that.

"Shoot me over an email of any issues you find in the apartment. I'll get them fixed right away and add them to your paperwork, just in case. I did a walk-through this morning and found everything to be in working order, but it's still important you do the same in case you spot something I didn't."

"I'll be back after work later and will check everything out. I won't be staying here for a few days, though."

He smiles, but I know I'm rambling, and this man couldn't care less if I am going to use the apartment or not. The only thing he cares about is getting his rent check on time every month.

"Whatever you'd like, Miss Gallo."

I thank him with a firm handshake, something my dad taught me to always do, and excuse myself because I only have a few minutes to make it to the shop and not be late.

I blast the radio as I drive to Inked, weaving in and out of traffic, belting out the lyrics to "Truth Hurts."

The day just started, but it can't possibly get any freaking better. I have the keys to my new place, and I am headed to my new job. I've dreamed about this moment for so many years, it feels surreal to finally be living it.

CHAPTER
SIX
PIKE

"ANY QUESTIONS?" my new boss asks after giving me the rundown on how he likes shit to go.

I can't blame the man. He is the owner. He spent years with his family building up Inked to be the most sought-after tattoo parlor in the state of Florida. Their reputation is what drew me to this place. Well, that and starting over after shit went south in the last place I settled down.

"Nothing yet."

"My kid is starting today too. She's been interning during her summer breaks, but today, she officially has a chair. So, you won't be the only newbie in the place."

"Cool."

Fucking great. The first week at any new place is hard, but add in the owner's kid, and shit can become a whole lot more complicated in a hurry.

"She's bossy as fuck, but just remember she's not your boss, I am."

I nod because what he's saying is technically true, but I'm pretty sure the kid will have his ear. If I fuck up and get off on the wrong foot with her, she can and probably will make my life miserable. I have to decide if I want to make friends with her, whoever the hell she is, or if I want to steer clear of her entirely to lessen the chances I'll get my ass canned in a heartbeat.

"I put you and her next to each other. I figure you two can help each other out. I know you're not new to this business and the craft, but sometimes people become intimidated working with so many family members."

I rub the back of my neck and try to pull on a smile. "It won't be a problem," I mutter, but nothing about the way I say the words is convincing.

"I'll be right next to you two, so I can be close if you have issues or questions."

Maybe I'm in over my head here. Working at a place like this, one with a crazy-good reputation, has always been a goal. No one wants to work at a run-down shop, scraping by and waiting for new clients to walk in the door. Inked has a two-month wait before someone can plop their ass in a chair and get the tat they've been craving.

The front door opens, and a beautiful woman steps inside, carrying a box of donuts and talking so fast on her phone, I can barely make out the words she's saying.

"That's Izzy, my sister. She's a ballbuster, so watch out for that one." Joe, my boss, laughs. "She may look small and weak, but the girl will no sooner have your balls in her hands, making you wish you could black out from the pain."

My eyes widen. "I'll steer clear of her, then."

I can't stop looking at her, though. There's something familiar in the way she talks, hand moving through the air like the person on the other end can actually see her. She's wearing a skintight white skirt, a pair of kick-ass boots with a heel long and pointy enough, she could do some damage with the fucking thing if she wanted. For an older woman, she's smoking hot.

Joe laughs louder. "There's no such thing. Once you're on her radar, you're on it. There's no hiding. So, prepare for that because, guarantee, she'll have her sights set on you at some point. I just hope, for your sake, she lets you get your feet wet before she decides to make a pet project out of you."

"Sounds great," I mumble, finally tearing my gaze away from the person who's going on my list of people to avoid while working here. "I'm sure we'll be great friends."

"Just don't get too chummy. She'll have you on the ground, begging for mercy, but it's her husband who will have you pleading for your very life."

Sounds fantastic. "Got it."

Izzy places the donuts on the front counter before telling the person on the phone she'll talk to him later. As soon as she ends the call and tosses her phone next to the donuts, her eyes are on me. "Well, well. I see the new kid finally showed."

"Ma'am," I greet and avoid correcting her on the fact that I'm nowhere near close to being a kid.

I'm twenty-seven and have been on my own for over a decade, with no one around to look out for me even longer than that. But I do the smart thing and keep my mouth shut.

"Ma'am?" Her mouth gapes open. "For real? What do I look like, your mama?"

I can't hold back the smirk as I run my fingers through my hair, trying to do something...anything...not to put my goddamn foot in my mouth. "No, ma'am. My mama looks nothing like you."

I can feel the judgment in them as she tries to make a decision if she likes me or wants to rip out my throat already with her blood-red fingernails.

"He just had to poke that bear," Joe mumbles behind me.

"I brought donuts for you assholes. That goes for you too, *kid*." She smiles.

I know she's going to call me that forever, just like she'll always be ma'am to me because that's how I was raised. As a Southern man, you don't have good manners unless you call a lady a proper name out of respect. I may have shit parents, but my grandmother taught me to be a gentleman. Because if I didn't, she'd smack me right upside the head.

I glance back at my boss, but he only shakes his head slowly like I need to let the conversation die and take what she's saying like a man. I make a quick note that Izzy, who's also Joe's sister, is the one who rules the roost.

"Where's my baby girl?" Izzy asks as she walks by us. "I thought she'd be early."

"She had to pick up the keys to her new place before work, but I'm sure she'll be here any minute."

I head to my station, unpacking a few personal items and the tools I brought with me that I've carried from place to place for the last nine years.

"She's really moving out?"

"Yep. I can't convince her to stay."

I keep my head down and do my best not to listen, but I also want to know the family dynamics so I can figure out which land mines to avoid in the future. Plus, I never had a family that could stand one another in even small doses, let alone work together every day. The entire thing is fascinating and completely foreign.

"She's independent and grown, Joe. You had to know this was coming. Once she had a taste of freedom, how could she ever move back?" Izzy says, grabbing the only donut with sprinkles and then proceeding to pick one off and throw the pink sugar into her mouth.

Joe sighs. "I know, but she's my little girl. I thought I had a few more years of waking up to see that beautiful face." He leans back in his chair, crossing his arms. "You know what I miss the most?"

"Her attitude?" Izzy laughs.

"Hell no. I blame you for all her piss and vinegar, sister. I miss sitting with her at the kitchen table, drawing together and talking about life."

Izzy leans against the counter, still picking apart the donut and eating it in small bites. "You can still have those moments. They just won't be random."

Their gazes move toward the front of the shop as an engine roars, and a sleek black pickup pulls into a parking spot out front.

"She's here," Izzy says, tossing the massacred donut into the trash can and brushing her hands together. "Finally, some new life in this place. The kid here—" she tips her head to me "—and the other kid are just what we need to liven things up around here."

I grumble under my breath, busying myself again. I have my first client booked in thirty minutes, and it's a piece that'll take me all day plus another session to finish. My back's already aching thinking about the hours upon hours I'll be hunched over the woman's back, giving her the angel wings she's requested.

"Sorry I'm late," the female voice says, coming through the front door.

"No problem, doll," Izzy, her aunt, says.

I doubt I'd get the same response if I'd shown up late today too. But that's what you get for being family. Special privileges are the way it goes. Who knows if this girl has any real talent or if she rode on the coattails of her father, not earning the chair based on her skills.

"Thanks, Auntie," the girl says as she makes her way toward her father and me. "Hey, Daddy."

Joe rises from his chair as I watch his boots move across the floor in front of me toward a pair of sexy boots much like Izzy's. "Are you ready for your first day?" he asks her.

"I've been ready for this day since I was a little girl."

I'm sure she has. Most kids dream of following in their father's footsteps. I, for one, did not. My dad was the only attorney in a small town. He was also a bastard and not someone I ever wanted to be like. As soon as I could, I got out and as far away from him and my mother as possible.

"I have someone I'd like you to meet," Joe says, and I know it's my cue.

I stand slowly, running my hands down the front of my jeans before I finally lift my gaze upward.

No fucking way.

My eyes widen, and so do hers.

"Gigi, this is Pike." Joe motions toward me with his hand. "Pike, this is my little girl, Gigi."

Fuck me.

She looks like a deer in headlights as her mouth opens and closes, but no words come out.

She can't be here.

I run my fingers through my hair, staring at the beautiful girl I'd tasted and fucked more than once, but then she vanished without even leaving me a phone number. All I had was a first name and memories after Daytona last year. Hell, they were some great fucking memories too.

I narrow my eyes as I sweep my gaze from her face and down her body, remembering exactly how perfect her skin is underneath the scraps of cloth she's wearing. I don't linger on her body too long before I bring my eyes back to hers. "It's a pleasure to meet you, Gigi."

"Mm-hmm. You too, Pike," she says like the words are acid, stinging her tongue. She's staring at me as the shock wears off and the reality of what we've done in the past is hitting her square in the face.

"Do you two know each other?" Izzy asks as she walks to our side, staring at us, but neither of us looks at her because we're too busy gawking at each other.

"Don't be silly," Joe says, wrapping an arm around his *little girl.* "Pike isn't from around here. He's new in town."

I fucked the boss's daughter. Way to go, big man.

"Are you sure you don't know him?" Izzy asks Gigi.

Gigi shakes her head, eyes still locked on me. "Never met the gentleman," she says easily, lying without hesitation.

She doesn't know Pike the gentleman. She's well acquainted with Pike the man. She'd spent days in my bed, pleasuring me and taking what she wanted without apology.

"Iz, I had a question about the schedule. You got a minute before we get slammed?" Joe asks.

"Sure," Izzy says, drawing out the word but not moving as quickly as Joe does. I can feel her eyes on us for a moment before she finally steps away and follows Joe into the office.

Gigi and I stand here, staring at each other, listening to the slow march of her family members' feet across the tile until they're on the other side of the shop.

"It's far too quiet in here," Izzy yells before loud music fills the shop.

Fuck my life.

"Are you stalking me?" Gigi whispers, getting right up in my face.

"Don't be fucking crazy." I wave her off and walk back toward my chair.

Gigi's right on my ass, practically glued to my back. "Don't fucking lie to me. You came here on purpose."

I turn to face her, leaning my head down so our faces are close. "Babe," I whisper, staring straight into her eyes so she knows what I'm saying is one hundred percent the truth. "Let's get a few things straight. You're a great fuck and you have a hot little bod, but I'm not chasing a piece of ass all the way across the state because I need another taste. I'm also not planting roots and finding a new job just to get closer to that piece of ass either."

She blanches. "You're crude."

"I thought that's what you liked best about me. At least, that's what you said when you were riding my cock and moaning my name, baby."

CHAPTER
SEVEN
GIGI

HIS WORDS ARE like a punch to the gut. There's truth to what he's said, but that doesn't mean it isn't devastating. I'd thought about Pike for months after spring break last year. Months of lying awake in my bed, replaying all the naughty things we did together, touching myself to the memories.

I knew Pike wasn't a gentleman, but the words he just threw in my face prove that simple fact.

There was nothing about him that screamed manners in the time we spent together. But there was a sweet side to him when he wanted to show it, which wasn't very often in the short amount of time I spent in his bed. He was a conundrum to me. I knew very little about the man.

Even though we spent days together, we didn't talk too much about our personal lives. I knew a few basic details about the badass biker with a cock so damn good, he could charge admission for a single ride.

I raise my hand, about to strike him, when he grabs my wrist and holds it in midair. "You're an asshole, Pike," I hiss, ripping my hand from his grip. I take a step back, knowing I need more space between us. "I don't know what game you're playing, but I'm not interested in spending more time with you."

He smirks. The bastard actually smirks when I say those words. His gaze moves toward the office where my father and Izzy are talking. "Babe," he pauses and steps closer. "I don't play games. I don't need to." He lifts his hand and runs the backs of his fingers across my cheek, but I don't move away. "And based on the color of your cheeks and the way you're looking at me, I'd say you'd like to be back in my bed and riding my cock."

I slam my palm into his chest, knocking him backward because kneeing him in the balls isn't an option. At least, not now, but I'm not above using that move to bring him to his knees. Pike's not fazed in the slightest. He just stands there, still smirking like an asshole, looking just as delicious as he did fifteen months ago.

"I will not be *riding your cock* ever again, asshat. You scratched an itch when I needed you, but I'm so over this—" I wave my hand between us. "Whatever we had, no matter how short, is all we'll ever have. Don't even look at me sideways, or I'm going to make you wish you hadn't packed up your life for a fresh start. You may have skill, but that doesn't mean my daddy wouldn't fire your ass in a heartbeat. Especially if he knew…"

"How good I fucked you?" He raises an eyebrow.

The growl creeps up my throat and slides out from between my lips before I can stop the sound from leaving my body.

"Everything okay?" Aunt Izzy asks, stepping back into the room.

I nod and turn my face toward her. "Just talking about the shop," I lie.

Her eyes move between Pike and me, and I can tell by the look on her face, she isn't buying what I'm selling. "It looks like a little more than that," she says, running her fingers across her chin.

"Auntie, it's just a little friendly competition between us. We're both starting on the same day, and neither of us wants to look like the bigger asshole...even if that's going to be Pike. You know how men are. They never like to be showed up by a woman."

Izzy walks between us and faces Pike. "Is that all this is?" She stares at him, watching his every facial feature for a tell. I know my aunt, and she misses *nothing*. One misstep and Pike's days could be numbered before he's even had a chance to finish unpacking his tools.

"That's all this is, ma'am."

Oh shit. There are things my aunt hates and then things she loathes. Being called ma'am is a surefire way to set the woman off like she's got a wick coming out of her ass, ready for ignition. She's going to blow like a Roman candle on the Fourth of July.

Her entire body stiffens. "Pike, sweetheart," she says, but her tone isn't friendly, "don't ever call me ma'am. I get where you're coming from, being a Southern gentleman and all."

I snort, but it dies as she glances over her shoulder at me for a moment.

"But around here, I'm Izzy, Iz, or boss. Do not ever, and I mean never, call me ma'am. Got it, kid?"

I pull my lips into my mouth, biting down on them to stop the laughter that's bubbling up the back of my throat. First, because Pike's getting his ass chewed out in the nicest way possible by my aunt, and second, because Izzy just called him a kid.

"I'm sorry, Izzy," Pike says without sarcasm. "I didn't mean to offend you."

"Your looks may get you a free pass with some women, but I'm not so easily charmed by a pretty face or that Southern drawl. Her daddy—" she pitches her thumb toward me "—will be even less impressed if you do something to piss off his daughter. So, word to the wise, kid, either steer clear of Gigi, or learn to make friends with her. You do something to make her mad, and it'll be your made bed you'll have to lie in as the door kicks you in the ass on the way out."

Pike nods, those beautiful green-blue eyes that have haunted my dreams for months showing no emotion. "Got it. Loud and clear, boss."

Izzy smacks her hands together and moves away from Pike. "My work here is done. We have a full schedule today, so it's time to get your asses in gear and your shit set before they walk through the door. No more time for girl talk. You two can finish your bullshit later. Got me?"

I'm staring at Pike, smirking because my aunt shut his shit down, but when I look at her, any glee I felt dies. She's staring right at me, looking like she knows something isn't on the up-and-up.

"There's no bullshit to finish later, Izzy. We're solid, and I don't have time for anything else. Bear's coming in this morning to get that piece he's always wanted."

"Who's Bear?" Pike asks.

"A real badass biker, Pike. You may want to take notes on how one acts instead of being a wannabe." I walk toward my chair and away from Izzy's penetrating stare.

"You two ready?" my dad asks, walking into the main room, completely oblivious to everything that's been happening. "I prepped your station last night, sweetheart. Figured it would make your first day less stressful."

I pop up on my tiptoes and kiss my dad on the cheek. "Thanks, Dad. You're the best." I wrap my arms around him and hug him tightly. I peer over his shoulder, catching Pike's eye and sticking my tongue out at him.

Not the most grown-up thing to do, but I don't care. I'm not into impressing Pike. I've already taken what I wanted, and now whatever we had, which was only a few days, is done. Over. Caput. Finished. There was no dipping my toes back in those waters again, no matter how fabulous the orgasms were.

And they were ridiculously great.

Every orgasm I'd had before Pike, I gave to myself. It had always been me and my hand until Pike rocked my world and showed me how it could be. Or should I say, how it should be.

"I'm here, baby girl," Bear yells as the bell above the door chimes so loud it's like my aunt purposely wants to scare the shit out of everyone every time it rings.

"Back here, Bear," I yell back, trying to be heard over the bell and the death metal my aunt feels is appropriate for this early hour.

By early, I mean noon. Nothing happens in the shop before noon. My family has a different idea of time. In college, I took the earliest classes possible so I'd have the rest of the day free. Now, I'm trying to reset my internal clock to be on Inked time.

"I'll grab Bear," Dad says as he pats me on the shoulder. "Get your shit together because Bear may love you, but don't put it past him to be on your ass on your first day."

I nod. "I'll be fine. I'm ready for whatever he's going to throw at me. You know I've spent my life handling men like him." I smile, because my father's friends aren't for the faint of heart, and I've perfected wrapping them around my little finger.

Bear's no exception. He and my dad go way back. They've been friends for almost thirty years, back to my dad's single life when he was an even bigger badass than he is now.

When I was little, Bear married my great-aunt Fran, my grandfather's sister. No one was happy about their relationship at first, and I remember more than a few screaming matches, but people calmed their shit after a while and gave them free rein to be happy. I love Bear and Aunt Fran together. She is absolutely perfect for him because I don't know if anyone else could *handle* Bear the way she does.

Bear may be a biker, but he is the very best kind of person. He is sweet beyond compare—but only if he likes you and you have a set of tits. He is a horndog. It doesn't matter how old he is or that his beard is almost completely gray, he's never lost his thirst for the females. But he is a one-woman guy, and that woman is my aunt Fran.

"Got a handout for your first client. Must be nice to ride on everyone's coattails," Pike says when we're alone again.

"Why don't you just fuck right off?" I glare at his reflection in the mirror. "I can't help it if my family owns this shop. I'm sorry that pisses you off so badly, but I earned this spot just as much as you did, Pike. So, get the fuck over yourself." I plop down in my chair, pulling the bottle of black ink out of the cabinet I stocked last week, ignoring whatever face I'm sure Pike's making at me.

"There she is," Bear says as he walks into the back, holding out his arms, waiting for me to jump into them like I did when I was a little girl. "Come and give me some love, baby girl."

"Hey, Uncle." I smile at Pike so he'll eat shit. I want him to know that I plan to have everyone eating out of my hands, whether they're related or not. The only person who's not going to like me is Pike, and for that...I don't give a shit. "I've missed you."

Bear hugs me tightly. "Not as much as I missed you."

Pike's gaze flicks upward as he slowly shakes his head, muttering something under his breath. I can't wipe the smile off my face, because knowing he's annoyed has me over-the-fucking-moon ecstatic.

I pull away, still holding on to Bear's arms. "You finally ready to let me scar you for life?"

Bear's eyes light up. "Been waiting for you to leave your mark on me for years, kid."

"Still putting it on your shoulder?" I ask.

"Well, it's either there or my ass. I figured I'd save your young eyes and stick with the shoulder."

I love my uncle, but there's no way in hell I'd tattoo his ass. I know it comes with the job. Men and women will walk through the door and ask for ink in places no human should have to see, but I am not prepared to go there with Bear. I'd never be able to sit across from him at another family dinner or holiday and not think about his pasty white ass.

"I have your design all ready." I grab my sketch pad from my bag and flip through the pages until I find his design. "I'm so excited for you to finally see it. I can make any changes you want." I tear out the page and hand it to him.

Bear holds the paper with both hands, gaze sweeping up and down and back up. His mouth twists at the corners, and his pink lips disappear, replaced by his white teeth. "Damn. You did good."

I let out the breath I've been holding because I wasn't sure if Bear would like the design, and I knew he wouldn't hold back. I may be his niece, but one thing Bear isn't is a liar. He doesn't sugarcoat shit. He doesn't spare anyone's feelings, and it's one of the things I love most about him.

I don't like people who are full of shit. Family or not, I want to be told the truth, and if Bear says it, I believe him.

"Do you want black or some color, Uncle?"

"Whatever you want, kiddo. Just not fucking pink." He shakes his head. "I fuckin' hate pink. No purple either. Not into having pansy-ass colors on my skin."

"No chick colors. I got it, Bear. You want it bigger or smaller than it is?" I ask, taking the paper from between his fingers.

"It's perfect. Let's get this show on the road. I have to be home in time to take your aunt Fran to dinner, or she'll have my balls in a sling, sweetheart."

"Get comfortable and take off your shirt. I'll be back in a minute, and we'll get started."

Bear sits down and pulls his shirt over his head before leaning back and throwing his hands behind his head, staring right at Pike. "What's your name, boy?"

I snort as I walk toward the back room to put the design on transfer paper.

"Name's Pike."

"Pike, huh? Where ya from?"

"Tennessee."

I stand close to the door, listening to them shoot the shit and trying to get whatever details I can on Pike.

"That your hog outside?" Bear asks.

"Yep."

"It's nice."

"You look like a man who knows his way around a machine, and that is one of the best."

"Had to cost you a pretty penny. I'm impressed someone your age could save enough for a classic like that."

"I don't spend my money on bullshit. I like a few things in life, and riding is one of them. I don't cheap out when it's something I want, and I wanted that bike since I was a kid."

Bear laughs. "A kid with an attitude. I don't know if this shop can take more, but you're going to fit right in here, Pike."

"So, Gigi's your niece?" Pike asks, and I move closer to the hall.

"By marriage. I've known her since she was born. She's like one of my own, and I can tell by the way you've been looking at her since I walked through the door, you better turn your eyes elsewhere."

"Ain't looking at her, man. She's not my type," Pike lies because from the way Pike fucked me, I'd say I was very much his type.

"She's every man's type," Bear tells him, calling him on his bullshit.

I laugh as I grab the paper, but I don't walk out of the back room yet. I'm enjoying this exchange way too much to interrupt.

"And I know her daddy, and he won't like you staring at his daughter like you want to devour her. So, word to the wise, kid. Look elsewhere. Don't shit where you eat, and do not—and I mean, absolutely do not—make goo-goo eyes at my niece, or you'll be packing up quicker than that young pecker of yours can come."

"Noted," Pike replies.

I cover my mouth to hide my laughter as I stroll back into my station, holding the design, ready to give Bear the best tattoo I can. I also plan to fuck with Pike as much as possible to make the day even more kick-ass.

CHAPTER
EIGHT

PIKE

MY CLIENT, Piper, has headphones on, and she's trying her best to last one more hour in my chair before she calls it a day. She's sweating profusely and on the verge of hyperventilation with her eyes squeezed tightly shut.

"It doesn't look like she's going to make it," Joe says, standing behind me and watching over my shoulder.

I don't look up. Every second is precious now, and I'm doing my best to finish the outline of the massive piece before Piper quits. "She said she can take it. I've asked her every ten minutes if she wants to tap out and finish another day."

"She pukes, you're cleaning that shit up," Joe tells me. "You have two hours before your next and last client arrives." He walks away, going to the front of the shop where everyone is standing around, shooting the shit.

Everyone except Gigi. She killed the design on Bear's shoulder and finished four other small pieces on various clients. Each design was better than the last. I'd assumed she'd gotten the chair because she was related and for no other reason. But I was wrong. The girl has talent and tons of it. I have nine more years under my belt than her, but she is so skilled, I would've guessed she'd been doing tattoos for years.

I glance up as Gigi feverishly types away on her phone, tongue poking out, sweeping across the corner of her mouth. She's barely said two words to me since our little chat before the shop opened. It's probably for the best anyway.

Of all the damn shops I could've planted new roots in, why in the hell did it have to be the one where I'd fucked the boss's daughter? I was psyched when I got the call that there was a free chair at Inked because they needed extra hands to keep up with the demand for their services. This is a dream job for me. Every artist wants to be at a place that's brimming with life.

That was my main reason for coming to Inked. That and starting over, getting away from the bullshit of the last five years, and finding a new place to call home.

"I'm done. Stop," Piper groans as she pulls off her head-phones, almost making me fuck up a wing tip.

I lean back, looking over the massive piece, knowing the shading will take a fraction of the time the outline did. "We can finish it when we do the shading."

Piper's facial features relax immediately as she sits up, holding her T-shirt against her chest. "I need a month before I can come back and go through this shit again."

I scrub my hand across my face, catching Gigi's eye as she watches us across the room. "Take all the time you need. When you're ready, we'll finish what we started. I've got nothing but time. Let me just cover this piece, and you can go."

Gigi's eyes narrow. I don't know if the words I just spoke were for Piper or Gigi. I don't plan on going anywhere, no matter how badly Gigi says she wants me to. What happened last year between us feels nowhere near finished either.

That's the biggest problem.

I didn't do a damn thing to the chick. At least, nothing she didn't beg for me to do to her. Yet, she's treating me like a piece of shit. A distant memory. A huge fucking mistake.

Piper pulls her shirt over her head as soon as I finish covering the back piece, facing away from me but giving Gigi the full view of her tits. "Can you put me down for one month from today? I want to have something solid in the books before I leave."

"I'll grab you a water and put you down." I stand, stretching my back and legs because they're stiff and ache like a motherfucker.

Piper follows me back to the front, standing on the other side of the counter as I pull up the scheduling software I've had five minutes of training in how to use.

"That piece is going to be killer when it's finished," Izzy tells Piper, chatting with her as I fumble my way through the screens, trying to find next month.

"I'll be happy when it's over. I always forget how much this shit hurts until my ass is in the chair and the needle is pulling at my flesh."

"But it's totally worth it. And Pike does some of the best damn line work I've seen in a long time. You'll be happy when the work is finished and you can show it off to the world."

Piper shakes her head. "This one is for me. I don't plan on showing it off."

"Oh?"

"My husband died last year, and this tattoo is for him."

Izzy gasps. "I'm so sorry. I didn't know."

I glance up as Piper gives Izzy a pained smile. "It's not something I share. I'm still not ready to talk about everything that happened. He always wanted me to get this tat, but I was too much of a pussy to do it until now."

"Well, it's beautiful," Izzy says, placing her hand over Piper's. "The tattoo and the sentiment."

Finally getting the computer program to work, I tell Piper, "There's a spot open on July 5th at noon if that works."

"It's fine." She nods quickly. "We'll be done after that?"

"Yes, ma'am."

I get the side-eye from Izzy, and Piper's face falters for a moment. What the fuck is it with the chicks around here? Why is ma'am such a shitty word? Where I come from, every woman is a ma'am. You'll get yourself smacked upside the head if you call a woman by any other name. But here, in the middle of fucking nowhere Florida, the women act like you're physically hurting them every time you speak the word.

"Just Piper, kid," she throws back my way, just like Izzy did.

"I keep telling him," Izzy says, giving me a satisfied smile.

I scribble the date and time on a business card before handing it to her. "I'll see you in a month, Piper."

"Thanks for helping me push through it today, Pike," she says as she heads toward the door.

I nod, smiling at the pretty lady whose face displays all the layers of pain and grief for the world to see.

"You have just enough time to grab something to eat," Joe says as he stands across the counter in the same spot Piper just was. "Why don't you take Gigi and go grab some dinner?"

"I'm fine." The last thing I need is to be alone with her tonight.

"You both need to eat. I have a client coming in, and no one else is free. Just take Gigi. She knows this area, and maybe you two can be friends. It's always nice to have someone at work to talk to who isn't related."

I don't want to tell him that she and I have nothing much to talk about. We could fuck like monkeys, but beyond that, I'm not sure we have much to say to each other. Based on our earlier conversation, I'd say there are no words left to be spoken.

"I can just grab something next door."

Joe shakes his head. "I want my kid to eat, and it's important to me that you two are friends."

"Joe, let the kids work their own shit out," Izzy tells him, grabbing on to his arm and handling him with her words and body. "You can't force them to like each other."

"Gigi!" Joe yells out like his sister didn't say anything to him.

Gigi's in the front, standing behind her father and glaring at me within a few seconds. "What's up, Dad?"

Joe dips his head in my direction, not turning around to see his kid. "Go with Pike and grab something to eat. Show him some of the local places that serve the good shit. No fast food."

"Go with Pike?" Gigi whispers. "Why?"

"I want you two to be friends."

"Are you fucking serious?" she whispers, eyes turning icy fucking cold, but she's staring at me and not her daddy. "For God's sake, why?"

Joe glances toward the ceiling, muttering under his breath. "Just do as I ask," he tells her.

She lifts her phone and shakes it in his direction as he turns toward her. "They have food delivery now, Dad. You don't actually have to go anywhere. I'll just order us something to eat."

If he knew what he was asking, if he knew what we'd done, he wouldn't be forcing her to leave this place with me. But I never plan on breathing a word of what we'd done to anyone. I'd have my ass booted from the shop, and my name blackballed from every tattoo place in the state.

"Just let her order in," Izzy says, looking at me and then at Gigi. "You know kids today, Joe. They don't like to actually do anything for themselves." Izzy laughs nervously.

By the way Izzy's acting, I reckon she's read something in our body language and has assumed we aren't the strangers we've made out to be. She seems like someone who can figure things out quickly and see through bullshit quicker than most.

"Grab me a burger from that place down on County Line. You know it's my favorite, and they don't deliver up here."

"That's fifteen minutes away," Gigi whines.

"It's a good fucking thing you both have over an hour, isn't it?" He shuts down any argument either of us can make on why we shouldn't head out alone.

Gigi curls her lip as she glances at me. "Fine. We'll go, but you've used up your asks for this week."

Joe takes a few steps toward his kid. I haven't moved an inch, just stood there, staring at them both. "I'm not asking as your father, baby girl. I'm telling you as your boss."

My eyes widen, and so do Gigi's.

"So, grab me my usual," he says, looking down at his kid, standing a foot away from her.

"Fine," she snaps.

"Oh lord," Izzy whispers and shakes her head. "Cluster-fuck. Total and complete clusterfuck."

I rub the back of my neck as I walk around the counter. "I can go alone," I tell Joe, not needing Gigi's pissy attitude because her daddy forced her to go with me. "I can find the joint and grab your food."

But any other words I have on the tip of my tongue die quickly as Joe glares at me. "No, you won't. She's going too. I don't know what bad blood you two have, if it's from both being new and starting on the same day, but this isn't a competition. This is a business, and you two have to work together. Whatever bullshit, imaginary beef you have ends here and now. Do you understand me?"

I nod because I'm not arguing with the boss. No way. No how. If he wants me to take a ride with his kid to hell and back to get him a bottle of water, I'll fucking do it. It's not like Gigi is hard to be around. Keeping my dick out of her might be an issue, but it isn't a hardship spending time with a pretty chick who could do more with that mouth than sass.

"I understand, Dad," she says softly. "I'll play nice."

Joe's lips turn up and his shoulders relax. "Now, get moving. I'm starving. Ask everyone else if they want anything before you go."

"I'll grab my keys."

"Oh no." Gigi shakes her head, still glaring at me like she wants to rip off my head. "I'm driving."

"Why?"

She crosses her arms, tilting her head to the side, eyes traveling up and down my body. "Let me guess," she says, her tone all full of piss and vinegar. "You have the bike, yeah?"

"Yeah."

"We're getting food for everyone, and I'm not fucking holding it while we weave in and out of traffic just because you want to take your bike."

I shrug. "I have a compartment."

"It's a big nope for me. We're taking my truck."

"Whatever makes you happy." I'm not going to stand here another ten minutes arguing about which form of transportation we're going to take. "I could give two shits how we get there as long as we get there."

"Smart kid," Joe says.

"Or the dumbest one ever," Izzy whispers before shaking her head at me.

Hopefully, whatever scenarios Izzy has swirling around in her head, she comes to me about before blowing up my life. She and Gigi are close. I can tell that from the short amount of time I've seen the two interact. If Gigi spills the beans, my ass will be on the back of my bike, searching for a new job and a new town...again.

"I'll meet you out front." Gigi tips her head toward the door. "Black truck."

I don't stick around. I need some air and to get my head on straight before I go anywhere with this chick. She has me all kinds of tangled up inside. My brain is going a million different directions, most of which are bad, but they all end up in the same place...with Gigi back in my bed, moaning my name, and begging for more.

Fuck.

The door doesn't close behind me as I step outside into the damp Florida air. I don't notice I'm not alone as I start to pace.

"I don't know what's going on, but whatever it is, you better find a way to fix it or move the fuck on," Izzy says.

I jump, clutching my chest. "Jesus fucking Christ. You scared the ever-loving hell out of me."

She marches up to me, craning her neck to look me in the eye. "Did you hear me?"

I nod. "Uh, yeah. I said you scared the shit out of me, Iz."

"Listen, kid." She points to the window of the shop. "Gigi's gunning for you. She doesn't like you, and she doesn't hate many people. So, whatever you did to fuck shit up, make it right. I don't want to lose you already, but she's family."

"Yeah. Yeah. I know how it goes." I run my hand through my hair and sigh.

"It's not my business. She's my niece and you're both adults, but mark my words, fix whatever you fucked up, or you won't be here more than a week."

I don't deny that there's history. I won't lie to Izzy again. She's smart. I won't be going into detail about all the ways I'm acquainted with her niece. I won't tell her how I know the way she tastes, how she kisses, and the perfect curve of her ass.

"I'll fix it." I jam my hands into my pockets, trying to figure out exactly how I'm going to do that.

Maybe I need to remind Gigi of how perfect we are together. I don't get why she's so fucking pissed. I did not stalk her across the state. Hell, I knew her first name but nothing else about the girl.

She lied to me, in fact.

First, based on the fact that she just graduated from college, her first lie was about her age. She told me she was twenty-two and was about to graduate last year. Second, she told me she was from Miami and stayed there to work. I know there were a million other lies she told me that week, but I wasn't exactly open and honest about my life or my past either.

We both knew what we were doing. The week in Daytona was all about pleasure. About being in the moment. Our pasts and futures didn't matter. The lies we told were of no consequence because there was nothing more than that moment, in that hotel, tangled in sheets and coated in sweat.

But now...our paths are intertwined. My fate and future lie in the hands of the boss's little girl, the same chick I'd banged until my legs barely worked anymore.

"Do whatever you need to do to make shit right," Izzy tells me before walking away and disappearing inside the shop, leaving me out front with my dick in my proverbial hands.

She said do *whatever*, but I wonder if the whatever includes being with her niece.

I know the spark is still there.

I caught Gigi staring at me more than once. Not with rage, but curiosity. Watching my hands as they touched Piper's back, maybe remembering the way they felt sliding across her skin.

Whatever there is between us...I'm not going to leave her alone until I find out.

CHAPTER
NINE

GIGI

FUCK. I love my dad, but come on. Why does he have to be so gung ho about the happy family vibe at the shop? What does it matter if I like Pike or not? I don't remember my dad going to this much trouble when they hired Kat. But what I do remember is my aunts going bananas about a young little hottie working so close to their men.

But now my dad wants us to be all kumbaya, holding hands, and one big, happy freaking family. If he only knew...

He'd fucking kill me, and then he'd murder Pike.

"We going to talk about this?" Pike asks from the passenger seat of my pickup truck.

"I think we said everything we needed to say already." I stare straight ahead, keeping my eyes on the road instead of on the hottie next to me.

Why the hell does he have to smell so good?

Pike shifts his body, but I don't dare sneak a glance. I know his eyes are on me and nowhere else. I can feel the weight of his gaze like a warm blanket, covering my skin. "Darlin'," he says with a hint of a Tennessee twang in his voice. "I have a lot more to say to you."

"Well, you talk, and maybe I'll listen while I drive." I

shrug one shoulder, wrapping my fingers tighter around the steering wheel. "It's not like I have a choice, do I?"

"I like a captive audience," he says sarcastically. "First, I didn't follow you. I'm not a stalker."

"That's what you say, but how do I know?"

"Gigi, how the fuck would I even find you?"

I shrug again. "Anything's possible."

"You told me your first name. You also told me you were from Miami, and the last time I checked, we're hundreds of miles away from there."

"There are other ways."

"What other ways?" He turns and his knee is almost touching mine, but I have nowhere to go. No way to fight back because he's making all the sense in the world, and it's aggravating as hell.

"I don't know. My uncle's a private investigator, and I'm sure he could've found me with very little to go on."

Pike laughs, and I can see him shake his head out of the corner of my eye. "Listen, babe."

I growl, which only makes Pike laugh. *Ugh.*

"You like darlin' better?"

"I don't like either. My name is Gigi or Giovanna," I correct him.

"Giovanna is kind of an uppity name, which right about now, suits you."

"I changed my mind." I reach for the radio because I'd rather listen to anything other than his sexy as all get-out voice.

He tightens his fingers around my wrist, peeling my hand away from the buttons on the console. "I didn't have anything to go on. I figured what we had was nice, but it wasn't anything that would go the distance. The last thing I'd do is stalk you to try to get another piece of that fine ass."

My gaze slides to his face for a moment before going back to the road. "Nice?" My voice is high, almost shrill. "What we had was *nice*?" I ask, grinding my teeth and ripping my hand from his grasp.

"Well, not really." He pauses, and he's lucky as hell I can't lunge across the seat and wrap my hands around that beautiful neck of his. "It was fucking spectacular. The shit you did…"

"Stop." I shake my head, grinding my teeth so hard, my jaw aches. "I was there. I don't need a play-by-play."

Pike laughs again, practically making my blood boil. "I'm just saying, I didn't track you down. I figured you had your fill and were through. So why would I bother to track you down?" He pauses, but I don't reply before he continues. "I don't chase pussy. Never have. Never will. It's not my style, darlin'."

"Thanks for that little nugget of truth, Pike."

"You're acting like I did you wrong. You were the one who just up and left without even so much as a goodbye."

I cringe when he says the last few words. I did do that to him. I told him I was running out for some coffee, and I didn't look back before I got in my car, picked up the girls, and headed back to FSU. But in all fairness, when I rolled over that morning and saw his phone with a text from some skank that read, "When you're done with the little girl, I'll be waiting for you," that shit set me right off. I knew I was just another piece of ass to him in a long line of pussy waiting to take my place.

For half a second, I thought we had something more than a casual fling, but that text reminded me I was nothing more than another notch on his bedpost.

"I waited in that hotel room for three hours before I figured you weren't coming back. I felt like a fuckin' fool too."

"I'm sorry."

I didn't take into account how he felt or if he'd even give a shit. I figured a clean break, no goodbye, no last kiss, and no more questions was the best way to end things with him. It was a coward move, but I'd never done anything like that in my life. I didn't know how to act or if there was a proper way to say *thanks for the cock, big man*.

"Who does that kind of shit?"

"Oh, please. I'm sure you've been with plenty of chicks who didn't kiss you goodbye."

"I've never had anyone run away without at least saying thanks."

My gaze moves from the red light to his face. He's staring at me with a hardness in his eyes, fingers moving across his beard. "Thanks?"

The corner of his mouth tips up, showing the white of his teeth nestled behind his facial hair. "Why not?"

I throw my head back and laugh. "I think you would've been the one saying thanks to me, buddy."

My words only make Pike laugh. God, he's so annoying. "I figured I gave you all the thanks you needed with so many orgasms you could barely walk when you went for that fake-me-out coffee."

I narrow my gaze on his handsome, smug face. "It's not like you're the only man on the planet who can give an orgasm. You're not God's gift to women, country boy. Hell, I can give myself an orgasm anytime."

"Do you think about me?" His smile grows wider.

I twist my lips, staying silent as I turn my eyes back to the road. I'm thankful we're two minutes from the burger shop because I need out of this truck and need distance between us. "Babe, when I'm touching myself, like really getting into it, fingers stroking away, and I'm craving to be filled…"

"Don't say things like that unless you want to be flat on your back, begging for my cock, sweetheart."

"You're so full of yourself." Fuck, he's so right.

We're trapped in the small cab of my truck, and he's so close to me, I can smell the musky soap on his skin. All the memories from that week come flooding back to me like the naughtiest and most vivid dream, but I push them aside, staying in the present with the more annoying version of Pike.

"Tell me you haven't thought about me once since you left Daytona, and I'll leave you be, chalking it all up to a good time and nothing more."

"I haven't thought about you once," I lie. "Have you thought about me?"

"Every. Damn. Day," he answers quickly, and I immediately regret asking him that question.

If I were being truthful, which I'm not because I'm not giving him any ammo, I've thought about him every damn day too. How could I not? After a week like we had, the way we had it, I couldn't think about anyone else but him.

He ruined me. I never thought I'd say those words, and I can barely admit them to myself sometimes. But he did. He ruined me completely.

Mallory had asked me before I met Pike if Erik was any good in bed. I said he was okay or maybe I said he was good, but now I know better. Pike did things to me that made my toes curl and my legs shake like I was having a seizure.

"We're here." I open the door and hop down from the truck's cab, leaving Pike behind as soon as I shut off the engine.

I move quickly, pulling open the door to the burger shop, trying to put as much space as possible between Pike and me. But no matter how quickly I move, he isn't far behind.

"We're not done," Pike says, almost plastered against my back in the impossibly busy restaurant.

I turn, glancing up and over my shoulder at him. "We are."

He leans forward, putting his face so close to mine, I can feel his warm breath tickle my skin. "I'm calling a truce for now, but that doesn't mean I don't want you in my bed again, lips on mine."

I suck in a long, deep breath, feeling a little dizzy, remembering how his lips felt like velvet even with that beard. "It's never going to happen." Quickly, I twist my head, staring up at the menu and silently cursing myself because I very much wouldn't mind being in his bed with his lips on mine again. "Asshole," I mutter softly.

"Welcome to Burger, Burger, Burger," the guy with the dopiest outfit ever says on the other side of the counter. The name is cheesy, the uniforms are even cheesier, but the burgers they make are the best in the county. "What can I get you?" he asks with a grin so large, I know it's fake as fuck because ain't no one that happy to be working in this joint.

"I'll take a Double Swiss and Mushroom, a large onion ring, and a medium diet lemonade."

"Diet?" Pike says in my ear. I elbow him because he's close, and I don't feel like getting into it with him in front of everyone.

"What do you want to eat, Pike?" I ask, not turning around, but instead giving the same fake-ass smile back to *Jim* —or at least, that's what his name tag says.

"Besides you?" Pike whispers in my ear, which earns him a second elbow to the gut. "I'll get what she's having." His voice is strained, the two good shots I got in clearly having an impact.

"For here or to go?" Jim, the cashier, asks with his smile still firmly planted on his pimply face.

"To go."

"Here," Pike says over me, and Jim nods. "We also do need a few other things to go." Pike's fingers graze my ass, and I jump but stop myself from smacking him when I see the yellow sheet of paper in his hands. He rattles off the order for everyone at the shop before handing Jim a wad of cash.

"You could've just asked me for the list," I snap.

Jesus. When did I become so bitchy?

Pike brings out the worst in me. That week in Daytona, I felt more like myself. I didn't have to be anyone else but who I was. Although I told a few lies because I didn't know Pike at all, I was truly me. I didn't have to put on a good face or act like some happy party girl, ready to do anything Mallory wanted so I didn't have to listen to her shit.

"My way was more fun." He smirks, eyes blazing as he stares at my snarled lips.

"We'll bring it out to you when it's ready," Jim says because, clearly, we're done and stopping the flow of traffic.

I stalk toward an empty table, plop down in the chair, and stare out the window.

"We can be civil," Pike says, sliding into the chair across from me. "I want this job, and I'm not looking to get canned before I've barely had a chance to start. Your dad won't fire you, but he'll toss my ass out in a fucking heartbeat. I'm not trying to piss you off."

"That's news to me, Pike, and by the way, I didn't get the job because I'm related. I've been working my ass off at the shop for years, earning that damn chair."

"Your line work is amazing," he says, complimenting me on something that isn't sexual for the first time. "Especially with the short time you've been tattooing. It's impressive, actually."

"Thanks. My dad taught me well."

"You're lucky," he says, leaning back in his chair and kicking one leg out so it's practically touching mine. "My father didn't teach me shit except how to be an asshole."

"Ah, it's genetic, then," I tease, reaching over and pulling a handful of napkins out of the container just so I have something else to do besides stare at him.

"Ha. Ha. Very funny. I'm not an asshole." He pauses. I risk a glance at him and quickly realize I shouldn't have. The teasing, happy-go-lucky guy from a few moments ago is gone,

and in his place is a man filled with sorrow and maybe...
regret. "Well, not one like my father, at least. We're nothing
alike. Thank fuck for small miracles."

"I'm sorry." I can't imagine growing up with a horrible
father.

Joseph Gallo may be overbearing, but he is so damn
loving that the amazing outweighs the bad. Sure, there were
times I wanted to scream at him about his ridiculous rules,
but I knew why he was being so over the top. He loves me.
He also thought he knew better than me, which he probably
did, although I'll never admit it.

I won the lottery the day I was born. I knew that much. I
have a father who adores me and a mother who is the
sweetest human being on the planet. I have an entire tribe of
people who are mine, looking out for me, loving me no
matter what shit I pull...and there's been a lot.

Pike shrugs one shoulder and then runs his fingers
through his impossibly messy, yet somehow perfect, dirty-
blond hair. "It is what it is. I put as much distance between
him and me as possible."

"But what about your mom?" I ask, unable to imagine not
being able to go home again.

"She's no better than him. Just a different type of asshole,
but still an asshole."

"That's harsh."

"If you knew them, you'd understand why I'm not being
harsh enough."

I stare at Pike, losing myself in his soulful eyes, wondering
what made me the lucky one to be born into a great family,
when there are others who got a shit deal the day they were
born.

"Two burgers, two onion rings, and two drinks," a girl
says at the side of our table, wearing the same hideous outfit
as Jim and looking no less ridiculous.

"That's us." I reach for the tray because she's staring at

Pike with wide eyes like a deer caught in headlights. She's not a deer and Pike's not a car, but she's no less mesmerized by him.

Yeah, girl, I know.

I take the tray from her hands, placing it on the table in front of us, but she doesn't move. She barely blinks, ignoring the fact that I'm sitting right here, like she's stuck to the floor, frozen in place.

"Can I get you anything else?" she asks him in an almost robotic voice.

"I think we're good," Pike says and looks at me, pleading with me with his eyes like I'm going to be able to chase this girl away. "You need anything else, darlin'?"

"I got everything I need," I reply, grabbing the burger from the paper basket, trying to ignore the weird girl who can't seem to do anything other than stare at Pike.

"Well," she says softly, blinking her eyelashes so quickly I'd think she has something stuck under her eyelid. "If you need anything, just ask for me." She smiles and points at her name tag. "Angie."

"Thanks, Angie," Pike says with a big smile, tipping his head to her. "I'll let you know if we need anything else. My girl and I are hungry."

Her top lip curls as Pike looks over at me, breaking the happy trance she was in and reminding her that he isn't alone. "Enjoy," she says flatly before stalking away from our table, thankfully leaving us in peace.

"Is it hard being you?" I tease him.

"Hard because people are nice?" he asks, grabbing his burger and holding it in front of his lush, soft lips.

"Hard because women seem to throw themselves at you."

"Sometimes it's great, while other times, it's a pain in the ass." He takes a big bite, chewing slowly, staring at me across the table as I do the same.

We sit like that, chewing and not speaking, but his eyes

say everything that needs to be said. I could lose myself in his eyes. The deep green like the Gulf of Mexico before a storm.

"Like the night I met you, that was one of the great times."

I'm mid-swallow, and the burger almost gets lodged in my throat, but I fight to get it down. "And when it's not so great?" I ask, wanting to talk about anything except us.

"Fuck," Pike mutters, burger in hand, cocky smile playing on his lips. "Who am I kidding? A face like this has its perks with very little downside."

I grab an onion ring and playfully throw it at his face, but Pike catches it before it can connect. "You're being an asshole again."

"Darlin', I'm always an asshole, but that's why you like me," he says with a straight face.

"Keep dreaming, buddy," I snarl and take another bite of my burger, chewing on my food and his words.

Do I like Pike?

I liked him enough to sleep with him…repeatedly.

I was attracted to him. That much was true.

I liked Daytona Pike way more than I like Inked Pike. But Daytona Pike also had an expiration date, whereas Inked Pike seems to be ready to settle in and stick around, putting down roots in my small town.

I can't chase him away. That would require me being open and honest with my father about what happened in Daytona and what went down between Pike and me.

Shit, my father didn't even know I went to Daytona, and the one thing he hates most is lying. I did my fair share of that in college, though. If they knew half the shit I'd pulled… Well, it's not like he could ground me. I don't live under his roof anymore and can make my own rules. But that doesn't mean my ass wouldn't get chewed out for the danger I'd put myself in.

I can't even imagine what he'd say about me sleeping with a stranger, let alone going to his hotel room where I could've been raped or murdered. I'm sure my father would immediately go to the worst-case scenario and all the ways I could've fucked up my life by sleeping with a stranger.

I didn't get an STD or end up with a lifelong reminder, waking me in the middle of the night to be fed. What I did get was the best damn sex of my life—and now a constant reminder sitting in the chair across from me.

"Finish up. We have to get back. I have a client in thirty minutes," Pike says as he glances at his phone.

I take two more bites, trying to keep my eyes on the table instead of on his muscular, ink-covered arms, flexing with each movement. When I lift my gaze to his face, he's watching me and knows exactly what I'm staring at. I'm totally busted.

"I'm done." I toss the burger back into the paper basket before shoving an onion ring in my mouth. "I'm ready when you are," I say while chewing, hoping to pull off being as unsexy as possible.

I know I need to put space between us. The spark, the chemistry, the pull I felt toward him in Daytona is still there. That scares the shit out of me too. I'd never felt that invisible force pushing me toward someone when I was with Erik or Keith, but it's so strong with Pike, I'm not sure I can escape it.

"You're still hot," he says like he sees through my plan. "Still give me wood, darlin', even with that mouthful of onion rings."

I'm out of my seat, tray in one hand and the to-go bag in the other before Pike can say another word. But I'm not alone for long. I don't even make it to the door before I can hear his heavy footsteps and feel the warmth of his body nearby.

"Fuck my life," I whisper into the glass door before pushing it open and stepping outside into the inferno that's a Florida summer day.

"Next time, we take my bike," he says, rounding the truck and opening my door before I can do it myself.

I stare up at him. "There won't be a next time." I stop myself from reaching out and running my fingertips along the coarse hair on his face.

Pike smiles, tipping his head and putting his face close to mine. "News flash, Gigi. Daytona was only the beginning."

CHAPTER
TEN

PIKE

"WHY COULDN'T you move to Nashville?" my grandmother asks as I stalk around my apartment searching for my boots. "There are plenty of places to work around here, sweetheart."

"Gram, it's still too close. I needed to put distance between myself and that shit-ass town."

"That mouth of yours, Pike. I know I didn't teach you to speak like that."

"Sorry, Gram." I pull on my boots as soon as I find them next to the couch.

"Nashville is two hundred miles from your daddy. It's not like you'd run into him."

My grandmother was the only saving grace I had as a child. She still is. How she's the same woman who raised my father, I'll never understand. Where she's sweet, he's cruel. Where she's soft, he's hard. It's like he decided to spite the world and do the opposite of anything Gram wanted for him.

"I know, Gram, I know."

"Just promise you'll come visit this old woman before I die," she says, laying on the guilt like she always does.

The woman has been talking about her death since I was

in middle school. At first, she used it as a means to control me. It worked like a fucking charm until I got smart enough to realize she wasn't dying anytime soon. Then, she used it as a way to guilt me into doing shit like being around my parents when I wanted to be anywhere else in the world than breathing the same air as them.

"I promise I'll come see you before fall."

"That's three months away, sweetheart. A woman of my age could meet her maker at any moment."

"Why don't you come here? I have a spare bedroom, and I can show you around where I live. Have you ever been to Florida, Gram?"

"No, and I have more humidity and heat than I can handle here. I don't need to come to Florida so I can get more."

I laugh as I step onto my patio with a cup of coffee, closing the screen door behind me because the bugs out here are ridiculous and bigger than most rats I've seen crawling around near the gutters of Nashville. "Don't be dramatic."

"I'm always dramatic."

"From your lips to God's ears."

"Lydia is here to take me to the store. Call me tomorrow, and let me know how you're settling in."

"Okay, Gram. Tell Lydia hello." I lean over the railing and rest the coffee mug on the top. "Talk soon. Don't die on me today."

"No one is promised time, Pike. Remember that," she says, hanging up without saying goodbye like she always does.

She'd just turn me off. When I was younger, it bothered me that she never said goodbye. She was the only person I knew who never uttered those words. She said they were too final and not meant for casual conversation. That was the hard part of Gram, but everything else about the woman was soft and loving.

"Beautiful morning, isn't it?"

I turn my head, coffee cup close to my lips, finding a buxom blonde in a silk robe. She's leaning against the railing of her patio which touches mine, only separated by some iron spindles. Her hand is wrapped around a mug, but the robe is open, nearly exposing her breasts.

"It's something." I don't let my gaze linger too long because I don't know this chick or if she has a man inside her apartment who'd be willing to go five rounds because I looked at his girl wrong.

"New here?" she asks, sliding closer but still leaning.

"Moved in last week."

She extends her free hand, but I don't move a muscle. "I'm Cadence, but my friends call me Cady like Katie."

She wiggles her fingers, not getting the clue that I'm not interested in niceties, especially at this hour. "Well, Cady like Katie, it's nice to meet you."

"I won't bite," she says with a small laugh.

I've known plenty of women like Cadence, and they always bite. They take their pound of flesh in the end, and I am not particularly looking to have any more scars.

"Pike." I take her hand, giving her a quick handshake and nothing more.

"Well, Pike, I'm always around if you're looking for company."

"Sorry, Cady, I'm a taken man," I lie because it's easier than telling her I'm not interested.

She doesn't look like a woman who takes no for an answer. The way she's staring at me, I can tell she wants a piece of me for breakfast.

"Such a shame," she whispers and withdraws her hand from mine. "But if you change your mind..."

"I know where to find you."

"Nice ink, by the way."

"Thanks." I leave out the part about being a tattoo artist. The last thing I need is Cady's ass planted in my chair at

Inked, tits hanging out, coming on to me in front of the entire Gallo family.

She gives me a once-over, eyes hungry and still burning as her gaze slides down my arms to my crotch. "You have a good day now, ya hear?"

"You too." I hold my breath, not daring to move until her screen door closes behind her.

I'm halfway back into my apartment, one leg still outside, when the patio door on the other side opens, and a familiar voice catches my attention.

"I know, Tamara. Can you believe this shit? Pike just shows up out of nowhere."

Well, fuck me.

If Gigi thought I was stalking her before, wait until she realizes I'm living next door to her. Out of all the places in this small-ass town, why in the fuck did she move in to my complex and right next door?

I pull my leg into the apartment but stay near the door and out of view. I don't dare shut the door because the last thing I want is for Gigi to see me or catch me listening to her.

"Yeah, he still looks delicious," she tells Tamara over the phone.

I fucking knew it.

"Tam, be serious for a minute here. Don't worry about Pike's big dick. Think of all the ways this shit can go south and bite me right in the ass."

There's nothing she can say now to wipe the big-ass grin off my face. Nothing. She can call me an asshole all she wants and pretend she doesn't want me, but I know the truth. She clearly told Tamara everything and is laying it all out for her again.

"You're so fucking funny." Gigi snorts but quickly sobers. "What if my dad finds out about Daytona? He'll fucking have my head."

Ah. The girl has a secret. Besides sleeping with me, her dad has no idea she was in Daytona last year for Bike Week. He'd probably shit a brick. I know if I had a daughter, I wouldn't let her anywhere near the place. Not when there're guys like me around. No fucking way would that ever happen.

I peek around the corner, getting a full view of Gigi's ass in the most spectacular pair of cutoff jean shorts ever. She's holding a coffee in one hand and her phone in the other, leaning against the railing near the corner.

"I can't sleep with him again."

I stand a little straighter.

"Because we work together, and Pike isn't the type of guy who settles down. I don't want to be someone's booty call forever, Tam. I want love. I want a relationship. I want what my parents have. What your parents have."

That's where she's wrong, but damn it, I can't set her straight right now. It would ruin everything that we built on yesterday. By the end of the day, she wasn't ready to rip out my throat. We'd made progress, and I wasn't going to do anything to fuck that up. And I most certainly wasn't going to scare the piss out of her by walking out on the patio and interrupting her most telling conversation.

"I'm not going for another ride on that cock just because I haven't been laid since the last time."

My eyes widen, and everything around me seems to disappear. Her words slam into me like a ton of bricks.

She hasn't slept with anyone else?

"My fling with Pike was a one-time thing because Mallory wouldn't shut the hell up about how I was a prude. I've embraced my prudishness now. I have exactly two notches on my bedpost, girl. Erik was a cheating asshole, and Pike is Pike. Best fucking sex of my life or not, I'm not rolling around with a man who can't commit."

To say I'm dumbfounded is an understatement. Very little surprises me in the world anymore, especially the shittiness.

But goddamn, I was only the second guy Gigi had ever slept with, and she hasn't been with anyone else since.

How is that even possible?

I know three things for sure in this moment.

First, Gigi isn't exactly what she seems. She's not a party girl and has never been one to sleep around. I was the exception and outside her norm.

Second, I still have a shot with Gigi. She wants love. She wants romance. I could do those. I could be whatever she wants me to be. She is that badass. She is soft and hard, sweet and salty, and everything I want in a chick. She has balls and a mouth on her that could break a man's heart or have him panting with need.

And third, I need to find a way to make Gigi mine without getting my ass shot by her badass father. I know I could break down Gigi's walls, but Joe... He is another story entirely.

"Trust me. The women basically throw themselves at Pike. They go all stupid around him. It's ridiculous." Gigi pauses for a moment. "I did not go stupid around him. Shut up, Tamara. He scratched an itch, and that's it."

I don't know what Tamara is saying, but I sure as fuck wish I could hear her. Having one side of the conversation is fine, but damn...I want it all. I wonder what she told her cousin. How open she'd been about the things we'd done and how fucking fantastic it had all been.

"I'm not full of shit," Gigi barks.

Oh, but she is. She hasn't been honest about a damn thing with me since the moment I met her, and she continued the lies yesterday. Her mouth was saying she hated me, but now, talking to Tamara, she's saying the opposite. I knew by the way Gigi stared at me that she still wanted me.

"Anyway, when are you getting here? My mom's flipping out because I'm living alone and I told her you're staying with me for the summer until school starts again."

Fuck. Tamara could be a wrench in my plans to win Gigi

over. But maybe not. From the sound of it, I think Tamara believes Gigi and I should be together, even if only sexually. I'll take what I can get, trying to win Gigi over piece by piece, orgasm by orgasm. Whatever it takes. I've never been a quitter, and when I see something I want, I go after it...full throttle.

"I'll have the place ready, but I'm only giving you two weeks to get your ass here. I don't know what the hell you're still doing up there."

I now have a timetable. I have two weeks to see what I can do to win the girl over before her cousin crashes the party. Maybe I can use the time to my advantage. If her parents, specifically her mother, don't like her living alone, maybe if they knew I lived next door, they'd feel better about her living arrangements. Knowing there was a friendly face and coworker right next door in case shit went bad wouldn't be a bad thing, would it?

"Dump Hank. He's a loser, Tam. You could do so much better, and you know it. You said you were breaking up with him a month ago, but there you are, staying at FSU for him." She pauses again, and I'm still plastered to the wall just inside the doorway. "You have two weeks to break his heart and get your ass here, or I'm telling your daddy you're there getting your brains banged out of that pretty little head."

I reach out, slowly sliding the patio door closed and engaging the lock. I keep my body out of sight, not knowing if she's looking but taking no chances either. I need to get to the shop, and I want to be out the door, on the back of my bike, before she has a chance to leave. The last thing I need is for her to find me here, thinking I'm following her ass around.

I have to find a way to let her know I'm living here without her also knowing I was listening in on her conversation.

It's a giant clusterfuck, but a damn good one too.

I'm halfway to my bike when a door opens behind me, and I freeze.

"Pike?" Gigi calls out. "Is that you?"

Fuck. I rub the back of my neck and turn to face her. "Hey." I wave with my other hand, keys dangling from my fingertips like a dope.

She looks stunning in the early morning sunlight, the rays shining around her hair and illuminating her like an angel. But the look on her face isn't sweet.

"What the hell are you doing here?" she asks as she stalks toward me, arms swinging at her sides with each hurried step.

"Headed to the shop." I wait in the empty parking spot next to my ride.

"No." She crosses her arms, the anger coming off her in waves. "I mean, what are you doing here at Sunshine Vista?"

"I live here," I answer flatly, laying out the truth.

"Here?" She points to the cement.

"There." I point toward the building. Our building.

She narrows her eyes. "Which one?"

"On the end."

Her eyes widen. "Right fucking next to me?"

My eyes widen too. "No shit. Really? What a crazy-ass coincidence."

Please for the love of God, I hope she didn't hear my sliding door close, figuring out I was listening to her conversation. I'd like to get to work with my balls intact and my voice in a normal octave.

"You say you're not stalking me. But for real, Pike, it sure as fuck seems like you are."

"I signed the lease two months ago, and I moved in last week. You?"

"I'm just moving in this week," she tells me, balling her fists at her sides, and I slide backward because she looks like she's about to throw down.

"Why here?"

"There're only two apartment complexes in this small-ass town. The other place was..."

"Gross," she finishes my sentence, and I nod.

"Wasn't going to plant my roots in a shithole like that. So, I wasn't stalking you. This was the only place within a twenty-mile radius that was worth renting. Nothing more. Now, you want a ride to work today or not?"

"Not," she hisses.

"Suit yourself."

"Pike, how would I explain why I'm on the back of your bike when we get to the shop? Think about it for a minute."

I slowly nod and swing a leg over my bike, sitting my ass down on the seat. "I wasn't thinking about much other than having you on the back of my bike, those sweet thighs rubbing against mine and your tits pressed against my back."

She tips her head toward the sky and groans, followed by a slew of curse words I haven't heard strung together in quite as creative a way before. "It's so not happening ever again," she tells me as she brings her gaze back to mine instead of the fluffy clouds floating above our heads.

Yeah, it will, darlin'. I don't utter those words out loud because she'll just deny how she's feeling and tell me I'm fucking crazy. But I heard her talk to Tamara, and I know the truth.

"Just go. I'm not ready for work yet. I have to do my makeup. I just ran out here to grab my makeup bag from my car."

My lip curls. "You don't need any of that shit on your face, babe. You're looking beautiful right now with the sunshine streaming through that brown hair of yours, kissing those cheeks."

Her cheeks turn a bright shade of pink, and the attitude that had been running all through her body seems to evaporate. "You're full of shit." She waves me off. "Go, and I'll be a few minutes behind you. Don't say anything about being here."

"Lips are sealed, darlin'."

"Gigi," she says as I throttle the engine, ready to take off.

"Sure thing, darlin' Gigi." I smirk, unable to hear her scream even though her mouth is open over the bike. I slide on my sunglasses, lift my chin to her, and walk the bike back slowly out of the parking spot.

She doesn't move from the spot she's standing in. Her eyes are on me, hands on her hips, body looking smoking hot in those jean shorts, showing off the perfect amount of leg. She looks like a goddess with her brown hair blowing in the soft breeze, watching me like a hawk as I pull away.

CHAPTER ELEVEN

GIGI

"WE'RE all going out after work to celebrate," Izzy says as I walk into the office to grab a cold drink after my last client of the evening finally leaves.

"I don't know," I mutter, reaching into the small fridge near the doorway. "I have a lot to do at the apartment, Auntie."

"We're celebrating you and Pike joining our team. So, there's no getting out of this one, kiddo."

I twist the lid off the soda as I turn around, gawking at my aunt as she sits at the desk. "I'm not new, and I don't think Pike will be here for very long."

She draws her eyebrows inward. "Why do you say that?"

I lift a shoulder. "Just a feeling I have."

She taps her fingernails against the wooden top. "Are you ready to tell me how you really know Pike?"

"I don't know what you're talking about."

I will deny the shit that happened between us for as long as humanly possible.

She pushes back from the desk and stalks toward me, crossing her arms, which is never a good sign. "I've been watching both of you for two days. Want to know what I see?"

"Not particularly."

She gets right in my face. "I see two people who know each other and know each other well."

I laugh, but it's a shrill, nervous one. My aunt's eyes flash, and I know I have to divert. "I don't know him. He's just hot, okay? It's been a while since I've been with anyone, and he's the only guy in the shop I'm not related to. It's that simple."

She stares at me, lips twisting like she's chewing on what I'm saying but not buying a word. "He is hot. I'll agree with you there, but there's more to the story. There's something you're not telling me. And about Pike..." She grabs my shoulders, moving closer. "He's sticking around, kid. He signed a one-year lease on that chair, and he's planting roots."

"Planting roots," I mumble because Pike has said those same words so many damn times over the last two days, I could scream.

"That man has been trying to get a chair here for three years, but we weren't ready for new blood. Now, we've got a spot for him, and he's staying as long as he wants unless he does something to fuck up majorly. But if he does, he still has to pay for that chair for the duration of his contract. So, settle in, sweetheart, the hottie's here to stay."

Three years? That kind of kills my theory that he tracked me down, following me halfway across the state to get me into bed again.

"Fuck," I hiss under my breath, and Izzy doesn't miss it.

"So, you might as well tell me how you know him and why you want him gone before those roots are firmly planted here."

I know if there's one person I can trust to understand everything that happened and how I feel about it, it's Aunt Izzy. She wouldn't judge me for sleeping with a stranger, but she'd probably give me a lecture about safe sex and other uncomfortable topics I didn't feel like talking to her about. Then, she'd probably lay into me about being in Daytona for Bike Week, which I don't feel like hearing. Not yet, at least.

"It's no big deal. We just ran into each other somewhere. He has an unforgettable face," I lie because it's easier than the truth.

I don't want to make waves for Pike. He didn't do anything wrong. I took what he gave, and then I ran away without so much as a goodbye. If anyone should be pissed, it's him. But he's not. He doesn't seem angry with me about the entire ordeal. Maybe I should tell him about the fact that I hadn't done anything like that before and I wasn't sure how to handle saying goodbye to a man I never planned to see again. But here he is, and he's not leaving anytime soon.

Izzy hasn't moved, and she's still staring at me like she's a human lie detector, ready to call bullshit. "That's it?"

"Yep." I stare her straight in the eye when I speak because doing anything else will be a dead giveaway.

"What bullshit are you two cooking up?" Uncle Mike asks as he walks in the room, scaring the shit out of me.

"Just talking to Gigi about today. Making sure she's comfortable and happy."

Mike collapses on the couch behind me, kicking his feet up on the small coffee table and putting his hands behind his head. "She's not new, Iz."

"Thank you." I wave my hand toward him, proving my point to my aunt.

"Well, she is, but she isn't," Izzy replies.

I roll my eyes. "I don't know why we have to go out to celebrate tonight."

Uncle Mike laughs. "After you have kids, you'll understand that you'll make any excuse necessary for a night out."

I cross my arms, feeling like my entire family is ganging up on me in some way. "I'm sure Auntie Mia would rather you be at home."

His laughter gets louder. "Mia will be asleep, and so will the kids. I'm sure she'll be lying in the middle of the bed, enjoying the extra space for a few more hours. Pike's finishing his last piece, so we're out of here in thirty. Want me to close out the register?"

"I got it," Izzy says before bringing that hard stare back to me. "We're not done, baby girl. I know you better than anyone, and there's something you aren't telling me."

"Oh, I love a good secret," Mike says from the couch.

"There's no secret, Uncle."

"Want me to hold her down, and you can tickle it out of her, sis?"

I put my hands on my hips and spin around to face my uncle. "I'm not five anymore. That won't work."

"Kid, you know your aunt. She's like a rabid dog when she gets something stuck in her craw. You might as well spill your guts now and make it easy on yourself. And in my mind, you're always going to be a little girl."

"There's nothing to tell. I'll go clean up my station so we can get this celebration happening earlier rather than later. I have a lot to do, and time's wasting away." I march out of the room, not giving them another chance to say anything more.

Pike, Anthony, and my dad are cleaning their stations, talking about bikes because what else would they be talking about.

"Gigi, Pike just told me something interesting," my dad says as soon as he spots me.

I stop dead like my feet have been nailed to the floor. My heart starts to pound out of control, pumping so fast, I'm pretty sure it's about to burst. "What?" I ask, wincing because I'm not sure I want to hear whatever my dad is about to say.

Pike's gaze locks on mine, and I'm ready to blurt out something, anything, to lessen the blow. Why in the fuck would Pike tell my dad about seeing me in Daytona? I thought he wanted to be here, and although starting on a lie isn't great, telling your boss you fucked his daughter is just plain stupid.

"He got a place over at Sunshine Vista. So, you two are neighbors now. That'll make your mom feel better, knowing someone is close by that can look out for you."

A slow grin spreads across Pike's face, and I immediately want to smack it off.

My eyes widen as my gaze moves to my father. "Look out for me?"

"Well, yeah." My dad nods, smiling because he doesn't know the truth. "Your mom doesn't like that you're going to be living on your own, and this will make her feel better."

"He could be a serial killer, Dad. We don't really know Pike that well, and anyway—" I smash my hands together, pulling at my fingers to keep my anger in check "—I'm twenty-one and can look out for myself."

My dad shakes his head. "You're also a girl who's living alone. I don't care if you're thirty, your mom is always going to be your mom. You know how she is, and with knowing Pike lives close, even if you don't ever need his help, she'll sleep better at night."

I love my father, but he still has some backward ways of thinking. He has three daughters and has taught us all how to defend ourselves and be independent, but here he is, talking about how my mom will sleep better knowing I have a guy nearby. A dick has nothing to do with safety. Knowing I've got a bullet for whatever dumb fuckers try to fuck with me is all the security I need.

"She should sleep better knowing I'll have my Glock in my nightstand, ready to shoot anyone who tries any shit."

Dad shakes his head, scrubbing his hands down his face and muttering a string of curse words under his breath. "First, you know she can't find out about the Glock."

"Dude, you never told Suzy about getting Gigi a gun?"

Anthony says, staring at my father with his mouth hanging open.

"Nope, and we're going to keep it that way," Dad tells him.

"You know how to shoot with that?" Pike asks, leaning back in his chair, eyes only on me.

"You want to find out?" I smirk.

Pike throws up his hands. "Maybe we can hit the range."

"That's a hard no." I turn back toward my dad. "I don't need a man to keep me safe. Not when I have Lola."

Anthony almost chokes on the water he's sipping. "You named your gun Lola?"

"Of course. What did you name yours?"

"I never named a gun, and I don't have any in the house anymore. Max would skin me alive if she found one with the kids in the house."

All the badass men in my life pretend to be in control, having shit on lockdown in their lives. But it's all a lie. The women in their beds have all the power. Anthony won't even keep a weapon in the house because he can't win an argument with my aunt because she holds the reins, as well as his balls.

"Well, Dad taught me how to shoot a long time ago. When I went away to FSU, he bought me Lola as a graduation present."

"Classy," Anthony says, earning him a glower from my father. "Couldn't get her a normal gift like money or a car?"

"He doesn't do anything normal," I add.

"That ain't no lie. Tamara hates guns," my uncle says, but he couldn't be further from the truth.

I chuckle because Tamara, Anthony's daughter and my cousin, so doesn't hate guns. She loved going to the range with me, especially when we needed to let off some steam around exam week. The girl actually has killer aim, a born natural for someone who never spent much time shooting.

"Lily has a gun," Mike says. "It's good for a girl to know how to defend herself."

Izzy walks into the main room, arms folded, head cocked, ready to go off. "You assholes act like we're weak. I never needed a gun to bring a man to his knees. Don't start acting like we're delicate flowers in need of rescue. You taught your girls how to fight just like you taught me. Lord help any man who fucks with a Gallo girl."

"You got a gun, Pike?" Anthony asks, diverting the conversation from the weakness of the Gallo women and back to guns.

"Nope." Pike shrugs. "I have my fists, and they're the only weapon I need. Used to have one when I was a kid, but haven't felt the need in years."

I roll my eyes again. That was such a bunch of macho crap spewing from his mouth.

"I got you covered, Pike, ya know...in case you need rescuing." I smirk.

Pike's body shakes with laughter. "You're a funny chick, Gigi."

"We're leaving in ten. Whatever isn't cleaned tonight will have to be done in the morning," Izzy announces to the entire room. "There's a cold drink with my name on it, and you Chatty Cathys are wasting time."

"We're moving as fast as we can, Mom," Anthony tells her, earning a glare back for his attempt at trying to make a funny.

Ten minutes later, Izzy's shooing us out of the shop, locking the door behind us.

"Want a lift?" Pike asks as he walks next to me into the parking lot.

I gawk at him. "Are you serious?"

"Well, yeah."

"Do you want a lift? Because I'm not going on the back of your bike tonight."

"Does that mean you'll get on the back another time?" he asks with his face covered in shadows, but his white smile is clearly visible.

"No."

"Why don't you ride with Gigi, Pike?" Izzy asks, and I know she's testing me. Seeing if I'll lose my shit, which I'm pretty close to doing. "Since we're going to be having a few drinks, one of you needs to stay sober enough to drive. Might as well use one car since you're going to the same place."

I open my mouth to argue, but Pike jumps right on in. "Good idea, boss."

"Just put your bike behind the shop. No one will mess with it," she adds, staring at me as I glare at her, but she's sporting the biggest smile. "Gigi will follow you back there."

I look to my dad for a rescue, but he's climbing on his bike, either completely oblivious to the conversation or he agrees with my aunt and just isn't saying anything.

"Works for me," Pike says, throwing a leg over the seat, looking all too happy about the turn of events.

"I'm sure it does," I mutter to myself before climbing in my truck and letting out a stream of curses as soon as I close the door.

My aunt, God love her, is testing my patience and doing what she does best...sticking her nose where it doesn't belong and meddling in other people's lives.

What else could possibly go wrong?

CHAPTER
TWELVE

PIKE

THERE ARE things I know for certain, and others I'd only assume. I know Joe Gallo loves Gigi more than just about anything, except for maybe his other daughters and his wife. The way he looks at his eldest daughter, it's like the sun and the moon rise and set on her very existence. I don't remember my parents, either one of them, ever looking at me the way he looks at her. I was more of a nuisance to them than a source of pride. I could do no right in their eyes, and they made sure to let me know how they felt on a daily basis.

Even from the short amount of time I've spent at Inked, I also know the Gallos are a tight-knit crew. They love being around one another, busting the others' balls about whatever they could find. I can't imagine having so many people willing to have my back about anything and everything.

The closest I got to having something like that wasn't from blood relations. When I turned eighteen and left Tennessee, I landed straight in the middle of a group of bikers who were hell-bent on making me one of their own. Spent three years riding with them as I worked at various tattoo shops all over Florida, trying to better my artistic craft and my line work. They treated me better than the two people who gave me life.

They didn't judge me, didn't expect anything but loyalty, and had my back no matter what shit went down. And there was shit. Plenty of it too. I was an angry kid with a massive chip on my shoulder, pissed off and ready to take on the world, no matter the consequences.

The guys adopted me in a way. As much as any group can when the person's not a child anymore. I was always open and honest, telling them the biker life wasn't for me. I had dreams, and nothing, not even my first real family, would derail me. When I finally found a shop that would hire me full-time, I started spending less and less time with the MC. They weren't happy, but they understood where my heart was, and it wasn't riding up and down the coast of Florida, wreaking havoc and raining down mayhem.

They weren't in my life on the daily, but I never said good-bye. I still met the guys every year at Bike Week, catching up like old friends who had a long history together. It was our own little fucked-up family reunion, because we had one another if no one else.

Over the last two days, I also realized Gigi's Aunt Izzy, the one with the giant attitude, liked to be in the know about *everything*. There wasn't a person's business she wasn't all up in. That included Gigi and now me since we were clearly throwing off some sort of vibe neither of us could hide, but we weren't about to fess up to anything either.

"This is my last beer," Mike says after he orders his second and another round, slipping a fifty to the waitress. "I finally feel as old as I am, and staying out late, partying my ass off, won't make for a happy Mike tomorrow."

From the little I know about Mike, he had dreams of being a fighter. He even lived out that dream, climbing to the top, getting the title, before marrying and calling it quits.

I'd thrown down with some pretty scary fuckers in my time, but no one quite as big as Mike Gallo. The man made every doorway seem small. But even with his imposing size, he has a kind smile and says shit that makes the smile slide easily across my lips.

"We're all leaving after this," Izzy announces, mothering us like she did all day at the shop. "This makes the second round, and anything more than this and none of us can drive."

"I'm good with the one," I add because although I'm not above mixing business with pleasure, I don't know these people well enough yet to match them drink for drink.

"Good, then you can drive Gigi home," Joe says from across the table with his daughter sitting right next to him, giving me the side-eye.

"I'm fine, Dad. It's only beer," she tells him and motions toward her half-empty glass sitting in front of her. "It's not like I'm about to chug the next one."

The first time I met Gigi, she had more than a beer in her system. The girl could drink and had an appetite for alcohol, like almost every college kid in the country.

"I'll make sure she gets home safely." I know it's going to aggravate her to no end that I'm willing to be her escort home.

"It's amazing I survived college without a ride home after a beer." She rolls her eyes, pushing her beer farther away with her top lip curling. "It takes more than that to get me tipsy."

Joe covers her hand as it lays on the table in front of them. "Just do your old man a favor. Give me peace of mind tonight and let Pike drive you."

"Why? Because he's a man?" she grumbles. "That's such bullshit, Dad, and you know it."

"Just be happy you have two sisters and not two brothers, Gigi. Your life could be worse. So much worse," Izzy adds, sliding her fingers through the water drops running down the side of her glass.

"Whatever," Gigi mutters, glaring at me across the table

like I'm trying to give her a hard time when I've done nothing but keep my mouth shut, letting our secret stay hidden.

"So, Pike," Anthony says, placing his phone on the table next to his beer. "What's your story?"

I blink a few times, staring at him in confusion because the question is loaded and totally open-ended. "My story?"

"Yeah." Anthony lifts his hand as his eyebrows pull downward. "You got any siblings? Parents still alive? What brought you so far away from home?"

"One brother. Ten years younger than me. My parents are very much alive and still in Tennessee, hopefully where they'll stay until they take their last breath." I push my beer glass to the side and lean over the table, clasping my hands together.

"Your folks planning a visit?" Izzy cocked an eyebrow, staring at me, waiting for more details than I gave. She was fishing. Always fishing.

"Nope. I haven't spoken to them in years." I catch Gigi's eye. "My grandmother raised me since I was thirteen."

"Years?" Gigi mutters. "I couldn't imagine going that long without talking to my parents."

"That's because you have good parents. No, great parents, Gigi. You grow up with shit parents, living the way I did, you ride away and don't look back. The last thing I need is to waste any more of my life on people who couldn't give a shit if I'm alive or dead."

Gigi's eyes widen in horror at the harshness of my words. "That's awful."

It isn't the first time I've seen the pity on someone's face when they realize I'd had a bad hand dealt to me before turning everything around and making it what I wanted.

"If I'd grown up with an ounce of what you've got—" I dip my head toward her father and waving a hand toward her aunt and uncles "—I probably wouldn't be sitting here, having a beer in another state, determined to plant new roots far enough away I could never run into my past either."

The pretty little waitress sets the beers down on the table, her eyes moving from one person to another but not saying a word because she can probably feel the vibe at the table has shifted.

"Keep it, doll," Mike says when the woman tries to hand him his change.

"You're too kind, Michael," she says as a giant smile spreads across her pouty lips. "If I didn't love Mia so much…"

"It still wouldn't happen, babe. While you're pretty and sweet, you're way too young for an old fart like me."

She snorts. "Always a charmer."

I'm thankful for her interruption. Most of the table is busy shuffling around the beer glasses, hopefully forgetting everything I said moments ago. Everyone except Gigi. Her eyes are pinned on me, sweeping over my face with the small little creases across her forehead more pronounced.

"What about your brother?" Gigi asks as soon as the waitress wanders off because the woman can't leave shit alone.

I shrug. "He was seven when I left home. It's not like we had a close relationship."

"But if your parents were that bad, don't you worry about him being with them when you're not there to protect him?"

I laugh and shake my head. "My parents were shit to me, but not that kid. They love him. Treated him like the king of the castle. He could literally do no wrong in their eyes. He's fine right where he is, and it's not like I could've just taken him when I left. The road is no place for a kid."

Before I took off, I thought about taking Austin with me, but I wasn't sure how I was going to feed myself, let alone a kid. I knew he'd be fine with my parents. They loved him way more than they ever loved me. They made sure I knew how much more on a daily basis too. My grandmother promised me she'd check in on Austin, and the moment their attitude went south and they started treating him like anything other than a little prince, she'd let me know. Then and only then would I go back for him, taking him wherever my ass ended up.

"Where have you been for the last nine years?" Gigi asks, leaning forward, resting her fist underneath her chin and studying me like I was a rarity instead of the norm.

"Here and there."

"Pike's been working at some of the best tattoo shops in Florida since he was twenty," Joe tells her, figuring my answer wouldn't satisfy his daughter.

"If they were so good, why is he here?" she asks like I'm not even at the table or able to answer.

"Because I only wanted to be at the best place, and that's Inked."

I hope it's enough for the conversation finally to shift away from me.

"And for the two years in between?" she asks like a blood-hound, suddenly interested in my life for the first time since I met her.

"He was hanging with the guys in the Disciples," Izzy throws out there like it is common knowledge and something I put on my resume, which I didn't, and I thought I'd covered my tracks enough that no one would find out. My gaze slides to Izzy, and she shrugs with a shitty smirk. "You didn't think I'd hire you without having my husband run a full back-ground check, did you?"

"So, you all knew, but hired me anyway?" I lean back in my chair, stunned as I look around the table, all eyes on me.

"When we let someone into the shop, we're not only letting them into our business, we're giving them access to our family. No one gets hired without a full work-up, no matter how fucking great their work is," Joe tells me, his face hard and unreadable.

"I was never a prospect," I reply, feeling like I need to explain my checkered past.

"We know," Izzy says, crossing her arms in front of her chest, leaning back like me. "You wouldn't be in that chair if you had been."

"How do you know?" I'm pretty sure the things she's saying and thinks she knows aren't public knowledge or part of any record. At least not something someone could find out without digging into my background, finding the filth I wanted to stay hidden.

"Babe," she says, a shit-eating grin spreading across her face. "My husband may be an investigator now, but he was a DEA agent working the MC scene all across the South. If there's something he needs to know about a person or any club in the country, he's going to find it and not stop until he does."

"He asked around about me?"

Izzy nods. "He went right to the source, had a sit-down with Tiny."

My shoulders slump, and I let out a long, exasperated sigh. "He went to Tiny?"

Izzy nods. "Yep. Got all the dirt."

I raise an eyebrow because I'm sure he got some dirt, but he didn't get the steaming pile of shit that was my time hanging with the Disciples. "Tiny isn't much of a talker."

"Tiny and James go way back, and my brother Thomas and he go even further. They picked Tiny's brain, got the dirt they could get, and were satisfied enough with what he had to say that I got the okay to offer you that seat." Izzy pauses for a moment, shifting in her chair, leaning forward with her elbows resting just off the table. "And just so you know, the Feds watch those clubs every second of every day. You're in the files. Your name is there, pictures of you at their compound, riding with them, causing the havoc only the Disciples cause. If Tiny hadn't vouched for you, telling my husband you were just a kid who needed a home and help, you wouldn't be sitting where you're sitting."

"Still don't like that shit one bit," Joe says, glancing down at his daughter as she gawks at me like she didn't know a damn thing about my past.

She may not have known about the Disciples, but she knew why I was at Bike Week. It's not like we met at the ice cream shop, sharing wanton glances as we licked our cones. We met at a biker rally. One of the biggest ones in the country for fuck's sake.

"I was never in the life, and I don't plan on ever being there either. Those guys took me in when I had nowhere to go. They gave me a bed and a place to belong at a time when I had nothing and no one. They were a solid in my life when all I had was chaos."

"They don't do that shit out of the goodness of their heart," Izzy says, clearly knowing a lot about the life from her husband. "I spent enough time around those guys to know that life comes with strings."

"You know a lot of bikers?" I ask, trying not to laugh because the woman may be scary, but she didn't seem the type to be hanging out at compounds, sucking the cocks of random bikers for kicks.

"Someday, if you stick around, maybe I'll tell you about the time I spent with the Sun Devils. But that day isn't today, kid."

My eyebrows shoot up. "I know enough about the Sun Devils that I'm not sure I want to know about what shit went down between you and them."

"The fucking Sun Devils," Joe groans. "I hate those fuckers. They caused enough shit with this family that if I ever see one of them again, I'll…"

"They're all put away, Joe. Calm your shit. They can't touch us now," Izzy tells him like he doesn't have a reason to worry, which isn't entirely true.

"They have a far reach, Iz. Even behind bars, those fuckers have eyes and ears on the ground. I'm waiting for the next time they come after this family. And besides, it's not like they have life sentences."

I swallow down the lump that's lodged in my throat, thinking about the Sun Devils and the carnage they'd spread across the South back in the day. "They came after the family?"

Joe nods, eyes steely and cold. "Kidnapped Izzy and, hell, Angel too, but in the end, they landed in the place they deserved. Should've known better than to mess with two DEA agents' family members, but they weren't always the brightest fucking bunch. They let their thirst for vengeance cloud their judgment and sealed their fate in pulling the shit they did."

"Happens a lot with men like that," Anthony adds as he lifts his beer glass to his lips.

The table goes on chatting about the Sun Devils as I sit there, staring at them in shock and amazement. I can't wrap my head around the fact that the MC went after the Gallos. They seem like the nicest people in the world, maybe wound a little tight and possibly a little too loving, but why the fuck would they come after them and kidnap two women who weren't even part of the world? It makes no sense. But then again, shit inside the MC world rarely made a bit of sense unless you were part of the life with axes to grind and anger to burn.

"I'm ready to go." Gigi stares at me across the table. "You ready?"

I nod, swallowing down the last sip of beer and pushing my seat back, standing. "Let's hit it."

"You two be careful on the way home," Joe says like he's said it a million times before.

A weird feeling crashes over me as Gigi waves goodbye. One of belonging. One of family. All about something I never had before but wished like hell I did. No one has ever given a shit if I got home okay or made it in one piece. The only person who cared was my grandmother, but she wasn't even that concerned, figuring I was a man who would somehow get myself through anything.

But Gigi grew up Gallo. She grew up surrounded by love, not knowing what it's like to have no one at her back. She is luckier than she could ever know, and I am kind of jealous of the life she's lived. The love she has. The acceptance that is freely given.

I'd give anything to have just a small sliver of that goodness in my life. I may not have been given it by birth, but I'll do whatever I have to do to get a little piece of it in my life now.

CHAPTER
THIRTEEN

GIGI

"I LOVE the last piece you did tonight," Pike says with his wrist on the steering wheel, looking like he's driven my truck a thousand times. The flash of oncoming traffic lights up his features, sending shadows across his face.

I stare at him in the relative darkness, taking in the slight bump on the bridge of his nose and the lushness of his lips. "I love when clients want me to design a piece. When they give me free rein to run with their thoughts and turn it into something original and meaningful."

"You nailed it. The coloring was spot-on too," he praises, and warmth blooms inside my chest.

"Thanks." I turn my head just as he turns his to look at me because I don't want him to know I'm staring at him. "I could use a little more practice at shading."

"Nah. It took me a couple years to get as good as you are now. In five years, you'll be featured in all the big magazines. Mark my words, Gigi."

"That's really nice of you to say, but you don't have to suck up to me. I don't plan on blowing up your world anytime soon, Pike."

He rolls the truck into the empty parking space in front of

our apartment building and stops, turning to me as he cuts the engine. "I figured if you were going to, you would've done it already."

"Oh," I whisper, glancing at him when he shifts, sliding a little closer to me. "What are you doing?"

"Just wanted to talk alone for a few minutes." Pike stares at me in the soft glow of the parking lot lights, and I practically have to will myself not to leap into his lap.

Even after fifteen months, the pull to him is so heavy, the attraction so deep, I have to remind myself he's not for me. We have very little in common except for where we live and what we do. He comes from a different life. One without a loving family but with the Disciples in his past.

"You can talk from over there." I tick my chin toward his side of the cab, because if he gets any closer…

He scoots closer, and I hold my breath. "What's going to happen?"

My fingers work the fringe on the bottom of my denim shorts, and I remind myself to breathe. "I just don't think it's a good idea."

The one thing I know about Pike is he won't do anything I don't want. If I tell him to back off and it's not going to happen, he'll leave me alone. But then I remember the way his mouth tastes, the sensation of his lips against mine, and how much I want to feel his body pressing mine into the mattress.

"Sometimes, the best things never are."

"What if we get caught?"

He cocks an eyebrow. "Your parents have surveillance set up?"

I shrug, laughing nervously because the way he's looking at me is nothing short of hot and needy. "I wouldn't put it past my mother. My father is overprotective, but my mother is downright smothering."

His gaze drops to my lips as I speak, and heat sparks

across my body. The needy ache I've felt for him since the moment I laid eyes on him again at Inked amplifies, and I'm pretty sure nothing but his touch will help chase the feeling away.

"Darlin'," he says, and my belly tumbles. I keep telling him how much I hate that word, but damn it, it's a lie. It's so much better than babe, and when Pike's saying it, there's nothing sweeter and it's a total turn-on. "Get your ass over here and kiss me already."

I gawk at him. It's like he's reading my mind because my body language doesn't exactly scream sex right now. I haven't moved an inch, too scared of what will happen if I do. The last time Pike and I kissed, we barely came up for air for almost a week. With my current dry spell, I'm confident it'll be much the same, but I don't have the luxury of time.

When I don't move, Pike slides closer until our knees are touching. "I'm going to kiss you, Gigi."

Oh God. Oh God. Oh God. Yes! Yes! Yes! I want to crawl into his lap, wrap my arms around his neck, and kiss the hell out of the man until I'm gasping for air.

"Pike," I whisper, my eyes locked on his mouth as his tongue pokes out, sweeping across his bottom lip. "I…"

The words don't make it out of my mouth before his hand is on my jaw, caressing my cheek with his thumb. "Tell me no, and I'll stop."

"Pike," I repeat like my brain is fried and his touch alone has rendered me completely and absolutely stupid.

He leans forward, eyes locked on mine, hand on my face as the shadows pass over his face when he moves his mouth closer.

"Yes," I whisper so quietly, I can barely hear myself over the loud thumping of my heart against the insides of my chest.

When his lips connect with mine, so velvety soft and warm, I can do nothing but open to him. The man is hard everywhere. Hard arms. Hard features. Hard eyes. Hard cock. But the one place he's soft is his lips. His mouth is demanding, just like the rest of him, as his lips press against mine. He tightens his fingers behind my neck, pulling me toward him, and my body moves on its own. Without thinking, I crawl into his lap, straddling him in the front seat of my truck in the very public parking lot of our building.

My arms go around his neck like they were always meant to be there as I settle into his lap, pressing my chest against his, loving the demanding way he's kissing me.

I could get lost in him.

I did actually.

Fifteen months ago, I'd been in this same position, tasting his lips, figuring I'd never see him again.

Wrong.

He slides a hand around my back, gripping my ass roughly as his tongue moves across my lips, and my skin starts to tingle everywhere like his mouth is the lighter fluid and his touch is the match. My body's on fire, burning for the man below me.

I grind my hips as I open my lips, giving him anything he wants. It's been so long since I've been touched like this. So long since I've felt this kind of need for anyone. In all honesty, I haven't wanted another man since the day I drove away from Daytona, telling myself Pike was nothing more than a fling.

Pike's fingers slide up the back of my neck before tangling in my hair, securing me to him even though I'm not going anywhere. I'm right where I want to be.

"I missed this," he murmurs against my lips, sending a jolt of white-hot electricity down my spine like a lightning bolt of need coursing through my system. "Missed how sweet you taste."

I moan and tighten the hold I have around his shoulders, latching my lips back on to his to stop him from talking. We talked all day. What we didn't do was kiss. Now isn't the time for chatter. Now's the time to get what I've been thinking about since the moment I laid eyes on him again.

A man clears his throat, and I freeze, my eyes flying open and going wide. We stare at each other, our mouths still touching, but not breathing.

"Excuse me," the man says, not giving two fucks that we're currently getting hot and heavy in the parking lot. "I'm looking for a Mr. Pike Moore."

Pike's lips move to the side, sliding off mine slowly, and I want to crawl through the open window and knee this guy in the balls for interrupting us. "I'm him."

The man reaches down, fishing something out of his pocket, and Pike's body stiffens under me. His hand is wrapped around my arms, hauling me off his body and to the other side of the truck, shielding me from whatever the man is about to do.

"I'm Special Agent Russo from the FBI. I was wondering if I could have a minute of your time." The man flashes his identification before snapping the leather wallet shut.

Pike growls. Flat-out growls like he's about to attack. "It's almost one in the morning, I'm sitting in the truck, having a nice time with my girl, and you pick now to bust my balls?"

The agent's eyes cut to me and then back to Pike. "Sorry for the bad timing, but I've been waiting around here all day for you, Mr. Moore."

"Bad timing," Pike mumbles, his hands balling into tight fists against his legs. "Understatement of the fucking year."

"I only need a moment of your time," the agent says, making no move like he's going to leave and let us finish what we began.

Pike's gaze moves to me. "Go inside, darlin'. I'll only need a minute."

"I'm not leaving." No man is going to tell me what to do,

and like fuck am I leaving Pike out here alone with an agent without finding out what the hell he wants.

"It's about your dad."

If I thought Pike was stiff before, he's hard as granite now. His movements are slow, letting the man's words wash over him, soaking into his soul. "Is he dead?"

"He wasn't the last time we had eyes on him."

Pike moves his hand to the steering wheel, making no attempt to get out of the truck as I sit next to him, not moving and barely breathing.

What the hell could the agent want with Pike if it has to do with his father? Whether Pike likes the man or not, I can't imagine a cop showing up, asking me questions about my own blood.

"I don't talk to my father, so I don't know how I can help." Pike's eyes burn as they come to me. "I'm busy with my girl, so if you could come back tomorrow, maybe, and I mean maybe, I'll talk to you."

"Sir," the agent says and shakes his head. "I'm not leaving until we talk. If I have to haul your ass downtown to FBI headquarters to do it, so be it."

My hand clamps over my mouth as I gasp, and I try to cover my horror at the entire situation. "Is that really necessary?" I mumble against my palm with wide eyes.

The agent nods. "Actually, let's take a drive. I'd like to speak to you in private. It'll be safer downtown."

"Like fuck," Pike hisses, hand tightening around my steering wheel like he's trying to choke the life out of it.

"Don't go."

I stick my nose where it doesn't belong, but that's always been my way.

"Ma'am, do you want to take a ride in the back of my car too? You can wait in the holding cell where we keep the *good* criminals." He winks.

Pike's out of the truck before the guy can straighten his

face again. "Leave her the fuck alone. If your beef is with me, keep it with me. Ya hear me?"

I lunge to the side, trying to grab on to his arm but miss, falling face first into the seat. "Let me call my uncle," I mutter into the fabric as I push myself upward to a sitting position.

Pike turns, his eyes flashing a warning that needs no words. I'm to call no one. "I'll be fine. Get your ass inside and lock the door." Pike ticks his head toward the apartment building like I'm just supposed to obey.

Is he for real? If the situation weren't so dire and the agent didn't look like such a giant douche, I'd laugh right in Pike's face. "Pike, I don't think…"

"He'll be fine, ma'am." The man dips his head, giving me a bullshit smile like I'm just going to take his word on that. He already said shitty things to me and hasn't been the nicest to Pike even though he's supposedly only wanted for questioning.

"Are you arresting him?" I blurt out as I slide across the truck, crawling to my feet just behind Pike.

The agent's gaze sweeps over Pike as he pulls at the cuffs of his dress shirt that are barely peeking out from his suit jacket. "Not yet, but stranger things have happened."

Well, isn't that reassuring?

"Just go inside, Gigi," Pike orders as I start to reach for my phone. "Call no one."

I let out a loud huff before jamming my phone back into my shorts pocket. "Fine."

"Let's go, son."

"Don't call me that. You're not my daddy," Pike says coldly.

"The longer you wait, the later it'll be when you get back."

Pike turns to me and grabs my hands, tangling his fingers with mine. "I'll text you when I'm back, darlin'. Don't worry. I'll be fine."

"I'll go with you." I take a step toward Pike before he tightens his grip, stopping me.

"Stay here in case I need you. Please," he begs with knitted brows.

What the fuck am I supposed to do from here? How can I help him if I'm thirty minutes away? He's crazy if he thinks I'm just going to stand by, twiddling my damn thumbs until he sends me a text message.

"Okay," I lie. "I promise," I lie again.

He exhales as his shoulders finally relax. "Thank you." He leans forward, placing his lips on my cheek and whispers, "I promise everything will be fine."

I don't know if I want to scream or cry as he releases me, backing up toward the agent, our eyes locked on each other. I want to beg him not to go. Beg him to stay here, but I know it's useless.

Pike folds himself into the back of the guy's unmarked car, staring at me through the window as the dickhead slams the door. I lift my hand and wave, wishing I could tell him everything will be okay. He may have whispered the words, but I know he didn't believe a word he spoke.

The agent smirks as he climbs into the front, revving the engine like that piece of shit Capri is a hot rod.

I walk toward the car, following as it slowly rolls toward the exit of the apartment complex. Pike turns in his seat, peering at me through the window, barely visible in the darkness.

I waste no time, grabbing my phone and dialing the only person I know who can help in this situation. The only one I know who can keep his mouth shut.

"It's fucking late. This shit better be good."

I wince. "Um, Uncle James. I need you." I look into the darkness as the taillights of the agent's car disappear.

CHAPTER
FOURTEEN
PIKE

THE SOUND of metal on concrete snaps me out of the haze from sitting too long in a quiet room at four in the morning. Fuck, I need to be at work in eight hours, and I'm nowhere near my place and need to get some damn sleep so I'm not useless tomorrow.

So far, the asshat agent hasn't said much but has come in to bust my balls every few minutes just as I'm nodding off. I assume it's all part of his genius master plan, trying to deprive me of sleep so I'll tell him whatever he's fishing for just so I can leave.

"Sorry," a new guy says, plopping down in the chair, almost spilling the coffee he's holding in one hand. "Didn't mean to wake you."

Fucker. "Can we just get this shit over with so I can get out of here?"

They took my phone as soon as I got here. I'm pretty sure there's probably dozens of texts from Gigi, possibly a few missed calls, all growing in levels of panic. I wasn't looking forward to having her chew my ear off for ordering her ass inside and telling her to mind her own business, even if I said it in a nice way. Or at least, the nicest way I knew how.

The man flips open a folder, fingers a few pages, staring down at the words. "Your father is Colton Moore?"

"Yes." I grit my teeth together, slouching over in the chair and rapping my fingertips on the metal table. "I thought we established this."

"I'm the new shift." He peers up for a moment as he turns a page. "Have you ever worked for the firm of Moore, Justice, and Sanders?"

I glare at this dumbass. "Do I look like a lawyer?"

"I guess that's a no," he says, pulling a pen from a pocket on the front of his shirt. "Have you ever spent time in his office?"

"Recently? I mean, my ass is in Florida, so that would be a no."

Is this guy fucking serious with these dumb-ass questions?

"Ever, kid. Have you ever spent time in his office?"

"When I was a kid, sure. He is my father."

He scribbles something on the paper, flipping to the next sheet. "Have you ever heard the name Dominic DiSantis?"

My face doesn't move because I've heard that name a million times in my life. Dirty Dom. That's how my father always referred to him, especially when talking with other friends and clients he'd bring back to the house. The man was a criminal and my father was his attorney, but half the shit my dad did for him wasn't covered under the umbrella of a normal attorney-client relationship.

They thought I was too young to understand when they'd talk in my presence. Just figured I was some dumb kid who was too busy pushing around the same shitty toy truck I'd had for three years to know what they were saying, but I heard every word and took it all in.

"I've heard the name," I tell the guy who is staring at me across the table, waiting for me to lie.

I'm pretty sure he already knows the answers to the questions. A quick background check would've told him I haven't lived in Tennessee in almost a decade, and being Colt's kid, of course I heard names I probably never should've heard.

He raises an eyebrow. "Care to elaborate?"

I raise mine right back. "Care to tell me why?"

The man sighs, leaning back in the chair, pushing the folder of papers toward the middle of the table. "Dominic DiSantis is a mobster."

I nod because anyone who's anyone and pays attention to the national news knows this shit. He was popped a year ago and is awaiting trial for money laundering and a whole long-ass list of shit I'm pretty sure he did.

"He's currently locked up and awaiting trial."

"Tell me something I don't know." I kick back, putting my hands behind my head, acting as chill as I can so I don't lose my shit. "Why did you haul me down here to tell me something I already know? This is bullshit, verging on harassment."

"Your father was on retainer with Dominic."

"I know," I bark, losing my patience.

"We believe your father may be involved in Mr. DiSantis's criminal enterprises."

I lean forward, resting my arms on the table and glare at this buffoon. "Whether my father is or isn't, I don't know how you think I can help. Do you know how close I am to my father?" I pause for a second, and just as he's about to say something stupid again, I continue. "I haven't spoken to my father in over ten years. I lived with my grandmother as soon as I started middle school because I couldn't be around the asshole another minute. He may be my blood, but that doesn't make him my family. I know you want to nail him and DiSantis, but there's nothing I can say to help you."

The agent crosses his arms, studying me. "Whether you've talked to him in ten years or not, you know things, were privy to things no one else was. If you're not willing to help us, maybe we should visit your little brother at summer camp and see if he's willing to help us."

I force myself to stay in my seat because all I want to do is lunge at the asshole and wrap my fingers around his neck until he begs for me to let go. "Leave Austin out of this."

"We're running out of options, Mr. Moore. Either you help us, or we'll have no other choice but to speak with Austin."

"Talk to my mother. I'm sure she'll flip on him if you offer her something she wants, like a new life and an unlimited bank account."

"She's dead, son."

I blink a few times, thinking I must have heard him wrong. "Excuse me?"

"Died this morning. Gunshot to the back of the head after she dropped Austin off at camp. We figured it was an execution, sending a message to your father from Mr. DiSantis."

My head spins with the news as it slams into my chest like a ton of bricks. *My mother is dead.* She and I had a tenuous relationship at best, but I wasn't her favorite and always seemed more like a burden than a blessing. She never once stopped my father from putting his hands on me. Never once stopped the man from treating me like an outcast in my own home. If she had a maternal instinct, it didn't appear until Austin was born.

I never went to summer camp. I never got shit as a kid. There wasn't a new toy in my room until the ones I had were so worn out they basically fell apart. I don't remember being hugged or snuggled, even if I was sick or bleeding. The two of them were worthless. The day my grandmother caught my father, hand raised, ready to strike me, she took me in and I never looked back.

"You think DiSantis killed my mother, and you track me down, harassing me for hours, and don't even bother to mention that shit until now?" I ball my hands into fists, wanting to punch this fucker straight in the face. "And you make me leave my girl alone and vulnerable so you can haul me down here, not even thinking it's a good idea to clue me the fuck in on the day's events?"

"We have no reason to believe your girlfriend is in danger."

"Pardon me if that isn't reassuring. Did you think my mother was in danger, or did you let her take one for the team?"

"Son…"

"Don't fucking call me that!" I yell, pushing back from the table and rising to my feet. "Don't ever fucking call me that. I want to talk to your superior."

The man's up, studying me as I pace around the room, running my hands through my hair to do something with them besides knock his lights out. "I don't think…"

"That seems to be the norm around here," I taunt, wishing he'd get pissed and swing on me just so I could land a good one on him.

He turns his back to me as the handle to the door turns and opens, and a man appears. "Agent Carson, the interview is over."

"Damn right, it is," I bark out, leering at the two men across the room from me.

"We weren't finished," Carson replies, turning and tossing his pen on the table that sits between us. "Just a few more minutes."

The other man shakes his head. "Can't let that happen. We have an issue."

"What kind of issue?"

"The Director called and isn't so happy about us bringing Mr. Moore in for questioning."

Carson stiffens. "How the hell does he know?"

The man gives a small shrug. "I guess the kid has a few connections. Calls were made. Favors exchanged, and we're to let him go or else…"

Connections? Favors? No one knows I'm here except for Gigi. *Fuck.* She didn't listen to a damn word I said. By now, the entire Gallo family probably knows my ass is downtown, sitting in FBI headquarters for some unknown reason. I'll have a lot of explaining to do and a lot of begging if I am going to be allowed to stay at Inked and at least finish out the contract on the chair I so badly want.

Fucking perfect. If shit wasn't fucked up enough already, my mom dead, my brother motherless, and my father who the fuck knows where, my job is in jeopardy because Gigi couldn't let me handle my own shit.

"What the fuck? The Director knows how important this case is." Carson throws out an arm in my direction. "And we're just supposed to let him go?"

The other man raises an eyebrow. "You want to call him at this hour and tell him you think he's wrong?"

Carson glances toward the ceiling and lets out a loud grunt. "Fuck. This is bullshit."

"It's *all* bullshit," I mutter, still pacing so I don't go ballistic about the entire situation, including the two assholes in the room with me.

"We're sorry about your mother, Mr. Moore," the new guy says like somehow his condolences are going to make anything better.

My mother cut ties with me years ago. The last time I talked to her, I was already living at the Disciples' compound, which she snubbed her nose at, reminding me that she thought I was a piece of trash before and always. That was the last time I said goodbye to her, and that time, I meant that word completely.

I should be crying, shedding a tear that the woman who gave birth to me is lying somewhere on a cold metal table, stiff and not breathing. But I can't bring myself to cry. I care, of course I do—she is family—but there's no love between us. There never will be now.

The thing I care most about is the fact that Gigi's out there and I don't know who's had eyes on me. If DiSantis was watching my parents close enough to off my mom, is he watching me too? Has he seen Gigi and me together? Would he use her to keep me quiet?

"You can go, Mr. Moore. If we need you further…"

I wave him off, pushing past Carson. "You know where to find me the next time you want to drop a bomb in my lap and harass me."

"The department truly is sorry," he says as I brush against him, wishing I could knock them both over as I make my way toward the sterile gray hallway.

"Save it. Just give me my phone and let me go."

"The receptionist at the front desk will give you your things before you leave."

I pause for a minute, waiting for someone to offer me a ride home, but they say nothing. I stalk down the hallway, happy to be heading toward freedom and to make my way back home to check on Gigi. I have to figure out what to do about her. Do I distance myself from her entirely? Distance myself from her family too? I don't want my father to put her and her entire family at risk because he's a money-grubbing asshole.

I'm staring at the floor, watching the black-and-white checkered pattern pass in a blur and thrilled as fuck to get out of here, even if I have to hitch a ride home with a stranger.

"Pike!" Gigi screeches.

I lift my head, catching sight of the beautiful brunette running toward me like we haven't seen each other in years. "Are you okay? Oh my God. I was so scared. I thought they were never going to let you go." Her gaze darts over my body, checking for some sign of wear and tear. "Did they hurt you? I was so worried, I didn't know what to do. I'm so sorry." She looks over her shoulder toward a man who doesn't look happy and is scarier than any dude in this place.

"I had to call someone. Don't be mad at me," she finally pleads, sucking in a breath because she hasn't given herself a chance to come up for air and stop talking long enough to breathe.

"I'm not mad, darlin'," I whisper, mindful of the man looking a little like a caged lion and totally pissed off to be here at this hour. I want to wrap her in my arms, steal her away from this place, and put her where I know no one will find her, but the way the man she came with is staring at me, at us, I know I'd better keep my hands to myself.

Gigi turns toward the tall, dark-haired man behind her. "This is James," she says and pulls me toward him, locking her fingers with mine. "My aunt Izzy's husband."

My eyes widen. "You called Izzy's husband?"

She nods, smiling at me like her decision made all the sense in the world. "Izzy's not stupid. She knows something is going on. Plus, James worked for the DEA, and I figured if anyone had connections with the FBI, it would be him. What else was I supposed to do? Just leave you here?" She squeezes my fingers and gives me the sweetest smile, like it's going to make all this shit okay.

Fucking great.

"Well, yeah." I pull my hand from her grip because Uncle James hasn't taken his eyes off our connection, and there's no happiness on his face. "I would've figured something out sooner or later."

James stands taller, crossing his arms as he spreads his legs farther apart. "You two about done?"

"We're done." I look the man in the eye because he deserves my respect. No matter what, he pulled my ass out of a jam, getting up in the middle of the night to help a person he didn't even know. "Can you just take us home?"

James shakes his head. "You two are going to my place. Izzy's waiting, and she's probably climbing the walls right about now. If I don't bring you there, she'll have my ass. And besides losing sleep, I don't need her chewing my ear off all morning about dropping you off at home."

"I'm sorry," Gigi says again.

"It's fine," I lie because what else am I supposed to say? Nothing about this night has been fine. From the moment the asshole interrupted our kiss until the moment I walked out of the interrogation room, nothing has been fine.

"We're coming, Uncle James." Gigi turns to me, grabbing my hand, giving my fingers a light squeeze. "Okay?" She stares up at me, looking for my confirmation.

I nod. I'm not sure if it's something I want Gigi to know because she'd flip her shit and rightfully so. Maybe I need to explain the situation to James, get his thoughts on what my next move should be and how we can shield Gigi from any potential blowback.

James practically punches the door open, walking into the thick night air with Gigi and me following behind him. She glances at me, giving me a small smile every few steps before staring at her uncle and frowning.

I know she has a lot to say. I know she wants to ask me everything, but she's holding back...for once. I have a lot to say too, but I'm not sure I can put everything into words just yet. There's so much swirling around my brain, I can barely make sense of it all.

"Pike, sit up front. You and I are going to talk," James says as we approach his kick-ass Challenger parked just outside the doorway since the place is deserted.

"Um," Gigi mumbles, wanting to say more but shutting her mouth when James turns his gaze toward her. "Got it. I'm in the back."

I fold the seat forward, letting her crawl into the impossibly small back seat, thankful I don't have to contort myself in crazy ways to sit next to her. I slide in under the watchful eye of James and stare straight ahead, feeling something strange wash over me.

"Seat belts, kids."

I don't argue with the man. I'm not stupid. I'm not even in the mood to tell him I'm not his kid because I'm almost certain he'd knock me upside the head, and I'd still have to put on my seat belt before he'd drive away. Right now, all I want is a place to lay my head, sort out my thoughts, and say goodbye to this day.

"How do you know DiSantis?" he asks before we're even out of the parking lot.

"I don't." I shrug, staring out the front window as the oncoming cars pass in a blur. "My father worked for him."

"That's it? You never did any side jobs for him?"

"That's it. I was a kid last time I was around him, fifteen years ago, maybe. I forgot about the guy until I saw he'd been arrested splattered on the front page of the newspaper."

James adjusts in his seat, leaning forward, holding the steering wheel with one hand. "The Director and I go way back. We have a history together. He told me what he could about the case, why they hauled you in for questioning, and what they're hoping to gain."

"I don't have anything to offer." I shrug, placing my elbow on the door, resting my head in my palm because I'm so exhausted, I'm fighting to stay awake in the darkness.

"They told me about your mom," James says softer, his voice laced with sorrow. "I'm sorry for your loss."

Gigi gasps behind me, and I straighten. "Oh my God. Pike, I'm so sorry." Her voice wavers like she's on the verge of tears, but there's no time for crying.

I ignore her, because there's more pressing shit than fretting over a woman who gave no shits about me. "I'm worried about Gigi and anyone who's around me right now. I could use your help in figuring out what my next move should be, sir."

"Why are you worried about me?"

This time, James ignores her. "We have a lot to figure out

and not a lot of time to do it. For the time being, the safest place for the two of you is at my house. You'll stay there until we know what we're dealing with. Got it?" James raises up, looking in the rearview mirror as we wait at a traffic light. "You hear me, Giovanna? I don't want any lip either."

Fan-fucking-tastic.

The night just went from bad to clusterfucked beyond belief.

CHAPTER FIFTEEN

GIGI

I YAWN for what might be the hundredth time in the thirty-minute drive home from the FBI headquarters. To say I'm tired is an understatement. I don't remember being this exhausted in my entire life. I never even pulled an all-nighter studying for college exams.

I've sat in relative silence as James and Pike talked around me, ignoring my every comment like I wasn't talking or even in the same car with them. They are both infuriating, cut from the same manly cloth, and it's annoying as hell.

"Be ready for the real grilling to start," James says as he pulls into the drive and his headlights land on Aunt Izzy.

She's pacing back and forth in the driveway, her head coming up as she's bathed in light from the car. The look on her face isn't friendly or even playful, but serious as a fucking heart attack and like she's ready to pounce at any second.

"Well, this should be fun," I mumble and wonder if I should've called Uncle Thomas instead. But I know Angel is shit at keeping secrets, and right now, I needed silence.

"Just let her say what she needs to say, answer what she wants to know, and you'll live to see the sunrise," James says, trying to make light of what totally isn't a funny situation.

I drag my hands down my face, trying to clear my mind and wake myself up for what's probably going to be hours of explaining and getting my ass chewed out.

"You handle your aunt while Pike and I talk in my office," James tells me as he cuts the engine and unlocks the car doors.

"Handle her?" I cackle, feeling loopy from exhaustion. "You know that's an impossibility, right?"

James's eyes slice to mine. "You're exactly like your aunt, kid. You two think alike. If I didn't know better, I'd think you were her daughter. You know how she thinks, so handle her. Tell her what you want, leave out what you can, and then get your ass to sleep." James turns toward the door as Izzy raps her fingers against the window before throwing her arms up in a *what the fuck* kind of way.

"I think I'm getting the better end of this deal," Pike says as he pushes open his door, climbs out, and pulls the lever to let me out of the crazy-small back seat.

"You so did," I whisper, brushing up against him as I crawl out, almost smacking my head before I find my footing. "I'll find you when you're done."

"You two better get your asses inside. You have a lot of explaining to do," Izzy announces before I've even stood straight and stretched my legs.

"I have a feeling I'm going to be done before you, darlin'," Pike says as the corner of his mouth quirks up.

I scowl because there's nothing even remotely amusing about the entire situation. From Pike being hauled downtown, the fact that his mother is dead and I have no fucking clue how or why, and that my aunt and uncle are now all up in my shit and Pike's too.

"Sweetheart," James says, grabbing Izzy by the waist and hauling her body against his. "Go easy on the kid. She's had a long, stressful night. She's tired."

Izzy glances at me over James's shoulder. "Good. She'll break easier that way."

"For fuck's sake," I mutter, rolling my eyes. "I'll tell you everything, Auntie, if you just let me sleep for a little while."

"Fat chance, missy. March your pretty little ass in the kitchen, and we'll have some coffee while we talk about all the shit you've left out."

Pike squeezes my hand, peering down at me. "Tell her what you want, Gigi. I have nothing else to hide. I'm pretty sure my ass is going to be fired anyway."

"Why?" I furrow my eyebrows as I glance up at him, my mouth hanging open.

"No one wants trouble coming to their door, especially from someone they don't know and just hired. Go with her. It'll all be better in the morning."

"Find me, okay? Promise me," I plead.

Pike nods, releasing my hand and pushing me toward my aunt. "Go."

Izzy's out of James's arms and around the Challenger within seconds, stalking toward me like a woman possessed. "Stop wasting time," she says, reaching for my arm and hauling me away from Pike like I'm a little girl again.

I glance over my shoulder, mouthing "I'm sorry" to Pike as I follow my aunt up the stairs to the front door of their house. He only waves, giving me a small smile like this is just another day and not one where his mother dies and his life may be at risk.

"Sit," Izzy says before I'm two steps into the kitchen, pointing at a chair near the island. "Coffee or water?"

"Coffee." I slump over, wishing she'd just give me a pillow and one hour to get a little sleep. But I know my aunt, and she ain't giving me nothing until I give her something in return.

She pours the coffee, her back to me, and I can almost hear

her thoughts and the line of questioning she's about to hurl at me.

"Before we start." I clear my throat, staring at her back, wishing like fuck I was anywhere but here. "Can you not tell my dad?"

Izzy sighs, placing the coffee carafe back on the warmer. "They already know."

I gasp, eyes widening, and suddenly feel more awake than I ever have in my entire life. "What?"

"There was an agent waiting at your parents' house when he got home from the bar tonight. He knows Pike was hauled in for questioning. But we left some things out like the fact that you called James in a complete panic, begging for someone to help a guy you claim to hate."

"I don't hate him," I mumble, crossing my arms over my chest, trying to figure out how to crawl out of this miserable mess.

"I know, baby girl," she says, sliding the coffee cup in front of me. "I used to look at your uncle James the same way. Girl," she laughs, shaking her head as she leans across the counter, facing me. "That man had me all kinds of crazy and my head all twisted."

I laugh because she says that like she's normal now and Uncle James's effect has worn off. He's the only man who can shut my aunt up when she's on a tirade, which is more often than not, especially lately.

"So, start at the beginning and tell me how you know Pike." She pins me with her gaze, and I swallow the lump that suddenly forms in my throat.

I glance down at the mug, wrapping my hands around the warm ceramic, wondering just how far back I should go and how detailed I should be. I'm not about to get graphic with my aunt because she's my aunt and I sure as fuck don't ask about her sex life, even if I have heard about it.

"Well…" I pause, stalling but knowing she would wait an eternity to hear the answer. "I met him last year."

Her eyes flash. "Where?"

"In Daytona."

"When?"

"Last year."

"No, smartass. When were you in Daytona? I don't remember you ever mentioning it to anyone."

I shift, squirming in the chair because Tamara and I swore each other to secrecy and hadn't broken our promise for fear of our parents flipping the fuck out. "We went there for spring break," I squeak, cringing at my voice and the look that shifts across my aunt's face.

"You went to Daytona for spring break last year?"

"Yeah." I nod slowly, holding her steely gaze.

"In March?"

I nod again because I figure there's nothing else I need to say, and I know more questions are coming.

She moves her coffee mug to the side, flattening her palms against the cold granite countertop. "Wasn't that Bike Week?"

I nod again, biting on my lip to stop myself from saying anything more.

"Are you fucking stupid, little girl?"

I shake my head, figuring words aren't necessary and knowing she is going to say enough for the both of us.

"You went to Daytona for spring break, which just happened to be Bike Week, alone, and didn't bother to tell anyone?" She sucks in a breath, looking like her head is about to pop off. "Do you know how goddamn dangerous that was?"

"I wasn't alone," I whisper, staring back down at my mug as I play with the handle.

"You were with Tamara, weren't you?" she says flatly because usually, wherever I go, Tamara isn't too far behind.

We're a package deal especially since Lily decided to go to Miami instead of FSU like Tam and me.

I nod again.

Izzy pushes away from the countertop, cursing into the air as she starts to pace again. "Of all the stupid shit you two could do…"

"We were safe. We made it back in one piece. Nothing bad happened, Auntie."

"Thank fuck," she blurts out, stopping on her heel and spinning her body to face me. "I've been to Bike Week. That shit ain't no joke, Gigi."

"You went there?" I ask, fascinated that my aunt ventured into the biker world, but I shouldn't be surprised. She did end up married to one of the most badass men I've ever known besides my father. "To Bike Week?"

"I was almost raped at Bike Week. If it weren't for your uncle Thomas and uncle James, I don't know what would've happened to me." She hangs her head for a moment and takes a deep breath. "But I was older and should've been wiser. You weren't even twenty-one yet, and Tamara isn't even twenty-one now, so explain to me what the fuck you two were doing at Bike Week?"

"Lying on the beach." I don't even believe my own shit because my voice rises like I'm asking a question instead of stating a fact. Dead giveaway and my aunt doesn't miss a fucking beat.

"Gigi," she says flatly. "Stop the bullshit. Lay it out, and I want the truth."

"We went for spring break, but we honestly didn't know it was Bike Week when we planned the trip. We found out as we pulled into town and noticed all hell had broken loose and everyone was covered in leather and tattoos."

"Even if you didn't know it was Bike Week, why did you lie about going to Daytona in the first place?"

I shrug. "We figured Dad would get pissed and Uncle

Anthony would throw a fit, so we just thought it would be easier."

Izzy chuckles softly, and I almost think she's going to let it drop, maybe let me go to sleep, but I'm dead wrong. "You should always let someone know where you are. You could've at least told me. A place like that at a time like that was risky, and you're lucky you two made it out unscathed."

"Yeah. I know that now." I'm trying to pacify her. "I'll never do it again."

"And how does Pike fit into—" she clears her throat "—lying on the beach in Daytona?"

"We ran into each other there," I lie and lift the mug to my lips, hoping to cover some of my face so she doesn't know I'm still not telling her the entire truth.

She straightens, crossing her arms in front of her as she stands there in a black tank top and yoga pants, her hair pulled into a tight, high ponytail. "So, you two ran into each other and then you looked like you saw a ghost when you ran into him again?" She narrows her eyes. "You think I'm going to believe that line of horseshit?"

"It's not horseshit," I mumble into my mug, staring at the black liquid because meeting her eyes is a little too much, especially when she's ready to start frothing at the mouth.

"You know the man better than just a quick passing hello. I wasn't born yesterday, Gigi. You better start telling me the truth, or I'll tell Joe about Daytona."

My eyes widen. "You wouldn't."

She drops a shoulder, a grin playing on her lips. "Sweetheart, I'll do whatever I need to do. It won't be my ass getting chewed out by him when he finds out."

I groan, knowing I'm not handling Izzy, but she sure as shit is handling me. Like a pro too. "Fine, we did more than run into each other."

"Did you drink together?"

"A little." I wince.

"Did he know you were underage?"

I shake my head. "We had fake IDs."

Izzy closes her eyes, pressing her fingers against her temples and rubbing. "Motherfucker," she whispers, drawing in a loud breath. "How many drinks did you have with Pike?"

"Which time?" I try to be funny even though I was also being honest.

She twists her mouth. "Stop being a smartass."

I shrug again. "The first night I met him, I think I had one drink."

"So, you weren't drunk?"

"Well…" I give her a nervous smile. "I may have been drinking before I met him. I said I only had one drink with him."

"On a scale of one to ten, ten being black-out drunk, where were you?"

"Before the drink with him or after?"

"For fuck's sake," she says, shaking her head, cursing again under her breath. "After you had the drink with him."

"A nine. I remember everything except for passing out, which I did because tequila." I laugh, trying to break the tension in the room, thinking Izzy will laugh because she's usually the fun one in my family.

She pulls her lips into her mouth, closing her eyes again, and groans. Clearly, I was wrong about the funny, and my aunt's sense of humor died somewhere between earlier tonight—or was that yesterday?—and right now. "You passed out with him, or were you with Tamara?" She's leaning over the counter, tapping her long black fingernails on the granite. "You can tell me, or I'll ask Tam when she comes home."

"I passed out with him." I don't want her questioning Tamara, and she'll find out anyway because Tam will crack like an egg under Izzy's pressure.

"Of all the stupid shit," she says, pushing off the counter and pacing again. "Did he hurt you?" Her eyes slice to mine.

I shake my head. "No, Auntie. He was a gentleman."

"A gentleman who took you back to his hotel room." She laughs. "You're priceless, kid."

"So, you've never had a one-night stand with a stranger?" I throw that right in her face because I've heard all about the night she met James at my parents' wedding. They weren't sipping coffee all night before she snuck right the fuck out of his room.

"We're not talking about me," she deflects. "Now, you had a drink with him, passed out, and then what? Don't leave anything out, or Pike will be out of this house and have his shit packed before your tired ass wakes up."

I take a deep breath and start at the beginning, telling my aunt every detail, minus all the crazy-amazing fucking we did. She doesn't need to know the details because she isn't my girlfriend, and it is already horrifying enough that I am telling her I slept with him. After what feels like I've been talking forever, I stop, finally looking at her in the eyes again. "That's it."

"Did you give him your phone number? Promise him anything?"

I shake my head. "He didn't even know my full name. Just knew me as Gigi, and I told him I was going for coffee one morning and never went back."

My aunt's face changes, and her eyes light up. "You said you were going for coffee?"

I nod, laughing a little and feeling guilty too. "I did. He said he waited for me for hours before realizing I wasn't coming back."

"You so should've been my kid," she says, holding her stomach, still laughing. "That's totally something I would've pulled back in my heyday."

"We're not talking about your heyday." I use air quotes on

the last two words. If there's anything more horrifying than telling your aunt about a guy you banged, it's hearing about the guys she banged when she was your age.

"I was young once."

"You still are." I suck up. Something I've always done with my aunt and has typically worked.

"You're a shit liar, baby girl."

"Don't fire Pike," I beg because her mood has changed, and this may be the only time I can beg her for mercy. "I promise he didn't do anything wrong."

"I need to talk to your uncle before I can make you a promise about Pike and his future at Inked."

"That's bullshit. I'm either an adult, or I'm not. You can't treat me like a girlfriend one minute, laughing about the way I left a guy with his dick literally in his hand, and then in the next breath, tell me you can't make me a promise until you discuss something with my uncle. Why not just throw Dad in there too?"

"Pike's future is going to be a family decision, Giovanna. We all own Inked. I don't get the final say in anything that happens to that man without the others getting to say their piece."

"Fucking great," I groan.

"I won't tell them about your spring break activities, but they will know what happened tonight and the world of shit surrounding Pike."

"You won't tell them that we were making out tonight, will you?"

When her eyes widen, I slap my hand over my mouth, realizing I hadn't told her about that and she had no way of knowing. *Fuck. Good going, dumbass.*

"I won't tell them about that either if you want Pike to still be breathing, but they're going to have questions, and you're going to have to woman up and answer them."

"Fine."

"But there will be lots of questions—especially now that Pike's worried about your safety."

Sounds like a fan-fucking-tastic time. I've always wanted to tell my dad about the lies I've told him and the guys—even though they've been limited—that I've banged. I'm totally looking forward to the most uncomfortable situation of my life. *Not.*

I would rather have my hair pulled out strand by strand while being tied to a chair of nails sticking in my ass than talk about any of this shit with the men in my family, especially my father.

"Speak of the devil," Izzy says as the door creaks behind me.

My eyes widen and I freeze, unable to move as if somehow I'll disappear and won't have to have this talk now instead of later.

"Giovanna," my father says, his voice washing over me like I'm a little kid again, waiting to be punished for my stupid shit.

I don't turn around because Joe Gallo is a sweet man, but every guy, even my dad, has his breaking point. I'm pretty sure I've punched right through that ceiling without even trying. "Hey, Daddy."

"You and me, outside."

"Just talk here and grab a cup of coffee. I'll go see what's taking Pike and James so long." Izzy catches my eye, giving me a small wink before she sashays right the fuck out of there, not even worried that my dad's going to blow a fucking gasket.

"Daddy…"

"Save it, baby girl."

I bow my head, staring at my coffee, and ready myself for the biggest ass-chewing of my life.

CHAPTER
SIXTEEN
PIKE

"WE HAVE A PROBLEM," James says into the phone, staring at me from across the desk with his lips set in a firm line. "You're the only man I could think to come to about the situation."

I bite the inside of my cheek, rubbing my hands against the wood of the chair my ass has been planted in for hours, taking James's questions in rapid-fire succession.

"I know what fucking time it is, but I couldn't wait until your old ass decided to get out of bed."

My mouth falls open. No one has ever talked to Tiny, the President of the Disciples MC, that way. At least, I'd never heard them do it, because Tiny would've pounded their face in until they were black and blue, sucking their food through a straw for the next two months.

James laughs. "You never were an early bird, ya old fuck."

I blink a few times, wondering who the fuck James is to Tiny, and how they know each other well enough that they can laugh while insulting the hell out of each other.

"I have your kid Pike here." James pauses, eyes sweeping over my face. "Yeah, he's in one piece, alive and breathing, sitting right in front of me."

I begged James not to call Tiny. Pleaded with him not to get the Disciples MC involved, but he told me not to be a fucking moron and picked up the phone like it meant nothing to call in a favor.

"Just sit there and keep your mouth shut," James told me before he dialed Tiny's number from memory, surprising the fuck out of me.

So, here I sit, watching James as he takes my business into his own hands, giving help where I didn't ask. But this isn't just about me; this is about his niece and the pile of shit she landed in just by being near me.

"He has an issue with DiSantis and needs somewhere to lie low." James taps the pen he's holding against the pad of paper he'd been taking notes on like he was working my case too. "Couldn't think of anyone with enough manpower and weapons, outside of law enforcement, who would look after the kids except you and the boys."

I shake my head, surprised James is asking Tiny for help. Not just Tiny, but a motorcycle club that has many wearing the badge shaking in their fancy, polished boots.

"It's serious. Pike's mom ain't breathing no more because of the shit his father's in with DiSantis."

I close my eyes, rubbing my fingers into the corners, wondering where the fuck my normal life has gone. Now, my mother's dead, lying somewhere cold with a bullet lodged in the back of her head. My brother's God knows where, hopefully with my grandmother, and my dad's gone missing because he's a fucking coward and a criminal.

"My niece is involved too, Tiny. She'll need safe haven and a guarantee you'll protect her with your life. I'm trusting you more than I've ever trusted anyone who isn't blood by asking you for this favor."

That shit ain't no lie.

Gigi said her uncle worked for the DEA but had since

retired, now owning a private investigation firm. But from the sounds of it, he's not entirely out of the game.

"I'll owe you, and you know I always pay my debts," James tells him, still staring at me with a look I can't quite place, and I'm not sure I'd want to even if I could.

"I'll drive them over after nightfall. You're going to have to keep them out of sight until this shit blows over. I don't want them traceable. No eyes can fall on them. The FBI has already questioned Pike, and I don't want them getting their hands on him again. No man, no matter how much he hates his father, should be put in this position. Just keep them safe, and I'll come for them when shit blows over."

"James." I want to argue with him because I'm not sure hiding out with a badass biker crew at their compound is the best idea.

He covers the phone with his hand, mouthing, "Not now. Just keep quiet."

I raise my eyebrows and twist my lips, biting back the words I want to say so badly.

"We'll be there around one. Be ready for us. I'm dropping them off at our meeting place and heading out. I'll have two cars following, making sure no one is on our tail. I want them untraceable."

James leans back, laughing with Tiny before he presses his finger to the phone screen, ending the call. "Go get some sleep. You have a long day and night ahead of you," he tells me, not even wanting to discuss the plans he made on my behalf.

I don't move because I'm not ready and I'm sure as fuck not used to being ordered around. "How exactly do you know Tiny? Because from what I can tell, neither of you run in the same circles."

"You know I worked for the DEA, yeah?"

I nod.

"We most certainly weren't friends back in the day, but

there was a mutual respect because I wasn't out to pop him or his club for the dumb bullshit they were pulling back then. The Sun Devils were our target, and they were the mortal enemy of the Disciples. Let's just say Tiny was happy to see that MC put behind bars."

"Wait, he helped you?"

James shakes his head. "Fuck no. He's not a narc, but when I started my own company and needed information, I went to Tiny, made peace, and paid him for intel I couldn't get through any legal channels."

"That's it? You paid him for information, and now you're sending us there, thinking Tiny's going to protect us?"

James studies me as he leans forward, putting his palms together, elbows on the desk, and his mouth resting on the tips of his fingers. "When I went to Tiny about you because Izzy asked me to look into your past before she took you on, I'd never heard the man speak so highly about someone who wasn't a brother." He drops his hands to his desk, squaring his shoulders, eyes still on me. "He talked about you like you were his own kid. A man like Tiny doesn't do that unless you crawled under his skin and made him feel shit he hasn't felt in years. You're up to your neck in shit, and by default, so is my niece. You need to hide out, lie low until shit with your father and DiSantis blows over. I can't think of a better place to put you than a spot that has enough brute force and an arsenal to handle an attack if the man is stupid enough to go after you inside their compound."

"I'd think a man like you would have us under FBI protection instead of the Disciples."

James gives a slow shake of his head. "Even though I worked for the government back in the day, I know how corrupt the system is and how easily people can be bought. I'm not putting my niece somewhere unless I know they can handle the blowback."

I've got nothing left to say. What he's saying is true. If

DiSantis wants me dead, I'm a sitting duck unless I hide out, and there's no better place to disappear from radar than at the Disciples' compound.

"Now the sun's up, the day's already fucked because I've been up for hours, and I'll have to listen to Izzy for an eternity as she tears me a new asshole. We'll roll out just after sunset. You tell no one where you're headed, and I mean no one. Not even your grandmother, Pike."

I nod. "I won't tell a soul. Gigi's safety is all that matters."

"If DiSantis's men come…"

"I'd throw myself in front of a bullet if it meant she'd be okay."

She wouldn't be in this shit if it weren't for me.

"I'll hold you to that. If you don't, I'll make you wish you had taken that bullet instead of what I'd do to you."

I stand, rubbing my hands down the front of my jeans, feeling the day's events finally starting to wash over me. "Understood, James."

"Now, go. I have shit to do," he says, not moving from his chair and lifting his chin toward the door.

I turn the knob, swinging open the door, and come face-to-face with Gigi's father. Our eyes lock, and I wait for his fist to make a beeline for my jaw, but he just stands there, staring at me. "We'll have words when this is done," he says, all joy gone from his voice.

"Yes, sir."

"Now, get gone so I can talk to my brother-in-law." He ticks his head toward the empty hallway. "It's best if I'm not around you right now."

By the hardness in his jaw and the coldness in his stare, I'm guessing he knows what went down with Gigi and me in Daytona. This isn't a conversation I want to have with him after being up all night. It's actually not a conversation I want to have with him anytime, but it's one that's going to come whether I like it or not. It's also not a conversation I've ever had to have with a woman's father because relationships weren't really my thing and the women I've slept with were usually older and not so attached to their fathers.

"Got it."

"Izzy's waiting for you in the kitchen," he says, brushing past me and stalking into James's office before slamming the door right in my face.

I expected nothing less. If Gigi were my kid and I were face-to-face with a guy who'd done the shit I did to her, I'd want to rip his fucking throat out with my bare hands. I couldn't fault the man.

I make my way down the long hallway and head toward Izzy's voice. If she weren't talking, I'm not sure I ever would've found the kitchen because the house is probably the biggest one I've ever stepped foot inside.

"There you are," Izzy says as soon as she sees me rounding the corner. "I was beginning to think James was never going to let you out of that room."

Gigi's sitting at the kitchen table, quickly running her fingertips over her cheeks. "I'll show him to his room," Gigi says to Izzy with her back to me.

Izzy raises an eyebrow, eyes moving from me to Gigi. "Your dad is still here. Watch your step, little girl. If you want Pike to still be breathing when the sun sets, don't get cute and try to crawl into his bed, curling yourself around the man for comfort."

So, Gigi did spill our entire sordid, although brief, history together. I'm surprised she kept her shit together this long, even though it's only been two days. I'm sure it was impossible for her to maintain the lie about not knowing me, especially after she lost her shit tonight once I was taken in for questioning. Even more, she was probably shaken up after hearing the shit James and I said in the car. All that together was just enough to have Gigi blabbing every last detail.

"Got it, Auntie." Gigi finds her footing before turning

around, showing me her tear-stained cheeks and red, puffy eyes.

"You okay?" I ask as my eyes sweep across her face, knowing I'd caused her tears.

She nods. "Let me show you to your room," she says, ignoring the look I'm giving her and the fact that she's been crying. She dips her head toward another hallway, adding to the maze that is James and Izzy's house. "We'll talk after we get some sleep. I want to know that you're okay."

I walk inches behind her, following her wherever she's taking me because I don't care if it's a closet, as long as there's enough space for me to stretch my legs and close my eyes. "I don't know how I feel just yet. Shit's pretty fucked up, and now you've been pulled into the same mess."

She stops near an open doorway, leaning against the wall, staring up at me with glassy, bloodshot eyes. "I'm sure Uncle James has a plan."

Reaching out, I wipe away a tear that's resting near the edge of her lashes, ready to fall. "Do you know what his plan is, darlin'?"

She shakes her head, not moving away from my touch when I let my hand linger.

"He's sending us to the Disciples' compound to lie low."

Her eyes grow big as saucers. "He's what?"

I nod, just as fucking shocked by that reality as she is. "He said it's the safest place. Can't say I disagree with him either, but the compound isn't a place for a girl like you."

She wrinkles her nose. "A girl like me?"

I sweep my thumb just under her cheekbone, loving the softness against my skin. "You're good, Gigi. Pure, even. The Disciples' compound is no place for a lady."

Gigi's eyes sparkle, and she snorts in the most unladylike way. "I've been around bikers my entire life, Pike. I think I can handle whatever happens at their compound without losing my shit and rockin' myself in a corner."

"These aren't recreational bikers, Gigi. They're hard-core. They live the life. All full of violence, mayhem, booze, drugs, and so much pussy, it'll make your head spin."

She wraps her hand around my wrist and pulls my arm away from her. "You used to live there, yeah?"

I nod.

"We'll be safe there. And right about now, I could use a big fucking drink, so the compound sounds like a good place to get lost and forget all this shit."

"I don't think James is sending us there to party, babe."

She draws her lower lip between her teeth, biting the tender flesh gently. "Then he should send us to a convent. I'm not going into that compound to sit in a dark room day and night, playing the role of a scared little girl. I'm letting my hair down, immersing myself in whatever they have to offer for however long they're offering it. You don't like it? Then you can sit in that dark room alone."

Oh fuckin' boy. This girl is clueless about so much. She's probably binged every motorcycle show available online, thinking she knows how bikers are. But even Hollywood glorifies the life. If she thinks she can handle watching a guy do blow off some chick's ass while she's stretched out on the pool table for everyone to watch, so be it. She's going to get a hard lesson in the real MC life, and it may be eye-opening if not entertaining.

"Just know I'm not leaving your side. You're out of your room, I'm on you like glue."

She grins. "I'm counting on that, Pike."

"But first, we gotta live long enough to get to that compound." I grab her by the shoulder, moving her away from my doorway. "Now, you need to get gone so I can get some sleep before your father finds you outside my room and I end up next to my mother."

Gigi stares up at me, eyes glistening in the bright light. "You want to talk about her?"

I shake my head. "Another time. Maybe once we're settled, but not tonight."

"Okay, but I'm always here to talk," she says sweetly, and I want to wrap my body around hers, surrounding myself with the goodness and warmth only she can offer.

"Night, darlin'." I fight the urge to plant my lips on hers, letting all the day's shit leak out into that kiss.

"Night, Pike," she whispers and takes a step back, staring at me like she's pleading with me to give her what I want to, but I can't because I want to live to breathe another day. "I'll be right next door."

"Got it." I dip my chin, waiting for her to disappear through her doorway before I take a step inside the bedroom, ready for this day to be fucking over with.

Tomorrow starts a whole new shitshow. One filled with Gigi's family, Tiny and the Disciples, and us running for our lives, ducking for cover in a den of sin.

CHAPTER
SEVENTEEN

GIGI

"DON'T you think this is excessive?" I ask Uncle Thomas, which earns me a hard stare in the rearview mirror. "I mean, seven cars behind us is a bit extreme. Even you have to agree with me." I turn to Pike, but he doesn't say a word because he's not rocking any boat, especially not after the way my uncles and father gave him shit before we left Izzy's house.

"Seven cars and twenty men is not excessive when you're dealing with a man like DiSantis," Uncle James says as he sits beside Uncle Thomas in the front seat of the car.

Pike's hand finds mine in the darkness, and he squeezes my fingers. "They're just being safe."

"Don't give me no shit, little girl," James barks.

That's my new name…little girl. I thought I'd grown out of it about the time I started to grow tits, but now it's back, and I have a feeling it's not going anywhere either.

"If I get word that you try to leave that compound…"

"You'll spank me?" I sass, smirking as soon as his eyes cut to mine in the mirror again.

Uncle James and Izzy get their freak on. I know all about their sex life now, after finding his profile on a BDSM website I'd used for research when I had to write a paper for my sexual psychology class at FSU. The textbook only went so deep, and the library was absolutely no help because many of the books they carried were by men who preferred the missionary position and knew nothing of real kink. So, I went right to the source, clicking my way through the biggest kinkster site I could find.

A few clicks later and I was on Master James's page, looking at shit I could never unsee and learning things I never wanted to know. That's not something you can just wipe out of your head. Can't erase the images and words with any amount of alcohol, and I should know because I tried and failed.

"Fucking hell," Thomas mutters, shaking his head. "You have a mouth on you sometimes."

"I'm just practicing for my stint at the Disciples' compound. I figure I can't walk in there all meek and mild. I have to be balls to the wall, ready to sling some shit with the best of them. Yeah?"

Pike's eyes flash as I glance at him with a big smile. "Fuck," he groans, which only makes my smile even bigger.

"It's best if you just stay in your room," James says, like that's going to fucking happen.

So, I keep poking because I have to do something to pass the time, and this drive has officially turned into the longest one of my life. "Why didn't you just lock us up instead, Uncle James? I mean, if you want us to be prisoners, why not just keep us home, locked in our rooms like the little kids you think we are?"

"I get you're pissed, kid, but I don't need your lip right now when I'm trying to do everything to keep you and Pike alive. You don't like the situation?" He pauses, but I don't fill the silence. "Too fucking bad. Sometimes, as adults, we have to do shit we don't want to do so we can live another day. You think a jail cell is going to be better than the compound?" He barks out a bitter laugh. "You have a lot to fucking learn."

"Three minutes out," Thomas says into the phone, sending a voice text to everyone who's following behind.

"Still all clear," my father's voice says back.

And I mean everyone. Not only are my other uncles and Dad in the cars behind us, but so are the guys from ALFA. Even Uncle Bear tagged along for the ride because he's down with anything that could end up with his ass shot. The man is crazy, searching for danger and driving my great-aunt Fran absolutely batshit crazy.

"I promise I won't cause trouble," I say softly, knowing my fate is sealed and our imprisonment within the walls of the compound probably won't be as bad as I'm making out.

"Just stick by Pike. He lived at the compound for a few years and knows what situations to steer you clear of."

"So, you want me at Pike's side at all times?" I clarify because it's sounding like I have the stamp of approval to be in Pike's bed.

"Gigi," James warns, knowing where I'm going, because of course he does.

"She's trying to get me killed," Pike whispers.

I squeeze his fingers, trying to hide my laughter because this shit is heavy. I'm using the only coping mechanism I have...my humor and my sarcasm.

Who wants to be running for their life?

Not me.

Who wants to hide out because there might be a bullet with their name on it?

Again, not me.

The only upside to this entire situation is that I'll have Pike at my side. But if he thinks he's bossing me around like I'm his woman, he has another thing coming.

"Let's go over a few things before you step out of this car."

"Of course." I roll my eyes, getting a hand squeeze from

Pike because he's not happy either, but somehow, he's remained silent.

"Absolutely no drugs."

"Uncle James."

"I'm serious, Gigi. They're into some heavy shit there. Stuff is just lying around, easy to get, and even easier to take. If I get word that you're sniffing coke or taking some shit you shouldn't be taking, I'll have your ass back in this car so fast…"

"I promise, Uncle. I've never taken anything before, and I don't plan to start now."

Pike raises his eyebrows because my admission has to be shocking to everyone in the car, especially him. I mean, what person my age hasn't at least dabbled in drugs besides me? Probably no one except Tamara. It has to do with the way our parents raised us and the fear of them finding out and the ass-chewing we'd both get over it after a very lengthy and boring-as-fuck punishment.

"No drinking either," Uncle Thomas adds.

My mouth drops open, and I gawk at the back of their heads, blinking like somehow it'll make those words any easier to swallow. "You've got to give me something. I'm old enough to drink and it's legal, so I don't understand the issue."

"Cut the girl some slack," Uncle James says, which shocks the hell out of me and Thomas too.

"Are you serious right now? She's going to be in the middle of a crazy scene, and you're giving her the okay to drink?"

"She's grown, Thomas. We can't stop her from drinking."

"Or doing drugs," I add because fucking with them is too easy, and maybe if I fuck with them enough, Thomas will relent on the drinking. "But I promise I won't get drunk."

"Just don't do anything stupid. Stay inside and out of sight."

"I'll sit at the bar day and night." I smile, earning me a few curse words from all three in the car.

"They're here," James says, ticking his chin out the windshield at a long-ass line of bikes and an unmarked, windowless van parked in an abandoned lot.

"Guess we're doing this," I whisper, glancing at Pike as he stares back at me.

"We're going to be okay," Pike says sweetly, squeezing my fingers gently. "I promise."

I believe what he's saying, and from the huge army waiting for us, I believe they'll do what's necessary to keep us safe. Unless DiSantis brings an actual army, they'll have a hard time outnumbering the men waiting in the parking lot and probably even more still back at the compound.

"Out," Uncle Thomas barks as soon as he throws the engine into park, letting it idle. "We're making this quick. Drop and dash."

Uncle James helps me from the back seat, looking no less badass than the other men standing in this parking lot. "Behave, Gigi," he warns before releasing my hand. "I love you and don't want anything bad to happen to you. Something goes sideways, and we're all going to be in the shit."

I swallow the lump his words cause to lodge in my throat. The last thing I want is for my entire family to be in the proverbial shit because I slept with a guy who has a questionable father and a possible order for his assassination.

"I'll be good. I promise," I rasp.

He gives me a quick nod before stalking toward a giant man with a potbelly, no doubt caused by all types of excessive drinking. I assume it's Tiny because that would make total sense as there's nothing small about him.

My father is at my side before I can follow Uncle James. "This is it," he says, balling his hands into fists as his eyes dart to Pike and then back at me. "I've said what I needed to say."

I don't correct him and tell him it was more of a lecture than a good old-fashioned chat. My dad chewed my ear off for hours about my trip to Daytona and throwing myself in the path of countless bikers and into the arms of one in particular.

"I'm sorry this is happening, Daddy. I never meant to cause any trouble."

His face softens. "Baby, sometimes trouble finds us, no matter how hard we try to stay away. This isn't your fault. It's not Pike's fault either."

I blink up at him in surprise. "You're not pissed anymore?"

His jaw ticks, which answers my question before he even opens his mouth. "I'm not happy about any of this. Pike and I will be having a long talk when you two are back home."

So, he is still pissed, but at least he isn't talking about murdering the guy anymore. In my book, that's progress. For my dad, that's a huge step. The man has the patience of a saint sometimes, but when it comes to men and his daughters, he has zero. I've probably had it easier than my sisters will because I'm like the trial kid where they can fuck up and see what works, tweaking their plans for the next in line. Luna and Rosie aren't going to stand a chance, but they're crafty little shits even at their age and will adapt easily before my father knows what hit him.

"Go easy on him, Daddy."

My father's eyebrows draw together, causing the wrinkles on his forehead to deepen. "You want me to go easy on Pike?"

"Yo, we gonna do this, or what? Eyes are everywhere, and I don't feel like being a sitting duck," Tiny yells across the parking lot.

"Gigi," Pike calls, motioning for me to move my ass before things start to get heated.

"I'm coming." I wave and stare back up into my father's piercing eyes. "Pike's no different from you, and I'm no different from Mom." I pop up on my tiptoes, planting a kiss on my father's cheek and throwing my arms around his shoulders, squeezing him tightly. "Well, maybe I'm a little different from Mom because I have two kick-ass parents."

"Baby," he whispers, wrapping his arms around my back and holding me so tight, I can barely breathe. "Go. Stay safe. Don't do anything stupid."

I nod, pulling out of his embrace ever so slowly. "I love you, Daddy."

"I love you too, baby girl. One call a day to me on the burner phone. You understand?"

"I'll call around noon every day. I promise." I start to walk backward. "But don't worry so much. I won't do anything stupid, and these guys—" I pitch my thumb over my shoulder toward the horde of badass bikers "—will keep us safe."

"Tiny, Gigi. Gigi, Tiny," James says, looking between the two of us as I walk toward them, almost faltering when I get close enough to realize the true size of Tiny.

"Holy fuck," I whisper. "Well, aren't you a big fella." I wink, throwing that out there because I know bikers, and they love a compliment.

Tiny's lip twitches ever so slightly, but the man keeps up his tough-guy exterior with his arms crossed, making him look even bigger and downright scary. "She'll do fine," he tells James like I'm not even standing here.

James extends his hand to Tiny, and the men shake as I turn my gaze toward Pike, who's also shaking hands with a man about his age and his size, but with a bald head and a tattoo across his forehead that does nothing except make him look so frightening, I can't imagine getting pussy is real easy.

"You." Tiny juts his chin at me as soon as we make eye contact. "Ass in the van. We gotta roll."

"And Pike?" I ask, because where he's going, so am I, whether Tiny or any of these other bikers agrees.

"He's in the van too. Can't have you bein' seen before we get you within our walls."

"Sure thing, boss man." I smile at the big guy, because if it's the last thing I do, I'll get the old bastard to smile back.

"She's a handful," Uncle James tells him, shrugging his shoulders and throwing out his arms like he doesn't know how to handle me and is sorry to put me off on someone else.

"I got a kid her age, but mine isn't so...pleasant. Anyway, Pike will keep her ass in line, and if he doesn't, I'll make sure she's under control."

I roll my eyes at their conversation, and Pike mutters, "Good fuckin' luck," at my side.

"Let's get this shitshow on the road, boys." I wave my hand in the air and look at Pike with a smirk. "This is going to be one hell of a time."

Pike keeps step with me as I stalk toward the van. "This isn't a vacation, darlin'."

"Don't give a fuck. We're spending time in a biker compound, and I plan to enjoy the fuck out of it because I'm not spending all day in my room worrying about some asshole trying to kill us. Now turn around, put a smile on your face, and wave to my family." I spin on my heels just outside the back door of the van, my eyes sweeping across the line of cars brimming with my family and the ALFA guys. I wave a little too happily, which earns me more than one glower. "Bye, I love you," I call out, knowing they'd all cuss me out if they could and probably will the next time they see me.

My father's near the car, talking to Uncle Thomas, shaking his head at my antics, knowing shit isn't going to be as PG as he hopes. "Just behave, kid," he yells out, knowing damn well there's a snowball's chance in hell that's going to happen. "Now, get your ass in the van, and get the fuck out of here."

I salute him before crawling inside, nestling against the

side wall of the filthy van. They could've at least cleaned up a little bit seeing as they were going to be transporting two people in here instead of whatever the fuck was here before us.

"We're only twenty minutes away," Pike says as he settles next to me, legs outstretched and his shoulder touching mine.

"Good, I could use a drink." I plaster a smile on my face because I don't want my father or uncles to know I'm terrified.

"Already?" he asks, staring at me as the doors slam shut.

"Already?" I gawk at Pike, happy I don't have to put on a good show anymore. "We're in some deep shit, Pike. What the fuck do you mean, already? Don't you want to drink that shit away?"

Pike shakes his head. "I have to stay focused. Shit can happen at any time, and I don't want to be three sheets to the goddamn wind when all hell breaks loose. They come for you, I need to be ready. I'll throw myself in front of whatever they hurl in our direction, shielding you so you can walk away without a scratch."

My mouth's hanging open as I blink at Pike like I'm trying to focus, but everything's crystal clear. "You'd give your life for me?" I whisper as Tiny slams the front door, shrouding us in darkness.

"I'd give everything for you, darlin'."

CHAPTER
EIGHTEEN

PIKE

"THIS PLACE IS like Disney World for crack whores, career criminals, and lost souls," Gigi says casually at my side, almost making me spit my mouthful of beer across the bar.

"Keep your voice down." I wipe my lips with the back of my hand, glancing around to figure out if anyone overheard.

"They can't hear above this classic rock, Pike. Half of them are probably hard of hearing, and the other half are so trashed, they're probably unable to form coherent thoughts."

"You're on a roll tonight, sweetheart." I lift my mug, glancing over my shoulder at a few guys who are sitting close, most likely assigned the task of keeping an eye on us while we're under their protection.

I'll have to talk to Tiny about that. While I appreciate his concern and security, when we're within these walls, hidden from view, we don't need extra eyes on us, watching our every move. Gigi most certainly doesn't need any men loitering near her, making her feel any more uncomfortable than she already does.

"They your friends?"

I shake my head. "Nope. Never seen them before. I

haven't been around here in years. Based on the lack of patches, I'd say they're prospects."

"Oh. I saw that on television," she says, confirming everything I assumed she thought this place would be. "How long do they have to do that?"

"As long as Tiny and the guys want them to."

"There's no time limit?"

"Babe, this isn't a job. Bikers don't put time on anything unless there's money involved."

"Where's the little fucker?" a familiar voice says, and we both turn, watching him finish tucking his cock into his pants before he zips his fly.

"I guess you're the little fucker, yeah?" Gigi giggles, peering at me over her shoulder.

I set my beer down, climbing off the stool to greet Morris before he sets eyes on Gigi and tries to get his hands on her too. "Morris. Lookin' good, man."

"Morris?" Gigi asks, not hiding her shock that the guy with the crazy-ass salt-and-pepper hair and goatee to match doesn't have a biker name like the rest of the guys.

Morris shakes my hand and pulls me in for a bear hug before slapping my back so hard, I'm almost winded. "Who's this fine piece of ass you brought with you, kid?"

"This is Gigi, my girl, Morris. Don't start no shit, and there won't be no shit."

A slow, wide smile spreads across Morris's face, showing his white teeth with a big enough gap between the two front ones it's hard to mistake him for someone else.

Morris throws his hands up as he steps away from me, and his eyes sweep over Gigi again. "Wait a second, isn't she the chick from…"

"Yeah, man. Don't say it. It's a long-ass story."

"Hello," Gigi calls out, waving her hand at Morris and me because we're talking about her like she isn't sitting right there, and she hates nothing more than being ignored.

Morris slides next to her, moving onto the barstool so smoothly, it's like he practiced the maneuver a thousand times. "You're even more beautiful than the last time I laid eyes on you."

She blinks at him in confusion, moving back slightly when he reaches for her hand and brings it to his lips. "I'm sorry, I don't remember..."

"You probably don't remember a lot, mama. You were pretty trashed the night I met you—and damn fucking mouthy too." Morris laughs, placing a soft kiss on the top of her hand and getting a growl from me.

Gigi laughs, looking like a little kid next to the old man who will stick his dick in just about anything as long as he can get off. "It was spring break. I was letting loose."

"And so you did, sweetheart." Morris grins, eyes only on her and not on me at all.

Gigi grabs her drink as soon as Morris releases her hand and rests her chin in the palm of her free hand, elbow propped against the bar. "Why Morris? Why don't you have a tough name like the rest of the guys?"

Morris grins at Gigi, motioning to the prospect behind the bar for a drink, but he never breaks eye contact with her. "Because every MC has a Tiny, Rooster, Reaper, and so on, but only the Disciples have a Morris."

Gigi's nose wrinkles. "That's the reason?"

"Doll, I'm one of a kind. Who wants to be lumped in with those sorry fuckers when you can be the only one?"

Gigi shrugs, lifting the drink to her lips, and his eyes follow the movement. It's time to shut down the flirtfest Morris is having with my girl, so I slide in behind her, wrapping my arm around her middle and hauling her ass backward so she's pressed flush against me.

"You happy to see me, baby?" she asks playfully, tossing a glance over her shoulder.

"I figured I needed to remind Morris who you belong to,

darlin'," I whisper in her ear, causing her to shiver, but my gaze is on Morris. "I don't want this dirty old man to get the wrong idea."

"My head only has room for wrong ideas," Morris says with a laugh. "Now, let's celebrate you comin' home, asswad, and get shit-faced drunk, telling stories about back in the day."

Gigi bounces on her stool, sending shock waves through my system from the way her ass is rubbing on my cock. "Fuck yeah. That's the best idea I've heard tonight."

"Gigi doesn't want to hear about all that boring shit, Morris," I hiss, because he's trying to start trouble.

It's what he's best at after all. If shit's going down, Morris is smack-dab in the middle, stirring the pot, making sure the shit stays moving.

"I very much want to hear about the *good old days,* baby. Hush your mouth." Gigi throws a wink at me over her shoulder.

"I could spend all night telling Pike stories."

"Don't you have a woman to satisfy?" I raise an eyebrow.

Morris shakes his head, grabbing the beer as soon as the redheaded prospect sets the bottle in front of him. "She's , passed out. Figurin' the session we just had, she'll be out for a couple of hours if she even wakes up at all."

"You're a dirty old man, Morris." Gigi grips my knee like she's going to keep me quiet.

"He's old, all right," I mutter, reaching for my beer with the hand that isn't locked around her waist because nothing is going to make me let go of her.

"I think this calls for tequila," Gigi says to Morris, scooting backward, knowing exactly what she's doing because she's always thinking ahead.

"My kinda girl." Morris smirks.

"Maybe we should just go to bed." I want her out of the common room because the real shit hasn't even begun. The night's young, and the guys aren't as shit-faced as she thinks.

"No, Pike. We're not going anywhere until *we* catch up with Morris here. So, settle in, cowboy, and get comfortable."

Morris is laughing so hard, he's almost falling off his stool. "I can see why you like this one so much, kid. She's mouthy and bares those kitten claws."

"Morris, baby," Gigi replies, laying her hand on his arm. "I'm not a kitten, sweetheart."

Morris tips his head toward her, grinning like I've never seen the man grin before. "See, mouthy as fuck."

I look toward the ceiling, cursing under my breath. The long night just became longer because once these two get going, there's no stopping them until someone's passed out.

"Three tequilas," Gigi tells the prospect as he walks by, delivering a handful of beers to the guys at the other end of the bar.

"Long-ass fucking night," I whisper, pulling on my beer, swallowing down the bitter liquid along with the sour taste this entire evening is leaving in my mouth.

"Have a fucking sense of humor, Pike. Did you lose your balls somewhere around Orlando?"

Gigi chuckles, turning her head so her lips are so close to mine, I could silence her with a kiss. "Let me have a little fun, Pike. I know you have a past. Hell, so do I. I don't know a lot about you, and I want to hear what Morris has to say. Don't shit on my parade. Ya dig?"

"I dig." That's not the end of the conversation even if she wants it to be. "Just remember whatever he says—" I jut my chin toward him "—is probably bullshit."

"I never bullshit," Morris interrupts, staring at me over the lip of his beer bottle. "Well, almost never."

"If you learn something you don't like tonight, you tuck that shit away and forget about it. I'm not the same punk kid I was when I lived here, surrounded by these men, five years ago. You dig?"

"I dig." Her eyes sparkle and drop to my mouth, and she pulls the corner of her bottom lip between her teeth, making me want to haul her ass into the back room and slide something else between those beautiful lips. "Now, Morris," she says, turning away from me quickly because she knows exactly what's on my mind. "Start at the beginning. How did Pike end up living with the Disciples? Didn't know you guys welcomed anyone into your world."

Morris snaps his fingers at the prospect who's still fumbling around behind the bar and hasn't delivered the tequila Gigi ordered. "We don't usually take in strays."

I roll my eyes because I know he's going to lay the shit on way thicker than it really went down. The reality of the situation is much more boring than he's going to tell her. He's going to glorify the entire thing, probably saying he rescued me from the side of the road like a wounded animal.

"We were pulling this job up in Jacksonville," he starts, at least getting that part right, but I know it's about to go sideways. "Some crazy-ass shit went down, guns came out."

"For fucking real?" Gigi gasps.

"For real, kid. Then this dumbass—" he ticks his chin toward me "—decides he's going to jump in front of one of the bullets, because his slow Tennessee ass can't move fast enough to get the fuck down."

Gigi turns, looking at me with wide eyes. "The scar on your shoulder?"

I nod, gritting my teeth because one of the fuckers shot me, not giving a fuck that I was an innocent bystander in the entire thing. I was filling my tank with gas, minding my own business, when they decided to open fire. I didn't have a chance to duck before I took one in the upper right shoulder.

"When shit died down, Pike was still standing there, holding his arm, glaring at me like it was my fault he was bleeding. We had words, and the fucking punk didn't care that I had a gun in my hand because he kept barking at me about how I put a hole in his body." Morris laughs, running his fingers through the tip of his goatee. He pauses when the kid finally sets down three tequila shots but is still moving like he has lead in his shoes. "About fucking time," Morris barks, shooing the guy away when he lingers a little too long. "What are we drinking to, kids?"

Gigi hands me a shot but doesn't give me her eyes. "To new friends and old times," she tells him, lifting her shot in the air. They clink glasses as I watch Gigi throw back the tequila like she's been doing it for years. "Now, finish the story. What happened after he had words with you?"

"I figured the kid had a pair of balls on him so freaking big he could be something to us. So, I had two choices."

"What were they?" she asks, not giving him a chance to finish.

"I could end his life right there, or bring his sorry, bleeding ass back here to get patched up and figure out what to do with his mouthy ass afterward."

"Aww," she coos. "You totally rescued him."

"He fucking shot me." I scowl.

Morris places his hand on his chest, trying his best to look innocent. "I did not shoot your ass, kid. Wasn't my bullet you jumped in front of that night."

"Don't mind him." Gigi jerks her thumb at me, and I tighten my hold around her waist, reminding her these men aren't playthings.

Morris may not have been the one who shot me, but someone in this room fucking did. They didn't give two shits that I was innocent with piss-poor timing, filling my tank when they decided to play cops and robbers at the gas station in a seedy part of town.

There isn't a man in this room who hasn't drawn blood from another human being without so much as a backward glance at the carnage they inflicted or the death they left in their wake. They give zero fucks about human life. Their world revolves around money, drugs, pussy, and the brother-hood—and not in that order either.

"And..." She leans forward, hanging on his every word.

"So, this kid..." He laughs, shaking his head like he doesn't even believe what he's about to say. "He's yelling at me, poking me in the shoulder while I've got my gun in one hand like I'm just going to stand here and take his shit. I didn't know what to do, so I punched him right where he got hit, sending his ass to the floor in a flurry of curse words that would make the devil himself blush."

"You fucking punched him in his injured shoulder?"

Morris shrugs. "The kid wouldn't shut up about how I shot him. Figured I'd give him something to be angry with me about, plus, I needed him to shut the fuck up for a few minutes so I could get his ass into the back of the van."

"Did you know you were going to keep him?" she asks.

"What the fuck?" I hiss, shaking my head. "I wasn't a puppy, Gigi."

"Shut up," she tells me. "Morris and I are talking."

"Three more tequilas," I tell the prospect, figuring the only way I'm going to get her to stop talking to Morris is to get her so shit-faced drunk, she'll pass the fuck out.

"Welcome to the party, Pike," Gigi teases, wiggling her ass right against my dick.

I flatten my palm against her stomach, moving my mouth near her ear. "Be careful, darlin'. I'm not above throwing you over my shoulder and hauling your ass into my room and putting something in that sassy little mouth of yours."

"Is that a promise or a threat?" she asks with a wicked gleam in her eyes.

"Both."

I've never been more serious in my life.

"Such a big talker," she teases.

I do the only thing I can. Moving quickly, I throw her over my shoulder like a sack of potatoes and march toward my old room.

"Put me down!" she screeches. "Help!"

No one pays any attention to her pleas for help. I even get a few high fives as I carry her ass to the back, ready to do exactly what I promised.

CHAPTER NINETEEN

GIGI

HE HAS one hand on my ass, only moving the damn thing when he smacks the hands of the other assholes in the room.

I wiggle, trying like hell to get out of his hold and off his shoulder, but that only causes him to tighten his grip around my leg.

"You're not getting out of this one, darlin'," he drawls, stalking on heavy feet, making my tits smack against his back with every step.

"You're an asshole."

"Speaking of asshole," he says, running a finger along the crease of my ass as we finally make it to the hallway.

I stiffen, squeezing my ass cheeks together as tightly as possible. "Don't you fucking dare!" I screech, lifting my head and catching sight of all the guys in the compound, laughing and watching us with total amusement. I give the biker assholes my middle finger, scowling at them for reveling in the spectacle Pike is putting on, even though I know I'm not helping it. "You're not touching my ass!"

"I promise you'll love it." His hand massages my cheeks, but I have them on lockdown, just like they're going to stay. "I'll make you want it always."

That's the problem. I know if Pike does it, I'll love the hell out of it. There hasn't been anything he's done to my body that I didn't want more of, craving it since the second I ran for coffee and never went back. He's skilled and generous, unlike anyone I've been with before…although my list is super-short and kind of embarrassing.

I reach down, trying to get my hands on his ass so I can pinch him hard enough that maybe I'll be able to break free. "The only thing I want is for you to put me down and let me finish my drink," I grit out, stretching as far as I can, but it's no use. His body is too long for my short everything even to get near anything worth pinching.

"You're done drinking," he says like he's the boss, which is laughable.

I go limp, knowing there's no use. I'm going nowhere except where Pike is taking me. "Where the fuck is your room? Another county?"

Pike laughs, making my body shake with his. "We're almost there, baby. You in a hurry to have my cock in you?"

A door opens, and Pike comes to a dead stop. "Calling it a night?" a man asks, and I crane my neck, trying to see, but damn my size.

"Takin' my woman to bed. Won't be back out until the mornin'."

"Morris put your shit back out and cleaned. Should feel like home for you, kid. You enjoy yourself."

I growl. "Hello, wanna help me here?"

The man laughs, moving around Pike, and crouches down to my level. "Looks like you're doing just fine, sweetheart," Tiny says.

"You're all fuckers," I hiss, which only gets me a small laugh and a headshake from Tiny as he goes back to standing on the other side of Pike and away from me.

"You got your hands full with this one, son. I hope you know what you're doing."

"Just reminding her who she belongs to, Tiny. You have a good night," Pike says.

Who she belongs to? Ugh. My father says shit like that all the time about my mother. Come to think of it, every man in my family says macho bullshit like that, and I roll my eyes every time.

Pike starts moving and I lift my head, catching Tiny's smile, the first one I've seen him crack since I met him tonight. Badass MC biker president or not, he gets a middle finger too before Pike turns a corner, opens a door, and we're suddenly in darkness.

"Will you put me down now?"

"Nope," he replies as he switches on the light, making everything in the tiny space visible. "Well, fuck."

I press my hands to his lower back, lifting my head up farther than before, and try to take in the sparse room covered with all things Pike. There are posters and artwork lining the walls, a twin bed along a black-painted wall, some furniture that had to be secondhand, and not one goddamn window for any type of natural light. "Is this a closet?"

My closet at my parents' place is twice as big as his *bedroom*. I couldn't imagine living in here on a daily basis without going a little mad from the lack of sunlight and the fact that it's the size of a prison cell.

"It has everything we need, babe." He finally relaxes his hold on my leg, allowing me to slide down his front, relishing the way his hardness feels against my body.

When my feet touch the floor, Pike's hands are on my hips and his eyes are on mine. He's so beautiful like this. Hair wild, his green eyes burning with need, and those lips begging for mine. "Pike." I'm trying to kill a little time now that we're alone, I know there's no turning back.

Pike shakes his head. "Been thinking about this since you left me," he says, and my breath catches in my throat. "Been thinking about the softness of your skin…" He runs his finger along the top edge of my jean shorts and across the sensitive skin on my stomach.

Goose bumps form everywhere, scattering across my flesh like they're reaching for his touch. "Pike," I say again, but my voice is needy. Even I can hear the way his touch affects me, and I'm sure it isn't lost on him either.

"Tell me to stop, and I will," he says, licking his lips, and my gaze drops to his mouth, remembering all the ways he brought me pleasure. He bends his neck, bringing those lips to my mouth, whispering, "I need you, darlin'."

I'm a goner. It's easier to pretend I hate him when he's not about to kiss me, staring at me like he's been in a desert without water and I'm the oasis.

"Kiss me," I whisper, staring into his eyes, losing myself a little more.

I barely get the words out before his lips crash down on mine, his hand sliding to my ass and pulling me flush against him. In the last fifteen months, I haven't forgotten how he tasted or the velvety softness of his tongue, no matter how hard I tried.

I slide my hands up his arms, tangling my fingers in his hair, holding him to me like he's my lifeline. My knees weaken as his tongue sweeps into my mouth, giving me exactly what I've craved and wanted since Daytona.

Pike turns, slamming the door behind us, but I don't even flinch at the noise because I'm too lost in the way he's kissing me to care about anything else around us. The world could crumble, and I wouldn't move from this spot, away from his body, away from his lips.

His hands are on my ass, lifting me in the air. I wrap my legs around his waist like they were always meant to be there as he walks us backward.

The kiss deepens, becoming more demanding as his hands move to my back, sliding up my tank top, finding my bra strap. I'm in his lap, his cock to my pussy, separated only by our clothes as he sits on the bed, working quickly to unclasp my bra.

I pull back, gasping for air as I stare at the handsome man underneath me. "Did you bring protection?" I whisper.

Pike nods as he grabs the bottom of my tank top, and I lift my hands because I want this more than anything right now.

"You knew I'd sleep with you?" I ask through the material as the cool air hits my skin and the bra goes with the shirt, both thrown to the floor behind me.

"I hoped," he says. His hungry eyes travel across my skin for a moment before he pulls my head back down, pressing his lips to mine.

I move my hands to his sides, reaching under the thin T-shirt, wanting and needing his warmth and hardness.

I've touched myself hundreds of times since I last was in his arms, trying to recreate the feeling only he'd given me. I'd failed miserably. Nothing could replicate the way he touched me, how he kissed me, or the way he made me melt into his body.

As I lift his shirt, our mouths separate and I lean back, taking in his ink and the lines of his taut stomach and firm shoulders. I only get a glimpse before Pike flips me, putting me on my back, and crawls between my legs, settling in like he's always meant to be there.

The sense of shame and uncertainty I had every time I was with Erik isn't there with Pike. I have no doubts he likes what he sees and loves everything he feels. I'm not ashamed of my nudity, and any worries I had about my inexperience were wiped away after our time together in Daytona.

Pike lifts up on one arm, staring down at me like I'm a goddess. "Dreamed about having you under me again, darlin'."

I run my fingers through the coarse hair of his beard, staring up at the man I know is about to give me so much pleasure, I'm not sure I'll ever recover. "Me too," I confess, because there's no reason to pretend otherwise.

He runs his hand down my neck, along my collarbone, over the swell of my breast. My eyes drift closed, and I sigh, letting every sensation wash over me, memorizing each touch in case I never feel them again.

Warmth covers my nipple, and I open my eyes, peering down my body and finding Pike with his mouth attached. A small moan escapes my lips as our eyes lock, and the pleasure his tongue's delivering shoots straight between my legs, making me squirm.

Without moving his mouth, Pike shuffles over, resting his front to my side. His hand is at my shorts, working the button and zipper quickly, and I lift my ass because I want nothing more than to feel whatever he's about to give.

My shorts and the fancy lace undies I wore just in case this would happen are thrown to the end of the bed, discarded without even a glance. He moves his hand to my mound, cupping my pussy, making the ache turn into a burning throb.

"More, Pike," I beg. My insides are like a raging inferno, and only his fingers can extinguish the flame.

He doesn't tease me or make me beg any more than I already have as he slides his fingers between my legs, and I rock into his touch.

"Greedy," he murmurs against my breast, and I can't argue with him.

I'm greedy as hell when it comes to him. I'm even needier, which should make me worry, but I want an orgasm so badly, I don't bother to think too much.

My knees fall to the bed as his fingers slide back and forth, capturing my wetness. I lift my ass, wanting more than he's giving, growing increasingly impatient with each pass of his fingers.

He slides one finger slowly inside, filling me, but it's not enough. I want more. I need more. I want the delicious ache of being filled, stuffed, owned. I arch my back, pushing my bottom toward his hand, letting him know I want more than he's giving.

I don't have to wait long before he adds another finger, stretching me more than I've been stretched since the last time I was in his bed.

Pike is exceptional at finger-fucking. Like, the best of the best. Or at least, the best I've ever had. He knows how to work every spot, sending me soaring over the edge faster than I ever have before.

My fingers fist the soft blanket, squeezing until my knuckles turn white as if it'll help the orgasm I want so badly to come easier.

"My girl wants this," Pike whispers against my skin, eyes moving to my face with a smile.

I seal my eyes shut, pushing my nipple against his lips, hoping he'll get the hint. He doesn't. He keeps staring, fingers working in and out of me, his thumb brushing against my clit with not enough pressure to have me singing the high notes, praising his work, and for the waves to rock my body.

"My girl needs this," he says, pressing the pad of his thumb flat against my clit.

I inch my bottom upward, rolling my hips, trying to get his thumb to move in the way I need to give me the damn orgasm.

"Enough with the *my girl* stuff and put your mouth to better use."

Pike's smile widens, and he slides down my body, fingers still inside me, thumb not giving me what I want. He settles his shoulders between my legs and pushes my legs farther apart. "Been waiting forever to taste you."

"For fuck's sake," I groan, bucking against his fingers because they've stopped although they're still inside me. "You have two seconds to put your..."

Heaven. That's what it feels like when Pike swipes his

tongue over my clit, rolling the tip around to trace the outside.

"Fuck yeah..." I drop my head back, closing my eyes and letting the sensations wash over me.

The warmth of his mouth.

The wetness of his lips.

The hardness of his fingers.

It all works together in perfect harmony and is everything I remember.

He curls his fingers, rubbing my G-spot as he seals his lips around my cunt in the most perfect way. "God, yes, right there."

The goose bumps from earlier return as every fiber of my being seems to be standing at attention, wanting this as badly as I do.

I open one eye, staring down my body again and loving the sight. There's nothing sexier than Pike nestled between my legs, eating like he's a starved man, fucking me like it's his sole purpose in life, and me...lying back and taking it all in.

Pike is right. I am a greedy lover. I won't apologize for it either. I'd lie here all night with him like this, orgasm after orgasm crashing over me if Pike would let that happen. But then again, I don't know of any man who is that giving.

My toes curl and my legs strain, trying to make the orgasm quicker. "Don't stop!"

His mouth is gone, and I groan my frustration. "Let it happen, darlin'. Don't force it."

I raise up on my elbow, glaring at the man whose lips are glistening from all his hard work. "Hey, Dr. Ruth, can you get back to suckin' and fuckin' without so much talk?"

"She's bossy too," he whispers, smiling up at me, mumbling something else to himself before his lips are back on my clit.

I collapse back onto the bed, trying to relax and let it

happen naturally, because Pike's right...it's always better when it isn't forced.

Within seconds, my toes curl again, but this time, I don't strain, chasing it. His fingers move faster, his lips suck harder, tongue flicking against my flesh as my muscles tighten on their own and all the breath in my lungs vanishes.

"Yes! Yes! Yes!" I scream, wrapping my fingers around the blanket again as my body shakes out of control. "Fuck yes!"

Pike doesn't slow. He doesn't allow the orgasm to wane. He pulls me from one orgasm straight into another, leaving me gasping for air and limp.

I'm in so much fucking trouble, and this time, there's no way out.

CHAPTER
TWENTY

PIKE

"WHAT'S YOUR NAME, HONEY?" a woman leans on the bar next to me, ass sticking out like she's looking for attention. Attention I won't be giving her beyond answering her question.

"Pike."

"You new around here?" she drawls, pushing her tits forward with the arm that's tucked under her chest.

"Nope."

"I've never seen you."

"Midge, leave the kid alone," Tiny says, stalking past us and around the bar. "He's an old-timer, but he's been gone for a while. He's not a brother, but a friend, and completely off-limits."

She snarls, but by the time he looks at her, her face is neutral. "I was just saying hello and introducing myself." She smiles at Tiny and straightens, allowing her tits and everything else to go back to normal, thanks to gravity. "I'm Morris's old lady."

"No shit?"

Morris never seemed like the type to settle down, especially not with someone so close to his own age.

"He doesn't know it yet, but I will be." She winks.

I hate to tell the lady, but Morris isn't settling down for no one. I don't care if she was a *Playboy* centerfold, the man couldn't stick to one pussy if his life depended on it. He is all about variety and excess, rarely dipping his wick in the same well twice.

"Get lost, Midge. We got shit to talk about, and you have work to do." Tiny glares down at the small woman with so many wrinkles, she looks like she was taken out of the dryer after staying in there too long.

"Yes, sir, big man," she says, throwing me a smile before stalking off with a sway of her hips.

Tiny glances toward the ceiling and sighs. "She ain't nothing but fucking trouble."

"Why keep her around?"

"She ain't got anywhere else to go, and she's a damn fine maid too."

"You finally hired someone to clean?" I look around the place, noticing it's not any neater than the last time I was here.

The floor is dirty, my boots stick to the tile in some spots, old alcohol acting like glue. Beer bottles are everywhere, but it's been a long night and the guys were celebrating my return, even if most of them didn't give two shits. They'd use any excuse to have a party.

"She cleans for beer and cock."

My eyebrows go up. "Interesting arrangement."

Tiny grabs a beer from the cooler, holds it out to me, and I take it before he grabs another one. "Where's the girl?"

I twist the top and take a swig, needing something to quench the thirst Gigi caused because the girl is insatiable. "Sleeping."

Tiny grins as he lifts the beer to his lips. "I like her."

Again, I raise my eyebrows. Tiny doesn't like many

people. Most of the time, I never thought he liked me. "You do?"

He nods. "She's a good fit for you. Unlike that other skank… What was her name?"

"Which one?" I laugh a little, but there's truth in what I'm saying.

I may not have been a brother or a prospect, but I had just as much pussy in my bed as every guy in this place. Somehow, the men here let me take advantage of all the perks without risking my life or requiring the oath bullshit they all swore to one another.

"What are you doing up?" I ask him because it's almost morning, but I haven't slept a wink.

"I'm not up. I'm headed to bed, but I had a few loose ends to tie up." He leans against the bar across from me, taking another swig of his beer. "I have eyes and ears out all over the state. No one's looking for you or the girl. Hopefully in a few days, you two can get back to your lives without looking over your shoulder."

"I'm sorry about this, Tiny. If I would've known James…"

Tiny waves me off. "If you're in any kind of shit, I want you calling me. If you need help, pick up the goddamn phone. I thought we made this clear to you when we saw you in Daytona. You may not live here anymore, but you'll always be part of our family."

"I don't know what I did to deserve any of this." I grip the neck of the bottle, swiping my thumb down the glass. "I don't see you taking in any other strays."

Tiny laughs. "You're a good kid. If I had a son, I'd want him to be just like you, Pike. Instead, I got a daughter because I've done bad shit in my life and the big guy found a way to pay me back. You needed help and had a pair of balls and a mouth back then." He laughs louder, shaking his head. "Hell, ya still do. I thought I'd convince you to be one of us, to join the brotherhood, but when I knew it was hopeless, I couldn't just toss your ass out into the street."

"You really could've. My parents didn't give two fucks what happened to me, and they're my own blood, Tiny. You have no duty to help me or even protect us right now."

Tiny's laugh dies and he moves closer, leaning into my space. "Family is more than blood, kid. Shit goes down in your life and you need backup, you call me. Now, you have James in your life and his people, which is good, but I'll always be here for you."

"James seems decent."

Tiny's laughter is back. "He's an asshole. One of the biggest fucking dicks I've ever met, but he's solid. When he speaks, it's the truth coming out of his lips. Shit went down years ago between us, but we made our peace. And when I need help, something I can't call on the guys to do, I call James and his guys."

"I don't want to know."

Tiny nods. "Trust me, you don't, but if that girl is his family, James will pull you into the fold."

"I work for her dad."

Tiny's eyes widen. "My man's fucking the boss's kid? You got a bigger set of balls on you than I thought."

"Or I'm dumb as a fuckin' brick. It's debatable at this point." I crack a smile, trying to make light of the situation, but none of it's funny. "And her life may be in danger because of that very fact. I'm pretty sure her father wants to rip my dick off and shove it down my throat, but we gotta make it out of here in one piece for that to happen."

"I'll make sure you live," Tiny promises, and I believe he'll do everything in his power to keep us alive.

"Thanks, T."

"Now, as a father to daughters, let me give you a little advice."

"I'm listening."

"Treat her good and make her happy. A father has many weapons, and if the guy is a douche and treats her like shit, he doesn't need to bring out the big guns to drive them apart. But if the guy is good and makes her happy, in bed and out, not even a nuclear weapon or her father's unhappiness can make her leave you. You make it right with her, her father will fall in line."

I shrug. "He's pretty pissed, and if I didn't know better, I'd think he was part of an MC too. He's friendly, but I know there's more to him than meets the eye."

"City was never in an MC," Tiny says.

"City?" I ask because that's not a name I know him by.

Tiny raises his hands. "Joe Gallo, dumbass."

I tick my chin toward Tiny. "How the hell do you know Joe?"

"He did a tat of mine back in the day, and I know all about him and that family from working with James and Thomas. He's solid. Never been in an MC, but he has been around the biking world for years. He keeps to himself. Dedicated to his family and isn't afraid to go to any length to protect them."

"Yep. That's him."

"I wish you fuckin' luck with that one," he says before he tips his head back, polishing off the rest of his beer.

"Thanks for the encouragement," I grumble because I know the shit hasn't even started. Once we step foot outside this compound, the danger gone, a new risk awaits, and it'll be directed only at me.

"Get some shut-eye. You look like shit."

I run my fingers down my beard, smiling at the old bastard. "Still lookin' better than you," I tease him as I climb off the stool and toss the rest of my beer in the trash as I walk toward the hallway.

When I open my door, Gigi's passed out, blankets half off her body, breasts sticking out, and taking up the entire twin bed like she's slept there her whole life.

I undress, pulling her over to one side, careful not to let her fall before I climb in next to her and tug her against my body. Her skin smells of sex and vanilla as I nuzzle my face into her neck, tightening my arms around her.

"Pike," she whispers.

"Shh, darlin'. Go back to sleep," I whisper back.

She turns in my arms, lying flat on her back, and blinks up at me. "Where were you?"

"Just talkin' with Tiny."

"Is everything okay?" She fights back a yawn but loses, covering her mouth with her hand. She closes her eyes, turning again and burrowing her face in my chest then throwing her leg over my hip.

"Everything's good." My fingers find her spine, tracing the straight line down her skin. "Don't worry. We're safe."

"Are you sad coming back here?"

"No. It's like going home again, although a fucked-up home, after being gone for a while. I'm comfortable here, but I worry about you being in a place like this."

She laughs against my skin. "Clearly you've never been in a frat house."

"Can't say that I have."

"The guys are bigger and scarier, but there is just as much drinking and naked bodies at a frat party as there was here tonight."

"How many frat parties have you been to?"

"A lot," she whispers. "Too many to remember."

I tighten my arms around her, and I don't like hearing about her in a place with so many drinks or naked people, but I know we both lived lives before we met. The thought of another man touching her makes my stomach knot.

"No more though, yeah?" I ask, letting my jealousy shine a little.

She laughs softly. "There's no time for frat parties. I figure this is like the last big hurrah, being at the compound. I'm going to use the time to party my ass off because adulting is going to suck and it's forever."

"You party as much as you want while we're here, but I'm going to be with you every step of the way. So, don't get any crazy ideas."

She pulls her head back, staring up at me with a smile. "What do you consider a crazy idea?"

"You're here with me and only in my bed. No one else."

Her smile grows wider. "Would you be jealous?"

I sigh, figuring I have to lay shit out because she's testing me. "Darlin', we both have pasts, but we're living in the now. I don't know if I have one hour or one hundred years, but whatever time I got, I want you where you are right now."

She blinks a few times, staring at me like I'm speaking a foreign language she can't understand. "I'm down with the now, but what makes you think you want to spend one hundred years with me where I am?"

"We got something special."

"Orgasms don't make a relationship." She rolls her eyes.

"They don't hurt either." I smirk. "But I've also been around enough wrong women to know when I've found the right one."

"Pike," she says softly, reaching her hand up between us and resting her fingers on my beard. "I'm not as...experienced as you."

"Really?" I say even though I knew that fact the first time she was in my bed. It's not hard to tell the difference. I knew back then Gigi Gallo wasn't an easy girl and didn't give her body away to just anyone. Why she decided to offer herself up to me in Daytona, I'll never know, nor do I give a fuck. It happened, and I haven't stopped thanking my dumbass luck for being in the right place at the right time since then.

She pulls at the hairs near my chin, toying with the tips. "I've only had a few boyfriends, and those relationships were complete disasters. How do I know we won't be the same?"

I press my lips to her forehead, wishing we could stay here, this way, forever. "There's no way to tell if we'll work out, but that doesn't mean I don't want to do whatever I can to hold on to whatever this is. All I can promise is that I'll treat you good, be loyal to you always, and give you as many orgasms as you want."

"As many as I want?" she whispers into my neck, fingers still playing with my beard.

"As many as you want," I repeat.

"I never had one with someone else before you," she confesses. Her voice is so soft and quiet, I almost don't hear her.

The statement doesn't shock me. So many women never get off with their partner, and half the time, the guys don't even try. They think that by getting theirs, they did enough, and if it doesn't happen for the chick, it isn't their fucking problem. I've never been that way. Can't even begin to understand that way of thinking.

"But you did with me, yeah?"

"Every time."

"That has to count for something. What if you don't stay with me, and no guy ever gets you off again?" It's a lie, but one I can use to my advantage since she has very little experience, and all of it before me was absolute shit.

"I do have a vibrator, so it's not like I'd never come again."

"I got a hand too, but it doesn't mean I'd be happy jacking off for the rest of my life."

She tips her head back, a smile back on her face. "Can I watch?"

My eyebrows draw together as I stare back at her. "Watch what?"

"You know." She waggles her eyebrows. "Watch you jack off. It would be the hottest thing ever."

"You going to give me that ass?" I ask, waggling my

eyebrows just like she did. "Because that would be the hottest thing ever."

Her nose scrunches. "Um, no."

"A little more tequila and I bet you'd say yes."

She lets out a loud huff and flattens her lips. "You let me watch you jack off and give me enough tequila, and I'll think about giving you my ass."

I roll her to her back, and I'm on top of her quickly. "See, darlin'. We work well together. Communication and negotiation are important in every relationship."

"You just want my ass, Pike."

"I want all of you, Gigi." I slide between her legs. "But right now, I want that sweet cunt squeezing my cock until we both pass out."

"That I can do," she promises.

CHAPTER
TWENTY-ONE
GIGI

THE COMPOUND IS MASSIVE. Not just the main building—everything is supersized. The ten-foot-high walls around the perimeter seem excessive, but I wouldn't be shocked if there was a moat on the other side of the gate either.

"Don't get any ideas, girl," cautions one of the men who's been following me around like he's my shadow.

I pull my hand back, letting the dusty green curtains fall back into place, and scrunch my nose. "Where would I go? Seriously, it's like Fort Knox out there."

The guy pulls a toothpick from his lips, sliding the same hand through his blond hair. "You look crafty and as if you'd claw your way over that wall like a superhero or some shit."

The double doors leading into a room that's set up like something you'd see in a corporate office creak, and the men file out, but there's no Pike, Morris, or Tiny. The looks on the men's faces don't give me much solace that this shit is over and we can finally go home. They called an emergency meeting an hour ago, telling me I wasn't allowed to attend even though my life was on the line and anything they said in there could either save me or end shit in a bad way.

To say I was pissed was an understatement. Even though I am a girl, I never have been treated like one by my family. We are all equals. It doesn't matter what you have between your legs, your opinion and thoughts count for something and are always taken into consideration.

The Disciples don't feel the same way. There is a macho hierarchy where the women cook, fuck, and suck dick, but beyond that, they aren't needed or wanted.

Thank God Pike didn't pick up on that shit when he lived here. He has enough of an attitude; I couldn't take the sexism on top of the rest of him.

The men scatter in opposite directions, pulling their guns from their waistbands as they walk. *Great.* Whatever they talked about has them on edge, because I haven't seen weapons out in the open in such numbers except for on television.

"What do you think's happening?" I ask Mr. Toothpick because he's the only one who's bothered to talk to me today besides Pike.

He shrugs. "My ass is out here with you, so I'm not in the know."

"They didn't clue you in?"

"They clue me in when they want me to be clued in."

The man talks in riddles, and he wouldn't be half bad-looking if he cut his long hair and trimmed his beard so it wasn't so scraggly.

"Gigi." Morris's voice booms through the open space, drawing my gaze. "Get your ass in here."

I smile at Toothpick. "Guess I'm going to be clued in before you," I taunt him because it's the only form of entertainment I have, and I'm feeling bitchy.

He snarls, waving me off. "Lucky you," he mutters and slides the toothpick back between his lips.

Morris is standing in the doorway, leaning against the frame, eyes on me like my ass is moving too slow for him.

"You out for a stroll?" he asks, confirming I am, in fact, moving too slow. But I have one speed, and it's sloth.

"The scenery lacks a certain charm." I smile, looking up at the big guy I've grown fond of in the short time I've been at the compound.

I can understand why Pike liked him even if he thought the guy shot him. I'm not sure I'd ever get over everything that happened, like him punching Pike in his injured shoulder, but men are cut from a different cloth like that.

"I'll make sure to call HGTV and see if we can get a makeover," Morris jokes, following me through the double doors.

Tiny's at the far end of the table, Pike next to him, both men staring at me as Morris closes the doors behind us. "Is everything okay?" I ask, walking slower than before because the looks on their faces say shit is far from okay.

Pike pulls out the chair next to him, and Tiny motions for me to sit. I do it quick, like my ass is suddenly on fire and only the chair can put out the flames.

Pike throws his arm around the back, turning his head to face me. I give him a timid smile. "What happened?"

As Pike opens his mouth, ready to tell me what I want to know, Tiny clears his throat. "There was an attempted hit on Pike's father last night."

I gasp, because this shit is far too real. His mother is dead, and his father was in hiding, just like us. But somehow, it sounds like he didn't come out unscathed.

Tiny leans back, eyeing me. "As far as we can tell, he's alive."

"That's good, right?" I ask, swallowing the lump that's back in my throat.

"DiSantis isn't taking his time. The next twenty-four hours will tell us if Pike or you are a target. So far, there's been no movement toward either of you. I spoke to James this morning, and he said it's quiet over there. He's had his boys sitting outside your apartments, parked outside Inked, and ears everywhere in that shithole town listening for chatter."

"And?"

Tiny drags his hand down his face, maybe not used to being questioned about anything. He probably lays shit out and people just take what he has to say and soak it in. But I'm not built that way. I question everything, and just when the person thinks they're done, I want to know more.

"We're ready in case they come here, looking for either of you."

"You really think they're here?"

Tiny shrugs. "Don't know. I'm sending out some guys to see if there's anyone new around, asking too many questions. The next few hours are critical."

"And if they hear nothing, can we go?"

"If we hear nothing, James and I will make the call on if your ass can walk outside those walls tonight."

"Okay," I whisper, knowing there's no point in arguing about who gets to determine our fate.

"DiSantis isn't a fool. I'm sure he did his homework, and if he's after Pike, he figured he'd come here for cover from the hell storm he's raining down."

"I can do another day standing on my head." I lean back into Pike's arm that's still flung across the back of my chair. I stare at Tiny, looking to him for some comfort.

"Just lie low. Maybe stay in Pike's room as much as possible. If shit goes down, I'd rather you be in a room with no windows than out there." He jerks his head toward the door. "I'm sure you can find ways to keep yourselves occupied." He winks.

I let out a nervous laugh. "Nothing gets me hotter than knowing I may be taking my last breath."

Tiny swipes his hand across his lips, muttering obscenities. "Take a nap, play Scrabble or some shit, but keep yourselves out of sight."

"Scrabble?" I scrunch my nose. "Poker maybe." I tap my chin, thinking of ways to entertain ourselves. "Strip poker works too." I turn to Pike, who's pale as a ghost. "You okay, baby?"

He gives me a small smile, hiding whatever passes across his eyes. "I'm great, darlin'."

His answer comes too easy, and I wonder what I'm not being told. Maybe he's in shock, mourning the loss of his mother and the possible death of his father.

"Now, you two get gone. I have shit to do, and the sooner this is over, the better," Tiny announces, pushing back from the table and climbing to his feet.

"You know you're going to miss me," I tell Tiny, standing and craning my neck to look up at him.

"Kid, the next time I see your face, I expect it to be under happier circumstances."

"Me too, Tiny. Me too."

Pike's on his feet, arm around my shoulders like he needs to be physically touching me at all times. I turn my head, looking at his face, soaking him in. "Why don't we grab a bottle of Jack before we head back?"

If the day goes to shit, I'm going to need something hard to chase away the fear that's settled into my bones. I've been good at keeping it under wraps. I've pretended to be sleeping, when half the time, I'm paralyzed by fear, waiting for the bad guys to come crashing through the doors, ready to take us out.

"I think we should stay clearheaded," Pike says, moving me toward the doorway right behind Tiny. "If something happens and I'm shit-faced…"

"We'll stay sober." I reach up and touch his hand that's closed around my shoulder.

Tiny puts out his hand, stopping us from walking to Pike's room. "Here." He pulls a gun from his waistband and holds it in front of us. "Take this. If you don't need it, great.

If you do, at least you have it. You remember how to shoot it?"

"I'll never forget," Pike says as he wraps his hand around the handle, holding it like he's done it a million times.

"Shit goes south, you shoot at anything coming your way."

Pike nods at Tiny, and I'm feeling a little left out again. "Do I get a gun?"

Tiny's eyes twinkle, but his expression doesn't change. "Absolutely not."

"This is bullshit."

"As is life," Tiny teases.

Pike moves one hand to the small of my back, the other one still holding the gun. "Come on. Let's let the guys do their shit so we can get out of here sooner rather than later."

"Fine, but I'm grabbing the Jack." I stalk away from him and push past Morris before Pike has a chance to usher me toward his room.

"Fuckin' women," Morris mutters loud enough for me to hear even though my legs are moving faster than before. "Now she's Jackie Joyner-Kersee."

I don't know who Jackie is, but she has to be badass if he thinks I'm anything like her. I'm so not chill right now as I stride across to the bar, throwing myself over the top, and reaching underneath to find a bottle of Jack. Once I have it in hand, I slide back down, turning to face the three of them, all of whom are staring at me with a look of amusement.

"Good luck," Morris says to Pike, slapping him on the back as I throw them a quick glance before striding down the hallway, cracking the top of the bottle open.

"You comin'?" I call out when Pike's not right behind me, hanging on me like he was a few minutes ago.

Tiny and Morris laugh their asses off, but I don't turn around to see if Pike's following me or not. I'm cranky and starting to go a little stir-crazy, missing the sunshine on my skin. All I can hope for now is that today's our last day in captivity and we walk out of here breathing.

———

Half a bottle of Jack and four hours later, I'm sitting on the edge of Pike's bed, wrapped in a blanket and nothing more. He's naked, pacing near the door like he's a caged animal, gun on the dresser.

"You okay?" I ask him, watching the muscles of his body flex and relax with each step.

His body is long, sleek, and sculpted. His legs are longer than his torso, all brought together with the most spectacular ass I've ever seen on a man.

"Just thinking."

I lean back, still staring at his nakedness because I can. "About?"

"How my family has fallen to shit because of the stupid, greedy things my father's done. But then there's you—" he motions a hand toward me "—and that part of my life feels like it's finally falling into place."

"I'm sorry about your mom and dad."

I can't imagine something happening to mine. I wouldn't even be able to get out of bed, let alone form coherent thoughts. My world revolves around my family. Always has, and I can't imagine that ever changing. I didn't even leave the state to attend college because I wanted to be close enough to go home whenever I missed everybody. Which ended up being more often than I'd expected.

Pike shakes his head. "I feel like I should be crying or at least be sadder than I am. They're my parents after all. They brought me into this world, but Gigi, they weren't good to me. There wasn't a day that went by where I didn't feel like I was a burden to them. Do you know how it is to be a little kid, playing with your old-ass toy truck that is falling apart, knowing you're not wanted." He looks at me, and I shake my head. "Of course, you don't. You have the Gallos. They love you. They worship the ground you walk on and would do anything for you if you asked."

"I'm sorry."

Those are the only words I have because I know I was lucky the day I was born. I could've very easily been born into a shit-ass family where I was just another mouth to feed. But I wasn't. I hit the proverbial jackpot. Not only do I have amazing parents, but my aunts and uncles are the bomb too.

"I'd give my left nut to have something good like that in my life."

I'm on my feet, walking toward him. "I wouldn't like that because I'm kind of partial to your left nut." I'm using humor because it's the only thing I can do. "Your right one just doesn't do it for me."

Pike grabs me as the blanket I have wrapped around myself falls to the floor. "You're such an asshole." He laughs, holding me tightly, skin against skin.

"But you love me."

"I do," he replies, running his fingers down my spine. "More than I have anyone in a long time."

"Pike." I'm breathless, wondering if he meant to say that, wondering if he'll take them back. "Is it a little too soon to say those words?"

He peers down at me, a swirl of emotion in his eyes. "I didn't just meet you, darlin'. After you left, I dreamed of no one but you. When I saw you walk into Inked, I couldn't believe my goddamn eyes. We've only spent two weeks together in total, but I feel like I've known you since the day you walked up to me and asked me for my number—and let me say, you never gave me yours."

"Well..." I don't know what to say to all that. If I were honest, I've thought about Pike a lot since the day I walked out the door for that nonexistent cup of coffee.

"You're young. Maybe you're not ready to say how you feel, but I've lived enough to know when there's something good in my life and something I don't want to let go of again."

"Um," I mumble, my vision blurring because this beautiful man, one who doesn't always share his feelings, is spilling his guts like water over Niagara Falls.

"I'll give you all the time in the world to figure out if it's how you feel too, but until then, you're my girl and only my girl. You're mine, Gigi Gallo."

My stomach flutters at the way he says those words and at the intensity in his gaze. I've heard my father utter those words a thousand times to my mother, and every time, I'd roll my eyes. But now I understand how it made her feel. I understand why those words made her smile and go all gooey in the knees, because in this moment, I am finding it difficult to stand.

"Okay," I whisper.

"Okay?" He raises an eyebrow.

I nod. "I'm yours." I brush my hand across the beautiful back dimples he has just above his ass. "But as long as we're staking claims, you're mine too, Pike Moore. No other women are in your bed or on the back of your bike. If we're doing this, we're doing it right."

Pike's sadness from earlier is gone, replaced by a big, toothy smile. He slides his hand up my back, cupping my neck. "In the shittiest week of my life, you've somehow found a way to make me the happiest man alive."

I don't get a chance to reply and tell him I feel the same before his lips crash down on mine, stealing my words and my breath.

CHAPTER
TWENTY-TWO

PIKE

MY EYES FLY open as a cold hand covers my mouth. "Pike," Morris tries to whisper, but being quiet has never been his thing. "Men are on the perimeter."

I blink up at him as I lift myself, letting his words slide over me, penetrating the haze I still have from the dream I was just in a minute ago.

Gigi shifts in my arms. "What's wrong?" She goes stiff as soon as she lays eyes on Morris, who's hovering above us.

"Get your asses up and be ready." Morris moves toward the door, but he's still staring at us, a worried look on his face. "Shit's about to go down."

Gigi rises next to me, holding the sheet over her chest. "Fuck. For real?" Her eyes are wide, and I can see the fear all over her face.

Morris doesn't answer as he disappears into the hallway. The only sounds are his heavy footsteps and those of his brothers moving around the compound as the door clicks behind him.

"Get dressed and go into my closet." I move my chin toward the door on the other side of the room. "Don't come out under any circumstances. And when I say any circumstances, I mean, don't come out until you hear me, Tiny, or Morris calling your name."

She scurries to her feet, gathering her clothes off the floor where I'd thrown them last night. "Don't come out under any circumstances," she repeats my words, pulling her shirt over her head and then moving for her pants. "Pike, what if…"

I shake my head, zipping my jeans. "No ifs. If you don't know the voice, don't come out. Stay quiet, and no matter what, don't cry. I don't want these fuckers finding you."

"Don't get yourself shot, okay? No jumping in front of bullets for me."

I stalk up to her, grabbing her neck and hauling her lips to mine. "Darlin', I'll do whatever it takes to get you back to your family and keep you breathing."

"I'd never be able to…"

I don't let her finish the statement before my mouth closes over hers, taking what I can get for what might be the last time. If shit goes south, which it could and probably will, I may never have another chance to kiss her beautiful mouth and feel her in my arms again.

I break away, even though I want to hold her like this forever and forget the shit that's going on outside this room.

"Go." I run my finger along her chin, memorizing every dip of her lips. "Get in the closet. Go all the way to the back and hide behind my things."

She nods, walking back slowly, dragging her hand down my arm until just our fingertips are touching. "Be safe and don't be a hero."

I've never wanted to be the hero, but I want to be hers. I'm not sure I've ever wanted to be anything more that in this very moment. No one would get by me and get to her. Not as long as I still have air in my lungs and the ability to move.

"Go, Gigi," I order her, pulling on my boots, gun by my side on the bed, my body facing the hallway.

A wave of emotion passes across her face as she opens the

door to the closet and steps inside. I lift my chin at her, and she gives me a pained smile before finally closing the door, disappearing into the darkness.

I grab the gun, but I stay on the edge of the bed, knowing whoever comes through that door is going to get one of my bullets. I won't hesitate to pull the trigger, and the brothers here know better than to walk in here unannounced or without calling the all clear.

Gunfire rings through the building, sounding like fireworks on steroids and coming so fast it's like a hurricane of metal and fire.

A million thoughts cross through my mind as the shadow of boots passes by the door, heading toward the main room where the majority of the bullets are flying.

These guys, the ones I thought of like family, are hauling ass toward the gunfire, shielding us from their spray.

We're the intended targets, but they're willing to put their lives on the line so we can breathe another day. They live for shit like this. They crave danger, not giving a fuck if they live or die as long as they enjoy every minute of the time they're here, walking this earth.

I hold my breath, knowing someone's going to come through the door if anyone has survived. I pray—something I haven't done since I was living with my grandmother—hoping like hell we get out of here unscathed. Not just us, but the men putting their lives on the line as I sit in the dark, protecting my girl and waiting for hell to come to me.

I've lived through a hail of bullets before, but I had never been the intended target. I've been shot, and I sure as fuck am not looking forward to feeling the hot metal slice through my skin again. But I also want to live, having more to live for than ever before.

My father's sins were following me. His curse was the only thing he gave me besides his name. But after tonight, after the gunfire ends, no matter which side comes out on top, his time in my life will end as well.

The shouts of the men I know are barely audible over the gunfire as it grows louder, coming close to us. I prepare myself, lifting the gun toward the door, poised to shoot anyone who enters. My hand doesn't shake, even though I've never shot a man before. I've held a gun hundreds of times growing up in Tennessee, but never have I been more prepared to use it to kill another person than I am right now.

My body stiffens as a door slams nearby. Clearly, someone's searching and got through the front line. I lift my other hand, gripping my forearm to steady the gun because if I shoot, I sure as fuck ain't missing.

"Keep lookin'!" a man yells. "I know he's here."

He is me, and I'm thankful they haven't said anything about Gigi. I'm their intended target and not the scared girl hiding in my closet probably losing her shit but following my orders nonetheless.

A single shot rings out in the hallway, sounding more like a firework popping and echoing through the tiny corridor. The knob on my door turns, illuminating my room with just enough light to see the outline of a man. I squeeze the trigger, not hesitating to fire as he lifts his arm, ready to take me out too. But my shot is quicker, and the man falls backward, a clean shot right in his head.

"Don't shoot," another man says, but my ears are still ringing from the shot I just fired. "Pike." I can't see him because he hasn't shown his face, probably not wanting the same fate as the dead bastard on the dirty-ass floor.

The gun's still pointed at the door, my hand not as steady as it was, but I'll take out any other bastard that tries to walk inside. I keep my mouth shut, not knowing who's calling my name or their intentions.

"It's Morris. Don't shoot," he says. "They're gone. All

dead but a few already out the door and running for the hills."

"They're gone?" I ask, not moving a muscle because I can't.

"Just this one cocksucker got by us, but you handled his ass. Three more made it out, but men are after them, making sure they don't get wherever they're going."

"Morris?" I ask because my mind is hazy and all I can see is the puddle of blood oozing out of the man's body.

"Yeah, kid. It's me. Put the gun down. The shit's over." He's still hiding, taking no chances with me.

I don't blame him. It's not every day a man takes the life of another. Morris knows I've never done it and how it changes a man.

My hand drops as I take my finger off the trigger, but I'm not ready to put it down. It's like the metal has fused to my hand, becoming one with me. I'm in shock. I know it. I know my body is trying to catch up with what my mind already knows. I shot a man. I took a life.

"Is it down?"

"Yeah," I call back to Morris. "Come in."

He steps over the man's body, flipping the switch on the wall and bathing the room in light. "Nice shot," he says as soon as his eyes land on the man with a bullet clean through his forehead. "I always knew you had it in you."

"Can I come out?" Gigi says from the closet, no doubt hearing our voices but unable to wait for the all clear. The girl only has so much patience to follow orders, which is maddening, but at least she stayed in there long enough to keep her ass alive.

"Come out, girl," Morris tells her before I can. "It's over."

I'm on my feet and at my closet before she has a chance to see the dead guy on the floor. I grab her face, keeping her eyes on me. "You okay, baby?"

She nods, eyes glistening as she stares up at me. "I'm

okay," she whispers, but her voice wavers. "When I heard the shot go off…" Her lip quivers, and her voice breaks, not finishing the statement.

"I'm fine. We're fine." I hold her gaze, trying to keep my shit together so I can convince her that what I'm saying is true.

"Yo!" Morris yells, making Gigi jump. "We got a body over here."

Gigi tries to look around me, but I hold her face, forcing her to look at me and nowhere else. "Don't look. You don't want to have that burned on your brain."

"Did you do it?" she asks, her voice whisper-soft, the quiver still on her lips.

I nod, rubbing my thumb across her cheek. "It was him or us, and I wasn't about to end what we have. I told you I'd do anything to protect you, and I did what I needed to do."

"You killed a man."

I nod again because I did. I pulled that trigger without an ounce of hesitation, thinking of him as the enemy and not a human being. I didn't give a fuck if he had a wife and kids. He wanted to kill us, and for that alone, he deserved the bullet he got.

The tears in her eyes build and fall when she blinks. "You protected me?" she whispers as her hands find my sides, gripping me like she needs to touch me to stay upright.

"I'll always protect you." I know my words are true. "I told you that, darlin'."

Boots are behind me, shadows moving around the room as the guys bend down, hauling the dead guy from the doorway. "Take him outside with the others," Morris says. "We'll deal with them together. And get Midge in here to help clean up this mess." There are a few grunts of understanding, followed by Morris's shadow growing in size on the wall behind Gigi. "I'll give you two some time to talk and some privacy."

I nod, not turning around because I'm not taking my eyes off my girl. She needs me. More than she needed me before this shit went down. She heard too much, knew too much, and that shit would mess with her head.

When I peer over my shoulder, there's only a small amount of blood visible near the doorway. The majority of the guy's brains and blood landed in the hallway just outside my door and out of sight.

I reach down, lifting Gigi into my arms, carrying her toward the bed. Her head moves to my shoulder, arms around my neck as I cradle her tightly, wishing she'd never had to experience this. I brought this to her door. My father brought this to mine.

"We're safe now." I sit on the edge of the bed, resting her ass in my lap, still holding her close. "No one's going to hurt you."

"I've never been so scared in my life, Pike." Her fingers toy with the hair on the back of my neck, sending a shock wave of feelings through my system. "Not just for me, but for you. I was so worried that..."

"Shh, baby. It's over. Stop thinking about it. I'm breathing. You're breathing. There's nothing else that matters right now."

"What about the guys?"

"I don't know what happened out there, and I'm not ready to find out. Tiny will call for us when he's ready to tell us what we need to know and what he wants to tell." I brush my lips across her forehead, needing to feel her softness and be reminded of all the good there is in life to replace the bad I've just done. "All that matters is you're okay."

"Do you think they'll come back?" she whispers, toying with the collar of my T-shirt, grazing my skin with her fingernails.

"I don't know if there'll be anyone to come back. If any of them made it out, the others went after them on foot. They don't have much of a chance on all this land with the Disciples on the hunt."

"I guess that's a good thing."

"It's a good thing for us, but not for them."

We're both thankful to be alive. I may have lived within these compound walls for years, but we'd never been attacked and I'd never been in what sounded like a battle zone. My body trembles slightly as the adrenaline that has been coursing through me starts to wear off.

"Do you think we'll ever get to go home?"

I run my hand up her back and nuzzle my face in her neck, needing her smell, her softness to keep me grounded. "We will, darlin'. DiSantis isn't stupid enough to lose all his men trying to kill someone who doesn't know dick about his business. I don't know how many came here tonight, but based on the sounds, I'd say he lost too many to try to come after me again."

"Kid?" Tiny calls, knocking on my door but not entering the room. "You two decent?"

Gigi laughs, and the sound is like angels singing, making all the shit that happened seem like it was part of a distant past.

"Yeah, Tiny. We're good."

The door creaks, and Tiny sticks his head in the room. "Just talked to James."

"Oh shit," Gigi whispers, and her laughter dies. "We may have survived the gun battle, but now we have to figure out how to make it through my family."

"He's on his way with a few of her uncles and her father. They'll be here in a few hours. Get your shit together. You two are heading back."

I gawk at Tiny as he wipes his bloodied hand with a towel. "But what about DiSantis?"

Tiny shrugs with a smile. "Fucker's dead. Someone went after him tonight before the hit went down. Took a blade across his neck just before lights-out. He ain't gonna bother you again."

I let out a heavy breath like a weight has been lifted off my back that I didn't know was there. "That's it? He's dead. It's over?" I repeat like the words haven't sunk in.

"Yup. Dead as a fucking doornail. You have three hours before the guys get here to collect you two."

He starts to close the door, but I have shit to say and not a lot of time to say it. "Tiny," I call out, causing him to stop. "Thank you for tonight and everything."

Tiny nods, still wiping the blood because there're so many dead bodies out there, I'm sure there's blood on everything. "You are family, kid, and we take care of our own. I meant what I said earlier, you need backup or safe haven, you come here. Nowhere else."

I nod. "Nowhere else."

"Now get some rest. You made it through one hit squad, but you're about to be in front of another. I have a feeling you're going to get an earful on the way back."

"I won't let them say anything to you." Gigi gazes up at me from my lap.

"You're cute, darlin'. If they want to lay into me, let them. I can take it. It's not like they're going to be shooting bullets at me. I can handle a little angry talk. Let them get it off their chests, and I'll take it like a man. They're probably worried out of their minds."

"A little angry talk?" she says, laughing with every word. "I know you're used to badass bikers, but these are Gallo men. They may not wear patches or ride a hog, but I'm telling you now, they're just as fuckin' scary. A little angry talk." She bursts into a fit of giggles, knowing her family way better than I do. "We're going to get our asses chewed out for a living, and you're going to wish you were lying in that heap of bodies outside."

"Come on. We're alive. How bad can they honestly be?"

CHAPTER
TWENTY-THREE

GIGI

I SLAM back two shots of Jack as Morris yells that two cars are approaching. The same two cars that are carrying my family. The same two cars that not only carry my family, but men so pissed off, I'm pretty sure they broke every speed record to get here.

I know what awaits me. I've seen my dad and Uncle James angry before, but it was never pointed at me. I figure if I am going to make it through the long-ass drive home, I need a little liquor to make me more agreeable and less likely to argue back.

"You ready?" Pike asks at my side, holding out his hand to me.

"I don't think I'll ever be ready." I try to smile, but it's impossible knowing my dad is nearby, probably foaming at the mouth.

"It won't be that bad," he says with a straight face because he only knows my dad and uncles as the chill guys they can be sometimes and not the raving lunatics they can be when someone in the family is in danger.

"I'll remind you that you said that." I grab the bottle of

Jack and try to pour myself another drink before Pike takes it from my hands.

"This won't make things better."

I try to pull the bottle out of his grip, but it won't budge as we play tug-of-war. "I beg to differ."

"Get your asses moving," Morris yells out, standing at the open door of the building, glancing back at us as we're locked around the bottle of Jack.

"Fuckin' fine." I let go, knowing it's a lost cause and we're out of time.

"The girl lives, sees death, but the attitude never leaves," Morris mutters, glancing up at the dark sky and shaking his head.

I walk away from Pike, stalking toward Morris, the guy I've grown fond of over the last few days. "Thanks for everything, big guy."

He blushes as he tips his head down to look at me. "Don't be a stranger, kid. Make sure to keep that boy in line, ya hear?"

I laugh, nodding at him as I wrap my arm around his middle. "I promise to make sure he walks the straight and narrow."

Morris's arm is around me immediately, holding me tightly. "Maybe I'll come visit. I could use another piece."

"I'd love that."

"You two done?" Tiny says, stalking by the doorway, heading toward the headlights.

I release Morris and practically run up to Tiny, hurling myself against him. He stumbles back like he's in shock and not used to being hugged. "Thank you for everything, Tiny."

Tiny pats my back but doesn't give me the rib-crushing embrace Morris just did. "Anytime, girl. Now, give me a minute with the boy."

I stare up at him, craning my neck all the way back to meet his eyes. "Can you make sure they don't kill Pike?"

"Can't promise anything when it comes to James," he says, amusement lighting up his face.

"It was worth a shot." I shrug and pop up on my toes to just reach his cheek.

Tiny doesn't move as I kiss his cheek and then step away. He looks a little shell-shocked, which is funny because he's so big and burly, but my little kiss seems to have knocked the badass right out of him and left him speechless.

Two cars pull in, gravel flying from the speed and hurling in all directions as they slam on the brakes. We're like deer, frozen in the headlights.

I was scared as hell in the closet, listening to the screams and gunfire going off everywhere. You'd think facing my family would be nothing after that, but nope. I'm just as scared as I was a few hours ago.

"Just stay calm," Morris calls out as Pike walks up next to me.

"You ready for this?" I ask, looking over at him, ignoring the sound of the car doors opening and boots hitting gravel.

"I don't know," he says before his eyes go to where my family stands.

I turn my head slowly, soaking in my uncle James, who looks like he's about ready to tear a man's jugular clean through his neck. My uncle Thomas, who looks just as pissed and no less scary. And then there's my daddy and Bear, looking like caged animals, shifting slightly like they're unable to stand still or all their fury would cause them to combust.

"Hey," I call out, putting on a smile and trying to act like our asses didn't almost get shot tonight. "I missed you guys." I slowly move in their direction, gaze going between all four men, trying to see if I could make their badass exteriors crack.

My dad rushes toward me, putting his eyes on no one and nothing but me. My slow walk turns into a full-on run until we're close enough that I leap into his arms, and he catches me like he used to when I was a little girl.

"I love you, Daddy." I feel like a kid again and finally safe in my father's arms.

"Baby girl," he whispers, holding my head with one hand and squeezing my body with his other arm. "I've never been so scared in all my fucking life and never more thankful than I am right now."

I bury my face in his neck, holding on to him like I don't think I've ever held him before. "I'm sorry," I whisper. "I'm sorry I had you worried."

"We'll talk about it in the car," he says.

Oh goodie.

Car talks have never been my favorite. I'm like a trapped animal and a captive audience with no escape or talking my way out of whatever my dad wants to put down. I freaking hate every minute of the car chats. They are the most suck-tastic things ever because they are so effective at breaking me.

"Joe," Pike says, walking up behind me, but my daddy's body goes stiff underneath me.

"Get your ass in the car with James and Thomas. I want to talk to my *daughter* alone."

Goodie times two.

"Yes, sir," Pike says without even arguing.

He probably knows it's a lost cause. There isn't any arguing with a Gallo man on a good day, but in a moment like this and with the anger on my dad's face, there is no way in hell Pike or I would win that argument.

My feet are back on the ground as Pike turns his back and is walking toward James and Thomas where they chat with Tiny and Morris.

"Let's get out of here," Bear says, giving me a wink instead of saying anything else.

I'm sure he wants all the details, but he isn't going to ask about shit when my dad's in a mood. And I'm pretty damn sure my dad's mood isn't going away anytime soon either.

"Daddy, can't Pike come with us, please?" I pitch my thumb over my shoulder toward the five guys.

"I want to talk to you alone, and James wants to debrief Pike." My father shakes his head. "They know the way home."

I hang my head, dragging my feet through the gravel as I make my way toward the car. I know I'm going to get my ass chewed out, but I'll live. It won't be the first time my father has read me the riot act about something.

But Pike may not be so lucky.

I turn toward Pike as I open the car door, giving him a small wave and pained smile when our eyes lock. He waves back, tipping his chin like shit is cool, but he's freaking clueless.

I don't know much about his dad and know even less about his entire family. But what he's about to deal with will, no doubt, be nothing he's prepared for or expects.

"We're out!" my dad yells across the parking lot, not bothering to wait for a response before he's climbing in the passenger seat.

"This should be fun." Bear catches my eye in the rearview mirror, always trying to make light of heavy shit.

No other words are spoken as Bear revs the engine, taking off the same way they came in...fast. I twist my fingers, staring out the window at the endless trees flying by in a blur as we exit the compound.

Maybe my dad is too pissed to even talk. Maybe he's too happy I'm alive to rip me a new asshole. Anything is possible. How can he be mad when we didn't do anything wrong, nor did we do anything to cause the clusterfuck of chaos that landed at our feet?

The silence is killing me. I figure maybe this is an instance where I've got to rip the Band-Aid off quickly and get it over with. Waiting just makes it worse, and I can't sit here in silence for the next two hours. "So…"

"Don't *so* me, little girl," Dad says.

I widen my eyes at his clipped tone. "Okay," I whisper, slouching down in the seat and crossing my arms over my chest.

"You could've been killed." He turns in his seat so he can look at me. "You almost were…"

"But I wasn't."

His eyes harden. "Were there bullets flying within fifty feet of you?"

I shrug. Now, I'm pissed. And when I'm pissed, I dig my heels in and turn on the smartass. "I didn't have my tape measure."

He surges forward like he's going to leap over the seat and wrap his hands around my neck, choking the life right out of me. His eyes aren't hard anymore; his glare is blazing hot. "What did you just say? Say it again."

"Dad, you're being a little crazy and unreasonable. Where's my big, badass father?"

"Your big, badass father is dealing with a lot of feelings after men just tried to bust into an MC compound, raining down fire, in an attempt to take out my kid and end her life."

"They weren't trying to kill me," I say softly because I know he's about at his wits' end and he doesn't need my shit.

"I know. They were trying to kill Pike, who—" he pauses, twisting his lips up, and I know what he's about to say before the words spill from his mouth "—you didn't tell me was actually your boyfriend!"

He yells those words, the sound echoing through the car like a bomb blast. "He's not my boyfriend, Daddy."

I keep up with the Daddy bit because it's always worked in the past and usually helps to defuse his anger. This isn't the first time he's been pissed at me, but it is the most pissed he's ever been that I can remember.

Bear shakes his head, muttering something under his breath, and he catches my eye in the mirror. I don't know what he's trying to tell me, but I know instantly I fucked up.

"That's right," Dad says, nodding his head, eyebrows drawn down, and his top lip curling like he's smelled the biggest pile of shit. "He's not a boyfriend. He's a guy you fucked."

Uh oh. This isn't good. Damn. I can't backpedal my way out of this one. There're no more secrets at this point, and I lied right to my dad's face about Pike when Aunt Izzy confronted me at Inked.

I don't move. It's as if my ass is glued to the seat, and every muscle in my body locks up as if I'm paralyzed. The only thing I can do is stare at my father with wide eyes and say, "I'm sorry."

He tips his head back, staring at the ceiling of the car. "She's sorry." His shoulders rise and fall. "No big deal, Dad. I met a guy at Bike Week and slept with him even though he could've raped me and left my ass for dead."

"I'm grown and I was careful."

"Adults die too, Giovanna. How many times did I tell you under no circumstances were you allowed in Daytona during Bike Week?"

"It was a mistake. We went for spring break."

"And did you tell me you were going to Daytona for spring break?"

"Did you tell your parents everything when you were twenty?" I pause, returning his hard stare because I'm sick and tired of being treated like a little kid. "Oh, wait. No, you freakin' didn't. You were out riding your bike, bangin' broads without giving any fucks."

He turns his head like he didn't quite hear me. "You want to repeat that shit for me?"

"No."

He grinds his teeth, and I wince at the sound. "I didn't fucking think so," he growls.

"She finally says something smart," Bear mutters.

"When we get back, I forbid you to see him again."

He forbids me? I raise an eyebrow, ready to dig the hole I've already dug a little deeper. "So, you firing him or me? 'Cause other than that, I don't know how I'm not supposed to see him. Care to explain, Daddy?"

My father slides a hand down his face before his fingers crumple into a fist near his chin. "Did the bullets scramble your brains or some shit?"

"Nope." I shake my head. "I'm seeing clearer than I have in a long time."

"The way your mouth is talking, I'd say you're still in shock."

"Not in shock. I'm feeling more alive than ever. So, who's leaving?"

"Izzy won't fire him, and you're not going anywhere. You two can work together without dating."

"Okay." I nod, thinking over my next words carefully. "So, the guy who was just ready to take a bullet for me, the guy who put his body in the way, hiding me so he'd die instead of me…" I close my eyes, remembering the way my body shook when the door to Pike's room opened and I didn't know which person had died. "I'm just supposed to tell him to kick rocks because my *father*, who's also his *boss*, doesn't want me to see him again." I open my eyes and roll them because I know it'll piss off my dad something fierce. "Hey, Pike, thanks for almost dying for me and being willing to throw yourself in front of a bullet, but my *father* doesn't think you're good enough."

"I didn't say he wasn't a good person."

I cross my arms again, lifting one shoulder, staring my father straight in the eye. "Just not good enough for me, right?"

My father's entire face scrunches up like he's about to shit a brick and it's painful as fuck. "His life is dangerous, Gigi. Look at all the shit you've been through in a couple days of him being in your life."

"It's not trouble he brought to his door. It was *his* father's fault, and if it weren't for the men in Pike's past, he'd probably be dead and maybe me too." I pause and our eyes are locked in a silent tug-of-war, but I don't give him a chance to talk because I'm not done making my point. "Didn't something happen to Mom when you two were dating? Wasn't she almost…"

"It was different," he says quickly.

"Shit happens, Dad. Life happens. No matter how hard you try to protect someone, you can't stop the bad from getting through all the time. Pike's innocent in this, and the decision of if we're going to see each other again falls to Pike and me. And frankly—" I swallow because if he hasn't leaped over the seat yet, my next words may be the nail in the coffin "—it's none of your business."

He blinks like I've slapped him, and his mouth moves but nothing comes out.

"I'm not trying to be mean, and if I am, I'm sorry. But imagine if Grandma or Grandpa said you couldn't see Mom anymore."

"I love your mother."

"Maybe I love Pike."

My father laughs. "You just met the kid."

"How long after you met Mom did you know you had feelings for her? Real feelings…"

"Well…" He looks at Bear because Bear was there in the beginning, and I have zero doubt he'll call my dad on his shit if he tries to lie. "Honestly, I don't remember a time when I didn't love your mom."

"Then why does it matter that I just met him?" I use air quotes on the last three words because we both know I didn't just meet him, but I have had fifteen months to think about him and the way he makes me feel.

"I…" He pauses, staring at me like he doesn't know what to say and hates to tell me I'm right.

"The man would've died for me tonight, Daddy. How many guys would do that? Let me tell you. Not many. Guys my age are a bunch of pansy-asses who cry when they get a paper cut. Chivalry is fucking dead. Pike would've taken that bullet and died with a smile on his face knowing I was going to live to breathe another day."

"I…" he says again, but I don't let him finish before I go on because I have shit to get off my chest.

"Here's this guy with a mother who's dead because his father is an asshole. The same father who treated him like shit as a little kid and a mother who wasn't much better. For growing up the way he did, he turned out to be a freaking great guy. He's envious of me, you know. He sees how close we all are, how much we love each other, and he knows exactly what he missed out on growing up and even now. So whatever misconceived notions you have about Pike, you may as well forget them all until you get to know the real man underneath."

"She's kind of telling you how it is, City." Bear glances at him with a slight shrug. "Pike's not too far off from the man you were at that age. You had a good family behind you, but you weren't a choirboy."

My father glares at Bear. "You're not helping. Whose side are you on?"

"Don't ask me to pick a side because I'll always pick the girl."

My smile's so big, my cheeks hurt. This is why I love my uncle Bear. He can totally call my dad out on his shit, reminding him of the man he is and used to be. It doesn't hurt that he's always willing to have my back. Always. It doesn't matter that we're not blood; he's been in my life since the day

I was born and is just as much my uncle as any of my father's brothers.

"It's a fucking conspiracy," my father mutters, turning around to face the windshield.

"Just give him a chance, Dad. Give me a chance to live my own life and find my own happiness."

"I don't like it."

"I never asked if you did."

CHAPTER
TWENTY-FOUR
PIKE

"THREE LARGE BLACK COFFEES."

"Would you like sugar, sir?"

"I said black," James barks out the driver's window, arm slung over the door, looking chill as fuck but sounding like he's wound so tight, he could break at any moment.

"Black means no cream, but it doesn't mean no sugar," the woman on the other end of the drive-thru tries to explain, but James is in no mood.

"No cream. No sugar. Just coffee."

"Iced or hot?" she asks.

James looks at Thomas like he can't get over this shit, and Thomas laughs at James's misery. "Hot," he growls out the window, practically foaming at the mouth.

"Please pull around, sir."

"What the fuck happened to ordering a simple cup of coffee?"

Thomas shrugs. "Life's moving fast, old man."

"Get the fuck out of here with that old man shit."

Thomas glances down, staring at his phone. "Well, this should get interesting."

"What?" James asks as he inches the car forward in the long line.

"Mom's requiring Pike to be at today's family dinner."

"She what?" I ask, shocked and a little scared.

"Joe isn't going to be happy about that," James states the fucking obvious.

From the moment our eyes met at the compound, I knew Joe hated me now. I'm not even sure hate is a strong enough word for all the things he's feeling toward me. I can't blame the guy. I'd fucking hate me too.

"I'd give my left nut to be in that car with them." Thomas laughs. "Gigi's more like Izzy than Suzy. She's probably reading him the riot act."

"Maybe one of them isn't going to make it back alive," James jokes, sliding up to the drive-thru window, trying not to make eye contact with the lady behind the voice.

Seconds later, Thomas's phone rings, and Joe's voice comes through the car speakers. "Do you believe this shit?"

"You know Ma."

"Why on God's green earth would she want him there?"

James turns to me, shrugging and rolling his eyes while the guys talk about me like I'm not overhearing the entire conversation.

"You know Ma is always the peacemaker and sticks her nose in everyone's business."

"This is my kid," Joe says.

"And you're her kid," Thomas reminds him. "I think that trumps your thinking."

"Does she realize Gigi could've died?"

"I'm sure she does. Our wives told her everything, Joe," James tells him, and I know there're no secrets left in this family. "You know they can't keep a secret, and Ma could pull the truth out of anyone, especially them."

"Fuck," Joe hisses. "Drop Pike off at my house, and he can ride with us."

"Do I get a say in this?" I ask from the back seat, wishing I could get out and run, but it's impossible without a door in the back of this Challenger.

Thomas turns, glaring at me to shut the fuck up but without actually saying the words. He doesn't need to either. I get the message loud and clear.

"We'll drop him off and go. We'll only have a few hours to sleep before we have to be there," James says. "She doesn't care that we've crossed the state and come back in the same day."

"You know how she is... There's never a good reason to cancel a dinner. Bullets. Near-death experiences. Hell, not even a hurricane would stop her," Thomas tells them.

I tip my head back, staring out the back window at the sky painted with pinks and purples as the sun starts to rise over the horizon.

All I want to do is talk to Gigi and crawl into bed, leaving all the bad shit behind. But I have a feeling I don't get a choice in whether I attend family dinner since the big men in the front seat aren't finding a reason I can't go. The fact that Joe wants me at his house and is going to drive me there himself seals the deal.

"We're grabbing a quick cup of coffee, but we'll be at your place a few minutes after you," James says, handing the money over to the woman.

"I'll be there waiting," Joe says before disconnecting the call.

"Well, that wasn't so bad," Thomas says, turning his head to stare at me as I lift mine, forgetting the beautiful sunrise because although that wasn't so bad, it wasn't good either.

I laugh. "So bad? I'm pretty sure the man wants to kill me."

"Here's your *hot* and *black* coffees," the woman says, holding three cups in her hands, waiting for James to take them.

He hands one to me, then to Thomas, and takes the final one for himself. He doesn't say anything else to the woman. He's had a shit night like the rest of us and doesn't want to get into another argument over something as simple as a cup of coffee.

"That man," James says, placing his coffee in the cupholder before he rolls the car forward, "is a devoted father. He'd lay down his life for his family. Just like we would in his shoes."

"I would've taken a bullet tonight to save Gigi."

"We know that, kid. Hell, even Joe knows that. He knows everything that went down at the compound. Trust me, he's thankful that you helped get her out of there alive, but the man's out of his mind right now. Joe doesn't scare easily, but he's been a raving lunatic the last few days. He'll come around. Just give him some time and space to let him get his head on straight."

I rest the Styrofoam on my knee, letting his words settle deep. "Then maybe you should just drop me off at my place. Give everyone some space without me around, crowding shit."

Thomas shakes his head. "Ma wants you at her house, you'll be at her house."

I close my eyes, trying to picture the mother of these rough and tough men. She must be a powerful force if, even at their age, she's still the boss.

"And if Joe walks around there all broody and moody, she'll set his ass straight if she likes you."

"Why don't you two hate me?" I ask, lifting my head and prying the lid off the coffee.

Thomas laughs and shakes his head. "We've been in shit just as big as you were last night. You didn't cause what came at you, but we played a role in the hell we brought to our door. Our women were almost casualties too. We know how things easily spin out of control. That's life, kid."

"Hell, Izzy's been knee-deep in our bullshit so many times," James says, gunning the engine as soon as he's on the highway with nothing but open road before us. "But that was shit we brought on ourselves or she put into motion. Life happens. Shit happens. We rolled with it, and so did you. The family, including Joe, will get over what happened. And if you're lucky, they'll welcome you into the fold if that's what you're looking for."

"I want Gigi in my life." I figured I'd lay shit out for her uncles since they are here and I'm not going anywhere. "She's the best thing to ever happen to me. But the family..." I pause, wondering how to explain the shit I've been through and the lack of familial support I'd grown up with. "That isn't something I'm used to dealing with."

"I didn't grow up Gallo," James says, looking at me in the rearview mirror for a moment, "but they treat me as if I did. From the moment I stepped foot in her mother's house, I was welcomed as part of the family. Doesn't matter how you were raised, kid. Once you're in, you're one of them. One of us. Win over Ma Gallo and Suzy too, and you're in the fold."

"Gigi's mother is going to hate me." I'm never the guy a girl brings home to meet her mother.

Thomas laughs, smacking his leg. "You're just like Joe, and Suzy's crazy about that man. Suzy may seem straitlaced, but don't let her fool you. She'll take to you like glue if she sees her daughter's happy. You'll remind her of the man she fell in love with. The guy with the chip on his shoulder who's head over heels for a girl."

All of this is out of my comfort zone and territory I haven't ridden through before. I've never dealt with an entire family. I never gave a shit if people liked me, especially not a woman's parents. But this is different. I have to win over countless people, starting with her mother and then her grandmother before I could get everyone on board.

"You looked death in the eye last night and came out

alive," James says. "Facing our family will seem like a cakewalk."

"Yeah," I mutter, staring into the blackness of the coffee, not believing a goddamn word. Sure, I was scared when the gunfight was going on and the door to my old room opened, but I knew how to respond. Family...isn't something I'm used to.

"Just relax. We'll be at Joe's soon."

"Oh goodie," I mumble and sip my coffee.

Thomas and James laugh, clearly getting a kick out of my misery and knowing full well shit isn't going to be as easy as they make it out to be.

An hour later, I'm climbing out of the back of James's car, and I catch sight of Gigi on the front porch, hugging a blond woman tightly. I assume it's her mother because that's the only thing that makes sense, but there's very little resemblance between the two.

Joe's next to them, glaring at me like I'm the enemy, and not over the shit that went down, or the fact that he probably knows everything about what happened between Gigi and me in Daytona. Well, not everything because I'd be a dead man, but he knows enough that he has to want to at least break my legs.

"Pike!" Gigi yells as soon as she sees me. She moves away from her mother, running down the front steps, across the driveway, and leaps into my arms. "I was so worried about you." She holds me tightly, locking her hands behind my neck and staring up at me. "I thought maybe my uncles would leave you somewhere on the side of the road."

"I'm fine, darlin'." I push the hair away from her eyes, needing to see her face. "Your uncles were nice."

I didn't say they were friendly because, under the circumstances, it wasn't like hanging out with my buddies, but they weren't assholes either. They laid shit out for me, telling me how it is and how to get in everyone's good graces.

She smiles up at me. "They were nice?"

I nod. "They weren't mean."

"Huh. That's shocking." Her smile widens. "I want you to meet my mother."

"I'm sure she hates me, Gigi. Maybe I should just go back to my place."

Gigi shakes her head, tightening her hold around me. "Not happening, big guy. My mother is a cream puff. She's going to go bananas for you."

"Bananas?"

"Yeah." She smiles again but bigger this time. "My mom is sweet where my dad's rough. She's going to love you as much as I do."

I glance toward her parents. They're in a heated conversation. Her mother's eyes are on me, but her father's only paying attention to his woman. She slaps Joe's chest, eyes raking over me as a smile spreads across her face. She looks harmless. A mess of blond hair, fair skin, and a tiny little figure. Gigi gets her size from her mother, but everything else about her is all her daddy.

"I want to kiss you so badly right now." I rest my forehead on hers, trying to control myself because her father could very well end me right here.

"We'll sneak away once things settle down. Maybe at my grandmother's, we'll go for a walk or something. But for now, my mother's waiting, and I think her patience has just about worn out."

"Lead the way, darlin'."

She releases her grip on me and grabs my hand, pulling me toward the front porch as soon as her feet touch the ground. Joe ticks his chin toward Thomas and James before James peels out of the driveway like his ass is on fire.

Suzy, Gigi's mother, doesn't even glance toward the noise. Her eyes are locked on me, soaking me in, probably thinking the worst.

"So, you're Pike," she says with a small smile.

"Ma'am," I reply, squeezing Gigi's hand because this is almost as terrifying as the gun pointed at my head.

Her mother comes down the stairs, meeting us at the bottom. "Thank you for keeping my baby safe."

"Um, you're welcome." I nod because I don't know what else to say and I wasn't expecting those words or her kindness.

"Now, don't freak out. I know you're a badass biker and all, but this mama bear wants to give you a hug."

Gigi snorts as her father starts cursing. "Told ya," Gigi says, describing her mother perfectly.

"Hush it," Suzy tells her and holds out her arms for me.

I pause, gazing down at my girl, but she's smiling and jerking her chin toward her mama. "You better do what she says. She isn't as sweet as she seems, especially if you don't do what she asks."

"Seems to be a theme in this family." I let go of Gigi's hand and move into her mother's waiting arms.

Suzy's hug isn't soft. Her hold is pretty damn firm, especially for her size. "I can hear you two," Suzy says with a small chuckle. "I can also understand why my daughter likes you." Suzy pulls back, gazing up at me, eyes sweeping across my face. "You're just like her daddy."

My eyes go to Joe, who's now pacing on the porch, brooding about the fact that I'm being welcomed and still looking like he's ready to leap over the railing and murder me at any moment. "I don't know about that."

Suzy takes a step back, hands still on my arms, gazing up at me. "Sweetie, if you don't see the similarities between you and her daddy, you must be blind. Her first love was her father, and now my baby has found a man who's the spitting image of him." Joe's eyes are on me as she speaks, and his cursing gets louder. "Don't mind him. He has a lot of trouble dealing with his children growing up and sprouting wings."

"I do not." Joe stalks down the stairs, heading right toward us. "I have a problem with my daughter falling for a guy who's—"

"Exactly like you?" Suzy interrupts him.

Joe grunts. "I wouldn't go that far, sugar."

"He's a biker, has tattoos, piercings too. Probably a lady-killer with a chip on his shoulder and bossy as all hell."

"Yep." Gigi smiles.

"So, tell me, dear husband, how are you two different?" Suzy crosses her arms in front of her chest, staring at her husband, waiting for his response.

Joe waves his hand in my direction, and his eyebrows draw down. "He's…"

"What?" Suzy taps her foot, looking a little annoyed at this point, and the sweetness has all but disappeared.

"Shorter." Joe shrugs.

Suzy grabs his arm, plastering her body against his. "That's the best you can come up with, sweetheart?"

"Sugar…"

Suzy shakes her head. "Whatever you're feeling right now doesn't matter. Look at your daughter." She tips her head toward Gigi. "She's happy, Joe."

"Well…" Joe's eyes go to his daughter then to me before going back to his wife. "I won't say I'm happy about any of this."

"Would you ever be happy with any man she'd bring home? I remember you didn't like the other two either."

"They were spineless shits," he says quickly.

"And Pike is not."

"He's just so…so…"

"Like you," Suzy says with a smile, winking at her husband.

Gigi chuckles at my side, tangling her fingers with mine as she tugs me toward the front door, leaving her parents standing at the bottom of the steps. "We're going in. We've had a long night and could use a nap before Grandma's."

"Pike can take the couch in my office. Separate rooms," Joe says, "if you want Pike to live another day."

"You're cute, Dad." Gigi laughs as we walk into the house. "Don't listen to him," she tells me. "He's a bit overdramatic."

"But he's right, and this is his house, darlin'. If he wants my ass to sleep on the porch, that's where I'll sleep. We're under his roof, and he gets to set the rules."

"Fine." She rolls her eyes. "I'll show you where his office is."

"Thank you. Now, tell me about your grandma. I've had enough surprises this week to last me a lifetime."

Gigi nods her head down a hallway, and I follow her as she starts to walk. "She's fierce."

"Great," I mutter because the fierceness in this family has already been off the charts.

"She's tough too."

"Even better."

"But…" Gigi stops outside a closed door and leans against the wall, tangling her fingers with mine. "If you win her over, you have an ally for life. It doesn't hurt that she's the boss of everyone, including her sons."

"So, you're saying I have to win her heart?"

"You have to win her mind." Gigi smiles.

I've got this one in the bag. Winning over the ladies has never been a problem. I'm sure another fierce and tough Gallo won't be too hard…

CHAPTER TWENTY-FIVE

PIKE

WITH THE WAY Gigi described her grandma, and based on the size of her children, I expected the woman to be tall, sizable, and downright scary.

"Baby, I was so worried about you," her grandmother says, wrapping her arms around Gigi and squeezing her tightly.

"I'm fine, *Nonna*. Pike made sure of it."

Gigi's already working the woman, trying to put in a good word for me because, like she said, she's the boss. The ride over here was tense. I sat in the back of the SUV with Gigi, getting an icy glare from Joe in the rearview mirror as her two sisters chatted in the seats between us.

Her grandmother's eyes are on me as she embraces her granddaughter in the driveway. "This is the boy I've been hearing about?"

Gigi pulls away, glancing over her shoulder at me, a smile on her lips. "Yep, but don't believe anything *he*—" she dips her head toward her father who's stalking by and ignoring us all "—says. You know how Daddy has a tendency to fly off the handle and overreact."

Her grandmother laughs with a slow shake of her head.

"He's just worried about you, and sometimes his emotions get the better of him. Cut him some slack, sweetheart. Your daddy will come around, but you have to give him some time to adjust to the reality that you're no longer a little girl, but this beautiful and confident woman who's standing here today."

I smile because I already like this woman. She gives sound advice, and it doesn't sound like there's an ounce of judgment in her voice.

"I guess." Gigi shrugs and steps to the side, turning toward me. "But he should've come to this realization the day I graduated from high school."

I haven't moved a step. I'm too engrossed in their conversation, the way they look at each other and like each other. One taller and younger, one shorter and older, but of the same blood with the same eyes and mannerisms.

"You never stop being a parent, Giovanna. There's no off-switch once your children sprout their wings and fly away from the nest. We always worry. Always want the best for them. When they hurt, so do we. He's just doing what he thinks is best for you, even if he may be totally off base. Forcing something on him that he's not ready to face won't make changing his heart and mind any easier. Just give him time, and he'll come around and see the light. What's your mother say?"

I turn toward the SUV where Gigi's mother is on bended knee, speaking with the two younger girls. I can't imagine what it had to be like growing up a Gallo. Sure, they were all up in each other's business, which could be annoying, but there is so much love between them that the good had to outweigh the bad.

Gigi sighs. "Mom seems to be cool about Pike. She says he's the spitting image of Daddy."

I catch her grandmother's eye as she laughs. "Oh, that had to go over big with your father."

"Can you talk to him for me?" Gigi begs. "Please. You're the only one who can talk sense into him sometimes."

The woman's laughter grows louder. "Child, when it comes to a man loving his children, there's no talking sense into him. You have to give him time and make him see the light." Her grandmother's eyes rake up and down my body before landing back on my face. "So, you're the one causing all the fuss?"

"Ma'am." I dip my head, giving her a playful smile because my lady-killer smirk doesn't feel right. "I've heard so many great things about you."

"All lies, I'm sure." She waves her hand through the air and steps closer, squinting up at me as she cranes her neck. "Well, aren't you a looker?"

The smile on my face only gets bigger, because Grandma may be old, but she's a tiger. "You aren't so bad-looking yourself." I throw her a wink.

"And a charmer." She laughs. "You've caused quite a commotion in a family that's seen serenity for a long time."

"I'm sorry." My voice goes up as I speak, making it seem like I'm asking a question when I'm making a statement.

"Don't be." She shakes her head. "You're both alive and well. Life has a way of reminding everyone of the preciousness of everything. Sometimes we need to have things shaken up a little to bring everything back into focus. Now, let me get a better look at you." She lifts her hands and wiggles her fingers.

Gigi ticks her head toward her grandmother, widening her eyes when I don't move right away. I take a few steps, closing the space between us as the woman stares up at me like she's trying to see something that isn't there.

"Quite handsome," she says, and she takes me by surprise when she wraps her arms around me, embracing me like she did Gigi. "Strong too."

I laugh, biting my lip to stop myself from saying something inappropriate. "Thank you." Again, the words come out like a question as the woman's hands splay across my back.

"Hush, child. Let an old woman enjoy herself for a minute."

Gigi shrugs, throwing her hands upward as she giggles silently behind her grandmother.

"Oh boy." Suzy walks by us with her two daughters in tow, taking in the hug. "Welcome to the lion's den, Pike. I hope you're ready for what you're about to walk into," she calls out, not bothering to look back at us.

My body stiffens at her words. I've never met anyone's family. Especially not all at once. I knew half the people inside, already working with them for a few days or riding with them back and forth from the Disciples' compound. But there were a few who were still a mystery to me. I've had the Gallos in small doses, but this is going to be supersized and in my face.

"Don't listen to her. We're as good as they come. Now, wrap your arms around me, and give Grandma a hug."

All the worry I have vanishes, and it's replaced by the goodness of the woman wrapped around me and her grand-daughter, who is beaming at me like I walk on water. I do as I'm told, holding the woman tightly in my arms.

"Much better. Now," the woman whispers near my ear. "I'll give my blessing because I see depth in those eyes, but if you hurt my granddaughter, you won't have to worry about her father, Pike. I'll find you first and make you wish you'd never been born."

There's the fierceness I'd been warned about. The tough-ness I'd been told to expect. "Yes, ma'am."

"Grandma," she tells me like I'm already one of the family.

"Grandma," I repeat, glancing down and taking in her beauty, wondering what she looked like when she was younger. Is Gigi the spitting image of the hellion in my arms?

"Now, my sauce needs stirring, and there are more than a few curious women inside looking forward to laying eyes on you." She takes a step back and puts her hands on my chest, groping me through my T-shirt. "They're excited, while their husbands are not."

I tip my head back, drawing in a breath. "You're really selling me on walking through that door."

The woman laughs. "What lies on the other side of that door is all the goodness I brought into my life. I created it— not alone, mind you—and there's no better group of people on this earth. Once you're in, you're in forever. See this chip?" She touches my shoulder, drawing my attention downward. "Don't let it falter, but keep that shit in check and mind your elders."

"I know my place, ma'am." Her eyes narrow, and I immediately know my mistake. "Grandma."

"Not such a quick learner, but you'll get there," she teases and takes a step back. "I heard you almost took a bullet for my granddaughter."

"He was willing to die for me, *Nonna*." Gigi steps forward and tucks herself under my arm.

"I was only doing what was right, darlin'."

Her grandmother smiles at her, eyes moving between us, taking us in as a couple. "My granddaughter needs someone who's strong both in mind and body. She's not a weakling and will never be controlled, but if a man's willing to take a bullet for her, just like her daddy would under the same circumstances, she's not going to let that pass without snapping up the goodness and keeping it close."

"It's not like that, Grandma. I liked Pike before this all happened."

I glance down, eyes wide because I don't want to talk to her grandmother about our time in Daytona. I didn't want anyone to know, but it seems there are very few secrets in this family.

"I've heard all about spring break. I remember your aunt Izzy causing some chaos there a while back. Trouble seems to run in our blood along with our affinity for badass, bossy men."

Well, there it is. Grandma knows all about everything and everyone.

"Now, if we don't get our asses inside, the sauce will burn, and you know how much Grandpa hates when his meal is shot to hell. We wouldn't want your aunt Fran fixin' the meal in my absence, would we?"

Gigi looks up at me. "Aunt Fran is Bear's wife, and she's not the best cook."

Grandma starts toward the door, and we follow. "You're being nice. She's the world's worst cook, but she has a good heart and a nosy spirit about her."

When the front door opens, there are so many eyes on me, I almost trip over the top step. There's not a man in the bunch. Four women I've never seen before are gawking at me like I'm an exotic animal on display and only there for their amusement. The grandmother laughs, shaking her head as she walks past them, disappearing into the back of the house.

Gigi grips my side, still tucked under my arm. "Pike, this is my aunt Max," she points at a very beautiful, tall, and lanky black woman. "She's Uncle Anthony's wife."

"Girl, get it straight. He's my husband," Max corrects her and takes a step toward us, staring up at me. "You're causing a lot of trouble around here."

"I never meant to…"

Max waves me off. "Don't say it. It's been far too quiet around here for far too long. We needed a little excitement." Then she turns her eyes toward her niece. "You did well with this one." She angles her head at me, talking like I'm not standing right in front of them. "I can't wait to see your dad lose his shit."

Great. Not only am I here to be gawked at, but they're all banking on me pissing off her father for nothing more than sheer entertainment. The last thing I want to do is make Joe mad. It doesn't mean I'm going anywhere, but I don't want the man gunning for me my entire life.

"He already lost it, Auntie."

The two women laugh.

My gaze moves to the three ladies still staring at me, covering their mouths and whispering to one another. I catch a few words here and there. The only words I can make out are *fresh meat*.

"Your daddy was the biggest badass I knew, sweetheart, but his heart is even bigger. Give him time. He'll come around."

Gigi rolls her eyes. "I don't think you understand the depths of his…"

"Love?" Max finishes her statement. "He's not angry, Gigi. He's mourning the loss of his baby. I can understand how he feels. Every day, I see the misery in Anthony's eyes as Tamara grows up and pulls away."

Gigi gasps. "Oh my God. Where's Tam? I haven't talked to her since before all hell broke loose."

So, this is Tamara's mother. The cousin Gigi had gone to Daytona with after lying to their parents, and the same Tamara Gigi had a conversation with on the phone about my cock.

"She's in hiding." Max laughs. "Anthony knows about Daytona."

Gigi's eyes widen. "I'm sorry we lied."

"Eh." Max shrugs. "You two were just blowing off steam, but I wish you'd been honest about where you were going and what you were doing."

"Dad and Uncle Anthony wouldn't have let us go."

"You're a grown-ass woman, Giovanna. Your fathers can't tell you how to live your lives forever."

"Then why's Tamara hiding from her dad?"

Max laughs. "I didn't raise a stupid child. A strong one, for sure, but not stupid."

"Enough chitchat," a small, older woman says, pushing by Max and getting the evil eye. "I need to get my hands on this boy."

"Auntie Fran, go easy on him," Gigi says as the woman plasters her body against me, resting her head on my chest.

"Shh. Don't ruin this for me, girl. When you're my age, there're very few thrills left in life."

I stare down at the woman, staying still as she feels me up like she's blind and trying to figure out the dips and curves, memorizing my body.

"Bear's wife." Gigi shrugs because Fran isn't stopping the attention she's giving to my muscles.

"Don't ruin this for me," Fran says again, her fingers digging into my pecs. "God, to be young again."

I laugh because what the fuck else am I supposed to do with this small, older woman hanging on my body? Talk about awkward. But then, there's been no real normal around me in days. This is just another experience with this family, and I can't say it's a bad one either.

"If I were ten years younger…"

"He'd break you, Fran," a redhead says from behind her, and all the women giggle.

Fran's hands move to my arms, holding tight and squeezing until her fingernails practically dig into my skin. "No, he wouldn't. I have the biggest baddie of them all, and I'd say I broke him." She nuzzles her face deeper into my chest. "I think I could handle this kid."

"Um." I hold out my arms. I'm not going to hug the woman draped across me like I'm a blanket and she's in need of heat. I'm already treading in deep water, and any movement, even if it's innocent, could send me spiraling to the depths on my ass.

When Fran doesn't unstick herself, Gigi starts talking,

ignoring my new body ornament. She points toward the pretty redhead. "This is my aunt Angel. She's Thomas's wife."

"It's nice to meet you," she says with a friendly smile.

"You too." I smile back, wishing I could at least shake her hand, but there's Fran.

She moves her hand toward a woman with long wavy brown hair and big, beautiful eyes. "This is Mia." Gigi steps closer, looming over Fran but having zero effect. "She's a doctor and my uncle Mike's wife."

I'm impressed. Mike doesn't seem like the type of guy who'd marry a doctor. I'd read all about him, knew about his career as a fighter before giving it all up for love. Looking at her, I can understand why he walked away from the ring.

"It's a pleasure to meet you." I tip my head because it's all I can do with Fran still twisted around me like I'm her new favorite accessory.

Gigi's grandmother appears in the hallway, shaking her head as soon as she sees Fran. "Give the boy some space, ladies. He's not here for your entertainment. Especially you, Fran."

"I'm not moving," Fran says, latching on tighter, and I wonder if I'm going to have to pry the woman off my body.

"Fran?"

My gaze moves across the room to Bear, who's staring at Fran, arms crossed over his chest and jaw set tight. "You have thirty seconds to let that boy go, or..."

Fran doesn't budge, and she doesn't even look in his direction. "Or you'll what?" She looks up at me with a playful smirk and a quick wink, looking like she's loving every minute of hanging on me and antagonizing the big guy.

"You're not going to be able to sit comfortably for a week."

"You promise?" she teases, finally turning her head away from my body.

"Woman, you have ten seconds to let go of that boy and get your ass over here…"

"He's such a big talker," she says, looking up at me and not paying any more attention to her husband. "He's all bark and no bite."

"You want teeth, baby?"

She continues to ignore him. "I should really trade him in for a newer model."

She barely gets the words out before his arm is around her waist and then her body's in the air, landing on his shoulder. "Woman, I think you need me to remind you of who this fine ass," he says with a smack right on her behind for everyone to see, "belongs to."

The move reminds me of the way I hauled Gigi out of the bar area at the compound in front of all the guys. I gave zero fucks if I pissed her off, but I had a hell of a time doing it. Just like Bear is having while Fran grabs at his ass like a woman starved for cock.

"Sorry about that," Gigi says, "Fran can be a…"

"No worries. I think she's great. Everyone is so far."

"Well, you know my uncles, but let's see how they are after all the shit that went down. You ready to face them?"

I nod, but I want to say hell to the fucking no, I'm not ready. The ladies are always easier. The men, not so much. This group of moody and broody guys knows all about my past, the last week, and that I slept with their niece. "I'm ready."

CHAPTER
TWENTY-SIX

GIGI

"THAT WASN'T SO BAD, was it?" I ask Pike as we walk toward the line of trees in the backyard.

"Compared to what?" He looks over his shoulder like he's checking to see if anyone is following us.

"It could've been worse." I shrug, gazing up and into his beautiful green eyes.

"There's still time."

I wave him off because if they were going to cause a scene, they would've done it already. "They like to put on a big show, but they're all pussycats."

Ten years ago, they maybe would've chased Pike out of here, but they've become more chill with age. Plus, they know the harder they try to drive him away, the more I'll run toward him.

"Why don't you say that to their faces?"

I curl my fingers around his hand as he brushes some hair away from my shoulder. "Do you like them, at least?"

"Who? Your family?"

I nod.

"They're like a small army, but yeah. You were a lucky kid to have so many people surrounding you as you grew up. I never had anyone except my grandmother who I could count on and who gave a shit about me."

"I care about you now." I curl into his side as we stand in the shade and out of view of all the nosy Gallos who are probably plastered to the back windows, trying to keep an eye on us.

He pulls our hands in front of us as his face grows serious. "Now that everything's over, I wouldn't blame you if you want to go back to the way things were."

"The way things were?" I ask, confused and a little dumbfounded.

"Yeah," he says like we're talking about the weather and not about *us*. "We went through some scary, heavy shit together. We didn't know if we were going to make it another day, and sometimes that affects how we think. Now that we're alive and no one's coming after us, maybe we should take a step back and make sure this is what we both want."

I jerk my head like he physically struck me. "You want to break up?" I take a step back, tearing my hands from his. "You're saying that shit now? You've met my family, saved my life, and were willing to take a bullet for me, and now you're saying you want to break up and not be together anymore?"

Pike steps forward, reaching for me, but I move quickly, evading his touch. "I didn't mean it that way. Be reasonable, Gigi. Think about it."

My eyes widen. "Be reasonable?"

"Um, yeah."

"I can't believe after everything we've been through, you're saying this shit to me now."

"I don't regret anything. I would still take a bullet for you or do anything necessary to keep you safe."

I fold my arms in front of me, cocking one shoulder upward, and raise an eyebrow. "But now that the bad shit has passed, you don't want to date me?"

"I don't want you to have any regrets," he says softly, closing the space between us, but I don't allow him near enough to touch me. "You're young. You have your whole life ahead of you. You have a perfect family who wants only good shit for you. What the hell do you want with an older guy who has baggage and commitment issues?"

"You have commitment issues?"

"Darlin', I never stay in one place longer than a few years. My parents fucked me up. I'm always searching for something bigger and better. Looking for that place I can call home and find out where I belong. I've been traveling around for almost ten years, and I still haven't found it."

I wave my arms around, trying my best not to sock him straight in the jaw. "What the fuck was this last week?" My hand flies toward the house. "You just spent an hour charming my family, building the foundation that's necessary to be welcomed into the fold. Now, you're saying you don't have a place, and you want to up and run away like a pussy."

"I'm not being a pussy, Gigi. I'm giving you a chance to think about if this is what you want. The shit we went through the last few days can fuck with your head and make it hard to think. We were living in the moment, hoping to have more, but now it's over. Shit's gonna settle, and I don't want you to look back and regret the time you spent with me before you up and marry some guy worthy of you."

I scrunch my nose because compared to any pile of horseshit I've ever smelled before, this was far worse. "You've got to be shitting me right now! Why the fuck did you come here if you felt this way?"

"It's not like I had any choice in this," he yells back, throwing his hand toward my grandmother's house. "But I like you, Gigi. Hell, I love you. I'm truly, madly, deeply in fucking love with you, and I don't want to be another mistake in your life. You deserve more than a guy who's good at ink, with a fucked-up family, and not much to offer other than how I feel."

I inhale and slowly exhale, letting all his words seep in. I know this man loves me. He's said those words before. Sure, we were probably about to die, but the possibility of not taking another breath doesn't make a man say shit he isn't feeling.

"Have I ever asked you for anything?"

"No," he says.

"Have I ever forced you to do anything you didn't want to do?"

"No."

"Ever asked you about your bank account and what you could bring to our relationship besides yourself?"

"No."

"You're right, Pike. I'm a lucky girl to be surrounded by all this." I tick my head toward my grandparents' house. "But I could give two shits about money or anything else. My parents taught me about the real important things in life. They taught me about loyalty, love, and most of all, family. I don't care if I'm piss-poor as long as I have someone with me who'll love me and do everything in his power to keep on loving me."

He tips his head back, staring up at the trees. "I'm not a saint. When I look at you—" he glances back down at me "—I see everything that's pure. I see an untouched soul who's had a life of good. And in the short time I've known you, I've brought you a whole lot of bad. I don't want that for you. I don't want you to have a moment's sadness in your life. I never want to see the look on your face I saw the night in my room after I shot that guy. I don't want to know I'm the one who put that look on your face."

"Are you done yet?" I ask, tapping my foot and giving him a dirty look because I'm barely keeping my shit under control.

He nods, not adding more fuel to the wildfire he's already started. I stalk up to him, pressing my fingers into his chest, letting my fingernails dig into the skin underneath his black T-shirt.

"Now it's my turn to talk and for you to shut the fuck up."

He throws up his hands. "I won't..."

I dig a little harder. "My turn, Pike." I glare up at him, and the corners of his lips twitch. "You didn't bring the bad into my life. That was your father's sin, not yours. Stop blaming yourself for shit you couldn't control." He nods, but I keep going because I'm not giving him a second to argue. "As for the look on my face, I didn't care that the bastard who wanted to kill you was lying on that floor, blood oozing from his body."

He scowls. "You didn't?"

I shake my head, twisting my lips. "I kept looking at him, imagining what would've happened if your gun hadn't gone off first. How that could've been you lying on that floor, bleeding everywhere, having taken your last breath." I lean forward, dropping my hand and resting my forehead where I've just poked the hell out of him. "It would've killed me seeing you like that. Do you know how close you came to dying?"

His arms wrap around me, one hand flattening on my back. "But I didn't die, Gigi. We lived. We're standing here, under the sun, listening to the birds sing, just as alive as we were last week when things were normal and you were never in danger."

I slide my fingers under his shirt, running my hands along the soft skin at his sides. "We're standing here because you made sure I lived to see another day. If it weren't for you, I could be dead right now."

He shakes his head. "If it weren't for me, you never would've been in that situation."

"Shut up, Pike." I listen to the slow, steady beat of his

heart underneath his shirt. "I've never told another man besides my father that I loved him. I've had a few boyfriends, not many, but they never got the words from me."

"Never?" he asks as I tip my head up, seeing the shock all over his face.

"Never. You know why?"

"Why, darlin'?" he asks softly.

"Because they never got me. All they cared about was getting in my pants. Even Erik, my last boyfriend, I never saw a forever with. He was nice and all, but he didn't have what it takes to be with me for the long haul. My father and uncles would've chewed him up and spat him out. Hell, if someone would've come after us, I'm pretty sure Erik would've hurled me in front of a bullet to save his own ass."

Pike's hands are on my shoulders, pushing me backward so he can look at me. "That's what I'm talking about. You haven't had any good relationships in your life, babe. You can't compare what we have to those guys...and I use that term loosely. Every man you're with should be willing to die for you because you're his girl. You need to explore, sow those oats, before you decide you want a nobody like me in your bed every night."

"Pike, do you really love me?" I whisper, gazing up at him, my nails starting to press into his skin because he's beginning to piss me off again.

"I do," he says quickly.

"Then can you just shut the fuck up and see where this goes? I'm not ready to walk away. I don't want to date someone else, I don't want to find out what good and bad is out there because I've already found something good, someone good, and I don't want to let go because even if I find someone out there who'll love me, they'll never be you."

His hands cup my face, and I melt into his touch, wanting more, always wanting more. "I've never wanted anyone as badly as I want you. I've never felt so at peace with someone as I do you. I've never been surrounded by so much love as I have been with your family, even if they don't like me."

"They like you." I wish he'd shut up and kiss me already, but he doesn't.

"They're tolerating me, hoping I go away."

"Not everyone in that house grew up the way I did. They have pasts and skeletons in their closets too. It didn't change the way my family feels about them. The Gallos judge people on who they are, not what they did or how they grew up. All that matters is that we love one another. The men in my family are protective and overbearing, a little like you, and I know they'll love you and welcome you with open arms when they realize how good we are together."

"Gigi…"

"Pike, just kiss me already. And so help me God, if you try to break my heart again, I'm going to knee you so hard in the balls, you won't be able to sleep with another woman for months."

Pike smirks. "I kind of like my balls, babe."

"Me too." I smile. "Now, you better kiss me, or I'm going to leap into your arms and cause a scene that'll have my dad out here so fast…"

I don't get the rest of the words out before his mouth crashes down on mine, stealing away the threat I was ready to carry out if necessary.

My hands slide behind his neck as I plaster my body to his, kissing him with all the force I can muster on my tiptoes. I've been waiting hours for a moment alone to feel his lips on mine, tongue sliding inside my mouth, giving me his small moans and the warmth of his body.

"Don't you ever threaten to leave me again," I murmur into his mouth, needing him to say the words.

"Never again," he whispers, pulling back and gazing down at me. "You're mine now, darlin', and I hope you understand what that means."

"I'm hoping it means a lot of dirty shit." I wink, pulling his head down because his lips are looking lonely.

"Gigi. Pike. Dinner," Nonna yells from somewhere in the distance. "Get your bodies untangled and get your asses in here."

Pike rests his forehead against mine, trying to catch his breath as we both gasp for air. "We better go." I know Grandma's still watching and isn't going to go anywhere until we "untangle" ourselves and start marching our asses toward the house. "But we're finishing what we started as soon as we get home."

"Your place or mine?" he asks, waggling his eyebrows with a playful smirk.

"I don't have a bed."

"Darlin', I only need a wall."

Oh. My. God. Fuck yes!

CHAPTER
TWENTY-SEVEN

PIKE

"GIVE ME TEN MINUTES, and then come over. I'll leave the front door unlocked because I have a surprise for you."

I can't stop the smile on my face as I lean forward, brushing my lips across hers and squeezing her ass. "What kind of surprise, darlin'?"

She bats her eyelashes, smirking. "What kind of surprise would it be if I told you?"

"You're a tease."

She giggles when my fingers find the bottom edge of her jean shorts and my lips slide down to her neck. "Hey," she says, pushing against my chest. "If you don't stop doing that, I won't be able to let you out of my sight, and the entire night will be ruined."

"If I fucked you right now, it would ruin the night?"

She lets out a loud huff. "Well, no, but I want this time to be special."

"Baby, every time with you is special," I murmur against her skin before running my tongue from her ear to her collarbone. "I don't know if I can wait ten minutes."

She tries to wiggle out of my hold, but I grip her thighs, wanting to sink between them even though we're outside.

"You waited fifteen months, I think you'll survive another ten minutes," she says, pushing against my chest again. "Please, Pike."

I loosen my grip, allowing her to put space between us. "Well, since you said please. But get your surprise and come to my place. I have a bed."

"And walls too." She winks.

"Walls too, darlin'."

"Okay, I still need ten minutes. I'll grab the surprise and be over."

"Perfect." I try to grab her again, wanting to taste her lips or skin, but she isn't having any of it.

She backs away, shaking her head. "No touching."

I raise an eyebrow. "I hope that isn't part of the surprise because touching is required for what I have in mind."

"There will be touching," she says, still moving toward her front door. "But not until I say so."

"Not until you say so?" My mouth falls open, but I'm totally playing. I know this girl, and she doesn't play hard to get. I also know just the right buttons to push to have her begging for more than my touch.

There's a wicked gleam in her eyes. "Of course. I'm the boss."

"Naturally," I tease, but she is.

I learned today that every woman in her family is the boss too. It doesn't matter how big or tough the man is, his wife has the final say in how things go down. I loved their strength and that their husbands didn't care as long as their women were happy.

"Now, go." She shoos me with one hand and takes her keys out of her back pocket with the other. "I'll be quick."

I throw up my hands and turn toward my door. "I'm going. I'm going."

"Catch ya in ten," she says before disappearing into her apartment.

I step inside my place, flipping on the light and kicking off my boots, thankful as fuck to finally be home and still breathing. I wasn't sure I'd make it back, and after a long-ass day of travel and Gigi's family, I'm happy as shit for a little peace and quiet.

I strip off my clothes as I walk toward the bathroom, needing a shower and a reset after all the bullshit that went down the last few days. I don't waste too much time under the spray because my girl's coming over with a surprise that I'm hoping includes very little clothing and a whole lot of fucking.

After a quick wash, I dry off, pulling on a pair of sweat pants and nothing else. I don't see the need when I don't plan on having clothing on my body for very long.

I glance at the clock, realizing it's been ten minutes, but Gigi's nowhere to be found. I press my ear against our adjoining wall but only hear silence. I wait another minute, pacing a path down my hallway, back and forth between my bedroom and living room.

"You comin'?" I text her because I've never been a patient man.

I take five trips up and down the hallway, turning my phone over in my hand, waiting for her reply, but I get no response.

I'm out the door, knocking on hers. "Gigi!" I yell because it's not like her to promise one thing and do another.

It isn't like she could lie down and accidentally fall asleep. The girl just moved in and doesn't have any furniture in her place.

I try the handle and it's unlocked, but I hesitate for a second because I also don't want to walk in and scare the hell out of her, getting myself kicked in the balls in the process.

"Gigi!" I yell again, pounding louder this time, and when there's no response, I open the door, figuring a kick in the balls is worth knowing she's okay.

My foot connects with something, and it skids across the floor, slamming into the wall. I look over, realizing it's her cell phone, and my heart immediately slams into my chest like a brick.

"Gigi!" I yell again, but I only get my echo back and not another sound.

I frantically look in each room of the tiny space, searching for my girl, but find nothing. My hands are sweating and my heart's beating double time as I push open the door to her bedroom, catching sight of a person's back.

A back that isn't Gigi's.

I lunge for the man, turning him around, laying eyes on his mask-covered face. His eyes widen, the only part of his face that's visible before I rear back, hurling my fist through the air and connecting with his jaw.

"Pike!" Gigi screams, and I move my eyes toward her voice. She's in the corner, hands at her neck, huddled in a ball, and tears staining her cheeks.

I lay into the man who's staggering in front of me, whaling on him with my fists until he falls to the floor. I kick him in the ribs once, making sure he's out cold before I run to Gigi, kneeling in front of her. Her eyes are wide, and her cheeks are stained with tears.

"Are you okay?" I ask her, lifting her into my lap, checking over her body.

"I'm fine. He was hiding in here when I walked in," she says quickly, whimpering at the memory. "He... He..."

"Did he hurt you?"

She shakes her head and curls into my chest, gripping on to my T-shirt with her long fingers. "He put his hand over my mouth and hauled me back here, but he didn't have a chance to hurt me before you showed up."

"I'm so sorry, baby. I should've been here sooner."

"I'm okay," she whispers like she's trying to convince

herself or maybe just me, but by the way she's shaking, I'd say she's anything but okay. "We have to call the police."

"I will in a minute." My priority is making sure she's okay before I let her out of my arms.

"No, Pike. I don't want him waking up and coming after you. My heart can't take any more," she whispers. "Please." She crawls out of my lap, staggering, but catching herself on my shoulder. "I have some packing tape we can use to tie him up."

"You're crafty," I tease because right now, we could use a little lightness in our fucked-up week.

"You have no idea." She smiles, wiping away the tears from her cheeks. "I'll grab the tape, and you check the guy." She's out of the room before I have a chance to rise to my feet.

"Let's see who you are, motherfucker." I hunch down next to the man's face, staring at the asshole who went after my girl.

Gigi's back, holding a roll of packing tape, eyes pinned on the lifeless body on the floor. "You didn't kill him, did you?"

I shake my head and laugh, reaching for the man's mask. "Darlin', I may be strong, but my punch didn't kill him."

"Thank God," she mumbles.

When I pull the mask from his face, I'm knocked backward, falling on my ass.

"What's wrong?"

I shake my head, blinking like my brain doesn't believe what my eyes are seeing. "It's my father."

———

Gigi & Pike's story continues in <u>BURN</u> - now available.

Gigi Gallo had always been taught the importance of loyalty, love, and family. And when she falls head over heels for Pike Moore, a hottie biker with a troubled past, everything she learned will be put to the test. But when you love a Gallo, you never fight alone.

After his family secrets are revealed, Pike must figure out how to leave the past behind him and allow himself to be truly happy, finding his happily ever after.

Tap here to read Burn now or visit menofinked.com/burn for more information.

DON'T MISS OUT!

Join my newsletter for exclusive content, special freebies, and so much more. Click here to get on the list!

Do you want to have your very own SIGNED paperbacks on your bookshelf? Now you can get them! Tap here to check out Chelle Bliss Romance and stock up on paperback.

Join over 10,000 readers on Facebook in Chelle Bliss Books private reader group and talk books and all things reading. Tap here to come be part of the family!

Want to be the first to know about upcoming sales and new releases? Follow me on Bookbub

DISCREET COVERS & SIGNED BOOKS

Own your very own discreet edition of your favorite story.
Now available on Chelle's website or on your favorite
paperback retailer.

Purchase your very own signed copies
at *chelleblissromance.com*

GALLO FAMILY TREE

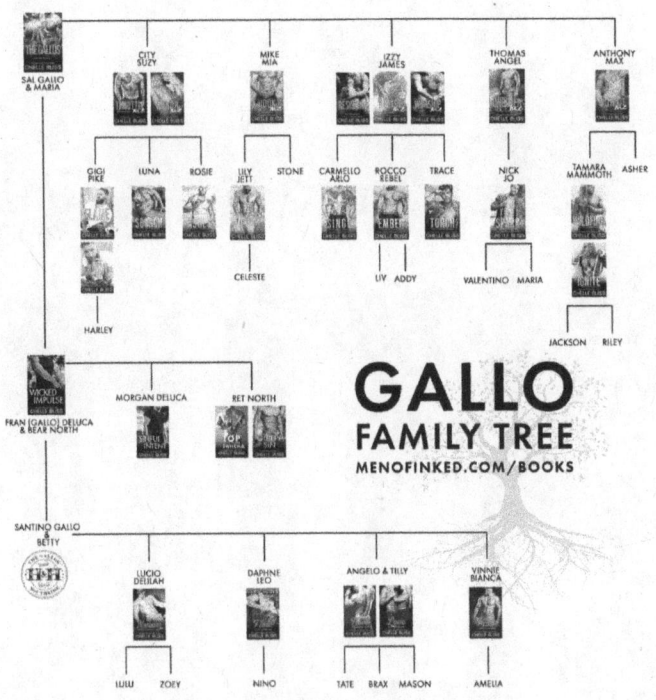

Want to learn more about my books or check out the Men of Inked family tree? Visit menofinked.com/books or menofinked.com/gallo-family-tree

ABOUT THE AUTHOR

I'm a full-time writer, time-waster extraordinaire, social media addict, coffee fiend, and ex-history teacher. *To learn more about my books, please visit menofinked.com.*

Want to stay up-to-date on the newest Men of Inked release and more? Join my newsletter at menofinked.com/news

Join over 10,000 readers on Facebook in Chelle Bliss Books private reader group and talk books and all things reading. Come be part of the family!

See the Gallo Family Tree at menofinked.com/books

Where to Follow Me:

facebook.com/authorchellebliss1

instagram.com/authorchellebliss

bookbub.com/authors/chelle-bliss

goodreads.com/chellebliss

amazon.com/author/chellebliss

twitter.com/ChelleBliss1

pinterest.com/chellebliss10

tiktok.com/@chelleblissauthor